MW01717260

Enemies

Stern was exhausted. The meeting had turned out to be much more than two old friends talking. Trudeau had his Trade Minister and two deputies in tow. They had been tipped off about Opel's interest in building a plant in Canada. Canada had grain and energy to sell, but wasn't sure if West Germany had the buying power or markets to compensate for the dollars that would be flowing back into Europe from the new plant. They had held his feet to the fire all afternoon.

Besides that, he was still fatigued by the trip from Bonn. He'd arrived in Montreal expecting a limo for the drive to Ottawa, but through a fluke, the car didn't show. Instead he caught the train, expecting to arrive at Union Station, a short walk to the hotel's lobby. But the city had decommissioned the building and erected a new Tremblay Road Station an annoying cab ride away.

Following the meeting, it was past 4 PM when he arrived in his room with the prospect of another session in the morning. *Scheisse!* He was too old for this! He'd tried to retire two years ago when Ludwig Erhard left office, but Kiesinger prevailed on him to stay on until he could find a suitable replacement in the Trade Commission.

The portfolio on his room desk reminded him he'd expected to trace the address of the owner this afternoon, but Trudeau's protracted meeting scotched that. Possibly there was more inside that would be a hint to the owner's destination this morning. Once more he unwound the string fastening.

Inside were drawings, *dozens* of them. Some were in ink, but most were pencil sketches, all spectacular in their realism and detail. One or two of them had been colorized. There were interiors, portraits, landscapes, and building exteriors. Many of the sketches were on standard, stiff writing paper, but also on small card stock, half as big.

The next thing Stern noticed were the dated initials *BDM* and title of each drawing in neat script. The drawings were in chronological order, ranging from June 1915 to October three years later. The first few were portraits. One of a man and a woman titled *Jocelyn Farm 6/1915*; he, with an axe at a chopping block. She was clutching something in her apron...*hen's eggs?* They faced each other, rather than the artist. A portion of a wooden farmhouse lurked in the background. Another sketch of a stocky young man, *Owen 4/1915;* another portrait of a young dark-complexioned boy in army uniform titled, *H. Gardinier 3/1916.* There was an April 1916 drawing of a building with the title, *Gouin St. Arena.* Here was a portrait of another boy in uniform, his light colored hair showing under his cap. Stern was drawn to the face. The signature read: *George K 5/1916.* Like the one of the Arena, and a number of others, it was done on good quality writing paper that carried an embossed *CRC* over a block-shaped cross. *Canadian Red Cross?*

Next in the chronology was a panoramic view of a field dotted with hundreds of tents. It was from a perspective of height, allowing detail of the nearest objects and the vastness of the expanse at the same time. It was brilliant. This one was dated 7/1916, entitled *Niagara Camp.*

He was impressed with the quality of the work. The portraits gave more than a sense of what the subject looked like; they seemed to look inside the person. He seemed to capture the subject's character, his worth as a human being. The landscapes and buildings were realistic to be sure, but they also told a story: a filthy doll left on the stoop of a gutted house, the pall of war haze over what once must have been a tranquil field. Then there were the depictions of the dead, so gruesome in their realism, yet no hint of voyeurism. These were poignant memorials to wasted youth.

There was no doubt. The drawings were a soldier's memoir of the Great War. They struck a chord that resonated with his own experiences of the time. He continued to peruse the collection until he came upon one that seemed somehow familiar. He reached to remove it from the others when it flipped over, revealing its opposite side. What he saw caused him to audibly gasp.

What They Are Saying About

Enemies

A wonderfully worthwhile read! Barnes induces deep and meaningful understanding of human nature in this well documented history from World War 1. The utterly absorbing tale delves deep into the hearts and minds of men of the trenches on both sides of the Siegfried Line as it wavers back and forth under oft-times inept leadership, at a dreadful cost of human life. He paints indelible mind pictures of men under pressure both physically and emotionally. This heady insight into the tribulations of the time brings us characters we understand as if kin.

A worthy piece of work in every aspect of tale telling.

Kev Richardson
historian, novelist, biographer

Other Works From The Pen Of

Richard Whitten Barnes

BRINK

What happens when a respected scientist loses everything, becomes homeless, then when on the road to recovery - is charged with murder?

THE CORYDON SNOW

In 1943, the SS Corydon Snow sails from Pearl Harbor on a voyage that will take it to the most dangerous battle areas of the Pacific.

A SCENT OF ALMOND

When Ontario Detective Andrea Blake investigates the newly discovered corpse of a man missing for two years, she gets way more than she bargains for: serial poisonings!

FORGOTTEN ROOTS

A tragedy from the War of 1812 emerges from the Canadian soil. Two hundred years later, Detective Andrea Blake finds the mystery thrust upon her to untangle…*Forgotten Roots*.

LUZON

America has broken Japan's "Purple" code, and a captured U.S. Navy officer knows it. Someone has to make sure the Japanese don't find out.

BAD MEDICINE

Inspector Andy Blake gets more than she bargains for when she returns to her Island home for R&R–a murder, and her old flame is in the thick of it.

Wings

ENEMIES

Richard Whitten Barnes

A Wings ePress, Inc.

Historical Novel

Wings ePress, Inc.

Edited by: Jeanne Smith
Copy Edited by: Camille Netherton
Senior Editor: Jeannie Smith
Executive Editor: Marilyn Kapp
Cover Artist: Trisha FitzGerald

Wings ePress Books
http://www.wings-press.com

ISBN 978-1-61309-822-6

Published In the United States Of America

December 2015

Wings ePress Inc.
403 Wallace Court
Richmond, KY 40475

Dedication

To the brave men of the Canadian Expeditionary Forces and the over four thousand from the Algoma, Ontario region who served.

~*~

In Memory Of

George H. Luehmann,
463d Regiment, 238th Infantry Division,
Imperial German Army

Robert W. Barnes
151st Artillery, 42d (Rainbow) Division
American Expeditionary Force

Acknowledgements

Two sources for researching *ENEMIES* were invaluable:

History of German WWI Divisions
U.S. Army War Office
1920

Canadian Expeditionary Force
1914-1919
Colonel G.W.L. Nicholson, CD

The above sources kept me true to the actual facts of the war, but it is through personal accounts that life is breathed into a story. I want to especially thank Jackileen Raines, Jeanne Basteris, and Holly Pook Sachdev for contributing background, documents and letters from their families. Carrie Uusitalo of the St. Joseph Island Museum was helpful as well.

Author's Note

November 11, 2018 will mark the hundredth anniversary of the end of World War One; "The War to End All Wars."

Yet, twenty years after the armistice Europe and Asia were on the threshold of another war exemplifying the treachery and hubris of man. The human species seems to have learned little since.

The "Great War" caused the deaths of ten million young men before they had a chance at life. A similar number were wounded under conditions unspeakable by today's standards of hygiene and medicine. Few readers of this generation have a clear idea of the hardships endured in that conflict. It is for that reason and the approaching anniversary that I set this as the era for *Enemies*.

I have chosen to tell the stories of two boys, both from similar backgrounds but separate allegiances to emphasize the blamelessness of all those young men sent so easily into peril by generals and politicians.

While *Enemies* is in no sense biographical and entirely fiction, I have done my best to adhere to the actual events and time line of the war on the western front. Dialogue and situations attributed to non-fictional characters are purely imaginary.

RWB

In Flanders Fields

In Flanders fields the poppies blow
Between the crosses, row on row,
That mark our place; and in the sky
The larks, still bravely singing, fly
Scarce heard amid the guns below.
We are the Dead. Short days ago
We lived, felt dawn, saw sunset glow,
Loved and were loved, and now we lie
In Flanders fields.
Take up our quarrel with the foe:
To you from failing hands we throw
The torch; be yours to hold it high.
If ye break faith with us who die
We shall not sleep, though poppies grow
In Flanders fields.

Lt. Colonel John McCrae
1872-1918

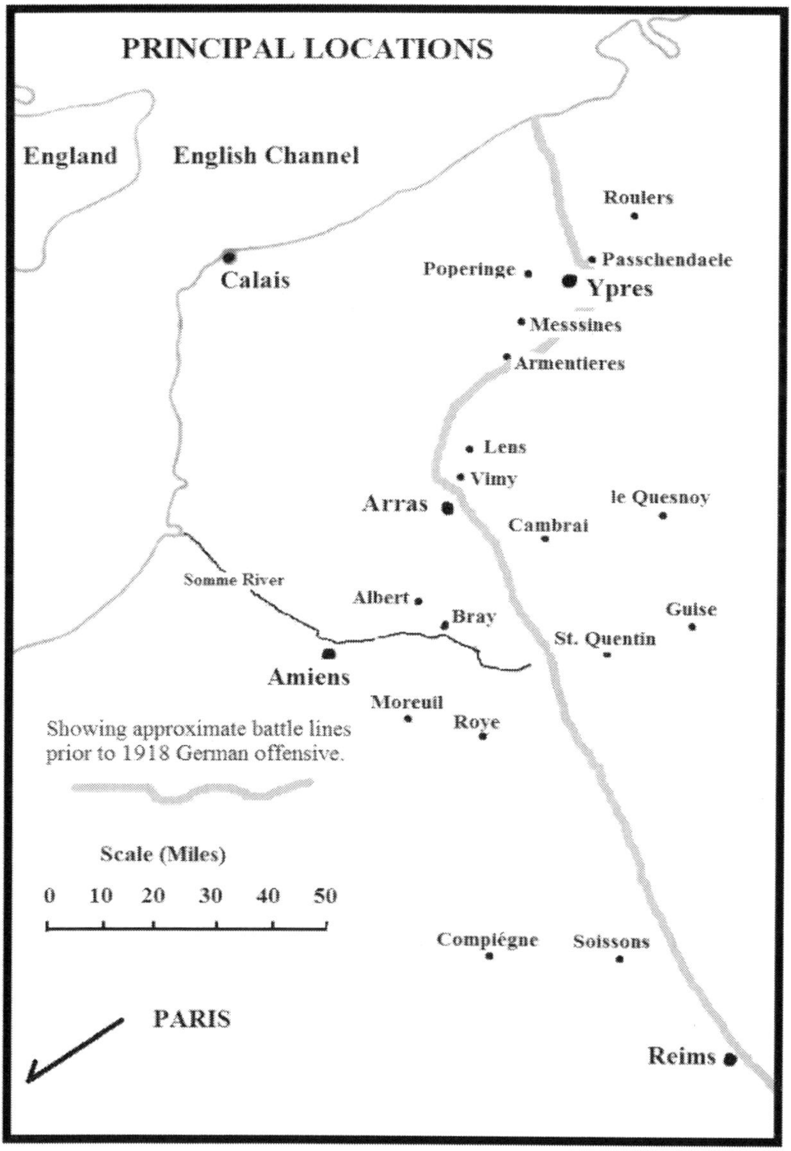
PRINCIPAL LOCATIONS
England
English Channel
Roulers
Passchendaele
Poperinge
Calais
Ypres
Messsines
Armentieres
Lens
Vimy
Arras
le Quesnoy
Cambrai
Somme River
Albert
Bray
Guise
St. Quentin
Amiens
Moreuil
Roye
Showing approximate battle lines prior to 1918 German offensive.
Scale (Miles)
0 10 20 30 40 50
Compiégne
Soissons
PARIS
Reims

One

November 11, 1968

Ottawa, Canada

Jürgen Stern had a clear view of the man from his breakfast table, and was fascinated. Possibly it was the red poppy on the gentleman's camel topcoat. It might have been because he looked to be close to Stern's own age of seventy. The man sat alone in the lobby of the Chateau Laurier Hotel, white hair under his fedora, a cane by his side, glancing repeatedly at his watch.

The flower wasn't unique on this eleventh day of November. The Canadians were even more patriotic than the Brits about the armistice of 1918. Remembrance Day poppies were on jackets and coats everywhere in the hotel and on the street this morning. It was the fiftieth anniversary of the signing.

"…and some more coffee, sir?" The waiter held a full pot at the ready.

"Please."

The act blocked his view of the lobby for mere seconds. When the cup was poured, the man in the lobby had left, probably to meet his appointment.

Stern was disappointed for some reason, and wasn't sure why. He continued to watch the vacated seat as he finished his coffee and signed his room number for the bill.

~ * ~

"Dad! Over here!" A black Volvo sedan was double-parked just past the taxi stand. A stylishly dressed woman in her forties waved from the open driver's door. "Where are your bags?"

"Just there, Melanie." The man in the fedora motioned to a bellman's cart.

Brian MacLennan loved his hard-charging lawyer daughter, but she could sometimes be a pain in the ass, and he knew he'd get a scolding for not being there waiting as she pulled up. It would be a long week, he thought, with her acting as the family matriarch at his son's wedding.

The bags were loaded and they were soon headed north out of the city. At once, Melanie was into relating the myriad of obstacles in the way of planning a rehearsal dinner at the bride's family summer home on Lac Saint Pierre, where it stood an hour north of the city, and from anywhere else. "What the hell were they thinking, having a November wedding at a summer cottage?"

"It's more of an estate than a cottage, I hear," Brian said. "Besides, you have four days to get it right."

Melanie had found a job in the government for her younger brother two years earlier. In the meantime he had met, and fallen in love with the daughter of a politically prominent Quebec family.

Brian let her go on while his mind drifted. He'd stayed overnight at the Laurier after flying up from Toronto to meet his daughter. She had suggested the sketches he made while serving with the Canadian Expeditionary Force in the First War as a wedding gift for his son. Colin had always loved looking at them.

Actually, it was a fine idea. They would mean a lot to Colin, so that was good. It had been years since Brian had looked at the drawings, and last night he'd stayed up late in the hotel room arranging them by date. Now, he wished he'd placed them in an album, or something more suitable as a gift than the battered old portfolio where he'd always kept them.

~ * ~

They'd been on the road for almost an hour before Melanie mentioned the drawings. "You did bring them, didn't you?"

"Of course." He glanced at the rear seat where his top coat and cane lay. *Not there. In the trunk with his bags?* He began to worry. Melanie in her own annoying way had begun chiding him about not paying attention to details since his wife's passing three years ago. He'd be damned if he was going to say anything about the drawings until he was sure. She'd insist on stopping to check the trunk. And then what if they weren't there? She'd make a fuss and be all over him for his carelessness. *If they're not in the trunk, the hotel will have them.*

~ * ~

"Doctor Stern." The man at the desk remembered his name from checking him in the previous day.

"Ah…yes," Stern smiled at the recognition. He placed a brown, time-worn portfolio on the counter. "It seems this was left in the lobby by a gentleman, but I don't see him. Perhaps if you keep it, he will return for it."

"There's no identification?"

"Not on the outside."

The deskman hunched his shoulders. "Well, then…"

Stern hesitated, but undid the string closure. Sure enough, inside the flap was an adhesive label bearing the address of a Toronto Company: *MacLennan, Esposito, and Assoc.*

"Let me check," the clerk said. "Yes. A Mr. Brian MacLennan checked out this morning. Would you like us to keep this?"

Stern hesitated, then declined; possibly due to the way he'd felt intrigued by the man—drawn to him. "I may have time to try contacting Mr. MacLennan after all."

Actually, he didn't. A week ago he'd received a call in his Bonn apartment from German Chancellor Kiesinger himself, requesting Stern to fly to Ottawa, and use his personal friendship with Canada's new Prime Minister, Pierre Trudeau, to pave the way for next January's trade talks between the two countries. He was due at Trudeau's chambers in an hour. The forgotten parcel would have to wait.

~ * ~

The fall colors had left the maples, and the leaves were falling in earnest. The Volvo entered the long driveway. Melanie tapped the Volvo's horn, and they came to a stop on the circular drive. A touch football game of half a dozen men and young boys was in progress on the lawn. Brian stepped out of the car, feeling his stiff leg complain from the trip. He took a moment to stretch it out while Melanie popped the trunk.

The drawings. He walked around to look inside the trunk. *Not there. Damn!*

"Dad!" Colin MacLennan strode away from the game, flashing his patented smile. He gave his sister a brotherly embrace and shook his father's hand. "Let me have your bags. I'll show you your room."

They chatted on the way; mostly Colin asking about the older man's health, and the trip up from Toronto.

Brian watched his athletic son effortlessly scale the stairs with a bag in each hand. He followed, feeling his own stiffness, convincing himself it was the damn knee, and not his seventy-two years that made him so goddam tired.

They arrived at a guest room overlooking the rear of the house and the lake.

"Quite fancy," he said. "Hardly a cottage."

"No," Colin said, and left it there.

Brian appraised his son for a few seconds, amazed how he reminded him of his brother Owen as a young man. "Your mother and I weren't sure you'd ever find the right girl."

"Thirty-six isn't that old. You were that age when I was born."

"Point taken. I'm looking forward to meeting Pamela's family." They stood there in awkward silence. "Well…look, I need to make a call." Brian pointed to an ornate-looking telephone. "Does that thing work?"

"Sure. Why don't you unpack and get comfortable? There are drinks on the rear patio in an hour…casual. You can meet the clan." Colin closed the door as he left.

Brian retrieved the hotel check-out receipt from his jacket and dialed the toll-free number.

"Front desk, please." He waited, wondering why it should take so long.

"Desk. This is Warren. How may I be of assistance?"

Brian explained having left a brown portfolio in the lobby at 7:30 this morning.

"I wasn't on duty until eight, sir, but let me check."

More waiting.

"I have nothing turned in, sir. Perhaps someone from the earlier shift will remember something. We have your address on file if we learn anything."

Brian replaced the phone, imagining how unlikely that would be. His first concern was not having the drawings to give to Colin and the flack he'd take from Melanie. The sketches had no monetary value, he was sure. But now that they were lost, he realized how precious they were to him.

~ * ~

Stern was exhausted. The meeting had turned out to be much more than two old friends talking. Trudeau had his Trade Minister and two deputies in tow. They had been tipped off about Opel's interest in building a plant in Canada. Canada had grain and energy to sell, but wasn't sure if West Germany had the buying power or markets to compensate for the dollars that would be flowing back into Europe from the new plant. They had held his feet to the fire all afternoon.

Besides that, he was still fatigued by the trip from Bonn. He'd arrived in Montreal expecting a limo for the drive to Ottawa, but through a fluke, the car didn't show. Instead he caught the train, expecting to arrive at Union Station, a short walk to the hotel's lobby. But the city had decommissioned the building and erected a new Tremblay Road Station an annoying cab ride away.

Following the meeting, it was past 4 PM when he arrived in his room with the prospect of another session in the morning. *Scheisse!* He was too old for this! He'd tried to retire two years ago when Ludwig Erhard left office, but Kiesinger prevailed on him to stay on until he could find a suitable replacement in the Trade Commission.

The portfolio on his room desk reminded him he'd expected to trace the address of the owner this afternoon, but Trudeau's protracted meeting scotched that. Possibly there was more inside that would be a hint to the owner's destination this morning. Once more he unwound the string fastening.

Inside were drawings, *dozens* of them. Some were in ink, but most were pencil sketches, all spectacular in their realism and detail. One or two of them had been colorized. There were interiors, portraits, landscapes, and building exteriors. Many of the sketches were on standard, stiff writing paper, but also on small card stock, half as big.

The next thing Stern noticed were the dated initials *BDM* and title of each drawing in neat script. The drawings were in chronological order, ranging from June 1915 to October three years later. The first few were portraits. One of a man and a woman titled *Jocelyn Farm 6/1915*; he, with an axe at a chopping block. She was clutching something in her apron...*hen's eggs?* They faced each other, rather than the artist. A portion of a wooden farmhouse lurked in the background. Another sketch of a stocky young man, *Owen 4/1915;* another portrait of a young dark-complexioned boy in army uniform titled, *H. Gardinier 3/1916.* There was an April 1916 drawing of a building with the title, *Gouin St. Arena.* Here was a portrait of another boy in uniform, his light colored hair showing under his cap. Stern was drawn to the face. The signature read: *George K 5/1916.* Like the one of the Arena, and a number of others, it was done on good quality writing paper that carried an embossed *CRC* over a block-shaped cross. *Canadian Red Cross?*

Next in the chronology was a panoramic view of a field dotted with hundreds of tents. It was from a perspective of height, allowing detail of the nearest objects and the vastness of the expanse at the same time. It was brilliant. This one was dated 7/1916, entitled *Niagara Camp.*

He was impressed with the quality of the work. The portraits gave more than a sense of what the subject looked like; they seemed to look inside the person. He seemed to capture the subject's character, his worth as a human being. The landscapes and buildings were realistic to be sure, but they also told a story: a filthy doll left on the stoop of a gutted house, the pall of war haze over what once must have been a tranquil field. Then there were the depictions of the dead, so gruesome in their realism, yet no hint of voyeurism. These were poignant memorials to wasted youth.

There was no doubt. The drawings were a soldier's memoir of the Great War. They struck a chord that resonated with his own experiences of the time. He continued to peruse the collection until he came upon one that seemed somehow familiar. He reached to remove it from the others when it flipped over, revealing its opposite side. What he saw caused him to audibly gasp.

~ * ~

"Good Day, *Bonjour,* MacLennan, Esposito."

Stern was about to state his business when the recording continued, "If you know your party's extension, press one. Otherwise press 'O.' *Si vous connaissez l'extension de votre partie , appuyez sur l'une. Sinon, appuyez...*"

He punched the zero.

"Good afternoon, MacLennan, Esposito. How may I direct your call?"

"Is Mr. MacLennan available, or perhaps one of his associates?"

"Mr. MacLennan has retired, sir. Can someone else be of assistance?"

Stern hesitated. The easiest thing to do was simply send the portfolio back to his company. The people there would know how to return it.

"How may I contact Mr. MacLennan?"

"I'm sorry, we can't give out personal information. Perhaps if you'll tell me—"

"Yes! I am Doctor Jürgen Stern. I will be in Canada only through tomorrow." He gave the woman his room number at the Chateau Laurier, asking her to have MacLennan contact him, and why. He disconnected and set the receiver down on the table next to the bed where the portfolio and several of the drawings were spread out. Once more he studied what he had seen, shaking his head in wonder.

Two

February 19, 1916
Jocelyn Farm

Talk at dinner was sparse. Long periods of silence were offset only by the clink of spoon against bowl or the heated house creaking in its battle against the harsh cold of the night. Brian's father set the mood, concentrating on his boiled lamb and canned potatoes, his mouth set in a grim line as he chewed; eyes downcast. The suspended kerosene lamp added to the effect in light and shadow on his face.

Brian toyed with his fork. Owen, oblivious of the tension, dug in to his food. He was four years younger than Brian—huskier and half a head taller than his brother's wiry frame.

"Any more greens, Ma?" Owen said.

Dora MacLennan rose and fetched the pot she'd pushed to the back of the woodstove. She doled out a spoon-full of spinach preserved from the previous summer's garden.

"I'm going to turn in then," Brian declared, pushing his plate away. He glanced at his father for approval. "It'll be early away tomorrow."

Thomas MacLennan said nothing. It had all been said—how he needed Brian, the oldest and cleverest, to take over the farm one day. He'd doubted Owen's ability at the task. There was no need for Brian to be a part of this war with Germany.

Brian felt he knew his brother better than his father did. Owen was seventeen, after all, a hard worker and strong as a bull.

"Success is hard work and inspiration," his father had said. Owen had both qualities. Brian lacked the inspiration for farming.

"Your books and sketches are all that inspire you," Thomas had said, and Brian agreed.

"That's right, Dad, and that's the problem."

The argument had been going on since the first contingent of men from the area volunteered for the CEF eighteen months ago in the summer of 1914. Brian had wanted to join then, but the volunteers were already trained and organized as the 51st Rifle infantry. Now, a second contingent was being raised in Sault Ste. Marie. Brian had registered at the post office, gotten his medical exam and was declared fit for duty. He was to report tomorrow in the "Soo."

Up in the room he and Owen shared, he was putting the last of his things together by candle light. A quiet rap at the door made him turn.

"Ma," he acknowledged.

"So it's final, then," she said.

"Yeah, ma. If it wasn't the war, I'd be off anyway."

She surveyed the small room the boys shared, covered with Brian's drawings. "You'll miss these."

He laughed. "I'm takin' my pencils. I can make more."

She picked up the few he seemed to be taking with him. "Good likeness of us all. I can see the affection for your father in this one."

"No more than for you, Ma." He put his arms around her frame so like his own, tightly wound and spare.

Dora MacLennan kissed her son He watched her quickly leave the room before allowing herself to weep.

~ * ~

The day promised to be sunny despite the bitter cold. Owen had hitched the mare to the sleigh for the trip to the north of the island and on to the mainland. Brian's mother and sister had said their tearful goodbyes; his father had not been present at the breakfast table. He stepped out onto the front porch, responding to the shock of the cold, and headed for the sleigh.

"Brian." His father's voice sounded paper thin in the desiccated air. The roughhewn figure of the man trudged its way through the snow from the barn.

Brian tossed his bag up to Owen and turned.

Thomas MacLennan removed a glove and reached into his coat pocket. "This here is all I've got of my father. I want you to take this with you and bring it back to me when you come home."

Brian knew about the knife. He knew it had been in the family forever. They said it was from Scotland. As a boy, Brian would find it and lovingly open its single blade from the knurled handle, then carefully replace it in the box on his father's chest of drawers.

"I…Dad…"

"Just take it."

He threw his arms around his father, surprising the other who was not easy with such signs of affection. The sense of the man's like response caused icy tears to form on Brian's cheek.

~ * ~

Owen kept a firm grip on the reins driving the sleigh down the steep hill to St. Joseph Island's village of Richards Landing. Brian's orders were to report to the 119th Algoma Overseas Infantry Battalion at the Soo Ice Arena Monday, February 21, 1916.

In the end, parting with his father had gone better than expected. Thomas' tough shell had softened somewhat, and Brian suspected his father felt a sense of pride in his son's fortitude.

The sun was up, and it was close to 9:00AM by the time they arrived at Richards Landing. Any other time of year, the *SS Premier* that plied the channel between Bruce Mines and The Soo three times a week, would have been the choice of transportation. But the cold December and January had halted her passage until the spring thaw. Today, Owen would drive the sleigh over the ice, and on to the new Canadian Pacific RR flag stop at Tarbut Crossing.

Once in town, they both knew there was one more good-bye. Owen stopped the sleigh a few doors down from John Richards' store and post office. When Brian hesitated, Owen practically shoved his older brother off onto a snowbank. Brian trudged to the door of the neat frame house which was opened before he could knock.

"Get in here, Brian MacLennan, before I catch a death of cold!" a cheery middle-aged woman admonished. She shut the door behind him as he stamped the snow from his boots. "Sarah's just…well, fixing her hair. She saw your sleigh from the window."

"Thank you, Mrs. White," he mumbled, embarrassed but pleased at her suggesting his visit might be special to Sarah.

She retreated into the house. It was a few minutes before he heard "Hello, Brian," in a soft but confident voice.

Brian had only recently built enough nerve to approach Sarah White. To him, she was the essence of elegance. Every boy in the township vied for her attention. She was younger than he by two years, and at nineteen, it was a miracle she was still unattached.

He had displayed some of his drawings at a crafts fair at the town hall last autumn, and she had been there. She'd admired his ability, and they talked about his wanting to go to school somewhere instead of farming. It soon became clear this girl was not only beautiful, she was knowledgeable in literature and art. He was smitten. He sketched her from memory and presented it to her one afternoon, fearing she'd be offended, but she wasn't.

"I heard at the post office about your signing up," she said.

"Yeah. I…can't stay. I'm meeting the train." He couldn't think. *He wanted to hold her.*

"I'll miss our talks," she said.

"Oh! I mean, yes?"

She smiled, and pulled something from the folds of her frock, handing it to him.

Brian stared, unbelieving, at the photograph mounted on stiff pasteboard. It was professionally taken, capturing the every detail of what made her so special. He stood there, speechless.

"Perhaps you'll think of me from time to time," she said.

"Sarah!" he stared at the picture, then at her. "I will," he croaked, and carefully slipped the photo into his breast pocket. "Well, then…" He motioned to the door and the waiting sleigh.

She reached to place a palm on his cheek.

"Be safe, Brian," were her last words.

~ * ~

A tree line—small firs crammed into holes drilled in the ice—marked the way across the frozen St. Joseph Channel to the mainland. It was a precaution. On windy days, blowing snow could obliterate the horizon, disorienting a traveler. It was a well-known occurrence to get disoriented and even lost, crossing the ice in a "white out." Today was crystal clear, but biting cold. The snow under the mare's hoofs squeaked against the ice.

Once across, it was less than a half hour's ride to Tarbut Crossing where three or four others waited, huddled under hoods and mufflers and stamping the cold from their feet. Owen jumped down from the sleigh to join Brian at the crossing. Each fumbled with words to say while they waited. Before long, the white smoke of a train could be seen far to the east.

"Take care, Brian. I know Dad would prefer it was me going and you on the farm."

"You know I'll never be a good farmer," Brian said. "He doesn't know it yet, but the farm's future is better off in your hands."

Soon, the engine was visible, blowing steam high and to either side in the cold air like a bellowing demon. Men were shaking hands and slapping shoulders. Brian and Owen awkwardly followed suit. The engine grudgingly groaned to a steamy halt, the vapor enveloping the waiting passengers.

And then, Brian was on the train with his single bag, waving at his brother from the vestibule, still aware of the photograph in his pocket as if it were on fire.

Three

Sault Ste. Marie, Ontario
Gouin St. Arena

Several in the coach were men his own age or younger. Older passengers looked on, bemused, as the post-pubescent boys jammed the aisles in mild horseplay, and going on about what they would do to “Fritz, or Heinie” when they had a chance. They were boys from all along the north shore of Lake Huron; towns like Espanola, Massey, Blind River, and Thessalon. Among the throng was a familiar figure.

His slicked-back hair, good looks and stylish coat set him apart from the crowd: Colby Wentworth. He was rich, or as rich as anyone was in these parts. He lived in Bruce Mines, but was a regular visitor to Richards Landing where his father’s lumber business had an office. He could be counted on to appear at most any event, talking it up with the girls. Brian resented him here.

He’d seen Wentworth talking and laughing with Sarah the last time he was in town. The experience rankled and continued until receiving the photograph from her very hands assuaged those feelings. Still, Wentworth’s mere presence took the edge off the excitement he’d felt.

“That you, MacLennan?”

A hand slapped his shoulder.

Brian recognized the husky, handsome boy, his lank brown hair long enough to cover the ears. Brian didn't know him well. The Kobak farm was isolated, and the family, though friendly enough, was a bit of a mystery to the other islanders. "Oh…Kobak, right? My brother helped on your haying last summer."

"Owen. Right. I somehow got food poisoning, and my father was frantic. Your dad wouldn't accept payment."

"There'll come a time when we get in a bind ourselves," Brian said. He noted Kobak's scarred leather valise. "Joining up?"

"Yeah, you?"

The ride in from the flag stop to Sault Ste. Marie took no more than forty minutes. They spent the time talking about their families, and respective farms. George Kobak had not attended school with boys his age, being home schooled by his mother. "It was just too far to go every day. My mother was a teacher in Austria."

Brian was glad to see George. The boy was a likeable chap with many of the same values for work and commitment that Brian admired. Brian had a vague idea where Austria was, but that was all. He learned the Kobaks had come to Canada in 1908 because of his father's disenchantment with the Austrian king, Franz Joseph I.

The train slowed. They could see olive uniformed men on the platform, their legs swaddled in cloth wrappings.

There were twenty-eight recruits on the train; some younger looking than Harry, but even a few in their thirties. A soldier with two stripes on his sleeve ordered them into columns, and marched them through the streets to the new ice rink on the dead-end that jutted off East Street.

Brian hadn't been to Sault Ste. Marie since the 1910 fire that gutted the building. It was much larger than he remembered. He craned his neck to see the peak of its triangular roof line. The effect was even more dramatic inside. There, desks were set up where they were told to wait in line, and sign in.

In the center of the arena, instructors were drilling recruits. Some were marching; others were practicing the manual of arms with dummy rifles made of pine. Brian could see young men in new—some ill-fitting—uniforms at the far end of the building where sleeping quarters had been constructed. Along one wall, new inductees were receiving blankets, shoes, boots, belts, and other gear to be stuffed in a duffle.

In line was a very familiar figure.

"Harry!" The boy, Harold Gardenier, had thick, black hair pulled back in a tie.

"You? For the CEF?" the boy said. "I heard your old man…"

"Well, I'm here," Brian cut him off.

"Your mother know about this?" Brian stared Harry in the eye.

"Sure!" He didn't blink, but Brian had doubts. Harry's mother fretted over the safety of two other boys serving in France, and grieved at her loss of them. Would she let her youngest go if she could help it?

Brian and Owen were as close to Harry as anyone. He would spend the summers on the Island working—mostly on the MacLennan farm. He was Métis—Native Canadian with some French ancestry—living near the Garden River with his large family. Harold Gardenier was the youngest of five brothers, the others having all volunteered with the 51st "Soo" Rifles in 1914. Tragically, two of the four had been reported missing and assumed dead in the battle of the Marne and at Ypres.

He introduced George Kobak.

"Where are our guns?" Harry asked.

"I think you'll have one soon enough," Brian answered.

They were issued their gear and assigned space in the barracks section. Thin mattresses were rolled upon hastily constructed bunks. Brian and Harry found two together.

"Hey, if it isn't the farm boy from St. Joe!"

Brian looked across the aisle to see the smirking face of Colby Wentworth. He nodded in reply, but resumed his conversation with Harry.

The bunks were sectioned off, twenty to a group. Animated talk in the bay suddenly stopped. He turned to see a slightly built, bandy-legged man in uniform, two stripes on his sleeve, standing in the entrance. He held a clip board between the crook of his arm and hip. His face had the look of someone who had seen it all.

"I want everyone out front in two ranks. Make it snappy!"

The men began to stir, finishing whatever task they'd been up to.

"Now!" he bellowed, in a voice that belied his bantam-like stature. That got men pushing against each other to get out of the bay and onto the drill area.

~ * ~

Light was dowsed at 10 PM except for the minimal glow from the new electric lamps in the arena's center. Brian was exhausted. After the roll call they learned they'd been designated 2nd Platoon of Company C, 119th Overseas Infantry Battalion. The corporal never told them his name, but proceeded to march them up and down the arena until the evening meal, and then for another two hours after. It had been seventeen hours since Brian had risen from his St. Joseph Island bed. It seemed like a week.

They'd discovered their corporal's name was Shanks, and had learned to fear him. Mistakes in their drills were met with draconian punishment—duck-walking among the worst. They learned their platoon officer had not yet been assigned, but the commanding officer of the 119th was a Lieutenant Colonel Rowland whom none of them had yet seen.

~ * ~

April, 1916

Two weeks of miserable rain at temperatures just above freezing preceded the bright Sunday that found Brian seated on a curb halfway down Gouin Street. The men had the day to themselves in anticipation of shipping out for more training.

Harry was off in town with his mother and a sister. Brian had decided to take advantage of the good weather by making a sketch of the arena on stationery supplied by the good ladies of the local Red Cross. It was good quality paper. The pencil took to it nicely.

"Well, well, MacLennan! What have we here?" Colby Wentworth and another man. He looked dashing in his uniform that somehow appeared tailored while Brian's felt too small in the jacket, and baggy in the seat. Wentworth's puttees were perfectly wrapped around his calf. Brian never quite got that process exactly right.

Wentworth's question was harmless enough, but said in such a condescending way, it rankled. Brian tried, but was at a loss for a tart rejoinder. He opted to say nothing.

The other man was one Brian had seen Wentworth talking with that day on the train, but was assigned to a different platoon. He was taller than Brian's brother Owen, and bigger. He had the face of a street tough. "You gonna kill the Hun with pictures?" the man grinned at his own wit, showing large, uneven teeth.

It was a stupid remark. Brian directed his comment to Wentworth. "Who is your ignorant friend, Colby?"

Wentworth laughed. "Whoa! Strong words from the farm lad."

The other man took a step forward, silent and menacing. Brian could smell his unwashed maleness. He wasn't intimidated, just annoyed. These two were spoiling the little free time he had on this perfect day. He wasn't a fighter, but growing up among a raft of farm kids, many much brawnier than his wiry one hundred-fifty pounds, he thought he might to be able to, at least fend off this thug.

"Just go away," he said, and watched Wentworth give the other a barely perceptible shake of the head.

"Let's go, Rupke. MacLennan's going to win back the Somme with his art."

The big man didn't move. He stared back at Brian with small dead eyes. Brian was put off by the ugly countenance, but was determined not to blink first, and concentrated on the bridge of the man's flat nose.

In the end, Wentworth succeeded in pulling the man named Rupke away.

~ * ~

May 1916
Niagara Camp

Harry Gardinier lovingly ran his hands over the stock and breech of the newly issued Ross Mk III rifle. Brian watched, amused, as Harry caressed the weapon. Like most north woods farm boys, Brian and George Kobak were well acquainted with a hunting rifle, and were decent shots.

Harry's family was dirt poor. The five boys did their best to work at odd jobs supplementing what their mother could make sewing for other families in Sault Ste. Marie. There was no money for firearms in the Gardinier home. Occasionally Brian would let Harry fire the MacLennans' weapon, but there was little time for entertainment when Harry was working there.

They had been at Niagara Camp for a month. The 119th was not alone. The camp teemed with replacement battalions from all over Ontario. There had been a shortage of weapons for the men, and the 119th had been training with dummy rifles. Today had been their first day on the firing range. It turned out Harry was a natural sharp-shooter. Already his rifle was cleaned and oiled. Brian was still struggling with the assembly of the complicated bolt and slide of the Mark III.

It was only their first day with weapons and men were complaining about them jamming. The problem was the .303 caliber ammunition manufactured in England for the Lee-Enfield rifle which was much more tolerant of variations in the size of the cartridge or the slightest bit of dirt. Brian's Ross had jammed today, however he thought it was a dream to fire when it was working properly. He would have to take better care in keeping it clean.

Brian, George and Harry had stuck together and the three friends had been assigned to a rifle squad, or *section* as referred to in the Canadian and British armies. To Brian's relief, Colby Wentworth drew duty in a machine gun squad along with his friend Rupke. Their training was separate for most of the day, except for time in the platoon drilling and marching. The two could be seen together in free moments. Brian discovered Rupke, like Wentworth, was from Bruce Mines, Ontario. Apparently Wentworth knew him through his father who employed the man in some way. Brian thought him despicable in manner, speech, and appearance.

The last month had been spent on physical training, trench construction, tunneling, and long marches from their camp at Niagara-on-the-Lake to any of the several sites within a ten mile radius. There was talk about a march all the way to Hamilton, a distance of almost fifty miles.

Brian finished cleaning his rifle and laid back on his cot, waiting for the mess call. Despite the frantic activity of the past month, he had not forgotten the photograph of Sarah White carefully secured in his pack. Her image was in mind constantly, and with it, the memory of Colby Wentworth's own seemingly convivial relationship with her.

He'd written Sarah, but there had been only one mail call since arriving at Niagara, one letter from his mother, but nothing from Sarah. He went over the scene in her house on the day he left the Island. *Had he misread her feelings? Was she only being kind?*

The tent was empty and offered a rare opportunity to steal a glance at Sarah's image. He slipped the picture from its place in his pack. Her face reassuringly gazed back at his. The bright, intelligent eyes of Sarah White assured him of her love. He lost himself in them for several moments.

"Who in hell do you think you are, MacLennan?"

Brian didn't have to look to know the voice of Wentworth. He dashed the photo back in its place.

"Where did you get that?" Wentworth's small white teeth were exposed in a grimace when Brian looked up. His face was flushed.

Brian didn't answer.

Immediately, Wentworth's face relaxed and the omnipresent smirk returned to his lips. "I suppose you think that's special."

"I don't know what you're talking about."

"Everyone in Algoma has that picture. Hell, *I* have one."

"You're a liar!

"And you're a sap!" He sneered with the remark as he pulled tent flap down and left.

~ * ~

It was after dark, and Brian was returning from the latrine, his mind on Wentworth's words. At first Brian dismissed the remarks as utterly false, but the lack of an answer to his letters to Sarah widened the fissure of doubt he fostered.

The punch to his stomach came from nowhere as he exited the latrine. He dropped to the ground, knees pulled up in pain while he fought for breath. A hard kick caught him in the kidneys. Brian never saw his assailant, but the same sour odor of Rupke was unmistakable.

~ * ~

Brian's eyes popped open at the first long notes of reveille. The attack of the previous night was forgotten until his first attempt to move. The pain was paralyzing. When the first blow to his solar plexus came, it knocked the breath from him so completely he was unable to draw another, and nearly lost consciousness. As a result he didn't feel the full effect of the kick to his rib cage. Somehow he stumbled into his tent and bed.

George was already pulling on his breeches. Harry was lacing his boots. "Better get a move on, Brian."

Trying to rise, the sharp pang caused Brian to cry out involuntarily. "Give me a hand."

"Whoa, chum! What's this, then?" Harry took Brian's arm and pulled his legs over onto the floor.

"Went for a pee last night. Someone must have seen me go, and waited for me to leave the latrine. I caught it good."

"Who? What reason?"

"I can only guess. Hand me my pants, will you?"

His two friends finished dressing, and discovered they'd have to do the same for Brian if he was going to make the morning formation.

The usual routine after morning roll call was a half hour of "policing" the grounds around the platoon before morning mess. This entailed ridding the area of the most minute weed, cigarette butt, toothpick, or anything else not put there by the Canadian Army. Corporal Shanks would typically follow his men around with invectives like "Make a clean sweep, you donkeys" or "I want to see nothing but ass holes and boot soles! Bend over and pick that shit up!"

Bending was impossible for Brian, and Shanks called him out. "You think everyone else is going to do this for you, MacLennan?" Shanks faced him nose to nose.

"I…got hurt, Corporal."

Harry came to Brian's defense. "It's true. Some bloke decked him last night, Corp'l."

Shanks gave Harry a dismissive glare, and said to Brian, "What did I tell you bozos about making trouble? You a trouble maker, MacLennan?"

"No, Corporal."

The bugle call for mess sounded. "I hear about you fighting again, I'll have your whole aching body in a sling. Move out!" Shanks abruptly turned and headed for the NCO mess.

"What happened last night?" George said on the way to the mess tent.

"I told you, I don't know."

"Yeah, but you have an idea. You have an idea, and so do I."

"You may be right," Brian said.

~ * ~

August 8, 1916
Halifax, Nova Scotia

The city of Halifax was alive in a sea of olive green uniforms. It had not been twenty-four hours since their Niagara Camp graduation ceremony and parade that they were loaded onto troop trains headed for the port city of Nova Scotia. They arrived early the next morning after the overnight trip. Upon detraining, recruits from Niagara Camp and elsewhere in Canada were directed to open shelters where the morning meal was served in their field mess kits, and where latrines were constructed nearby. The place was alive in a snarl of piers, cranes, ship's masts, and above all, humanity.

Remarkably, the troops were given free range of the city, and told to be back by noon mess. Brian, George, Harry and an older recruit from Sudbury, Ake Lankinen *(call me Lank),* wandered to the waterfront. The tops of the cranes they'd spied from the train station soared high overhead. The smell of rotting fish in the salt air warmth of the August morning was entirely foreign to the men. They walked north past a bridge to a large basin where ships lay at anchor so tightly spaced it was a wonder they could maneuver.

Near the wharf was a large building with the name OLAND BREWERIES Ltd. along one wall.

Lankinen remarked, "Hey! That's the *Moosehead* factory."

Brian had never tasted beer. His father was against alcohol in the house. Cider and beer were available at social events on St. Joseph Island, but there were few places to purchase beer other than in Marksville, where it was brought in from Thessalon, Bruce Mines or Sudbury.

Oak barrels were being loaded onto a motorized truck. "See if you can take one of those with you to France," Harry said, but the joke fell flat. They wandered back to the assembly area for the midday meal.

By late afternoon, they were marched to the quay where two ships lay alongside. They were directed to one bearing the name on the stern, *SS Matagama.* Brian had never seen any manmade thing so huge. It looked new compared to the other transports. Its twin stacks were painted gold, and tipped in black. Its black hull was sleek and free of the rust streaks of the other vessels in the harbor. Someone told him it was five hundred feet long, having been piloted down from its anchorage in the Basin the three men had viewed this morning.

They were lined up and marched up the gangway onto the deck. There, across the channel, Brian could easily see the nearby shore of the neighboring town of Dartmouth. *Such a narrow passage for these large ships!* For a farm boy from central Canada, it was fascinating.

His enthusiasm soon waned. Once aboard, the troops were crammed into bays and staterooms designed for peacetime passage, and converted for carrying troops in the most Spartan way. He and George managed berths together where they were stacked six high. George's was no more than a few inches above Brian's nose as he lay on his back. Turning over was problematic.

Shortly before leaving Niagara, a letter from Sarah had arrived. It was in response only to his first of three written to her. Her words were cordial, even warm, but noncommittal. It had been dated mid-June. The two he'd written since had confessed his feeling for her, and whether he might have expectations upon his return from service. He resigned himself to not knowing her feelings for a long time.

That night he lay in the berth listening to George breathe, still not knowing if the girl in the photograph was the love of his life, or simply a thoughtful girl who had been kind to a departing friend.

~ * ~

On their first morning at sea, Brian woke to find the relatively cool air from the ventilators had become warm and muggy. After a Spartan breakfast, the men were allowed on deck to find conditions just as humid.

"It's the Gulf Stream," Lankinen said. "Pushes warm water up here from Mexico."

Harry asked how he knew such things.

"We got schools in Sudbury, Shit for Brains."

"We *have* schools in the Soo, as well, smart ass," Harry came back.

Brian wasn't sure if Lank caught the grammar lesson, but stepped in with a change of subject. "I haven't seen Wentworth or his goon, Rupke."

Henry said, "You think it was Rupke jumped you that night at Niagara Camp, don't you?"

"Maybe. Forget it."

They strolled aft where the ship's props were laying down a trail of white froth back to Canada. The image was at once beautiful and unnerving. Who knew when, if ever, they would see home again?

Four

August 13, 1916
Neuhaus, Lower Saxony, Germany.

Jürgen Stern was riding high. It began with his matriculation into the adult competition at the regional *Schützenfest* near his home town, some one hundred kilometers northwest of Hamburg. Granted, the local shooting festival was not as grand as the ones in Bremen or Hanover, but for that summer he was king—literally. The *Shützenfestkonig* was crowned for the marksmanship competitions at the four day annual event.

He'd turned eighteen in July. Since his seventeenth birthday, he had been conscripted into the German Army Reserve, the *Landsturm,* and had already been given notice to report. But for this perfect Sunday culminating the festival, he was the toast of Neuhaus. The parade had commenced at the shooting grounds and proceeded the four kilometers into the town center with Jürgen leading the procession. Jürgen had no illusions about the honor. He knew the cream of the male population was away fighting in the fields of Turkey, Russia and France. Still, there was no diminishing the fact that he had competed with the adult group for the first time, and won!

They marched down Bahnhofstrasse, and people waved from their front doors and along the street. It was glorious weather. The warm breeze ruffled his straight, blond hair as it did the banners proclaiming his majestic status. Then the unimaginable happened. From a group of young girls, one of them ran to him, taking his arm. *Käthe*!

"Jürgen !" she giggled. "May I walk with the king?"

He beamed, thrilled by the attention from the popular and beautiful girl. "Of course! I am king, and order you to do so."

The onlookers applauded the attractive couple. Someone shouted "die Königin!"

Käthe exulted in her new title of *Queen,* and cheers went up from the others in the procession as they continued to the village square.

Käthe Von Helm came from a family that, centuries ago, owned all the land in the region along the Oste River, a tributary of the Elbe. Somehow other baronies had usurped the Von Helm power, leaving the family with their own estate, but little else than their name. Still, the Von Helms were socially important, and much better off than most of their neighbors.

She had always been popular, but had preferred the attention of boys older than Jürgen . He couldn't believe his good fortune. This girl with her long flaxen hair, skin like silk, had been unapproachable. Yet here she was.

When they reached the *Stadtplatz*, Jürgen was led to a dais where he was to be crowned. On a whim, he pulled Käthe with him. The others loved it, and cheered still more. When the coronation was completed, another remarkable thing happened. Before he could react, warm lips were pressed against his. Käthe! The crowd went wild.

~ * ~

They were together every day for the rest of the month. He would take her sailing in his gaff-rigged dingy he kept on the Oste River. They would go for long walks. It was wonderful. Ultimately the walks led to more.

They were alone having followed a trail along the Oste. Käthe wanted to rest and Jürgen suggested the shade of a large tree overhanging the water.

"No! Back here is cooler," she said. She led him away from the water to a copse of trees and knee-high grass. She lay down on the sweet grass, and lifted her hand to his. Jürgen came to her. Tender kisses, at first, then he began to explore with his hands, feeling the softness under her blouse. He was on fire, and Käthe didn't seem to resist, but he swore to himself he would not take liberties with this beautiful girl.

Her hand found his and moved it against her breast. Then slowly she guided it down to her thigh. He felt her warmth under the thin summer fabric which she pulled out of the way. The effect was electrifying.

"Hhhhuh…"

"Slowly," she instructed.

As if detached, having a will of its own, his hand moved upward. She released a soft sigh, her hand still on his. Jürgen wasn't sure what to do next, but she made it abundantly clear.

"Oh," she breathed, and her breaths came faster.

"Käthe , I…"

Then she took command, and Jürgen's inexperience was no longer.

~ * ~

The final few days of August melted away. Jürgen 's orders were to report to the army's District Muster Office in Hamburg on Monday, the fifth of September. He spent the weekend saying goodbye to his widowed father and relatives.

His mother had died from consumption less than two years before. It tore a big hole in the family. With Jürgen and his two younger brothers, his father had tried his best to keep life normal, but it would never be what it was. Their maiden aunt Berta was kind, but only a mild facsimile of her sister. His mother had been a sturdy woman who, Jürgen thought, could never have succumbed to sickness. Her personality had dominated the household. She reared her boys with an iron fist in a velvet glove.

Her loss was a terrible blow to Jürgen's father who numbly went through the motions of his job as captain on the Oste River ferry at Geversdorf. Jürgen, being two years older than the capricious twins, had been bearing much of the responsibility for helping his frail aunt with chores, but there was nothing to be done about the conscription. All German youths had known it was inevitable, war or no war.

~ * ~

On Sunday evening, he bicycled to the big house where the Von Helms resided. Käthe was the youngest and only daughter of three children. Her two brothers were much older. Jürgen had seen her parents from time to time in town and in nearby Otterndorf, which was closer to the Von Helm estate. They were austere and insular people, and Jürgen was apprehensive using the polished brass knocker of the elaborate door.

It was opened by a maid in a black uniform and starched white apron and cap.

"Uh, Jürgen Stern to see Fraulein Käthe."

She instructed him to wait. Minutes later, the woman he recognized as Frau Von Helm appeared.

"*Guten Abend,* I am Jürgen Stern. I wonder if I might see Käthe," he croaked, cap secure in both hands.

The tall woman held a cigarette. She arched a penciled brow. Her closed lips formed a thin smile, distorting her thin face to one side. "You are the ferryman's son, are you not?"

The question annoyed Jürgen. He considered the woman in her dated, yet expensive, clothes and exaggerated *hochdeutsch* speech. "I am a soldier coming to say goodbye to your daughter, Frau Von Helm." At once he was shocked by his own impertinence.

She turned away without a comment, but left the door open.

Jürgen stepped inside the foyer, his footsteps echoing on the slate floor. The house had an institutional aroma, somewhat like a museum or possibly a courthouse. A large, pendulum clock clicked the seconds away. Presently, Käthe appeared. She wore a lavender summer dress. She looked irresistible.

"What is it?" she asked.

"Well, Käthe…I'm leaving tomorrow…for Hamburg; for the army."

"I know, Jürgen. You already told me." After an awkward beat she added, "I hope you'll be safe."

"I will, Käthe, I'll come home, and we….

"And what, Jürgen?" She glance at the room where her mother sat smoking, a magazine in hand.

"And then…you know, I'll…be…home."

She kissed him lightly. "I must go now, Jürgen." She half turned to leave the foyer. "Something else?"

He said, "I love you, Käthe," and left, feeling like a fool.

~ * ~

A celebration of sorts was planned for Jürgen's last night, but no one's heart was in it. Aunt Berta's cooking was never as good as his mother's and was further hampered by the rationing's lack of enough meat for the stew she'd made and no cream for the apple torte. Jen's father stared glassy-eyed at his son for most of the meal, and the twins were uncharacteristically mute.

The next morning, Hans Stern said goodbye to his son at the Neuhaus Bahnhof, held him in an embrace for much longer than Jürgen could ever recall, then rode away on his bicycle to the ferry without looking back.

Five

September, 1916
Huron Camp, Bramshott Common, England

They had arrived in Liverpool on August 19 having survived eleven days of stomach churning weather aboard the *SS Matagama.* Brian swore he would never again allow himself be subjected to such conditions. His friends claimed to having experienced no such maladies and jokingly suggested Brian find himself a nice life in Europe if he had no plans to return home on a ship.

The scene in Liverpool was like Halifax, only one hundred times more hectic. There were soldiers, drays, stevedores, horses, vendors, and civilians teeming on the waterfront. Impressive buildings, one with a clock tower, another with a huge dome, lined the street. *If this was England, what must London be like?*

As usual, the army was hurry up and wait. They were marched off the ship and double-timed to a holding area near the rail terminal on Lime Street. There they waited in a drizzling rain for almost two hours before a train could be put together for their departure to *who knew where?* Once loaded, word passed down along the cars that their destination was a camp in the south of England.

Bramshott Camp turned out to be located in an area called Hampshire, and Brian thought it was charming. Narrow lanes lined with hedges through shady overhanging trees defined the villages in the area. In many ways, Hampshire reminded him of home; the rolling hills, narrow lanes and unassuming villages. All that was missing were the maple trees that dominated his island.

The camp was, for an army training facility, quite acceptable. Instead of tents, the men were assigned to wooden huts. They were divided into five sub-camps named for the Great Lakes of North America. The 119th Battalion became part of the 5th Canadian Division, and commenced a level of intensive training they had previously not known.

~ * ~

The area defined as the Bramshott Camp was modified to, as much as possible, approach the conditions the allies were experiencing along the western front. They had been at the camp for three weeks, with two of them in the field, away from the relative comfort of their wooden huts at Huron Camp.

Colby Wentworth's animosity toward Brian was extended to his friends, especially George. Somehow Wentworth had previously known about George Kobak's Austrian background. He began badgering George whenever he could, especially in front of others. The mess line was a favorite. It was something different each time.

"You sound like a Heinie, Kobak! I hear you're from Austria. That's Germany, right?

"What are you doing in *this* army, Kobak?"

"Kobak: What kind of a name is that? Sounds foreign to me."

"You sure you aren't a spy, Kobak?"

And so on. It was a relentless assault, one that George was helpless to do anything about without making matters worse. Brian, Harry and Lank did their best to shout Wentworth down, but he'd just laugh, and stop until the next time.

Oddly, something good came from it. The battalion leaders became aware of George's German language abilities, and assigned him to work in Battalion HQ as a clerk. No one was sure what his duties were, but suspected it had something to do with intelligence. Fortunately for the four friends, Kobak remained billeted with the C Company of the 119th. Everybody was happy for him; everybody except Wentworth, of course, but also George himself, who complained that he hadn't joined up to be a scribe in the rear lines.

~ * ~

The problems they had faced with the Canadian-made Ross MKIII rifle were exacerbated at Bramshott. The field conditions and duration made cleaning more difficult, and here all of the ammunition was intended for the more forgiving British Lee-Enfield weapon.

It was while they were huddled in a newly dug trench, cleaning these same rifles that word was passed along they'd be heading back to camp in one hour. Brian was nursing a gash in his shin from a coil of barbed wire he'd tangled with.

"Not soon enough," Harry muttered, taking his breech slide apart for the second time. "We spent the whole day without ammo in this here trench, and it still jams."

There's a rumor we're getting American rifles to replace ours," Brian said.

"And where are the bloody Yanks, anyway?" Harry said.

"Their president ran for election on a promise to stay out of the war."

"Where did you hear that?"

Brian's answer was cut short by Corporal Shank's bark. "Alright you lazy bastards, up off your arses and form up."

It was a relief after ten days of mostly light rain, overcast skies, and mud. They'd sleep dry tonight.

~ * ~

The return to camp was a shock—at least to Brian. They had heard some stories from personnel passing through the camp about another major battle having been waged in July and August along the Somme

River in northern France. Now, scores of wounded were said to be cramming the five hundred available beds in Connaught Hospital located there.

Brian had his sketch pad out, finishing a drawing he'd made of the stables and blacksmith shop. His leg was stretched out on his bunk with the intention of exposing his wound to the air. Shanks entered the hut and noticed Brian's leg.

"That looks bad, MacLennan. What are you doing about it?"

"Trying to let it heal, Corporal."

"That's *Sergeant*, to you soldier. Now, get your arse down to the hospital and get that thing cleaned out. I'm not having you go home for some goddamn nick before you get on the line."

Brian noticed the new stripes on Shanks' sleeve. "Right, Corp…Sergeant. Now?"

"Not *tomorrow,* ya twit. Move!"

Brian rolled down his breeches and loosely re-wrapped his bloodied puttee. He stowed his sketch with the others and headed off to the hospital. It was a good walk to the A3 Trunk Road where the hospital was situated, and Brian wondered at the wisdom of reopening the gash.

He arrived as a motor lorry with a large red cross on its side was pulling away. Inside the hospital was, if not chaos, frenzied activity. Nurses in their white caps and stiff collars over immaculate dresses and sometimes stained, white aprons were scurrying from one improvised cot to another while they performed admission evaluations on the newly delivered wounded. What Brian witnessed was beyond disturbing. These were not just wounded men, they were, for the most part, severely maimed. Missing limbs, horrible burns, disfigured faces were everywhere.

"What are you doing here, soldier?" A nurse, perhaps in her sixties, confronted him.

"I…well…I have this…" He felt utterly stupid asking aid for his cut while these men were suffering. “"Uh, you're busy." He turned to go.

The nurse held up her hand. She pulled a *lorgnette* from a chain on her apron and peered at Brian's bloodied puttee. "Sit there." She directed him to a chair by the door.

"My sergeant made me—"

"Do as I say, young man, and show me your wound." She left, and came back with a porcelain enameled pan filled with water and some dressings.

"Your sergeant did the right thing. This wound is filthy."

True, the gash still had bits of Hampshire soil embedded. She washed it thoroughly, applied something that stung like hell and taped on clean gauze.

Brian motioned toward the hallway. "These men…will they—"

"The men you see there are the lucky ones. They will likely live. The others have been taken to surgery. Now get back to your company. I have work to do."

Brian proffered a "Yes ma'am," and retreated.

As he walked back to his hut, the sound of the bugler playing retreat gave him a chill, reinforcing the feeling he took away from that hospital hallway.

~ * ~

It soon became apparent the 119th Infantry was not going anywhere soon. The new CEF 5th Division was created as a replacement and home guard unit. The 119th was assigned to it as a Replacement Battalion. Morale was sinking as a result.

The months of October and November were given over to intense training, most of it in the field. Exercises for as long as ten days at a time were held, with little more than an oil skin for cover. Once, in mid-November, they received orders to load up for the ship to France, but it was rescinded at the last minute.

Finally, on December 5, after four months in England, two platoons from Company C only, were loaded onto lorries for the short ride to Southampton. The weather was as foul as they'd seen, and Brian feared the worst for any voyage on a ship.

His fears were justified. They were going to the French port of Le Havre. The overnight passage was miserable, with the ship wallowing from starboard to port in a sea from directly abeam. The ship was loaded to capacity with other replacement units, and the men stood, packed like sardines for the overnight trip. The specter of the horribly wounded men at Connaught Hospital loomed throughout the sleepless night. Brian MacLennan was scared to death.

~ * ~

December 8, 1916
Le Havre, France

Horses, motor cars, trucks of every description—and a sea of olive green uniforms! The port of Le Havre seemed like the bees crawling on his mother's honey frames at home. Brian wondered how the ship would possibly be unloaded with all that activity. Unloaded they were, and marched in columns of four through the streets where the throng, accustomed to such activity, melted away from their approach.

A field where permanent tents had been evacuated for their use appeared and they were halted. During their training, Corporal—now Sergeant—Shanks had been the only constant authority for the 2nd Platoon of Company C. Temporary lieutenants had come and gone. Now a First Lieutenant Cross they knew from Bramshott seemed to be in charge of the platoon, with Shanks standing off to one side as they awaited orders from the company commander.

The CO of their newly formed company was a man Brian had never seen. He was a captain, who looked somewhat different than the officers he'd watched in England. Perhaps it was the casual way he wore his uniform. Smart, but not pretentious, like he'd seen it all before. He projected confidence.

He introduced himself as Captain Goode of the 10th Canadian Brigade, to which the company would be attached. His address was brief, acknowledging the protracted training the company had endured in Bramshott, and how they should be proud to have served under leadership Lt. Colonel Rowland provided the original 119th while training in England. Brian thought it was generous of this experienced captain for his words about Colonel Rowland who, like them, hadn't yet heard a shot fired in anger.

They were assigned to tents and given time to settle before being herded off to somewhere closer to the front. Others were joking and excited about getting into the action at last. Brian had the visions of the hospital to reflect on, and felt no such giddiness.

~ * ~

It was unusually warm. The woolen greatcoats were shed as the men lounged in their tents. Brian made sure his coat was on the cot provided, and not touching the ground. Stories about the lice were rampant and he was damned if he was going to endure anything like that.

It seemed the army did not know what to do with them as they spent two days standing formation for meaningless roll calls and duty assignments for "make-work" tasks. Then, on the third day, they were marched to the Gare du Havre train station. A steam locomotive stood huffing while they were loaded onto boxcars for the ninety kilometer trip to the city of Roen. The trip took three hours, but Brian felt they were now officially in France, officially in the war.

~ * ~

December 30, 1916

Bray sur Somme, France

"Is that it?" Lank whispered, as they viewed the small stream. "I pictured it bigger."

Brian agreed. All the talk about the battle of the Somme River and its importance as a line of defense went counter to his impression of the stream. It was hard to believe that here, just last autumn, hundreds of thousands were either killed or seriously wounded. The British and French had penetrated five or six miles into the German lines, but had failed to take a town that was critical to the enemy for their winter provisions.

George said, "Look at the marshy land on either side. You don't just march across that without a bridge."

Ahead was the town of Bray-sur-Somme, where the other three battalions of the brigade waited. From Rouen they had railed north until dismounting and marching east toward the line. Christmas Eve was spent on the march in a steady rain, and the next night drying their sodden greatcoats around a bonfire from scavenged wood.

As they were the last of the battalions to arrive, a wreck of a barn that had a hole in the roof was the only domicile available. Fortunately the rain had stopped, as the roof revealed a considerable amount of starry sky.

Since arriving at Le Havre, Brian had seen little of Wentworth or Rupke. He knew they were present at the first muster, but training for the machine gun squads kept them sequestered from the riflemen. Now, in the old barn, Brian heard the annoying voice of Wentworth boasting of one thing or another. Rupke, next to him, was paying no attention to Wentworth's oration, but looking directly at Brian.

~ * ~

They were at Bray over the new year getting a half day free. Brian had taken the time to sketch some of the surroundings, and was finishing a drawing after dinner when someone called, "Attention!"

Lieutenant Cross entered with their CO, Captain Goode. Goode strode forward, a swagger stick under his arm. He was a stocky but well-built man perhaps in his early forties, rusty hair under his cap. Word was he'd been a big-time lawyer in Toronto before the war.

"At ease! Please carry on, men," he said and began chatting with some of the troops. Brian returned to his work. A few minutes passed, and he sensed someone over his shoulder. His eye caught the boot and jodhpurs of an officer, rocketing him to attention.

"Rest easy, soldier. You're on your time now." Goode bade him to return to his drawing. "That's amazing," he said, pointing to the sketch of an artillery piece with its caisson attached. It was done on one of Brian's few remaining sheets of Red Cross stationery from home.

"You did that from memory?"

"Yes sir, I mean partly, sir. I draw the technical stuff, like how many spokes on the wheel, and get the proportions, then fill in later…sir."

"May I?" the captain asked, pointing to some of the other sketches.

Brian handed them to the officer.

"I know that place. It's the stable at Bramshott."

It was. Brian remained at attention.

"What's your name, soldier?"

"MacLennan, sir."

"Algoma boy?"

"St. Joseph Island, sir."

"Carry on, then," Goode said, and continued through the rest of the company, speaking here and there with his men.

Brian was a little embarrassed, but few of the other men seemed to notice or care about the exchange.

~ * ~

The battalion moved out for duty on the line near the ruined town of Albert. Brian was amazed at the extent of the trench system. Underground rooms had been cut into them, connecting trenches along the line and from forward observation posts back to rear command centers as well.

They spent over two weeks there, getting the feel of actual warfare. It was in every way as they had trained at Bramshott except for one thing: It was real, and that made it frightening. Standing guard at an observation post, knowing someone was out there wanting to kill you, changed everything. For the sixteen days, they were on edge, not knowing if a German charge was coming or not. Brian almost wished they would to break the tension.

They were pulled back to the town of Villers-au-Bois where they were billeted among the villagers' homes, spending the nights there and the days in maneuvers, and of all things, digging more tunnels.

Six

January, 3 1917
Hamburg, Germany
Landsturm Reception Facility

Jürgen waited in line for his photograph to be taken. It seemed waiting was all he'd done since reporting for service in the *Landsturm,* Germany's term for required military, the service of all young men. He'd reported to Hamburg in September to discover the facility almost empty of other recruits. A large group had recently shipped out to train somewhere, taking most of the cadre with them.

Uniforms were not yet available to issue, so the recruits, as they dribbled in, sat around much of the early days there in civilian clothes with little to do but fill out forms, receive orientation and keep the barracks clean.

Later new instructors were assigned, and physical training and drilling were commenced. It wasn't until the day after Christmas that the uniforms arrived. So it was that he waited in line in his new, woolen uniform waiting for his turn to be photographed and immortalized as a hero of the German Army.

It had not been until the completion of this preparatory drill and discipline that they were administered the oath. In groups of three, the men were told to raise their right hand while their left rested on the German colors. A representative from Berlin was expected to do the honors for God and Fatherland, but they learned this man was a minor official from Hamburg.

Then the official German Army photograph. When it was his turn, he stepped in front of the camera, handing a sergeant a card with his name, serial number and home address. In the rear of the set was a screen depicting an idyllic forest. Next to him was a pedestal upon which a book lay.

"Hold the book in your right hand, please," the photographer said.

Jürgen thought how silly this must appear—a callow boy trying to look like Friedrich Schiller posing at his estate—but he complied, resting his hand on the pedestal, gripping the book, chest out like a proud soldier.

"Hold still." The cap came off the lens and quickly replaced. "Next!"

Jürgen walked out into the large hall where the others were collecting their gear for the train ride north.

~ * ~

They were headed north from Hamburg to Neumünster sitting on a siding while the southbound came through. The coach, full of replacement recruits, was unheated, and they huddled together for warmth. Jürgen thought about past summers when his father would take the family east across the Oste and Elbe Rivers and the ferry to Glükstadt then on to Itzehoe in Schleswig-Holstein where a favorite uncle lived. It wasn't far from where they were headed that day.

With a jolt, the train began to move again, and pick up speed. A dusting of snow had covered the ground and branches of the fir trees. The overcast added to the bleak landscape that retreated from his view. He should have been excited at the prospect of this new adventure, but the news of the war was not good, despite the government propaganda. Rumors of a major defeat in Russia, the stalemate in Belgium, and the severely wounded boys from his and neighboring villages were now common signs of trouble at the front. Disturbing stories about the western allies' assault across the Somme River last summer were being circulated.

Jürgen had never understood the need for Germany to attack France. Or how it had anything to do with the assassination of some archduke in Bosnia. Attack Russia, perhaps; one could never trust the Russians. And now here he was, headed for the war as part of what some of the people at home were calling the Kaiser's cannon fodder.

His mood matched the melancholy of the passing landscape.

~ * ~

January, 1917
Lockstedt, Training Camp
Schleswig-Holstein, Germany

The train had ground to a shuddering halt at Neumünster when the men were assembled into ranks according to their assigned units. Jürgen joined the others assigned to the 463d Regiment, one of three regiments of the newly formed 238th Infantry Division.

The march to Lockstedt was extreme. A slender boy to whom Jürgen had spoken on the train, marched next to him. He wondered how he was handling the march. He'd noticed the boy in Hamburg, struggling with the physical training. It was tough going. Snow began to fall, small hard flakes with a bitter North Sea wind in their faces. The sixteen kilometer trip took them six hours. When they were ordered to halt, the boy was exhausted.

The Lockstedt camp consisted of well-maintained, brick barracks, mess halls and administration buildings. A Regiment consisted of twelve companies. The men were separated according to size, the tallest to the 1st, 5th, and 9th company of each regiment, and the shortest to the 4th, 8th and 12th. Jürgen never understood the logic of this. There was barely time for the troops to be fed and assigned to barracks before a bugle sounded tattoo for the night.

They were roused the next morning at 5AM. A *Feldwebel* named Büler was shouting "*Aufstehen*! *Schneller*! *Jetzt*!" banging a stick against the posts, and ordering the men at attention at the end of their straw mattress bunks.

The men were ordered to clean up their area and get ready for inspection in ten minutes, when they were flushed outside into the cold to stand for personal inspection while the barracks were inspected. They waited there until 6AM when a lieutenant named Stoner received Büler's report on the state of the Second Platoon, Company III of the 463d Regiment.

~ * ~

Büler, a newly made sergeant, was in charge of the fifty-four men in the platoon. A corporal, or *unteroffizier* named Koss, led the sixteen men in two sections, a *korporalschaft*, that included Jürgen Stern.

The men were informed in a fifteen minute dressing down how utterly ignorant, sloppy, and lacking in any form of discipline they were, and that Third Company, particularly second platoon, would be transformed into fighting soldiers in one of two ways: hard, or unbearable. It was up to them. Büler and Koss were as good as their words. The next weeks were horrible.

The winter in northern Germany is typically long and bleak. This year's signature was the bitter cold. Drills included weaponry, but also entrenching in the frozen ground, outdoor PT, obstacle courses, long marches. Almost any activity required heavy woolen coats and gloves, making the handling of a weapon nearly impossible.

The Mauser 98 rifle was a departure for Jürgen, accustomed to the lighter, wieldier sporting weapons of home. Adding the cumbersome *Steigenwehr* bayonet put another fifteen inches to it. The whole assembly was almost as tall as the average soldier, yet it was an accurate weapon, and Jürgen proved his prowess as a marksman early on.

~ * ~

In the bunk across from Jürgen's was the boy from that march from the train. He learned the boy was from the city of Stade, a little south of his own village of Neuhaus. His name was Alfred Hauser. Because of his slight build, the training was taking a toll, and he was becoming a target for derision and bullying among the other men. Jürgen admired Hauser's pluck in spite of the abuse, and came to the man's defense on more than a few occasions. This resulted, to an extent, in Jürgen's own alienation.

On one significant occasion, the platoon was running an obstacle course that included a six meter wall over which the men had to traverse. This meant teamwork, some boosting others, while those on top would help the ones below.

Alfred's turn to approach the wall came, but no one gave him a boost. Jürgen was already over and on his way when he heard the jeering. He doubled back to see his friend stranded, alone. *Unteroffizier* Koss was there, arms folded.

"What are you doing, Stern?"

Jürgen came to attention, but said nothing.

"Go ahead, boost your friend, but you must go over as well."

"I already did, *Unteroffizier*,"

"I don't expect an argument. I didn't see you."

Jürgen locked his hands together, motioning for Hauser to insert his foot, and easily boosted him to the top of the wooden bulwark. "Now you," Koss said.

Jürgen eyed Houser's frail body peering down. He looked like a mere boy. "Can you pull me, Alfred?"

"I think so," was his hesitant answer.

Jürgen took a running jump, sticking his boot on the wall as he did. Their hands caught, but their grip was lost, and he fell back.

"Again!" Koss said.

This time, their grips held, but Jürgen felt Hauser being pulled toward him and despaired. Then the feeling reversed, and Hauser was winning the tug of war. Jürgen let one hand free and grabbed the top of the wall. Hauser caught him by the collar, and pulled him up.

Koss gave them no time to celebrate, "Move out you two, and catch up with your comrades!"

~ * ~

Hauser's performance at the wall impressed Jürgen. There was more to the boy from Stade than the others perceived. To Koss' credit, he gave the men a tongue lashing for abandoning a fellow soldier on the obstacle course. The scolding did only a little to ease the abuse Houser continued to take with no complaint.

Jürgen and Hauser's friendship increased, but while not alienating him outright, served to set him apart. In addition, his prowess with the rifle was noticed by the cadre, who assigned him away for additional training as a sniper, or *heckenshüztze*—literally hedge-shooter. He was issued a scope for his M98 rifle, and spent considerable time away from the platoon honing his skill from varied positions and distances.

It turned out that Hauser was considered a violin prodigy at an early age. He had been accepted at the *Berlin Hochschule fur Musik* to study under the acclaimed teacher Willy Hess when he received his notice of conscription. No amount of entreaties from his parents or the conservatory was successful in gaining his deferment. Jürgen was the only person with whom Alfred shared this.

As the weeks progressed, the winter waned, and army life became more bearable. Büler and Koss turned out to be good leaders. They had both seen action at the Marne offensive in 1914, and had stern words for anyone who thought, as they had, that victory would be an easy matter for Germany. The lessons they had learned in their unsuccessful push to capture Paris were harsh, and they drilled their men incessantly on learning those lessons.

In time, army training did to Hauser what it was designed to do. It toughened him. Soon he, Jürgen, and as many as a half dozen others formed a nucleus of comrades. In their spare moments, they would visit the canteen where a beer could be purchased for five phennigs, not an inconsiderable sum on their seventy phennig pay.

It was an eclectic group of mostly apprentices at one skill or another, ranging from Veldstein the aspiring mason through the butcher's son Berg, Sternkopf the machinist apprentice, to the sensitive musician Alfred Hauser. Jürgen somehow naturally slipped into the role of moderator, using the interpersonal skills honed over young years dealing with the wide variety of people traveling on the Oste ferry.

~ * ~

April, 1917

The Siegfried Line, France.

After three months at the Lockstedt Camp, the day to entrain for the western front came on April 19. From the train window he watched the French landscape slide by through towns like Treves, Sedan, Naraur, Caudry, detraining at Cambrai. It seemed incredible to Jürgen that only one week ago he'd been safely back in the rolling farmland of the Schleswig-Holstein training camp.

"Where are we, *Feldwebel*?"

The usually self-contained Sgt. Brüle seemed nervous. They had only just detrained, formed up and were at ease, smoking.

He seemed to look past Jürgen when he answered. "It's a part of the front called the Siegfried Line. North of here is a town called Arras; to the south is Soissons. The line runs between the two. It's going to be shit keeping the Frenchies on their side of it."

Hoffner, the *gefreiter* of Jürgen's section overheard. "We'll make them eat our steel, *Feldwebel*!"

Brüle looked at Hoffner with tired eyes, but said nothing. Jürgen sensed this veteran from the French defense at the Marne River had seen enough to know that Hoffner's enthusiasm was naïve. The *gefreiter* took Brüle's silence as approval and, smirking, looked around to the others.

A German infantry platoon was broken down into eight-man sections, each having a lead man, *gefreiter*. He was usually a corporal, but sometimes a man from the unit given the acting responsibility without the rank. Such was the case with Hoffner, also a recent trainee. Nobody seemed to object. Jürgen certainly did not covet the position, though somewhat annoyed at Hoffner's easy presumption of his leadership.

For four days they settled in behind the lines, finding a covered trench recently vacated by another unit transferred elsewhere. Then on the twentieth of April, they were posted on the line near the tiny village of Bellicourt. It was there these untested replacements learned about trench warfare.

Spring rains had flooded the trenches to the point it was impossible to keep feet dry. The nights were still cold and sleep was obtained in fitful snatches. Comfort was the least of their problems. Although they experienced no major offenses by the Allied forces, they were constantly harassed by sniper, mortar and artillery fire.

It was here that Jürgen had his first battlefield experience. He was ordered to a post behind a small ridge overlooking a *Niemandsland* between the barbed wire of the two armies. From there he could see hints of activity on the Allied side. Per his training, he set out at once to sight his weapon. The M98 rifle was cumbersome as it was beautifully made, and very accurate. He fashioned a cradle with his pack and set his sights for 300 meters. Picking out a sandbag along the enemy's trench line, he squeezed off a round. It fell just short. Two clicks of the rear sight were enough to see the puff of dirt hit only centimeters to the right. He'd have to allow for that.

And then he waited for a target. It came sooner than he'd expected: something—a *helmet?*—appearing from time to time silhouetted at a spot along the trench. He trained his sights on that spot, and waited, the cross hair on his scope set just left of the target. Five minutes, six, then *there!* Without thinking, he squeezed the trigger, and the Mauser bucked. Through the scope, the target vaporized in a blur of red. Something—*the helmet!*—spiraled crazily and disappeared.

Jürgen felt numb. He stared at the vacated spot. Cold sweat formed on his lip and down his back. Growing up with guns of all kinds and the weeks of drilling with the Mauser never conditioned him for this: the killing of another human being. The ersatz eggs he'd consumed for breakfast were threatening to come up. His head swam. The vision of the killing reminded him as a boy with his friends using apples as targets, and seeing them explode.

Jürgen pulled his hands away from the rifle, seeing it as something foreign, evil. During his training he had wondered if he would have the nerve to use his bayonet against another man, and supposed he would in self-defense or even in a charge, if it meant the other man or himself. But he had never given this a thought, despite knowing what a sniper was meant to do. He spent the remainder of the day shooting, but hitting nothing of consequence.

The most dangerous job in the in trench warfare was that of messenger. These men were easy and prized targets as they scampered over the top from trench to trench. Interrupting the enemy's communication was a priority. The fastest, most nimble runner was usually chosen. For Company III of the 483d Regiment, one of those men was Alfred Hauser. Alfred sustained three near-misses in the time they were at Bellicourt. Jürgen had seen glimpses of enemy runners, but never hit one.

For thirty-one days they were posted at this section of the line. In that time Jürgen's company suffered one death and six injuries, all from mortar shrapnel.

Seven

April, 1917
Canadian Corps
Villers au Bois, France

They had never experienced a training exercise of this magnitude. A four mile wide mock-up was laid out on a field far removed from the front. All through February and March they had rehearsed a phased attack where objectives were delineated by colored tape. The attack was interrupted with timed pauses for support to be brought up from the rear. They were trained to advance no faster than a "walking artillery barrage" could be laid down in front of them.

When they weren't engaged thusly, they were put to work helping a strange collection of men construct an extensive array of tunnels in the chalky earth of the area. These were men from Northern England—miners, called Bantams—working with crews from the mining areas of the Pacific Islands, for the most part. These tunnels surpassed anything Brian could have imagined.

On one of the first days, Brian, having a bit of biscuit on a break from work, was sitting next to a Yorkshire man of about thirty. "This is all you do?" he asked.

The man gave him a brief glance; hard eyes behind a leathered visage. He didn't respond.

"Sorry," Brian said. "I didn't mean anything by that."

"That's right, old son. It's all I do. Been doin' it since the beginin'."

"Here?"

"Up and down the line, lad."

A moment passed while Brian thought about these words. "How far is that?"

The man laughed, a sort of cough. "Which way ye fancy?"

Brian hunched his shoulders.

"These here trenches will let ye walk all the way ta Switzerland, if ye don't mind swimmin' a few rivers. Same the other way to the sea."

There was no sign of mirth in the man's face, and Brian decided not to challenge the preposterous claim. No sense starting a fight over nothing.

"You think I'm jesting, fecking with yer."

Brian took a bite of his biscuit; hunched his shoulders again.

"All the way up and down the line, these trenches go; more'n four hunnerd mile." The man threw down his cigarette, picked up his shovel and returned to the new section of tunnel they were excavating under No Man's Land.

While drills and work were exhausting, the small farmhouse where Brian and part of his section were billeted could not have been more accommodating. The men stretched out on the floor while a fire in the old stove kept them warm and dry. The lady of the house, Madame Arnoult, was a war widow, having lost her husband at the Marne, and a son reportedly captured in the same battle. She would have a pot of coffee ready for the men, and even did some of their washing.

She had two daughters, the eldest named Genevieve, with dark brunette hair peeking out from under her kerchief, and a pair of laughing eyes that mesmerized George Kobak. He was smitten. Brian agreed there was a unique beauty about the girl and set out to make a sketch of her with her younger sister as they sat together mending stockings. Although the men knew there was little likelihood of ever seeing this family again. Brian promised George to copy a portrait sketch of Genevieve when he had time.

By now the troops knew that Canada's s role in the next offensive was to capture a four mile long ridge west of the village of Vimy. From there the Germans had dug in with fortifications protecting this vantage point that commanded the field of fire over the Allied positions. For any advance to be successful, Vimy Ridge must be taken and held. They were told how, in the previous year, the French had tried and failed with disastrous losses to capture this strategic stronghold of the enemy.

~ * ~

They were working on a section of the tunnel close to the front lines where a large room was being excavated in the chalky earth. Brian and his platoon were on a detail removing excavated waste when Sgt. Shanks called his name.

"Clean yourself up and report to Corps H.Q. Ask for Captain Goode," he announced.

Brian was dumfounded. He barely knew where to find the Headquarters site. *What had he done?* He hitched a ride back to Villers where he cleaned his boots and tried his best to wash the grime from his tunic, hands and face; all the while searching his mind for some infraction he might have committed.

The weather had been fair, and H.Q. was temporarily set up outside in a large tent at a place named Camblain l'Abbe. A soldier was guarding the tent's open flap where, inside, Brian could see nothing but officers' polished boots and insignias of rank.

"Private MacLennan reporting for Captain Goode," he said.

The soldier eyed his somewhat soiled presence with an air of distain. "Wait here."

Brian stood fidgeting with cap in hand for a minute or two while word was passed along inside. The soldier returned with a corporal who said, "Follow me."

He was led to the rear where a group of officers was looking down at a large table, and recognized Capt. Goode standing next to a man he knew to be the commander of the 10th Brigade

Another very tall, rather portly officer was holding forth, and had their attention. Brian waited until he was noticed. That officer was first to say something. "Is this your man, Captain?"

The other two officers turned to see. Goode said, "MacLennan, sir. I think he can do it."

"Soldier, take a look at this, and tell me if you can do what I have in mind," the tall officer said.

Brian obeyed, wondering what on earth it could be. On the table was a huge relief representation of a terrain. It had been fashioned from clay, apparently. Hills and ridges were there. Wooded areas were realistically represented; a few buildings. It was a remarkable undertaking.

Brian had nothing to say.

"Answer the general," Goode said.

"He can't, Captain, because he has no idea what I want from him."

General! Brian swallowed.

The general continued. "This is a representation of the ground over which our spring offensive will take place. It was prepared in part from existing maps, surveys, and recent photographs taken from our aeroplanes."

Brian nodded his understanding as the general continued.

"I have divided the field of engagement into a dozen sections representing various unit objectives, both intermediate and final. What I need are individual maps made from these delineated sections. I want them drawn to fit on cards like this." He pulled a piece of pasteboard from his tunic. It was slightly larger than the size of a penny postcard, only stiffer, stronger.

The three officers waited for a response. Brian looked at Goode, his most immediate commanding officer. "Sir, I don't know. I can try."

Goode said, "Suppose you do that, MacLennan. Draw a sample for General Currie."

This was the first time Brian had heard the tall officer's name or noticed the star and crown insignia of a Major General. "Yes, sir."

Currie smiled. "Captain Goode, will you take Private MacLennan to Operations, and show him the map I have marked up?"

~ * ~

The large map was mounted on one wall of the underground room that jutted off a tunnel that led to the front lines, over four miles to the east. On the map's surface were rectangles formed by push pins and colored string. Each square was labeled alpha-numerically.

"See if you can copy this section accurately, MacLennan." Goode pointed to a square labeled "G-7" taped to one of the four push pins. A few blank cards identical to the one the general had were nearby, along with pen, ink, and pencils.

Brian chose a card, a soft pencil and began to copy what he saw inside the rectangle.

When he was finished Goode said, "It looks fine to me. Do you think you could make a less detailed version? We can let the General choose."

Brian repeated the copy, leaving out the elevation lines.

Goode summoned a messenger to take them to General Currie. In a matter of minutes, the courier was back. The general was pleased, choosing the less detailed rendering.

"Now," Goode said, "here is what I want you to do."

~ * ~

It was the final rehearsal for the offensive, the Allies' attempt to break through the enemy's defensive line and possibly continue on to Berlin. Again the color-coded tape was strewn over the immense training ground well to the west of the Germans' prying eyes. This time, however, each man was issued a postcard-size map on stiff cardboard. Platoon leaders instructed their units on how to time their advances toward objectives on their individual maps. It was an unprecedented tactic.

Brian was surprised how well the maps he'd drawn onto the soft mimeograph paper were reproduced. The maps' labeled objectives were identified on the practice field with corresponding flags. The rehearsal lasted all day, completing the operation twice. The day of the offensive was still a secret, but everyone, down to the lowest private, knew it could only be hours away.

~ * ~

April 9, 1917

Allied Front lines West of Vimy Ridge

They had been overnight in the tunnel, trying their best to stay comfortable in the damp, close-to-freezing conditions. The same tunnel had conveyed them from miles to the rear, out of sight to the enemy. They knew the Germans had tunnels as well, but Brian doubted they'd have anything so extensive.

All four divisions of the Canadian Corps would be deployed on this operation the British were calling the Battle of Arras. On the Canadian's left flank was the British 1st Corps. On their right, the British 17th Corps. Brian's Replacement company was part of the 4th Canadian Division on the far left of the Canadian Corps.

Yesterday's Easter dinner, served piping hot, was forgotten. Lank and Henry had their knees pulled up to their chests in a futile attempt to stay warm. In lieu of a cap, Brian had wrapped his head with a strip of puttee that would fit under his steel helmet.

"You look like a bloody mummy," Henry said.

In the sparse light of the electric lamps strung along one wall, Brian suspected he did look rather ghoulish, but his head was warm. Despite that, he shivered, more from nerves, he knew, than the cold. "What time is it?"

Lank looked at a pocket watch he carried in his tunic. "Two or three minutes before four," he said.

Henry said, "Lucky bloody George, sittin' high and dry, hob-nobbin' with the brass."

"You know better than that, Harry," Brian admonished.

"Yeah. He's miserable about not goin' over the top. He's still lucky, though."

"I don't know what the hell I'm supposed to do with this little map," Lank said.

Henry snorted. "Bloody Finn! Didn't you listen? If something happens to Shanks, we're supposed to know the objectives and keep going."

An argument was snuffed by Captain Goode and Lieutenant Cross passing through the tunnel, patting each man on the shoulder, giving words of encouragement.

"Won't be long now; fine chap; any time now, men; keep that weapon dry." and so on. They passed through, but Goode turned to give Brian a last look.

Around 5:30, Cpl. Shanks came scrambling down the tunnel. "Any time now boys!"

Brian took one last look at his map, studying the first objective, a hillock four hundred yards from the tunnel opening.

"Not you, MacLennan. Captain says to report back to your tent and wait for his order."

Brian was incredulous. He looked helplessly at Lank and Harry.

"*Sarn*, I can't leave my mates!" He was almost in tears.

"You'll bloody well do what—"

Then all hell broke loose.

At first, Brian thought they were under attack. There were explosions of such intensity and frequency, it sounded like one continuous roar. But it was the Allied barrage. It lasted for several minutes, then suddenly stopped.

"Now!" Whistles signaled the command to go. All along the line, troops from four infantry divisions leapt from their trenches or poured out of forward tunnels exactly as they had been drilled.

Brian watched as men did what they had rehearsed so often; some over the top of their trench, others through an opening in the tunnel. Shanks' last words kept him frozen in place.

And then it was eerily quiet in the trench, the exuberant whoops of frightened soldiers having died away. Slowly he made his way back up the tunnel to wait at Villers where Company C was quartered. Brian MacLennan had never felt so miserable.

~ * ~

He had barely poked his head outside of the tunnel where it opened at the tiny village of Careny when he was practically accosted by a burly corporal. "Where in the goddam hell you think yer goin', Private?"

Brian panicked. He knew there were guards posted against deserters. He gasped, "Sergeant Stark—uh, Captain Goode—uh, I'm—"

"You ain't MacLennan, are ya?" The corporal had his nose two inches from Brian's.

"Yes!"

"Where the hell have you been? They been lookin' for ya over an hour!"

"I've been with my section. I was told—"

"Never mind that. Get yer arse over to Corps!"

By then, Brian knew the way to the HQ at Camplain-l'Abbe, just west of Villers, and followed the half mile of rutted road. It was snowing hard with a biting wind in his face. He thought about his friends and the rest of the platoon trying to manage in this weather where he could hardly see twenty yards. Then he thought about the Germans coping in the same conditions, only having it in their faces.

When he reached Canadian Corps HQ, he was eventually directed to a CEF Major Dutton who was in animated discourse with two other field grade officers moving markers around a map table. Brian waited patiently to be recognized. While doing so, he got the gist of their conversation. It seemed some things were going very well and others not so well.

At the far end of the area sat George Kobak, hunched over a field table, concentrating on some document or other. Brian decided it would be best not to bother him.

He looked at a clock on the wall—almost 7:00AM—ninety minutes since the order to attack. He could hear the barrage of the British and Canadian big guns, but they were not continuous as before. Still, the officers ignored his presence, and still he listened to their recounts of the battle.

"What is it, soldier?" One of the officers finally noticed him standing there.

"I'm MacLennan, sir. Captain Goode, sir, he told me to—"

"Here's your man, Major. Best get him started," the officer told one in the group who turned to observe Brian. He had a ruddy, round, bespectacled face, thinning brown hair, and a crisp moustache. "I'm Major Dutton. So you're our lad, are you?"

Brian supposed he was. He didn't reply, not knowing what to answer.

"Come here," Dutton said.

Brian edged up to the table.

"Seems your little maps have done the job—so far." The words did not seem congratulatory, only factual. He continued, pointing to the map table where as many as twenty moveable, numbered markers were spread along a jagged line. Brian recognized the red, blue and brown lines from their rehearsals and the big map of the previous day. "These represent battalions." Dutton went on to explain how some of the objectives of this morning had been changed and how new maps had to be provided to replacement troops.

"I'll need six more maps as soon as you can draw them. You should have been here two hours ago."

"I was at the line, sir, ready to go over the top with the Fourth Division."

"Bloody hell! You were supposed to report here."

"Sorry, sir."

"Not your doing, MacLennan. Glad you're safe. The Fourth is catching it in the teeth."

Brian noticed the markers at the northern end of the line had barely moved, while those on the southern and middle showed significant advances. Again his mind drifted to Harry and Lank.

He spent the next hour being briefed on the areas and specific objectives for each of the six new maps to be reproduced and distributed to replacement troops.

~ * ~

It was late afternoon when the new maps were completed and run off on the mimeo an hour ahead of his promised time. Brian had learned that the 4th Division had not achieved the same element of surprise as the other three Canadian divisions. After suffering an initial whipping, finally—and only after the Germans were running out of ammunition—were they able to gain their first objective. Losses were reported as "very high."

The new maps had new objectives for the town of Givenchy and a knob designated Hill 145 which, if captured, would overlook the whole of Vimy Ridge to the southwest. It was not until that night that Brian, allowed to remain in the command center, learned that the vital Hill 145 had been taken by the Canadians. He hoped the worst was over and Harry and Lank would be safe.

As replacement units were deployed, men from the first wave were returning. Brian waited to no avail for word of anyone from his unit returning. He could only speculate that they had either advanced too far for the replacements, or were pinned down somewhere. He did learn that the Germans had recaptured Hill 145. Finally, he was ordered back to his quarters at Villers with instructions to return the following morning at 8AM.

Eight

April 12, 1917
Canada Corp HQ
Camplain-l'Abbe, France

A British Royal Flying Corps Nieuport Scout circled in the sky to the northeast, keeping watch over a slower reconnaissance aircraft in the slate grey sky. By the end of the third day, the Canadians had achieved most of their objectives. The one remaining was the high ground on the north flank of the assault known as "The Pimple." Brian had heard nothing of Lank or Harry, except he knew they were deployed in that section with the 10th Brigade that was taking a beating from the heavily armed positions there.

When Brian reported to Corps on the morning of the eleventh, Major Dutton was waiting with assignments for additional maps. As exhausted troops returned from being replaced, they were relieved of their maps, and Brian had been given the job of securing them for disposal.

Between assignments he had little to do, and used the time to draw. The nearby artillery battery was one subject, as was the ruined row of buildings in Camplain-l'Abbe. The reverse side of the stiff cardboard maps was a perfect replacement for his used-up Red Cross stationery.

As the hours of the day passed, he heard snippets of information about the progress of the assault. The 1st and 2nd Divisions had achieved their objectives of the Brown Line by that afternoon. The 3rd was also successful in overtaking the town of Vimy that lay east of the ridge.

But the 4th was having its problems. Hill 145, which sat half way between the Allied lines and the Ridge, was heavily fortified. It was barely taken late in the day. The division's far left was bogged down from heavy fire from The Pimple. It had taken another day and help from the British on their left flank.

Brian was making a detailed map of the town of Givenchy-en-Gohelle just below the objective when he was told to stop. The Pimple had been taken. It was 6 PM.

Around 10 PM, he and George were off duty and began to recognize men from the 10th Brigade as they returned to their billets near Villers. Brian returned with George to the barn he and his company shared, and waited.

Brian handed one of the maps he'd made to George.

"So?" George had seen enough of them.

"Turn it over," Brian insisted.

"Oh!"

It was a portrait of Genevieve Arnoult. "It looks just like her! How did you do that?"

"I copied her face from the sketch with her sister."

George studied the pencil drawing for a while. Then, with a shy "thank you," placed it carefully inside his tunic.

Two or three men from the platoon wandered in, covered in grime, but not Harry. Then, shortly after 11 PM they were rewarded with the sight of Harry Gardinier's unmistakable frame at the entrance. They would not have recognized him otherwise. The chalky earth of Northern France caked his hair and caused his eyes to peer through the layer of dirt like shiny, black marbles.

"Harry!"

"Oh, God, Brian!"

Brian waited, but Harry stood there, unable to take another step. Tears began to wash down Harry's face, leaving streaks of exposed skin.

"Wh…what?" Brian whispered. "Harry, are you alright? Here, put your kit down and sit there." He led Harry to a hay rick where the boy collapsed, his Enfield still firmly in his grasp.

"Lank," Harry uttered, looking up into his friends gaze. "Boys, he's dead."

"Oh, Harry!" George gasped.

Harry began to shake as whatever adrenaline held him together began to wear off. The shaking escalated into sobs. Brian dropped to his knees, and put his arms around the heaving shoulders. When the sobbing stopped, Harry was fast asleep.

~ * ~

When Brian woke the next morning, there was already light peeking through the loft door. George had already left for duty at Battalion HQ. He was surprised to see the spot where Harry had lain to be empty. Sergeant Shanks was just entering from outside. "Sarn, have you seen Gardinier?"

"Washing Vimy Ridge off his neck, just outside," Shanks said.

Brian lowered his voice. "Is it true about Lank?"

The older man stared at Brian, who felt awkward in his clean tunic and boots fresh from four days in the command center. "Look around you, MacLennan. Thems you don't see are either dead or had something blown away. Yeah, Lankinen got it on the last day. Thought you'd have known by now."

It was true. The platoon, thirty-two men at last count, looked to have been decimated if he'd taken the time to count. "Oh, Jesus," he mumbled, but Shanks was gone.

By then, Brian felt the stares of the other men either going about their business or reclined on beds of hay, heads propped on backpacks. There were no comments, just the looks. He felt like yelling that he'd been ordered to leave the fight, but that seemed somehow…he had no word for it. *Shit.*

Harry slammed the door as he entered, looking much improved over the previous night. He perched on the same rick where Brian had led him a few hours earlier, and Brian followed. He waited for Harry to say something, but it was minutes before the boy from Garden River lifted his dark eyes from the floor.

"You alright, Brian?" he said.

"Me? For Crissake, Harry, me? It's *you* I'm worried about!"

"Lank was your mate more than me," Harry said.

With those words, Brian's sense of guilt for abandoning his friends in battle overwhelmed him. Tears came. "Harry, I'm so sorry. I should've been with you."

"Aw shit, Brian. You did what you were told. Hey, old man Shanks was all over that map of yours; said it was a smart idea. Hell, I even used the new one sent up yesterday. Saved my ass from getting' lost, honest."

Brian had already heard the officers and noncommissioned types praising the maps. General Currie's idea to issue them to individual soldiers was deemed a success. Still, Harry's words helped more.

"I heard the Fourth got it a lot worse than the other Divisions," Brian ventured, dying for Harry to tell what he'd done over the last few days. He needn't have worried. Harry seemed to have a need to verbalize those events.

"We got our asses handed to us on that first day out of the trench," Harry said. "Gotta hand it to Captain Goode, though. He stayed with us the whole way to that first German trench on your map."

Brian urged him to continue.

"The buggers on our right flank from the Twelfth Brigade--they got it the worst. Had to retreat back to our own trenches, the Huns hit them so hard." He went on to explain how the 10th Brigade had to veer right to support them, and their job of taking the 4th Division's most important objective; the high ground designated Hill 145.

Brian said, "Yeah, we heard about that. You were there?"

Harry closed his eyes and shook his head as if trying to erase a vision. "It was bloody awful. Some smart general decided not to shell a set of trenches without telling us. We had Germans popping up out of them, attacking our rear after we swept through. Cut down half our men before we ever reached the Hill."

He told how that objective had not been taken by nightfall, and how they'd had to fend off a German counter attack from the north in the pre-dawn of the next day.

"By then, the ground was one huge muddy crater after another. Blokes are being cut down trying to work around them, no shit. Worst of it is, we gotta keep pressing forward without helping some poor bugger."

He told of the 10th involved in securing the north side of Hill 145, while the 11th and 12th Brigades took the rest and stormed down the other side behind the retreating enemy the next day.

"That was on day three, and we thought we'd be relieved, but they sent us north to help the British take another hill they called 'The Pimple.'"

Brian said he knew all about that and had drawn a new map showing objectives and strongholds there.

"I guess the Tommies tried lots of times to take that pile of shit," Harry said.

Brian knew the Pimple was more than a pile of excrement. It commanded the whole valley west of Vimy Ridge, and was even more heavily fortified than Hill 145. "You were still with the Tenth?"

“Yeah, but we were assigned to a new battalion, the Forty-sixth.”

“Western Canada boys.”

“Yeah, good blokes. We had to lay low that night. Next day the bad weather got worse. I know we see some god awful weather back home. But this was a damn *gale* with sleet and snow! I think the Hun was surprised that anything on legs would be out in that, but we were, and at 5 AM, at that. It took us just three hours, but the Forty-sixth lost half their men.”

With that, Harry stopped talking, once more staring at his shoes.

Brian started, “Is that where…?” but he knew Ake Lankinen was on Harry’s mind as well.

Nine

May 20, 1917
The Roeux-Gavrille Line
Near Gavrelle, France

One month to the day after leaving Lockstedt Training Camp, the three regiments of the 238th Infantry Division were relieved from their spot on the line south of Arras, and sent a short distance north to an area east of Vimy, where they learned The Imperial German Army had lost a major battle protecting an important vantage point along a ridge east of the town. Several earlier successful attempts to repel the British ultimately failed to hold back a new offensive by Canadian troops.

But the Canadians had failed to break through the defenses and push through to Berlin as Allied propaganda had been promising. German forces had ceded ground in a strategy of bend, but do not break. The 238th would be part of that new defensive line that still held strong from the cities of Lens south to Roeux.

It was in that village of Roeux on the Scarpe River that Jürgen and his comrades first saw the scale and horror of modern warfare as foretold by their *feldwebel*. There, a field hospital had been erected, the flaps of the tents held open to invite fresh air, exposing the extent of the wounds, both in severity and number. Jürgen heard the

Canadians had caused much of the carnage through unprecedented use of artillery.

Amputations were carried out in plain sight. Severed limbs were visible in open receptacles. Men, still alive, but barely. Hardest for Jürgen to look at were the burn victims.

The division was marched through the town and on to a section of the line near the tiny settlement of Gavrelle. Here, another trench waited to be occupied.

~ * ~

They were assigned a place among the rear trenches. Jürgen was immediately given kitchen duty in the mess tent, separating him from his friends. After his duty, he exited the tent with his own dinner of some kind of meat in a gravy ladled over what looked like decent enough bread, and took it back to a spot behind the mess tent to eat, sitting cross-legged on a rare spot of grass. The evening was warm and a breeze from the east wafted the aroma of spring from the bucolic fields of northern France.

He finished the meal which was better than expected and leaned back against the canvas of the tent. It was the first time he could remember having a minute to himself since Lockstedt. His thought were rapidly drawn to Käthe Von Helm.

Even his first sight of her had made an impression. She must have been no more than fourteen years old, because he had seen her at church the Sunday he was confirmed. Käthe was the envy of the other girls her age, always dressed in beautiful winter woolens or gossamer summer dresses. Her hair was long and silky; not the braids of the poorer girls.

At first, she would come into Neuhaus with a maid or their gardener; never with a parent. Later as she grew older, she'd come by herself for some big event, like May Day or as on that wonderful day—*Shützenfest!*

Every boy Jürgen's age thought she was beyond approach, which is why, as she grew older, the more mature boys, and some *much* more mature, were her entourage. She seemed to have few, if any, girlfriends. But then, Jürgen had known what it was like to hold, to kiss, to—

"Off your backside, Private, and back to your unit, unless you want to scrub pots."

The goliath that was the mess sergeant and whom Jürgen had been avoiding all afternoon, towered over him, hairy arms crossed against his stained apron. Without a word, Jürgen scrambled back to the trenches before the man changed his mind.

~ * ~

The 238th found itself thrown into the line at the Scarpe River, only a few miles south of Vimy where the Canadians had gained the high ground, thus a strategic advantage in the region. At least that's what Feldwebel Büler told them. Jürgen had to admire the crusty old soldier. He admired the man's ability to command respect with an economy of words in his curious Austrian idiom.

The 238th was acquiring the nickname *Die Kommunionkinder*—communion children—as if they had only recently been deemed adults by the church. Most of them had never been more than a few kilometers from their northern villages. For them, thirty-eight year old Büler was, indeed, a phenomenon.

The swagger upon detraining in France was rapidly dissipating among the troops. The short stint in the line at Bellicourt and the gruesome encounters with the wounded and dying from recent battles were taking their toll. Jürgen was as frightened as anyone.

"These trenches look like they have always been here," he heard Hoffner say.

It was true. The sides of the trenches were reinforced with branches intricately woven together. Niches called *unterständen* were carved into the sides for protection against the elements and artillery. Wooden walkways to keep boots out of the water looked well-constructed.

Corporal Koss was quick to admonish, "Don't get used to this. It's a support trench. The forward trenches are for the likes of us.

They soon found out for themselves. A stint of duty on the second day had most of the 463d Regiment looking across *niemannsland* at the Allied lines less than a thousand meters away. Jürgen was assigned as a lookout while others maintained position in case of attack.

"Who are they, *Feldwebel?*" Jürgen asked when Büler was walking past his post. "I mean, are they the Canadians?" The intensity of the Canadian offensive at Vimy Ridge had spread among all the German units.

Büler said, "No. They're British. Maybe Seventeenth Corps. That's what I hear. Why do you care? Just do your job. It doesn't matter who you have to kill in order to keep yourself alive."

Büler's simple logic hit home. Repulsive or not, Jürgen had come to the conclusion he would not hesitate to pull the trigger of his rifle if faced by an oncoming enemy soldier.

~ * ~

May 24, 1917

They were in that trench for five days with no action, not even enemy mortar harassment. Then word came that the 463d would be assigned on a raid to take two key positions west of the line. One was a rail station on the Lens-Arras line, the other a Chemical factory nearby. Both served as fortified positions having a high value for either side.

Jürgen and Alfred were huddled against the trench wall sheltered from the miserably damp wind from the west. Jürgen puffed on his clay pipe with the last bit of tobacco from his pack.

A remnant of daylight illuminated the fine features of Alfred's face. "When do we go, I wonder?"

"They should tell us soon enough," Jürgen said. "I suppose I'm more concerned with the 'how' than the 'when'." As a replacement division they had trained in trench combat, not in raids through streets and buildings.

An hour later, Jürgen was scraping the bowl of his pipe when Koss assembled his two sections.

"Our battalion has been assigned to take back the chemical works."

"Take *back?*" Hoffner remarked.

Koss glared at him for the interruption, but clarified his statement. "We lost it to the British last winter. Those buildings control a large portion of *niemannsland.* We want them back."

Hoffner lowered his eyes, and Koss continued. "The plan is to take them back for good. We do that by first securing the buildings, followed by a full attack on their trenches by the rest of the Regiment. Taking those buildings is key to the success of the attack."

Jürgen asked the obvious question when Koss had finished. "Once we take the building, how do we hold it?"

"We do what the Canadians did to us last month. Our artillery will lay down a carpet of scorched earth between the buildings and their lines as our troops advance. We will make sure the buildings are in our hands until that time."

Koss' explanation seemed solid, and Jürgen felt better. He wanted to ask how long they had to hold the captured buildings, but thought he'd already gone too far.

"We move out at oh-three-hundred hours. When we go, you follow me until I gave you further orders." He advised the sixteen men comprising the two sections of his *korporalshaft* to get some rest while they could.

~ * ~

They were in position where Büler, then Koss led them. Someone coughed. "*Ruhig, du dummer Wichser!*" Hoffman whispered. The skies had cleared, dropping the temperature to near freezing. In the thin slice of a waning moon, Jürgen could barely make out the broken silhouette of the building. He trembled from the air's chill as well as his nerves.

There were living, breathing, *armed* troops in there. While he waited for a signal to attack, he thought of them—boys like himself—probably scared. Then he put the thought out of mind. He could not afford the luxury of compassion.

The order to move in came as a simple *now! "Jetzt!"* Büler hissed.

They moved at a walk in concert with other units of their battalion, waiting for return fire, an alarm—something!

The building's crumbled walls became clearer. Jürgen could see the entire first floor intact behind thick stone. No wonder it had stood and remained a bastion of sorts.

Then it came: a shout, "Shite! The ficken Huns!" From Jürgen's left, a light machine gun opened up casing sparks to fly on the heavy stone façade. Others followed; rifle fire and LMG noise.

"Keep moving!" Büler could be heard over the din.

Jürgen pointed his weapon, but had no target until a muzzle flash shown from the building. A hail of fire descended on that spot. He added a round or two as well.

They advanced until Koss yelled, "Now to the wall! *Schnell*!"

Jürgen obeyed, finding himself by an opening—once a window—now a toothless maw. Inside was no target, only pitch blackness. He pulled his single grenade from his belt, thinking there was no better time to use it.

He unscrewed the cap at the end of the long wooden handle and yanked hard on the weighted cord that dropped out of the hollow. He counted off two of the five seconds he knew the fuse had to burn—just as in training—and hurled it.

The explosion sent debris back into his face. The sound of it brought cheers from the others. Someone yelled, "Inside!" and most of Company III of the 463d Infantry regiment poured inside, firing their weapons at anything at all.

It was over almost before it began. They lost one man from the first platoon. Inside were seventeen bodies and twenty-two frightened English soldiers. Jürgen was surprised at how lightly the place was defended.

He heard an officer laugh. "A shitty replacement company did this! My God, you English should be ashamed!"

It was then that Jürgen felt the first sense of German pride since holding the colors and swearing allegiance to the Fatherland. Perhaps it was true: *Gott ist mit uns!*

~ * ~

The prisoners were removed back to Roeux and beyond. Rations were brought up from the line for the one hundred ninety men of Company III chosen to guard the building. It was noon, May 25, 1917.

Jürgen looked out on the landscape of *Niemandsland.* It was a strategic bunker, alright. Inside, the large building consisted of a basement that had been built for storage, but reinforced with massive steel beams to support the heavy equipment of the first floor—that equipment supposedly torn out for scrap to make weapons of war.

The basement was excellent protection against all but the heaviest of direct hits from artillery. From this position, they could survey 360° of open field. The rail station was but a few hundred meters away. It, too, had been secured, albeit with higher casualties.

Signalmen were laying telephone wire back to the east. Soon communications would be in place. It was a complete victory.

"I told you the English are no match for well-trained Germans." Hoffner, the acting *Gefreiter,* strutted like a rooster while Jürgen and the others in his eight-man section took their turns at the watch. No one responded. Jürgen thought he'd wait to strut when the promised attack on the British trenches was successful. He felt exposed here. The attack was to be preceded by an artillery barrage. It was hard waiting for one to commence with Hoffner going on like that. His prideful talk was unnerving.

The sun fell away to the west and dusk settled in on their first full day there. Still no sign of retaliation by the British. At 1800, he was relieved from the watch and joined Alfred eating from a tin of rations marked *Fleischkonserve.* Jürgen pulled a packet of biscuits from his coat and began to gnaw on the hardened mass.

"What's going to happen, Jürgen?"

"I guess we will attack the enemy. We wouldn't have risked taking these positions for nothing. We'll know for sure if the bombing starts up."

Darkness came, but the night was silent.

~ * ~

Jürgen woke from a deep sleep to the sound. He felt, more than heard it. The earth trembled, and debris ran down the sides of the walls that were still standing.

"A barrage!" someone called out.

Jürgen was confused, as the sound seemed to be strongest from the wrong direction. He gazed out onto the cratered fields. The pre-dawn light was too dim to reveal anything.

The shouting of orders began. "Full alert! Man your posts!"

"Hurry! Do as you're told!" Hoffner yelled. He looked frightened.

The loudest noise sounded like it was coming from their own lines. Büler appeared, exhorting his platoon to be alert. "An artillery battle and it sounds like we're getting the worst of it. The bastards preempted us!"

It was already rumored that the Allied artillery had been built up to unprecedented size for the recent operations at Vimy Ridge and the Scarpe River. Soon it was obvious to all that the sound of exploding ordinance was coming from the east. "Our guns have retreated out of range," an officer was heard to announce. At the same time, a lookout called "Enemy!"

At first, Jürgen could see nothing from his vantage. Then he saw a line of troops running to take up positions to the north. From the south end of the building came another report of troop movement. They were flanked on both sides.

"What are they doing?" someone called.

"Quiet!" Jürgen heard Büler order.

The line of enemy was now apparent as sunlight touched tips of the leafless trees. Light artillery could be seen moving into position.

We are finished, Jürgen thought. He looked at Koss who was watching from the same hole in the wall. The corporal, who had already experienced defeat at the Marne River, had resignation in his eyes, but the lack of panic was reassuring.

"What now, *Unteroffizier*?" Jürgen asked.

Koss gave him a steady gaze. "We follow orders, Stern," and left to say something to Büler and Lieutenant Stoner, who were eyeing both flanks. The first artillery shell hit at 0800. The tallest part of the wall still standing showered bricks and mortar. Then came a hail of machine gun and rifle fire. Jürgen could hear the signature short bursts of the British Lewis guns.

Men began to fall wounded or dead. By 0820, with fire coming from both flanks, it was hopeless. The order to retreat was given.

Jürgen found Hoffner pushing Alfred and a man named Scribner through a hole in the east wall, and followed. "Oh Christ! Run!" he yelled after them as they fled into the maelstrom of relentless crossfire.

They had gone fewer than fifty meters when Scribner fell, half his face blown away. "Oh God!" he heard Alfred shout over the intense noise. Another fifty meters, and Hoffner went down, a gash in his thigh seeping crimson. Alfred went back to help him.

Jürgen cried, "Alfred! We can't stop!" to no avail.

Alfred Hauser grabbed Hoffner's arm, and wound it around his shoulder, trying to lift him to his feet. A rock inches from them exploded from a hit. Jürgen ran back to the pair and got Hoffner's other arm, dragged him to his feet away from the withering fire.

Somehow the three men tumbled into the forward trench of the Roeux-Gavrille German position.

Alfred looked up into Jürgen's face and grinned, unaware of the crease in his steel helmet from a British bullet.

Ten

Canadian Corps Headquarters
Villers au Bois, France
June 6, 1917

The mail came this day, a letter from his mother; his second from home. Owen was proving Brian right by exceeding his father's expectations in managing the farm. His mother's words were full of optimism and encouragement, but he could sense, or perhaps only imagine, the worry in them.

In vain, he looked for a letter from Sarah White. He'd written to her often. At first, some bold words about his feelings for her, but there were no replies, and his last few had become more tempered about his feelings. It had been weeks since he'd ventured to write to her again.

Thinking of Sarah made him wonder if Colby Wentworth was right and she had feelings for him instead. The idea made him cringe. He felt his face flush.

He'd see Wentworth from time to time, but knew Colby was in a machine gun platoon and even quartered separately. When they did encounter each other, the same smug smirk was there, as if he knew something Brian didn't.

"MacLennan!" Brian heard his name called in Shanks' inimitable croak. He looked up from his sketch of a ruined cottage to see his feisty NCO, hands on hips, not two feet away.

"When I holler, you jump, soldier."

"Sorry, Sergeant, I had my head somewhere else."

Shanks ignored the excuse. "Get your arse up to Corps. Captain Goode wants you."

"Right, Sarn." He put his drawing away, and trudged the two hundred yards through the mud to Corps Headquarters. Since the assault on Vimy Ridge, there had been two more actions along the Scarpe River in towns east of Vimy. Brian had made his maps of the areas around the towns of Arleux and Fresnoy for the troops. He'd heard talk of similar actions planned further north toward the city of Lens.

As before, Captain Goode was receiving intelligence from senior officers, all of them bent over a map table. "There you are, MacLennan," Goode said, accepted Brian's salute, and led him away from the others.

"I want to thank you for your service, but I'm returning you to regular duty."

The words were a surprise—and a tremendous relief. He liked making the maps, but hated seeing his friends return from battle filthy and exhausted while he looked on in his spotless uniform.

Goode continued. "Sorry, but an experienced cartographer has been given the job. Frankly, I thought yours were just fine, but—"

"Very good, sir!" Brian snapped another salute, happy at the thought of returning to his mates.

"Well, then…carry on, MacLennan."

Brian did a crisp about face, and returned to his platoon's billet. Shanks was still there briefing the men on their next assignment. He was pretty sure what it was, because he'd copied the maps himself.

Shanks must have known about Brian's reassignment back to duty. "MacLennan, you still know how to use an Enfield?" He didn't wait for an answer. "Listen up. I'm not going through this again!"

He went on to tell about their part in an operation up the Souchez River toward Lens. During May several raids in the area south of

Lens had been only partially successful. A small village and other objectives had been taken and briefly held, but accurate enemy artillery had succeeded in driving the Canadians back to their original lines. A full out attack on the trench that guarded Lens and its southern suburb of Avion would, if successful, provide a permanent gain.

For this action, a full rehearsal was to be held the next day on taped ground as they had done for Vimy Ridge. Brian had kept one of the small maps he'd prepared for the attack. On its reverse was the sketch of the cottage he'd been working on when relieved.

The attack was along a four mile bulge in the line around Avion and along the Souchez River that ran east/west south of Lens. The objective was to destroy German emplacements, kill or capture the enemy, then fall back before German artillery had a chance to respond. The difference between this and previous raids was the scale. Ten Canadian battalions plus a British Division north of the river would be deployed.

~ * ~

June 8, 1917

Brian followed Harry as their company moved single file along the trench into position, their Enfields fixed with bayonets. They were assigned temporarily to the 75th Battalion. Their objectives were German emplacements along the Lens-Arras Road. Royal Air Service had reported machine gun and mortar units set up in a deepened ditch along the road's edge north of a brewery building being used by the enemy for observation. These had been overrun in previous raids but subsequently re-established.

Darkness had fallen. Without an audible signal to attack, the battalions simultaneously and silently crept from their trenches. There was no pre-battle artillery barrage to announce their intentions, but every unit advanced on a run.

The full moon gave meagre light through a thin overcast, allowing the men to keep together. They ran for perhaps a hundred yards before the first enemy fire came from the tiny village to their right, but it was not directed at Brian's company. Another fifty yards and more firing came from straight ahead. Brian heard the *zip* of a bullet past his ear. A shout of pain came from his left, and the sound of a body hitting the ground. Now he could see muzzle flashes in the distance. They'd been spotted.

"Keep moving!" Lieutenant Cross' voice shouted from just ahead. He could not be seen as thickened overcast doused the moon's light. Other similar orders could be heard, right and left.

He made his profile as low as possible, holding on for dear life to his Enfield. Earlier rains made the pulverized earth muddy and the sticky clay weighed like lead on his feet. His legs burned.

The rifle fire increased. A machine gun started up. Another man on his left dropped. *Was that Harry?* He called Harry's name, but no response. The whole scene became surreal in the darkness. The only way to tell which way to go were the enemy gun flashes.

After another twenty-five yards of scuttling along the mud, the sky brightened, and he saw the shallow swale that was noted on his map. It was their first objective. From where he lay, he was protected from direct fire that was increasing rapidly. An explosion to his right could not have been five yards away. It deafened him, and the fallout of mud and dirt was so dense he lost all sight. "Keep moving!" came the order again. Another explosion. Again, a rain of French clay, this time someone's forearm and hand, a wedding band still attached. A steel helmet rolled nearby. He had an urge to flee, tempered by not being sure which way to go.

"Move, MacLennan!" It was Shanks' gravelly croak, and it had never sounded better. A hand pushed on Brian's rump, and he resumed his crawl.

"No artillery, my arse!" Shanks yelled. "They sure got mortars!"

Another explosion, but this one behind their forward progress. At the crest of the rise, Brian surprisingly could see the road just thirty or forty yards ahead. As the moon peeked out from behind a cloud, he could see a machine gun position so clearly he could make out individual soldiers, some in helmets, and others in soft caps.

The familiar *thunk* of a mortar shell being launched and the commensurate puff of smoke came from the same ditch. He turned to report it to Shanks, but the sergeant was gone, off to exhort some other frightened soldier.

What was he supposed to do? *The objective is to kill or capture the enemy and destroy their equipment.* The words were clear, but how? The ditch was too far away for a grenade from where he lay flat on the ground.

A sweep of automatic fire passed immediately overhead. He could hear the bullets as they passed… *pft-pft-pft-pft!* sure that if he even peeked over the ridge he'd be killed—but he *must*. Another blast of machine gun fire. Brian peeked to see the gunner finish his sweep from left to right. After a few seconds another sweep, this time from right to left. The pattern was repeated.

He could not sit here and cower. He'd have to chance it. The next wave came as the gunner strafed the top of the rise. *Now!*

Brian rose and charged while arming the fuse of his grenade. He lobbed it in a high arc at the trench. He could see the gunner stop shooting as he and his partner watched the grenade descend, then scramble for cover. For two long seconds nothing happened as Brian continued his rush. A bright flash and pressure wave brought him to his knees, making him lose his rifle. He picked it up and stumbled forward into the trench. Tears filled his eyes, almost blinding him.

Two bodies lay next to the overturned machine gun. One of them moved, and Brian fell forward on his rifle as the bayonet drove through the boy's chest.

Time slowed. The boy's eyes gazed skyward, then rolled back into his head. He was a husky blond-headed boy, Brian's brother's age. *Oh Jesus! Oh Jesus!* Fear and nausea combined to well up in his gut. He was paralyzed. *Think!*

The top of a building was visible down the road to the south. *The Brewery.* Brian knew it was an objective of the raid, He moved toward it down the deepened ditch, and more sounds of machine gun fire. Head down, he rounded a slight curve to spot another pair of gunners twenty yards off. He raised his Enfield and shot, dropping the gunner. The man's partner, wide eyed, dropped behind the body of the gunner draped over his weapon. Brian fired again, but heard the sickening *click* as the rifle misfired. His next image was that of the German heaving what he recognized as a "potato masher" grenade. He dove for the floor of the ditch.

The shock hit him like an anvil dropping on his chest, and then he felt nothing.

~ * ~

"Follow the light, can you soldier?" An older man's voice. Flashes of light morphed into a single source moving back and forth. Brian struggled to watch its movement.

"He's coming out of it."

He could feel discomfort in his buttock. The light stopped flashing. In its place, a man's mustached face peered down at him, a grey and white-clad nurse by his side.

"Put him in C Ward," the man said. He wore an apron, no longer white, but smeared with brownish red.

"Yes sir," she replied, and they both turned to leave.

"You alright, chum?" Another face peered down, this time one he recognized from his platoon; a man named Adam Moyer.

"I suppose I'm alive."

"You're alive alright. Got a hunk of that grenade up your arse, and a concussion, but not enough to send you home."

"What about…how did the—"

"The raid?? Good enough, I guess. They went all the way to the Avion trench and Part of Lens." Moyer kept talking, telling Brian about details from the raid. He began to drop back into sleep, hearing Moyer's voice drone.

The nurse returned with a soldier bearing a medic's arm band. She directed Moyer, who kept up the chatter, to help transfer Brian onto a gurney and then to another tent.

"Let this poor boy get some sleep now," she scolded.

Moyer left with assurances he would return.

"I couldn't shut that guy up," Brian slurred to the medic.

"He's just excited," the man replied.

"About what?"

"Saving your life. He carried your ass out of a ditch and all the way back to our lines." The medic adjusted Brian's pillow, saw to it he had water at bedside, and left.

Eleven

August 15, 1917
West of Lens, France

The trenches roasted under the sun bearing down from directly overhead. Fetid vapors rose from the puddles under the duckboards. There was no escaping it.

Brian strained to keep awake as he gazed across no-man's-land to the rise that was tomorrow's objective. Heat waves rising from the tortured earth made the few miserable sticks that were once trees shimmy like exotic dancers.

He glanced over to where Harry and Adam Moyer were pressed up against one side of the trench where a sliver of shade offered but granted no protection from the heat. Moyer had more or less replaced Ake Lankinen in their quartet of comrades since Brian's return from the hospital.

Brian liked Moyer immensely. The man, in his unassuming way, dismissed what he had done that night two months earlier. Since returning to duty the previous week, he'd been on minor scouting parties with Moyer. But for the most part, the war for the Canadian Corps had been recently quiet.

They knew that was going to change. Four brigades had been training for a week to capture the high ground on which Brian was staring, designated Hill70. As a replacement company, Brian's was assigned to one of the two brigades that would flank the hill on its right, entering the suburbs of Lens which lay to the south.

There was a tap on his helmet. "Noon, chum." A boy soldier with the haggard face of a man grinned through a cigarette in his lips. It was his relief.

Brian stood down from his post and joined his friends, leaning his Enfield against the wooden frame of the trench wall, slouching down next to it. He opened a can of the soldier's staple, *Maconochie Army Ration,* a stew that was intended to be eaten hot. Brian was probably the only man known to his friends who could stomach it cold.

Harry held one of the postcard-sized maps issued for tomorrow's assault. "Not as good as yours were."

Brian didn't comment, but privately agreed. The cartographer had added minutia such as elevation lines and landscape details superfluous to the needs of the infantryman. Brian's had been simple: The unit's objectives, numbered in order, laid out in relation to the home trenches with a yardage scale at the bottom.

"You ready for this?" Moyer asked, shooing away a rat that was boldly eyeing Brian's stew.

Brian considered the question. It would be the Canadian's biggest action since Vimy Ridge, but his concussion and shrapnel wound had healed fully. "You worried you'll have to tote me out again?"

Moyer reddened. "No, Mac…I didn't…"

"He didn't mean nothing, Brian," Harry said.

"I know. Sorry. It's just so blazing hot I can't act right." He studied his own map. The hamlets of St. Édouard and St. Émile were to the south of Hill 70. They had to be taken and held while the main attack of the summit and beyond went as planned. Fighting for these towns, which had been reduced to rubble, was mainly to engage the enemy, preventing more resources from resisting the main assault. Brian wondered if that was worth the loss of life on both sides that would inevitably occur.

Moyer read his mind. "We take that hill; it just moves the line fifteen hundred yards to the east. That's all. Then it's the same old shit. Sometimes I wonder what the hell our generals are using for brains."

Brian smirked. "Lucky for us The Hun has generals, too!"

Harry guffawed. "That assumes we *hold* the hill."

Brian nodded. "Fact is we only have three of our divisions engaged. They say Fritz has his whole Sixth Army out there. I'm thinking this might be a diversion to keep them occupied while the British are planning something bigger."

Moyer peered out on the horizon. "Now you're scaring me, MacLennan."

"I have the feeling you don't scare too easily, Adam."

Moyer glance around at the use of his first name. "Where did you learn that?"

"On the dressing station report," Brian admitted. "The medic there said you're from Manitoulin Island. Where did you train?"

It turned out that a large group of the 119th Algoma Battalion was from Manitoulin. Somehow neither Brian nor Harry had met Moyer in Niagara.

"A fellow islander!" Brian said.

"Not really," Harry put in, "now they got them a bridge to the mainland."

"Really?" Brian said.

"*Not* really," Adam Moyer said, "Well kind of. It's a rail bridge they put in five, six years ago. You can't use it for a wagon or walk across. It's a pivotal contraption that stays open until a train comes along.

"How do your folks make a living?" Brian asked.

"Same as yours, I suppose. Lots of farming there. My dad and I log, mostly."

"Got a girl back there, Moyer?" Harry smirked.

"Bet your ass, Gardinier!"

And that's how they spent the afternoon as all soldiers do: waiting, talking of home, of girls, out-thinking their officers, forgetting about their fear.

~ * ~

They watched troops from the 1st Division clamber from their trenches behind a rolling barrage in the pre-dawn light of August 15. As the sky brightened, aeroplanes from the Royal Air Service roamed, directing artillery fire. The shelling was constant, and almost as loud as the Vimy Ridge barrage of last April.

"When do we go?" Harry asked nobody in particular.

Brian was sketching the scene on the back of his map while Company C waited in the trench. "Not until those villages are taken and we're called to relieve."

"So those bastards get all the glory," Harry said.

Moyer lit another cigarette. "*Glory*! Shit I just want to survive. That's what I'm thinking."

By 8 AM the artillery barrage quieted to only directed fire, called in by forward observers and returned aircraft. One hour later, word came for them to march to the village of Cité St. Édouard. The crest of Hill 70 had been taken successfully.

They followed along a rail spur that had been badly treated by the artillery. Twisted rails and cratered road bed were interspersed with undisturbed sections of track. Haze from the burning oil of smoke bombs lingered over the fields. Along the road were shattered gun carriages, caissons, and mangled horses, their mouths agape in last minute anguish.

Soon, with the rise of Hill 70 on their left, they could see the roofs of the city of Lens on their right. They entered St. Édouard around 10 AM. There was almost nothing left of the place, from where its citizens had long since fled, mostly to Arras, they supposed.

Brian wondered about those citizens, and if they ever would, or could, return to the life they knew. He doubted it. This war was destroying more than houses, shops, and roads. It was obliterating a culture.

Already preparations were being made for an expected counterattack. Horses were drawing up the eighteen pound guns of the field artillery they'd marched with. Positions along the north, east, and south edges of the village were being hardened. They learned how the first wave overwhelmed the enemy who, for the most part, had retreated, and were assumed to be regrouping.

Almost immediately, as feared, the counterattack materialized. To the south, and over a slight rise, came a line of infantry. The eighteen pounders and mortar units had set up and begun getting their range. Soon the artillery began to produce gaps in the enemy lines, but on they came. The order to fix bayonets was given and repeated around the rim of the village.

"We're in for a cock-up," Adam Moyer called out over the cannons and shouting of orders.

Brian fixed his bayonet. The memory of that great spike entering the chest of a boy returned. He watched the enemy advance over the pock-marked field, the gloriously blue sky of the otherwise beautiful summer day at their backs. The mortars started pumping their projectiles into the sky, having found their range. Brian could see individuals falling, or taking cover, he couldn't tell which.

On they came. Soon they were within rifle range. "Fire at will," came an anonymous order. He fired off two rounds, but saw no results. A second wave of enemy soldiers appeared over the rise.

Above the din he could hear a frightened voice reciting the Lord's Prayer. It was somehow comforting, despite his liturgical doubts. He squeezed off two more rounds and saw a man, perhaps a hundred yards away, go down—*so much more sterile way of killing than the bayonetting of that boy in the roadside ditch last June.*

The two sides had different advantages. To be sure, the Germans had the numbers, possibly two to one. But the Canadians had the cover of the ruined town and additional artillery support from the top of the newly captured Hill 70.

The Germans were relentless in their attack, despite their lack of cover. At fifty yards, machine gun platoons opened fire and slowed the first wave, but by then the second wave was at hand.

Brian reloaded, and emptied a clip as enemy soldiers reached the low wall where he and his company had been posted. The wide-eyed face of a helmeted German appeared while Brian slammed a new clip into his weapon. The man almost fell on him as he pulled the trigger. Another grey uniform hurled itself over the wall only to be caught by his bayonet.

A red rage burst in Brian's head—more from disgust and fear than from hatred. Killing had become easier. It was a demon beneath his rib cage, taunting him to join in the mayhem. Fighting turned hand-to-hand, except for those still firing from cover.

What seemed like an hour, but not fifteen minutes later, the upper hand was gained, and the enemy retreated toward Lens ahead of relentless fire.

This round went to the Canadians at the cost of heavy losses. Casualties in C Company were forty. Half of those were killed. Brian knew them all, two of them well. He would never be the same.

~ * ~

They held the village for another 24 hours. Surely they'd be told to pull back to the Canadian lines. The hill was taken, and the little hamlet of Cité St. Édouard had no more tactical importance.

They were wrong. The taking of Hill 70, and the success in repulsing the German contingent from Lille convinced someone in the Canadian command to march on Lille itself.

A medical unit was evacuating the Canadian dead and wounded, one hundred-eighty casualties in all. Brian watched the wagons wobble down the rutted road. Another train of troops and equipment came up the same road from the rear. Light artillery, mortar and machine gun platoons joined what appeared to be another eight hundred to a thousand troops.

He and Harry were sharing a cigarette in their section of the perimeter. Lieutenant Cross was nearby, taking a long pull from his canteen when they heard a familiar voice.

"Lieutenant Cross, sir," It was George Kobak.

"George!" Harry called, but Kobak was all business.

"What is it, Private?" Cross screwed the top back on his canteen.

"I need to speak with Captain Goode," George said.

Cross seemed to consider the request before realizing it might be something important, and said, "I'll take you to him."

They were away for several minutes while Brian and Harry pondered what that was all about. Moyer walked over to the two. "The stench is getting to me," he said, holding a cloth to his face.

Harry nodded. "That and the flies. We should give this pile of bricks back to Fritz and let him pick up his dead."

The streets of the destroyed town were filled with troops. Officers and NCOs shouted orders, trying to keep discipline in their commands amongst the rubble of Cité St. Édouard. Lieutenant Cross returned with Captain Goode, who assembled the entire company outside the ruins of a bakery.

"Now listen up," Goode began his instructions to Company C. "Our battalion will be part of an attack on the city of Lens. We will be part of the Fourth Infantry Division's attack of the city. We will be on the right flank of the Brigade."

It would mean moving the battalion out of this village in a wide counter-clockwise arc around Lens to the right of 4th Division's position.

They formed up and moved southeast for about two miles to where they'd been assigned alongside another one of the Fourth's battalions. After about an hour of confusion, they began their march toward the German lines.

"Who are these guys?" Moyer wondered aloud.

"Don't know," Brian said. "Think that battalion's from Vancouver, though. Seem like good enough chaps. They seem happy to have us."

"Spreads the odds, the more of us there are," Harry said.

They were advancing over open terrain in a one mile-wide portion of no-man's-land.

The Division's artillery started up. They could hear the shriek of the eighteen pounders from guns that had been drawn up to positions close behind. Explosions began to erupt ahead. Plumes of dirt and smoke rose up from over the rise.

An explosion lifted the earth and more than one soldier into the air not fifty feet away. They all went to ground as dirt rained down. Instinctively the three friends spread out as if to ensure against their mutual demise.

We've been zeroed in on, Brian thought, as the whole company hunkered down in a shallow ditch. The Germans must have had a battery of mortars, because the bombardment continued for several minutes with no let-up. It was so intense Brian wanted to bury his head in the soft dirt…his feelings were beyond fear as he waited for death. *My God, make it stop!* He felt his bowels begin to liquefy and knew he was about to foul himself. The bombardment—or *minenwerfer*—abruptly ended, but after many minutes of murderous intensity.

Shelling from their own lines increased. The infantry of the 4th Division and supporting units were in full run. Brian straggled forward. A double line of barbed wire was just below the crest of a rise. Orders were given to take cover. The most likely place there in the open was an old (or not so old) shell crater. Brian watched in awe as designated men bravely scuttled forward with wire cutters, adding gaps in the wire where the shelling had failed. Some were left there, lifeless, hanging on the wire they had just cut. In a matter of minutes, the whistle to advance was given. They rushed for the openings in the wire, pulling the coils aside as they passed.

Then, once more, all hell broke loose. This time, machine gun fire from multiple positions, and it was directed on the gaps. Soon men were tripping over their fallen mates in order to get through.

Brian was one of the first of twenty or so who made it through, finding cover with three others behind the roots of an overturned tree. The machine guns were spread some fifty yards apart, forming the German's first line of defense with enfiladed fire.

One of their group, a corporal from the 46th, took charge. "Look here, boys. We ain't gonna live if we don't take out that nest up there."

Brian looked at the other two: one of them a kid he didn't know, scared out of his mind, the other a man from first platoon, much like himself—scared, but rational.

"What you have in mind, Corporal?" Brian shouted over the combined noise of the shelling and machine gun chatter.

"Those Huns gotta reload sometime. When they do, we rush in behind 'em and pay a visit to their back door."

It didn't sound like much of a plan to Brian, but then what else was there to do? They waited while the *minenwerfer* continued to rain down on the Canadians who had drawn back from the wire, and the machine guns continued to mow down anything that moved. He thought about Adam's words about sensing a "cock-up." If this wasn't it, he couldn't guess what was.

As predicted, the machine gun stopped.

"Now or never, lads!" the corporal hissed."

To Brian's surprise, the soldier who had seemed so frightened, drew a breath, set his jaw and leapt from cover up the rise. Brian felt himself respond, and followed as if his legs had control of his brain. The sound of the others' feet slapping the ground was close behind.

Just then intense small arms fire commenced from the crest of the rise where the Germans had been entrenched and waiting. Most of it seemed to be directed over the wire at the dug-in Canadians. Then, friendly artillery fire began finding its range on the German trench.

The nearby machine gun started up again, joining their comrades down the line.

The corporal motioned Brian to approach the gun emplacement from the opposite side, along with the young troop. The corporal and the other man would approach from the other side.

As they ran, Brian felt a bullet rip through his backpack. The machine gun position was surrounded by sandbags on all sides. The gunner was strafing back and forth. One of the men was cooling the barrel with a wet towel. Two others were handling ammunition. It was one of those who spotted them. He got off a shot, killing the man from first platoon, and paid for it in kind. The three remaining Canadians emptied their clips into the dugout. The gunner slumped against his weapon, causing the barrel to point awkwardly into the uncaring summer sky.

"Gas!" came a cry from somewhere. The word was the same in German as English. Brian paused to determine the origin of the alarm.

"Let's go!" The corporal shoved him in the back.

But Brian stood transfixed as a greenish cloud crept over the crest where enemy troops in masks began to descend toward them.

"Now!" the corporal shouted, and was well away toward the wire.

Brian and the young troop followed in his dust. He fumbled in vain to open the flap of his gas mask bag, bounding down the hill. Puffs of dust exploded around them. At the gap, the corporal went down, his helmet being the only part of him to make it through.

Together, Brian and his companion soldier leapt over the body of the nameless corporal, their leader just minutes ago. The barbed wire caught Brian's arm, tearing away a patch of cloth and adding a three inch gash on his shoulder.

His throat began to burn before he thought to put the mask he held in his hand to his face. Ahead, the whole 4th Army was in retreat from the gas. He looked to find the young soldier who had been so brave, but the boy had either fallen, or was off in a different direction.

They ran and ran until the fickle wind shifted the gas away from the southeastern boundary of Lens, France.

Twelve

Late September 1917
In transit to Roulers, Flanders

He could smell her, feel her breath on his cheek. Käthe Von Helm's breast was soft under his touch. He gently, lovingly moved down over her satin-smooth belly to the reward waiting there. It was… the boxcar rumbled over a trestle, arousing Jürgen from his reverie. He lifted his gaze to the scene. Forty tired and hungry soldiers, heads bobbing to the jostling sway of the train.

They were headed north. The rumor was liberty in Antwerp, but he didn't believe it. Exaggerated stories of good times and easy women were being spread by young men no older or worldly than he. Wishful thinking was more like it, he thought.

His eyes found Hoffner asleep on the straw-covered floor by the big sliding door. He'd been released from the dressing station and declared fit for duty. Alfred Hauser had visited him over the three weeks of his recovery, and they'd become close. It was a strange friendship; Alfred the sensitive, delicate featured musician, and Hoffner, the often crass, boastful, know-it-all.

Sun slanted in through an opening by the door, illuminating Berg, Sternkopf, and Veldstein gambling for cigarettes on the dirty floor boards. The heat and the monotonous motion of the boxcar caused him to drop into a half-sleep once more.

They had held the Roeux-Gavrelle line for four months until a day ago when they were relieved by a Bavarian unit. After the attack on the chemical works and rail station, followed by the failed attempt to overwhelm the British 17 Corps, they dug in at their original trenches, suffering constant harassment and casualties from artillery and night raids.

The commanders were obdurate in maintaining a strategy of a defensive war, hoping to defeat the enemy through attrition. Jürgen could not see how that was working, in the least.

For every victory and for every defeat, it seemed the losses on both sides were equal. The British were bringing in troops from their entire empire: Australians, New Zealanders, Indians, South Africans, and of course, the Canadians. Now it seemed the Americans had entered the war as well. *Beat them by attrition? How could we?*

The train rocked on for another two hours, stopping on a siding once or twice to let a southbound train or lone engine pass. It was late afternoon when it slowed for the last time. Jürgen peeked through a crack to see a sign announce the town of Roulers.

"Must be Belgium," he said to himself, aloud.

"More specifically, Flanders." The voice was Feldwebel Büler's.

"What's the difference?" he asked the older man.

"In the north, Belgians are more like the Dutch. They even speak it."

"It looks like a busy place." Jürgen had his face to the crack. "How long are we here, Feldwebel?"

Büler laughed. "They don't consult sergeants on those matters, Stern. You'll do much better in the army by putting one foot in front of the other, and not concerning yourself so much with the future."

It was a cynical outlook, but Jürgen knew he was right. It was how he'd learned to cope over the past months of paralyzing fear, watching comrades die, their bodies wrenched apart by a mortar shell, or rendered lifeless by a sniper's bullet. So far, his little group of friends had come through unscathed, save minor injuries from flying shrapnel. They all suffered from poor nutrition, dysentery, and lack of sleep. Their saving grace at Gavrelle had been the well-built trenches. Only direct or near hits had caused most of the fatalities.

~ * ~

They detrained to find a town with some shops still operating, but many already destroyed or abandoned and looted. They marched to an assembly area where, nearby, they were assigned to quarters in an abandoned factory, and immediately dismissed until evening rations could be found for the two hundred-twenty hungry men of Company III.

Jürgen, along with Hauser, Berg, and Hoffner, wandered off down the main street of the town. It was busy with military vehicles, horse drawn carts, and soldiers. Hoffner, despite his humbling experience at Gavrelle, assumed his leadership role, and led the excursion, making instructional comments about this or that.

But it was Jürgen who had been endowed with an innate mien of leadership, and the others naturally gravitated to him as they walked. He couldn't help but notice what a charming town Roulers had once been. The shops, such as cobblers, drapers, haberdashers were all dark or destroyed. Curiously, the *estaminets* seemed to be going strong. They counted at least three operating in various stages of repair.

"Who has money?" Jürgen asked.

They managed to pool together some French centimes and German pfennigs, and entered a door under a sign advertising "De Drei Koningen."

At once, they were uncomfortable. Two of the four tables were occupied with officers.

Alfred whispered, "We'd better go."

The officers at the near table looked their way, but said nothing.

"No," Jürgen said. "Pull up some chairs over there. We'll order some good *pils*."

To his relief, the proprietor wiped his hands on a soiled apron and approached.

"*Heren*?" the man's eyes darted to the officers' tables.

"How much for beer?" Jürgen inquired in German.

The man gave him the price, which was thankfully just within their resources.

"Yes! Four beers, please."

The beer was drawn, and served in clay mugs.

"Not bad," Berg, the oldest, said.

Jürgen had been used to drinking at home since he turned fifteen, and agreed with Berg. It seemed there were some things even this miserable war could not affect. "A little warm, but my first since Lockstedt."

They soon settled into a somewhat exaggerated conviviality stimulated by their first freedom of any kind since enlistment.

Hoffner said, "I say to hell with our dinner. We'll just drink it!"

Berg laughed. "You're the one with no money!"

"I'll pay you all back. I'm good for it!" Hoffner's face reddened under his blond, almost platinum hair.

"If we ever get paid," Hauser said, sipping gingerly at his mug.

Hoffner noticed. "Not a drinker, Alfred! Don't they have beer in Stade?"

"Don't worry about me, Heinz. When yours is gone, I'll still be drinking."

The banter continued until, as Hauser predicted, their mugs were dry. It was time to pay. On the table their shared coins were counted out, and the proprietor came over to collect.

"You, men!"

Four heads turned to see one of the officers approaching. His tunic displayed the braided collar board of a field officer—two pips indicating an *oberst*, or full colonel.

They shot to their feet, wide-eyed.

"What is your unit?"

They looked to Hoffner, their *gefreiter* and nominal leader, but he was speechless, mouth agape.

"Two hundred thirty-eighth Infantry, sir. Four thirty-six Regiment," Jürgen replied. "We have just arrived from the Roeux-Gavrelle line, *Oberst*."

The colonel said nothing, but waited as the proprietor scraped up the coins from the table. "Herr Dykstra. Bring these brave soldiers another round and add it to my bill. They are the heart and soul of The Fatherland. And be generous with your draft, Dykstra." He returned to his table without another word.

The men waited for their beer in silence before Alfred said, "Those officers—they look so confident. Do you suppose they know if Germany will win this war?"

"What do you mean, 'if?'" Hoffner scoffed. "Haven't you seen the buildup of troops and guns here? Germany will march to Paris by Christmas."

Jürgen hunched his shoulders. "Remember that big blast that shook the earth back in June? Feldwebel Büler says it was miles north of Lens, yet we still felt it. He says thousands of our men died when the English detonated several large mines at once and won a major victory near the town of Messines."

"Hoffner could be right," Berg said. "If we weren't strong, they would have continued on after such a victory, but we held."

Jürgen couldn't deny he had wondered why the enemy hadn't pressed their advantage, if the explosion at Messines was so devastating. "One thing is sure," he said. "They haven't brought us up here for nothing. Something big is about to happen."

"Now you are making sense." Hoffner took a last gulp of beer.

"Are you frightened, Jürgen?" Alfred cocked his head slightly.

Jürgen considered how to answer the question, but was preempted by a very close-by explosion. Dust filtered down from the ceiling and glassware rattled on shelves behind the bar. The four soldiers found themselves taking cover were they could. Oddly the officers hadn't moved except to brush bits of plaster from their uniforms.

One, a junior officer, called to them. "You boys must get used to city life. That was just Tommy sending us a good night kiss!" The others chuckled appreciatively.

"Let's drink up and go," Jürgen said. "I'm hungry."

~ * ~

They stayed in Roulers for three more days with little to do but "stand to" each morning and evening. The increasing military traffic in and out of town was obvious. Troops from other units, including the two other regiments of their own division, were pouring in. It was becoming clear that Jürgen's earlier speculation about an imminent battle was correct.

Moving an infantry division from one place to another is a logistical nightmare. In 1917 the typical German division was composed of over eight thousand men plus officers. It had taken a month to arrange the move of the 238th from Northern France to Flanders, and another four days to communicate with, and assemble, the three regiments for a march en masse a mere ten kilometers to the west. For Jürgen and his friends, the word *west* confirmed they would be taking part in the immense preparations that were taking place.

They set out on a march through town, and by noon they were encamped on the eastern slope of a hill near what remained of the village of West Roosebeke. Here there was no shelter against the steady rain that began on the afternoon of their arrival.

Latrines had to be dug, canvas tents were distributed (typically not until after the rain had started), one to every four troops. Mess facilities were set up, one for each battalion of eight hundred sixty men. There were no pre-dug trenches there. It was merely a holding area, to be sure.

They lived thus for the next week, hunkered down, trying in vain to keep their weapons dry. Adding to their misery was a new wave of dysentery among the men. Long queues formed for a turn to straddle the boards thrown over the latrine pits.

And the rain increased.

Thirteen

October, 1917
Ypres, Belgium

What was left of the original brigade was barely recognizable to Brian. Since the attack on Lens and Hill 70, replacements had come to fill losses going back to the Vimy Ridge offensive. That Ake Lankinen was the only casualty (other than himself) among his closest friends was hard to believe.

In an unprecedented act of transparency, they were informed the entire Hill 70 operation had been a feint to draw the enemy's resources away from Flanders, where the next big drive would be. What was not said, but was well rumored, was the feint did little to create the desired outcome. This, at the expense of almost ten thousand Allied casualties. A period of inactivity followed up and down the northern sector of the Western Front. Idleness is the soldier's enemy, and morale had hit a low point.

Early October was passed doing the mind-numbing tasks associated with moving the entire Canadian Corps from northern France to a position east of Ypres, replacing British and Anzac units. The entire support organization had to be re-deployed…supply depots, dressing stations, mess facilities, command centers. All of this carried out by the rank and file, slogging through rain-mired country roads. The artillery suffered the most. The distance of not more than thirty miles might as well have been several hundred. The men knew there had been two previous "battles to end the war" at Ypres (Wipers, they called it) and were not easily inspired that this would be any different.

~ * ~

The city of Ypres was, after being three years near the front lines, reduced to nothing that resembled its storied glory. Brian's unit had stopped there while receiving rations and line assignments. He took time to sketch what was left of the famous Cloth Hall, a magnificent building that dated back to the thirteenth century. Much of it was completely destroyed by German bombing, but the famous tower hadn't been leveled.

He'd managed to scavenge more map cards from the Hill 70 attack, and had been using one of them for the Cloth Hall. The sketch and his pencils were stowed in his pack, and he was on his way for the mess wagon when he literally ran into Colby Wentworth.

"Easy there, McLennan! What's the hurry?"

Christ! Wentworth. "Just on my way to the mess."

"You'd better hurry. They're shutting down soon."

Brian said nothing, but commenced on his way.

Wentworth called after him, "By the way, McLennan, have you heard from Sarah?"

Brian stopped. The words hit him like a cudgel. He turned. "Why…would you care?"

"Oh, no reason. Just thought you'd like news from home. She says all the ladies of the Women's Institute are knitting scarves and socks for the boys."

Brian turned on his heel, continuing on his way. His face was flushed, his ears ringing as if he'd taken a blow to the head.

~ * ~

They arrived on the line on 18 October, replacing the 2nd Anzac Corps with orders to take and hold the high ridge between the town of Passchendaele and the village of Westroosebeke. Their position was little different from that of the British in the spring of 1915. It was an objective the British had failed at twice before, and had become almost an obsession of British Field Marshal Douglas Haig's. General Currie was given the task of doing the impossible.

Currie was against the plan, feeling the weather and terrain was not conducive for an attack, and the potential loss of life not worth the small chance of a breakthrough. Haig prevailed.

Once more, General Currie was meticulous in his planning. Once more he was issuing the postcard maps to the men, but Brian was excused from this duty again for which he was grateful. If this was to be the "big one," he wanted to be with his comrades.

Outside of Ypres they had rehearsed what was to occur on the field. As in past Canadian involvements, objectives were laid out in the form of colored lines. Key reference points were designated; the foundation of a farmhouse, the remnants of a church, the mangled rail line to Roulers.

It was along these tracks where Brian's battalion was assigned, supporting the 46th Battalion of the 4th Division. This was the far right flank of the Canadian Corps. The men knew the 46th well, having fought alongside them at Vimy, and Hill 70.

As the weather turned cooler, one of the first things the men noticed was the greatcoats of the Ypres veterans. They were short; knee length instead of at the issued mid-calf, and they soon discovered why. The sticky, yellow Flanders mud would gather at the skirt and add considerable weight to the coat. By then, the high command had turned a blind eye to the practice of cutting off as much as a foot from the skirts. After only days in the area, Brian and his mates followed suit.

His first impression of the now famous Ypres salient was the utter lack of any sign of a former civilization. There was not a man-made structure standing, nor a tree or bush. The entire front was an ocean of grey-yellow mud pocked with huge, water-filled craters as far as a man could see.

On the 22nd of October, the barrage of German positions commenced. The men knew it could be hours or a few days before the assault began, but begin it would.

~ * ~

October 25. 1917
Near Moorslede, Belgium

The 10th Bavarian Regiment had been replaced by units of the *Gruppe Ypres,* fresh infantry to which the 238th Division was juxtaposed for the expected allied offensive. For four days, the shelling along their lines had been almost unbearable. The men were becoming inured to seeing whole platoons dismembered by a direct hit, or a solitary hunk of shrapnel tear into a man standing nearby.

Jürgen heard the increased shelling was due to the exhausted Anzac troops being replaced by the artillery minded Canadians. It made no difference to him. Both had reputations of being dogged fighters. But the damned shelling! It was constant. The village of Moorslede was rubble, hardly a building standing. Lately the British aeroplanes had gained superiority over Flanders. They were flying bombers with impunity, and with pinpoint accuracy.

The battle lines, as usual, were static, or nearly so. Each side would lose hundreds, even thousands of men for a few yards of real estate. *Real estate!* The land was nothing but rain-soaked pulverized earth with craters so deep and close together as to make it impossible to traverse in a straight line.

The men were completely spent. The rain-soaked soil stuck and sucked at their boots. The slightest wound or misstep could cause a man to fall into a crater, many of them chest-deep in water. Without help it was impossible to extricate oneself. Many wounded or disoriented drowned in the chaos of the battle, but the Germans, with the high ground, were told they had it better than the attacking Canadians.

The 238th had been assigned to retake a wooded area the maps called Decline Copse. They had been slogging in the ditches along the Ypres-Roulers rail line making dugouts and machine gun emplacements. With the increased enemy shelling over the past three days, the task was like living in hell.

Jürgen looked around at his comrades. Hoffner had been killed the day they arrived on the line, Sternkopf removed to the rear with a foot blown away. Half the men were replacements he barely knew. Where was the bravado of Lockstedt just months ago? Jürgen did not think he had the energy to fight when it came time, and they knew that was inevitable. The enemy does not waste munitions unless it is preparing to attack. He was wet clear through to his skin and covered in the slippery clay of Flanders.

His name was called, and he jerked as he came alert. "Stern!"

It was Lieutenant Stoner.

"Stern—you are the sharpshooter?"

He hadn't been assigned to a *heckenshüztze* post since his first weeks of active duty. He blinked, saluting. "Yes, Lieutenant!"

Stoner consulted a map. "Three hundred meters down the track is a rail station. Go down there and set up a post. We expect penetration from the enemy tomorrow, latest. You will be our first alert. Pick off an officer, if you can. That should slow their advance while they figure out next in command. You can identify an officer. He'll be carrying a pistol instead of a rifle." He pointed to the station on the map where what looked like a wooded area was shown nearby. "You can make it into those woods, then back to our position."

Jürgen swallowed hard. There was no arguing with the lieutenant. Corporal Koss, the *unteroffizier,* perhaps. Not even Sergeant Büler, the strict but fair *feldwebel.* This sounded like a suicide mission.

"Yes, Lieutenant! At once!" He saluted.

"Get some water and food for the night, Stern." Stoner returned the salute and strode away with a task for some other *volunteer.*

~ * ~

Jürgen sighted his scope down the track. He had a clear view sitting in the shadows well back of the second story window. It was perfect, his rifle resting on a crate he'd found on the tracks below. What was not so perfect was the fact that the "thick" woods on the map had become a denuded collection of sticks, their branches and leaves having been blown away by relentless barrages. His chances of using the woods for cover were almost nil. The station was still standing only because of thick stone walls and the lack of a direct hit. Its interior stairwell was barely intact.

In the distance, he thought he could see the wire of the Canadian lines. He'd been told they were just hundreds of meters away. It was almost dark. Not even the Canadians would begin an offensive at night. He settled in for a long night, trying not to think of what might come in the morning.

~ * ~

October 26. 1917
Near Moorslede, Belgium

Jürgen stared out into the black. He'd been dozing, and the realization shocked him into alertness. Something was different. It was the silence. The incessant rain had stopped, as had the sound of the enemy's big guns. He had no idea what time it was, carefully making his way to the window and listening. Nothing.

The end of the barrage meant the attack was imminent. Possibly forty-five minutes passed, and then something. He could barely make out shapes in the predawn light. *It's the attack!* Before he could find a target, he could hear footsteps already directly below.

How could he shoot when he had no clear target? Shuffling sounds came from inside the building. He returned to his rifle, taking it with him under the crate he'd used as its mount. *Don't even breathe.*

He waited for the sound of footsteps on the stairs, but none came, only the sound of a thousand boots crunching on the ground, possibly the whicker of a horse, a whispered command. Then, as quickly as they had come, they were gone, having passed through to the east.

He tried to come to grips with the fact he had failed in both his objectives…the most damaging was not engaging the enemy, thereby depriving his unit forewarning of the enemy's advance. Only a few minutes later, he heard the first sounds of small arms fire and its crescendo into all-out battle.

Jürgen was miserable and at a loss for what to do. *I am now in enemy territory.* He emerged from his hiding place and strode to the window. The morning was brightening, revealing a pitiful landscape of twisted rails and cratered earth, all shrouded in ground fog.

But there was something else…the figure of a lone man following the rail bed, and coming toward the station. He carried no rifle. *An officer!* Jürgen quietly checked the breach of his Mauser for a seated round. This was his belated chance to make up, even partially, for his failure. *Come closer!*

The man was walking, head down, picking his way through the detritus of the destroyed rail tracks. Jürgen sighted for the head, a sure kill, and squeezed the trigger.

The sound of the gun echoed in the empty room. Under the window, Jürgen saw the man drop face down, arms outstretched. His saucer-shaped helmet spun away like a top.

Got him.

He took the rifle down to the first floor to get a better look. There he was, not five meters from the doorway. He laid aside his weapon and ran to the prone figure, turning the body over. This was no officer!

Jürgen had no idea who else might be following the man. *Get him out of sight.* He dragged the body into the station and retrieved his rifle, thinking about what to do. He took time to look at the soldier he'd killed. Canadian, alright, the collar pin with the maple leaves surrounding the number 119. *Better check his pockets.*

Yes. There was something in each breast pocket of the tunic. One was a letter written under what looked like a military letterhead, and signed by someone with the title: Commander, the word almost identical to the one in German.

Jürgen could speak some English, but the writer's longhand script was illegible to him. He put the letter in his own pocket. The other item was a postcard-sized map on stiff cardboard. None of the locations or notations on it seemed to have anything to do with this area. Among them was a road with an arrow labeled "TO LENS." That was miles from here…useless.

He noticed something on the reverse side, a drawing—that of a girl. She was beautiful, and Jürgen thought of Käthe as he had done often over the past months while holed up in some miserable trench or dugout.

There was a soft exhale that emanated from the soldier's body. A death rattle? Jürgen put his fingers to the man's open mouth, but could not be sure. He chambered a round into the Mauser, and pointed it at the temple.

No. He couldn't. This would be murder, not war. The man was probably dead anyway. He stuffed the map into his pocket with the other, and fled into what meagre cover the woods and the fog might provide.

Fourteen

October 26, 1917
Canadian Corps
Near Zonnebeke, Belgium

They huddled together, keeping warm under a rubber sheet in their shell crater. The men had been moved as far forward as possible overnight in preparation for the assault.

Brian's company was temporarily attached to the 4th Army's 46th Battalion, responsible for the Corps' right flank. Their first objective in the coming battle was to follow the old Ypres-Rouelers rail line (roughly northeast) to a German strongpoint established near a wood indicated on the map as Decline Copse.

Harry Gardenier cradled his rifle, keeping it clear of the mud. "I got a bad feeling this time, Brian old boy. I'm thinkin' it wouldn't be so bad to be Kobak, nice and dry back in Corps HQ."

"Shut the hell up, Harry." Adam Moyer poked the rubber sheet with the tip of his barrel and peered out into the dark. "Rain's let up; only a mist."

Brian thought of George, and remembered how miserable he had felt when his mates went off to fight, and he stayed back making maps. He climbed up the side of the crater in an effort to keep his feet out of the water.

Harry noticed. "My socks are already wet."

"To hell with your socks. Think about getting your ass back in one piece!" Moyer said.

Brian was about to comment when the whistled signal came. It was 5:40 AM.

"This is it, boys!" they heard Sgt. Shanks call from the next crater. That was the last order they heard. Silently, thousands of men emerged from their dugouts, craters, and trenches along a two hundred yard line and began their part of General Currie's plan to assault the Passchendaele Ridge. Twice before it had ended in failure.

For a while, the men skirted water-filled craters walking on wooden grates laid by the engineers, but those were soon gone. They picked their way, often single file, occasionally having to help a man who'd stumbled into one of the holes as dangerous as quicksand. They trudged in silence, only the sucking step on the man ahead to be heard. Keeping that man in sight was the only way to know where to go.

When they came to the rail bed, the going got easier. Brian followed a horse laden with two Vickers machine guns. They'd been walking for less than a quarter hour when the indistinct shape of a building loomed ahead. By then, the battalion had spread out over a wide swath. Lt. Cross held up a hand, signaling a halt. They waited, but no enemy activity ensued. Cautiously Cross advanced, and they followed. As they passed the ruined train station, Brian noticed a few of the troops nosing around on the ground floor, but he continued up the rail bed.

They'd gone another one or two hundred yards when the first shot rang out. In the foggy, first light of day he couldn't be sure from which side it was fired, but other shots followed.

The advancing troops were frantically searching for cover. Brian found an overturned railroad hand car, and was joined by two others, neither from his company. He could see muzzle flashes through the ground fog. Others began returning fire.

xplode among them. One landed behind them, hrapnel hard against the hand car inches from

of the others.

It was Sgt. Shanks, already leading the way forward, his bayonet prodding the mist. Brian knew to stay there would be lethal. He and the others reluctantly followed. He snapped on his bayonet.

Increased shooting from ahead, this time augmented by machine gun. A cry of pain from his right as a man went down, then another. Still Shanks edged forward, signaling his platoon to follow. Mortar explosions continued at their rear, confirming Shanks' wisdom in moving forward.

A second machine gun started up, forcing the Canadians to ground. Brian crawled forward to where Shanks lay flat.

"You okay, Sarn?"

Shanks spit a clot of Flanders soil from his mouth "Think so. You see that M-G?" He motioned to a spot where bursts of fire were coming.

Brian nodded.

"You and me are gonna shut it down."

Brian had no idea how that might be accomplished, but waited for Shanks to continue. The sergeant pointed to Brian and to the right of the machine gun. Then he pointed to himself and to the gun's left. Brian nodded his comprehension of what he assumed his NCO had in mind.

Between bursts of fire, Brian crawled through mounds of dirt hurled up by earlier shelling. At times he'd been sure he was spotted, and would lie flat in the wet soil, waiting for the fatal bullet that did not come. Inch by inch he wormed his way to a depression about five yards to the right of the gun emplacement, and waited. Surely Shanks would take the lead. This was his idea, after all.

From opposite the machine gun nest came the unmistaka of a British Enfield rifle firing as fast as the weapon would Shouts in German rose from the nest.

Now! Brian sprang from his spot to see a crew of three. Two of them were intent on repelling Shanks fire, but the other caught sight of Brian who, in turn, squeezed off a round, finding the man's chest. The other two turned their attention to their fallen comrade, and to Brian. One had a pistol, fired and missed when Brian dropped to the ground.

More shots from Shanks' gun sounded.

"Let's go!" the sergeant yelled.

Brian rose to see three dead soldiers in their well-constructed M-G nest.

"Stay low." Shanks pointed in the direction of their own troops. "Friendly fire." They were in danger of being mistaken for the enemy. "We'll get the other one now," Shanks called over his shoulder.

The noise of battle was intense. The insect buzz of a bullet passing close by was a much too common occurrence. He followed Shanks to where they'd heard the second machine gun, only to find it abandoned. Brian saw two helmets appear over a mound of dirt. Canadian helmets. Shanks waved to them. Others followed.

"They've pulled back," Shanks said to one of the men, a lieutenant whom Brian did not recognize.

The officer had no chance to respond before they were thrown to the ground by an explosion just yards away. For long seconds, Brian could hear nothing. He checked to see if he had all his parts. Amazingly, he still grasped his rifle. One of the soldiers was badly wounded. Another explosion not far away.

"That's mortar fire on their old position," the lieutenant called. "Keep moving on, and get out of here!" He blew on his whistle, signaling his men to follow.

Brian looked back to the wounded man, but Shanks pulled at his sleeve. "Move it, McLennan."

~ * ~

The pitiful remains of what might have been an attractive wood was now nothing but a collection of ugly boles looking like they'd been jabbed into the ground by some giant hand.

It was not yet 8:00 AM and they had, albeit with significant casualties, driven the enemy from their hold on Decline Copse. The copse was on higher ground, and by taking it, they'd deprived the enemy of an excellent defensive position.

Brian expected them to dig in here, but soon orders came for them to keep advancing. It took fifteen minutes for all the units to get the new marching orders.

The 46th battalion was emerging from the copse en masse when the shelling started. Perhaps twenty huge explosions hit them within a few seconds and continued in intense bombardment. "Those are big guns!" someone yelled. It was clear they'd been lured into an artillery trap. The only option was to retreat. By 9:00 AM they were dug in not far past their morning position. Decline Copse was back in enemy hands.

~ * ~

October 26
238th Battalion
North of Decline Copse

Horst Veldstein huffed as he ran. Jürgen watched him tumble into the newly dug trench. The men were sprinting back to this secure position after their cursory defense of the Copse.

"Let them take it," Jürgen had heard the commander declare, "Our artillery is trained on their coordinates. Their casualties will be devastating."

It was part of the new German philosophy of "flexible defense," and it was taking its toll on the enemy. They'd been ordered to make a showing, then fall back, luring the enemy into an artillery ambush.

"Will it work?" Berg wondered aloud.

No one replied, all wondering the same thing. The rain had returned in earnest, and the temperature was not far above freezing.

His friends were happy to see him alive.

"What did they say to you when you returned, Jürgen?" Alfred asked, looking out across the field to the edge of the Copse.

"Ah…I was supposed to have picked off two or three of them, starting a lot of shooting that would be a signal to you. I couldn't, though. It was too dark to see."

"Are you in trouble?"

"No, I shot and got something from a messenger that must have been important, the way the brass reacted."

"What was it?" Berg said.

"Couldn't read it. I did see something about October thirtieth, though."

Alfred turned to look at Jürgen. "I hope we are all here in three days."

The morose words were sentiments shared by all. Until then, the 238th had been posted mostly in support roles, sharing the miseries of life in the trenches, but spared the worst of the fighting. This defense of the Passchendaele Ridge had put an end to that.

Twice before, the first time exactly three years ago, the enemy had made major offensives driving east from Ypres. Thousands were dead as a result. This time the 463d Regiment, including Jürgen's company, was in the advance. Sooner or later hell would come.

~ * ~

When Jürgen had reported to his commanders that morning, he noticed a formidable array of artillery dug in well hidden behind a long swale. As the men waited in silence, the guns suddenly went off in unison. They could hear the shells scream as they passed overhead and black bursts began peppering the Copse and surrounds. Jürgen wondered how the merest of living things could survive the barrage, much less a soldier.

The shelling continued for fifteen minutes, then abruptly stopped when the order was given to charge the inflicted area with fixed bayonets.

They shot out of the shallow trenches and poured across the field, not knowing who or what would be dug in to meet them. To their surprise, the resistance was only a rear guard posted to slow their progress and allow an orderly fallback. By 9:00 AM, Decline Copse was back in German hands.

~ * ~

October 27

Canadian Corps

Sergeant Shanks was dead. In the chaos of falling back out of that denuded woods, and out of range of the German artillery, the units had become scattered. Brian lost contact with all but Harry, who stuck to him like a magnet. He knew the casualties were high, he and Harry having to all but carry a wounded man back to their lines. But they hadn't heard of Shanks' death until late the previous night by Captain Goode.

All in all, the company had forty-seven casualties, fourteen of them fatal. It was little consolation to learn those numbers were deemed moderate, considering the dire circumstances they had been lured into.

British aeroplanes had since spotted the German artillery and the Canadian guns were pounding them as the 44th Battalion and units of the Australian 2nd Army were back at Decline Copse in an attempt to retake it.

The loss of Shanks hit Brian harder than he would have anticipated. He respected the bandy-legged leprechaun of a man, but their joint experience with the German machine gun made his death much more personal.

"I haven't seen Kobak," Adam Moyer mentioned as they were in line rinsing out their mess kits.

"I'm afraid Corps has him busy translating and running errands," Brian said, still thinking of Shanks.

Harry shook his head. "Yeah, but the man's got to sleep and eat. Wonder where he is."

~ * ~

October 29, 1917

Near Decline Copse

A cold drizzle fell in the darkness. Jürgen pulled the tarp over Alfred and himself as they waited for the signal to go. The successful defense of the Copse on the 26th had been overturned the very next day when fresh Canadian and Australian troops surprised Bavarian units who'd been posted to hold it.

With their superior defensive position, the Bavarians had put up a fierce fight, but the Australians had found the German guns with their own artillery and their superior numbers prevailed by the night of the 27th.

The enemy seemed satisfied to have consolidated its position and not press farther the entire day of Sunday, 28 October.

Jürgen knew yesterday was Sunday only because the Bavarians kept a chaplain ministering to their papist needs. It had not been since his confirmation—his mother's dying wish—that Jürgen had seen the inside of a church.

That meant this was Monday, a fact he would not have known or cared about, as the days melted into an amorphous mass of sameness. Would today be unique? He thought about that. Late last night, Lieutenant Stoner told his platoon he'd volunteered along with the first platoon to conduct a night raid on the Copse. The idea was that a force of less than one hundred men could penetrate the enemy before being noticed. An intelligence report maintained the enemy's Australian faction had pulled out, leaving the Canadians with only one, possibly two companies in place. Stoner said it was worth an attempt to surprise them with a two pronged raid.

They set out well before daylight, relying on what light the moon could filter through the overcast and the short distance they had to traverse. 2nd Platoon was to approach from the east, storming the

Copse at exactly 4:45 AM. If all went well, they would overwhelm the outer perimeter and—at best—drive the enemy from their position. At worst, they could possibly capture an officer or two for interrogation.

With fixed bayonet, Jürgen picked his way in the meager light, following the footfalls ahead. Sooner than expected, the first straggly trees of their destination appeared.

In less than a minute, and before the planned attack, sounds of engagement erupted. They'd been detected. Shots rang out. English words, "Raid! Raid!" were echoed down the line. *So much for surprise.*

"Keep moving! *Geradeaus!"*" Stoner's panicked voice ordered.

Jürgen bumped into the man in front of him, stumbling in the dark and falling on his rifle. More shooting. He got to his feet in time to see the flash of a rifle, and he fired in that direction, not knowing if he'd hit anything. *This is insane!*

An explosion that sounded like a grenade joined the increasing small arms fire. More explosions followed. He saw the dark shape of a man rushing toward him. Instinctively he extended the sharp blade of his bayonet, and felt it penetrate. He heard a soft *oof!* The man did not fall, but disappeared into the dark.

There were more of the enemy among the skeletal trees. Stoner yelled, "Fall back!" Jürgen wasn't sure which way to run, having been turned around in the dark. He thrashed his way through the tree trunks, somehow making it into a clearing. Someone ran past him. He followed, eventually finding a friendly trench.

It was some time later before Jürgen learned of Lieutenant Stoner's death from Sergeant Büler. Obviously the information about the enemy's strength and preparedness was faulty. The whole affair had been a disaster from start to finish.

Fifteen

October 29, 1917
Canadian Corps

Since the attack of the 26th, the engineers and sappers had been expending resources, laying down wooden planking around the mud and water-filled craters of the newly won territory. This in anticipation of Phase 2 of General Currier's plan to take the high ground at Passchendaele. Every last man available was put to work in supporting this work. Without the planking, the allies knew from experience that men, horses, and vehicles of any kind would be unable to move across the landscape.

The concern among Brian and his friends was for the whereabouts of George Kobak, constantly on their thoughts and in their conversation.

"He's on a secret mission, maybe," Harry said, unloading one end of a twelve foot plank from a motor truck, and loading it onto a mule-drawn cart. A cold rain dripped off the end of the animal's muzzle.

Brian held the other end of the plank, and let it drop onto the cart. "He's a translator, not a spy."

The cart was nearly loaded when a soldier approached the work detail. "One of you named McLennan?"

Brian identified himself, and was led to the Corps headquarters tent where Captain Goode sat at a corner desk. Two soldiers stood at ease nearby. Brian recognized one of them from the attack along the rail bed three days before.

"Good to see you again, McLennan," Goode said after the requisite salutations were concluded.

"Thank you, sir."

"These two soldiers have just given me their rendition of events at Decline Copse on the twenty-sixth. I have written it up, and will present it to General Currie's staff for consideration. I am sure it will be approved.

Brian was confused. What now? His mind raced.

Goode continued. "Your actions and those of Sgt. Shanks in destroying an enemy machine gun emplacement saved untold lives, and were key to the successful outcome of the mission. I am recommending you for the Victoria Cross."

Brian was stunned. Getting at the machine gun was Shanks' idea, and he said as much.

"That's not what these two soldiers say."

One of them spoke up. "We agreed, Lem and me, sir. We was pinned down by that gun, see? No ways we coulda made it if that gun had kept it up, sir. We seen him crawlin' right toward that gunner, sir."

Goode thanked and dismissed the two men, motioning for Brian to remain.

"McLennan, the mark of a leader is initiative. You've demonstrated the kind of initiative that inspires men to follow. I'm promoting you to the rank of corporal, and assigning you to lead your section. I know you won't disappoint me."

It took time for the words to sink in. Nothing could have been further from his expectations.

"I…no, sir."

"Report to Lieutenant Cross. He's waiting to give you a briefing on tomorrow's mission."

Tomorrow! "Yes sir." Brian saluted and made an about face, exiting the tent. He was lightheaded as if he'd had too much to drink.

It was all too much. He'd have never stormed the machine gun without the leadership of Sgt. Shanks, just as he would not have rushed to the MG nest at Lens without the bravery of the unknown corporal. Both men had died, yet he lived to receive a medal for it.

He made his way to Lieutenant Cross who had a dugout he'd commandeered from an Anzac counterpart on a rare dry patch of ground. As Brian walked, he noticed two Australian soldiers, one of them an officer, escorting a hatless man in Canadian uniform, shuffling head down between them.

It looked like... *Was it George?*

~ * ~

"Looking for the lieutenant, sir," Brian said to the officer who apparently shared the living space with Cross.

"Just left for somewhere, who knows? Said he'd be back in an hour. What is it you want, soldier?"

"I thought he'd be expecting me, sir. I'll come back."

The officer returned to the book he'd been reading without a comment.

It was 11:45 AM. The mess would open in a quarter hour. He decided to return to the work party. Harry and three others were loading the last of the planks.

"Hold on to the reins of that bloody mule if you want to help," Harry called in greeting. "What was that all about?"

Brian wanted Lieutenant Cross to be first to announce his promotion. "I think Shanks is getting a medal for that business along the rail line."

"Lotta good that does him now." Harry wrestled with a crate of nails.

Brian wondered if a posthumous Victoria Cross would comfort whomever Elmo Shanks had waiting for him back in Sault Ste. Marie.

"Did you ask about George?"

"No. I…saw him."

Harry dropped what he was doing, and moved to where Brian held the mule. "You seen him? Keep on talking."

Brian described the scene of the hatless George being escorted with bowed head between what looked like two guards. "It sure looked like him."

"You're not sure?"

"No…yes! It was him. He looked dazed, that's all."

"You think he deserted?"

Brian couldn't conceive of George Kobak as a coward or a traitor. "No! It's got to be something else."

The two friends looked for a sign in one another's face, but no saw clue for what that might be.

~ * ~

"Grab that stool and sit, McLennan." Lieutenant Cross, a big-city boy from Toronto had the suave good looks and polish of the university man he was. He poured a cup of coffee from one of the new *Thermos* flasks being made in America; offered it to Brian.

The hot liquid felt good on this raw, rainy, late October day. "Thank you, sir."

"Soldier, I don't know what you did to make corporal in less than a year, but I trust the major's judgment."

"Major, sir?" Brian hadn't paid attention to the pips on Goode's tunic.

"Since, hmm, three days ago," Cross said. He let Brian take another sip of the coffee before beginning his briefing.

"In a battlefield environment, there's no time to train you in every aspect of your new duties and responsibilities. So, you and I will be spending as much free time together as possible from here on. Today all I can do is advise you of your main responsibility and that is the well-being of your men, whether in battle or not.

"Your primary duty is to obey orders, and to see that your men do as well." Cross went on to explain the differences between Brian's *personal* responsibilities and *command* responsibilities.

By the time Cross was done, Brian wasn't sure he wished to be an NCO at all.

"Now, about tomorrow," Cross said. "The attack is set for shortly after five AM." He reached for a stack of the, by now, familiar postcard-maps so well favored by General Currie, handing one to Brian.

Brian noticed the objectives had changed from those of the 26th. The red and blue line had advanced several hundred yards in places. A new green line encompassing the town of Passchendaele was added. Objectives such as *Vienna Cottage, Crest Farm, Graf House* were notated.

On Brian's copy, Cross drew a series of arrows. "We will be inserted on the line with the *Patricias*." He referred to The Princess Patricia Light Infantry Regiment, originally made up almost entirely from Canadian veterans of the Boer War. They had entered the war from the very beginning, serving with valor in almost every engagement since.

Their ranks had been decimated over the three years and filled with replacements. Major Goode's company would be temporarily under the command of Lieutenant Colonel Adamson, commander of the *Patricias*.

"I know these men from Vimy, sir. They're good."

"Tomorrow you will stay in communication with me at all times. Designate a runner for that. If something happens to me, Sergeant Tilly will assume command of the platoon."

Cross spent another hour going over their main objective: the taking and holding of a strategic crossroads at *Meetcheele*, a mere dot on the map.

In time, Cross stood, signaling an end to the briefing. "I'll announce your promotion this evening when we stand to. That'll give you some time to be with your section.

~ * ~

“Dismissed!” The order came from Major Goode who had just instructed the men of Company B about the next day’s attack. They were to assemble with their section leaders at 4 AM and proceed to the jumping off positions by 4:30 under the cover of an intense artillery barrage. The signal to attack would come sometime after 5 AM.

Lt. Cross had already announced Brian’s promotion to corporal and as the new leader of Sgt. Shanks’ ten man section. The reaction was more positive than not. The men had caught wind of Brian’s nomination for the VC which ameliorated any feelings of jealousy that might have prevailed. More importantly, Harry Gardinier and Adam Moyer seemed pleased. The newly sewn stripes glared like flashing beacons, or so it seemed to Brian.

He called for the men to congregate, and explained to them, as best he could, the objectives of the coming day, and how they might achieve them.

Later, after mess, he prevailed on a favorite cook for a dozen hard rolls. He’d pass them out to his new charges in the morning, thinking they’d be needing something then.

Sixteen

October 30, 1917
Meetcheele, Belgium

"Where are we?" Sternkopf asked.

"Some little village in Belgium. Why does it matter to you?" someone countered.

In the first hours of the new day, it was still pitch black. The 463d Regiment had marched that night the two kilometers north from their position near Decline Copse, a trek made arduous by the mud and intermittent light as clouds drifted across a half moon. Meetcheele was more of a crossroads and a few houses than a village. But it was a vital artery in the transfer of men and equipment from the rear and all along the frontier.

"Quiet down, you men!" Sgt. Büler appeared in the darkness. He had been given command of the platoon after Stoner's death, elevating Koss from *gruppe* to section leader. "Now listen well."

He told them about new intelligence they'd received of a new thrust by the Canadians on the 30th. Jürgen wondered if the orders he had taken from the wounded soldier were the source of that intelligence.

"Our job," Büler went on, "is to blunt that thrust by occupying positions in front of our lines, inflecting as many casualties as possible before pulling back to the trenches. The Tommies won't expect resistance so soon. With luck it will confuse them enough to repel the attack. When we've done our job, we'll be pulled back behind the lines."

To Jürgen it sounded like a death sentence. They would be positioned in front of the trenches? Terms like "cannon fodder" and "sacrificial lambs" had been tossed around the company. The words held the ring of truth.

As they continued west toward the trenches, the number and sizes of the craters increased, making it slow going in the dark. They passed by a line of blockhouses, each with a slit on the two west-facing corners for machine guns. It was reassuring to see the muzzle of the MG-08 guns protruding from each slit.

Arriving at the forward trench, they found it well manned. Soldiers bearing the insignia of a Bavarian regiment were trying to catch the last hours of sleep before daylight.

"Why aren't those bastards the ones being sent out into no-man's-land? Why us, for God's sake?" It was Berg's question and a good one.

"Shut up, Berg." Koss said, but there was a tremor in his voice, and everyone knew Berg had a point. The story about plugging a gap in the line was a lie. They would be thrown to the wolves in order to slow down the expected attack.

Duckboards were thrown over the trench along their sector for the companies of the 463d. The two hundred men of Company III crossed near a blockhouse situated on a slight rise at the rear. Platoon leaders led their men to positions among the craters. Here the earth was a morass of slimy clay. The drainage was nonexistent, making the craters watery graves for the hapless or wounded troop. More than one man from Company III had to be pulled out after a careless step.

Somehow the platoon leaders organized their men along a line parallel to the trench. Section leaders were instructed to dig in where a flat piece of ground existed. Nevertheless, water began to seep into the newly dug holes.

Koss had found a spot between two large craters that were only partially filled with water. The space was barely long enough for the nine of them, and Jürgen took his shovel to excavate another meter of space at one end.

He was almost finished when the western sky lit up like a sunrise.

"Shit!" Koss cried.

The flashes were followed by the drumroll of a hundred cannons. Seconds later a shell lifted the earth into the sky in a brain-numbing explosion. Dirt and water rained down. That one was followed by others until they were surrounded by a hell so intense Jürgen thought death might be preferable. This was insanity. They could do nothing but hug the floor of their hastily dug trench, becoming one with the drenched earth. Fallout from the explosions rained down. One gut-wrenching shock after another made Jürgen want to scream for it to stop. Others did scream—some from fright or pain, others in death.

The eternal barrage was, in fact, over in five minutes. It was the first of a series of salvos that would follow ahead of the approaching enemy. Jürgen's ears were ringing. He could not hear the last of the explosions, but could feel them wrench his intestines with every hit. He shook the caked earth from himself and looked around. Alfred, wide-eyed, was moving his mouth, but Jürgen heard nothing.

It was like the battlefield had gone silent. Alfred, too, pointed to his ears, shaking his head. Jürgen looked for survivors. He saw one or two helmeted heads poke up from the landscape like groundhogs. He waited for more but the survivors were few. Impossible! Where were they? He moved along his own trench, Alfred following. The back of a helmet protruded from the earth. Jürgen and Alfred found Koss barely alive, having almost suffocated. The ditch followed into a crater where they had taken a direct hit. Nothing was left. No human could have survived. The whole section! Just three survivors.

"No!" Alfred mouthed and Jürgen understood. They returned to find Koss surveying the carnage. The corporal was saying something Jürgen couldn't understand, but from his pointing it was clear they were returning to the relative safety of the main trench and machine gun blockhouses.

A clot of earth exploded next to Koss' shoulder. Then Jürgen felt something graze his helmet. A bullet. All three glanced to the west. There they were, the flat helmets of the enemy creeping low over the muddy terrain, shooting at anything that moved.

Again, Koss motioned for them to follow. He crawled along the trench to the newly excavated crater, then made a dash for the nearest hole toward their lines. Bullets pounded into the mud at their feet as they dived from one pockmark in the land to the next. Once Koss fell waist high into the muck of a crater, and had to be pulled out, but they made it back to the trench.

It was deserted.

"What in God's name…? Koss' words were faint as Jürgen's hearing slowly returned.

The trench seemed to be intact, untouched by the first salvo. That trench, once crammed with elite Bavarian professional soldiers, had been stripped clean. They had pulled out en masse.

"Come on," Jürgen said. "We have no business here. We can't even fire our mud-fouled weapons."

The machine guns commenced firing on the attackers. *Thank God for the blockhouses!* They found a communication trench leading to the rear and ran for their lives, pulling the still-dazed Koss along. It was an inglorious day for the 463d Infantry regiment.

~ * ~

They found the remnants of Company II and a few from their own who had survived and slipped away, resting at the side of the road near a bridge. A sign chiseled into the stone identified the stream as Lekkerboterbeek. The stream was gurgling happily away, headed west to feed the morass that was the battlefield at Meetcheele. The group from Company II was comprised of its commander, *Hauptman* Krauss, and six privates. Two others were from Company III that Jürgen knew only slightly. In their care was a badly wounded man on a litter fashioned by running long sticks through four field jackets from an unknown source. Dead comrades, perhaps.

"We are Second Platoon of Company Three, sir," Koss reported.

"Where are the others?" The captain gazed hopefully back down the road.

"I don't know, Hauptman. We're all that's left from our section."

Kraus appeared resigned to accept Koss' report, but the words hit Jürgen hard. The reality of Feldwebel Büler, Veldstein, Hoffner, Berg, Sternkopf being dead only set in at that moment. Why had he and these few others been spared?

"Corporal, you and your group can relieve these men with the litter for a kilometer or two. They are barely walking themselves."

Jürgen and Alfred took the first stint as the captain led the ragged remnants of the 463d Regiment to the east, and safety.

~ * ~

They were in the ruined shell of what had been a West-Roosebeke café. Jürgen remembered camping near the village a month earlier. The roof was still intact, offering protection from the drizzle that had started up. Others began straggling in; beaten, war-weary faces on young men not much more than boys. Jürgen looked across to where Alfred slumped against the bricks, the same weary look in his eyes.

Koss drank from his canteen, and wiped his mouth on his sleeve. "I wouldn't turn down something to eat."

It was an understatement. Jürgen felt his own pang of hunger, realizing they hadn't been fed since a dried biscuit and weak coffee the morning before. They had been given West-Roosebeke as a regrouping location, but somehow the high command failed to have any kind of services waiting for them. That included medics for the wounded.

"Stern," Koss said, interrupting Jürgen's thoughts of food. "The pair of you saved my life out there. Thank you."

The words were unexpected, giving Jürgen pause. German army NCOs did not expose their vulnerable sides. "It was our duty, *Unteroffizier.*"

"My first name is Gerhard."

Jürgen wasn't sure if this was an invitation to use his Christian name, or just a comment. "Where is your home...Gerhard?"

"Ludwigshaven, by Manheim," Koss said.

Jürgen shook his head.

Koss smiled. "A big city. You've seen the airships?"

"The Zeppelins?" Jürgen had actually seen one flying from Hamburg to the North Sea.

"Zeppelin is a competitor to my father's company, Schütte-Lenz."

"Your father owns an airship company?"

"No, but he's an engineer there. They make mostly for the military."

Jürgen wondered if Koss' father could have found some way to secure a deferment for his son, and asked him about it.

"Yes. They offered me a job, even though I hadn't finished my schooling."

Jürgen discovered Koss wasn't that much older than himself.

"But you were at the Marne!"

"My family wanted me to take the job, but that would have been impossible. A young man has to make a choice: put his life in danger, or live the rest of it in disgrace."

Jürgen knew a man in his town who had wangled a deferment. It was true. People were cordial, but he was never included in social activities. His friends didn't want to be painted with the same brush.

"And the Marne: How bad..." He saw Koss' eyes drop to the floor. "Sorry."

Koss looked off in space. "We were too sure of an early win, so close to Paris. We had no conception of the resolve the French could marshal."

"But you made it."

Koss did not reply, but Jürgen could see the hurt in his eyes.

The moment was broken by Captain Krause's shouting about the lack of food and water there. He was incensed, but there was nothing he could do about it. Jürgen overheard him commiserating with another officer; words that were, if not treasonous, certainly defeatist. It was another inkling that their glorious victory over the enemy might be fleeting.

It was obvious the Bavarians had cleared out unscathed. Not one of them was to be seen. There could not have been more than half the four hundred men that the 463d Regiment put into the line making it back to the rendezvous. Jürgen wondered if the rest of the front had taken the same beating as did the defense of the Meetcheele crossroads.

Seventeen

Canadian Corps Line
October 30, 1917

The skies had cleared overnight, cold air having driven the overcast inland, exposing a crystal clear half-moon with intermittent clouds. Picture a moonscape of gray pockmarked with craters ranging from five to twenty feet across, every inch of the ground having been pulverized by three years of heavy artillery shells. Drench it all in rain having fallen days on end, forming a quagmire in soil that was already famous for its lowland swamps.

Brian walked up and down the slit trench the platoon had dug into the soggy earth, talking to his men and distributing the rolls he'd secured from last night's mess. He was doing his best to emulate Shanks who always saw to the welfare of his men.

He could see how these men—boys, actually—had changed over the past months. By then, all of them had lived through experiences unimaginable to most humans. Seeing a man at your side dismembered does something to either harden or break you.

Talking to the men, he could sense their fear. Despite their bravado, he could hear their shallow breath, the clipped, high pitch of their voices. In a way it was comforting to know he wasn't alone in sensing this day would be their worst yet.

For the better part of an hour, the Canadian artillery had been pounding the enemy, focusing on their reported gun emplacements and forward trenches. Without warning, the sound of shells screaming overhead ceased, and a whistle sounded.

"Now, mates!" Brian shouted, echoing similar cries down the line.

They clambered up the ladders and onto the wooden walkways the sappers had laid down overnight. The moon was just bright enough to expose the ugly wasteland of gaping craters filled waist high with mud and water. It was a monochromatic world devoid of anything worth fighting for. In the relative silence, the sound of thousands of boots on the boards and the odor of cordite was all that filled the air.

Oddly, there was no returning fire from the German artillery. They made their way around the craters this way until the wooden planks ran out. Then the way was harder. Boots sunk into the mire, slowing every step. The possibility of sliding into a crater increased significantly. Brian wondered when the German guns would start up. It must have been five minutes since the whistle to go over the top.

A single cloud drifted slowly past the moon, throwing the landscape into darkness. Someone made a cry of distress, and the sound of a body hitting the mud followed. "Help me," someone said from up ahead.

Brian was on him in a few strides where a man was already extending a rifle butt to another who'd slid down the side of a crater. Troops piled up in back of Brian as the fallen man slithered out of the hole on hands and knees, his own rifle hopelessly fouled with mud.

"Move it," someone whispered from the rear.

The minutes were ticking away, and still no fire from the enemy. *It must be close to ten minutes we've been exposed out here,* Brian thought. The thought was no sooner born when the unmistakable sound of a German 77mm. shell splitting the atmosphere was followed by the sharp report of the gun from behind the enemy lines, cries of wounded men in its wake. They called them Whizz Bangs because you could hear the shell before the sound of the cannon. It was the first of many, as the German artillery recovered.

"Keep moving," Brian said to his section, trying to keep Lt. Cross in view on his left. He figured they'd progressed maybe a hundred yards across no-man's-land with another fifty to go. Then the craters would become farther apart.

"Moving as fast as the bloke in front of me," a voice from ahead said.

The explosions came in waves. Showers of mud were everywhere. Men would fall, but there was no time nor or opportunity to give aid. The only priority was to reach the German lines. A wounded man was on his own; a dead man's problems were over.

The cloud passed and Brian could see the German wire that had been breached by the Canadian guns. "Run for it!" he yelled. Immediately bursts of machine gun and small arms fire erupted from the blackness ahead.

"Down!" someone shouted, and Brian repeated the order.

Then, "Keep moving," he said to his men, who were bunched behind and to his right. As they inched forward, he made sure they did not try to return fire before finding cover, although others were stopping long enough to shoot at muzzle flashes in the darkness.

They reached the wire a little ahead of many of the other Princess Pat units, having found a patch of dry ground and a good sized gap in the coils. Ahead, the wreck of a cart and a dead horse looked like good cover, and he signaled his men to get there.

"In a sprint, lads, after the next burst from that M-G."

On Brian's "Now!" they sprang, running for their lives. "Oh!" A cry of pain, and someone went down, as small arms fire crackled.

"Move up!" Brian yelled, throwing himself down behind the rotting horse. The smell was nauseating, but it was cover. Others hit the dirt, using the cart and horse as protection.

Cross had told Brian of the Germans' latest tactic of using a lightly held perimeter of small arms and machine gun nests as a first line of defense, inflicting as much damage as possible, thus slowing down the advance on their better-protected fortified lines, where their permanent trenches and concrete machine gun emplacements would be. "Pill Boxes," the British called them. It was these that must be destroyed if they were to successfully advance on Passchendaele Ridge.

"Danny got hit," Brian heard a voice say.

"Mortimer?" Brian yelled back.

"Right."

"Killed?"

"Don't know."

The machine gun started up again. The bullets hammered into the cart and thumped into the carcass of the horse.

"They've spotted us," Brian heard Moyer say. He knew they couldn't stay there forever.

"Who has the best throwing arm?" he called.

"Janowski," someone said.

"Okay, Janowski, think you can throw a grenade on that nest?"

There was a pause. "Not sure. It's pretty far."

"No matter," Brian called back. "When I say so, throw it. It'll at least make 'em duck. When I say 'go,' we all charge that nest at the same time you throw. Everyone got that?"

Answers of assent were mixed with the sound of the machine gun and small arms.

Brian watched as a tall, raw-boned blonde pulled a Mills grenade from his pack. He gave the soldier a nod and the pin was removed from the spring-loaded fuse lever.

A burst of fire ended from the nest, and Brian shouted, "Go!" They scrambled from cover as the grenade made a slow, high arc coming down five yards short of the nest. It was a beautiful throw, possibly forty yards.

The explosion raised dirt and smoke, the latter lingering in the windless dark. It quieted the rifle fire as well. Men from other sections of Cross' platoon followed Brian's. Without being told, Janowski threw another grenade, which detonated in the midst of the gun's crew.

In the dim light return rifle fire was mixed with the sight of retreating enemy soldiers.

"Go!" Brian urged his men, but the entire platoon followed into the German lines—killing, being killed.

~ * ~

They'd found a shallow bunker the Germans had constructed, and used it as a place to regroup. Brian counted his men: Wells, Selby, and Mortimer dead or missing. Three out of ten men, and the sun was barely up.

In the open ground beyond the wire, the battle became largely hand-to-hand, extracting the enemy from their craters and entrenchments. This was combat of the most primal kind—face to face with a young man not much different from you, seeing the fear in his eyes, reflecting your own.

Brian found a way to demonize the enemy, forcing himself to hate them. To do otherwise was a death sentence, and he exhorted his men to do the same. "Kill those bastards or they'll kill you!" It was an easy sell.

Farther ahead, up the valley, the Germans had posted snipers as the Canadians scrambled from one mud hole to the next. The air was saturated with the sound of gunfire. Too often the wasp-like buzz of a bullet would zip past the ear so close a man could feel the wind of it.

The going was increasingly sloppy. Everyone was covered in the slippery muck. Keeping it out of the rifle breach was a matter of self-preservation. Progress was measured in feet, groveling along the ground. A lifted head in order to see was an invitation for a bullet. The hated bomb craters were their only cover.

As they moved again, Brian struggled to keep in contact with his men and Lt. Cross. He dove into the next crater followed only by Harry and a man named Taylor. Two Germans were waiting for them, but they were dead. New machine gun fire racked them inches above the ground.

The sky was light enough to see their new tormenter, a pill box on higher ground about a hundred yards ahead, just to the rear of some freshly dug trenches. It was clear those trenches would have to be taken before the pill box could be silenced.

They were inserted between the Princess Patricias and the 49th Battalion. To his right, Brian saw the "Pats" crawling from their craters like scorpions. Three of the five made it to the next one. Their bravery was an inspiration.

"Harry, Taylor! We can't spend the war here!"

"The hell we can't!" Taylor yelled over the din.

The machine gun noise rose and fell over the background crackle of small arms. Brian decided to follow the lead of the Patricias and make a dash for the crater he'd spotted ten yards ahead, and to his left. There was a lull from the pill box, and Brian shouted "Go!" not knowing if the others would follow. They did.

With rifles slung on their backs, they skittered on all fours, actually diving head first into the empty crater knee high in water. Bullets pounded the earth while they took cover on the far side.

"You alright?" he asked the others.

Taylor looked fine, except for his expression of terror. Harry had a tear in his tunic, and was bleeding.

"Yeah," Harry said.

"You're not! Shit! Let me see." Brian cut open the tunic with the knife his father had given him, seemingly a lifetime ago, to find a wound contaminated with fibers and dirt.

"Never felt it," Harry said.

"Here," Taylor held out a white handkerchief. It was embroidered with the letter T. "My ma stuffed it in my bag when I left home.

Brian took it and tied it tightly around the arm. "That'll have to do."

"Now what?" Harry said.

"We keep doing what we've been doing, I suppose. Can't go backwards. You ready, Taylor?"

"Rather not," the man said.

Brian smiled at the man's mirth in the face of their probable deaths. To the right and left of them Canadians were scuttling forward, many dropping, felled by a bullet from the vicious fusillade. He signaled to the rear for his section to keep advancing, not knowing if they could hear or see him. They dashed to where a large tree had fallen years before. They could only stay there for minutes before the gun from the pill box picked it to pieces.

"There!" he pointed to another shallow pit where a head peered out.

"That ain't a Battle Bowler!" Taylor cried, using the British term for their dishpan-shaped helmets.

Sure enough, two helmeted silhouettes were German and appeared peeking to the west.

Brian said, "I want that hole more than they do."

"They ain't lookin' this way," Harry said. "We can jump 'em."

"Come out shooting, then." Brian checked his bayonet was once more secure on his Enfield. "Go!"

The two Germans, focused on the Canadians to Brian's right, were caught unawares, and had no chance. One was dead from one of the three rifles and the other from the bayonet of Harry Gardinier. Once more the three were safe for the present. This was a crater that had been significantly enhanced. Sand bags had been piled up on the western side. Boards had been thrown across the inevitable puddle at the bottom.

"Comfy," Taylor said.

Harry was relieving one of the dead Germans of his rifle. "This boy's a sniper," he said, holding up the Mauser with scope attached. He slung his own weapon over his pack, and sighted through the scope toward the east. A bullet raised an explosion of earth in his face.

"Get down, ya silly twit!" Taylor said. The words weren't spoken before he caught a bullet of his own. It hit him square in the chest.

His face had the look of confusion, as if he couldn't process what had happened, then realization, and he was dead.

Instantly a mortar hit close by, then another, sending a piece of shrapnel careening off Brian's helmet.

They had to move. There was no time to mourn. They crawled, using smoke from the mortars as cover, not knowing what lay ahead, until they tumbled into a trench lined with wooden supports and floor boards. It was empty.

"They're gone!" Harry whispered.

Brian lifted a finger to his lips, motioning Harry to check the trench to his left while going to the right. Hastily abandoned gear: ammunition canisters, a mortar, ration containers, were all he found.

A body came hurtling over the top, almost on top of him. It was a lieutenant from the Patricias.

"Looks abandoned, sir." Brian said.

Another man dropped down, this one none other than Adam Moyer.

"Where are the others?" Brian asked him.

"Pinned down by that pill box. We lost Henderson and Wells."

That meant four of his section already dead—five if Mortimer's was more than a wound. It was a nightmare. "That leaves just Sweeny and Person out there." Brian thought aloud. He told Adam about Taylor.

Harry showed up with Sweeny and Person in tow. "I found these two malingering down there." They all exchanged hugs and slaps on the back.

The lieutenant was assembling his men, and Brian asked him where he'd like him to post his section.

"That boy know how to use that sniper's rifle?" He nodded at Harry.

Moyer didn't wait for Brian to answer. "You bet your ass—your life, sir."

The lieutenant spoke to Brian. Fan your men to the left until you run into your own troops or from the 49th." To Harry he said, "You say with me until I figure how to knock out that pill box."

~ * ~

"Thought we lost you, sir." Brian admitted his loss of contact with the platoon leader, noting his eyes were red from crying.

"How many of you are there?" Cross ignored Brian's words.

"Six, counting me."

Cross paused, seeming to process the news of still more dead under his command. "Right then, McLennan, take your men to our left flank. Turner is there with what's left of his section. Deploy to his right. We've got to plug the gap between the forty-ninth and the Patricias.

Brian told Cross about Harry's being commandeered. Cross gave a slight nod of recognition as he consulted his mud spattered map.

"We're about here." He pointed to a spot, possibly 500 yards west of the crossroads near *Meetcheele.* "We may get separated again, but that's our objective. Keep me on your right and Turner on your left. Advance when I signal."

There would be no advance in this sector with that pill box dominating, but Brian did what he was told, spreading his men over the thirty yards that separated Turner and Cross.

They waited for the signal but the only sound came from the rattle of machine guns up and down the line. Clothes were drenched, hands red and raw clutching their weapons. There were whistles to advance but none from Lieutenant Cross nor the Princess Patricia officer. Then the closest machine gun fell silent followed first by shouts of celebration, then the whistles to attack.

"Over the top, boys!" Brian yelled, and they sprang from their watery ditch, heading for an objective they could not see. The ground fell away into a wide swale filled with more mud and more craters, larger than before.

The bones of what had been a farm lay two hundred yards ahead. A storm of small arms fire came from that direction. He led his men toward it. Once more the only means of advance was slogging through the muck from crater to crater. This time they were occupied with the enemy.

~ * ~

They were sheltered by the crumbling remains of the farm's hearth. Harry had shown up minutes earlier after searching all day for the platoon.

"Bravest thing I ever seen," Harry said for the second time, staring at the ground as if replaying the experience, speaking softly while narrating what he saw. Brian and Moyer listened while he told how the Princess Patricia lieutenant sacrificed his life by drawing fire while his sergeant sneaked around its rear and dispatched its occupants with his pistol. "That gun was pickin' us off like nuthin' to it in that shallow ditch," he said.

It had taken Harry well into midafternoon to find the squad. Brian, in trying to rescue Turner's section from being cut off, ventured a hundred yards to the left of his intended path. Turner was dead, as well as all but four of his section. A platoon from the 49th Battalion helped to repel the enemy, but not before Person was killed, and Sweeny wounded.

As a result, Brian brought Turner's four into his section, and they forged ahead toward the crossroads. Increasingly, the going got easier. The German perimeter was breaking apart. Captured machine guns were turned around to harass the fleeing enemy. On higher ground, the craters were drier and fewer.

Both sides seemed thankful for a brief hiatus. The Canadians were digging in, anticipating a counterattack at daybreak. The rain had started again. It would be a wet, cold night.

Brian had gathered the few sticks he could find, found some unburned wood in the hearth, and began fumbling his way toward making a fire.

"Here, white boy! Let an Indian show you how to get that going!"

To their delight, a small flame started up, and Harry began adding pieces of the sticks to it.

Moyer, with more than his share of Métis acquaintances on Manitoulin, commented. "Indian? With a name like Gardinier?"

Harry's white teeth reflected the fledgling fire in the dark. "There may be a frog in my family back when, but I wouldn't know. You can call me "Wa-agosh" instead of Gardinier, if you want.

Moyer laughed and repeated the name. "What does *that* mean?"

"Fox. I might change it after all this."

"Well, *Fox*, how is life in Sault Ste. Marie? Our Métis seem to be doing okay."

The question seemed to take the mirth out of the conversation.

"Probably about as well as with your Manitoulin friends," Harry said in a deadpan.

"It ought to be okay." Moyer pressed. "Hell, you got the Indian Act going for you. Free education—"

Harry cut him off. "Free. And worth every penny." After a pause he went on. "A Canadian First Nation citizen can go to a camp somewhere, usually hundreds of miles away from his family, to forget his culture, and learn how to talk and dress like a white man, or he can stay home and attend a rundown shack on his reservation and learn almost nothing. That's the 'free education.'"

"Christ, Harry—"Moyer began.

"No, it's okay. You asked how life was. I'm doing alright."

Brian had never heard Harry so…what was the word? Erudite? He would never see the boy from the Garden River Reservation in the same way.

They talked some more but the meager fire was soon out, and they huddled the best they could, waiting out the night.

~ * ~

October 31, 1917

The counterattack never came. By 10:00 AM of the next day, a company of replacements arrived with orders for Major Goode to return with his men for a rest. They made their way back through the muddy, treeless fields. The craters, some full to the brim with water, were littered with the dead of both sides as they picked their way around them. More than one tank sat mired in the mud, unable to move. One of the behemoths was half submerged in a crater.

Brian recognized a face; one from the old Algoma Battalion. It stared up from the grey water at the passerby, mouth agape in a grimace. "Oh my God!" he heard Janowski say. Brian shivered.

Replacements threading the opposite way through the craters were lugging duckboards sections, reminiscent of men bearing their crosses on the way to Golgotha.

In their condition, the slog back through the mud was exhausting. The mud sucked at every footfall. It was hard to believe they had come all this way under fire, but in time they arrived back at the Canadian lines. Transports were waiting—trucks of all kinds, farm wagons drawn by overworked, horses or mules—all overloaded to the extreme as they lumbered away over the planked roads.

"Where they takin' us?" Harry asked.

"Wipers," someone said, using the soldier's argot for Ypres.

"If the Huns haven't leveled it," someone else added.

Eighteen

November 8, 1917
Ypres, Belgium

The weather had cleared, but winter was in the air. Brian turned up the collar of his newly issued overcoat against the wind.

Upon arrival in Ypres, the men had been directed to delousing tents and showers. The showers were heated, but barely. Still, it was a luxury to have the grime of war washed away. They were issued clean uniforms that had to be traded amongst the men to arrive at a reasonable fit.

"Me bloody pants is too tight under me armpits!" one wag joked.

They were fed their first hot food since the attack and given a week's rest in the city.

Today he was inching along in a line of men waiting to vote.

The Canadian parliamentary election, a contentious one at that, was slated for December 17. Robert Borden's Conservative Party was in favor of a conscription of men for the army, while the Liberals, headed by Sir Wilfred Laurier, were against. The majority Conservatives were garnering every vote possible, trusting the mail-in votes of the soldiers would go their way. The recently passed Military Voters Act allowed soldiers under 21 to vote.

Brian had just come from the Ypres dressing station where Harry was recovering from his wound. It had become infected and was being treated with Dankin's Solution, a mixture of bleach and boric acid. To his surprise, in Harry's tent was the new man, Mortimer, they had assumed had been killed. He'd been hit in the foot and fallen into a crater. It wasn't until replacements were called forward that he was found clinging to a root.

The second phase of the attack on Passchendaele Ridge had been a success. Holding the crossroads at Meetcheele was one of the key factors in the allies' ability to push on. By November 6, they had taken the town itself, and beyond. Unfortunately, the Germans had, again, pulled back into a strong defensive position that precluded the war-ending breakthrough some had hoped for.

In the end, over two hundred thousand allied, and a similar number of German casualties paid the price for perhaps two miles of farm land along a six mile front. The officers were saying they were winning the war. Maybe so, but it was hard to tell from Brian's perspective.

The so-called successful campaign had been waged in the worst weather and over the worst terrain imaginable for an aggressor. On the contrary, the same conditions were much to the defenders' advantage. Reports from captured soldiers confirmed their leaders' rejoicing over every rainy mud-filled day.

~ * ~

What was left of Brian's company was billeted in the basement of a church near the bombed out ruins of the *Lakenhalle,* or Cloth Hall, that Brian had sketched on that first day. The Hall had been the center of Flemish trade since its construction in the thirteenth century. Today it was nothing but a shell. Nothing stood but the skeletal outline of its signature tower.

Replacements from the 8th Reserve Battalion in England were filling out the Company's ranks. Some were from the original 119th Algoma Battalion still attached to the 5th Army in England. Brian's 2nd Platoon gained seven, almost bringing it up to full roster. Brian recognized one or two.

The company commanders had been away at Corps Headquarters. Rumor was that a new campaign was being planned for the near term, probably before Christmas. It was from one of these meetings that Major Goode returned to find Brian waiting outside the church.

Returning Brian's salute, Goode said, "McLennan. Something?"

"Yes sir. Private Kobak, sir. I'm wondering how…where he is."

Goode turned to consider his newest N.C.O. with the freshly sewn corporal stripes. "You're chums from home, are you?"

"From St. Joseph Island, near Sault Ste. Marie."

"How well do you know Private Kobak?"

Brian hesitated. *Compared to anyone except Harry, quite well, but George led an insular life on the Island. How well did he really know him?* "Well enough, sir."

"Hmm. Your friend is being court-martialed for desertion.

That last word was a blow. Brian looked for a sign—any gesture from his C.O. that this didn't apply to George Kobak.

"Desertion." He exhaled the word.

"The hearing is Monday, at ten AM," Goode said. "I've been assigned to present his defense."

Brian remembered talk of Goode being a Toronto lawyer before the war. He waited for the major to make his point.

"It would be helpful to have you as a character witness in his defense.

That caught Brian off guard. Granted, George was raised just a few miles from the McLennan farm. But they knew each other from the occasional meetings at the market, perhaps or in town on a holiday. They hadn't become close friends until joining up.

"Yes, sir. I'll be glad to. Anyone in our platoon would."

"I think a person from his home town would be best. Come inside, and we'll talk."

~ * ~

The house sat at the western edge of Ypres where the shelling had been less dense. One wing was gutted, but the Corps had offices here and carried out other functions. One of those was a Field General Court Marshal.

As Brian entered, soldiers were converting the old dining room by spreading blankets on the tables where the officers of the court would sit. In a few minutes a rudimentary courtroom was established.

He waited for several minutes, unsure of what to do, before Major Goode strode in carrying a leather valise. He nodded at Brian, but sat at one of the tables, spreading a file and note pad in front of him. The night before, Goode had had Brian tell him everything he knew about George Kobak from the day his family arrived on St. Joseph Island to the last time they had spoken.

One by one the panel of three officers filed in, headed by a colonel from the Judge Advocate General office. The room settled down as it emptied of all but possibly a dozen souls. Goode motioned for Brian to take a chair against the wall.

At the other end of Goode's table, another officer with the three shoulder pips of a captain sat. The two men acknowledged one another. The senior officer at the head table introduced Goode to the prosecuting officer as Captain Cooper from the JAG office, and returned to conferring with his judges.

Meanwhile, accompanied by two guards, George Kobak was seated in a straight back chair next to Goode. He seemed to have physically changed; morphed in a matter of days from the hale, 180 pound farm boy/soldier for King and Country to this diminished figure in both stature and bearing. Brian tried to catch his eye, but Kobak stared straight ahead, looking at nothing in particular.

"This court is now convened!" the senior judge announced in clear baritone. "Gentlemen," he said to the two counsels, "I am Colonel Ivan Pern. My associates are Majors Short and Collins," pointing out each as he spoke. "We are here to adjudicate the matter of Private George L. Kobak, to be tried under Section Four of the Army Act for deserting His Majesty's Service, or attempting same. "How does the defendant plead?"

Major Goode rose. “The defendant pleads ‘not guilty,’ sir.”

“Thank you, Major Goode. Captain Cooper, are you prepared to prosecute this case?”

He was blond, smartly dressed in his creaseless uniform, his riding boots oiled to a luster. “I am, sir. The evidence will show the defendant willfully deserted his assignment in the vicinity west of Decline Copse on the morning of October twenty-six. He had been dispatched to deliver orders of a secret and critical nature to the Forty-sixth Battalion Commander or his representative. The Battalion never got those orders that were vital to phase two of the Passchendaele campaign. Later the defendant was found behind enemy lines by a unit of the First Australian Division.”

“Thank you, Captain. You may proceed with your evidence.”

First, Cooper called on a Major Nix of the Corps Staff. He testified giving a document for Kobak to deliver to the command at a location where the 46th Battalion was purported to be. Cooper then called on the aide to the 46th Battalion commander to witness the fact that they had never seen Kobak, nor anyone else from Corps with special orders on that day.

He then produced two men wearing the belted tunics and holding slouch hats of the Australian AIF. They testified finding a bare-headed soldier walking purposefully in enemy territory at approximately 1030 hours on 26 October. They challenged him, and he did not stop nor raise his hands in surrender. They subdued him, recognized the Canadian insignia, and turned the man over to their superiors. Both pointed to George Kobak when asked to identify the man. Another witness from the Canadian Military Police testified to Kobak’s belligerent attitude upon being questioned.

Goode began his defense by cross-examining Cooper’s witnesses. He got the 46th Battalion aide to admit the orders could have been delivered to someone, since Kobak was instructed to find the highest ranking officer in the event the commander was not available. But the aide was adamant that the intended orders reached no one, and the

46th did not get the benefit of the intelligence the orders were later revealed to contain.

Goode tried to get the Aussies to admit they had no idea which way Kobak was heading, but was thwarted by one's reply, "Well now! 'E was 'eddin' the direction ta where the Krauts was, wasn't 'e?"

Colonel Pern, a smile on his lips, rapped an ash tray on the table to restore order as laughter erupted.

The only witness for the defense was Brian. He duly took his place on the stand, giving Goode a litany of all the best things he knew about George Kobak.

Then Cooper had his turn at cross. "How well do you know Private Kobak?"

"As I told Major Goode…pretty well."

"You were from the same town?"

"The same island, yes."

"St. Joseph. That's a really big island, isn't it?"

Brian began to feel alarm. *What's going on?*

Cooper stepped closer. "So, you were pretty close friends back then?"

"We…knew each other."

"Then, not that well, you're saying."

"I know him well enough now, and he is…" Brian searched for an attribute. "…a fine fellow!" *How stupid that sounded!* He tried to recover, but Cooper preempted him.

"Thank you, that's all."

Goode asked a few more questions, but all Brian could say was that the rest of the section got along well with George.

"Other witnesses, Major?" Colonel Pern asked. He had an annoying habit of fiddling with his fountain pen, which he flipped in and out through his fingers like a mini baton.

Goode emitted an audible sigh. "Sir, I'd like to examine the defendant."

Brian saw something in George's face that indicated this might not have been planned. It was the first sign of animation in his friend's demeanor since the beginning of the trial.

George looked around the room, ultimately locking eyes with Brian, then took the stand.

"Now then," Goode began, "tell us about that morning when you were *rescued*." Brian thought the use of that word was ingenious on Goode's part.

George looked up at the ornate ceiling of the old house, remembering the day. "It was still dark, maybe six AM. I'd been up all night translating captured documents and the personal letters of the enemy soldiers. Major Nix called me into his room. He was holding a sealed document, asking me if I wanted to volunteer for an assignment that he said might be 'rather dangerous.'"

"And you accepted?" Goode asked.

"Right away, sir. It's hard seeing my mates go over the top while I sit back behind the lines at Corps."

"What were you specifically told to do?"

"As the gentleman said," George indicated Captain Cooper, "I was to catch up with the Forty-sixth on their way up the rail line to Rouelers. I was to find their commander in the field, and deliver the sealed order. If not, then to the highest ranking officer I could find."

"And did you?"

"No, sir."

Goode waited, then prompted, "What happened that caused you to fail?"

"Not sure, sir. I was trying to catch up with the Forty-sixth by following the rail bed in the fog. Last thing I remember was a building of some sort up ahead. The day was just starting to brighten up. I hesitated, but thought it must be safe since our boys must've just passed through."

"And then?"

"That's all I remember until I woke up. My head hurt really bad, sir. I mean I couldn't even think straight. I knew I had to keep walking, but somehow lost the rail bed. Then I got lost, and...well, I didn't know which direction was east."

"How much time had passed?"

"Don't know, sir. It was much brighter, but I couldn't see the sun, so I guessed. I knew I shouldn't go back to our lines without doing my duty."

"What did you do with the sealed orders?" Goode turned to face Cooper as he asked the question.

"I didn't do anything. I thought I still had them with me when I was arrested, and they asked me what I was up to."

Goode returned to his chair. "Thank you, Private Kobak."

Colonel Pern said, "Captain, you may cross."

Cooper made a show of rising slowly, as if deliberating on his next words. "*Kobak*...that's a new name to me. Polish?"

"Hungarian, sir."

The prosecutor repeated the word and let that sink in for the panel's consideration. "I understand you are fluent in German. How is that?"

"My...parents...uh, we speak it at home."

"Oh! Then they aren't Canadian?"

"They are, sir..."George began.

"But born where?"

Brian saw George redden.

"Near Vienna," he mumbled.

Cooper turned to the panel when he said, "Pals of Franz Joseph, perhaps."

George exploded. "NO!"

Pern rapped his ashtray loudly on the table. "Quiet! Major Goode, control your charge."

The room settled down, and Cooper continued with a line of questions about Koback's *so called* injury and why there was no physical evidence of a wound.

"I don't know," George said. "Doc said I could have had a concussion without a wound."

Cooper allowed that was possible, but asked, "How is it you receive a concussion out of thin air. You admitted no one was around. You said the building was 'safe,' I believe."

Goode objected. "Private Kobak has no way of giving an informed answer to that question."

Cooper said, "And we are to believe that you woke up and did not notice the sealed orders were missing?"

"The paper was in my tunic pocket, sir. I didn't think…"

"That's all I have for now," Cooper said to the panel. "I'd like to call another witness, Private Wentworth."

Brian gasped. From where he stood in the vestibule, Colby Wentworth confidently strode into the room and replaced the stunned George Kobak in the witness chair.

After Wentworth was sworn in, Cooper asked, "So, Private Wentworth, tell us where you are from."

"Bruce Mines, Ontario."

"And where is that?"

"In Algoma, near St. Joe Island." Wentworth looked around the room, smiling.

"Are you familiar with the defendant?"

"Hardly knew him at all, and I probably spent more time there than at home."

"Why is that?"

"My father has a business there. I grew up knowing most of the Island children."

"But not Private Kobak."

"No, he seems to have been schooled at home. Nobody knew him well."

"Yet Corporal McLennan testified as to Kobak's character."

"That would be a mystery to me. I rarely saw either McLennan or Kobak in town."

"Thank you, Private." Cooper said. "That's all."

Goode rose. "I have a question for the witness." Pern nodded and he continued. "You used the term 'in town.' What town is that?"

"Richards Landing…sir."

"And where is that located on the island?"

Wentworth thought. "Well, on the north side, I guess."

"Indeed. And where does Private Kobak live?"

Wentworth was stumped. "I guess I don't know."

"I'll tell you," Goode said, but was informing the panel. "At the far south of that thirty mile long island. And where does Corporal McLennan live?"

Wentworth blinked. "On a farm somewhere."

"I'll tell you that, too. In the middle of the Island, probably closer to Private Kobak's home than 'in town,' as you said." Goode returned to his seat. "That's all I have for this man."

Brian thought Goode had won that exchange, but doubted it would make much of a difference.

Cooper stood. "The prosecution rests, Gentlemen."

Goode rose, and called as witness the doctor who examined George upon his arrest. The man testified that the accused *could* have received a blow that rendered him senseless without a visible wound, but was forced to admit under cross-examination that it would be more unlikely than so.

Goode rested the defense.

"Thank you, gentlemen," Pern said, standing. All followed suit. "This court-marshal will reconvene at fourteen hundred hours, at which time a verdict and sentencing will be handed down. You are dismissed until that time."

Goode and Cooper saluted, and gathered their papers. The guards escorted George out. Wentworth hightailed it without a glance to Brian.

"What's the worst case, sir?" Brian asked his C.O.

"This is a Field General Court Marshal. In the case of desertion, it has the power to exact the death sentence."

Good's words set of Brian's teeth on edge. The wait until 2 PM would be intolerable.

~ * ~

There were fewer people now, only the panel, Goode, Cooper and George Kobak, his guards standing at Parade Rest nearby. George stood at attention in front of the three judges. Major Goode had, at Brian's pleadings, allowed him as far as the vestibule looking in on the proceedings.

Brian, upon leaving the morning trial, had visited Harry in the dressing station, giving him a rundown on what had transpired.

"They're either gonna shoot him, or let him go; no in between. And I don't see 'em lettin' him go." That was Harry's cheery analysis.

Brian could hear the sound of shuffled of papers bouncing off the ceiling of the big room followed by Pern's sonorous voice: "In the matter of Private George L. Kobak and the charge of Desertion, this court has come to a decision. The defendant is guilty of 'Failure to Repair' to his post. In our opinion, the prosecution gave ample evidence of desertion, but we found the evidence to be circumstantial. On the other hand, the defense was unable to provide convincing evidence of innocence. One thing was clear to the court…the accused did not carry out his assignment. This is mitigated by the fact of his volunteering for the mission.

"For failure to return to post in a timely manner, we find the accused guilty of bad conduct, and will receive a discharge from the Canadian Expeditionary Forces being stipulated as such. This court is now adjourned."

Brian watched George's shoulders slump, not knowing if it was from relief at not being shot for desertion, or from the humility of a Bad Conduct Discharge.

The two guards caught him up, and summarily whisked him away. Just like that, George Kobak was gone, not to return.

~ * ~

The following days were filled with the training of replacements. Platoon leaders were given the job, which of course included the skill of advancing with a "walking" bombardment that was so successful at Vimy Ridge. However, the new concept of tank warfare in concert with the infantry was a training necessity for all. The tank's contribution at Passchendaele was almost negated by the terrain and weather, but armor was expected to be a major factor in battles to come.

The 4th Division was slated to return to its position near Lens now that the Ypres salient had been reduced and the high ground gained. Harry Gardinier learned he would be returned to duty with his unit, despite having thought he'd received his "Blighty," the Tommy's term for a ticket back to England.

The Flanders front was relatively calm by then. The Allies had pushed the Germans back from the high ground advantage they had enjoyed from the start of the war, but their line hadn't buckled. Defensive positions to the rear were bolstered to prevent an all-out Allied breakthrough.

Rumors about a separate German-Russian armistice were flying. Should that happen, surely hordes of troops would be transferred to the west. Countering this would be the arrival of the Americans, already beginning to show up farther south. The front would not be calm for long.

~ * ~

December 3, 1917
Ypres, Belgium

The olive green Sunbeam truck with its red cross emblazoned on a white circle rumbled west on the Ypres-Poperinghe Road. Brian sat next to the driver as the older man wrestled the wheel over the ruts.

After George Kobak's trial Brian had let a week-end go by before attempting to revisit Harry at the dressing station, only to find him gone. It was a mystery. Harry had seemed to be resting comfortably on his last visit. It took him most of a day to discover Harry had developed a fever and was removed to the Casualty Clearing Station (CCS) at Poperinghe.

That was a week ago. Brian's company had been kept busy fortifying defenses along the newly established front lines. Then, at the insistence of Major Goode, they were relieved by replacement troops and awarded another ten day leave.

It wasn't more than a dozen miles to this town that housed the CCS, but the going was slow over the road rutted by November rains. The cots in the back of the truck were empty. The Clearing Station and its staff had officially packed up, moving elsewhere along the front as those facilities were designed to do.

It was Brian's first time to "POP," the soldier's sobriquet for the city. His first impression as the truck rolled into town was the number of people, civilian and military, carrying on life as if there were no war just over the hill. Despite some bombed structures, commerce was in full tilt. The shops were open, including one or two pubs, or *estaminets,* as they were called there and in France.

His second impression was more intense. They passed through the center of town on their way to the CCS on the western edge. There, in close proximity, was a huge field filled with crosses so close together they seemed to touch.

How could there be so many dead in just this corner of the war? For a moment Brian forgot how the war ever started, then remembered the assassinations in Serbia. Were these lives so valueless that they could be sacrificed for two Austrian Royals? He was still shaken as he entered the nearly vacated building. An unattended reception desk stood in the vestibule.

"Mate!" he called to a soldier on crutches.

He was a small man, looking smart in his pressed uniform, despite his missing foot. The soldier gave him an inquiring glance.

"Looking to pick up some chaps from my company."

"Thems well enough for duty are in the lounge down there." He pointed down the hallway. "Just a few of us waitn' to ship home."

Brian thanked him and found the room, a smoke-filled chamber featuring a piano and a dart board, both of which were in use. He saw Harry at once, his ebony shock of straight hair among the other twenty or so men.

The piano and gaggle of singers were well into their version of "Mademoiselle from Armentieres," and trying to compete with Henry's boisterous friends at the dart board. As a result, Brian's call was unheeded.

"Are you losing again?" He gave Harry a nudge from behind.

"Brian!" Harry laughed. "Gentlemen, this here is our bad-ass section leader, and my best friend, Corporal MacLennan!"

A mixture of mock jeers and muttered welcomes were returned, and the game continued.

"Let's get out of this madhouse where we can talk," Harry said. "What are you doing here?"

Brian explained catching a ride on the very ambulance dispatched to pick up Private Harry Gardinier and two others for their return to duty. "I lost track of you. What happened?"

"My wound wouldn't heal. They tried everything. I was 'bipped' with paraffin and some stuff called bismuth. That didn't work, so they cut away some of the infected area and sent me here."

Brian had heard about the last one called "Debridement," where dead flesh was excised from the wound. "You look fine to me now."

"They shipped me here where they have…I mean *had* these X-ray machines that can look inside you. Found out I still had a hunk of metal in me. Once they got that out, the bismuth stuff did the job."

"What happened to Moyer?"

"That ding on his foot earned him a 'blighty' and a trip home." Harry referred to the British soldiers' term for England, and by extension, a return ticket there.

Harry's words turned Brian's own thoughts to home. He hadn't thought of Sarah White during the insanity of the Passchendaele battle and George's trial, but he could not visualize home without the image of that morning in her parlor and her hand on his cheek. That had given him so much to look forward to, only resulting in the disappointment of her not returning his letters. He'd tried to get over it but could not.

"Lucky bloke, I'd say," Harry continued.

"What…oh, yeah. On his way by now. I thought that ticket might be yours."

Harry snorted. "Docs fixed me up too good. What now?"

"You're coming back to C Company. You heard about George?"

"Yeah. This place hears all the court-marshal news. The executions are carried out right here in POP. He dodged that verdict, but they still labeled him a deserter. I don't believe it."

"I don't either," Brian said. He pictured George returning home to his farm on the Island; discredited, dishonored. It was sickening.

"You have transportation?" Harry asked.

"For you and two others." Brian gave Harry the names.

"I'll round them up, get my kit and some letters the lads will want mailed."

Harry returned from the noisy day room with two jovial sorts from the 4th Army, arm in arm still singing… *Hinky-Dinky Parlez Vous* after one of the song's endless verses.

~ * ~

They rode back to Ypres in the ambulance…Brian, Harry, and the only two other CEF soldiers among those being returned to duty. They were all dropped off at the dressing station, on their own getting back to their respective units.

"I've got to mail these letters at the FPO," Harry said, referring to the Canadian Postal Corps Field Post Office.

The facility was housed in a theater, only partially damaged from shelling since 1914. It handled all the Canadian mail in Belgium.

A low wall behind the counter revealed workers sorting mail. There was an open bay at the rear where a truck was unloading olive green duffels filled with mail. Harry deposited his letters with the clerk. They were turning to leave when Brian spotted a familiar figure climb back on the truck. The face was obscured but the man's gait and toss of his head were unique. *That was Wentworth?* It was too unlikely. Wentworth was in a machine gun company. He dismissed the notion. They hitched a ride the short distance back to camp where Harry, popular among their Company, was greeted enthusiastically.

Just before evening mess, they were ordered to "stand to." Ever since the successful campaign to take control of the Passchendaele Ridge, they had wondered where they'd be sent if anywhere at all. The speculation ended when Major Goode announced they would continue their support role with the 4th army that was returning to their previous station west of Lens.

That occasioned an audible and collective groan of disappointment. Flanders duty, with its mud and bad weather, had been miserable, but the rat- and louse-ridden trenches at Lens and Hill 70 were worse. At least the shell holes there weren't filled with neck-high water. Familiarity breeds contempt, Brian thought, and they were more than familiar with the trenches in the chalky clay of Lens.

Nineteen

March 19, 1918
Near St. Quentin, France

The defeat at Passchendaele was devastating, not only for Jürgen's regiment, but the whole of Germany's northern divisions. The 238th Infantry Battalion suffered more than fifty percent casualties. They were rested in a village east of Rouelers for a week, then entrained for the one hundred-fifty mile trip south to St. Benoite, a small town near St. Quentin. There they trained with replacements whose numbers were yet insufficient to produce a full regimental complement. What would have added up to shattered morale was buoyed by the news of victory on the Russian front.

Second Platoon had a new leader, Heinrich Lutz, a newly commissioned 2d Lieutenant, or *feldweblelleutnant.* Jürgen did not envy this man, not much older than himself. The army was massing for something big, and Lutz would be thrown into the thick of it. That his own new role of *gefreiter* increased his peril hadn't hit home.

The code word "Michael" was rumored to be the big offensive that would drive the German army through to the English Channel, Paris, and victory. The official name heard was *Kaiserschlacht*, the Emperor's Battle. After years of stalemate and false hopes, the thought was exhilarating.

Tonight they were enjoying sausage for dinner. It was the first real meal they'd known since Rouelers. Tomorrow, they were told, they would march to the line. That meant the attack would probably be the following morning. Earlier in the day, Jürgen had seen more artillery being put in place than ever before. It seemed the predictions of something big happening were coming true.

They would be part of the 18th Army, whose main objective was the city of Amiens, the major transportation center for the Allies. Everything traveling north and south went through Amiens.

~ * ~

From St. Benoite it was only a 5km march to Grugies, a tiny crossroads that had been a village before having the bad luck to be located yards from the front lines of The Great War. There was not a single building standing. The weather had reversed itself from a promising spring day to an overcast, cold mist.

They arrived at the trenches around 6 PM, having had only a modest breakfast of oatmeal doled out by a humorless mess staff. Dinner would be making do with their own rations. One of the new replacements, tall with curly brown hair, had a fire started with scarce firewood he had somehow wangled. He was holding an open can over the small flame. Jürgen was impressed with this clever conscript from Bremen. His name was Feldenhauer. What caught Jürgen's attention was the man's quiet acceptance; making the best of any situation. The fire was an example.

"Mind if I share, Feldenhauer?"

"Of course, *Gefreiter*."

"Jürgen is fine. I haven't really earned the title."

Feldenhauer smiled. "Rudi."

Jürgen held his open can of pork over the flame. Soon the fat sizzled, making the usually unpalatable contents smell surprisingly good.

"Where's your home, Rudi?"

"Bremen."

"Really?" Jürgen enthused. "I'm from a Neuhaus, just south of Cuxhaven; so close to Bremen, but I've never had the chance to go there."

"Why the interest in Bremen? Hamburg is just as close, and more interesting."

"Why, the competitions, of course!"

Feldenhauer frowned, shook his head. "Competitions?"

"Your Shützenfest! One of the best in Germany. What an honor to win there!"

Feldenhauer made a wry smile. "I suppose," he said, but let the subject drop.

They watched the flames and ate their warmed rations.

"You have a trade, Rudi?"

"I worked at the brewery!"

Jürgen could see a spark of enthusiasm in his answer. "The *Braueri Beck*?"

"None other. I'm there three years. I'll make it my career if I live through this. How about you?"

The question bothered Jürgen. He'd asked it of himself many times, wondering if he was good at anything besides shooting at targets. "I've no idea. More schooling is what I need, if I could find a way to pay for it. That isn't likely. I'll probably wind up working on the Oste, or if I'm lucky, the Elbe ferry."

Feldenhauer waited a bit before saying, "If I wanted something, I wouldn't let anything stop me. You only have one life. You have the power to either grab it, or accept what the world hands you. Figure out a way to go to whatever school you want."

Jürgen supposed he was right. Wise words, but hard to put into practice.

"Frightened about tomorrow, Rudi?"

"Apprehensive," he replied. "Too green to be scared. You?"

Jürgen searched for something clever to put Feldenhauer at ease, but failed. "We have hundreds of thousands of men from seventy-two divisions ready to attack an unsuspecting enemy…but yes…yes, Rudi. I'm scared."

~ * ~

March 21, 1918

The first of the big guns Jürgen had seen being positioned announced the first day of the *Kaiserschlacht.* It was 4:40 AM.

Jürgen had been fast asleep, but felt the ground shudder as other guns joined in to commence battle with the British 3rd and 5th armies. He knew it would go on for a while until they pounded the enemy's command/control locations, artillery emplacements, and probable front line positions.

The first wave of troops would be special shock troops--*Stoßtruppen*, the most seasoned and fit men creamed away from their units. Their job would be to chop holes in the enemy defenses by avoiding strongholds, and penetrate deep while regular troops followed up, consolidating the ground gained. Jürgen wondered what kind of man it was that lasted long enough in this war to be considered both seasoned and fit. If he was seasoned, he was certainly not fit, he thought.

It would be another hour before the 238th Infantry would deploy. All the troops would be traveling light in order to enhance mobility. The usual heavy pack of the German soldier was left behind. At first light, the fog was unusually thick when Lieutenant Lutz led his men into the killing field.

It wasn't long before they sensed that things seemed to be going quite well. The terrain, though pockmarked from years of bombardment, was not the sodden morass of Belgium. They moved swiftly over the chalky soil, surprising pockets of British resistance as they loomed up, unseen, in the dense fog. The British perimeter was too dispersed to halt the wave of German troops. By late afternoon, after the fog had lifted, the British were in retreat after sustaining considerable casualties and dead.

"If it continues like this," Koss said, "we'll be swimming in the Channel by June."

~ * ~

Day two of the offensive was almost a copy of the first, including the heavy fog. The British 5th Army was pulling back, although inflicting more casualties on the advancing German troops than at first. News from farther south was also good. They were advancing on the city of Noyon toward Paris, as the British 3rd had to fall back lest they be flanked by the 5th Army's retreat. Yet they inflicted considerable casualties on the Germans in the face of losing Noyon.

By day three, the 238th was near Roye, a city southeast of their main objective, Amiens. This was farther west than any German soldier had been since the first incursion in 1914. Then, news came that their 7th Army had thrust deep into the Allies' heart, delving almost to the town of Riems, one hundred-fifty kilometers from the outskirts of Paris. This time, it seemed, the officers were right. *We could win this war, after all.*

Despite their success, the 18th Army had outpaced their supply, running low on munitions and, more importantly, food. There were no mess facilities at end of the day, and what food was available came from the pockets of the individual soldier.

Jürgen had been out of canned rations since day two. He nibbled on his biscuit in order to ration it. Water was another issue. The British had ceded ground that was almost devoid of resources. Out here there was no population to plunder…except for that town that lay just to the west: Roye.

~ * ~

March 25,1918
Roye, France

Their thrust had been northwest along the Somme basin; territory that, two years earlier, had cost many thousands of lives on both sides. This time, unprepared as the British were for an attack at this part of the front, they had inflicted serious casualties on the Germans, who by then had gained control of Albert, not far to the northwest of Amiens. Along the route, stubborn resistance existed in British strongholds, *redoubts,* that were bypassed by the shock troops. Each of these had to be neutralized, costing substantial casualties on both sides, but the *Kaiserschlacht* continued.

Jürgen Stern had never really known hunger, nor had any of his eight men—until now. Their rapid progress toward Amiens could be celebrated some other time. Right then, food, and in many cases, water were on everyone's mind.

Roye was a small town fifty kilometers southeast of Amiens. It had been spared excessive destruction despite it being an industrial city. As a result, it was thought to be still well provisioned owing to its proximity to Amiens and an ongoing economy.

Lieutenant Lutz led his men into town down the Grand Rue. Jürgen's first indication that something was not quite right was the shouting. It sounded like a large football match, a sustained clamor. He could hear it build up ahead where the street took a bend into the town center.

The units marching ahead began breaking into a run despite warnings from their officers.

Koss cautioned, "Stay in formation!"

Lutz echoed the order to the entire platoon.

It was useless. Units behind them began to break up and run for the market that came into view as they rounded the bend. The scene that unfolded was chaotic. Shops, especially those advertising anything to consume, were being mobbed. Wire grates were wrenched from closed store fronts; boarded windows torn away. An entire army had broken discipline, overwhelming the place.

By night fall of the following day, total order had yet to be restored among the ranks. Some wise general officer had opted to let the men sate themselves in lieu of any support from the rear. Now, with too many of their horses slaughtered for meat, the 238th Infantry had lost mobility, and worse, discipline.

The looting was short-lived. The spare provisions of Roye were insufficient to slake the hunger of an entire division. By the time the

463d Regiment arrived in the town center, there was nothing left to loot had Jürgen and his section opted in.

In the cathedral city of Albert forty km. to the north, and barely thirty from Amiens itself, the looting and near-rioting had occurred on a larger scale. As a result, more than twenty-four hours were required to reinstate discipline and procure supplies. This gave the British 5th Army a breather, allowing them to harden their defenses of the city. It would be harder going now.

~ * ~

March 28, 1918
Moreuil, France

From Roye they marched to Rollet, where they were regrouped with artillery units of the 238th. Rollet was on a good road south of Amiens, enabling the big guns to keep up with the infantry.

They had camped overnight, having received only meagre rations following the fiasco at Roye. The morning fog made the cold penetrate to the bone.

"Get ready to move out!" an order came.

Jürgen shed the large blanket he shared with Alfred and Feldenhauer. It was one thing he'd managed to scavenge in Roye; a quilt someone had lovingly crafted in a time and place unimaginably foreign to their present circumstances. He tried to remember his home, and the handiwork of his mother and grandmother, but could not. It was simply too remote of a concept.

Again, they were formed up and on the road. After a day's march, a crossroad sign pointed north reading: MOREUIL 4KM. Soon after, they were disbursed into a moving front of perhaps a kilometer wide, cautiously approaching the town. The 463d Regiment was positioned to the right of the road, marching over fallow fields. In the distance, Jürgen could see the village rooftops. A road led away to the east, beyond which was a line of thick woods.

He felt exposed. Anything could be hiding in wait among those trees, despite scouting reports to the contrary. They halted five hundred meters from the road while advance patrols confirmed the woods were undefended. It was Moreuil Wood, according to a map of the area, about one kilometer deep and half again as wide. They entered it among seasoned units of the 23rd Saxon Division, and were assigned positions that commanded the field west of the wood where the road continued north along the Avre River to meet the Somme at Amiens.

As darkness arrived, the men began to complain once more about the lack of rations. Friends were sharing what they carried, but it was clear they could not continue much longer without resupply.

"We should be digging in here," Alfred said. "It's a perfect defensive position."

Jürgen agreed, but saw no effort at establishing anything permanent.

"We're not staying here." Koss overheard the talk.

"I can't walk another kilometer," Feldenhauer said.

"You'll have to, I'm afraid," Koss said. "The *Kaiserschlacht* is an offensive to end the war. There should be no more trenches."

That night, the little food that could be commandeered from the town of Moreuil was barely enough for an army, but the men were fed something. Water from the Avre filled their canteens. It would have to be enough to sustain them until they were able to appropriate the resources of Amiens.

"God willing we get there," Alfred said.

~ * ~

That night was considerably warmer, and the men rested well under their oiled tarpaulins and blankets. Jürgen woke to see the sun painting the trees' new growth a bright green against the blue Picardy sky. One could forget the war for a brief moment.

He'd relieved himself, and was having a breakfast of last night's remains when sporadic shooting sounded from the northern edge of the wood.

Word was spread that an enemy patrol had engaged their northern perimeter and retreated. At once they were ordered into defensive positions. They had the advantage if there was to be an attack. The trees were dense enough to supply excellent cover. Still, Jürgen wondered why their leaders didn't use this time to organize an offensive toward Amiens. This seemed counter to what Koss had been saying the previous night.

The sun was well up when they heard a crescendo of gunfire from the north. Jürgen peered out onto the open field, but could see nothing but the occasional bird pecking for nest straw. The view across the road to the river was like a still life painting.

"You hear that?" Feldenhauer said from his post five meters away.

"What?"

"Listen!"

It sounded like the rumble of distant thunder. *Horses running?* The only horses Jürgen had seen lately were the tired dray horses hauling the field pieces; certainly not likely to be running anywhere. Also, these were held well south of the wood.

The answer was revealed when, from their right, at full gallop came mounted troops, some of them wielding sabers, a vision out of the Napoleonic Wars. There were hundreds of them wheeling around to bear down on the woods from the west.

"Fire!" an order was shouted, and Jürgen did, but missed the bobbing target he'd chosen. He chambered another round from the five round clip, this time taking down a horse, but the rider got up to continue his charge on foot only to be felled by someone else's bullet.

In seconds, the cavalry charge was into the woods, shooting and hacking at anyone and everyone. Jürgen fumbled with his bayonet, hoping he wouldn't be killed as he did. It clicked in place in time for him to use the trunk of a tree to parry the thrust of a sword.

It was mayhem. They'd had brief encounters with hand to hand combat, but nothing like this. In the din of the shouting and gunfire, he could hear the same from elsewhere in the wood. They'd been attacked on all sides!

As afraid for his life as Jürgen was, he could see the terror in the eyes of the horsemen as well. They had rushed headlong into the woods, likely knowing they were outnumbered by an Army and surrounded as soon as they entered. Soon the sabers were neglected in favor of rifle and, better, pistol.

Jürgen was surprised by his calm in this melee, which was devolving into separate skirmishes throughout the wood. Killing another man up close cannot easily be done by a healthy mind unless done in the fog of battle. Here it was different from that first sickening experience of one year ago at Bellicourt on sniper duty. That was a cold and calculated kill with time to think about it before and after the event. This was fighting for your life.

So it was when he dropped the young trooper out of his saddle with a 7.9mm bullet from his Mauser, he felt a tinge of remorse, but had no time to vomit as he'd done that day on the Siegfried Line. He had lost all contact with his own company, much less his section. As the fighting continued through the morning, he noticed two things. These men were all Canadians. This so soon after engaging them in Flanders. His second notion was that fewer and fewer horses were involved. The enemy must have realized their ineffectiveness among the close quarters of the trees.

By afternoon, despite being outnumbered, the Canadians were able to push the Germans to the southern limits of Moreuil Wood, having commenced an artillery attack, and even directed aerial bombing by the Royal Flying Service.

At day's end, the 23rd Saxon Division and support units were forced to retreat out of range of the shelling, well south of Moreuil. The enemy had gained full control of Moreuil wood.

~ * ~

Jürgen was exhausted and hungry. There was no fight left in him. He wandered around the army's rear position along the Avre looking for anyone from the 463d Regiment, and for something to eat. He found both. Standing in the rear of a food line were Rudi Feldenhauer and Alfred Hauser. They stared at him, amazement obvious in their faces.

"You were reported dead."

"Not yet, but just about," Jürgen said.

Feldenhauer avoided Jürgen' eyes. "Koss is dead," he said. "I was there."

Alfred move two steps forward in pace with the food line. "I'm alive because of him, that's all I'll say."

Jürgen was deeply saddened. Koss had been in the war since 1914. He'd barely survived the Marne battle, according to Sgt. Büler. Jürgen remembered his leadership at the chemical factory near Gavrille, and their close scrape at Passchendaele. Who would remember his deeds after this nameless skirmish?

"Back of the line!" a soldier complained to Jürgen, arousing him from his thoughts. He took his place there, shuffling forward and thinking of *Unteroffizier* Gerhard Koss, his corporal since training camp in Lockstedt, a lifetime ago.

Twenty

May 30, 1918

Cernay lès Reims, France

Jürgen trudged in the double file, avoiding the wheel of the gun carriage sharing the road. It was still dark, and already the day promised to be unseasonably hot. His stomach felt hollow. Despite the ration of thin porridge last night, he felt weak with hunger. The supply lines from St. Quentin were all but shut down.

They were marching east from Cernay toward Reims after being relocated well to the south last April when the attack on Amiens had bogged down. This was in preparation for a major offensive to take the important city of Reims and other Territory north of the Marne River.

Their failure to hold Moreuil Wood had since been reversed by fresh troops. German units again held that key outpost. As a result of that news and of huge German guns actually shelling parts of Paris, morale crept up a notch. Perhaps victory was in sight. At the moment, victory would be something substantial to eat.

Today's attack would be a feint to test the strength of the enemy east of Reims. They were to probe the city's defenses before drawing back. Feint or not, Jürgen knew a man could easily get himself killed in a skirmish like this.

They were just two of the three regiments of the 238th Division along with parts of the 62nd Field artillery. So it was more of a raid than a battle.

"I don't like the feel of this," Alfred said as they were being broken down into discrete units of two companies, each with a sector to probe.

Their bivouac at Cernay was just 4km from the outskirts of the city where the French 4th Army had dug in a double line of trenches, according to scouting reports. They would have to rely on cover from the terrain to effect any surprise. The French, supported by newly arrived units from America, had cleared two hundred meters in front of their lines of any cover. Alfred's misgivings were entirely justified, Jürgen thought.

It was still dark, and Jürgen was relieved when the order came to move on the trenches. To do so in the light of day would be suicide.

The two companies III and IV advanced over the field at a trot. Although they were undermanned, there was no way they could adequately muffle the sound of four hundred men in full stride.

They got closer than expected before the first machine gun flashes began, forcing them to the ground. Jürgen estimated they were as close as fifty meters. Another machine gun started up, and both fired blindly into the darkness. The sound of rifle fire added a rhythmic counterpoint to the brutal MG bursts. Jürgen knew reinforcements would be pouring in from the rear trench. If they were going to get within hand grenade range, it had better be now.

The orange burst of a friendly artillery shell momentarily brightened the landscape. Jürgen saw one brave soldier dart closer with a grenade. Seconds later the burst of it exploding looked to be well short of the forward trench.

Support from the enemy's rear must have been alert, because new muzzle flashes began to fill the atmosphere with bullets. Enemy Stokes mortars began to find their range. There was no doubt that just two infantry companies and one artillery battery were not going to penetrate the enemy line—at least in this sector.

In less than thirty minutes, whistles signaling a retreat sounded. In the process, forty five of the 390 man contingent never made it out. The rest of the two regiments had similar results. There was no doubt that the French were well prepared to defend Reims.

~ * ~

July 15, 1918

Cernay lès Reims, France

Jürgen had seen the enemy tanks in Flanders. They were great lumbering things. They had seemed so menacing before getting bogged down in mud and the huge water-filled craters. But these captured British tanks would be operating in much better conditions. For one, the terrain here had not been shelled constantly as had the fields east of Ypres. Then there was this dry summer weather. Where the wet conditions at Passchendaele had favored the defender, these favored the attacker.

The probes carried out May 30 must have convinced the high command that any attack on Reims would have to be with every piece of armament available. The attack would be on two simultaneous fronts, east and west of the city. The 238th Division would be one held back in reserve. Only their artillery would join the attack on the city's east.

The entire 1st and 3rd Armies would attack from the east. Jürgen and Feldenhauer watched in the dark as the tanks rumbled away, their big diesel engines growling like hungry lions. Hundreds of field guns followed, the larger guns already in place and trained on the line of trenches kilometers away.

Just before dawn, a *Feuerwaltze*—a walking barrage learned from the Canadians—would lead the infantry over the enemy trenches. Everything was meticulously planned. The taking of Reims would be a devastating blow to the French and their allies, both tactically and psychologically. "I'm glad it's not me going," Feldenhauer said. "I'm not as afraid as I'm too hungry to march there."

Jürgen felt the same. He'd noticed Alfred, slight of build to start, become alarmingly thin. Yet, he was the most stoic of all about their dearth of rations. Now there was nothing to do but wait to be called forward for the final taking of prisoners and the occupation of Reims, France.

~ * ~

It was noon when the first reports of the attack came back to the bivouac at Cernay. It was a disaster. The official report was delivered to Generals Von Boehm and Eben, but the messenger's driver had his own story to tell.

Contrary to the experiences of the May 30 probe, the trenches had been abandoned. Exhilarated, the two armies' poured over them headlong toward the city. There, they set up their field guns in preparation for the final attack when pre-aimed artillery of unprecedented density and over the entire front surprised them. They had been lured into a killing field. By 1100 it was obvious the city would not fall, but the fighting continued in order to protect their retreat.

By nightfall they heard that the western campaign went off better, but the city was still in the hands of the French 4th Army and their American divisions. It was a staggering defeat.

Twenty-one

August 8, 1918
Amiens, France

"Quiet, you two!" Brian hissed at a pair of replacements assigned to his section while at Lens. They had been marching since nightfall, a sliver of moon barely visible in the blackness above. Friendly territory or not, their movement was strictly secret. Tomorrow's attack had to be a complete surprise, and there had been credible reports of spying.

Brian's company was reassigned to 4th Army's 11th Brigade. Earlier on the previous day, they were told how tomorrow would go. A combined force of British, Australian, Canadian and French would launch a simultaneous attack along a forty mile front with the intent of pushing the enemy back all the way to the Hindenburg line at St Quentin.

The German spring offensive had advanced west almost to Amiens, and as far south as the Marne River. But the British had held at Amiens and the French, with help from the newly arrived Americans, had hurled them back north away from the Marne cities of Reims and Chateau Thierry.

By the time the brigade was encamped in a field west of the city, it was 2 AM. They were told to get some rest as they would not be part of the initial attack scheduled to begin in a few hours. Their time would come later.

Then, at 4:20 AM, they heard the first big guns of the artillery.

"Holy Christ!" Harry said from a corner of the shelter he, Brian and Janowski shared.

Brian felt the ground shake as batteries from the combined armies simultaneously erupted. There was no use trying to sleep.

"When do we go?" Janowski asked Brian.

"Don't know. Later today, I suppose." They'd been told the 1st, 2nd, and 3rd Divisions would be in the first wave with the Aussies on their left flank and the French on their right. The front extended from Albert in the north to Mondidier to the south. Forty divisions would take part in the attack.

"Don't be in such a hurry, Janowski," Harry said.

"That's just what I'm not. What I'm thinking is: the more we do this, the worse our chances. I'd rather have my foot shot off, or get sent home like Kobak than bleed to death out there."

Harry scoffed, "You don't want to end up like Kobak!"

"Maybe not." Janowski pondered that thought, and said, "It shouldn't be like that. He got singled out because of his Austrian family. My parents came from Krakow, which is still under Austrian rule. They left for the same reasons as George's family, I'll bet."

Brian broke in. "He said it was because they couldn't stand what the emperor was doing."

"Exactly! My dad hates Franz-Joseph, or whatever his name is."

"Hated," Brian said. "I think he died a few years back."

"Good," Janowski said.

Despite the barrage, Brian finally did fall back to sleep until aroused by their new platoon leader, a fresh faced, bespectacled Lieutenant MacLeod, newly arrived from the 5th Reserve Division in England. He was replacing Lieutenant Cross, who'd been promoted up to captain and a company of his own.

By 7:30 they were fed and briefed on the day's objectives. Maps were distributed showing the road heading east-southeast out of Amiens toward Roye, thirty miles away.

Brian gathered his squad around. "We're relieving a brigade of the Third Army when they reach their objective, that green line on the map. So far, they've had the Huns skedaddling, but they seem to be digging in here." He pointed to a village along the road named Le Quesnel. "Our job will be the dotted blue line and to secure that town by tonight."

He checked that his section carried only the necessities to ensure mobility: haversack, 200 rounds of ammunition, gas mask, water bottle, "iron rations" of canned Maconochie Stew & biscuits, entrenching tool, two Mills bombs, and two sand bags. A password, Landovery Castle, was drilled into their collective memory, and Brian felt his section was as prepared as any in the 4th Division.

"What's 'Landovery Castle'?" Peck, a new man from southern Ontario asked.

"Christ, Peck," Harry said. "Our hospital ship that went down last month!"

It was big news, widely promulgated by the command. Over two hundred-fifty were lost, including fourteen of the beloved Canadian nursing sisters, when the ship was torpedoed. It was a well-chosen password meant to instill resolve among the men.

The whistle to move out came at 9:45 AM.

~ * ~

The Canadian Corps' part in the Allied attack was to push the enemy back along two diverging roads out of Amiens. The road to Saint Quentin ran due east, while the road to Roye and beyond stretched more southeasterly. It was along the Roye road that Brian's unit was assigned.

Throughout the rest of the morning, the units of the 4th replaced their 3rd Division counterparts. Despite having lost several tanks to heavy machine gun and artillery fire, the 3rd Division had surpassed the green line objective by noon, outpacing the French 31st Corps assigned south of the road. Brian overheard two senior officers complaining how their right flank was exposed as a result.

Lt. MacLeod had them dig in where a 3rd Div. unit had relinquished its position. Brian had no sooner gotten his section in place when they began taking mortar fire. For several minutes, confusion reigned while the source of the attack was determined. Ultimately, the sound of the mortars being launched was heard from south of the Roye Road.

"That steeple's gotta be how they're sighting on us!" someone shouted.

Then, "MacLeod, Brewster! Take your platoons over to that village and shut those bastards down!"

Brian saw the alarm in the eyes behind MacLeod's round lenses. The man had barely set foot on French soil. To his credit he did not hesitate, but responded with a crisp "Yes sir!"

A brief word with the 1st Platoon leader and MacLeod ordered, "Second Platoon! Follow me!" but the tremor in his voice belied the confidence he sought.

The two officers led their men to a rill no larger than a ditch that ran under a tiny wooden bridge on the road. Brian glanced at his map, noting the steeple was situated in the village of Mézières-en-Santerre, and from the scale looked to be about six to seven hundred yards away.

The morning fog had lifted, and the two platoons were wisely led along the rill until it bore away from the village to the west, requiring them to scramble behind sparse vegetation to avoid being seen.

"If you can't see that steeple, they can't see you," Brewster reminded.

~ * ~

It took them an hour, duck-walking, darting from cover to cover in broad daylight. They approached the uninhabited town from the east, checking for manned outposts.

"I'm thinkin' the Bosh are lookin' west for the Frenchies," Harry whispered.

"Let's hope," Brian said. He could see the front of the church—more a chapel than anything—about eighty yards down a lane from where MacLeod positioned them.

First section was on the other side of the lane, while Brewster's platoon remained south of the town. The two platoon leaders had cooked up a plan that Brian thought was credible. They flipped a coin to see which of them would draw fire from the steeple while the other attacked it and the mortar emplacement. MacLeod got the latter of the two. Either would be extremely dangerous.

"When first platoon starts firing, we go," Brian whispered to his men. He worried about the lack of intelligence on the whereabouts of the mortar team. It was probably within shouting distance of the steeple unless the Germans had telephone lines this far out.

Right on time, rifle fire commenced from Lt. Brewster's platoon.

"Time to go," MacLeod announced.

They hugged both edges of the cobbled lane dodging around obstacles, an overturned cart, a smashed chest of drawers—the detritus of war. The steeple was in view. Brian could see bits of its masonry shatter as it received rifle fire. MacLeod signaled for a dash to the building's rear entrance.

They got no farther than the corner of a shop, its window smashed under a sign, *Boulangerie* in faded lettering. Down the intersecting lane, the mortar battery was at work. The Canadians were seen, as well, and were immediately under fire. Someone, Brian could not tell who, went down before they could find cover.

"Hurley!" MacLeod called to his runner. "Circle back and tell Lt. Brewster where we are and where that mortar battery is."

A terrified Hurley spared no time skedaddling back the way they'd come.

Their presence did not deter the mortar team from their harassment of the Canadians across the Amiens-Roye Road. They ducked back around the building. MacLeod was standing next to Brian, his chest heaving, cherubic face drawn tight with indecision.

"We can't hesitate," Brian said to no one in particular, as a piece of the shop's brickwork disintegrated from a German bullet "We've got to do something."

The words or the bullet brought MacLeod out of his daze. He stared into Brian's eyes for a moment, then his voice was steady, and his words concise.

"Alright Corporal, here's what we'll do." He directed Brian to choose one man to make a dash for the church while the rest of the platoon engaged the mortar bunker.

Brian swallowed hard, wishing he'd kept his mouth shut. He saw Harry had overheard. His friend met his glance and nodded.

MacLeod looked back down the lane one more time as if hoping to see Brewster's platoon. "That's it, then," he said.

~ * ~

They heard a single shot followed by a fusillade of rifle fire, and bolted from behind the shop across the square. It went well for the first ten yards or so, but a lull in friendly fire brought the sound of bullets stinging the air like bees, and throwing up shards of stone from the cobbles. Brian felt his pack take a hit, the force of which almost knocked him down.

Harry was two strides in front, running for dear life, holding on to his tin hat. Then they were scrambling up the steps to the door. Brian wondered for the first time if the door might be locked. If so, they were dead men, but Harry tugged it open, and Brian dove in behind him.

They paused, transfixed. The cool interior looked oddly serene, as if there had been no war here for the last four years. The figures of Christ and the Virgin looked down on them sadly, like parents disappointed in their children and their antics.

Brian stood for a moment, unsure where to go, but Harry saw the door in the tiny narthex leading to the steeple, and tugged at Brian's sleeve. The door opened noiselessly, and they closed it behind them, shutting out the last sounds of gunfire.

There were no stairs, but a ladder leading to a level just below the open belfry. Brian started up, but Harry held his arm.

"You got a plan?"

"No," was Brian's reply. He hadn't, but nothing would be accomplished down here. He kept climbing.

They reached the platform, clearly hearing voices above them, probably giving coordinates to the team in their sandbagged bunker. *Or calling for help,* Brian thought. Then from above, the "crack" of a rifle shot. One of them was sniping at the platoon.

The room, about eight feet square, tapered up to the belfry which was around six feet on a side. A shaft of light shown down through an access to which a stout ladder led. Harry looked helplessly to Brian, who was momentarily at a loss for the next move. There had been no time to think. Brian took stock of what they had at their disposal to use. *The Mills bombs!*

But how to use them? He removed one of the two from his belt, and showed it to Harry, pointing to the belfry. Harry shrugged and followed suit. Brian motioned Harry to one side of the ladder, and they ascended, side by side. They climbed to just below the belfry floor of stout planks. The voices were clearer; words sounding like numbers being called out. They could hear muffled, sporadic shooting below.

With one arm around the ladder, Brian pulled the retaining pin from the grenade. The Mills bomb had a spring lever that, when released, ignited a seven second fuse. He motioned for Harry to toss his bomb through the access hole. White with fear, Harry worked the pin loose, took careful aim, and lobbed the bomb up into the belfry.

Pandemonium began above as Harry flew down the ladder, calling for Brian to follow. Brian heard the scuffle and shouting as the occupants dealt with the emergency. He pulled his pin, counted to four and tossed his bomb.

He slid down the ladder, landing on Harry as both grenades exploded, sending a shower of wood splinters down on them. The concussion in the small confines was deafening.

Thick dust cleared, exposing the green-clad limb of a man hanging from the access. Harry was exhilarated. His white teeth showed in a wide grin. Brian felt ill as they scuttled down the bottom ladder to the ground.

~ * ~

The destruction of the steeple resulted in not only the cessation of mortar fire, but the surrender of the five men in the battery.

"That steeple flew apart like a popped balloon," Janowski said, making their way back across the Roye Road. "Didn't take 'em a minute to start waving a white towel at us."

The prisoners were combined with the hundreds of others surrendered in this morning's fighting, and sent to the rear. It had been easy going for the Canadian Corps so far. But the enemy had recovered and their defense was stiffening.

~ * ~

The 11th Brigade had made progress in the hours it took to neutralize the mortar fire from Mézières. Major Goode and the rest of their unit were found a mile or more to the east. With the help of the Mark II tanks, they had cleared out the village of Beaucourt-en-Santerre, but seemed stalled when Brewster and MacLeod returned with their platoons.

Flat countryside had morphed into rolling hills and small wooded areas. They were receiving increasing fire from the wooded areas and a ridge that ran north-south in front of them. Proceeding slowly now, the commanders surveyed the defensive obstacles guarding the towns of Le Quesnel and Caix.

The first was a copse of trees. Enemy machine guns and mortar batteries were dug in there, and would have to be dealt with. It was a good quarter mile to the east.

"Take your men along the south side of those trees. Third section will join you along with two machine gun squads," Lt. MacLeod said. "When you hear our mortars commence, wait two minutes and attack. Others will be doing the same from the north and west."

Brian located a rise due south of the trees and headed for it, along with the third section. They did not get far. An explosion erupted not twenty yards ahead, taking down two men from the third.

"Get down!" Brian shouted to his men. The only cover was in the craters from the morning's shelling, and Brian followed Janowski into one of them. They were scant protection from shrapnel, but all there was to be had. They literally landed on top of two men. It wasn't a warm reception.

"Get the fuck out of here!" one of them yelled. He was a big man, cradling a machine gun in his arms.

Brian focused on the man's face. "Rupke!" It was Colby Wentworth's oafish friend. The other man was unfamiliar.

Rupke's small eyes under a thick brow stared back at Brian. He shouted over the noise of exploding ordinance. "Move it, I said!"

"Where's Wentworth?" Brian shouted. "I thought you were a team!"

"That yellow bastard weaseled his self a nice safe staff job six months ago. Now, clear the hell out of this here crater if ya know what's healthy."

Janowski shouted, "He's right, Brian. We're too exposed here!"

Dirt and clots of turf rained down from a nearby blast, bring with it more invective from Rupke and the other man.

Brian gave Janowski a nod, and they scrambled over the rim. They hadn't gone five yards when another huge blast landed behind, throwing them to the earth, face first.

Conciousness returned to Brian as he saw Janowski, his helmet a yard away, moving his lips trying to be heard over Brian's ringing ears.

"Are you alright?" he called to Janowski, who seemed concerned about something. He was pointing to Brian's legs.

Brian twisted around at his left leg which seemed perfectly fine. Another blast shook the earth and filled the air with chaos. Again, Janowski pointed to Brian's legs, this time pulling at him to return to the crater.

"No," Brian shouted. "Keep moving!" and began to rise, but the right leg would not respond. Only then did he see the large gash in his red-stained puttees.

Janowski had him under the arms and was dragging him back to the crater. The last thing Brian remembered before passing out was the smoking, empty crater where a boot, bits of fabric and the tripod for a Vickers machine gun were the only occupants. The crater had received a direct hit.

~ * ~

September 15, 1918
Quincy-Basse, France
20km north of Soissons

"You shut your mouth, Schreiber, or I'll shoot you myself!" Jürgen could hardly believe his own words, but the man's talk of desertion had to be stemmed.

Starting with the failure at Reims, a series of setbacks for the *Kaiserschlacht* had commenced. Word came that the Spring Offensive that had begun so well had bogged down elsewhere along the Marne River. The French and Americans had prevailed at Chateau Thierry. What had stopped the German Army from reaching Paris in 1914 stopped them now. They had outrun their re-supply capabilities. The attrition of troops, ordnance, and most importantly, rations severely crippled their ability to fight. The last of these was the major cause of talk like that of Schreiber.

They had held on to a defensive position at Cernay lès Reims until the August 20. Since Reims they had been on the line at Leuilly north of Soissons when the French and a division of Negro soldiers from America broke through, overrunning German positions, seizing artillery pieces, and their few tanks. An uncoordinated retreat resulted in many hundreds of German prisoners taken.

Marching north into the tiny crossroads called Quincy-Basse, Jürgen felt the same gnawing in his gut as the others. But by then—after a year of fighting, seeing his friends and mentors die, after barely surviving himself—he felt too invested to give up. New replacements like Schreiber could not understand this.

It was almost dark when they halted at a farm outside the village and were told to get rations from a lorry parked nearby. The rations consisted of water and canned biscuits only. It was worse than nothing, as the men were in need of some real food. Their complaining was becoming a serious morale problem.

They took their three cans per troop back to a dry well where Jürgen bedded his section down for the night. It was not to be. They were ordered to prepare a defense of the crossroads deemed vital by someone in command who, thought Jürgen, must know why.

A whole division of hungry, exhausted men began digging in. They did not finish until first light of the next day. The expected attack never came.

It proved to be a short respite, but the added day's preparations paid off as they were able to hold off a series of raids over the next week. After that the enemy seemed to be satisfied with their gains, having fish to fry elsewhere.

The conditions for fighting were unbearable. Over and above the hunger was the heat. A constant vigil was required as the enemy would sporadically probe in raids for intelligence. The lulls would let the men focus on their hunger and the vermin that plagued them, especially the fleas that seemed to thrive in the environment.

Jürgen watched Alfred as he tried in vain to rid his *Tornister* knapsack of the pests. Alfred Hauser, the frail, sensitive artist, had become a tough wiry soldier—one Jürgen would trust with his life.

"I think, Alfred…" Jürgen started, "…this war is almost over. What will you do?"

This earned Jürgen a quizzical look. Alfred paused before answering.

"I had plans, but that door may have shut. Honestly, I don't know."

"But your music…"

Alfred looked at his toughened hands. Grime was ground into the callouses and under his nails. "I don't know," he repeated.

It troubled Jürgen to see his friend reduced to such a state. "You must have been very good to be accepted at the *Hochschule*. When did you begin to study the violin?"

Alfred produced a derisive snort. "I had one handed to me before I could go to the toilet alone!"

"But you liked playing?"

"I love…loved it, but it wasn't easy in a town like Stade. I'm a Jew, Jürgen. I've been bullied all my life, whether about my violin or my religion or being called a sissy."

"You're no sissy, Alfred. I've been to war with you."

Tears welled up in Alfred's eyes.

"What? What did I say?"

Alfred hesitated to say anything. Then, "They called me worse words than *sissy*. The thing is: they were right!"

Jürgen recalled one or two boys in Neuhaus and nearby Cadenberge whom he'd tormented because of their effeminate ways, and felt ashamed. "Alfred, my good friend, promise me you will go back to your music when you return home. I've never known a finer man than you."

~ * ~

The following days were filled with a succession of enemy raids, night probes meant to harass and destroy morale. Duty on the picket line was extremely dangerous, and the occurrence of a lone sentry not returning from his outpost was common. Jürgen was getting increasingly disenchanted with their commanders, the ones directing their movements. The Quincy area appeared to have no strategic value. What was the use of trying to defend an imaginary line in the sand? He knew they were too weak to effect a meaningful attack on their own. Their artillery, someone had said, was too low on munitions to support an offensive.

As if the high command had been reading his mind, on October 12 they were ordered to quietly pull out of the area in the cover of darkness, marching 20 km. east to Crepe, where they were put on trucks for what Jürgen came to realize was a full retreat. When they disembarked the trucks, they realized they had travelled far north and east of the once-impregnable Hindenburg Line that ran through Saint Quentin.

"Where are we?" Feldenhauer was shaking the sleep out of his head as he tumbled off the bed of the truck.

Alfred pointed to a sign hanging askew from a post. The letters G U I S E were battered, but visible. A barrel-shaped, medieval castle dominated the landscape of the otherwise featureless village. What was there was mostly ruins from fighting four years earlier. Once more Jürgen questioned the wisdom of digging in and defending such a seemingly inconsequential plot of Picardy.

Twenty-two

September 15, 1918
Avonmouth, Severn Estuary
England

His fever had returned. For a moment Brian forgot where he was until a sister who watched him wake from a fitful sleep told him the ship would dock momentarily. From a tray she took a damp towel, and pressed it to his forehead.

"Docking," Brian repeated.

"Bristol," the nurse repeated.

Brian tried to process the word while he focused on the red cross of the woman's pinafore. "Bristol?"

"England, young man. Now be patient, if you can. It will be some time before we can get you all ashore.

He remembered then, being loaded on the steamer at Le Havre after being shifted from dressing stations to two field hospitals, and finally to the hospital ship.

The action at Amiens and the Scarpe River soon after had taxed the Allies' medical facilities to their limits. Brian had lain unattended for a day after receiving his wound. The delay nearly cost him his leg, if not his life. Even now, saving the leg was at issue.

He remembered nothing, having to be told of Jannowski carrying him over his shoulders to the rear until finding a team with an empty litter. He woke up with searing pain in the right thigh. For twelve hours he received only attempts to clean the wound, but nothing for the pain. Morphine had run out by the time Brian arrived.

Because he was not in immediate peril of death, he was regulated to a holding area, and waited in pain. Then a series of mix-ups sent him not to a field hospital, but yet to another dressing station. Further confusion resulted in his being trundled to two different field hospitals before being, at last, sedated and transferred to the HMHS Dieppe, a 273-foot steamer requisitioned by the Royal Navy for hospital service, and bound for England.

The sister knew what she was talking about. It took another ninety minutes before it was Brian's turn to be carried down the covered gangway to the wharf at Avonmouth and a waiting lorry.

For a soldier who had known nothing for months but fetid trenches, field hospitals, and the stinking hold of a ship, the sea breeze and tangy promise of an English autumn was elixir. He slept the whole hour's drive to Bristol.

~ * ~

Brian and Owen were cutting wood, one on each end of a long, two-handled saw. Sarah was there, sometimes sitting in his mother's rocker on the porch, sometimes standing next to Owen. He wished Owen would stop so he could talk to Sarah. *He needed to talk to Sarah!* But the saw kept going and he was compelled to pull back on the blade biting into the log that seemed impervious to their efforts.

He wanted to stop. He wanted to talk to Sarah—ask her why she never wrote. Then Owen wasn't there, and it was Colby Wentworth grinning back, and so was Sarah. She was teasing him, calling his name. "Brian! Brian! Wake up." He was hot—burning, in fact. *Stop the saw!* "Brian!" He felt his face cool. It was wonderful. Someone shook him. He opened his eyes to see a girl's face, but it wasn't Sarah.

"Brian," the face said. "It's alright. Wake up, now."

He looked past the girl to a tall, domed ceiling and arched windows on the far brick wall where sunlight directed yellow shafts of illumination through the room. There were beds lined up against the wall and on either side.

She was pressing a cool compress against his cheeks and forehead. “You were having quite a time of it, Brian. My name is Ann, one of your nurses. We’ve been a little concerned about your fever.”

His gaze rested once more on hers. Eyes that were older than her youthful face. *Blue? Green?* Remnants of childhood freckles across her narrow nose, hair of ginger. It was her voice, he realized, that reminded him of Sarah, but they resembled one another in no other way.

He whispered, “Sarah.”

“No dear, Ann. Is Sarah your…”

He closed his eyes, slowly shaking his head, “No.”

The burning in his leg returned him to the present. “My leg.”

“Don’t worry about your leg,” she said, which of course was impossible.

He tried sitting up to look at the offending pain, but his legs were covered, and the effort excruciating.

The girl gently pushed him back onto the pillow. “Your leg is being cared for, Brian.”

He tried to resist, but was too exhausted, and gave in to whatever it was they’d given him for the pain.

~ * ~

October 6, 1918
Bruce Cole Military Hospital
Bristol, England

In 1914 when the German army swept over Belgium, thousands of families were displaced and the lucky ones found refuge in Britain. The Bruce Cole Recreation Centre, built just six years earlier for the employees of a large sweets manufacturer, was turned over to house some of those families until they could be relocated. One of those families was that of Doctor Adriaan Martins.

When the building was converted into a military hospital, Dr. Martins stayed on, partly in gratitude, partly for the meagre salary. He was a large man in both stature and voice. The floor of the B Ward was large, as hospitals go, and Dr. Martins' voice would resonate from the first bed to the last. No one's malady or progress was a secret after he made his rounds. He had a high forehead, despite having retained all of his hair after his more than sixty years. Bushy eyebrows of black and grey shrouded eyes that looked down to where Brian sat propped in his bed.

"You are going to keep your leg, my man," he said in his heavy Flemish accent. "But if you are going to walk on it, you are going to do exactly what I and your nurses say."

Brian looked to Ann who, hands pressed against her pinafore, assumed the air of a task master.

"That means much work. Painful work," Martins said.

Brian's eyes remained on Ann. "Then I guess that's what I'll have to do, Doc."

Martins took the nurse aside, but Brian had no trouble hearing the doctor review instructions for the first week of his recovery.

"When do we start?" he asked when she returned and Martins had continued down the ward.

"Right now."

"Now," he repeated, not believing.

She pulled off his sheet and removed a device that had his leg immobilized.

Brian noticed his bare toes stained with iodine, treatment for his touch of trench foot, a debilitating condition shared by most who had spent days on end in trenches and ankle deep, fetid water.

"You have to stretch your leg muscles," she said and held her hand an inch or two from his heel. "Touch my hand with your foot."

"What?"

"Go on, do it!"

He pushed away with his leg, but the pain shot from knee to ankle. "I can't!"

"You will, or spend the rest of your life in a wheel chair. Now try again."

He tried again with the same result. "Hurts like hell," he complained.

"Half an inch," she insisted.

Again, he tried, groaning in agony and frustration.

"You did it!" she said. And he had. "Tomorrow morning you do one inch."

~ * ~

The therapy consisted mostly of learning how to bear weight on the leg and stretching what muscle hadn't been destroyed. The stretching of his muscle relied on the original game of pushing his foot out straight. Ann would reward his successes with a foot massage. It was a strong incentive. Being able to bear the weight of his body was accomplished by endless walking, first hobbling down the line of beds in the ward, then outside in the recreational field that fronted the columned façade of the one-time concert hall.

After three weeks he was walking unassisted with a cane, albeit slowly.

He increasingly looked forward to his daily sessions with Ann, whose last name, he'd learned, was Prichard. He especially enjoyed their walks around the recreational field when the weather allowed. They gave time to ask her about herself, which he was constantly doing and she was ever equivocating.

It was on one of these walks, with coats buttoned high against a nip in the wind off the estuary that Brian's infatuation with her emerged. They were sitting on the stone bench at the far end of the field.

"You have a…friend at home?"

She laughed. "You mean a boyfriend?"

He smiled sheepishly.

She didn't answer his question. "And you, I'm sure, have a girl waiting—Sarah?"

Startled, he said, "How would you know?"

"Your first day here. You were dreaming. Tell me about her."

Brian looked down at his feet, hands in his jacket pockets. "She's just a girl in my town."

"A special girl, I think."

"You could think that. I don't."

She put her hand on his arm. "I'm sorry. Did you get one of those letters that—"

He cut her off with a derisive laugh, "No! I *didn't* get a letter," and limped off down the walk toward the building.

He waited for her that next day, watching her work with the influx of new men. Instead, Dr. Martins came by to tell him he was well enough to take his exercise unaccompanied, and perform his stretching on his own. *Did she ask to be relieved as my therapist?*

~ * ~

In the weeks that followed, men were being released to make room for new wounded soldiers of battles with names of Selle, Cambrai, Le Cateau, as the Allies continued their rout of the Germans' heralded Spring Offensive. Despite the Allies' successes, casualties poured into the English hospitals.

He jealously watched her attending the others, all the while regretting his petulant outburst. It wasn't until one afternoon when he'd just returned from an hour on the outside balcony, that he looked up and saw her at the end of his bed. Her tapered fingers rested on the footboard, her rust colored hair soft against her cheek, smiling her smile. *Perfect.*

"How are you doing, Brian?"

"I was hoping…I mean, I'm glad to see you."

It was an awkward moment that she let pass. "I've been watching your progress. You should be going home soon."

No! I need to talk with you. "I'm sure that's too soon! Ann, I…"

"We need the beds, soldier, and you're looking mighty fit—except for that." She moved to straighten the collar of his hospital robe. Her hair brushed his face, hair that carried her own subtle scent. He found her arm, and pulled her mouth to his. For a delicious moment she lingered, then gently pulled away.

"Ann…" he started, not knowing what else to say.

The mouth he'd just kissed smiled. "No, Brian. You can't mean it."

"But I do! I love—"

She touched her fingers to his unfinished words. "You can't."

"I'll stay in England!"

"Brian! Stop! You're alone. You're hurt—in your body and your heart. You don't know me. You can't possibly love me."

"You're engaged? You've got someone!"

She didn't answer, but smiled and shook her head. "I'll see you tomorrow. There are others to see now."

And she continued down the aisle from bed to bed, adjusting pillows, a kind word, checking charts. He watched until she quit the ward.

~ * ~

The next morning two nurses arrived and began stripping his bed.

"It's fine, sister. They were changed just yesterday."

"We're packing you off to the outpatient ward, corporal," said the older one with a pince-nez clipped to her apron. "We need your bed."

A helplessness bordering on panic seized him. *Ann!* He had to talk to her; explain his rash behavior. They were shipping him out without giving him the chance. He searched the ward, but she was nowhere in sight. He watched, powerless to stop the nurses from destroying his link to Ann Prichard.

~ * ~

November 3, 1918

The vast majority of the patients at Bruce Cole Hospital were British with a sprinkling of Australians and Canadians. Men were being discharged to their homes in the British Isles, but the colonials had to wait for manifests to be filled for the troop ships.

Twice, Brian got a glimpse of Ann while out on the recreational field and taking fresh air on the balcony. But each time she was gone before he could reach her. He cursed his leg and the cumbersome cane.

He never saw her again.

His stay in the outpatient ward was short-lived. On the second day, he received orders to entrain for London, reporting to the 18th Canadian Reserve Battalion, then on to Portsmouth for ocean transfer back to Canada. It all went so fast and with so much bureaucratic nonsense he barely had time to think about the girl with the ginger hair.

Twenty-three

November 3, 1918
Guise, France

This time Jürgen was wrong about the importance of the territory around Guise. The village was on the main road between the German supply depot of Saint Quentin and the new command post of La Capelle, twenty kilometers to the east. Just as important was its position as the southern anchor of a defensive line that ran fifty km. due north to Le Quesnay, a medieval city that had seen many wars through the ages.

The new defensive line was set after a major Allied offensive along the Selle River that nearly caused the collapse of the German Army in Northern France. That was a week ago. Thousands of weak, hungry, dejected German soldiers were taken prisoner. Casualties were unknown, but assumed to be enormous.

A valiant attempt to mount a counterattack had failed. Their command post at La Cateau was lost. General Ludendorff established this most recent defensive line as an attempt to halt further Allied advance.

There was consensus among the troops this stand had to hold or there would be nowhere left for retreat. La Capelle was only twenty km. from the Belgian border.

The supply situation was perilous. Munitions needed for the counterattack at the Sambre River had sapped the other units. Food was limited to biscuits and even water had to be taken from the canals and boiled.

"We could, at least, raid the cottages in the western towns," Alfred said. He was dissolving a biscuit in a tin of water, making a kind of gruel that could be more easily eaten.

Jürgen watched the faces of his men as he gnawed on his own hardtack. Feldenhauer had recently stopped talking altogether, his usual quick quip about events silenced.

Schreiber, one of the new men, stared westward with terrified eyes, as if a French or Canadian tank might appear over the horizon. His left foot was in constant motion, beating out a tattoo in the dirt.

He scanned the other three new men, none of them over seventeen years old. They'd had a taste of combat at Leuilly-Ternay, but they all knew what was to come must be worse.

His section, or *Gruppe,* of nine men was down to six, resulting in longer watches, increased exposure to danger. He wondered if the new men knew how small their chances were.

The sun dropped below the trees, causing a chill in the air. Jürgen scrunched down in the trench he'd had his section dig and fortify. He pulled his tunic collar tight and shut his eyes to the war, and what was left of November 3.

~ * ~

Dawn came crisp and clear with a blanket of dew. Jürgen expected it would also have brought the French Army, but it did not.

Commotion down the line soon was revealed to be a mess team passing down the trenches with hot coffee and small rations of bacon. It was like Christmas.

It turned out not to be real coffee, but satisfied better than the water, and the bacon was real—from a source Jürgen could not imagine. He hadn't seen a live pig in months.

Around 9 AM word came that the Allies were attacking on the north end of the line at Le Quesnoy. The fighting was reported to be fierce.

All morning they waited for word from scouts of the enemy's position and apparent intentions. Intelligence reported the French 1st Army had overrun the village of Origny-Sante, just 12km to the southeast. They were speeding, unabated, towards Guise, part of them flanking the town to the south. It was terrible news.

~ * ~

The French came so fast they outran their artillery. On they came, confident by their early successes. The 238th artillery had their guns set to fire at short and point-blank range. The French tanks were the first to engage and were soon disabused of an early victory by the 10.5 cm. field cannons. The first wave of attackers came, despite the tank losses, in overwhelming numbers.

But the line held, and by sundown Guise was still in German hands.

Jürgen checked on his men, amazed they were all alive. The work they'd done in preparing the trench had paid off. Gerber, one of the new men, had a metal splinter in his shoulder, but insisted it was superficial and went to the aid station for first aid. Even Schreiber was settled down.

Jürgen's men had been tested and had come through it, toughened.

~ * ~

After a night of fitful sleep punctuated by sentry duty, the next day's fighting began before the sun showed. This time the French artillery was well in place. The first explosion found its mark shortly after 5 AM, killing some of the artillery horses and two men. Then hell erupted. Jürgen and his men were pressed against the wall of their ditch for thirty minutes while the bombardment continued. The air was thick with shrapnel.

Then the shelling stopped as suddenly as it started. Jürgen knew the real fighting was about to start.

"Casualties?" he called to his section.

One by one his soldiers called to him, only five responses.

"Schreiber?"

Alfred answered. "Schreiber's dead.

From down the line came a shout, "Here they come!" on top of Alfred's words.

Jürgen could barely see them surmounting a slight rise about three hundred yards out. Their overwhelming numbers gave him a feeling he would not survive the day. It had a calming influence on his nerves, and he shared it with his men.

"This is it, my friends. It's been my pleasure to know you. Let's die like German sons."

"Up yours, Stern!" Feldenhauer shouted, "I'm not dying for anyone!"

Other retorts followed, making Jürgen smile at their pluck.

Their sandbags began to *pup! thup!* as they did their job stopping small arms and machine gun fire. It was time to shoot back. Jürgen had a slot between two of the bags where he mounted his scoped Mauser. They all had a limited number of ammunition clips. He instructed his men to take single shots at clear targets, only. That was easier said than done with a massive army climbing down your throat.

In this way, the defenses held until late morning when the French decided to dig in and commence a mortar barrage. Again, there was nothing to do but hunker down against a direct hit. As bad as the artillery barrage had been, Jürgen thought this was worse. Many of the mortar shells were set with time fuses, showering their contents of anti-personnel shrapnel down upon them. Jürgen dragged a sandbag down on top of himself during the worst of it.

By mid-afternoon the barrage stopped, and the enemy mounted a full-out bayonet charge. Jürgen had no idea how many of his men were alive, but stood up on his perch to fire. The welcome sound of nearby firing cheered him considerably. His section was holding off the charge. Only once, a fearless French boy reached their trench, his bayonet poised, only to catch a bullet in the throat for his heroic effort.

The assault lasted until dusk, when the enemy slipped back over the rise. Jürgen did another count of his men. Alfred peered back at him, cradling his weapon as if it were his lover.

"You alright?"

Alfred blinked and nodded affirmation.

Feldenhauer was badly wounded, his right arm shattered.

"Rudi!"

The man stared back at him, a sad, accepting smile on his face.

"Medic!" Jürgen shouted, only to hear other shouts for corpsmen up and down the line. Feldenhauer was not bleeding badly, so an artery must have been missed. He would likely live.

Schreiber's body lay where he'd taken shrapnel to the head in this morning's barrage. Next to him lay Schönemann, his face nearly obliterated by a French bullet. Gerber was still alive, but shaken. Just three of his section left.

He returned to Feldenhauer. "Rudi, can you walk?"

"Christ! I don't know, Stern. I hadn't any plans to travel."

"I'm getting you to a dressing station. The war's over for you, my friend."

"Shit! The war's over, period," Feldenhauer said.

~ * ~

As night arrived, orders came with it to abandon the town. The village of Thérache just southeast of them had fallen, completely exposing their left flank. Fighting tomorrow would be suicide.

Jürgen and his men were assigned to the units covering the retreat. The few exchanges of small arms fire took place in the early hours of November 6, but ultimately the French First Army entered the town without further bloodshed.

On the road to La Capelle, passing through the village of Buironfosse, Jürgen thought about Rudi Feldenhauer's words. Maybe he is right. *This war is over.*

~ * ~

November 7, 1918
La Capelle, France

What was left of the 238th Infantry camped overnight in a fallow field east of this town, there being no billeting room there for an additional combat division of over five thousand troops. La Capelle was still largely intact, having been far enough behind the Hindenburg Line to avoid shelling. As a consequence it was a popular place for a military man's leave, and many of the houses had been confiscated by officers for their headquarters and personal billets.

On the following morning, rations were sent out from town to the encamped division. It was only weak coffee and a chunk of brown bread, but with it came shocking news. A week earlier, sailors in the German port of Kiel had refused to return to sea. It was a full mutiny, and sparked other protests throughout the country over the failure of the Kaiser's leadership. The word "revolution" was being heard around the mess line. They learned that the army's inability to provision the troops extended to the entire nation, largely due to an effective blockade of trade from the Americas.

It was discouraging news. How fast the fortunes of those first heady days of the *Kaiserschlacht* when the German army was rushing toward Paris and the coast! Jürgen surveyed his section. With the exception of Alfred Hauser, every man he'd trained with was dead or terribly wounded. How had he come this far unscathed?

Before noon they were ordered to continue their "withdrawal" (never a retreat) to a position on the other side of La Capelle. Marching through the streets, Jürgen noticed for the first time in this war the presence of German civilians, well dressed dignitaries, stepping out of staff cars parking at an attractive villa. It seemed as if something momentous were about to occur. He craned his head to see, but the column marched on.

~ * ~

November 9, 1918

Discipline among the troops was breaking down. Word of rioting in Berlin added to the perennial malady of the soldier: *nothing to do*. Then, that evening came the devastating news handed down through the chain of command that Kaiser Wilhelm II had abdicated. A temporary government had been formed, and was suing for peace with the allies.

For Jürgen, the first pangs of despair on hearing of his country's capitulation soon dissolved into thoughts of home. The little town of Neuhaus that for months had seemed a lifetime away was clarifying in his mind's eye. The tile roofs, the cobbled streets, the *Shützenfest*, the *Stadtplatz*, Papa, and…*Käthe!*

~ * ~

November 11, 1918

Compiègne, France

4:30 AM. Mathias Ertzberger was exhausted. First, the ten hours it took to motor from La Capelle near the French-Belgian border across war-torn Picardy to the train that brought them to this rail siding in the forest was all he could bear. Then the grueling negotiations and the intransigent demands of the Allies, especially that pompous ass, Foch!

If the Reichstag and the Kaiser had listened to him a year ago, he'd never have been in such a position of weakness. He'd pleaded for a negotiated peace, but had been hooted down, even received threats of treason. Here, with Germany's back to the wall, the Central Powers in shambles, they expected him to salvage something out of this. But now came the instructions from Hindenburg himself: sign the document without further argument! *Scheiße! They could have sent a schoolboy on such an errand!*

A knock came on his compartment door.

"They are convened, Herr Ertzberger," the aide announced.

Ertzberger rose heavily, set his spectacles on his face, checked in the tiny mirror over the washbasin that his cravat and moustache were in order, and led the aide down the narrow aisle of the railroad carriage to the adjoining car.

At 5 PM, after the documents were laid out for the signatories on the small table, he added his name to the document that would end the hostilities between the Allies and the nation of Germany. It would become operational at 11 AM, six hours hence.

Twenty-four

November 12, 1918
RMS Victorian

Brian paced alone at the rail of the huge liner, only a few feet shorter than the famous *Titanic* that tragically sank six years earlier. The Royal Navy had requisitioned her in 1914 for service as a troop carrier. Her civilian service to Canada continued, for the most part, to and from that country.

The *Victorian's* manifest was made up almost entirely of troops returning for medical discharge, the vast majority of them having been recovering from an epidemic of influenza that was being tagged, "Spanish Flu," although Spain denied any connection with the origin of the disease. Suffice to say, it took a greater toll than the enemy among many of the units fighting on either side.

While Brian carried his cane, he was not totally dependent on it, preferring to strengthen the leg by not favoring it. It felt good out on the pre-dawn deck; never mind the bite in the salt air. Yesterday's celebrations on hearing of the armistice erupted into reveling as much as could be expected without the aid of alcohol. Card and dice games of chance continued into the wee hours.

Brian did not partake. Whether it was a case of his withdrawal from the morphine or from the therapeutics of Ann Prichard, both having been recently denied him, he did not know. He simply felt like being alone. While most of the ship still slept, he watched as the low smudge of the North American continent appeared in the first light of this Tuesday morning. It frightened him, a feeling of unease. The land mass represented a new chapter in his life, and he hadn't the slightest idea how he was going to fill it.

~ * ~

November 12, 1918
Halifax, Nova Scotia

The troops, especially the Canadians, had certainly heard about the explosion, almost a year ago, in Halifax Harbor. As Brian understood, two ships got their signals mixed, and collided. One of them was chock full of high explosives. The blast caused horrific damage to the other ships in the harbor, the city of Halifax and the community of Dartmouth on opposite side.

But what he saw was orders of magnitude worse than his imagination. Everywhere, even eleven months later, block after block of flattened houses, twisted metal, gutted buildings, interspersed with new construction as far as the eye could see. Most of the repairs were near the wharf where the priority for maintaining port facilities was critical.

Still standing, but worse for wear, was the Oland Brewery that he, Harry, George Kobak, and Ake Lankinen had noted on their brief stroll of the city over two years earlier. As far as he knew, Harry had survived at least through the Amiens fight. Poor George had been sent home in shame, swearing his innocence. Brian believed him, but tell that to the folks at home. Then Lank: he hadn't thought of him in months. Ake Lankinin died on the slopes of Vimy Ridge, barely weeks after arriving in France. A shroud of guilt crept over him, the artist and map maker, while his chums risked their necks.

The *Victorian* unloaded her cargo of troops. Some were assigned to transient barracks, and some, like Brian, to the Halifax military hospital for an examination and, as in his case, discharge. Back pay totaling $52.50 and a rail pass home had him on a crammed train heading west by November 15.

He was going home.

Twenty-five

November 18, 1918
Jocelyn Farm
St. Joseph Island, Ontario

The noon sun sat low in the southern sky, adding scant warmth to the late autumn day. The last of the desiccated maple leaves clung, unwilling to fall from the big front yard tree, as Brian made his way up the two wheel ruts leading to his house.

He'd arrived in Sault Ste. Marie on the previous morning, but had to wait until today to catch the *SS Premier* on its return journey to Bruce Mines. It made a short call at Richards Landing to drop off mail, provisions for the Island—and Brian MacLennan, veteran soldier.

Two teen-aged boys, busy with the boat's lines, paid little attention to the soldier carrying a duffle and cane. Brian took his time walking the two hundred yards to the town center. Passing the front door of Sarah White's house, he kept his eyes straight ahead on John Richard's post office and general store sign. There, after pats on the back and "well done" by the store's regulars, he had no trouble accepting a lift up the "mountain" to the MacLennan farm.

"Don't mind sayin', lad. We were surprised to see ya," the old man had said, driving his team up the 20th Side Road. "Folks were talkin' you didn't make it."

The yard was empty. Even the odd hen was snug in her coop. He felt strange mounting the three steps to the porch. It seemed he'd been gone forever, yet not a thing had been added, or subtracted where two rockers and a small table stood sentinel there since he could remember.

Setting his duffle down, he pushed the door open with his cane. "Ma?"

The mantle clock ticked in the silence, its small, brass pendulum dutifully marching on behind the glass door. There was no use calling again. The tiny house consisted of one large room under the four small bedrooms carved out of what space there was at the top of the stairs. She'd have heard. Sometimes his mother helped in the field, especially around haying time, but it was a bit late for that.

He started up the stairs, got halfway up and heard the back door slap. When he returned, there she was, a block of ice in her apron, still smeared with wet sawdust.

"Praise God!" She stared, unbelieving. The ice dropped to the floor, skittering under the table.

They held each other for long moments until Dora MacLennan was able to speak. "I'll get your father."

"No need, Ma. He's busy, I'll bet."

She paid no attention, retreating to the back porch to bang on the forged triangle they used for emergencies. "Thomas! Owen!" Her clear soprano cut through the sigh of the wind through the maples.

~ * ~

He'd thrown a blanket and bridle on Alice, retired recently from the plow. The mare was a bit frisky, happy to be out of her shed and tended to break into a trot from time to time. Brian estimated a ninety minute ride to the Kobak farm.

Answering the alarm, Thomas MacLennan had rushed into the house, his wide-brimmed hat in hand, searching for the calamity he assumed had occurred. True to form, he maintained his stolid composure on seeing his son, even after eying the cane propped against the staircase. But when Brian reached in his pocket for his father's knurled handle knife, and held it out, Thomas' eyes grew red-rimmed. Shortly, Owen followed into the room, bursting with joyous energy, lifting everyone.

The horse knew the route. The MacLennan family had become friends with the Kobaks soon after Brian enlisted, mainly through Owen's having helped on their farm at times, since their only son was at war. Alice had made several trips there. At length she turned into the lane leading to a small, but immaculate house on land that had to have only been cleared in the ten years since Karl Kobak homesteaded it.

In the yard next to a handsome barn, a man was splitting logs. A row of neatly stacked firewood stood under the eaves of the barn. Brian's approach caused the man to cease his labor.

"You are Brian," he said in his accented English. "I know this horse, and Owen has no other brothers."

"Yes sir. I'm here to see George. You're Mr. Kobak?"

Karl Kobak nodded in the affirmative, and pointed. "He is out there, clearing."

Brian saw a team of two horses being worked on the far side of a large, fallow field.

"Thank you, sir," Brian said, and turned to go, but hesitated at the senior Kobak's words.

"He may not be pleased to see you."

At that Brian gave Alice a nudge with his heel, heading her away.

George Kobak was engaged in re-deploying a stout chain around the thick girth of a tree stump, having chopped anew at its roots. He goaded the team to pull, and the stump nearly pulled free, exposing the rocky soil below. Brian jumped from his mount, seized George's axe, gave the offending root a whack, releasing the team, tackle, and stump in concert. "A two-man job, I'd say," he intoned.

George wiped his forehead with the back of his glove, and considered the intrusion. "Seems you survived." His face revealed no emotion.

"Yeah…and Harry, far as I know. Moyer got his blighty and ticket home." Brian's eyes scanned the large field from the tree line back to the house and barn, aware that all had been cleared by hand exactly as George was doing now. "Looks like you could use some help."

I'm fine," George said, leading the team to the next newly cut stump.

Brian followed with the axe and shovel. "George, I never got a chance to say…" His words were interrupted.

"Look. I'm fine. I don't need help. Nice of you, and all that."

Brian started to object.

"Look! I'm well used to being alone. The whole Island's given me a wide berth since…" He didn't finish.

That stopped Brian momentarily. He knew George would be sensitive about returning early from service for no apparent reason. But he failed to consider how living in a confined community where everyone knew everyone else's business could be a toxic atmosphere in such a case.

"George, let me tell you something. You have nothing to be ashamed of. You told me what happened over there. I believed you, and I don't mind saying so to anyone who'll listen. Now, I am back home without the least idea of what to do with my life, and you're my only friend left on this island, it seems."

Kobak said nothing as Brian picked up the spade, limped to the next stump, and began digging.

~ * ~

December, 1918

The first of the young men of St. Joseph Island began drifting home as their units mustered them out of service. Many would not return until well into 1919. Thirteen had been listed as killed in action.

Brian's friendship with George Kobak developed as only comrades can who have known war together. Visions of bloated corpses, slain friends, a starving, displaced citizenry; the others could not possibly know. For separate reasons, they shied from social contact, particularly trips into either Marksville, or Richards Landing. That could go on for only so long, however.

Christmas was approaching. Owen had been going on about the linen chest he was building for his mother at a friend's workshop. He had an initialed straight razor made for his father since the summer, and pestered Brian about his plans.

Thomas refused to take back his pocket knife Brian had carried all through northern France. Brian thought to replace it for a similar one he'd seen at the Kentvale store. But for his mother, he wanted something really personal.

There had been another fire in Richards Landing since he'd left for the war; not as severe as the one eleven years earlier, but some shops were badly damaged. He'd seen something in the window of a newly rebuilt shop that first day back. Dora MacLennan had long auburn hair she kept in place with her combs. What he'd seen was a blue comb inlayed with mother-of-pearl. He had to have it for her.

And that is why he found himself in the "Landing" on this unseasonably warm day. With his mother's gift purchased, he stepped out onto the street to wait for Owen's return from the post office. Then what he dreaded might happen, did.

Francine White, not Owen, exited the post office. She spotted Brian across the street immediately. Reluctantly, he stepped off the wooden walk, and crossed to her.

"Mrs. White." He removed his cap.

Her tone was as flat as her expression. "Hello, Brian. I heard you came home. We're happy for your folks."

This was the woman who so ebulliently welcomed him into her home the last time he'd seen her.

"Well…thank you."

Her eyes dropped to the dirt road. "We heard you…"

"No ma'am, I wasn't killed."

She fidgeted with her shawl, clearly perplexed. Neither knew how to break the awkward silence.

"…I'm waiting for my brother, you see," he managed, finally. He touched the bill of his cap. "It's good to see you, again, Mrs. White," and returned to the wagon for Owen to join him.

He watched her return to her home, looking once over her shoulder, then quickening her pace.

~ * ~

Riding back up toward the Marksville road and home, Brian asked Owen about his reported demise in the war.

"It was going around town since August. I had to keep it from the folks," Owen said.

"Yeah, I heard. Today, and my first day back. No clue where that idea got started."

"Oh, I do! Old John Richards told me." Owen slapped the reins which made no difference in Alice's pace. "Old man Wentworth got a letter from his son, Colby. It said he thought Brian MacLennan caught it in Amiens. The story took off, and folks assumed the worst. Don't blame 'em. So many of our chaps got killed so early in the war—they just assumed."

Brian thought, *Wentworth!* It was just like him to assume—or hope—the worst, and report it home.

"I saw you talking to Mrs. White," Owen said.

Brian kept his eyes on Alice's tail swishing side to side.

"You ask about Sarah?" Owen prodded.

"Nope."

"Good, because she's not here."

Brian turned his head to confirm his brother was serious.

"Seems you never returned any of her letters, so when her ma's sister got sick last summer, she volunteered to take care of her aunt down in Barrie, near Lake Simcoe."

At first Brian's mind was a blur. He had agonized over every word in his letters to her. *And she never got them?*

As Alice's steady clip continued, things began to fall in place, all seeming to revolve around Colby Wentworth: Colby's jealous behavior at Niagara Camp, and probable related beating by his goon of a friend, Rupke. That encounter in Ypres when Colby asked if he'd heard from Sarah, suggesting that he, Wentworth, certainly had. And Rupke's probable last words on earth claiming Colby Wentworth to have long since wormed his way out of combat duty. *The appearance of Wentworth at the shipping dock of the mail center.*

A deer and her two fawns bolted across the road, causing Alice to briefly shy, but Brian did not notice. His mind was on Sarah White.

Twenty-six

January 9, 1969
Mississauga, Ontario

The dusk came early with an overcast sky. The Ford LTD station wagon turned off Sawanaga Trail into the driveway and the motion light flooded the yard. It slid to a stop as the garage door opened and closed behind. Brian MacLennan was home.

Through the door into the kitchen he dragged his bag. The house had the familiar scent of home and the feeling of him never leaving, though it had been a month since he'd driven to Toronto Pearson International for the short flight to Ottawa. He'd expected to stay just for the week of Colin's wedding then return, but Melanie had insisted she spend Christmas with them. *"The girls see so little of you since mom passed."* So he figured what the hell.

Brian loved the kids, but unfortunately never gained a rapport with Melanie's husband, a lobbyist for the mining industry. They were cordial, but personality opposites; Brian the artistic optimist, Ian Rand the pragmatic pessimist. The girls loved their grandpa well enough, but at fifteen and seventeen, were more interested in boys, Elvis, and their 8Track stereo, in that order. Christmas was less about them and more about Ian and Melanie entertaining their influential Ottawa friends. He didn't blame them. Their life was much like his as he did what was necessary to build his design firm from nothing.

He walked through the darkening rooms wondering why they had put off selling the place and finding an apartment or townhouse closer in towards Toronto. It was, and had been, entirely too big for the two of them since Colin left home over fifteen years ago. It seemed so obvious, but their children had urged them not to, pleading it was "the family nucleus" that held them all together.

Brian dumped his suitcase on the queen-sized bed, ignoring the blinking light of the message machine, made an urgent stop in the bathroom, and began to get out of his traveling clothes. It was darker when he re-entered the bedroom. Glass sliders looked out onto the fairway of the country club plunged into darkness despite the inch of snow.

The blinking red light continued to nag, and he gave in. The first message was from his old secretary, Maggie Hitchens, asking him to call at the office when convenient. That was time stamped November 11, the day after he arrived in Ottawa. The next from the *Toronto Star* soliciting his subscription, two political surveys, and the last, time stamped January 7, with a message in an accented voice:

"Yes...yes, Mr. MacLennan, I am Jürgen Stern. I am in Toronto on business, but would like to meet with you. Perhaps you can call me after six anytime this week at the King Edward. Thank you."

He'd call the office in the morning. It couldn't be serious, or they'd have tried to reach him at Melanie's...that is if he'd thought to tell them where he'd gone. The other message was intriguing, though. He got the King Edward number from the phone book in the nightstand, and dialed.

January 10, 1969
Toronto, Canada

Jürgen Stern was uneasy on more than one count: Kurt Kiesinger had only one month left as Germany's Prime Minister. Scoring a new Opel plant in Canada would help validate his Grand Coalition and ward off a defeat by Willy Brandt's Social Democrats in the coming election. Kiesinger had begged Stern to return to Ottawa and use his personal friendship with Pierre Trudeau. The meetings in November were not promising. Jürgen had the sense that further talk was futile.

He'd agreed to make the effort largely because he wanted to make this side trip to Toronto, and felt a little disingenuous as a result. He could have refused, having recently and officially retired.

Ultimately, his unease was likely due to his attempt to contact this man, MacLennan, who had seemed cordial enough on the phone, but for all Jürgen knew, cared little about the past, and would consider meeting a waste of time. MacLennan had returned his call last night around nine, and was surprised to hear about the drawings after Jürgen told about finding them in the lobby of the Chateau Laurier. MacLennan hadn't heard from his office about their receiving them.

"They have no value," MacLennan had said, "but were meant as a gift to my son who admired them. I am happy to pay you something for their return, though."

Jürgen was quick to dispel the idea he was interested in money, and may have overdone the protestations. Despite the awkward conversation, MacLennan agreed to a meeting today at 2 PM in the lobby of the King Edward. Jürgen would be wearing a poppy in his lapel he'd kept from Remembrance Day in Ottawa.

He sat in one of the lobby couches, glancing back and forth between his watch and the door. Five minutes early, he heard, "Mr. Stern?"

Jürgen stood. The man was slender, slightly shorter than Jen's hundred-eighty centimeters, but solid musculature. Curly white hair with black strands interspersed. A cane in one hand and raincoat in the other. MacLennan obviously had not come in from the street door.

"Ah! Yes! I am Jürgen Stern, and you are Mr. MacLennan. I am so pleased to meet you." Jürgen proffered his card he'd had at the ready.

MacLennan took his time reading it. "So, *Doctor* Stern. Minister for Economics and Development. I'm impressed."

"An old card. I am recently retired," Jürgen said.

"What brings you to Canada, Doctor Stern?"

"Please, I prefer Jürgen. I am here for a meeting next week in Ottawa, but have taken my own time to visit Toronto for our meeting." He noticed MacLennan held his raincoat draped over a large mailing envelope.

MacLennan slipped the card in his shirt pocket, and said "Jürgen it is, then. My name's Brian. Let's have a drink."

"In here," Jürgen said, pointing to the lounge. He thought he might like this Canadian and his informal mannerisms.

They found a quiet booth. "So what is it about my scribblings that's brought you to Toronto?" Brian said after they'd ordered drinks.

Jürgen gestured toward the manila envelope. "Is that them?"

"Ha! Yes. My one-time secretary had a message waiting for me last night. I picked them up on the way here. By the way, thank you for returning them. They were a wedding present for my son. I'm surprised anyone cares about the first war anymore, yet he seems to."

Jürgen said, "It was my pleasure." He hesitated before continuing. "I must admit, I looked at the drawings quite carefully. At first it was because I admired their quality. You…are quite gifted, I feel."

Brian said nothing; shifted uneasily.

"It was the maps—one in particular—that shocked me."

"Just one?"

"There were one or two others of the same map, but different drawings on the reverse. One was a map that was familiar to me." From his breast pocket, Jürgen removed an envelope and handed it to Brian.

A waiter in red waistcoat brought their drinks, and left.

"This is it?" Brian asked, receiving no reply.

Jürgen watched Brian's face as he removed the drawing. It revealed little until he turned the card over from the map to the sketch. A sad smile slowly developed.

"My heavens. How in hell did you come by this?"

Jürgen leaned back in the booth they shared. "I was there. Not *there*," he said, pointing to the map. "I think that must have been a map of Vimy Ridge by the April, 1917 date, and the town of Villers-au-Bois labeled. I was a little farther south at the time. You Canadians scared us to death." He watched Brian gaze off for a moment.

"The girl… her name was Genevieve. Don't ask why I remember," Brian said. He looked Jürgen square in the eye. "I asked you how you got this."

Jürgen carefully placed his palms on the table. "I killed the man who carried it." The words tumbled out involuntarily.

Brian's eyes returned not to the map, but the girl's face. "George," he whispered.

"Excuse me?"

Brian continued to stare at the drawing. "Kobak, George Kobak."

Jürgen waited, knowing there must be more.

"Again, how did you get this?"

Jürgen told him about his sentry stint in the Ypres-Roulers train station near the town of Moorslede.

"You were there?" Brian said, a little too loudly.

Jürgen nodded, and went on. "It was thick fog that morning. A large enemy unit came out of nowhere, and passed right under my second story sniper's window. I hid, but soon after they were gone, another soldier came alone. He carried no rifle, so I assumed he was either an officer or a courier. Either way, it was my duty to shoot him. It turned out he *was* a courier. I took papers from him my officers said were important. The map was of no value in the Ypres salient, so I was allowed to keep it."

"All these years." Brian finished the thought.

"She was a beauty, and it was a lucky souvenir for me of that day. I should have been discovered by your soldiers that day and killed."

"And you thought you killed him."

"It was a clear shot to the head. I was a good marksman."

Brian took a sip of his single malt. "You'll be interested to learn he is *not* dead, but a doting grandfather living in northern Ontario."

"*Mein Gott*…my God! He is alive." Jürgen held his hands to his face. "In that filthy war I killed some of your countrymen, but my memory of pulling the trigger on that day has…it has stayed with me. Perhaps another reason I could not destroy that drawing. I thought *he* may have sketched it; perhaps of his wife or sweetheart."

"It wasn't. He barely knew her. It was a young French girl he—we all—fancied. I sketched her, and he asked for the drawing."

"And the maps on the backs of the drawings?"

"Drawing paper was hard to find. The maps were on good card stock. I used anything I could find to make my sketches."

"And the girl; did she…"

"Genevieve. Survive? Who knows? I like to think so."

They sat in the darkened lounge sipping their drinks, both digesting what they'd shared.

"There's more to this, you know," Brian said, finally.

Jürgen's eyebrows lifted, eager to hear, and Brian began to tell of George Kobak and his trial for desertion.

~ * ~

Brian watched Stern's reactions as he told about his time in Flanders. Only slightly taller than Brian's 5'8," Stern had thinning hair that had once been blond, but had faded to dishwater, and was combed straight back from his forehead. He'd grown a paunch, but appeared to be hale enough. He was intensely interested in what Brian was saying.

"You were actually in Decline Copse!" Jürgen Stern said, for the second time.

"Us…and the Aussies," Brian said.

"I lost my platoon leader there," Jürgen said.

"And I, my sergeant, a good man, and I'm alive because of him." Brian paused, and went on. "It was a few days after that; George Kobak had been missing, and we wondered where the hell he was. He was assigned to Staff as an interpreter, and some of us wondered if he'd been sent somewhere else. Then here he comes with two guards escorting him back from the Aussie camp. They'd found him behind your lines, east of the Copse."

Jürgen said, "I was sure he was either dead or dying. If he was behind our lines, I am sure he was disoriented. You don't take a Mauser bullet in the head, then go on to spy for the enemy."

They talked at length about their experiences in the miserable conditions of Flanders in October of 1917. Brian, of his unit's capturing the Meetcheele crossroads, Jürgen of the improbable coincidence of being there as well.

"We were sent forward into shallow trenches to blunt your advance, while the Bavarians held the main trenches guarding the crossroads," Jürgen said. "We caught hell out there. Your Artillery had zeroed in on us. There was nothing to do but wait it out. Only three from our section survived. When we retreated back to the main trench, the Bavarians had gone, the pigs!"

They spoke of their experiences in Picardy, Brian's being shortened by his wound in the Amiens battle. Jürgen told of his euphoria in the early days of the German *Kaiserschlacht*, and the disgrace of those last days retreating behind the Hindenburg Line, and ultimate capitulation.

Jürgen told of returning home to his town in Lower Saxony. “We were mustered out near Aachen two weeks after the armistice, given rail passes, and told we were on our own from there. I had built up a picture in my mind of my return home. When I left I was a minor celebrity, having won a shooting contest. I foolishly thought there might be some kind of reception for me. Of course, I wasn’t the only one returning, and the village had nothing to offer any of us. The Allied embargo had successfully starved not only the German Army, but its citizens as well.”

“Did you have a wife then?” Brian had no idea of the man’s age.

Jürgen laughed. “I had high aspirations. She kept me company for many nights in France. But it was not to be.”

He told Brian about bicycling his second day home to the large estate of the Von Helm family. How the once trimmed lawns and perfect flower garden inside the circular driveway were shabby and overgrown. Dry autumn leaves were left unswept under the portico at the front door. Instead of the usual servant answering his knock, Frau Von Helm answered, still dressed in her expensive, outdated frock. Her haughty, severe features he’d remembered were now drawn and fatigued.

“I’ve come to see Käthe,” he’d said.

“Then you had better go to Bremen where she is living with her fifty year old lover.”

Jürgen laughed again. “She slammed the door in my face; the door, and my dreams of Käthe in my bed.”

Brian commented, “You seem to have done alright for yourself.”

Another laugh, this time rueful. “I was mortified. I couldn’t leave the village soon enough. I had a cousin in Denmark where I got a job as a laborer, and took classes at university in Copenhagen. It’s a long story, but six years later, I had a degree in economics, found work in a ministry of the fledgling Weimar Republic, and…met the mother of my two children. Life progressed from there.”

The more they talked, the more Brian liked this man. Yes, their backgrounds were similar—boys from tiny, rural communities, both entering late in the war into replacement regiments. But it was also a genuineness about the man, his candor in the telling of his own foibles, and those of his wartime commanders. Brian countered with the insanity of the Allied generals insisting on the Passchendaele offensive under the worst possible conditions; thousands of lives lost for a few hundred yards of real estate, only to be ceded back in a few months. Three times over the course of the war, the Ypres salient had been pounded into pulverized, toxic, waist-high slime—one huge Flanders graveyard for both combatants.

It was getting toward dinner time, and the bar was filling up with pre-prandial drinkers. Jürgen noticed Brian's body language signaling his thoughts about leaving.

"What are you intending to do with the drawing?" he asked.

Brian was gesturing for a check. "I don't think you realize how important your story will be to my friend."

"You mean the 'George' you speak of?"

"Exactly. I intend to give your *souvenir* to him. It should, at least, be a comfort to him and his family. It corroborates his story the court martial didn't believe."

"You're sending it to him?"

"I'm going to hand it to him. I haven't seen him for a while. Now is a good time."

"Can it wait?" Jürgen had his hand on Brian's arm, as if he were leaving this minute.

"What?"

"I have a week at most in Ottawa. After that I am free. I'd like to go with you, and meet your friend."

He watched Brian consider this. It was a forward request. The two Canadians had been comrades in arms. That was the kind of fellowship into which one could not easily be invited. Across the booth Brian was obviously weighing the pros and cons.

Then he spoke. “We could fly there, but by the time spent waiting at the airports, and renting a car, we might as well drive. Can you be ready a week from tomorrow? It’s a Saturday.”

Jürgen assured him he could.

“Bring some outdoor clothes. You can’t go traipsing through a snowy barnyard in those shoes, either. We’ll be taking a chance with the weather whether we fly or drive.”

~ * ~

January 18, 1969

Brian hadn’t spoken with Owen nor his wife, Trina, in over a month. He was relieved when it was she who answered the telephone and was more than just *okay* with the visit. She invited Brian and his friend to stay at the farm. “There’s tons of room, as you know,” she’d said.

There was. Their daughter, Nina, was married, and their son, Owen Jr., was teaching chemistry in Thunder Bay. Owen Sr. had proved his father wrong by making the MacLennan property enough of a success to send both children to university.

“We’ll drive up next Saturday,” he’d said. “Might be evening before we arrive.”

Jürgen called Brian Thursday night, and Brian told him to check out of his hotel and spend Friday night in Mississauga at his home. They packed Brian’s station wagon that night, and were on the road, coffee in hand, by 7 AM for the ten hour drive.

They drove in relative silence for the first hour as Brian negotiated the week-end traffic of greater Toronto. Then Brian pressed Jürgen about his career, and how he’d gotten to his position.

“I became noticed, I suppose; was posted around to different embassies. People thought I might be a spy, but no, I was *really* one of those commercial attaches. I returned to Denmark in thirty-eight as Hitler was doing his disgusting thing, achieved my doctorate, published some economic theories certain people thought worth reading. I spent the war teaching in Canada and returned to Germany in forty-seven. I've been in government ever since.

"And you are here for…"

"Along the way I met, and became friends with your Prime Minister, Pierre Trudeau when I lectured at the University of Montreal. He was a law student there. I thought he was brilliant—and so did he—so we hit it off, so to speak. I'm here to use my 'influence' about a trade deal, but I don't think it will bear fruit."

Jürgen let a few miles slip by before asking, "And you; how did a soldier boy from a farming family end up owning a large industrial design firm?"

"A girl," Brian said after some thought.

"Well, then?" Jürgen said, after Brian's silence.

"Just that I knew I had naught to offer anyone without a trade, and it wasn't going to be farming. I set out for the big city, and Toronto looked mighty big to me. Got a job running errands for a tool and die company. They found I was pretty good on a drafting board, and before long I was a draftsman. Then I had an idea for making a special kind of cabinet hinge, but kept it to myself until the owner caught me working on it one night after work."

"Did he sack you?"

"He could have, or even declared my design belonged to the company, but he backed my idea by investing start-up money for forty-nine percent of anything that came of it. His name was Esposito, and his son bought my fifty-one percent eighteen months ago. You could say my career hinged on that investment." Brian held his nose at the pun that was as old as the company.

They talked like that; about children and their problems, perils of the cold war, last November's close election of Richard Nixon, North Viet Nam finally joining the Paris peace talks, the launch of Apollo 8 to orbit the moon. The miles melted away.

~ * ~

After stopping for a late, but leisurely lunch in Sudbury, they pulled off Highway 17 around 6 PM for the short ride to the St. Joseph Island ferry and the trip over the swirling water of the St. Joseph Channel. For Jürgen it was a world apart from the ferry trips over the docile Oste River or even the wide and tranquil Elbe River of his youth. The sharp image of his father at the helm of his ferry momentarily flashed and disappeared.

Brian was waving to someone he knew, and Jürgen wondered how often he returned to this remote place where Lakes Superior and Huron were joined. The sun was low in the sky, making a recent snowfall glow yellow, mottled with the shadows of pine and maple. It was magical.

A recently plowed gravel road took them up into the higher elevations of the island where a mailbox read MacLennan under the red flag. The house stood out in sharp contrast against the snow, reflecting the sun that hung just over the tops of the trees.

"Quite an impressive place, Brian." Jürgen was admiring the well maintained fencing, and neat barnyard. A tractor and what Jürgen imagined was some kind of haying machine stood parked next to a like-new barn.

"It's a far cry from the house I grew up in." Brian pointed. "That's the original part of the house. Owen added the rest." He touched the car's horn, bringing a huge man out from behind the house, a Swedish saw in hand.

The men were introduced. Jürgen thought Owen must be well over six feet. He had arms the size of his brother's thighs, and a thick but lean torso.

"You *are* brothers?" Jürgen said, looking from one man to the other.

Owen laughed. "Brian stopped growing."

"As most adults do," Brian added. "Owen just kept going."

"Let's get out of the cold," Owen said.

Inside, the house was decorated in light colors and hardwood trim. A scent of something delicious emanated from the kitchen followed by Owen's wife whom he introduced as Katrina.

She gave him a look, and said to Jürgen, "Please, it's Trina."

Most of the night was spent with Owen catching up Brian with the business of the farm, which intrigued Jürgen, who had never pulled a weed in his life. He learned from Trina that, years earlier, Brian had loaned his brother a substantial sum of money toward modernizing the farm. That loan was paid back, but the couple never forgot the generosity.

~ * ~

Brian and Jürgen headed out after a late breakfast of sausage and eggs from the MacLennan hens. By the time they reached the foot of the island, they had to follow the snow plow that was still working on a much less improved road to the Kobak farm. A sign advertising *Kobak Maple Syrup* hung at the opening to the long driveway that was freshly plowed to the house, a modern looking ranch. Three other smaller buildings stood in the rear of the property, lined up like soldiers. A late model Chevy truck was parked there, from which a tall, slender man was just alighting. Turning at the sound of the car, he waved, peering through the windscreen to see who might be inside. Brian stepped out, and the two men embraced.

"What the hell have you been up to?" George Kobak asked his friend.

"Trying to cope with retirement, my late-blooming son, and my bossy daughter…not necessarily in that order." Brian motioned to Jürgen who had followed onto the driveway. "I'd like you to meet someone I've had the pleasure of knowing a short time."

Jürgen stuck out his hand. "Jürgen Stern. It's a pleasure to meet you, Mr. Kobak."

Kobak took off his glove and took Jürgen's hand. "Well, thank you, Mr. Stern." He glanced to Brian, eyebrows raised in question.

Brian said, "Does Doris have a pot of coffee in there?"

"Doris is still at church in some damn committee or other. She'll be home in an hour or so, but I know how to throw grounds in a pot. Come on in."

As they were removing hats and coats, George said, "So, Mr. Stern, you're from Germany?"

"It is an accent I cannot hide, sir, nor wish to deny."

There was a moment when no one said a thing. Brian tried, but could not utter a word that wouldn't sound trite or gratuitous. George put the percolator on the burner, and the three men sat around the kitchen table.

Empathizing with Jürgen's discomfort, Brian began. "Jürgen was at Passchendaele, George."

Kobak stiffened. They had not mentioned the war to each other since that day after Brian's return in 1918.

Jürgen said, "Brian, perhaps you should just show it to him."

From his inside jacket pocket, Brian retrieved the card, still enclosed in the King Edward Hotel envelope.

"What's this, then?" George said, accepting it.

The other two sat tacitly.

Kobak's reaction was of immediate, palpable recognition. His nostrils flared, lips drawn tight. His grim face transformed into one of confusion. He looked to Brian for clarity, but Brian's eyes shifted to Jürgen.

"How?" was all George could say.

Then Jürgen started from the beginning… his 238th Infantry Division being sent to Flanders, his regiment being posted at the ruined Ypres-Roulen rail line, his sentry post in the abandoned train station, the single bullet from his Mauser rifle that felled an enemy courier, the taking of the courier's papers.

George held the card by its edges as if it might disintegrate. He then saw Jürgen for the first time as more than a guest in his house. Here was living proof that he had been wounded, disoriented, and lost behind enemy lines.

To Jürgen he said, "I was court marshaled. They didn't prove I was a traitor, or even a deserter. But they didn't acquit me either. I have lived under that cloud ever since. My children have been bullied because of it. This is a place where everyone knows the others' business." He paused, and said. "All these years I have carried the weight of those accusations. I thank you for coming forward, even now."

Jürgen asked, "What do you intend to do with this?"

George considered the question as the percolator began its staccato rhythm. "Probably nothing. This is proof to nobody but me, but it is something I can share with my family. This and your story.

The three men talked about their days in Flanders, about Genevieve, about fallen friends, until George's wife came home. She cried as she heard the news, as he did, holding her head to his chest.

Brian and Jürgen stayed only a short time after that, letting the Kobaks have their happiness together.

January 22, 1969

The station wagon was headed down that same road where, over fifty years ago, Brian and Owen drove the sleigh to the rail stop on the mainland.

"I don't know why you insist on flying," Brian said to Jürgen.

"I need to get back, and you need to spend time with Owen and Trina. It's enough that you're driving me to the airport."

"It's just an hour or so to the Soo, and Trina gave me a list of things to pick up while I'm there. You're doing them a favor."

After only a few miles, Brian said, "We have time to spare. There's someone I'd like you to meet."

The car made a left turn into, of all places, a cemetery, its headstones all wearing fresh caps of white snow. Jürgen followed Brian to a plain granite marker where Brian hunkered down, and touched the name. He knelt like that for just a few seconds, and rose.

"She was a good one, Jürgen." He moved so Jürgen could read the inscription.

> Sarah White MacLennan
> February 2, 1898 – April 8, 1965
> Devoted Wife and Mother

"Was she the girl you spoke of?" Jürgen asked.

Brian nodded. "Oh, she was the girl, alright."

~ * ~

The 4 PM flight to Toronto was called. Brian and Jürgen promised to keep in touch, both knowing those promises were harder to keep than not.

"I feel good about the visit," Jürgen said, "I think it was worthwhile."

Brian agreed. "It was a comfort to them. I just wish the court martial had never happened, but there's nothing we can do about that."

Jürgen shrugged. “I guess,” as he stepped out onto the tarmac, waving goodbye over his shoulder. An eddy of snow swirled in the cold. He took a last look back as he climbed up to the open door of the plane and was gone.

Twenty-seven

May 19, 1969
Bonn, Germany

Jürgen cut the switch to the bathroom light, and tightened the sash of his bathrobe. It had been a tiring day at the ministry convincing the committee he would *not* go to South Korea, despite their entreaties. It was time for younger men to take the helm. He walked to his desk to extinguish the lamp, and took one last look at the letter he'd finished.

Dr. J.V.Stern
232 Romersrasse
Bonn, Germany

20 May, 1969
The Right Honourable Pierre E. Trudeau
Office of the Prime Minister
86 Wellington Street
Ottawa, Canada

Dear Pierre,

Time certainly does fly. I have owed you this letter before now. I have been trying desperately to extricate myself from government duties, having "retired" these many months.

I certainly appreciate your position on the Opel plant, and believe I have convinced the ministry here to forego their efforts in this regard for a time when the currency issue is more in balance.

As to the matter of the honorable discharge for that WWI soldier, your assistance was invaluable. I appreciate your seeing the evidence as being conclusive in his favour on the basis of my testimony, and your subsequent request to the Ministry of Defence.

As always, I am your friend and servant,

Jürgen.

He sealed it and affixed the stamp, so it would be ready to mail in the morning.

~*~

June 14, 1970

St Joseph Island, Ontario

The Chevy pickup ground to a halt and George Kobak stepped out at his mailbox after an errand to town. He thumbed the letters; a flyer, the newspaper, a bill or two, an envelope from some ministry or other.

He drove up the long stone driveway, parked, and went inside.

"That you?" Doris Kobak called.

"Who else?" he called back, sorting through the mail. Power company bill, a *North Shore Sentinel,* a Simpson Sears flyer, and the envelope from…He opened it.

CANADA

Ministry of National Defence

Mr. George L. Kobak

Route 3
St. Joseph Island, Ontario
Dear Mr. Kobak,

It is my honor to inform you of the decision of the Ministry to award you an honorable discharge for your patriotic service to the Canadian Government and its citizens during your service for the period December 1915 to November 1917 (enclosed).

On behalf of a grateful country, thank you, and congratulations.

(Signed)
Léo Cadieux
Minister

Aufgrund des Zutreffens der aufgelisteten Eigenschaften, ergeben sich eine ganze Reihe von Problemen im Zusammenhang mit der Qualitätsbeurteilung von Lehrveranstaltungen. Analysiert man Lehrveranstaltungen nach Potential- und Prozeßqualitäten, so lassen sich folgende Dimensionen der Angebotsspezifikation unterscheiden[7] :

- **Personen**, die als Lehrende tätig werden;
  Qualität ist dabei nicht nur über Potentialqualitäten wie fachliches Wissen und Kompetenz zu definieren, sondern schließt wesentliche Prozeßqualitäten in Sinne der rhetorischen und pädagogisch-didaktischen Fähigkeiten, der Interaktionsfähigkeit, der sozialen Kompetenz u.a.m. mit ein.

- die Rolle der Studierenden als **"externer Faktor"** bei einer Lehrveranstaltung;
  Ihre Inputqualitäten (u.a. Allgemeinwissen, Vorkenntnisse, praktische Erfahrungen, Erfolg bei Einstiegsklausuren), Persönlichkeit, Integrationswilligkeit (Mitarbeit), Interaktivität mit Kollegen (bei Diskussionen oder Gruppenarbeiten erwünscht, bei Vorlesungen unerwünscht), Lernfähigkeit, Motivation etc.

- **Materielle Hilfsmittel** der Lehrveranstaltung und das **Leistungsumfeld;**
  Darunter fallen Größe und Ausstattung der Hörsäle (Sitzplätze, Computerarbeitsplätze etc.), technische Hilfsmittel zur Gestaltung der Lehrveranstaltung (u.a. Overheadprojektor, Videokamera und -rekorder, Diaprojektor), Licht, Raumklima, Arbeitsunterlagen (Begleitliteratur, Skripten) u.a.m.

- **Prozesse.**
  Im Sinne organisatorischer Merkmale durch Zeitpunkt und Zeitdauer der Veranstaltung oder als Abläufe und Gestaltungselemente für den Lehrveranstaltungsprozeß (Lehrveranstaltungsstil, Gruppengröße, Eingehen auf studentische Fragestellungen und Probleme, Kontaktqualität), Gestaltungsfragen wie Klarheit, Nachvollziehbarkeit, Strukturiertheit, logischer Aufbau u.a.m.

Um die Rolle der personenbezogenen Adjunktivität bei Lehrveranstaltungen zu hinterfragen, d.h. die Dimension „Person“ als eine der zentralen Einflußgrößen auf die Zufriedenheit der Studierenden zu extrahieren, eignet sich der gewählte Studiengang aufgrund folgender spezifischer Eigenschaften für ein quasi-experimentelles Untersuchungsdesign:

---

[7] Vgl. Scharitzer (1994), S. 46ff.

- kleine Klassengrößen mit ca. 25 Studierenden,
- hoch-standardisierte Ausbildungsinhalte,
- homogene Vorkenntnisse und
- parallele Führung der Lehrveranstaltungen.

Experimentelle empirische Untersuchungsdesigns in der Dienstleistungsforschung zum Thema „Kundenzufriedenheit" sind sehr selten[8], da außerhalb des Labors kaum Bedingungen hergestellt werden können, bei denen anhand standardisierter Leistungen bei Variation entsprechender Variablen eine kausale Wirkung auf den Output beobachtet werden kann.

Die Entscheidung, die Eigenschaft der Adjunktivität einer Leistung, exemplarisch an der herausragenden Bedeutung der Person des Vortragenden einer Lehrveranstaltungen nachzuweisen, resultiert aus dem spezifischen Studienaufbau des betrachteten Fachhochschulstudiengangs für „Wirtschaftsberatende Berufe".

Das in Abschnitt 4.3 detailliert analysierte Beispiel der Einführungslehrveranstaltungen für "Marketing", verdeutlicht diese Standardisierung, da es sich bei diesen Einzelveranstaltungen um ein gemeinsam von fünf ReferentInnen entwickeltes Ausbildungsprogramm handelt. Die „Marketing-Lehrveranstaltungen" des Grundstudiums sind gekennzeichnet durch

- idente Inhalte und Anschauungsbeispiele (Praxisfälle),
- idente Stundenbilder,
- idente Literaturgrundlage,
- idente Foliensätze zur Lehrveranstaltungsunterstützung,
- ReferentInnen aus dem selben „Marketinginstitut" der WU-Wien, die vertraut mit den Lehrinhalten sind und
- eine gemeinsame Erarbeitung des Lehrveranstaltungskonzeptes und der -inhalte.

Diese Standardisierungsmerkmale können als typisches Beispiel einer Dienstleistung gesehen werden, bei denen die Ressourcen und die Leistungsfähigkeit durch Vervielfältigung der Angebotspotentiale vermehrt werden sollen.

Die Lehrveranstaltungen wurden exakt zum selben Zeitpunkt (Blockveranstaltung am Nachmittag) parallel von fünf verschiedenen ReferentInnen angeboten.

---

[8] Vgl. bspw. Bitner (1990).

Der Vorteil dieser Versuchsanordnung liegt in der Tatsache, daß versucht werden kann, die Person des Vortragenden als die einzige variable Größe zu isolieren, sofern das in einer Nicht-Labor-Situation überhaupt möglich ist.

3.2. Erhebungsdesign der Lehrveranstaltungsevaluation

Die Lehrveranstaltungsevaluation aller Einzelveranstaltungen stellt wie bereits erwähnt eine der Säulen im Qualitätssicherungssystem des Fachhochschulstudiengangs in Wr. Neustadt dar. Als Instrumente werden eingesetzt:

- „Blitzlichtartige" Beurteilungen nach etwa einem Drittel der gehaltenen Lehrveranstaltung,
- in regelmäßigen Abständen stattfindende Qualitätszirkel und
- eine Bewertung jedes Lehrbeauftragten durch die Studierenden mittels eines schriftlichen vollstandardisierten Fragebogens am Ende jeder Lehrveranstaltung.

Für die dargestellte Forschungsfrage war die schriftliche Bewertung am Ende jeder Lehrveranstaltung Grundlage der empirischen Analysen. Bei dieser Befragung wurde eine Vollerhebung durchgeführt. Dazu wurden in der letzten Veranstaltungseinheit alle anwesenden Studenten gebeten, eine Beurteilung der entsprechenden Lehrveranstaltung mittels Fragebogen durchzuführen. Um die Anonymität der Untersuchung zu gewährleisten mußte jeder der Lehrveranstaltungsleiter während des Ausfüllens den Hörsaal verlassen. Die Bewertungsbögen wurden von den Studierenden direkt der Fachhochschuladministration übermittelt. Schlußendlich stand für die Auswertung das Datenmaterial des gesamten Studienjahres 1995/1996 zur Verfügung.

Der eingesetzte Fragebogen[9] war folgendermaßen strukturiert: 26 Fragen zu Merkmalen der Lehrveranstaltung aus den Bereichen Person des Vortragenden, Organisation der Veranstaltung, Struktur und Vermittlung der Inhalte; eine Frage zur Gesamtzufriedenheit und zwei Fragen zur Vorbildung bzw. wieviele Jahre der Schulabschluß zurückliegt. Alle Fragen wurden geschlossen gestellt und waren auf einer 5-teiligen Skala (1=trifft völlig, 5= trifft nicht zu) zu beantworten. Die Zuordnung zu den einzelnen ReferentInnen

9 Anmerkung: Der verwendete Fragebogen wurde nicht von den Autoren entwickelt. Anpassungen und Veränderungen für die gegenständlichen Untersuchungsfragen waren aus Gründen der Vergleichbarkeit der Daten mit anderen Studiengängen seitens der Administration nicht möglich.

(Lehrveranstaltungen) war aufgrund entsprechender Kategorisierungsvariablen bei jedem Fragebogen gewährleistet.

Im Beobachtungszeitraum (September 1995 bis April 1996) wurden in 91 Lehrveranstaltungen insgesamt 3108 Bewertungen durchgeführt. Bei allen Erhebungen kam derselbe Fragebogen zum Einsatz.

3.3. Selektion der Lehrveranstaltungen

Eine Bearbeitung der aus der Vollerhebung im Studienjahr 1995/96 erhobenen Daten war ohne eine vorhergehende Segmentierung der Fälle nicht zweckmäßig. Zu unterschiedlich präsentierte sich das gesamte LV-Angebot des Grundstudiums des Fachhochschulstudiengangs.

Die Lehrveranstaltungen wurden daher nach folgenden Kriterien kategorisiert:

- **Zugehörigkeit zum Studiengang**:

In die zu analysierende Datenbasis wurden ausschließlich Veranstaltungen aus dem betriebswirtschaftlich orientierten Studiengang „Wirtschaftsberatende Berufe" einbezogen. Der zweite vor Ort angebotene Studiengang für „Präzisions-, System,- und Informationstechnik" wurde von den weiteren Analysen ausgeschlossen.

- **Fächer**:

Im Grundstudium des Studiengangs „Wirtschaftsberatende Berufe" sind

- betriebswirtschaftliche Lehrveranstaltungen (Rechnungswesen, Finanzierung, Marketing, Personal und Organisation, Materialwirtschaft und Logistik)
- volkswirtschaftliche Lehrveranstaltungen
- Rechtsfächer
- Wirtschaftssprache „Englisch"
- EDV sowie
- Persönlichkeitsbildende Fächer (Kommunikations- und Kooperationstraining, Präsentationstechnik, Moderationstechnik, Verhandlungstechnik etc.)

enthalten.

Aufgrund des besseren Einblicks und um eine Vergleichbarkeit der Lehrveranstaltungen zu gewährleisten, wurde eine Einschränkung auf betriebswirtschaftlich orientierte Veranstaltungen vorgenommen.

- **Lehrveranstaltungstyp**:

Die laut Studienplan vorgeschriebenen Lehrveranstaltungen lassen sich in Vorlesungseinheiten (große Hörerzahl, wenig Interaktion mit dem Vortragenden) und Übungen (25-30 Teilnehmer, hohe Interaktion mit dem Vortragenden, aktives Einbringen der Teilnehmer) unterscheiden. Es erschien für die gewählte Fragestellung nicht notwendig eine Differenzierung in Vorlesungen und Übungen vorzunehmen.

3.4. Prüfhypothesen

Zur Prüfung der Adjunktivität bzw. zum Nachweis des „Halo-Effektes“ bei der Zufriedenheitsbeurteilung wurden folgende Kernhypothesen formuliert.

H1: Nachweis adjunktiver Merkmale bei Lehrveranstaltungen

Unter den Potentialqualitäten zur Beschreibung der Kundenzufriedenheit mit einer Lehrveranstaltung, nimmt der Faktor „Person des Lehrenden“ eine dominierende Stellung gegenüber allen anderen Gestaltungsmerkmalen ein.

H2: Nachweis eines Halo-Effektes bei der Lehrveranstaltungsevaluation

Standardisierte Elemente einer Lehrveranstaltung (Inhalte, Unterlagen, organisatorische Rahmenbedingungen) werden weitgehend unabhängig von der Person des Lehrbeauftragten beurteilt.

4. Ergebnisse

4.1. Zusammensetzung der Stichprobe

Für die Bestimmung der **Qualitätsdimensionen bei Lehrveranstaltungen** (Abschnitt 4.2) wurde der Erhebungszeitraum September 1995 bis April 1996 gewählt und insgesamt 1093 Fragebögen in die Auswertungen einbezogen. Es wurde eine Reduktion auf ausschließlich betriebswirtschaftliche Lehrveranstaltungen (60% Vorlesungen und 40 % Übungsveranstaltungen) des ersten Studienabschnittes des Studiengangs „Wirtschaftsberatende Berufe“ vorgenommen. Diese Einschränkung bedeutet, daß die Stichprobe Lehrveranstaltungen aus Rechnungswesen, Marketing, Personal, Führung und Organisation, sowie Materialwirtschaft und Logistik beinhaltet.

Für die Analysen im Zusammenhang mit dem **Nachweis eines bestehenden Halo-Effektes** wurde die Stichprobe begrenzt auf die Lehrveranstaltungen „Marketing“, da nur bei diesen die notwendigen quasi-experimentellen Bedingungen (Standardisierungen) kontrolliert werden konnten. Die Auswertungen in Abschnitt 4.3 beziehen sich auf fünf Vortragende mit insgesamt 120 Fällen im Sommersemester 1996.

4.2. Qualitätsdimensionen bei Lehrveranstaltungen

Zur Ermittlung der Qualitätsdimensionen der Lehrveranstaltungen und zur Prüfung der Hypothese 1 wurde eine explorative Faktorenanalyse über sämtliche Bewertungsitems mit Varimax Rotation gerechnet. Die Ergebnisse der Faktorenanalyse zeigen eine fünf Faktorenstruktur mit einer Gesamtvarianzerklärung von 61,5.

Factor	Eigenvalue	Pct of Var	Cum Pct
1	10,81260	41,6	41,6
2	1,48712	5,7	47,3
3	1,34675	5,2	52,5
4	1,22043	4,7	57,2
5	1,13415	4,4	61,5

Tab. 1: Faktorstruktur und deren Varianzerklärung

	Factor 1	Factor 2	Factor 3	Factor 4	Factor 5
n=1093 ***Reliability*** *(Cronbach Alpha)*	,93	,86	,79	,67	,76
Faktor 1: Persönlichkeit					
Erläuterung komplizierter Sachverhalte (V7)	.76				
Tempo des Vortrags (V8)	.73				
Eingehen auf Studentenfragen (V12)	.71				
Angenehme Atmosphäre (V20)	.68				
Kontakt zwischen LV-Leiter und Studenten (V19)	.67				
Klare Ausdrucksweise (V14)	.67				
Sachliche Kompetenz (V13)	.56				
Vertiefung in Übungen (V6)	.55				
Akustische Verständlichkeit (V15)	.50				
Angemessene Hausaufgaben (V4)	.43				
Klarer Praxisbezug (V3)	.41				
Faktor 2: Methodik, Didaktik, Pädagogik					
Transparente Leistungsbeurteilung (V2)		.64			
Nutzung der Unterrichtsmaterialen (V10)		.63			
Verständliche Unterlagen (V9)		.58			
Einsatz von Hilfsmitteln (Folien, Kopien, ...) (V11)		.57			
Klare Lehrveranstaltungsziele (V1)		.56			
Übersichtlichkeit und Gliederung des Lehrstoffs (V5)		.53			
Faktor 3: Lehrziel					
Neuigkeit der Lehrinhalte (V16)			.78		
Spätere Anwendbarkeit des Gelernten (V17)			.60		
Abstimmung mit anderen Lehrveranstaltungen (V18)			.56		
Faktor 4: organisatorische Rahmenbedingungen					
Optimaler Klassenraum (V26)				.73	
Optimale Teilnehmerzahl (V25)				.72	
Veranstaltungsform (Doppelstunde, Block) (V 27)				.55	
Faktor 5: Prüfung					
Angemessener Umfang des Prüfungsstoffes (V23)					.75
Gute Prüfungsvorbereitung durch LV (V22)					.72
Gerechte Leistungsbeurteilung (V24)					.40

Tab. 2: Qualitätsdimensionen der Lehrveranstaltungsbeurteilung

Auffallend bei der Analyse der Daten ist die hohe Varianzerklärung des **Faktors 1** (41,6%). Dieser Faktor umfaßt Items, die sich auf die Person des Lehrveranstaltungsleiters beziehen. Es geht dabei insbesondere um solche Merkmale, die zeigen, wie ein Lehrbeauftragter seine persönlichen Potentiale (Kompetenz, Erfahrung, sozialer Umgang, Wissen) bei der Leistungserbringung einsetzt.

Beim **zweiten Faktor**, handelt es sich in erster Linie um Kriterien, die sich auf die didaktischen Hilfsmittel zur Unterstützung der Lehrveranstaltung beziehen. Im Gegensatz zum Persönlichkeitsfaktor zeichnen sich diese Items durch wesentlich größere Standardisierungsmöglichkeiten aus. Maßnahmen zur Qualitätssicherung können bereits in der Lehrveranstaltungsvorbereitung gesetzt werden.

Faktor 3 bezieht sich auf die Aktualität der Inhalte, deren spätere Anwendbarkeit und Vernetzung mit anderen Lehrveranstaltungen des Studienplans. Obwohl das Untersuchungsdesign sich auf die Prozeßevaluation beschränkt, repräsentiert dieser Faktor, neben Faktor 5, der prüfungsbezogene Variablen enthält, am stärksten eine Ergebnisorientierung. Die Bewertungen dieses Faktors sind mit einer Unsicherheit behaftet, da zu hinterfragen ist, ob die Studenten, die sich noch in der Ausbildung befinden, eine geeignete Beurteilungsgrundlage für die Beantwortung der Kriterien haben. Es ist zu vermuten, daß eine schlüssige Bewertung dieser Items erst nach entsprechender Erfahrung im Rahmen der beruflichen Praxis möglich ist.

Faktor 4 subsumiert die organisatorischen Rahmenbedingungen von Lehrveranstaltungen. Diese sind im wesentlichen durch die Studiengangsleitung und die Lehrveranstaltungsplanung der Fachhochschule vorgegeben. Aus der Sicht der Lehrbeauftragten stellen sie eine nicht beeinflußbare Größe, die weder durch die Person noch durch die individuelle Lehrveranstaltungsgestaltung veränderbar sind.

Faktor 5 beinhaltet Fragen in Zusammenhang mit der Leistungsbeurteilung und Prüfungsabhaltung. Bei der Analyse und Interpretation der Ergebnisse dieses Faktors muß darauf hingewiesen werden, daß die Beurteilung dieser Dimension vor dem Prüfungstermin stattgefunden hat. Ähnlich wie bei Faktor 3 sind die Ergebnisse daher als Erwartungen der StudentInnen zu interpretieren, ohne, daß diese auf gemachte Erfahrungen im Zusammenhang mit einer bereits stattgefundenen Prüfung zurückgreifen konnten.

Die Ergebnisse der 5-Faktor-Struktur werden auch durch das Qualitätsmodell von Grönroos[10] gestützt, der zwischen der „technischen“ (Grundlagen zur Erbringung der Leistung) und der „funktionalen“ Qualität (Fähigkeit der Umsetzung der Potentialqualitäten im Leistungsprozeß) einer Leistung unterscheidet. Diese Differenzierung ist insbesondere aus der Betrachtung der Wirtschaftspädagogik von zentraler Bedeutung, da damit die Grenzen der Erlernbarkeit und Weitergabe von Wissen aufgezeigt werden. Weitere vergleichbare Unterscheidungen findet man auch bei anderen Autoren[11] , die zwischen Struktur-, Prozeß- und Ergebnisqualität unterscheiden.

Für die Errechung der relativen Bedeutung der einzelnen Qualitätsdimensionen für Lehrveranstaltungen wurde als Verfahren eine multiple Regressionsanalyse gewählt. Zur Berechnung

---

[10] Vgl. Grönroos (1983), S. 10.

[11] Vgl. Parasuraman et al. (1985), S. 42; Meyer/Mattmüller (1987).

der Regressionsfunktion wurde das Globalmaß für die Gesamtzufriedenheit (Gesamteindruck der Lehrveranstaltung) als abhängige Variable und die fünf Qualitätsfaktoren als unabhängige Größen herangezogen. Die Faktoren wurden nach der Varimax-Rotation der Faktorenanalyse als Score-Variable pro Faktor anhand einer Funktion von SPSS-Windows ermittelt. Das Ergebnis dieser Berechnung ist nachstehender Abbildung 1 dargestellt. Dabei wurde durch die Regressionsanalyse ein R^2 von .64 für die fünf Faktoren ermittelt, die Berechnung der Anteile erfolgte durch die Umrechnung der Beta-Werte.

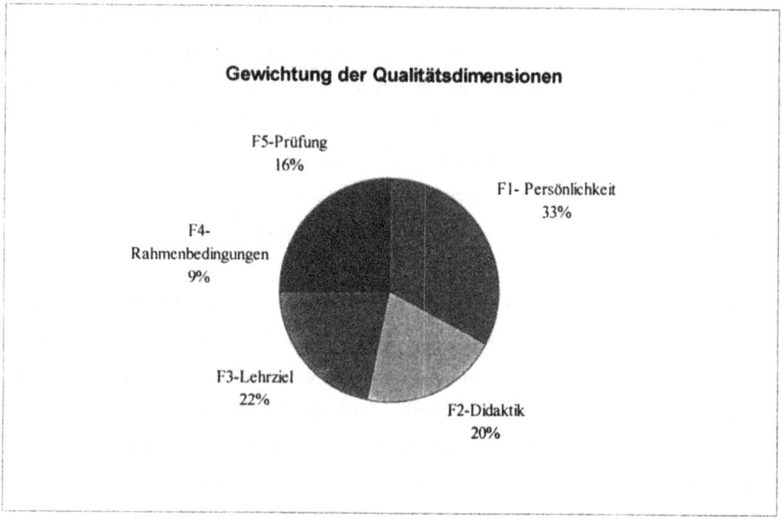

Abb. 1: Gewichtung der Qualitätsdimensionen

4.3. Halo-Effekt bei Lehrveranstaltungsevaluationen

Böhler[12] definiert das Phänomen des „Halo-Effekts" als „bei der Gestaltung des Fragebogens zu berücksichtigender Ausstrahlungseffekt vorhergehender Themen bzw. Fragen, so daß die Gedanken des Befragten systematisch in eine bestimmte Richtung gedrängt werden und die nachfolgenden Antworten verzerren."

12 Böhler (1992), S. 388.

Die Vermutung existierender Ausstrahlungseffekte einzelner Qualitätsbeurteilungsmerkmale auf andere, resultierte aus den Einzelergebnissen der Evaluation der fünf Lehrveranstaltungsleiter im Fachbereich „Marketing“. Anlaß zu detaillierten Analysen gab die Entdeckung, daß die Auswertungsprofile der fünf ReferentInnen der Einführungslehrveranstaltung „Marketing“ sehr unterschiedliche Ergebnisse zeigten. Nicht nur, daß die personenbezogenen Kriterien (Faktor 1) signifikante Beurteilungsunterschiede aufwiesen, zeigten auch fast alle standardisierten Lehrveranstaltungselemente große Abweichungen in der Studentenbewertung. Auffallend war dabei, daß sich offensichtlich dieser Effekt bei zwei Gruppen besonders zeigte: Drei Lehrbeauftragte, die bereits mehrjährige Hörsaalerfahrung hatten, erhielten signifikant bessere Durchschnittswerte bei der Beurteilung als zwei jüngere Kollegen mit geringer Lehrerfahrung. Daher wurde eine Unterscheidung in zwei Gruppen vorgenommen und diese einer weiteren Analyse unterzogen. Die nachstehende Tabelle zeigt in einer Gegenüberstellung den Vergleich der Mittelwerte dieser beiden Gruppen. Als Teststatistik wurde ein T-Test herangezogen, der wie aus den Daten ersichtlich, nur bei zwei Variablen keine signifikanten Mittelwertunterschiede aufweist.

Das vorliegende Ergebnis zeigt, daß von der Person des Lehrveranstaltungsleiters auch fast alle anderen Beurteilungskriterien wesentlich beeinflußt werden. Dies ist vor allem ein überraschendes Ergebnis, wenn man sich das eingangs dargestellte Untersuchungsdesign vergegenwärtigt. Die Konzeption der Einführungslehrveranstaltung „Marketing“ war so aufgebaut, daß im Sinne einer Qualitätssicherung versucht wurde, über die Einzellehrveranstaltung hinausgehend einen stark standardisierten Veranstaltungstyp zu konzipieren. Damit sollte v.a. den eher unerfahrenen Kollegen Unterstützung durch eine starke Struktur gegeben werden. Es bestand daher in Bezug auf die Evaluationsergebnisse der Einzellehrveranstaltungen die Vermutung, daß zwar in der Qualitätsdimension „Person des Lehrveranstaltungsleiters“ unterschiedliche Bewertungen der Zufriedenheit zu erwarten waren, daß aber bei den standardisierten Lehrveranstaltungselementen homogenere Bewertungen vorliegen müßten.

Analysiert man vor diesem Hintergrund die in der Tabelle 3 dargestellten Ergebnisse der Faktoren 2, 3 und 4, so muß Prüfhypothese 2 „Standardisierte Elemente einer Lehrveranstaltung werden nicht unabhängig von der Person des Lehrbeauftragten beurteilt“ in 11 von 12 Kriterien verworfen werden. Wie sich zeigt, ist selbst die Beurteilung standardisierter Lehrveranstaltungselemente nicht unabhängig von der wechselnden Personen des Vortragenden. So ergab beispielsweise die Beurteilung des Klassenraums (V26) trotz gleich großer Klassenräume mit gleicher Ausstattung signifikant schlechtere Werte bei den unerfahrenen

Kollegen ($\alpha<0.001$). Die Einzelergebnisse bezogen auf die beiden Referentengruppen streuten auf einer fünfteiligen Notenskala von 1,9 bis 2,7. Das gleiche Ergebnis zeigte sich auch bei der Beurteilung der Unterlagen. Auch hier wichen die Mittelwerte in Bezug auf die Verständlichkeit (V9) und die übersichtliche Gliederung des Lehrstoffes (V5) stark von einander ab und zeigten abhängig von den Referenten signifikante Unterschiede. Alle drei exemplarischen Beispiele zeigen deutlich, daß der Versuch der Qualitätssicherung über eine weitestgehende Standardisierung im Bereich der Hilfsmittel und den Rahmenbedingungen nur eingeschränkt möglich und die Wirkung dieser Maßnahmen im Einzelfall zu prüfen ist.

n=120	Gruppe 1 „mit Erfahrung“	Gruppe 2 „ohne Erfahrung“	T-Test Sig.
Faktor 1: Persönlichkeit	mean	mean	
Erläuterung komplizierter Sachverhalte (V7)	1,9	3,0	,000
Tempo des Vortrags (V8)	1,5	2,4	,000
Eingehen auf Studentenfragen (V12)	1,5	2,3	,000
Angenehme Atmosphäre (V20)	2,0	3,3	,000
Kontakt zwischen LV-Leiter und Studenten (V19)	1,9	3,3	,000
Klare Ausdrucksweise (V14)	1,5	2,6	,000
Sachliche Kompetenz (V13)	1,5	2,9	,000
Vertiefung in Übungen (V6)	1,8	2,8	,000
Akustische Verständlichkeit (V15)	1,3	1,8	,000
Angemessene Hausaufgaben (V4)	2,4	2,7	,243
Klarer Praxisbezug (V3)	1,7	2,3	,000
Faktor 2: Methodik, Didaktik, Pädagogik			
Transparente Leistungsbeurteilung (V2)	2,3	2,9	,002
Nutzung der Unterrichtsmaterialen (V10)	2,7	3,0	,288
Verständliche Unterlagen (V9)	1,8	2,5	,000
Einsatz von Hilfsmitteln (Folien, Kopien, ...) (V11)	1,6	1,9	,025
Klare Lehrveranstaltungsziele (V1)	2,3	3,8	,000
Übersichtlichkeit und Gliederung des Lehrstoffs (V5)	2,1	3,2	,000
Faktor 3: Lehrziel			
Neuigkeit der Lehrinhalte (V16)	2,2	2,8	,002
Spätere Anwendbarkeit des Gelernten (V17)	2,1	2,9	,000
Abstimmung mit anderen Lehrveranstaltungen (V18)	2,4	3,2	,000
Faktor 4: organisatorische Rahmenbedingungen			
Optimaler Klassenraum (V26)	1,9	2,7	,000
Optimale Teilnehmerzahl (V25)	1,7	2,3	,001
Veranstaltungsform (Doppelstunde, Block) (V 27)	3,4	3,8	,048
Faktor 5: Prüfung			
Zu diesem Faktor konnten bei der Lehrveranstaltung „Marketing“ noch keine Beobachtungen gemacht werden, da eine Prüfung noch nicht stattgefunden hatte.			

Tab. 3: Vergleich der beiden Referentengruppen in einem Auswertungsprofil (Mittelwerte)/Signifikanztest

Für die Interpretation der vorliegenden Ergebnisse scheinen zwei Erklärungsvarianten möglich: Erstens wäre denkbar, daß sich die beiden jungen Kollegen nicht an das vereinbarte

Lehrveranstaltungskonzept gehalten und dadurch auch keine Vorteile aus der Standardisierung und dem Input der erfahrenen Kollegen gezogen haben. Ein zweiter Erklärungsansatz, der nach Rücksprache mit den Kollegen jedoch eher zutreffen dürfte, ist der, daß bei diesem Untersuchungsdesign Halo-Effekte im klassischen Sinn nachgewiesen werden konnten. Die Vermutung liegt nahe, daß es aufgrund der dominierenden Bedeutung des Faktors „Persönlichkeit des Referenten" zu Ausstrahlungen auf die anderen Beurteilungskriterien gekommen ist, so daß diese Antworten deutlich von der tendenziell schlechteren Gesamtbeurteilung gefärbt wurden.

Folgt man dem zweiten Erklärungsmuster, so bedeutet das, daß bei der Ableitung von Verbesserungsmaßnahmen aus Evaluationsergebnissen darauf geachtet werden muß, daß nicht voreilig unrichtige Schlüsse gezogen werden, im Sinne einer Bekämpfung der Symptome anstelle der Ursachen. Würde man in unserem exemplarischen Fall fordern, daß bspw. die bei den unerfahrenen Lehrveranstaltungsleitern signifikant schlechter beurteilten Unterlagen zu verbessern sind, oder würde man als organisatorische Maßnahmen eine andere Hörsaalgröße fordern, so ist zu bezweifeln, daß ohne Verbesserungen bei den persönlichkeitsabhängigen Werten eine deutliche Veränderung der Kundenzufriedenheit eintritt. Nicht zuletzt ist auch vor dem Hintergrund der hohen Gewichtung des Faktors 1 im Hinblick auf Zufriedenheit der Studenten die Bedeutung anderer Gestaltungsmöglichkeiten einer Lehrveranstaltung zu relativieren.

4.4. Adjunktiviät einer Dienstleistung und die Grenzen der Standardisierung

Aus den Ergebnissen gezeigt am Beispiel einer Lehrveranstaltung betreffend den Nachweis der personenbezogenen Adjunktivität lassen sich eine ganze Reihe von verallgemeinerbaren Implikationen für Gestaltungsentscheidungen einer Dienstleistung ableiten:

- Bei Dienstleistungen, bei denen die wesentlichen Potential- und Prozeßqualitäten von der Person des Leistungserbringers abhängig sind, wird auch das Qualitätsurteil der Gesamtleistung durch diese dominiert. Als eine Folge ergibt sich für die Qualitätssicherung das Problem im Umgang mit Leistungsschwankungen (z.B. schlechte Tagesverfassung), sowie im Falle einer Verhinderung oder Fluktuation die Frage der Nachbesetzung.

- Ein spezieller Problembereich betrifft die Duplizierung von Leistungsfähigkeiten. Der im Handelsmarketing gängige Filialisierungsansatz durch mehrfaches Anbieten einer standardisierten Faktorkombination ist bei vorliegender Adjunktivität nur eingeschränkt möglich. Dieses führt aufgrund von Ressourcenengpässen, die in der Leistungsfähigkeit und eingeschränkten Verfügbarkeit von Personen begründet sind, zu einer Abhängigkeit von wichtigen Leistungsträgern und schränkt gleichzeitig Expansionsvorhaben ein.

- Der in einigen Branchen sichtbare Trend, standardisierbare Leistungspakete personenunabhängig anzubieten (bspw. Angebot einer Lehrveranstaltung auf CD-ROM), muß vor dem Hintergrund der Ergebnisse der Lehrveranstaltungsanalyse auch kritisch hinterfragt werden. Bei Substitution des Dienstleistungspersonals durch technische Hilfsmittel und Kommunikationsmedien verzichtet der Anbieter auf möglicherweise wettbewerbsentscheidende Differenzierungsmöglichkeiten. Eine Gefahr liegt auch darin, daß ein erzielter Know-How-Vorsprung von einem Mittbewerber leichter kopiert werden kann, als personengebundene Fähigkeiten. In diesem Fall sind Kostenvorteile genau in Hinblick auf die genannten Risiken abzuwägen, bevor eine Entscheidung getroffen werden kann.

- Die Adjuktivität von personenbezogenen Merkmalen kann andererseits auch als USP vermarktet werden, der Profilierungsmöglichkeiten durch die Einzigartigkeit und Unverwechselbarkeit des Leistungsangebotes bietet.

5. Resümee und Forschungsausblick

In Bezug auf die der Arbeit zugrundeliegenden Kernhypothesen ist abschließend folgende Schlußfolgerung zu ziehen: Die von Scheuch postulierte Hypothese der Adjunktivität als Merkmal von Dienstleistungen, bei denen die Leistungsfähigkeit stark von der Person des Erbringers abhängt, konnte mit dem verfügbaren Datenmaterial eindeutig bestätigt werden. Betrachtet man dieses Ergebnis in Verbindung mit den Erkenntnisse in Bezug auf den festgestellten Halo-Effekt durch das Erhebungsdesign, läßt sich für Anbieter von Lehr- bzw. Seminarveranstaltungen als Fazit ableiten, daß Maßnahmen der Qualitätssicherung über Standardisierung von Ausbildungsinhalten und Durchführungskriterien nicht zwingend zu einer Verbesserung der Qualitätswahrnehmung aus Kundensicht führen.

Als Konsequenz dieser Aussage müssen die Möglichkeiten und Grenzen der pädagogischen Ausbildung für Vortragende relativiert werden. Es ist im Einzelfall zu analysieren, ob Schulungs- und Trainingsmaßnahmen zu einer deutlichen Verbesserung des Evaluationsergebnisses führen, da gerade Veränderungen im Bereich persönlichkeitsabhängiger Bewertungen des Referenten vielfach nur eingeschränkt möglich sind.

Erweitert man diese Schlußfolgerung auf andere Branchen mit ähnlichen Charakteristika der Leistung, so ist im Rahmen der sehr aktuellen Diskussion zur Qualitätssicherung - bspw. in Zusammenhang mit der ISO-Zertifizierung - die grundsätzliche Frage zu stellen, inwieweit personengebundene Leistungsfähigkeiten gesichert und als Ressource dauerhaft verfügbar gemacht werden können. Aus den vorliegenden Ergebnisse kann weiters abgeleitet werden, daß Qualitätssicherung durch Standardisierung vor allem bei vorliegender Adjunktivität nicht für alle Branchen gleichermaßen geeignet scheint.

In welchem Ausmaß personenbezogene Adjunktiviät zur bestimmenden Einflußgröße in Hinblick auf die wahrgenommene Leistung durch den Kunden wird, ist fallspezifisch zu untersuchen. Dieser Nachweis wird in manchen Bereichen schwierig zu führen sein. Es ist daher die Forderung an die Marketingforschung zu stellen, sich vermehrt auf quasi-experimentelle Untersuchungsdesigns, wie es hier dargestellt wurde, einzulassen bzw. danach zu suchen, um personenspezifische Einflüsse unter ceteris-paribus Bedingungen analysieren zu können.

An der Schnittstelle zum Personalmarketing stellt die Adjunktivität auch ein Personalmanagementproblem dar. Sowohl die Akquisition als auch Qualifizierung geeigneter Mitarbeiter, sowie die Bindung von personenabhängigen Erfolgspotentialen stellen vor allem bei hoher Mitarbeiterfluktuation oder bei starkem Wachstum Unternehmen vor entscheidende Probleme.

Den Abschluß bilden zwei methodengeleitete Feststellung zum Thema Zufriedenheitsforschung: Ist in Branchen der Nachweis der Dominanz des Faktors „Person" auf die Wahrnehmungsbeurteilung einer Dienstleistung festzustellen, so sollten die Ergebnisse vor dem Hintergrund möglicher Halo-Effekte kritisch hinterfragt werden. Dieser störende Einfluß kann die Bewertungen sowohl in positiver wie auch in negativer Hinsicht verzerren, was eine valide Interpretation von Kundenzufriedenheitsanalysen erschwert.
In diesem Zusammenhang sollte auch eine weitere Störgröße hinterfragt werden: die Reihenfolgeeffekte bei der Fragebatterie der Qualitätsmerkmale. Bei der vorliegenden Auswertung

mußte, wie bereits erwähnt, auf einen standardisierten Fragebogen zurückgegriffen werden. Bei einem weiteren empirischen Erhebungsschritt wäre es daher interessant, verschiedene Fragebogenvarianten mit einer unterschiedlichen Anordnung der Fragen zu entwickeln, um sie auf Auswirkungen in Hinblick auf die Antworttendenzen abzutesten zu können.

6. Literatur

Bagozzi, R.P. (1996), The Role of Arousal in the Creation and Control of the Halo Effect in Attitude Models, in: Psychology & Marketing, Vol. 13 (May 1996), S. 235-264

Bitner, M. J. (1990), Evaluating Service and Encounters: The Effects of Physical Surroundings and Employee Responses, in: Journal of Marketing, Vol. 54 (April 1990), S. 69-82

Böhler, H.(1992), Halo-Effekt, in: Diller, H. (Hrsg.): Vahlens Großes Marketing-Lexikon, Vahlen/Beck, München, S. 388

Chmielewicz, K. (1969), Wirtschaftsgut und Rechnungswesen, in: ZfbF, 1969, Heft 2/3, S. 85ff

Corsten, H. (1988), Betriebswirtschaftslehre der Dienstleistungsunternehmungen, Oldenbourg, München 1988

Grönroos, Ch. (1983), Innovative Marketing Strategies and Organization Structures for Service Firms, in: Berry, L.L./Shostack, G.L./Upah, G.D.: Emerging Perspectives on Services Marketing, AMA Proceeding Series, Chicago 1983, S. 9-21

Maleri, R. (1994), Grundlagen der Dienstleistungsproduktion, 3. vollst. überarb. Aufl., Springer 1994

Meyer, Anton (1983), Dienstleistungs-Marketing, Forkel-Verlag, Augsburg 1993

Meyer, A./**Mattmüller**, R. (1987), Qualität von Dienstleistungen, in: Marketing ZFP, Heft 3, August 1987, S. 187-195

Nisbett R.E./**Wilson**, T.D. (1977), The Halo Effect: Evidence of Unconscious Alteration of Judgements. in: Journal of Personality and Social Psychology, Vol. 35, S. 250-256

Parasuraman, A./**Zeithaml**, V.A./**Berry** L.L. (1985), A Conceptual Model of Service Quality and Its Implications for Future Research, in: Journal of Marketing, Vol. 49 (Fall 1985), S. 41-50

Scharitzer, D. (1994), Dienstleistungsqualität - Kundenzufriedenheit. Schriftenreihe "Forschungsergebnisse der Wirtschaftsuniversität Wien", herausgegeben von Topritzhofer, E., Service Fachverlag, Wien 1994

Scheuch, F. (1982), Dienstleistungsmarketing, Verlag Vahlen, 1982

Zeithaml, V.A./**Parasuraman**, A./**Berry**, L.L. (1985), Problems and Strategies in Services Marketing, in: Journal of Marketing, Vol. 49 (Spring 1985), S. 33-46

Herbert Woratschek*

CONJOINT MEASUREMENT - EIN DURCHBRUCH BEI DER PREISENTSCHEIDUNG IM DIENSTLEISTUNGSBEREICH?

Inhalt

---

* Prof. Dr. Herbert Woratschek, Universität Bayreuth, Lehrstuhl für Betriebswirtschaftslehre VIII, Dienstleistungsmanagement, 95440 Bayreuth

1. Problemstellung

Das Conjoint Measurement ist ein Verfahren zur Schätzung der Präferenzen von Konsumenten. Es wurde erstmals in den 70er Jahren in Amerika für die Schätzung von Präferenzen verwandt.[1] Allerdings wurde die Methode erst in den 80er Jahren für preispolitische Analysen in Deutschland eingesetzt.[2] Simon und Kucher haben 1987 im Harvard Manager ihre preispolitische Analyse unter dem Titel "Conjoint Measurement - Ein Durchbruch bei der Preisentscheidung" veröffentlicht.[3]

Die Aktualität des Themas dokumentiert sich in einem Boom empirischer Anwendungen der Conjoint-Analyse in den letzten zwei bis drei Jahren in Deutschland. 1994 haben Bauer/Herrmann/Mengen ihren Ansatz, den sie "Conjoint + Cost" nennen, in der ZfB vorgestellt.[4] In diesem Ansatz integrieren sie die Kosten von Produktvarianten in die Conjoint Analyse.

Die Empirie-Euphorie der letzten Jahre bezüglich der Conjoint-Analyse lassen eine kritische Reflexion aus theoretischer Sicht in den Hintergrund treten. Ein Verfahren kann nicht losgelöst von den spezifischen Gegebenheiten des Untersuchungsgegenstandes auf seine Eignung hin beurteilt werden. Daher soll beurteilt werden, ob der besagte Durchbruch bei der Preisentscheidung im Dienstleistungsbereich als gelungen zu bezeichnen ist.

Die Diskussion um die Abgrenzung von Sachgütern und Dienstleistungen hat gezeigt, daß es aus ökonomischer Sicht nicht sinnvoll ist, diese voneinander zu trennen, da ohnehin in fast allen Fällen Kombinationen aus den drei Komponenten abgesetzt werden. Aus dieser Erkenntnis heraus, wird zunächst eine informationsökonomisch fundierte Typologie der Dienstleistungen zugrundegelegt, deren Abgrenzungskriterien von zentraler marketing-politischer Bedeutung sind.[5] Anhand dieser Typologie kann die Eignung verschiedener Marketing-Instrumente und hier die Eignung des Conjoint Measurement vorgenommen werden.

---

1 Vgl. zu einem Überblick empirischer Conjoint Studien z.B. Cattin/Wittink (1982).

2 Vgl. z.B. Albers (1983) und (1989); Kucher (1985); Dichtl/Thomas (1986).

3 Vgl. Kucher/Simon (1987).

4 Vgl. Bauer/Herrmann/Mengen (1994). Der Ansatz wird als Innovation (S. 85) eingeführt. Im Rahmen der Produktlinienoptimierung wurden in der amerikanischen Literatur merkmalsbezogene bzw. variantenbezogene Kosten bereits seit längerem integriert. Vgl. Green/Krieger (1985); Kohli/Sukumar (1990) und Green/Krieger (1992). Ein Überblick findet sich bei Gaul/Aust/Baier (1995).

5 Vgl. Woratschek (1996), S. 34.

2. Typologie der Dienstleistungen

Dienstleistungen können kumulativ nach dem Grad der Individualisierung, der Integrativität und der Verhaltensunsicherheit unterschieden werden.

Der Individualisierungsgrad ordnet die Dienstleistungen auf einem Kontinuum ein, dessen Extremausprägungen standardisiert und maßgeschneidert sind.[6] Die Auswirkunken des Individualisierungsgrades auf die Kosten einer Unternehmung sind unmittelbar einleuchtend.

Die Integrativität bezieht sich auf das Ausmaß, in dem der Kunde selbst oder Produktionsfaktoren des Kunden in den Produktionsprozeß eingebunden werden.[7] Beim Friseur oder der Akupunktur muß der Kunde sich selbst einbringen, damit die Dienstleistung erstellt werden kann. Auch hier lassen sich die Dienstleistungen auf einem Kontinuum abbilden, dessen Pole autonome und hoch integrative Produktionsprozesse darstellen.[8] Die Integrativität bezieht sich also auf das jeweilige Ausmaß der für die Produktion notwendigen Kooperation zwischen den Marktpartnern.

Der Grad der Verhaltensunsicherheit bezieht sich auf die Unsicherheiten über die Leistungsfähigkeiten und den Leistungswillen der Marktpartner. Hierin sind auch die Unsicherheiten über die Produktqualität einbezogen. Verhaltensunsicherheit und Integrativität sind nicht vollständig unabhängig voneinander. Einerseits spielt bei einer hohen Integrativität die Unsicherheit des Kunden über das Verhalten des Anbieters eine größere Rolle als bei niedrigerer Integrativität. Andererseits wird durch die Dauer einer Geschäftsverbindung die Verhaltensunsicherheit bei bleibender hoher Integrativität abgebaut.

Bei einfachen Konsumgütern ist die Qualität bei Vertragsabschluß leichter zu beurteilen als bei komplexen Dienstleistungen, die häufig erst noch produziert werden müssen. Beim Privatunterricht hängt die Qualität nach Vertragsabschluß von den Leistungsfähigkeiten und dem Leistungswillen des Anbieters ab. Leistungsfähigkeiten sind in diesem Zusammenhang z.B. Einfühlungsvermögen und Didaktik. Leistungswillen kommt in der Anstrengung zum Ausdruck.

---

6 Vgl. Meffert (1994), S. 524-525 und Meffert/Bruhn (1995), S. 30-35.

7 Vgl. Engelhardt/Kleinaltenkamp/Reckenfelderbäumer (1993), S. 415.

8 Vgl. Engelhardt/Kleinaltenkamp/Reckenfelderbäumer (1993), S. 417.

Das Conjoint Measurement soll nach seiner Eignung für die beiden Extremausprägungen in der beschriebenen Typologie beurteilt werden, die in der Abbildung 1 grau unterlegt sind.

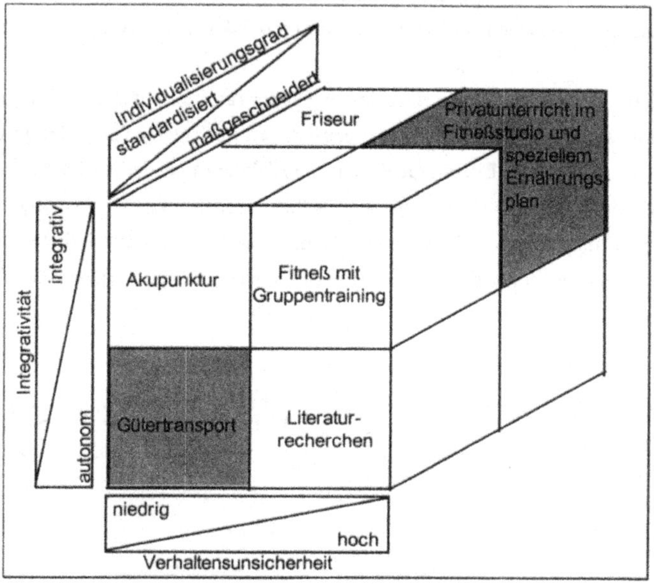

Abbildung 1: Typologie von Dienstleistungen

3. Conjoint Measurement

Beim Conjoint Measurement werden den Versuchspersonen verschiedene Produktvarianten vorgegeben, in denen das Produkt der betrachteten Unternehmung und die Konkurrenzprodukte enthalten sind. Dies geschieht anhand der Vorgabe von Mustern, Modellen, Bildern oder verbalen Beschreibungen. Am Beispiel eines Fitneßstudios soll diese Vorgehensweise gezeigt werden.[9]

---

[9] Der Vortrag des Workshops bezog sich auf ein anderes Beispiel aus der Dienstleistungsbranche, in dem verbale Stimuli mit einem Bild kombiniert den Probanden zur Beurteilung vorgelegt wurden.

3.1. Untersuchungsdesign

Es können, wie in diesem Beispiel, den Versuchspersonen Produktkarten vorgelegt werden. Auf jeder Karte wird eine Variante beschrieben. In diesem vereinfachten Beispiel werden verbale Stimuli den Probanden zur Beurteilung auf Produktkarten vorgelegt.

Die Produktkarten enthalten verbale Beschreibungen der für die Kaufentscheidung relevanten Produkteigenschaften. Die Festlegung der Eigenschaften im Untersuchungsdesign tritt leider in den meisten empirischen Literaturquellen in den Hintergrund und es bleibt unklar nach welchen Kriterien die Eigenschaften ausgewählt werden. Es ist wichtig, daß nur Eigenschaften in das Design aufgenommen werden, die kaufrelevant sind. Hierzu gibt es verschiedene Methoden in der Konsumentenforschung wie, z.B. das Repetory Grid[10] und die Elicitation-Technik.[11]

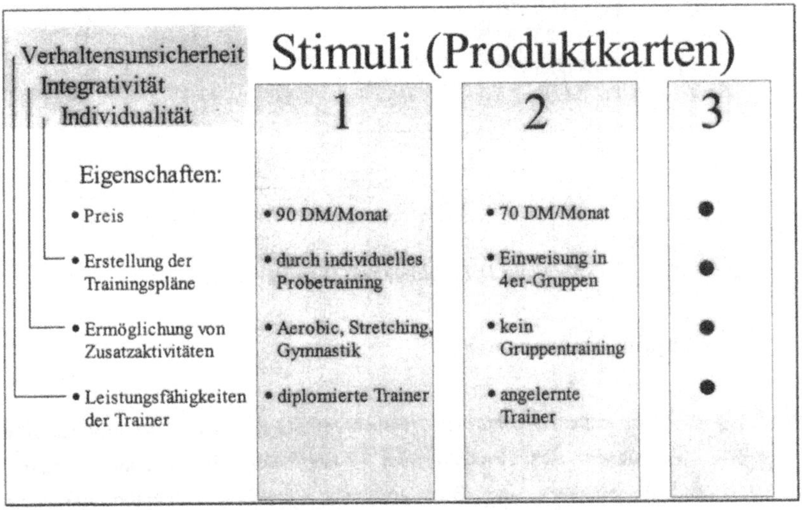

Abbildung 2: Stimuli im Conjoint Measurement

Beim Repetory Grid, werden drei Produktmarken ausgewählt, von denen der Kunde ein Paar auswählen soll, das sich von der dritten Marke weitgehend unterscheidet. Danach soll er die unterscheidenden Merkmale benennen. Sobald keine Unterschiede mehr genannt werden

---

[10] Vgl. z.B. Müller-Hagedorn/Vornberger (1979), S. 185-207.

[11] Vgl. z.B. Böhler (1979), S. 270.

können, wird dieser Vorgang mit einer neuen Markentriade solange wiederholt bis keine diskriminierenden Eigenschaften mehr genannt werden können. Fraglich dabei ist, ob die genannten Eigenschaften wirklich für die Kaufentscheidung relevant sind, da durch das Verfahren häufig eine übermäßige Konzentration auf Unterschiede erzeugt wird, die bei realem Kaufverhalten in diesem Ausmaß nicht gegeben ist. Bei der Elicitation-Technik soll der Kunde spontan relevante Eigenschaften benennen und es werden die am häufigsten genannten Merkmale in das Untersuchungsdesign aufgenommen. Ich glaube, daß die Abbildung realen Kaufverhaltens besser gelingt, wenn die Eigenschaften theoriegeleitet erfolgt, d.h. diese Techniken durch typologiegestützte Überlegungen ergänzt werden. Dabei kann z.B. der hohe Individualisierungsgrad dazu führen, daß diesbezügliche Eigenschaften wie z.B. die Art der Erstellung der Trainingspläne in das Design aufgenommen werden.

Wichtig ist, daß der Preis im Rahmen des Conjoint Measurement als eine von vielen Produkteigenschaft in das Untersuchungsdesign aufgenommen wird. Die Produktvarianten werden generiert, indem alle möglichen Ausprägungen der einzelnen Eigenschaften miteinander kombiniert werden. Die Varianten bzw. die unterschiedlichen Produktkarten werden den Probanden vorgelegt. Die Aufgabenstellung für die Probanden könnte lauten: "Bitte bringen Sie die Produktkarten in eine Reihenfolge, die Ihrer Präferenz entspricht. Legen Sie die Karte mit dem Fitneßstudio, das Ihnen am liebsten ist nach vorne. Das am wenigsten geliebte Fitneßstudio ordnen Sie ganz hinten ein."

Diese Form der Erfassung der Präferenzen nennt man Ranking. Es gibt auch hier unterschiedliche Techniken. Beim Rating sollen die Probanden ihre Präferenz für die einzelnen Varianten durch Ankreuzen auf einer Skala zum Ausdruck bringen. Das Ergebnis der empirischen Untersuchung ist eine individuelle Präferenzreihenfolge der vorgelegten Produktvarianten. Aus dieser empirischen Präferenzreihenfolge sollen metrische Nutzenfunktionen auf individueller Basis geschätzt werden. Hierzu ist es notwendig ein Nutzenmodell zu spezifizieren, dessen Parameter geschätzt werden.

3.2. Nutzenmodell und Schätzmethode

Es gibt verschiedene Nutzenmodelle im Rahmen einer Conjoint-Analyse, die hier nicht im einzelnen dargestellt werden sollen. Die Ausführungen beschränken sich auf die anerkanntermaßen flexibelste Variante, dem Teilnutzenmodell. Im Gegensatz zu den Varianten "Idealvektormodell" und "Idealpunktmodell" können Eigenschaften auf Nominalskalenniveau geschätzt werden, d.h. es können auch Eigenschaften berücksichtigt

werden, für die nicht einmal eine ordinale Reihenfolge angegeben werden kann, wie z.B. die Eigenschaft "Leistungsfähigkeiten der Trainer" mit den Ausprägungen "diplomierte Trainer" oder "angelernte Trainer". Desweiteren muß kein bestimmter Funktionstyp für die Teilnutzenfunktionen wie in den anderen Varianten vorgegeben werden. Häufig wird daher in empirischen Anwendungen das Teilnutzenmodell spezifiziert:

$$U = \sum_{n=1}^{N}\sum_{m=1}^{M} u_{nm}x_{nm} \; mit \; x_{nm} = \begin{cases} 1 & wenn\ die\ Eigenschaft\ n\ in\ der\ Ausprägung\ m\ vorliegt \\ 0 & sonst \end{cases}$$

mit Unternehmen für den Gesamtnutzen eines Probanden (auf den Index für die Probanden wurde aus Vereinfachungsgründen verzchtet), n für die Eigenschaft, m für die Ausprägung der Eigenschaft und x für die Hilfsvariable

Für jede Variante des vorgelegten Fitneßstudios, d.h. jedem Stimulus, kann der Gesamtnutzenwert eines Probanden aus dem Nutzenmodell ermittelt werden. Der Gesamtnutzen kommt zustande, indem die Teilnutzenwerte einer jeden Eigenschaftsausprägung des betrachteten Stimulus addiert werden. Nur wenn die spezifizierte Ausprägung auf der Produktkarte enthalten ist, geht der zugehörige Teilnutzenwert in die Bildung des Gesamtnutzenwertes als Summand ein. Wenn diese nicht vorliegt, wird die Hilfsvariable 0 und der Teilnutzenwert (genauer: das Produkt aus Hilfsvariable und Teilnutzenwert) bestimmt somit nicht den Gesamtnutzenwert.

Der Teilnutzenwert u drückt die Bewertung des Probanden für die entsprechende Eigenschaftsausprägung aus. Dieser kann als Regressionskoeffizient der Hilfsvariablen betrachtet werden. Die Gesamtnutzenwerte sind durch die empirisch erhobene Reihenfolge gegeben. Die Teilnutzenwerte werden aus den empirisch erhobenen Reihenfolgen geschätzt. Hierzu wird in der Regel die monotone Regression und das Gradientenverfahren angewandt. Als Ergebnis der Schätzung erhält man für jeden Probanden eine metrische Nutzenfunktion, die die empirischen Rangdaten möglichst gut wiedergibt. Dies bedeutet, daß stark präferierte Stimuli höhere Nutzenwerte erhalten als schwach präferierte Stimuli.

Da der Preis als eine Eigenschaft in das Teiluntzenmodell eingeht, kann der Teilnutzenwert für den Preis geschätzt werden. Für die Bestimmung gewinnoptimaler Preise reicht die Kenntnis der Teilnutzenwerte des Preises, d.h. der Preiswichtigkeit, für einzelne Probanden nicht aus. Die indiviudellen Nutzenfunktionen müssen zu einer Preisreaktion aggregiert werden.

3.3. Modellierung der Preisreaktion

Die Aggregation erfolgt im Conjoint Measurement zum einen durch die First Choice-Regel und zum anderen durch die Attraktionsregel.

Bei der First Choice-Regel wird unterstellt, daß jeder Konsument seinen Nutzen maximiert. Jede Variante, die dem Angebot der betrachteten Unternehmung oder der Konkurrenz entspricht, wird mit dem Nutzenmodell des Probanden konfrontiert. Es wird dabei unterstellt, daß der Proband die für ihn nutzenmaximale Variante wählt. Der Anteil der Konsumenten, die das Fitneßstudio i* als nutzenmaximal empfinden, wird als Marktanteil dieses Fitneßstudios in der Stichprobe interpretiert. Stufen z.B. von 60 von 100 Probanden i* als nutzenmaximal ein, beträgt der Marktanteil von i* 60%.

Der geschätzte Marktanteil ergibt sich demzufolge:

$$\hat{m}_{i^*} = \frac{\#\left\{ k \middle| U_{i^*k}^{max} \right\}}{K}$$

*mit als geschätzter Marktanteil von Fitneßstudio i**
und den Konsumenten k=1,...,K.

Es ist offensichtlich, daß diese Regel nicht geeignet ist, Dienstleistungen mit einem hohen Grad an Verhaltensunsicherheit und hoher Integrativität abzubilden. Bei diesen Dienstleistungen kann nicht davon ausgegangen werden, daß ein deterministischer Zusammenhang zwischen gemessenem Nutzen und dem Kaufverhalten gegeben ist. Situative Faktoren führen dazu, daß z.B. aus Zeitdruck ein Produkt gewählt wird, das die "zweite Lösung" darstellt. Persönliche Präferenzen, die im Laufe von Gesprächen vor Vertragsabschluß gebildet werden, führen zur Auswahl eines Fitneßstudios, das nicht dem gemessenem Nutzenmaximum entspricht.

Aus dieser Kritik hat sich die Attraktionsregel etabliert, die einen stochastischen Zusammenhang zwischen gemessenen Nutzen und dem Kaufverhalten modelliert. Die Attraktionsregel unterstellt eine Kaufwahrscheinlichkeit für die einzelnen Produkte. Die Kaufwahrscheinlichkeit ist hierbei als das Verhältnis des Nutzens von i* zu der Summe aller Nutzen aus den möglichen Alternativen definiert:

$$w_{i^*k} = \frac{U_{i^*k}}{\sum_i U_{ik}} \quad mit\ i, i^* \in A\ und\ i \neq i^*$$

mit A als Menge der Anbieter i= 1,...,I und w als Wahrscheinlichkeit dafür, daß k die Dienstleistung von i in Anspruch nimmt.*

Die durchschnittliche Kaufwahrscheinlichkeit wird als Marktanteil des Anbieters i* in der Stichprobe definiert:

$$\hat{m}_{i^*} = \frac{1}{K}\sum_{k=1}^{K} w_{i^*k}$$

Ein in der Literatur zum Conjoint Measurement selten diskutiertes Problem ist die Hochrechnung des Marktanteils in der Stichprobe auf den betrachteten, relevanten Markt. Hier wird häufig von einer repräsentativen Stichprobe ausgegangen und der Marktanteil der Stichprobe als prognostizierter Marktanteil der Gesamtheit angesehen. Dieses Problem muß m.E. im Rahmen von Conjoint-Analysen intensiver diskutiert werden, um Fehlprognosen zu reduzieren.

Unabhängig davon, welche der beiden grundlegenden Aggregationsregeln im Conjoint Measurement zum Einsatz kommt, können für die betrachtete Variante des Fitneßstudios Marktanteile ermittelt werden. Da der Preis eine Eigenschaft dieser Variante darstellt, kann dieser sukzessive variiert werden, und somit punktweise eine Preisabsatzfunktion bzw. eine Marktanteilsfunktion ermittelt werden. Die resultierenden Preisabsatzfunktionen unterscheiden sich in Abhängigkeit der gewählten Aggregationsregel.

Aus der ermittelten Preisabsatzfunktion läßt sich eine Erlösfunktion ableiten. Kennt man die Kostenfunktion in Abhängigkeit der Absatzmenge, läßt sich ein gewinnoptimaler Preis bestimmen für das Angebot des betrachteten Fitneßstudios bestimmen. Kucher und Simon bestimmen in einer Studie von 1987 den gewinnoptimalen Preis auf Basis einer aus dem Conjoint Measurement abgeleiteten Preisabsatzfunktion[12]. Dabei sind prinzipiell drei Vorgehensweisen denkbar:

1. Für jeden Preispunkt wird zunächst ceteris paribus der Marktanteil bestimmt. Auf dieser Basis werden die Erlöse berechnet. Der Preis mit dem höchsten Gewinn wird gewählt.

---

12 Vgl. Kucher/Simon (1987), S. 30-32.

2. Die Preisabsatzfunktion wird zwischen den Preispunkten als stückweise linear angenommen und die Erlösfunktion bestimmt. Die Gewinnfunktion wird ermittelt, indem die Kostenfunktion zugeordnet wird. Das Gewinnoptimum wird analytisch berechnet.

3. Die ermittelten Preis-Marktanteilskombinationen bilden den Dateninput für eine weitere Regression[13].

Die beiden ersten Vorgehensweisen entsprechen der Grundidee von Kucher/Simon und unterscheiden sich nur durch den Berechnungsmodus. Wenn Preisschwellen existieren, ist die Annahme der stückweisen Linearität inadäquat und kann zu erheblichen Prognosefehlern führen. Da die Nutzenfunktion im Conjoint Measurement lediglich punktweise definiert ist, wenn das Teilnutzenmodell zugrunde liegt, ist die erste Vorgehensweise theoretisch besser abgesichert.

Im linken Teil der Abbildung 3 ist die erste Vorgehensweise skizziert. Auf der Basis individueller Nutzenfunktionen wird zunächst ein anzusprechendes Kundensegment für das Angebot i* identifiziert. Für dieses Segment schätzt man die individuelle Preisabsatzfunktion. Dies geschieht, indem die erste Preisausprägung mit dem individuellen Nutzenmodell des Konsumenten 1 konfrontiert wird. Das Konkurrenzangebot bleibt dabei konstant. Auf dieser Basis ist für den Konsumenten 1 die Kaufwahrscheinlichkeit ermittelbar. Diese Berechnung erfolgt für alle Konsumenten. Aus den individuellen Kaufwahrscheinlichkeiten berechnet sich der Markanteil und der Erlös. Der Erlös ist gleich Marktanteil mal Marktvolumen mal Preis. Die Kosten müssen in Abhängigkeit des Marktanteils ermittelt werden. Auf dieser Basis läßt sich für die entsprechende Preisausprägung der Gewinn bestimmen. Diese Rechenschritte werden für jede untersuchte Preisausprägung wiederholt, so daß für jede Preisausprägung der Gewinn errechnet ist. Es wird der Preis für i* gesetzt, der den höchsten Gewinn verspricht.

Bei der beschriebenen Konzeption wird eine Vorgehensweise gewählt, die dem Denken in Preislagen entspricht. Die Qualität für i* wird definiert und ein gewinnoptimaler Preis bestimmt. Denkbar wäre aber auch eine gleichzeitige Variierung von Qualität und Preis. Es ist möglich, daß die Gewinnsituation sich verbessert, wenn nicht nur der Preis, sondern auch die Qualität variiert wird. Die simultane Variation von Preis und Qualität ist für den 1994 vorgestellten Conjoint + Cost-Ansatz kennzeichnend[14], der im folgenden dargestellt wird.

---

[13] Vgl. zu einer solchen Vorgehensweise Albers (1983), S. 222-224.

[14] Vgl. Bauer/Herrmann/Mengen (1994).

4. Conjoint Measurement und Kosten

Ausgangspunkt von Conjoint + Cost ist wiederum die Ermittlung individueller Nutzenfunktionen durch das Conjoint Measurement. Allerdings werden die einzelnen Nutzenmodelle mit jeder denkbaren Variante konfrontiert, d.h. im genannten Beispiel wird das Fitneßstudio mit allen möglichen unterschiedlichen Eigenschaftsausprägungen getestet. Bei diesem Vorgang bleibt das Konkurrenzangebot wiederum konstant.

Die Vorgehensweise ist im rechten Teil der Abbildung 3 gezeigt. Für jede denkbare Produktvariante s=1,...,S werden die individuellen Kaufwahrscheinlichkeiten ermittelt und die resultierenden Gewinne errechnet. Hierzu beginnt man mit einer konkreten Variante, dem Stimulus s=1. Dieser Stimulus wird im Vergleich zum Konkurrenzangebot durch das Nutzenmodell auf individueller Basis bewertet und die individuelle Kaufwahrscheinlichkeit wird ermittelt. Dieser Vorgang ist für jeden Konsumenten durchzuführen und auf dieser Basis sind Marktanteile und Erlöse zu bestimmen. Um die Gewinne zu ermitteln, müssen Kostendaten einer jeden Variante bekannt sein. Dies bedeutet, daß Conjoint + Cost eine Matrix mit merkmalsbezogenen Kosten voraussetzt. Die Gewinne sind unter diesen Voraussetzungen für jede Variante ermittelbar.

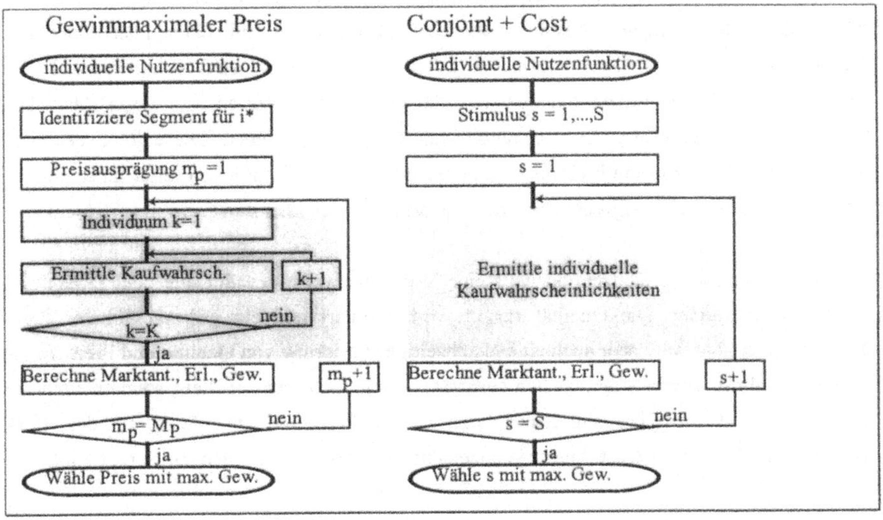

Abbildung 3: Ablaufdiagramme der Conjoint-Analyse

Dieser Rechenvorgang erfolgt für jeden Stimulus. Es wird dann die Variante bzw. die Leistung eines Fitneßstudios angeboten, die den maximalen Gewinn verspricht. Für eine begrenzte Anzahl von Merkmalsausprägungen ist der Rechenaufwand mit der heutigen Technologie enumerativ zu bewältigen. Durch Conjoint + Cost ist es prinzipiell möglich Qualität und Preis simultan festzulegen.

5. Beurteilung der Conjoint Analyse

5.1. Grundlegende Kritik

Das dem Conjoint Measurement zugrundeliegende Nutzenmodell ist in der häufig spezifizierten Form des Teilnutzenmodells linear additiv. Die inhaltlichen Konsequenzen dieser Formalstruktur liegen darin, daß die Eigenschaften in Bezug auf den resultierenden Gesamtnutzen vollständig kompensatorisch sind. Dies bedeutet, daß ein Nachteil bezüglich einer Eigenschaft durch einen Vorteil einer anderen Eigenschaft ausgeglichen werden kann. Es werden im Conjoint-Nutzenmodell demzufolge keine K.O.-Kriterien abgebildet. Bei einem Fitneßstudio bedeutet dies, daß die Unfreundlichkeit des Personals durch die Qualifikationen des Trainers aufgefangen werden können. Mangelnde Freundlichkeit während kann aber ein K.O.-Kriterium sein. Insbesondere kann auch der Preis ein solches K.O.-Kriterium sein. Dies ist aber im linear additiven Nutzenmodell nicht abbildbar.

Budgetrestriktionen werden ebenfalls nicht abgebildet, da der Preis im Conjoint Measurement eine disnutzenstiftende Eigenschaft ist. Wenn ein Konsument maximal 80 DM einen Monatsbeitrag ausgeben kann, dieser aber 100 DM beträgt, wird das Angebot nicht in Anspruch genommen werden, auch wenn es den maximalen Nutzen stiften würde.

Eine wesentliche Einschränkung der Anwendungsmöglichkeiten ergibt sich daraus, daß nur wenige Eigenschaften in die Analyse eingehen dürfen, da die Anzahl der zu beurteilenden Produktkarten exponentiell in Abhängigkeit der Merkmalsausprägungen steigt.

In dem bereits angeführten Beispiel wurden für das Fitneßstudio vier Eigenschaften als relevant erachtet. Wenn man für jede dieser vier Eigenschaften nur fünf Ausprägungen berücksichtigt, ergeben sich bereits 1024 Produktkarten, die der Proband in eine Reihenfolge bringen soll. Es ist unmittelbar einsichtig, daß der Proband mit einer solchen Aufgabe

überfordert ist. In der Regel wird der Proband vereinfachte Entscheidungsregeln anwenden und die Validität der ermittelten Nutzenfunktion ist in Frage zu stellen.

Anzahl der möglichen Stimuli bei n Eigenschaften mit je m Ausprägungen

m \ n	2	3	4	5	6
2	4	8	16	32	64
3	9	27	81	243	729
4	16	64	256	1024	4096
5	25	125	625	3125	15625
6	36	216	1296	7776	46656
7	49	343	2401	16807	117649
8	64	512	4096	32768	262144

s < 20

Abbildung 4: Dilemma des Conjoint Measurement

In der Literatur wird versucht, dieses Problem zu lösen, indem fraktionierte oder Designs zur Verfügung verwendet werden.[15] Fraktionierte Designs sind Untersuchungsanordnungen, die die Komplexität der Bewertungsaufgabe für den Probanden reduzieren. Sie sind mit dem Verzicht auf die Aufdeckung von Interaktionseffekten verbunden. Es werden Produktkarten ausgesondert, die für die Schätzung nicht wesentlich sind und Eigenschaftskombinationen, die ohnehin unrealistisch sind, z.B. ein Fitneßstudio mit individuellem Trainings- und Ernährungsplan, diplomierten Trainern, einer großen Anzahl von Zusatzangeboten und niedrigem Preis. Unabhängig von der konkreten Ausgestaltung des fraktionierten Designs, geht die Komplexitätsreduktion zu Lasten der Validität. Besonders problematisch dürfte dies bei der hier beispielhaft gezeigten Anwendung sein, wenn man bedenkt, daß für die Auswahl eines Fitneßstudios weitere Eigenschaften wie z.B. Gerätevielfalt, Studioatmosphäre, Öffnungszeiten und Qualität der Sanitäranlagen relevant sein dürften.

Wenn man desweiteren bedenkt, daß ein Proband maximal 20 Profile sinnvoll bewerten kann, bleibt das Problem strukturell erhalten, selbst wenn man fraktionierte Designs verwendet. Abbildung 4 zeigt eindrucksvoll wie stark die Anzahl der Produktkarten ohne

[15] Vgl. Addelman (1962), S. 21-46 und Green (1974), S. 61-68.

Berücksichtigung fraktionierter Designs in Abhängigkeit der Anzahl der Eigenschaften und der Anzahl der Eigenschaftsausprägungen wächst. Einerseits ist für die Validität der Schätzung individueller Nutzenfunktionen eine hohe Anzahl von Eigenschaftsausprägungen und damit der Stimuli notwendig. Andererseits führt aber eine hohe Anzahl von Stimuli zu einer Überforderung der Probanden. Dies kann als Dilemma des Conjoint Measurement bezeichnet werden.

Es ist ebenfalls wichtig, daß die für das Untersuchungsdesign ausgesuchten Eigenschaften relevant für die Kaufentscheidung der Konsumenten sind und vollständig die Kaufentscheidung bestimmen. Es ist möglich, daß aber aufgrund der Komplexität der Beurteilung eines Fitneßstudios, nicht die einzelnen Komponenten bewertet werden, sondern der Konsument seine Entscheidung sich vereinfacht. Dabei kann er z.B. auf einen ihm bekannten Sportlehrer vertrauen. Er wählt dann das von seinem Bekannten empfohlene Fitneßstudio. In solchen Fällen bildet das Conjoint-Nutzenmodell die Entscheidungsituation nicht adäquat ab. Inbesondere bei Dienstleistungen mit niedrigem Involvement dürfte der Kunde vereinfachte Entscheidungsregeln anwenden, die nicht dem im Conjoint-Nutzenmodell unterstellten Trade-Off der Eigenschaftsausprägungen entsprechen. Das Abwägen verschiedener Merkmale einer Dienstleistung setzt ein hohes Involvement der Kunden voraus.

Ein weiterer Punkt ist die im Conjoint Measurement ermittelte relative Wichtigkeit einer Eigenschaft, z.B. der Preiswichtigkeit. Die ermittelte Preiswichtigkeit hängt von der Anzahl der zu berücksichtigten Merkmalsausprägungen ab.

Um dies zu verdeutlichen stelle man sich ein vereinfachtes Nutzenmodell vor, bei dem die Trainingsplan und der Preis als relevante Eigenschaften in die Untersuchung eingehen. Die zu diesem Nutzenmodell gehörigen Teilnutzenwerte sind der Abbildung 5 zu entnehmen. Zunächst berücksichtigen wir für den Preis drei Ausprägungen und für die Erstellung des Trainingsplans zwei Ausprägungen. Die ermittelte relative Preiswichtigkeit kommt im Teilnutzenmodell in der relativen Spannweite der Teilnutzenwerte zum Ausdruck. Dies führt dazu, daß die Wichtigkeit des Preise errechnet werden kann: $(5-3)/[(5-3)+(5-1)] = 2/(2+4)=2/6=1/3$.

Stellen man sich ein alternatives Untersuchungsdesign vor, bei dem fünf Ausprägungen für den Preis berücksichtigt werden und ansonsten alles andere unverändert bleibt, d.h. die Probanden entscheiden unter den gleichen Nutzenvorstellungen und der Trainingsplan wird weiterhin mit zwei Ausprägungen in der Analyse berücksichtigt. Angenommen, die "wahre" Teilnutzenfunktion verläuft monoton wie in Abbildung 5. Dann errechnet sich die relative Preiswichtigkeit: $(5-1)/((5-1)+4)= 4/(4+4)=4/8=1/2$. Die Preiswichtigkeit verändert sich

demzufolge von 1/3 auf 1/2. Diese Veränderung ist ausschließlich darauf zurückzuführen, daß mehr Ausprägungen der Eigenschaft Preis im Design berücksichtigt werden.

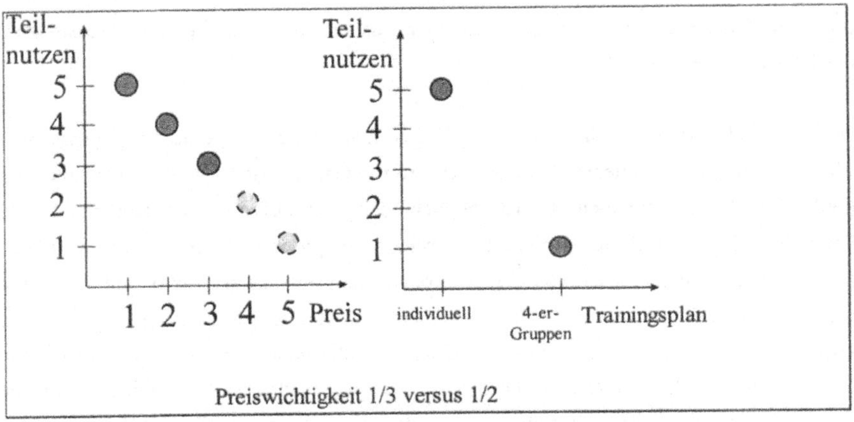

Abbildung 5: Verzerrung der relativen Wichtigkeit einer Eigenschaft

Dies bedeutet, daß die Wichtigkeit der einzelnen Eigenschaften von der Anzahl der im Design berücksichtigten Ausprägungen abhängen kann. Der Forscher steuert somit durch die Festlegung der Anzahl der Ausprägungen die relative Wichtigkeit der einzelnen Eigenschaften. Um korrekte relative Wichtigkeiten zu ermitteln müßte er im Prinzip die "wahre" Spannbreite der Teilnutzenwerte bereits vor der Analyse kennen.

5.2. Conjoint-Preis-Analyse und Typologiefit

Da im Teilnutzenmodell alle stetigen Variablen diskretisiert werden, werden in der Conjoint Analyse zwangsläufig Informationen vernichtet.[16] Dieser Informationsverlust führt bei der Ableitung von Preisabsatzfunktionen dazu, daß diese nur punktweise ermittelt werden. Daraus folgt, daß man die ermittelte Preisabsatzfunktion auch nur punktweise interpretieren darf und nicht über den gesamten Verlauf. Insbesondere wenn Preisschwellen existieren kann der Fehler groß sein, wenn man die ermittelte Preisabsatzfunktion stetig interpretiert.

16 Vgl. Balderjahn (1994), S. 17.

In der Literatur wird darüber hinaus die formale Kritik geäußert, daß die Rechenoperation der Attraktionsregel ratioskalierte Nutzenwerte erfordern.[17] Eigentlich ist beim Conjoint Measurement das Ratioskalenniveau nicht gegeben. Die Nutzenwerte sind allenfalls intervallskaliert. Die inhaltliche Bedeutung dieser formalen Kritik muß jedoch ebenfalls verdeutlicht werden, damit dem Anwender klar ist, welche Annahmen hinter der Anwendung der Attraktionsregel stehen.

Die individuelle Kaufwahrscheinlichkeit wird bei der Attraktionsregel als Quotient gebildet. Es wird der individuelle Nutzen einer Alternative ins Verhältnis zur Summe der Nutzenwerte aller Alternativen gesetzt. Um einen solchen prozentualen Nutzen zu bilden, müßte sichergestellt sein, daß jeder Proband einen absoluten Bezugspunkt hat, an dem er alle Objekte in seinem jeweiligen Wert bemessen kann. Darüber hinaus müßte das Meßverfahren diesen Bezugspunkt erfassen. Dies ist im Conjoint Measurement nicht der Fall. Die Formulierung der Kaufwahrscheinlichkeit in Abhängigkeit vom relativen Nutzen ist somit inhaltlich nicht begründbar.

Zur Schätzung des Marktanteils werden die individuellen prozentualen Nutzenwerte über alle Probanden addiert. Es werden somit individuelle Nutzenwerte miteinander verknüpft, ohne daß sichergestellt ist, daß die individuellen Nutzenwerte auf der gleichen Skaleneinheit gemessen werden. Der Nutzenwert für i* für einen Probanden kann nicht mit dem Nutzenwert für i* eines anderen Probanden verglichen werden. Dies gilt auch für die relativen Nutzenwerte, da nicht sichergestellt ist, daß alle Individuen den gleichen absoluten Bezugspunkt in der Wertbemessung zugrunde legen. Es wird implizit ein interindividueller Nutzenvergleich bei der Attraktionsregel unterstellt. Das Problem des interindividuellen Nutzenvergleichs läßt sich auch nicht durch die häufig in der Literatur vorgenommene Normierung auf ein Intervall von 0 bis 1 beseitigen. Je nachdem welche individuelle Maßeinheit dem Probanden vorschwebt, erhält ein Stimuli unterschiedliche Positionen in diesem Intervall, so daß die Problematik unterschiedlicher Maßstäbe für den individuellen Nutzen nicht beseitigt ist. Die Attraktionsregel ist aus diesen Gründen abzulehnen.

Die verbleibende First Choice-Regel erscheint grundsätzlich geeignet, wenn man an Dienstleistungen denkt, die mit einer geringen Verhaltensunsicherheit verbunden sind. Für diesen Typ von Dienstleistungen könnte die Formulierung eines deterministischen Zusammenhangs zwischen gemessenem Nutzen und dem Kaufverhalten vertretbar sein. Allerdings kommt die Formulierung eines deterministischen Zusammenhangs für Dienstleistungen mit hoher Unsicherheit über die Qualität der Dienstleistung, die

---

[17] Vgl. Green/Rao (1971), S. 355 und Balderjahn (1994), S. 16.

Leistungsfähigkeiten und den Leistungswillen des Anbieters nicht in Frage. Für diese Dienstleistungen ist die stochastische Formulierung des Zusammenhangs notwendig. Wenn man die Attraktionsregel ablehnt, ist die Conjoint-Analyse allenfalls für die Untersuchung von Dienstleistungen mit niedrigem Grad an Verhaltensunsicherheit geeignet. Die Eignung der Conjoint-Analyse hängt also von der Position in der eingangs vorgestellten Typologie der Dienstleistungen ab, die noch von den Komponenten Integrativität und Individualität abhängt.

Hoch integrative Dienstleistungen bestehen aus einer Vielzahl von Kontakten zwischen Anbieter und Nachfrager, da ein hohes Maß an Kommunikation zwischen den Partnern notwendig ist. Wenn z.B. für ein Fitneßstudio die Freundlichkeit pauschal beurteilt wird, so kann die Beurteilung ein Ergebnis der Erfahrungen an verschiedenen Kontaktpunkte während des Prozesses der Leistungserstellung sein. Die begrüßende Person kann einen sehr freundlichen Empfang bereiten, der durch die Unfreundlichkeit des Trainers zunichte gemacht wird. Wie bewertet der Konsument den Anbieter bezüglich der Freundlichkeit?

Die hohe Integrativität erfordert die Berücksichtigung der Eigenschaftsmessung in den einzelnen Stufen der Leistungserstellung, wie dies bei der ereignisorientierten Qualitätsmessung[18] geschieht. Wenn man die verschiedenen Stufen der Leistungserstellung im eigenschaftsorientierten Conjoint Measurement erfassen wollte, resultiert daraus eine relativ hohe Anzahl von Eigenschaften im Design, die aufgrund des vorher beschriebenen Dilemmas des Conjoint Measurement nicht berücksichtigt werden kann. Das Conjoint Measurement ist somit für hoch integrative Dienstleistungen kaum geeignet.

Individuell erbrachte Dienstleistungen haben eine Variation der Eigenschaftsausprägungen in Abhängigkeit der individuellen Kundenwünsche zur Folge. Es gibt bei individuellen Dienstleistungen nicht ein bestimmtes Set an konkreten Eigenschaftsausprägungen, das diese kennzeichnet. Allenfalls ließe sich eine individuelle Dienstleistung über den Grad der Fähigkeit des Anbieters beschreiben, auf individuelle Wünsche zu reagieren. Derartig grobe Formulierungen lassen große Interpretationsspielräume der Probanden zu, die sich wiederum auf die geäußerte Präferenzreihenfolge und somit auf die gemessene Nutzenfunktion auswirkt. Ein unspezifisch gemessener Nutzenwert ist aufgrund des hohen Aggregationsniveaus der zugrundeliegenden Eigenschaften nur beschränkt tauglich für die Prognose des Kaufverhaltens.

Für Dienstleistungen mit niedriger Integrativität und niedrigem Grad der Verhaltensunsicherheit ist das Conjoint Measurement m.E. meistens vertretbar, da die

---

[18] Vgl. zur ereignisorietierten Qualitätsmessung z.B. Stauss/Hentschel (1990), S. 232-259.

Beschränkung auf wenige Eigenschaften und die Konkretisierung der Ausprägungen plausibel ist sowie ein deterministischer Zusammenhang zwischen gemessenem Nutzen und dem Kaufverhalten die Entscheidungssituation hinreichend modelliert. Für Diensleistungen mit hoher Verhaltensunsicherheit, hoher Integrativitäg und hohem Induvidualitätsgrad ist das Conjoint Measurement ungeeignet.

5.3. Wettbewerb und Kosten

Die Ableitung gewinnoptimaler Preise erfordert die Berücksichtigung der Kostensituation der betrachteten Unternehmung. Der Conjoint + Cost-Ansatz behandelt nicht die Probleme, die mit einer merkmalsbezogenen Kostenzurechnung behaftet sind. Der Hinweis der Vertreter des Conjoint + Cost-Ansatzes darauf, daß die Daten "aus dem internen Rechnungswesen" stammen[19] genügt keineswegs. Das interne Rechnungswesen stellt in der Praxis merkmalsbezogene Kostendaten nicht bereit.[20]

Fröhling schlägt als Ausweg die Einbindung von Verfahren der Variantenkalkulation in Conjoint + Cost vor.[21] Selbst wenn man merkmalsbezogene Kosten in der Conjoint-Preis-Analyse sinnvoll integrieren kann, erfolgt die Ableitung gewinnoptimaler Preise immer unter der Bedingung konstanter Konkurrenzangebote. Allerdings können preispolitische Maßnahmen Konkurrenzreaktionen auslösen, die im Extremfall zu ruinösem Wettbewerb führen und somit keinesfalls gewinnoptimal nach erfolgter Konkurrenzreaktion für die betrachtete Unternehmung sind. Demzufolge ist es notwendig, daß Konkurrenzreaktionen in die Conjoint-Analyse einbezogen werden.

Aus der Oligopol- und der Spieltheorie weiß man, daß es eine Vielzahl möglicher Reaktionsweisen der Konkurrenz gibt. Ein Konkurrent kann nicht nur mit preispolitschen Maßnahmen, sondern zudem mit der Qualtitätsvariationen reagieren. Stabile Marktlösungen, die zudem noch gewinnoptimal sind, existieren nicht für jede Konstellation auf einem Markt. Das Auffinden eines globalen Gewinnmaximums scheitert an der Komplexität der Realität.

---

19 Vgl. Bauer/Herrmann/Gutschke (1995), S. 1443.

20 Vgl. Fröhling (1994), S. 1150.

21 Vgl. Fröhling (1994), S. 1150.

Daher ist notwendig, wenn man Konkurrenzreaktionen in die Conjoint-Analyse einbezieht, die Komplexität zu reduzieren. Keinesfalls dürfen aufgrund der Komplexität mögliche Konkurrenzreaktionen außer Acht gelassen werden.

Darüber hinaus tritt im Dienstleistungsbereich der Kunde selbst als potentieller Konkurrent auf. Viele Dienstleistungen können durch Eigenleistungen der Kunden ersetzt werden. Die Möglichkeit einer solchen "Make or Buy"-Entscheidung wird in der Conjoint Anlayse vernachlässigt. Insbesondere bei zu teuren einfachen Dienstleistungen ist der jeweilige Anbieter ständig durch die Ausschaltung seiner eigenen Kunden bedroht.

6. Fazit

Die Conjoint Anlayse ist für die Preisanalyse von Dienstleistungen geeignet, wenn folgende Bedingungen erfüllt sind:

1. Es werden Absatzleistungen mit niedriger Integrativität und niedriger Verhaltensunsicherheit untersucht (Typologiefit).

2. Die notwendigerweise geringe Anzahl der modellierten Eigenschaften bestimmt die Kaufentscheidung vollständig.

3. Die Auswahlentscheidung ist mit hohem Involvement der Konsumenten verbunden.

4. Die Auswahlentscheidung ist nicht vom Typ "Make or Buy".

5. Für die Gewinnberechnung erfolgt eine kostentheoretische Anbindung auf Basis merkmalsbezogener Kosten.

6. Das Konkurrenzverhalten wird in die Analyse einbezogen.

Diese Bedingungen sind in den meisten empirischen Studien zum Conjoint Measurement nicht erfüllt. Das Conjoint Measurement hat somit keinen Durchbruch bei der Preisentscheidung erzielt. Es ist allenfalls ein kleiner Schritt getan, um die Preisbereitschaft der Nachfrager besser zu erforschen.

Es muß somit vor der leichtfertigen Anwendung der Conjoint Analyse gewarnt werden. Die empirische Umsetzung wird durch eine Vielzahl an leicht zu bedienenden Programmen erleichtert, die immer ein Rechenergebnis liefern. Diese Programme warnen jedoch nicht vor dem unzweckmäßigen Einsatz der Conjoint Analyse. Ein unzweckmäßiger Einsatz kann erhebliche Falschprognosen von Preisreaktionen der Nachfrager zur Folge haben.

7. Literatur

ADDELMAN, Sidney: Orthogonal Main-effect Plans for Asymmetrical Factorial Experiments, in: Technometrics, 1962, S. 21-46.

ALBERS, Sönke: Gewinnorientierte Neuproduktpositionierung in einem Eigenschaftsraum, in: ZfbF, Jg. 41, 1989, S. 186-209.

ALBERS, Sönke: Schätzung von Nachfragereaktionen auf Variationen des Tarif- und Leistungsangebots im öffentlichen Personennahverkehr, in: Zeitschrift für Verkehrswissenschaft, Jg. 54, 1983, S. 207-230.

BALDERJAHN, Ingo: Der Einsatz der Conjoint-Analyse zur empirischen Bestimmung von Preisresponsefunktionen, in: Marketing ZFP, Jg. 16, 1994, S. 12-20.

BAUER, Hans H./HERRMANN, Andreas/GUTSCHKE, Jens: Grundprobleme und Perspektiven einer gewinnmaximalen Produktgestaltung mittels des Conjoint+Cost-Ansatzes, in: ZfB, Jg. 65, 1995, S. 1443-1451.

BAUER, Hans H./HERRMANN, Andreas/MENGEN, Andreas: Eine Methode zur gewinnmaximalen Produktgestaltung auf der Basis des Conjoint Measurement, in: ZfB, Jg. 64, 1994, S. 81-94.

BÖHLER, Heymo: Beachtete Produktalternativen und ihre relevante Eigenschaften im Kaufentscheidungsprozeß von Konsumenten, in: Meffert, Heribert/Steffenhagen, Hartwig/Freter, Hermann (Hrsg.): Konsumentenverhalten und Information, Wiesbaden 1979, S. 261-289.

CATTIN, Philippe/WITTINK, Dick R.: Commercial Use of Conjoint Analysis: a Survey, in: Journal of Marketing, Vol. 46, 1982, S. 44-53.

DICHTL, Erwin/THOMAS, Uwe: Der Einsatz des Conjoint Measurement im Rahmen der Verpackungsmarktforschung, in: Marketing ZFP, Jg. 8, 1986, Heft 1, S. 27-33.

ENGELHARDT, Werner H./KLEINALTENKAMP, Michael/RECKENFELDERBÄUMER, Martin: Leistungsbündel als Absatzobjekte, in: ZfbF, Jg. 45, 1993, S. 395-426.

FRÖHLING, Oliver: Verbesserungsmöglichkeiten und Entwicklungsperspektiven von Conjoint+Cost, in: ZfB, Jg. 64, 1994, S. 1143-1164.

GAUL, Wolfgang/AUST, Eberhard/BAIER, Daniel: Gewinnorientierte Produktliniengestaltung unter Berücksichtigung des Kundennutzens, in: ZfB, Jg. 65, 1995, S. 835-855.

GREEN, Paul E./KRIEGER, Abba M.: An Application of a Product Positioning Model to Pharmaceutical Products, in: Marketing Science, Vol. 11, 1992, S. 117-132.

GREEN, Paul E./**KRIEGER**, Abba M.: Models and Heuristics for Product Line Selection, in: Marketing Science, Vol. 4, 1985, S. 1-19.

GREEN, Paul E./**RAO**, Vithala R.: Conjoint Measurement for Quantifying Judgmental Data, in: Journal of Marketing Research, Vol. 8, 1971, S. 355-363.

GREEN, Paul E.: On the design of choice experiments involving multifactor alternatives, in: Journal of Consumer Research, 1974, S. 61-68.

KOHLI, R./**SUKUMAR**, R.: Heuristics for Product-Line Design Using Conjoint Analysis, in: Marketing Science, Vol. 36, 1990, S. 1464-1478.

KUCHER, Eckhard/**SIMON**, Hermann: Conjoint-Measurement - Durchbruch bei der Preisentscheidung, in: Harvard manager, 1987, 3. Quartal, S. 28-36.

KUCHER, Eckhard: Scannerdaten und Preissensitivität bei Konsumgütern, Wiesbaden 1985.

MEFFERT, Heribert/**BRUHN**, Manfred: Dienstleistungsmarketing: Grundlagen, Konzepte, Methoden, Wiesbaden 1995.

MEFFERT, Heribert: Marktorientierte Führung von Dienstleistungsunternehmen - neuere Entwicklungen in Theorie und Praxis, in: DBW 1994, S. 519-541.

MÜLLER-HAGEDORN, Lothar/**VORNBERGER**, Eva: Die Eignung der Grid-Methode für die Suche nach einstellungsrelevanten Dimensionen, in: Meffert, Heribert/Steffenhagen, Hartwig/Freter, Hermann (Hrsg.): Konsumentenverhalten und Information, Wiesbaden 1979, S. 185-208.

STAUSS, Bernd/**HENTSCHEL**, Bert: Verfahren der Problementdeckung und -analyse im Qualitätsmanagement von Dienstleistungsunternehmen, in: Jahrbuch der Absatz- und Verbrauchsforschung, 1990, S. 232-259.

WORATSCHEK, Herbert: Die Typologisierung von Dienstleistungen aus informationsökonomischer Sicht, in: "der markt" - Zeitschrift für Absatzwirtschaft und Marketing, 1996, Heft 1, S. 59-71

Mihai Calciu/Franck Delagrande*

ATTRACTIVENESS SENSITIVE VERSUS ATTRACTIVENESS NEUTRAL TERRITORIAL MARKET PARTITIONS

Comparative analysis and congruence measures in the case of bank agencies in an intrabrand context

Contents

---

* Université des Sciences et Technologies de Lille, Ecole Universitaire d'Ingeneur de Lille (EUDIL), Cité Scientifique, F-59655 Villeneuve d'Ascq

1. Introduction

Unlike other service firms which, by definition, lack patent protection for their products, banks have historically had a certain monopoly for the services they offered. This monopoly vanishes under the pressure of deregulation and technology and causes fundamental change in the way retail banks territorially compete.

J.E.G. Bateson (1995) considers that services firms have four basic choices when competing territorially, these choices result from four possible combinations of static and mobile clients and servuction systems.

During a long period of time when regulations and state control limited products, pricing and location, banks had a static servuction system and were **competing for reach** with customers considered mobile within a relatively big urban area.

In France the deregulation process started by liberalising opening and location of agencies, 1966-67 (M. Zollinger, 1992). The approach to competition changed. The servuction system became mobile in order to attract (drain) "static" customers. In those years banks started **competing for geography**. The number of agencies increased from 8000 in 1967 to more than 25000 in 1984 when it seemed to stabilise. France became one of most "bancarised" countries of the world, with less than 1300 inhabitants per bank counter, with more than 99% of the French customers of a credit institution and 96% of them having a cheque account.

This geographic expansion came to saturation in the nineties due to competition (especially the one from non bank actors like insurance companies and big retailers) favoured by further deregulation of prices and products and due to technology.

Credit cards, telephone banking and direct marketing techniques are subtly moving banks towards a situation were **competing for market share** is less dependent on geography.

Under these circumstances banks are feeling the burden of too large and not enough specialised (differentiated) retail networks. They are closing agencies and restructuring the network. To do this, management needs methods and tools to appreciate territorial performance and estimate market areas for their retail networks.

In this paper we apply an attractiveness sensitive method to divide a market territory among the agencies of a bank within a big metropolitan area , using outlet patronage and performance data. We analyse the sensitivity of the method compared to attractiveness neutral methods and suggest some measures of congruence between managerially defined market territories and computed market territories (using our method or other methods).

2. Geometric approximations of market areas

Estimating trade areas is central to sales forecasting, to shop location, relocation or dismantling, to management of retail networks. Many services are highly dependent upon location and available trade area.

There is a variety of methods to estimate trade areas of an outlet. All rely on some measure of accessibility, based on the consumer's travel time, distance, of cost or a combination of these. To evaluate accessibility some use simple geometric approximations based on Euclidean (straight line) measurement on distance others rely on more detailed (and costly) often survey based techniques to register travel patterns and deriving there from the travel cost (time, distance, etc.).

In this paper we focus on geometric approximations that consider the market place as a simple flat surface where the distance is the straight line geometric distance. The methods whose validity and sensitivity we empirically test here rely on such geometric simplifications.

Ghosh and McLafferty (1987) in their review of trade area estimation methods consider three approaches: the **space-ratio method** that uses the relative selling space to determine the market area, the **proximal area method** that uses Dirichlet(1850) or Thiessen and Alter (1911) polygons to compute the nearest distance area around an outlet, and a method based on Reilly's Law of Retail Gravitation.

The **space-sales method** uses initial circular approximations of trade area, subjective or experience based radii equal to expected travel distance to separate the total market area. It then estimates the distribution of buying power within the joint market area using secondary or internal data and finally divides the joint area among outlets proportionally to size of each outlet in the total retail space.

The **proximal area method** defines nearest point polygons around each outlet based on the nearest centre hypothesis of classical central places theory (Christaller, 1935, Lösch 1954). It identifies for each outlet the nearest neighbouring outlets (normally using some nearest point triangulation) and intersects bisectors to the imaginary adjacent lines linking the outlet to the neighbours. In this way the method demarcates the area that is closer to an outlet than to any other.

The method based on **Reilly's Law of Retail Gravitation** is demarcating trade areas for outlets fixing the boundary between two neighbouring outlets there where attractiveness of the two outlets is equal. The formula used was derived by analogy to the Newtonian law of planetary attraction. It states that shoppers from an area between two cities are attracted by each city in direct proportion to the city's population and in inverse proportion of the square of the distance between the shopper's location and the city. We suggest an extended formulation of this relation in formulas (1) and (4).

3. Spatial choice models

Despite their relative empirical success these methods have one major limitation, which is the lack of underlying theory to explain consumer spatial choice behaviour.

Luce's (1959) fundamental choice axiom which states that individuals select among alternatives probabilistically in relation to the utilities offered by each choice, inspired probabilistic models of spatial choice that have gained large acceptance.

Huff (1964, 1966) was the first to suggest a probabilistic formulation of a spatial choice model. His model states that the probability that a customer patronises a facility is proportional to its floor area and inversely proportional to a power of the distance to it. Nakanishi and Cooper's (1974) multiplicative competition interaction (MCI) model replaces the floor area by a product of factors. Attractiveness is now an aggregate of more variables: image of the facility (Stanley and Sewall, 1976), appearance, price, service (Jain and Mahajan, 1979), proximity to other centres (Hansen and Weinberg, 1979), transportation modes (Gautschi 1981). Nakanishi and Cooper's log transformation procedures made it possible to estimate model parameters by ordinary least squares.

4. Introducing attractiveness and probability in the nearest centre approach (the gravity polygons)

In Calciu and Salerno (1996) we introduced a new method for partitioning the market area among outlets, which is sensitive to the distance from consumers to outlets and to some measure for outlet attractiveness. The method computes what we called "gravity polygons" dividing the area into nearest point triangles (Delaunay triangles) uniting the nearest outlets. The same triangulation can be used to compute Voronoi polygons (1907, 1908) , known also as Thiessen, Alter polygons or Dirichlet polygons (in Hilbert and Cohn-Vosson, 1990).

In a **nearest points triangle** or Delaunay (1932, 1934) triangle the attraction limits between two points are fixed on each edge bilaterally. We suggested a general formula for computing the attraction limit between two points A and B of a triangle (limit noted L_{AB}):

$$L_{AB} = \frac{1}{1+\left(\frac{a_B}{a_A}\right)^{\beta}} \qquad (1)$$

where a_A and a_B are attractiveness indexes of the points A and B and β is the elasticity coefficient towards distance. We also suggested that the attractiveness index and the value of β can be fixed using spatial choice models (the gravity model of Reilly 1931, Huff's model 1964, the MCI model of Nakanishi and Cooper, 1974) or a direct utility assignment model.

In this paper we adapt the formula (1) to make it able to accept previously calibrated spatial choice model parameters.

We suggest a probabilistic approach to the attraction limit between two outlets considering that this limit can be fixed on a straight line in point i, where the probability of patronising the outlet A and the one of patronising the outlet B are equal.

To compute the probability of a point i to patronise an outlet j we use Nakanishi, Cooper's (74) generalisation of Huff's (64) model:

$$p_{ij} = \frac{d_{ij}{}^{\lambda}\prod_{k} a_{kj}{}^{\beta k}}{\sum_{j} d_{ij}{}^{\lambda}\prod_{k} a_{kj}{}^{\beta k}} \qquad (2)$$

where:

d_{ij} = distance (or other measure of spatial separation) between consumers in point i and outlet j

λ = parameter reflecting consumer patronage sensitivity du to distance.

a_{kg} = marketing variable k (where k = 1, 2 .. K) for outlet j and

β_k = parameter reflecting consumer patronage sensitivity due to variable k.

so the limit between A and B can be derived form the following expression

$$p_{iA} = \frac{d_{iA}{}^{\lambda}\prod_{k} a_{kA}{}^{\beta k}}{\sum_{j} d_{ij}{}^{\lambda}\prod_{k} a_{kj}{}^{\beta k}} = \frac{d_{iB}{}^{\lambda}\prod_{k} a_{kB}{}^{\beta k}}{\sum_{j} d_{ij}{}^{\lambda}\prod_{k} a_{kj}{}^{\beta k}} = p_{iB} \qquad (3)$$

that symbolises the point i with equal probability of patronising outlet A and B

Here from we obtain the formula for the attraction limit between A and B (L_{AB}) seen from A as a fraction of the distance between A and B:

$$L_{AB} = \frac{1}{1 + \left(\frac{\prod_{k} a_{kA}{}^{\beta k}}{\prod_{k} a_{kB}{}^{\beta k}} \right)^{1/\lambda}} \qquad (4)$$

It is easy to see that the bigger the value of λ the bigger the influence of distance and smaller the effect of marketing variables. For big λs the L_{AB} tends towards 0.5, meaning the middle of the distance between A and B.

For the polygonal partition of the market areas this corresponds to the special case of Voronoi polygons (Figure 1 a.) while gravity polygons are, in this case, a more flexible approach (Figure 1. b).

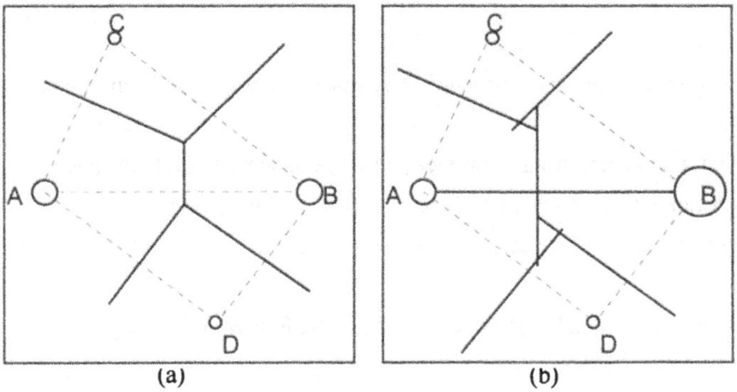

Fig. 1 :. Attraction limit to obtain Voronoi polygons and gravity polygons (a) When attraction limit tends towards 0.5 it intersects the straight line between A and B through the middle and Voronoi polygons are obtained, if attraction limit is variable along AB gravity polygons are obtained.

Using the gravity polygons and this probabilistic definition of the attraction limit we hope to obtain market areas for each outlet, so that relative probability of the consumers within this area and patronising the outlet should be bigger than the probabilities of patronising other surrounding outlets.

In this way managers can obtain quick market area estimations that are sensitive to marketing variables, and use them as tools in managing services retail networks.

In the rest of the paper we calibrate several MCI models using a big matrix of outlet patronage by census tract, in which 36552 flows between the 70 outlets and 5600 census tracts are identified. We test the predictive accuracy of the models and use them to perform sensitivity analysis on market area partitions obtained with the "gravity polygons" method.

To evaluate the market area partitions we suggest some measures for geographic congruence of managerial and computed market areas.

5. Estimating attractiveness parameters

5.1. The data

Our data deal with the retail network of a bank in a large metropolitan area in France. The network consists of 70 bank agencies, (with 1 to 20 employees) and covers an area containing 5600 census tracts representing a population of nearly one million inhabitants (ANNEX 1, Map 1). The agencies were dispersed over the territory with densities proportional to the ones of the population.

The data used in the study include patronage data concerning number of persons from each census tract patronising each agency. Marketing data concerning each agency included total accounts and total active accounts at the moment of the study.

Other attractiveness variables were screened but rejected due to weak relationship with the criterion variable of outlet patronage probability.

In the end the matrix of outlet patronage by tract included 29770 patronage directions (flows) with intensities ranging from 1 to 480 customers per flow. In this way the travel directions towards 60 retail outlets of the bank for 206535 people were identified. This matrix is a valuable means to study clients spatial choice behaviour because it offers complete geographic coverage and gives information about actual outlet patronage and not only intentions.

Unfortunately we had only patronage data for each census tract and no information about actual sales, which could have revealed more accurate flows.

5.2. Multiple choice model specification

Estimation of attractiveness sensitive market area partitions, supposes previous estimation of the sensitivity of patronage to the outlet's location and to nonlocational marketing variables. MCI model are very flexible in incorporating multiple indicators of attractiveness and proximity and computationally easy to estimate.

Two model forms were tested using the available data a simple model, the basic spatial model having as unique explanatory variable distance and an extended spatial model including besides distance a set of available nonlocational variables.

The **basic spatial model** assumes equal attractiveness for each outlet, implying that the outlet's market potential depends uniquely on proximity to consumers. It is expressed by the following relation:

$$p_{ij} = \frac{d_{ij}^{\lambda}}{\sum_{j} d_{ij}^{\lambda}} \qquad (5)$$

where:

d_{ij} = distance (or other measure of spatial separation) between consumers in point i and outlet j

λ = parameter reflecting consumer patronage sensitivity du to distance.

The **extended spatial model** adds nonlocational variables, essentially marketing variables, whose effect on patronage is assumed similar among all outlets.

The model is :

$$p_{ij} = \frac{d_{ij}^{\lambda} \prod_{k} a_{kj}^{\beta k}}{\sum_{j} d_{ij}^{\lambda} \prod_{k} a_{kj}^{\beta k}} \qquad (6)$$

where:

d_{ij} = distance (or other measure of spatial separation) between consumers in point i and outlet j

λ = parameter reflecting consumer patronage sensitivity du to distance.

a_{kg} = marketing variable k (where k = 1, 2 .. K) for outlet j and

β_k = parameter reflecting consumer patronage sensitivity due to variable k.

5.3. Results

The parameters for the two models one without and the other one with marketing variables were estimated. Log-centering transformation was applied to data before estimation by ordinary least squares.

Results in table 1, show that the model with marketing variables fits data better than the one without, proving that marketing variables increase predictive ability of the basic spatial model. Unfortunately the contribution of marketing variables, we could use, was not very significant compared to the one of distance. This proves the dominant role of distance in explaining patronage probability for the retail network of the analysed bank. It shows that the services offered by this network are perceived as proximity services.

The overwhelming role of distance in consumers' spatial choice for this kind of service, makes the main objective of this paper difficult to prove. It isn't easy to show that a method for dividing a market area among outlets, which reflects attractiveness of outlets, the "gravity polygons" is better than one who doesn't (Voronoi polygons), when the market is not sensitive to outlet attractiveness.

	Model without marketing variables	**Model with marketing variables**
Parameters:		
Distance	-0,969193 [a]	-0,996125 [a]
	(0,004931)	(0,004767)
Total new accounts (TAC0693)		0,539773 [a]
		(0,039676)
Total current accounts (TCL0693)		-0,045664 [b]
		(0,024170)
Predictive Accuracy		
Adjusted R^2	0,51380	,55331

[a] $p < 0.001$; [b] $p < 0.05$

Tab. 1: Parameter Estimates for Multiplicative Competitive Interaction

Total credits (TOTPR)	-0,004924 [c]
	(0,011927)
Turnover per Employee	0,004011 [c]
(ENCEMPL)	(0,011525)
Employees	0,002763 [c]
	(0,022597)

[c] rejected variables because not significant

Tab. 2: Estimated parameters for other marketing variables screened but rejected due to week relationship to consumer spatial choice.

6. Polygonal market partition using estimated parameters

6.1. Descriptive analysis of patronage flows

The geographical analysis of the patronage flows using the Geographic Information System (GIS) MapInfo on an PC computer and some self programmed procedures in MapBasic offered an interesting view on travel patterns toward the outlets forming the retail network of the analysed bank. From each census tract customers were patronising an average of 7 outlets, the number of outlets patronised from each tract varying from 1 to 39. The 74 outlets situated in this metropolitan area were attracting people from 5600 census tracts. Each outlet had customers originating from 33 to 1640 census tracts, with an average of 468 census tracts per outlet. The number of customers visiting each outlet varied from 41 to 16213, with an average of 3246 customers per outlet. Although travelling patterns varied a lot some proximity behaviour could already be observed from initial graphical analysis. Statistical analysis of the distribution of travelled distances gave a better insight to patronage behaviour.

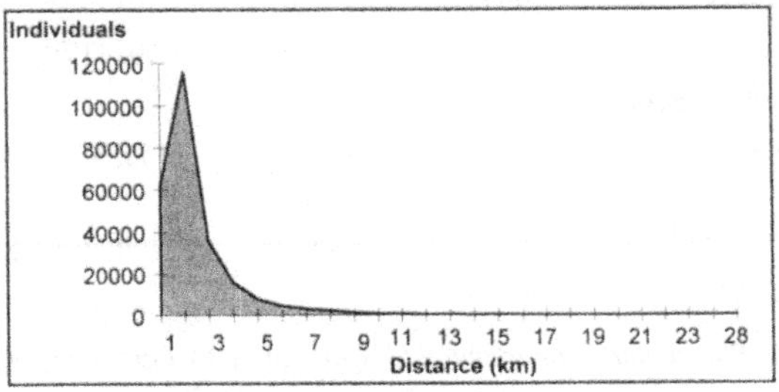

Fig. 2: Distances travelled by individuals to outlets (km)

Figure 2 shows that the majority of the travelled distances is concentrating towards the minimum in a range which varied between 0 and 28 kilometres. The average distance travelled by the 254744 customers first analysed was 1,5 km. Nearly three quarters of the customers (70%) travelled less than 2 km and only 10% of the customers travelled more than 4 km.

The majority of the analysed outlets seemed to drain their part of proximity customers (see ANNEX 1, Map 2 and 3). This means that even if there are big differences between the analysed outlets, and if some of the bigger and more accessible once are attracting customers from remote places, they all act as proximity agents too. Therefore we used them all in our study, although a finer central place theory based analysis should have distinguished and separated proximity agencies from agencies with larger attraction fields and belonging to higher levels in the hierarchy of central places.

The proximity buying behaviour could also be highlighted by applying our attractiveness sensitive market partition method.

6.2. Attractiveness sensitive market partition

The best fitting MCI model was selected to build an attractiveness index based on previously estimated parameters and to compute attractiveness scores for each of 70 outlets taken into account. Attraction limits and "gravity polygons" were computed (ANNEX 1, Maps 4 to 7) applying the formula (4). The algorithm for computing "gravity polygons" was written in C++ programming Language and implemented as a function in a DLL (Dynamic Link Library) and introduced as an option to the MapInfo GIS using MapBasic.

An attractiveness sensitive market partition resulted, consisting of 70 "gravity polygons" out of which 54 were retained for further analysis[1] .

The 54 market areas captured within their borders 12,7% of the total flows and 51,69% of the paths travelled by the 206535 customers. This proved that although more than 87% of the patronage flows were exceeding the frontiers of each market area, in terms of intensity of these flows (number of customers) the gravity polygons were able to circumscribe the

[1] Marginal outlets with their polygonal market areas have been deliberately eliminated, because the polygonal market areas computed for them were to big due to clipping reasons

majority of the paths travelled. Such a good concentration of paths travelled, could be estimated from high correlation of patronage probability with distance that came out from estimating parameters of the MCI Model.

Testing the quality of this attractiveness sensitive partition could be better put in evidence by comparing it to a partition not taking into account other variables than distance. The data of the study show high relationship of patronage probability to distance and low relationship to other variables including marketing variables. This makes it difficult to prove the advantage of our method. Despite this situation we still try to find some evidence of better behaviour of the "gravity polygons" method compared to methods neutral to attractiveness.

6.3. Comparison to a market partition neutral to attractiveness

"Gravity polygons", when sensitivity to distance is high, converge toward Voronoi polygons that fix attraction limit between two neighbouring outlets at the middle. At first view, in the analysed case, Voronoi polygons seemed to perform slightly better than "gravity polygons" in capturing patronage flows and travel paths. But the difference is really very small, Voronoi polygons circumscribe 13,05% of the total flows and 51,74% of the individual travel paths compared to 12,68% of the patronage flows and 51,68% of the travel paths for the "gravity polygons".

Despite this very slight difference we can prove that gravity polygons are more efficient.
First, compared to their surface they capture more paths. If the surface filled by the two partitions was the same (the surface of the Voronoi polygons partition is 1,05255 bigger than the "gravity polygons" partition) then Voronoi polygons would capture only 12,04% of the flows and 49,15% of the individual paths compared to the 12,68% of the flows and 51,68% of the individual paths of the "gravity polygons" (ANNEX 1, Maps 8 to 11).

Second, analysing the flow map (ANNEX 1, Maps 4 to 7) several particular situations appear were the superiority of "gravity polygons" is obvious while the opposite cant be observed.
Third, the method we chose to compute "gravity polygons" is deliberately avoiding overlapping of market territories, by leaving free space between market areas that is no man's land (see Figure 1 b) and for the partition of which we didn't suggest a solution yet. Finding a solution for dividing these territories between neighbouring gravity polygons using similar

attractiveness sensitive rules, could increase the capacity of this partition to capture the main flows.

Applying the "gravity polygons" method to data from other retail networks or other services or industries where customers' spatial behaviour is more sensitive to marketing variables would probably be useful in showing the advantages of this method.

6.4. Measuring congruence of market areas

Affecting market territory to outlets is an important decision when managing a retail network. Attractiveness sensitive market partitioning methods could be a useful managerial tool for affecting territory and evaluating territorial performance.

In an intrabrand network, partition of market areas among outlets is often needed, in order to control the local impact of the outlets and their proximity performance. Therefore it is desirable to define market areas around each outlets that hopefully don't overlap. Avoiding overlapping is not so important when performing bulky quantitative analysis. The extent of overlapping could become crucial, in qualitative analysis, when taking into account each outlet's specialisation and level in a hierarchy of outlets:

Outspread market areas, obviously including the market areas of several other outlets testify different travel paths, people considering to visit that outlet on their travel path to work, on their shopping tours in the centre of towns, or on the main roads. Such outlets belong to a different hierarchical level within a retail network and should be treated separately from outlets with spatially concentrated market areas which rely heavily on customers proximity behaviour. This hierarchical separation is consistent with central place theory, the "best known and most widely accepted" (Mason and Mayer 1981) theory of the location and spacing of retail centres.

When affecting sales territory to outlets management should consider the size of the catchment area and the distance the customers are willing to travel to use the service and distinguish between proximity outlets and higher level outlets.

The simplest way of affecting market areas to proximity outlets in the analysed case was to affect the census tracts to the outlet that attracted the main flow of customers. A managerial market partition was obtained with quite contiguous territories for each outlet.

In order to compare managerially decided market partitions among outlets to attractiveness sensitive market partitions obtained by our method and to asses their consistency, we suggest a market area congruence indicator.

The indicator uses a confusion matrix approach. The lines of the matrix represent the market areas of the actual partition (managerial partition) and the columns represent the market areas of the computed partition. The method counts the number of census tracts falling within each couple of market areas (managerial and computed), filling the corresponding cases of the matrix. The entries on the diagonal of the matrix represent the hit rate or the proportion of the coincidentally included census tracts in both definitions of the market areas for the same outlet. The ratio of the sum of hit rates to the number of census tracts gives an overall measure of congruence of the two partitions.

We developed a MapBasic program to implement this indicator and applied it to a sample area. 55% congruence was obtained when a territorial inclusion operator was used to asses that one census tract belonged to a certain area. Congruence was much higher when only census tract's centroid inclusion into area was considered. This is logically obvious because in the first case all marginal census tracts that were not entirely within the tested area were excluded, lowering the hit rate.

7. Conclusions

In this paper a probabilistic formulation of the attraction limit between two neighbouring retail outlets has been suggested by integrating probabilistic spatial choice models. This attraction limit has then been used to obtain an attractiveness sensitive territorial market partition among retail outlets of a bank using the gravity polygons method.
Attractiveness sensitive and attractiveness neutral territorial market partition methods (Gravity polygons versus Voronoi polygons) have been compared, using a large database, including a big outlet patronage matrix.

The lack of pertinent marketing variables to describe outlet attractiveness and the overwhelming role of distance in explaining patronage behaviour of individuals made it difficult to prove the overall superiority of the attractiveness sensitive method. However in many individual situations the better performance of "gravity polygons" in defining the catchment area of an outlet was largely shown.

The geographic congruence measure we suggested, applied to compare attractiveness sensitive to attractiveness neutral market partitions or to managerial market partitions can help to reveal inconsistencies in managerial partitions or to reveal inconsistencies in the qualitative separation of proximity outlets from outlets higher in the retail hierarchy.

The results show that some additional empirical and theoretical support is needed in order to turn gravity polygons into an efficient territorial market partitioning method. Empirical support should be found in patronage data for retail outlets from other services or industries. Some additional theoretical elements from the central places theory, especially those concerning the hierarchy of central places can be better integrated in this approach. Clustering retail outlets on consumer patronage behaviour could reveal different levels in the hierarchies of retail outlets e.g. rural and urban outlets and the urban outlets could also be separated in proximity outlets and central outlets. Calibrating separate spatial choice models for each group of outlets would probably reveal different elasticities with distance and different priorities for marketing variables, confirming retail network specialisation. In this way better territorial market partition could probably be obtained, where higher level retail outlets would contain within their catchment area the sales territory of several lower level outlets.

8. References

Bateson, J.E.G. (1995): Managing Services Marketing. Text and Readings, 3rd Edition

Calciu, M.; **Salerno, F.** (1996): A new Approach to Spatial Management of Retail Networks, based on German School's Central Place Theory. Application to Bank Location, Working paper, First French-German Workshop on Services Marketing, Innsbruck, 2.28-3.1.1996

Christaller, W. (1935): Die zentralen Orte in Süddeutschland, Jena, G. Fischer

Craig, C. Samuel; **Ghosh,** Avijit; **McLafferty,** Sara (1984): Models of Retail Location Process: A Review, in: Journal of Retailing, Vol.60, No.1, Spring, S. 5-36

Delaunay, B. (1932): Neue Darstellung der geometrischen Krystallographie, in: Zeitschrift für Krystallographie, Vol.84, S.109-149

Delaunay, B. (1934): Sur la sphère vide, in: Izv.Akad.Nauk SSSR Otdelenie Matemat.Estestvennyka Nauk Vol.7, S.793-800

Dirichlet, G.L. (1850): Über die Reduktion der positiven quadratischen Formen mit drei unbestimmten ganzen Zahlen, in: Journal für angewandte Mathematik, Vol. 40, S.216

Gautschi, D.A. (1981): Specification of Patronage Models for Retail Center Choice, in: Journal of Marketing Research, Vol. 18, S.162-174

Ghosh, A.; **McLafferty**, S.L. (1987): Location Strategies for Retail and Service Firms, Lexington, MA: Lexington Books, S.64-88

Hansen, M.M.; **Weinberg** C.B. (1979): Retail Market Share in a Competitive Environment, in: Journal of Retailing, Vol. 55 (Spring) , S.37-46

Hilbert, S.; **Cohn-Vosson,** S. (1990): Geometry and Imagination, Chelsea Publishing Company, New York 1990

Huff, D.L. (1964): Defining and Estimating a Trade Area, in: Journal of Marketing, Vol. 28: S.34-38

Huff, D.L. (1966): A Programmed Solution for Trading for Approximating an Optimum Retail Location, in: Land Economics, Vol. 42, S.293-303

Huff, D.L. (1981): Retail Location Theory, in: R. Stampf et E. Hirschman (Hrsg.), Theory in Retailing: Traditional and Non Traditional Sources, Chicago: American Marketing Association

JAIN, A.K.; **MAHAJAN,** V.(1979): Evaluating the Competitive Environment in Retailing Using Multiplicative Competitive Interactive Models, in: Sheth (Hrsg.) Research in Marketing, Greenwich 1979

LÖSCH, A. (1954): The Economics of Location, New Haven, Conn.: Yale University Press

LUCE, R. (1959): Individual Choice Behaviour, John Wiley & Sons, New York 1959

MASON, J.B.; **MAYER,** M.L. (1981): Modern Retailing Theory and Practice, Piano, Tex, Business Publication

NAKANISHI, M.; **COOPER,** L.G. (1974): Parameter Estimate for Multiplicative Interactive Choice Model: Least Squares Approach, in: Journal of Marketing Research, Vol.11, S.303-311

REILY, W.J. (1931): The Law of Retail Gravitation, Knickerbocker Press, New York 1931

STANLEY, T.J.; **SEWALL,** M.A. (1976): Image Inputs to a Probabilistic Model: Predicting Retail Potential, in: Journal of Marketing, Vol.40, S.48-53

THIESSEN, A.H.; **ALTER,** J.C. (1911): Precipitation Averages for Large Areas, in: Monthly Weather Review, Vol. 39, S.1082-1084

VORONOI, G. (1907): Nouvelles applications des paramètres continus à la théorie des formes quadratiques. Premier memoire: Sur quelques propriètes des formes quadratiques parfaites, in: J. Angew. Math. Vol. 133, S.97-178

VORONOI, G. (1908): Nouvelles applications des paramètres continus à la théorie des formes quadratiques. Deuxième mémoire: Recherches sur les parallélloédres primitifs, in: J. Angew. Math. Vol. 134, S.167-171

ZOLLINGER, M. (1992): "Marketing bancaire", Eyrolles, Paris 1992, S.66-67

9. ANNEX 1

Maps and tables illustrating the analysis of market areas and patronage flows in a metropolitan area

CONTENTS

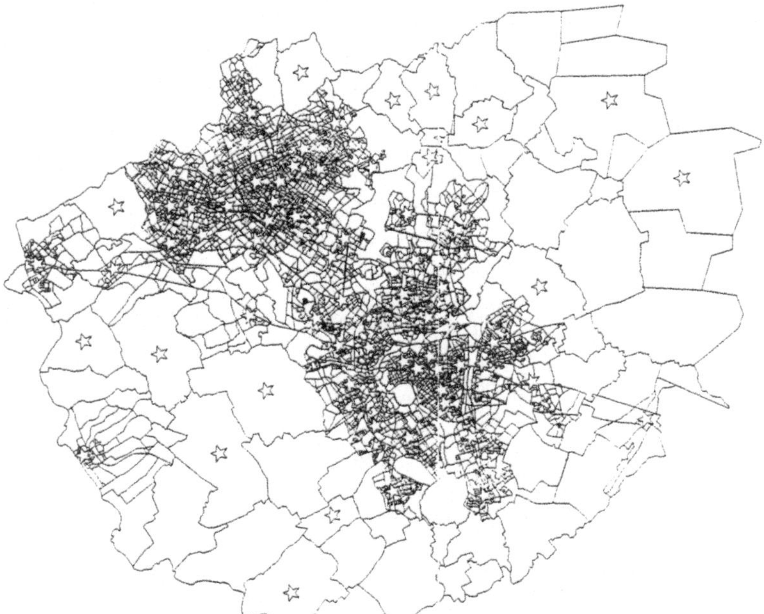

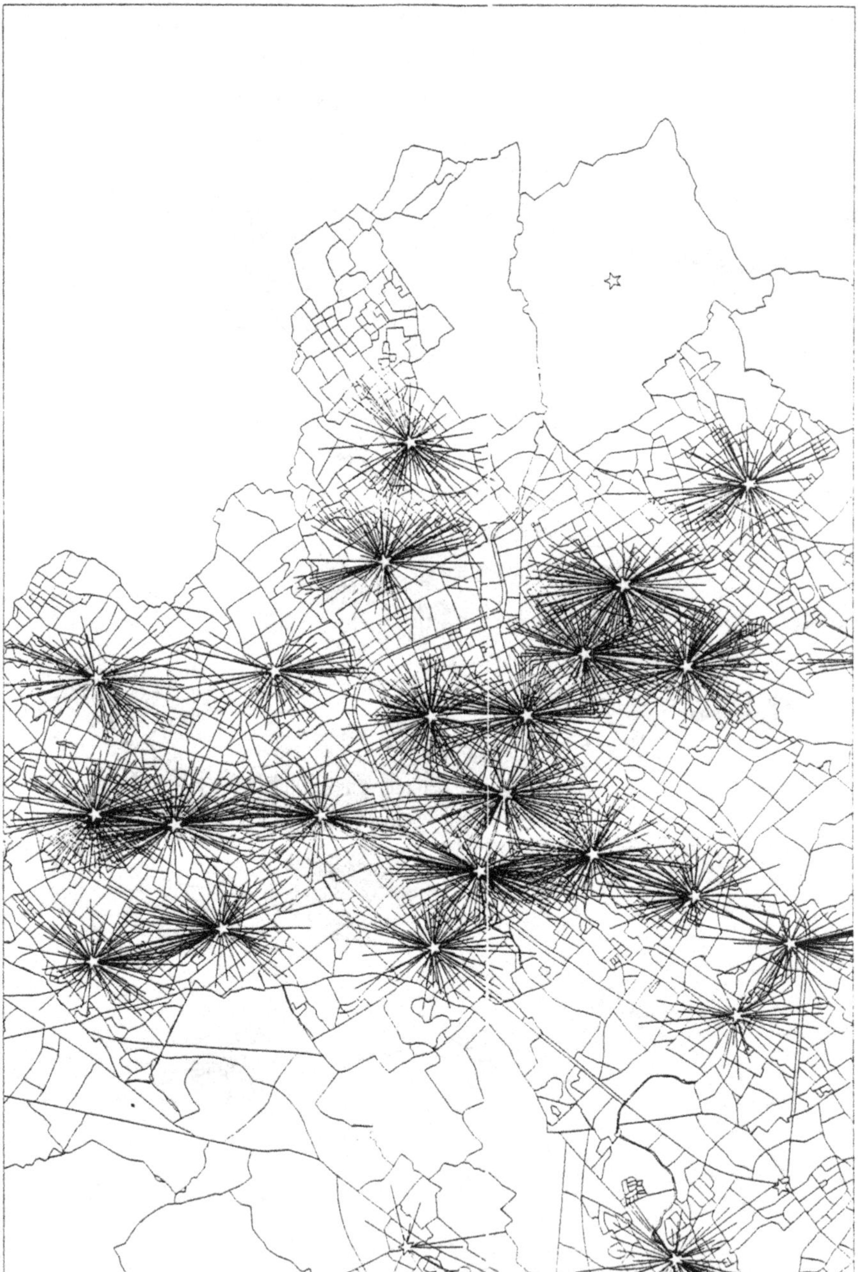

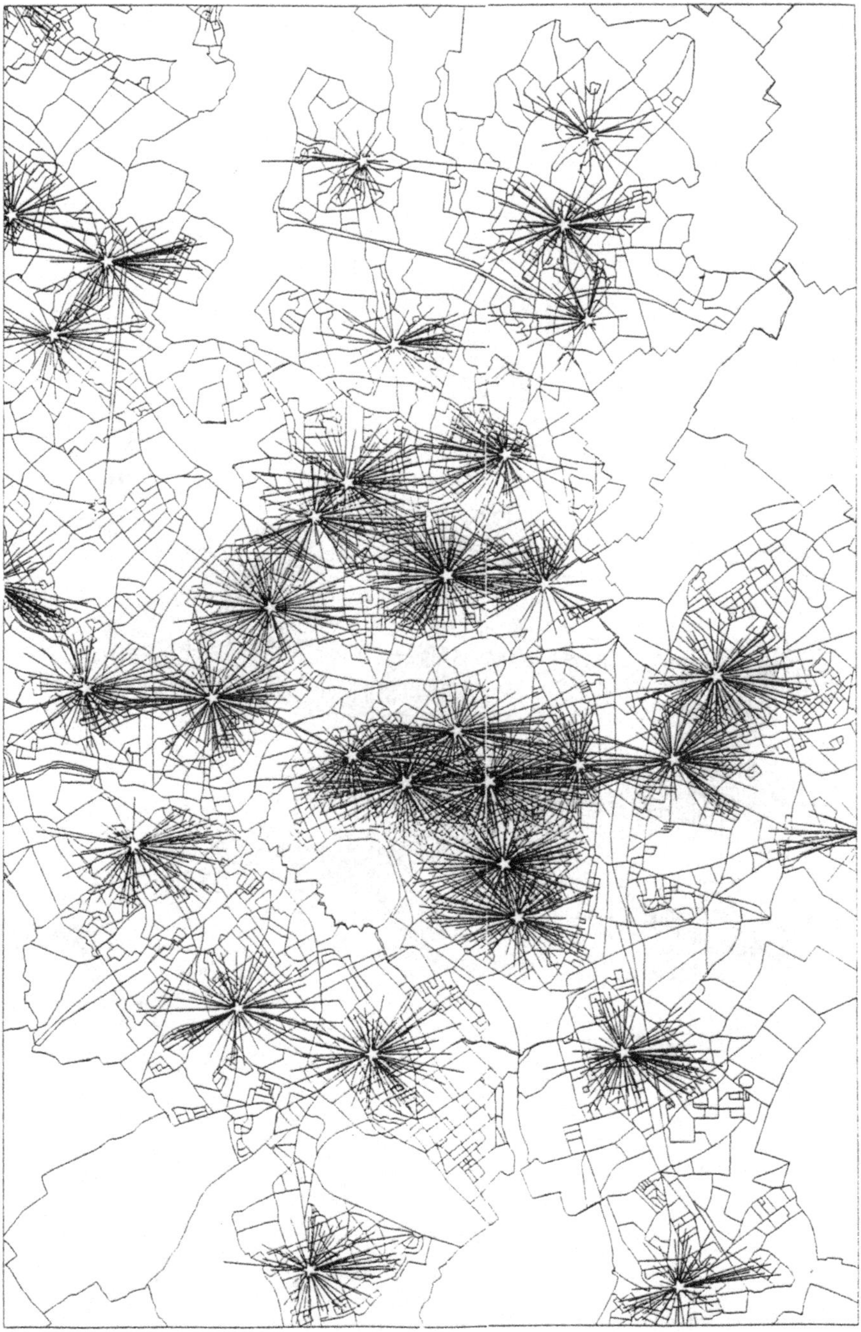

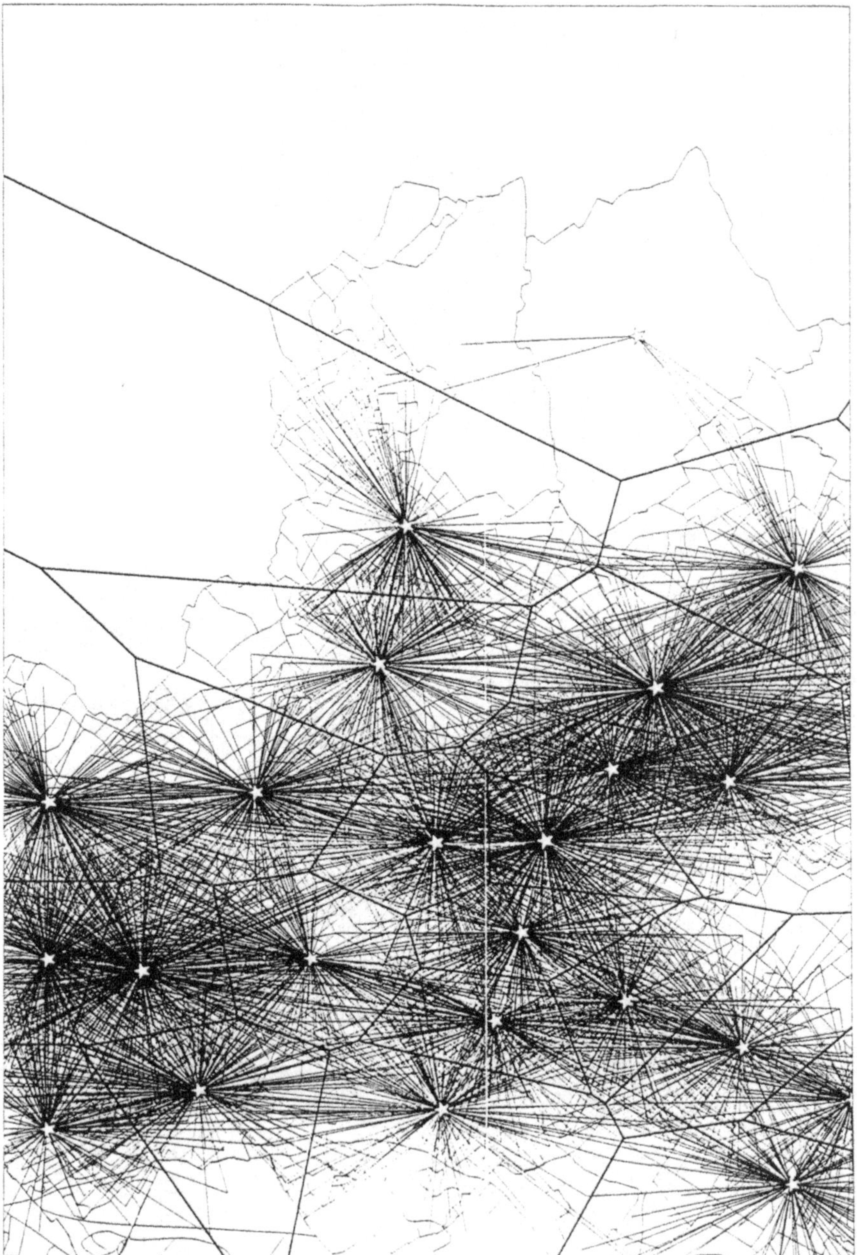

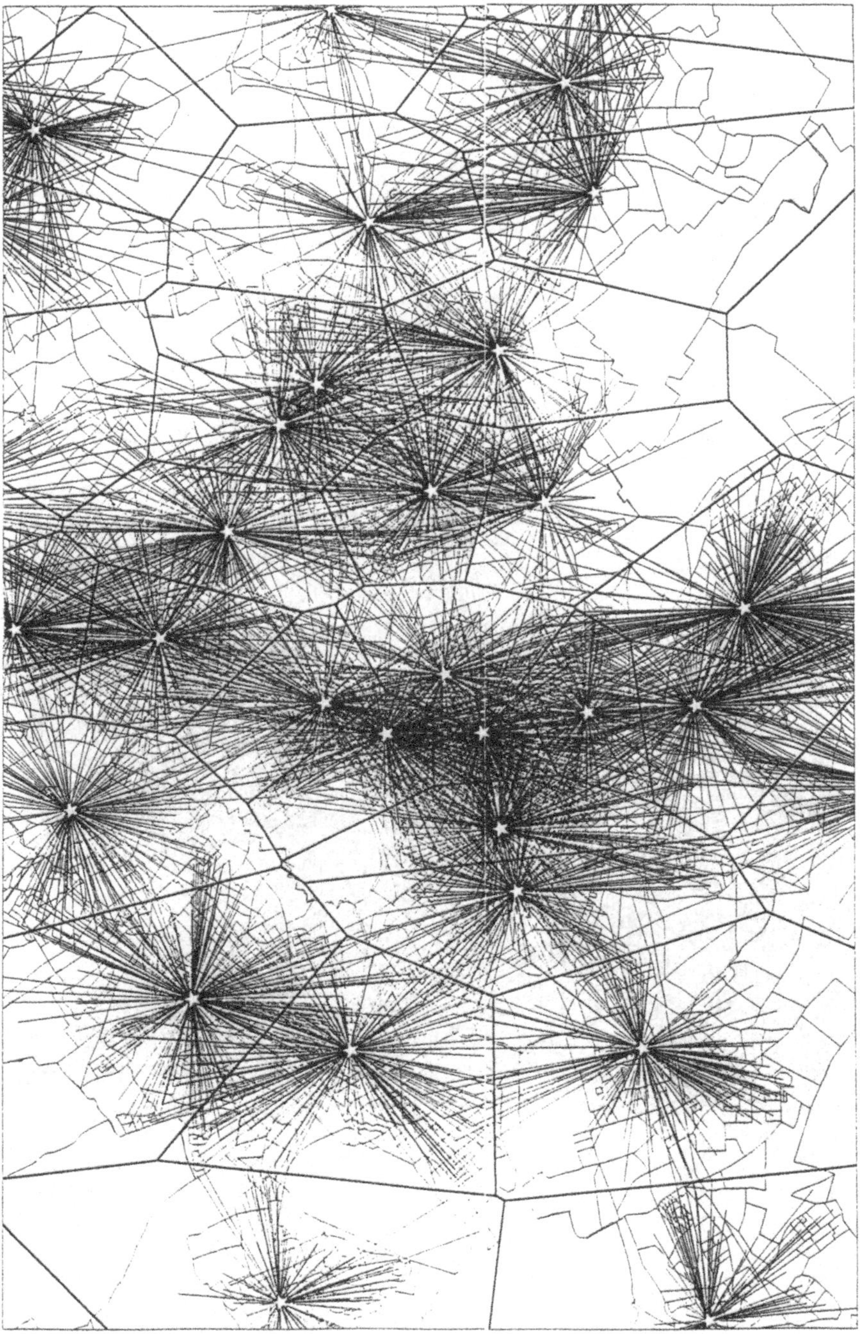

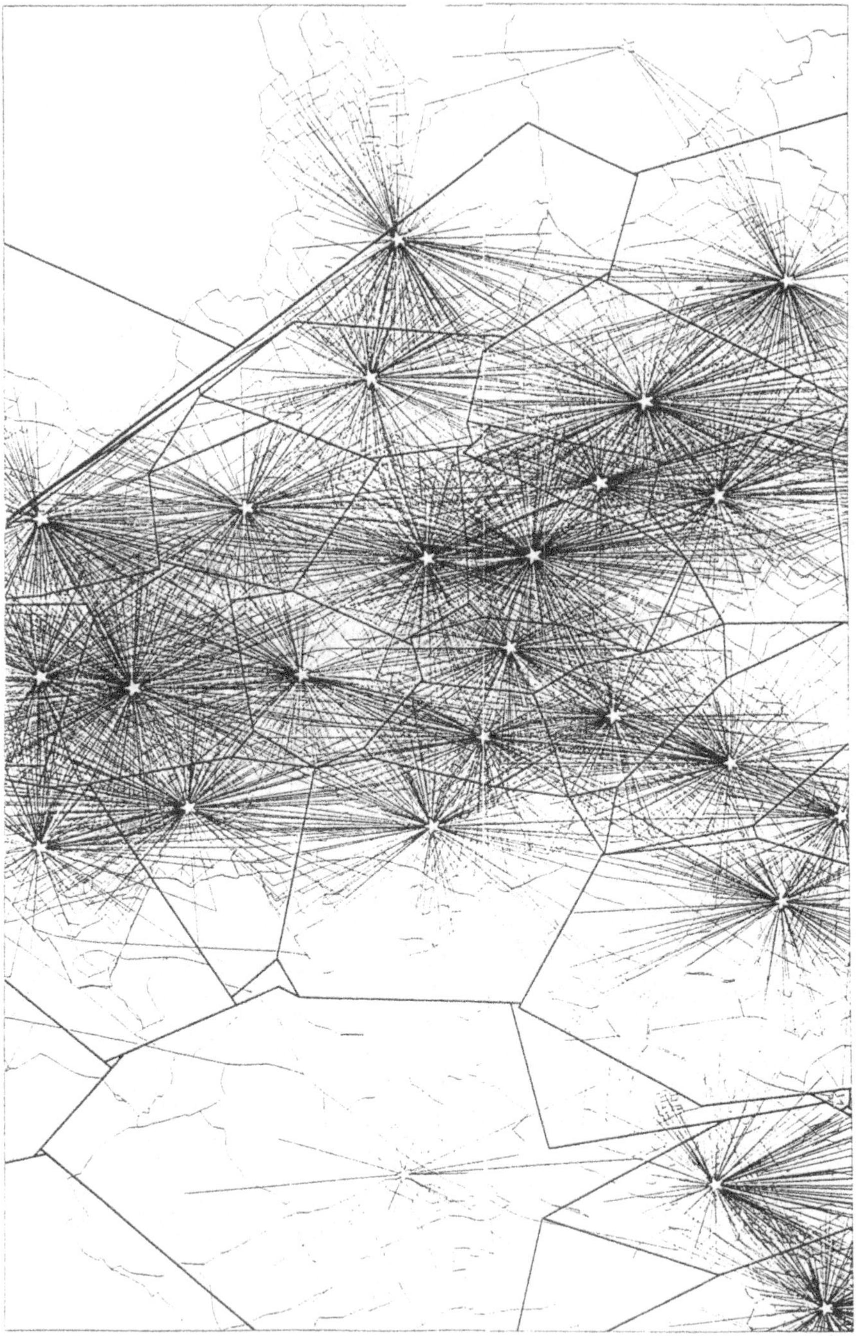

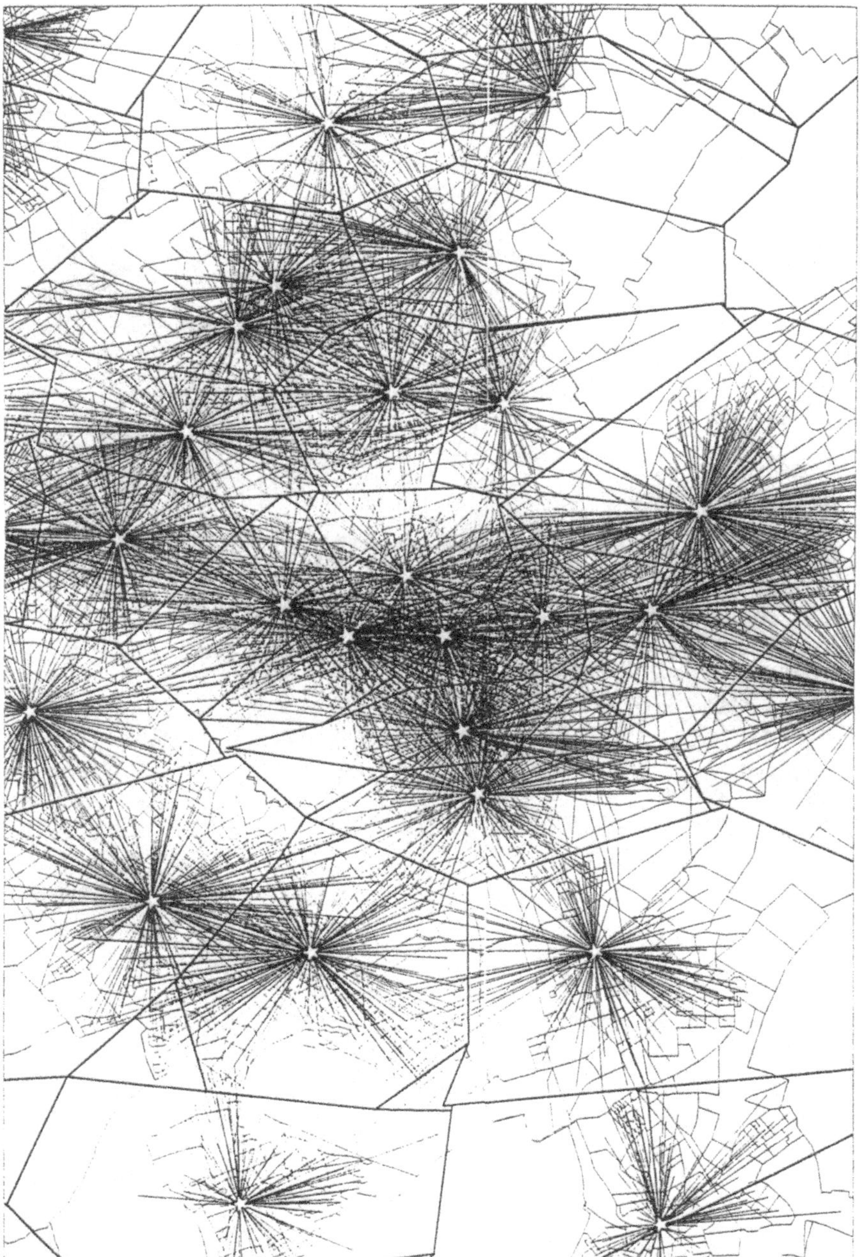

PJTOGRVO

AGE	FLOWS	CLIENTS	VOROFLOW	VOROCLIENT	GRAVIFLOW	GRAVICLIEN	Grav_Are	VoroArea	Voro/Grav_Area	PJVOROFLOW	PJGRAVIFLO	AdjPJVorFl	PJVOROCLIE	PJGRAVICLI	AdjPJVorCli
802	1181	3440.00	58	710.00	59	698.00	0.7186	0.689	0.9588	5.00	5.08	5.30019	20.64	20.29	21.53
803	804	3194.00	88	2002.00	80	1883.00	1,10906	1,39954	1,26192	14,57	13,25	10,496	82,68	58,33	49,67
811	813	3605.00	114	2064.00	123	2219.00	0,84299	0,73709	0,87438	18,60	20,07	22,9481	57,25	61,55	65,48
812	675	6577.00	160	4920.00	157	4897.00	2,01633	1,86453	0,92471	23,70	23,26	25,1529	74,81	74,46	80,90
813	770	3541.00	103	1357.00	97	1325.00	0,60518	0,8286	1,36919	13,38	12,60	9,20061	38,32	37,42	27,99
815	425	3326.00	35	1197.00	31	1079.00	0,60245	0,57654	0,957	8,24	7,29	7,62189	35,99	32,44	37,61
816	1411	6602.00	86	1189.00	78	1094.00	0,45631	0,54895	1,20301	6,09	5,53	4,59512	18,01	16,57	14,97
817	546	4906.00	97	3561.00	98	3631.00	0,61704	0,78496	0,96073	17,70	17,88	18,6141	72,58	74,01	75,55
818	582	6286.00	85	2670.00	85	2823.00	1,41249	1,63437	1,15708	14,60	14,60	12,6221	42,48	44,91	38,71
819	498	5630.00	123	4089.00	126	3953.00	4,16878	3,37147	0,80874	24,70	25,30	31,2846	72,63	70,21	89,80
820	484	4544.00	121	3732.00	122	3762.00	3,99235	3,94572	0,98832	25,00	25,21	25,5045	82,13	82,79	83,10
821	487	4308.00	81	2192.00	74	2023.00	0,8482	0,8728	1,029	16,63	15,20	14,7668	50,68	46,96	49,45
822	716	2433.00	50	1063.00	43	997.00	0,60166	0,69742	1,15916	6,98	6,01	5,18097	43,69	40,98	37,69
823	557	5778.00	168	4187.00	174	4724.00	2,33824	2,31539	0,99023	30,16	31,24	31,5471	72,12	81,76	72,83
825	358	3151.00	105	2302.00	97	2025.00	2,16942	2,31367	1,06649	29,33	27,09	25,4057	73,06	64,27	68,50
827	442	2556.00	79	1556.00	77	1530.00	1,48458	1,37971	0,92936	17,87	17,42	18,7449	60,88	59,86	65,50
828	353	2416.00	60	1672.00	59	1643.00	0,97617	0,83968	0,86036	17,00	16,71	19,4262	69,21	68,00	80,44
829	389	3758.00	95	2606.00	83	2466.00	2,40435	4,52841	1,88342	24,42	21,34	11,3287	69,38	65,65	36,84
830	383	2064.00	61	1271.00	55	1174.00	1,04745	1,27124	1,21365	15,93	14,36	11,8323	61,58	56,88	50,74
831	454	3090.00	90	2097.00	86	2046.00	1,47797	1,57341	1,06458	19,82	18,94	17,7937	67,86	66,21	63,75
832	406	3121.00	79	2292.00	72	2233.00	0,90038	0,94935	1,05438	19,46	17,73	16,6194	73,44	71,55	69,65
840	401	1207.00	19	277.00	17	253.00	4.58145	5,59511	1,22661	4,74	4,24	3,4562	22,95	20,96	18,71
841	420	1745.00	77	917.00	60	808.00	0,26918	0,53482	1,84944	18,33	14,29	7,72434	52,55	46,19	28,41
801	824	4003.00	84	2083.00	85	2090.00	1,23799	1,14802	0,92733	10,26	10,42	11,233	52,04	52,21	56,11
802	412	3200.00	85	2399.00	82	2392.00	0,59532	0,7657	1,2862	20,63	19,90	15,4742	74,97	74,75	58,29
804	228	840.00	22	297.00	17	252.00	0.8848	1,75595	1,98458	9,65	7,46	3,75705	46,41	39,38	23,38
805	431	945.00	22	179.00	17	126.00	0.63914	1,16681	1,39049	5,10	3,94	2,83664	18,94	13,33	13,62
810	155	1338.00	38	1117.00	34	1069.00	1,31687	2,1499	1,63258	24,52	21,94	13,4361	83,48	79,90	51,14
820	1840	12205.00	49	1156.00	76	2018.00	0,72795	0,53037	0,72858	2,99	4,63	6,36049	9,47	16,53	13,00
821	831	6460.00	117	3226.00	139	3519.00	1,29375	1,0703	0,82729	14,08	16,73	20,219	49,94	54,47	60,36
822	745	5006.00	108	2928.00	106	2900.00	0,73907	0,70396	0,95249	14,50	14,23	14,9379	58,49	57,93	61,41
823	526	2306.00	70	950.00	44	750.00	0,33213	0,56752	1,70872	13,31	8,37	4,89549	42,50	32,52	24,87
826	520	3715.00	129	2365.00	112	2093.00	0,96561	1,17497	1,21682	24,81	21,54	17,7006	63,66	56,34	52,32
827	451	2646.00	81	1596.00	57	1189.00	0,3237	0,53382	1,64852	17,96	12,64	7,66683	60,32	44,94	36,59
836	403	3503.00	51	2165.00	47	1892.00	3,70447	2,17297	0,58658	12,66	11,66	19,8822	61,80	54,01	105,36
838	479	4821.00	103	3625.00	102	3695.00	2,87886	2,20292	0,76521	21,50	21,29	27,8283	75,19	76,64	98,26
848	135	353.00	26	117.00	22	106.00	3,59324	4,83317	1,34507	19,26	16,30	12,1155	33,14	30,03	24,64
863	440	3610.00	59	2106.00	65	2232.00	1,43374	1,40948	0,98308	13,41	14,77	15,027	58,34	61,83	59,34
865	362	3562.00	50	2761.00	51	2764.00	1,72069	1,6042	0,9323	13,81	14,09	15,1114	77,08	77,18	82,68
866	402	1118.00	40	343.00	39	330.00	1,08756	1,1787	1,0838	9,95	9,70	8,95135	30,68	29,52	28,31
867	525	2900.00	24	1311.00	23	1310.00	1,34293	1,9129	1,42442	4,57	4,38	3,0756	45,21	45,17	31,74
950	407	2050.00	64	1310.00	61	1247.00	0,45599	0,56767	1,24492	15,72	14,99	12,0391	63,90	60,83	51,33
951	423	3866.00	87	2916.00	84	2676.00	1,99472	2,15591	1,08081	20,57	19,86	18,3734	75,43	69,22	69,79
954	413	3425.00	25	2245.00	26	2246.00	5,14276	4,71071	0,91599	6,05	6,30	6,87279	65,55	65,58	71,56
956	207	339.00	1	11.00	1	11.00	6,04749	5,93668	0,98171	0,48	0,48	0,49209	3,24	3,24	3,31
957	490	4015.00	69	2564.00	71	2573.00	2,06487	2,07693	1,00584	14,08	14,49	14,4057	63,86	64,08	63,49
959	401	4913.00	31	3513.00	30	3506.00	4,38106	3,9657	0,90519	7,73	7,48	8,26487	71,50	71,36	78,99
961	590	3101.00	75	1693.00	58	1585.00	0,75986	0,89015	1,17146	12,71	9,83	8,39184	54,60	51,44	46,60
962	470	3301.00	71	2068.00	53	1750.00	1,02006	1,26704	1,24212	15,11	11,28	9,07849	62,59	53,01	50,39
965	471	4677.00	202	6680.00	90	3209.00	0,80689	0,91954	1,13962	42,89	19,11	16,7673	142,83	68,61	125,33
969	1261	16213.00	78	3150.00	124	4876.00	1,04476	0,64741	0,61968	6,19	9,63	15,6687	19,43	28,84	31,35
Tota	*27579*	*########*	*3875*	*106805,00*	*3649*	*103480,00*	*84,58*	*89,27*	*1,05551*	*14,05*	*13,23*	*12,5353*	*54,62*	*52,92*	*51,75*
Min	135	339.00	1	11.00	1	11.00	0,29	0,53		0,48	0,48	0,49	3,24	3,24	3,31
Max	1640	16213.00	202	6680,00	174	4897.00	6,05	5,94		42,89	31,24	31,55	142,83	82,79	125,33
Mea	541	3833,86	76	2094,22	72	2029,02	1,66	1,75			14,16				
	Non coincident polygons														
801	1044.00	3801			64.00	1105,00	0,32062		1		6,130268199			29.07	
835	130	234.00	8.00	46.00				12,8414	1	6,153846154			19.66		
845	57	78.00	2,00	4.00				10,0495	1	3.50877193			5,13		
808	412	839.00			12.00	46.00	2,9608	1,92969	1		2,912621359			5.48	
963	548	6056.00			49,00	2124.00	0,70548		1		8.941605838			35.07	
Tota	*2191*	*11008*	*10*	*50*	*125*	*3275*			*1*	*0,46*	*5,71*		*0,45*	*29,75*	*0,45*
Tota	28770	206535	3885	106855	3774	106755			1,05255	13,05	12,68	12,0443	51,74	51,69	49,15

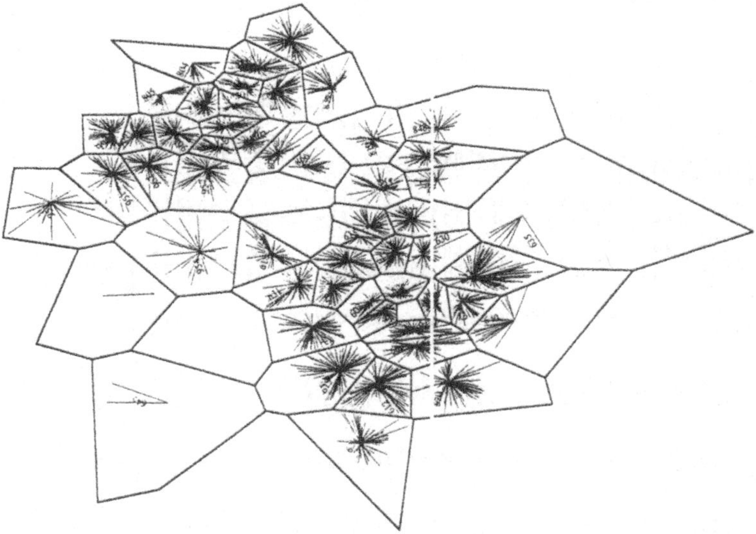

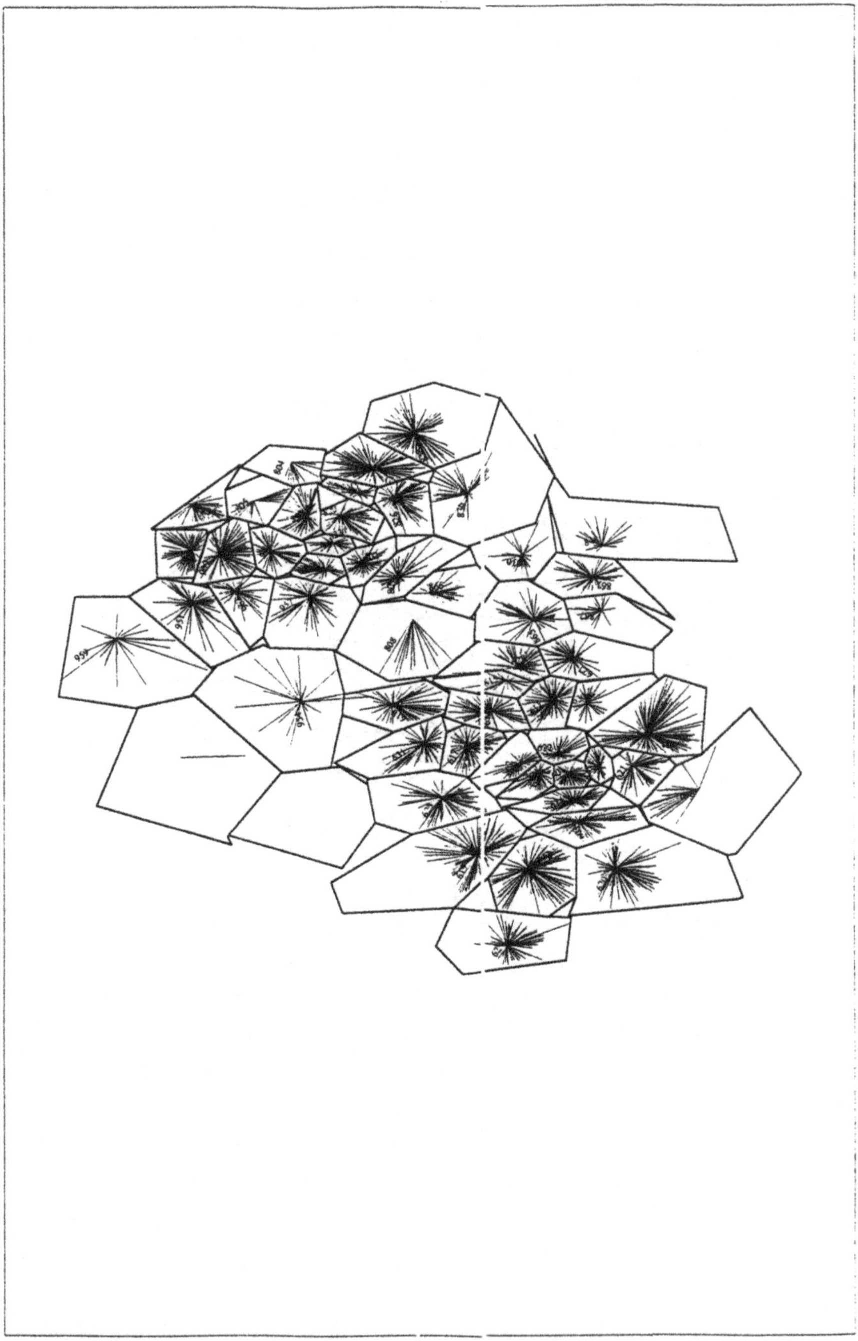

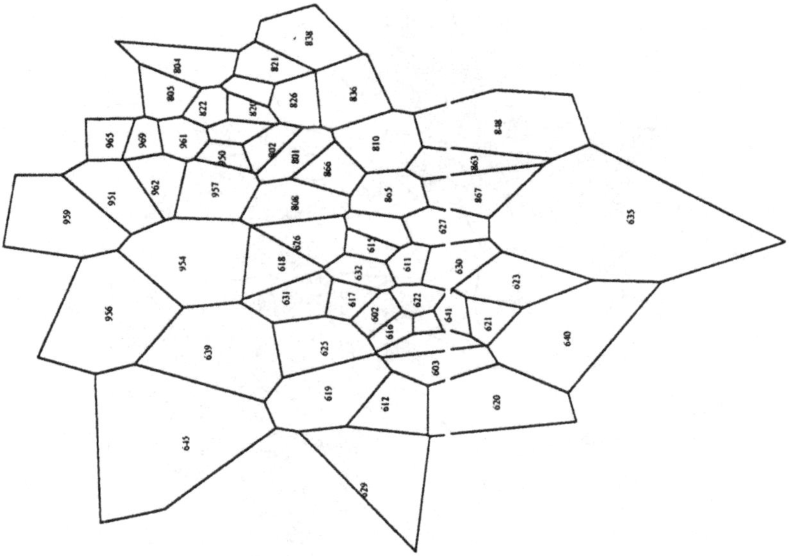
629
645
612
619
620
603
625
639
640
621
616
641
602
617
631
956
623
622
630
611
632
618
954
626
627
635
959
867
865
808
957
962
951
863
866
801
802
810
961
969
965
848
822
836
826
803
821
804
838

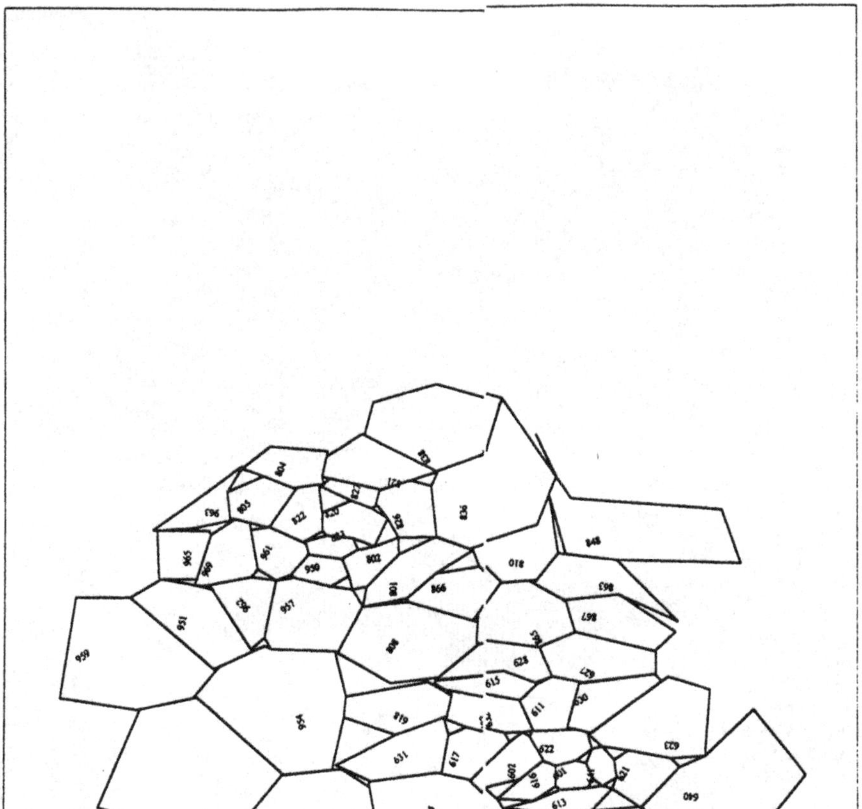

Michael Paul/Stephan Paul*

ILLOYALITÄT ALS CHANCE?

Zu alternativen Wegen des Geschäftsbeziehungsmanagements im Privatkundengeschäft von Banken und deren Anforderungen an das Controlling

Inhalt

* Dipl.-Ök. Michael Paul ist wissenschaftlicher Mitarbeiter am Lehrstuhl für Angewandte Betriebswirtschaftslehre III (Marketing), Dr. Stephan Paul wissenschaftlicher Assistent am Lehrstuhl für Angewandte Betriebswirtschaftslehre II (Finanzierung und Kreditwirtschaft), Ruhr-Universität Bochum. - Die beiden Autoren widmen diesen Beitrag ihren Eltern und ihrem Bruder mit Dank für die vielfältige Unterstützung ihrer bisherigen Arbeit.

1. Einleitung

Widmete man sich im Spätsommer 1996 bei der Urlaubslektüre den Hochglanzmagazinen der überregionalen Zeitungen, so begegnete man einem freundlichen Herrn, der die Leser aufforderte:

„Bleiben Sie bei Ihrer Bank. Aber testen Sie unsere Immobilienfinanzierung. Sicher gibt es gute Gründe, Ihrer Bank die Treue zu halten. Mindestens ebenso gute Argumente sprechen aber dafür, in Sachen Baugeld mit der Vereinsbank fremdzugehen."[1]

Vergegenwärtigt man sich, daß es seit Jahrzehnten ein Kernelement der Marketing-Aktivitäten deutscher Kreditinstitute ist, die Loyalität ihrer Kunden zu stärken, so kann nur der erste Teil der Botschaft (und auch nur vordergründig) beruhigen („Bleiben Sie..."). Die unverblümte Animation zum Seitensprung („in Sachen Baugeld ... fremdgehen") setzt dagegen bewußt auf die Illoyalität bestimmter Nachfragergruppen und schlägt damit einen für die Bankenwerbung bislang ungewohnten Ton an.

Im folgenden wird die Theorie der Bankloyalität kurz rekapituliert (2.) und sodann gefragt, ob empirische Hinweise für eine Auflösung traditioneller Bindungen bestehen (3.). Im Anschluß daran werden die Geschäftsbeziehungen im Privatkundengeschäft der Banken detaillierter beleuchtet und drei Haupttypen von Bankkunden herausgearbeitet (4.). Nach der Diskussion der Möglichkeiten der Erfolgsmessung bei Geschäftsbeziehungen (5.) werden aus der Kundentypologisierung resultierende, strategische Stoßrichtungen für das Geschäftsbeziehungsmanagement vorgestellt, die eine entsprechende Ausgestaltung des Bank-Controlling erfordern (6.). In diesen Zusammenhang eingebrachte, aktuelle Beispiele aus der Kreditwirtschaft (7.) lassen daran zweifeln, daß die Planung, Steuerung und Kontrolle der Geschäftsbeziehungen bereits hinreichend systematisch erfolgt.

2. Zur Theorie der Bankloyalität

Vor knapp 30 Jahren wurde aus der Theorie der Markentreue (Brand Loyality) von SÜCHTING die Theorie der Bankloyalität entwickelt. Unter der Bankloyalität verstand er *die Bereitschaft eines Wirtschaftssubjektes, dauerhaft die Leistungen eines bestimmten Kreditinstituts*

[1] Süddeutsche Zeitung Magazin, Nr. 39 v. 27. 9. 1996, S. 4f.

nachzufragen.[2] Von zentraler Bedeutung ist dabei die Auffassung, daß die zunehmende (positive) Erfahrung mit einem Kreditinstitut zu wachsender Treue gegenüber diesem führt. Seine Ursache findet dieser Lerneffekt im spezifischen Charakter der Bankleistung. Unabhängig von ihrer vielgestaltigen (im IV. Abschnitt näher beleuchteten) Ausprägung vom Sparbuch über die Baufinanzierung bis zur umfassenden Vermögensbetreuung ist diese doch aus Sicht des Kunden

- besonders *erklärungsbedürftig*, da es sich um eine abstrakte, immaterielle Leistung handelt und

- besonders *vertrauensempfindlich*, da sie auf Geld gerichtet ist und den Kunden mehr oder weniger lang bindet.

Der Bankmitarbeiter kann deshalb als der zentrale Präferenzenträger angesehen werden, der dem Kunden über die Kompliziertheit der Leistung hinweghilft und sein Mißtrauen abbaut. „Die fachliche Kompetenz und die persönliche Akzeptanz des Betreuers prägen das Bild des Kunden von der Bank und seine Entscheidung, bei welcher Bank er seine Geschäfte abwickelt."[3] Nicht die Produkte im engeren Sinne, sondern den Bankmitarbeiter lernt der Kunde im Zeitablauf kennen.[4] Hierdurch wächst das Vertrauen, das den Kunden an die Bank bindet, sein Entscheidungsprozeß erfordert zunehmend weniger Aufwand für Überlegung und Informationssuche. Durch die wachsende (noch einmal: positive) Erfahrung des Kunden im Umgang mit dem Bankmitarbeiter verläuft die Abnahme neuer Leistungen zunehmend automatisch, ohne Prüfung von Anbieteralternativen ab. Im Gegenteil: Ein lange mit einem Kreditinstitut zusammenarbeitender Kunde wird wenig geneigt sein, seine Bankverbindung zu wechseln, da dieses mit Lästigkeiten und Kosten verbunden ist. Als Handlungsempfehlung wurde dementsprechend herausgearbeitet, diejenigen absatzpolitischen Maßnahmen zu forcieren, die das menschliche Element als Berater und Verkäufer den Kunden gegenüber möglichst intensiv zum Einsatz bringen.

Den Einstieg wählten die Kreditinstitute dabei zumeist über das Girokonto, um auf der Basis dieses „Informationspools" Cross-selling, also ein Verkaufen über das gesamte (relevante) Sortiment hinweg zu betreiben. Das jüngste Beispiel dieser Strategie lieferte die vielbeachtete Kampagne der BfG Bank AG, die den Privatkunden seit Anfang 1996 ein entgeltfreies

---

2 Vgl. Süchting (1967 und 1972).

3 Schütte (1991), S. 219.

4 Vgl. Süchting/Boening (1971).

(„kostenloses") Girokonto anbietet, bei dem für die Kontoführung, das Telefonbanking, die Euroscheck- sowie eine Kreditkarte keine Preise erhoben werden. Bei der Einführung hieß es:

„Der Kampf um den Kunden beginn(t) beim Girokonto. (Die BfG Bank) setzt bewußt auf die Akquisition von Neukunden und die Erträge aus dem Cross-selling. Aus Erfahrung wisse man, daß ein Kunde mit Gehaltskonto im Rahmen seiner Hauptbankverbindung etwa zwei weitere Produkte bei seiner Bank in Anspruch nehme. Hiervon will die BfG Bank gezielt profitieren. Um den Wegfall der Gebühreneinnahmen aus den derzeitigen Girokonten zu kompensieren - er wird auf 20 Mill. DM beziffert - benötigt man im ersten Jahr 60.000 Neukunden."[5]

Offenbar sind also derzeit beide strategische Stoßrichtungen im Privatkundengeschäft zu erkennen: Das unverminderte, ja eher noch verstärkte Setzen auf die umfassende Beziehung (Beispiel BfG) sowie das Herausschneiden eines Teils aus der Gesamtbeziehung (Beispiel Vereinsbank).

3. Empirische Hinweise auf eine nachlassende Bankloyalität

Angesichts der zentralen Rolle, die die Bankloyalität nach den bisherigen Ausführungen spielt, ist es erstaunlich, daß empirische Untersuchungen zu diesem Thema bislang kaum vorliegen. Zwar könnte man sich mit der Annahme trösten, einzelne Kreditinstitute würden doch sicherlich Loyalitätsstudien in ihrer Kundschaft durchführen, diese lediglich nicht publizieren. POLAN berichtete in seiner Untersuchung 1995 jedoch, daß in keiner der von ihm betrachteten Großbanken die Loyalität und - spiegelbildlich - die Kundenabgänge systematisch analysiert werden.[6] In einem Pressegespräch stellte es die Deutsche Bank AG Anfang November 1996 als Innovation heraus, ihre Kunden zukünftig regelmäßig nach deren Zufriedenheit zu fragen.[7]

Dabei ist indes auch nicht eindeutig geklärt, mit Hilfe welcher Meßgrößen das Ausmaß an Bankloyalität quantifiziert werden kann. SEITZ hat vorgeschlagen, Zahl, Wechsel und Dauerhaftigkeit von Bankverbindungen zu betrachten - diese Daten werden ca. alle fünf Jahre

5 O.V.: Aggressive Strategie (1995).

6 Vgl. Polan (1995), S. 21f. und 204.

7 Vgl. o. V.: Deutsche Bank: Regelmäßige Kundenbefragungen (1996).

vom Spiegel-Verlag erhoben, wobei die Vergleichbarkeit der Zahlen durch die deutsche Wiedervereinigung gelitten hat.[8] Ähnliche Ergebnisse liefert das (allerdings nicht allgemein zugängliche) GfK-Finanzmarktpanel.[9]

Es zeigen sich folgende Entwicklungen:

- Die Zahl derjenigen privaten Haushalte, die mehr als eine Bankverbindung unterhalten, ist von 17% (1973) über 29% (1980) auf mittlerweile fast 40% gestiegen - dies deutet auf eine rückläufige Loyalität zu jeweils einer Bank als „Allein-Lieferant" hin.[10]
- Ihre Bankverbindung schon einmal gewechselt hatten 1980 lediglich 16% der privaten Haushalte, 1995 hat sich diese Zahl mit fast 30% bald verdoppelt. Auch dieses Kriterium weist auf eine gesunkene Bankloyalität hin und ist nicht allein durch die höhere Mobilität der Bankkunden (Wechsel der Bankverbindung durch Umzug) erklärbar.[11]
- WITT hat schon vor 10 Jahren gezeigt, daß der Anteil der Wechsler mit der Dauer der Beziehung abnimmt, wobei er den „kritischen Zeitpunkt" nach etwa 1,8 Jahren sah.[12] Eine jüngere, unveröffentlichte Studie eines deutschen Kreditinstituts bestätigt diesen Wert exakt.[13] Leider sind die Daten der regelmäßigen Spiegel-Studie nicht differenziert genug, um zu überprüfen, ob dieser Wert allgemeine Gültigkeit besitzt und sich in den letzten Jahren verschoben hat: die unterste Klasse wird als „Hauptbankverbindung kleiner fünf Jahre" zu global abgegrenzt.

Insbesondere aus dem Bereich der Unternehmensberatung werden häufig punktuelle Ergebnisse vorgestellt, deren Erhebungsweise allerdings regelmäßig nicht bekannt ist. Zwei Zahlen seien dennoch zur Illustration ausgewählt: Die „Kundenanbindungsquote" im Neugeschäft beträgt im Durchschnitt der Banken nur noch ca. 50%, so daß die Hälfte des Neugeschäfts zur Konkurrenz abwandert. Mittlerweile hat der durchschnittliche Bankkunde

---

8 Vgl. Seitz (1976) sowie Spiegel-Verlag (1980 - 1996); zu den davorliegenden Zahlen vgl. Becker (1975).

9 Vgl. Epple (1991).

10 Vgl. Spiegel-Verlag (1996). Nach dem GfK-Panel liegt diese Zahl sogar schon über 50% (Epple, 1991).

11 Vgl. Spiegel-Verlag (1996). Dem liegt ein Bild der Bankloyalität als ausschließliche Bindung an eine Bank zugrunde. Wie im weiteren noch gezeigt wird, muß diese Sichtweise relativiert werden. Wenn ein Kunde das Gesamtbündel „Bankleistung" aufschnürt und einzelne Angebote bei unterschiedlichen Banken nachfragt, kann er bezogen auf die einzelne Leistung und das jeweilige Institut durchaus loyal sein. Eine steigende Zahl von Bankverbindungen deutet aber darauf hin, daß das Band zwischen Kreditinstitut und Kunde immer dünner wird, was insgesamt schon als Illoyalität bezeichnet werden kann.

12 Vgl. Witt (1986).

13 Vgl. Polan (1995), S. 137.

14 Produkte bei insgesamt sieben Finanzdienstleistern (allerdings inkl. Versicherungen) im Bestand.[14]

Nimmt man die genannten Ergebnisse zusammen, so kann man - auch bei vorsichtiger Interpretation - doch von einer tendenziell rückläufigen Bankloyalität sprechen.[15]

Will man die illoyalen Nachfragergruppen näher bestimmen, so bieten sich aufgrund der nur schmalen Datenbasis lediglich die Kriterien Alter, Beruf und Einkommen an:

- Besonders illoyal sind die 30 - 49jährigen, bei denen 11% über mehr als drei Bankverbindungen verfügen. Ihre Bankverbindung bereits einmal gewechselt haben schon 34%, nur noch 65% besitzen dementsprechend noch ihre erste Bankverbindung. Jenseits eines Lebensalters von 50 gilt tendenziell: je älter, desto loyaler. In der Gruppe der über 65jährigen besitzen noch 82% ihre erste Bankverbindung.[16]

- Während 85% der Facharbeiter ihre Bankverbindung noch nicht gewechselt haben, sind dies bei Selbständigen und Angehörigen freier Berufe nur noch 74%. Bei letzteren verfügen auch 11% über mehr als eine Bankverbindung, während dieses in der Gruppe der Facharbeiter nur auf 5% zutrifft.[17]

- Mit zunehmendem Einkommen steigt die Zahl der Bankverbindungen. Bedienen sich noch knapp zwei Drittel der niedrig verdienenden Haushalte nur einer Bank, so sinkt diese Quote stetig bis zu einem Drittel der Haushalte, die netto 5000 DM und mehr monatlich verdienen. In dieser Gruppe verfügt jeder vierte Haushalt über drei und mehr Bankverbindungen.[18]

Dies leitet über zu der Frage nach den Ursachen der zurückgegangenen Bankloyalität. Einige wesentliche Trends seien schlaglichtartig genannt:

---

14 Vgl. Szallies (1996), S. 101.

15 Damit haben sich die zu Beginn der neunziger Jahre abgegebenen Prognosen bestätigt - vgl. Süchting (1991) sowie Epple (1991).

16 Vgl. Spiegel-Verlag (1996).

17 Vgl. Spiegel-Verlag (1996).

18 Vgl. Epple (1991), S. 549.

- Erstens besteht mittlerweile eine weitaus größere Zahl von Anbieteralternativen als noch vor 10 oder gar 20 Jahren. Den Privatkunden werden Finanzdienstleistungen immer stärker offeriert durch Tochterinstitute großer Industrie- (z.B. Automobilbanken) und Handelsunternehmen (z.B. Quelle-Bank). Zudem haben die Versicherungen ihren Anteil an der Geldvermögensbildung der privaten Haushalte auf über 25% ausweiten können.[19] Auch kommen viele Haushalte eher unbewußt in Kontakt zu anderen Banken - etwa durch den Kauf einer „Bahncard" mit Zahlungsfunktion, die den Besitzer zum Kunden der Citibank macht.

- Über dieses vermehrte Angebot kann sich der Private - zweitens - zunehmend schneller und kostengünstiger einen Überblick verschaffen - am ehesten bei den stark standardisierten Produkten wie Spar- und Termineinlagen. Der Weg über T-Online oder das Internet ermöglicht es, binnen kürzester Zeit Angebote quer durch Deutschland und darüber hinaus zu vergleichen. Diesem Weg gehört die Zukunft, da er für die nachwachsende Generation bereits heute selbstverständlich ist.[20]

  Die Markttransparenz wird in den letzten Jahren zudem erhöht durch Verbraucherverbände einerseits, Medien andererseits, die regelmäßig etwa Konditionenvergleiche von Musterkonten im Bereich des Zahlungsverkehrs verbreiten. Nach einer Allensbach-Umfrage halten es mittlerweile bei einer Anlagesumme von 10.000 DM bereits 46% der westdeutschen Bankkunden für ratsam, zunächst die Angebote verschiedener Banken miteinander zu vergleichen und erst dann zu entscheiden, wo das Geld tatsächlich angelegt wird.[21]

- Drittens wird die Bereitschaft, ein unter Preis/Leistungs-Gesichtspunkten günstigeres Angebot tatsächlich wahrzunehmen und dafür auch die angestammte Bank zu wechseln, zum einen durch den gestiegenen ökonomischen Bildungsgrad breiter Bevölkerungsschichten befördert. So ist die Quote der Abiturienten unter den privaten Haushalten auf mittlerweile 17% angestiegen. Die Aufgeklärtheit der Bankkunden zeigt sich in der Nachfrage nach renditestärkeren und zugleich liquideren Alternativen zur klassischen Bankeinlage wie etwa Geldmarktfonds oder Wertpapieren. Hielten die privaten Haushalte 1970 erst rd. 7% ihres Finanzvermögens in Form von Wertpapieren, so waren es 1994 bereits über 16%. Dazu trug auch bei, daß die überwiegend in der Nachkriegszeit

---

19 Vgl. zur Quantifizierung der nachlassenden Bankenintermediation auch St. Paul (1994).

20 Vgl. auch hierzu entsprechende Zahlen der Spiegel-Studie.

21 Vgl. Köcher (1997).

akkumulierten Vermögen nun verstärkt vererbt werden und die Privaten es sich somit erlauben können, vom reinen „Notfallsparen“ abzugehen. Zum anderen erzwingt die Arbeitsmarktlage in immer stärkerem Ausmaß die Mobilität der Arbeitnehmer. Von daher kann es nicht überraschen, daß auch der Wohnungswechsel häufig als Grund für den Wechsel der Bankverbindung genannt wird.

Nicht zuletzt trägt der - wenn auch nur schwer zu fassende - sogenannte „Wertewandel“ dazu bei, daß „Loyalität“ in der Gesellschaft immer weniger verwurzelt zu sein scheint - in bezug auf die Familien, Parteien und Gewerkschaften, die Kirche und eben (last but not least) die Bank.[22] Die Bedeutung des Vertrauensverhältnisses zum Bankmitarbeiter läßt nach, Problemlösungskompetenz und die „Angemessenheit“ des Preises werden vom Kunden bei seiner Kaufentscheidung stärker gewichtet.

Die Kreissparkasse Recklinghausen beispielsweise fand 1995 in einer mit der Bochumer Marktforschungsagentur TPC durchgeführten Befragung von 12.000 Kunden (= 11% ihrer Privatkunden) heraus, daß ein fester Ansprechpartner nur noch von gut der Hälfte der Privaten für „äußerst wichtig“ oder zumindest „wichtig“ gehalten wurde; bei den jungen Kunden spielte dieser Aspekt eine weitaus geringere Rolle als bei den älteren Kunden.[23]

Immer schwieriger wird daher die Bindung durch den langjährigen, persönlichen Kontakt zwischen Kunde und Bankmitarbeiter, die Basis der Bankloyalität wird brüchig.

4. Betrachtung der schwindenden Bankloyalität aus Sicht des Geschäftsbeziehungsmanagements

Angesichts des angesprochenen gesamtgesellschaftlichen Wertewandels ist die in der Kreditwirtschaft festzustellende, sinkende Loyalität ein branchenübergreifendes Phänomen. Immer mehr Unternehmen erkannten in diesem Zusammenhang, daß ein einseitiger Fokus auf Neukundengewinnung bei gleichzeitiger Abwanderung von Stammkunden auf Dauer negative Folgen für den Unternehmensgewinn haben kann; dementsprechend gewann der Begriff der „Kundenbindung“ an Bedeutung.[24]

---

22 Vgl. Wünsche/Swoboda (1994) sowie Klages (1987).

23 Vgl. Online - Mitarbeiterzeitschrift der Kreissparkasse Recklinghausen, 10/1995.

24 Vgl. zum Überblick Meyer/Oevermann (1995), Diller (1996), sowie Engelhardt/Freiling (1994 und 1995).

Mit Wurzeln im Investitionsgütermarketing der siebziger Jahren - damals mit anderen Begriffen umschrieben -, verstärkt seit Beginn der neunziger Jahre hat sich daher auch das Beziehungsmanagement zu einem wesentlichen Marketing-Konzept entwickelt.[25] Hierunter wird verstanden die „aufeinander abgestimmte Gesamtheit der Grundsätze, Leitbilder und Einzelmaßnahmen zur langfristig zielgerichteten Selektion, Anbahnung, Steuerung und Kontrolle von Geschäftsbeziehungen."[26]

Von besonderer Bedeutung ist dabei die investitionspolitische Perspektive: Geschäftsbeziehungen werden als Investitionsfelder betrachtet, die effizient, ressourcen- und zeitgerecht zu bearbeiten sind sowie die langfristige Bindung des Kunden sicherstellen sollen[27] - hier zeigen sich starke Berührungspunkte zwischen diesem Konzept des „Relationship-Marketing"[28] und der Theorie der Bankloyalität.[29]

Die theoretische Fundierung des Beziehungsmanagements durch die Institutionenökonomik[30] hat dazu beigetragen,

- Geschäftsbeziehungen zu typisieren,
- das Eingehen von Bindungen zu erklären,
- verschiedene Verhaltensweisen in Geschäftsbeziehungen zu anlysieren
- sowie auf Probleme des Managements von Geschäftsbeziehungen hinzuweisen.

Es bietet sich daher an, mit Hilfe dieses Rasters auch die zunehmende Illoyalität von Bankkunden zu beleuchten, sie aus der Perspektive des Beziehungsmanagements anzuschauen.

Nach PLINKE kann unter einer Geschäftsbeziehung eine Kette von Transaktionen zwischen zwei Partnern verstanden werden, die nicht zufällig ist, sondern einen inneren Zusammenhang aufweist[31] ; diesen stellt die Bindung der Partner aneinander dar.

---

25 Vgl. Diller/Kusterer (1988).

26 Diller (1995), Sp. 285.

27 Vgl. Plinke (1989).

28 Vgl. Plinke (1992).

29 Vgl. dazu auch Süchting (1992), S. 456f.

30 Vgl. Kleinaltenkamp (1994), Kleinaltenkamp/Marra (1995), speziell S. 112ff. und Schäfer (1995).

31 Vgl. Plinke (1989), S. 303ff., Plinke (1997) und Kleinaltenkamp/Plinke/Söllner (1996).

Analysiert man die Geschäftsbeziehungen von Banken zu ihren Kunden im Privatkundengeschäft, so fällt auf, daß sich unter dem Dach der Geschäftsbeziehung sehr unterschiedliche Transaktionen abspielen können; die abgesetzten Leistungsbündel weisen mitunter eine hohe Vielfalt auf. Je nach Untersuchungszweck lassen sie sich in bezug auf verschiedene Dimensionen systematisieren. Für die hier verfolgte Fragestellung kann zum einen im Hinblick auf die Dauer der Problemlösung unterschieden werden:[32]

- Die „Zeitpunktleistung"[33]: Sie wird nachgefragt für Probleme, die zu einem bestimmten Zeitpunkt auftreten und in diesem (i.d.R.) abschließend gelöst werden. Beispiele dafür sind Kredite für den Autokauf, den Hausbau, bestimmte Anlageentscheidungen etc. Für eine Anschaffung benötigt der Bankkunde in einem bestimmten Zeitpunkt Liquidität. Wenn die Bank ihm diese einräumt, ist das Problem gelöst. Zwar kann sich die Rückzahlung über einen längeren Zeitraum erstrecken, doch wenn es nicht zu Zahlungsaufschüben oder Kreditaufstockungen kommt, ist die Problemlösung beendet. - Wenn ein Anleger vor der Frage steht, wie er 100.000 DM für drei Monate anlegen kann, so wird ihm das Kreditinstitut möglicherweise eine Termineinlage für diesen Zeitraum empfehlen. Zwar sieht der Kunde in der Folge monatlich einen Auszug seines (Unter-)Kontos, doch wiederum ist die Problemlösung im Zeitpunkt des Absatzes der Termineinlage abgeschlossen. Hat der Kunde in einer späteren Periode erneut Anlagebedarf, so wird eine neue Beschaffungsentscheidung getroffen, je nachdem welche dann zugrundeliegenden Probleme bei dem Nachfrager auftreten. Damit ist bei derartigen Leistungen möglicherweise auch der Anbieter jedesmal wieder in Frage gestellt. Um Mißverständnissen vorzubeugen, sei noch einmal ausdrücklich betont: Der Begriff der „Zeitpunktleistung" stellt auf die Dauer der Problemlösung, nicht die Vertragslaufzeit ab.

- Die „Zeitraumleistung": Sie löst für den Nachfrager ein Problem, das dieser dauerhaft hat bzw. bei ihm immer wieder auftritt. Das Problem, den Zahlungsverkehr abzuwickeln, ist ein solches. Solange man in einer durch den bargeldlosen Geldverkehr geprägten Gesellschaft lebt, muß man ein Girokonto unterhalten, um mit dessen Hilfe daran teilzunehmen. Auch der in der Regel damit in Verbindung stehende Dispositionskredit ist eine solche Leistung. Durch Schwankungen im Einkommensstrom entsteht immer wieder der Bedarf nach zusätzlicher Liquidität für einen beschränkten Zeitraum. Der Bankkunde

---

32 Vgl. Süchting (1968), der von „kontakthäufigen bzw. -seltenen Leistungen" spricht, wobei der Kontakt über die eigentliche Problemlösung hinausgehen kann; insofern wird hier eine Fokussierung vorgenommen.

33 Vgl. zu einer ähnlichen Einteilung Corsten (1985), S. 122. Im Unterschied zu der hier vertretenen Auffassung bezieht Corsten diese Begriffe aber nur auf die Dauer des Leistungs*erstellungs*prozesses, nimmt also eher die Perspektive des Anbieters ein.

möchte aber dauerhaft Sicherheit, daß die Bank ihm diese in einem vereinbarten Rahmen auf Abruf zur Verfügung stellt. Die Zeitraumleistung besteht also im Grunde aus mehreren Transaktionen oder Teilleistungen, die in einem großen Leistungsbündel zusammengefaßt sind. Es gibt deshalb auch meist nur einen Vertrag, der lediglich Spielregeln, nicht aber die Details der Zeitraumleistung regelt. Eine solche Regelung wäre nämlich nur schwer möglich, da über den zunächst unbeschränkten Zeitraum, über den sich die Leistungserstellung erstreckt, nicht alle Zukunftslagen prognostizierbar sind. Als bekanntes Beispiel hierfür mag der Zinssatz für einen Dispositionskredit dienen. Üblicherweise wird beim Absatz dieser Leistung nur der Rahmen der Inanspruchnahme festgelegt, der Zins aber verändert sich entsprechend den Refinanzierungsmöglichkeiten der Bank.

Neben dem unbestimmten Zeitraum und der nur ungenauen Spezifizierung des Umfangs der Leistung ist für die Zeitraumleistungen typisch, daß der Nachfrager die Entscheidung über ihre Beschaffung nur in größeren Abständen, evtl. sogar lediglich einmal im Leben trifft. Solange er keine bessere Möglichkeit sieht oder die Wahl der Kontoverbindung für ihn wegen mangelnder Evidenz[34] kein Problem darstellt[35], wird er keinen neuen Beschaffungsprozeß einleiten. Dieses gilt - um ein weiteres Beispiel zu nennen - auch für die umfassende Vermögensverwaltung, bei der der Kundenbetreuer in regelmäßigem Kontakt mit dem Nachfrager steht, seine Vermögenssituation analysiert und Anlageempfehlungen gibt.

Im Hinblick auf die Bindungsmöglichkeiten des Kunden bietet sich darüber hinaus eine Unterteilung nach der Komplexität des zu lösenden Problems an, die sich auf die Intensität des Kontakts Bank/Kunde auswirkt:[36]

- Seine Lösungskompetenz kann der Anbieter bei komplexen Problemen und den auf sie zugeschnittenen („Individual"-)Leistungen wie dem Wertpapierkauf eines Privaten, der kurz vor der Pensionierung steht und sich mit ständig ändernden Steuergesetzen konfrontiert sieht, wesentlich stärker unter Beweis stellen als bei einer („Standard"-)

34 Vgl. zum Begriff der Evidenz Engelhardt/Schwab (1982).

35 Vgl. Stauss/Neuhaus (1995), die drei Kategorien loyaler Kunden unterscheiden: den fordernd zufriedenen Kunden, der wegen hoher Erwartungen schnell bereit ist, den Anbieter zu wechseln; den resignativ zufriedenen Kunden, der mangels besserer Alternativen nicht wechselt, bei einem überzeugend attraktiven Angebot aber wechselbereit ist und den stabil zufriedenen Kunden, der dauerhaft bei „seinem" Anbieter bleibt. Die Intervalle der Beschaffung von Zeitraumleistungen dürften vom ersten zum letzten Typen länger werden.

36 Daher spricht Süchting (1968) auch von mehr oder weniger „kontaktintensiven" Leistungen.

Lösung wie z.B. einer Termingeldanlage für drei Monate. In beiden Fällen handelt es sich in der Regel um "Zeitpunktleistungen", da der Bedarf des Nachfragers vollständig gedeckt wird. Dies bedeutet nicht, daß - um im Beispiel zu bleiben - der Private in Folgeperioden kein Geld mehr anlegt. Es wird jedoch hierfür ein neuer Vertrag erforderlich sein, so daß die Position des Anbieters nicht zementiert ist.

- Auch bei „Zeitraumleistungen" scheint eine Differenzierung erforderlich. Obwohl sich die Problemlösung sowohl bei einem Girokonto in Verbindung mit einem Dispokredit als auch bei einer umfassenden Vermögensbetreuung über mehrere Jahre oder gar Jahrzehnte erstrecken kann, ist die Bindungsmöglichkeit im zweiten Fall aufgrund des wesentlich höheren Komplexitätsgrades des Kundenproblems deutlich größer. Durch den intensiven Austausch erhält der Anbieter die Chance, sich eingehend zu präsentieren.

Zusammenfassend kann man also von folgender Typologie ausgehen:

		Komplexität des Problems	
		niedrig	*hoch*
Dauer der Problem-lösung	*in einem Zeitpunkt*	**Termingeldanlage**	**Wertpapierkauf u.B.d. Steuersituation**
	über mehrere Zeitpunkte	**Girokonto mit Dispositionskredit**	**Umfassende Vermögensbetreuung**

Abb. 1: Systematisierung von Bankleistungen im Privatkundengeschäft

Die Ausgangsthese der Strategieentwicklung in vielen Banken war, daß bestimmte Zeitraumleistungen eine gute Grundlage für den Aufbau und den Erhalt von Geschäftsbeziehungen darstellen. Speziell Girokonten wurden als Einstieg in eine engere Beziehung gesehen. Dabei ging - und geht (siehe die BfG Bank) - es darum, Nachfrageverbunde in einem Zeitpunkt (der Berufseinstieg bringt z.B. eine Reihe von gleichzeitig auftretenden Finanzierungs- und Geldanlageproblemen) und/oder über einen Zeitraum (aus bestimmten Einkommenssituationen ergeben sich über die Zeit miteinander verbundene Fragen der Geldanlage, der Altersvorsorge etc.) zu nutzen[37].

Hat sich der Nachfrager einmal dafür entschieden, sein Girokonto bei einer Bank zu eröffnen, so war dies über lange Zeit eine sehr dauerhafte Festlegung. Diese Dauerhaftigkeit und die immer wiederkehrenden Kontakte waren selbst bindend, gaben der Bank darüber hinaus aber

[37] Vgl. zu den Nachfrageverbunden Engelhardt (1976).

auch noch die Möglichkeit, zusätzliche Bindung aufzubauen. Je intensiver Kreditinstitute die sich ergebenden Kontakte und die daraus erwachsenden Informationen nutzten, desto besser konnten sie sich auf die Bedürfnisse einzelner Nachfrager einstellen. Die Nachfrager wiederum bauten darauf, besser verstanden und betreut zu werden als bei anderen Kreditinstituten, die erst wieder einen entsprechenden Erfahrungsfundus hätten aufbauen müssen. Gerade im Bereich der Kreditleistungen läßt sich das preis(mit)bestimmende Merkmal der Bonität nur schwer an ein anderes Institut transferieren, da es auf Erfahrungswerten der Vergangenheit basiert - der Nachfrager ist „informationell eingeschlossen."[38]

Aus dieser genauen Kenntnis der Verhältnisse des Bankkunden, so der zweite Teil dieser Idee, ließen sich weitere Angebote zielgerichtet an diese Nachfrager vermarkten. Verkürzt gesagt: Wenn die Bank die Entwicklung des Saldos auf dem Girokonto und die Einstellungen des Kunden eine Zeit lang kennt, fällt es ihr leichter, ihn auf bestimmte Anlagemöglichkeiten anzusprechen. Wenn der Nachfrager seinerseits ein Problem hat, wird er sich am ehesten an diejenige Bank wenden, die er über seine Kontoverbindung schon kennt - ideale Voraussetzungen also, um Cross-selling[39] zu betreiben. Insbesondere, wenn der Kunde Zeitpunktleistungen benötigt, muß nicht jedesmal ein neuer Akquisitionsprozeß durchlaufen werden. - Dies war im übrigen auch einer der Grundgedanken bei der Kreierung von sogenannten „Allfinanz"-Konzepten.

Für die Banken ergab sich aus dieser Vorstellung über das Marktgeschehen die Notwendigkeit, Girokonten zu gewinnen bzw. zu halten und darüber hinaus eine möglichst breite Palette an Leistungen anzubieten, um den Nachfrager umfassend bedienen zu können. Ziel war es dabei, Abwanderung bei einzelnen Leistungen als Gefährdung für die Geschäftsbeziehung zu verhindern; auch dies eines der Motive von „Allfinanz"-Strategien. Angestrebt wurde deshalb eine möglichst hohe Bankloyalität des Nachfragers, die sich entsprechend der eingangs gegebenen Definition so auswirken sollte, daß dieser sämtliche der aus seiner Sicht erforderlichen Bankleistungen bei seiner Hausbank beschafft.

Bei dieser Argumentation wurde dementsprechend unterstellt, daß *enge Bindungen und umfassende Geschäftsbeziehungen die Grundlage von Rentabilität* sind, weil:

[38] Vgl. Sharpe (1990), S. 1070 und Engelhardt/Freiling (1996), S. 147.

[39] Für den Bereich der Finanzdienstleistungs-Geschäftsbeziehungen hat Farny (1995, Sp. 2602f.) diese Option auch aus der Perspektive der Versicherungswirtschaft beleuchtet.

- das *Erlös*potential des Kunden besser ausgeschöpft werden kann,
- sich Einsparungen von Transaktions*kosten* z.B. für die Kundensuche, -einschätzung und -kontrolle ergeben
- sowie eine Ergebnis*stabilisierung* durch die Dauerhaftigkeit der Verbindung eintritt.

Wie unter 3. gezeigt, entsprechen aber die realen Verhältnisse im Finanzdienstleistungsmarkt für private Kunden nicht mehr den Annahmen, die dieser Argumentation zugrunde liegen. Insbesondere zwei zentrale Änderungen scheinen danach offensichtlich:

- Die Intervalle, in denen Bankkunden die Entscheidung über die Zeitraumleistungen (insbesondere die Girokonten) überdenken, sind kürzer geworden. Die Nachfrager sind bei Unzufriedenheit bereit, schneller als zuvor die Bankverbindung zu wechseln. Die Wirkung solcher Leistungen als Bindung an sich hat nachgelassen.

- Die Nachfrager sehen in der Bank, bei der sie ihr Girokonto unterhalten, nicht mehr unbedingt den ersten oder einzigen Ansprechpartner für ihre Finanzprobleme. Es gibt aus Sicht der Nachfrager mehrere Anbieter, mit denen sie ebenso gut über ihre Fragen reden können.

Durch diese Veränderungen sind auf einem gedachten Kontinuum drei Haupttypen von Bankkunden beobachtbar:

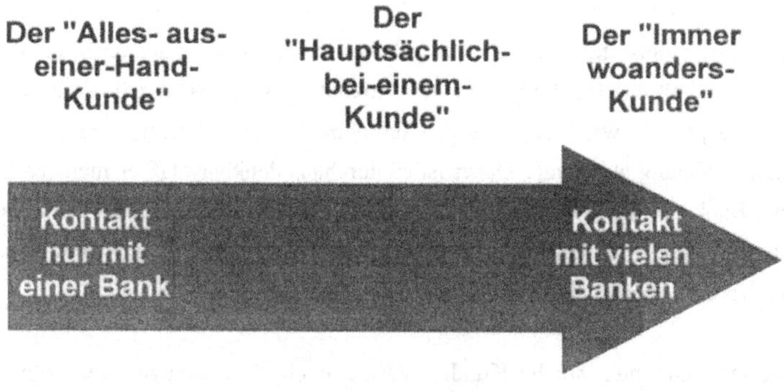

Abb. 2: Kundentypologie

- Der **„Alles-aus-einer-Hand-Kunde"** entspricht dabei dem, was bisher als Normalfall angesehen wurde. Er weist eine Loyalität zu seiner angestammten Bankverbindung auf, die so stark ist, daß er Bankleistungen nicht bei anderen Kreditinstituten beschaffen würde. Dabei sei zunächst dahingestellt, warum er so verfährt. Von mangelnder Information und

einem deshalb besonders stark ausgeprägten Risikoempfinden über Bequemlichkeit bis hin zur mangelnden Möglichkeit, überhaupt mehrere Bankleistungen abzunehmen, dürften hier sehr unterschiedliche Motive zu beobachten sein.

- Der **„Hauptsächlich-bei-einem-Kunde“** ist von diesem bisherigen Bild schon ein Stück entfernt. Zwar betrachtet er immer noch ein Institut als seine Haupt- oder Hausbank, bei der er möglicherweise auch die meisten Leistungen kauft. In Einzelfällen ist er aber bereit, diese auch bei anderen Banken zu beschaffen; sei es, daß er „seiner“ Bank bei den entsprechenden Problemen nicht die notwendige Kompetenz beimißt, sei es, daß er bei diesen Leistungen eine besonders hohe Preissensibilität aufweist und deshalb zu einem anderen Kreditinstitut wechselt. Es besteht also nach wie vor eine - vielleicht sogar durchaus enge - *grundsätzliche Bindung* an die Hausbank, doch bewirkt diese nicht mehr eine absolute, sondern nur noch eine beschränkte Loyalität. Der Nachfrager ist grundsätzlich an einer dauerhaften Geschäftsbeziehung interessiert; bei Angeboten, die ihm besser erscheinen als die der Hausbank, ist er aber auch bereit, Kontakt zu anderen Instituten aufzunehmen und somit aus Sicht der Hausbank im traditionellen Sinne „illoyal“ zu werden.

- Der **„Immer-woanders-Kunde“** schließlich stellt den genauen Gegentyp zum hergebrachten Nachfragerbild am anderen Ende dieses Kontinuums dar. Er fühlt sich nicht an ein einzelnes Institut gebunden, sondern entscheidet immer wieder neu und unabhängig von bestehenden Verbindungen über die Beschaffung der Bankleistungen. Zwar benötigt auch er Zeitraumleistungen, doch ist er jederzeit bereit, diese anderweitig in Anspruch zu nehmen. Er wählt das für ihn günstigste Girokonto aus und ist durch diese Entscheidung nicht vorgeprägt, was etwa die Aufnahme eines Kredits zum Kauf einer Eigentumswohnung anbelangt. Dabei ist es durchaus denkbar, daß er mehrere Leistungen bei einer Bank beschafft. Das wäre allerdings eher als Zufall anzusehen, da die betreffende Bank bei all' diesen Leistungen in den wesentlichen dem Nachfrager wichtigen Kriterien anderen Kreditinstituten überlegen sein müßte.

Die Banken betrachten solche Kunden stärker noch als diejenigen der vorhergehenden Kategorie durch die Brille der bisherigen Marktsicht als *„illoyal“*. Aus Sicht der Nachfrager kann aber eine Art *„selektiver Loyalität"* konstatiert werden: Solange Preis und/oder Qualität der Leistung den Kunden überzeugen, wird er *bei einem einzelnen Bankprodukt* loyal zu der anbietenden Bank stehen. Er weist lediglich *keine umfassende Loyalität* hinsichtlich aller nachgefragten Leistungen mehr auf, hat das

Gesamtleistungsbündel auseinandergeschnürt. Wichtig ist auch, daß jede Bank, mit der der Kunde Geschäfte tätigt, zu diesem eine Geschäftsbeziehung unterhält. Diese besteht lediglich aus weniger Transaktionen und Interaktionen als dies früher der Fall war. Die Banken haben auch zu diesen Nachfragern einen Kontakt, der sich für weitere Geschäfte nutzen ließe - dies ist allerdings wesentlich schwieriger als zuvor.[40]

5. Möglichkeiten der Erfolgsmessung bei Geschäftsbeziehungen

Diese „selektive Loyalität" muß indes nicht ein Weniger an Rentabilität bedeuten - wie auch umgekehrt eine starke, umfassende Bankloyalität und Rentabilität nicht gleichgesetzt werden können. POLAN systematisiert in Übertragung einer Idee von PLINKE vier potentielle Kundenattraktivitäts/Kundenbindungs-Kombinationen. Dabei erscheinen im hier gewählten Kontext besonders interessant die „A"-Kunden (in der folgenden Abbildung links oben), die zwar ein nur geringes Bindungspotential aufweisen, zugleich jedoch - gemessen an ihrem jährlichen Deckungsbeitrag - sehr attraktiv sind.

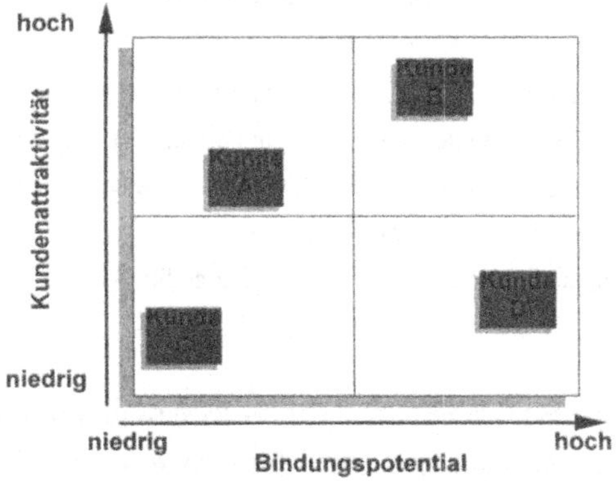

Abb. 3: Kundenattraktivitäts/Kundenbindungs-Portfolio[41]

Aussagekräftige empirische Studien zu diesem Zusammenhang sind bisher rar. Die Existenz von vier Kundenklassen wurde jedoch jüngst in der sorgfältigen Studie von HALLOWELL bestätigt. Die Befragung von 12.000 Kunden aus 59 Filialen einer Bank und ihre Kombination mit den Daten aus dem internen Rechnungswesen zeigte, daß es tatsächlich eine quantitativ

40 Von daher ist ein reines „transaction marketing" kaum vorstellbar; vgl. Wehrli/Jüttner (1994).

41 Polan (1995), S. 189. Vgl. zu den Vorläufern Plinke (1989), S. 316 sowie Diller/Götz (1991).

erhebliche Gruppe von Nachfragern gibt, deren Kundenbindung (dort gefaßt als Dauer und Tiefe = Cross-selling-Rate der Beziehung) nur gering ist, deren Attraktivität (gemessen als Aufwandsrentabilität) aber als hoch eingestuft werden kann (aufgrund der anderen Achseneinteilung in der folgenden Abbildung links unten):

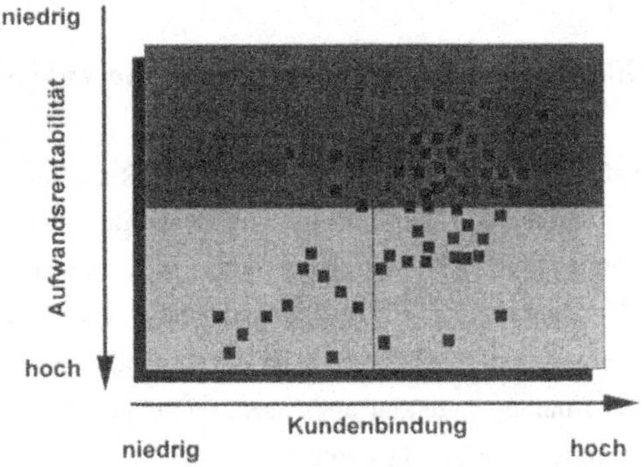

Abb. 4: Rentabilitäts/Bindungs-Portfolio[42]

Umgekehrt zeigt sich aber eben auch, daß ein Großteil der loyalen Kunden unattraktiv ist (Sektor rechts oben). Darauf deuten auch die (gleichwohl nur auf empirisch schmaler Basis gewonnenen) Hinweise aus anderen Studien, 50% der Privatkunden seien unprofitabel bzw. mit 10% der Kunden würden 100% des Gewinns erzielt.[43] In der deutschen Kreditwirtschaft gilt eine Faustformel, nach der 20% der Privatkunden für 80% der Erträge verantwortlich zeichnen sollen.[44]

Indes drängt sich der Eindruck auf, daß es in der Kreditwirtschaft (noch immer) *an systematischen Kundenergebnisrechnungen*[45] *als Ausgangsbasis für ein zielgerichtetes Beziehungsmanagement mangelt* bzw. die bereits existierenden Ansätze mit nicht unwesentlichen *Schwachstellen* behaftet sind. In dem 1995 erschienenen, beinahe 1.000seitigen „Handbuch Bankcontrolling" gibt es in diesem Zusammenhang lediglich den folgenden lapidaren Hinweis:

---

42 Vgl. Hallowell (1996), S. 35.

43 Vgl. Storbacka/Strandvik/Grönroos (1994).

44 Vgl. Polan (1995), S. 41.

45 Zu den Grundlagen der Kundenergebnisrechnung vgl. Plinke/Rese (1995).

„3.4.4 Führung von Kundenbeziehungen

Sogenannte Senior Banker und Account Manager sind für den Erfolgsbeitrag von Kundenbeziehungen verantwortlich. Insbesondere bei Großkunden ... setzt sich diese Beziehung aus diversen Dienstleistungen und Produkten zusammen, die in der Verantwortung mehrerer Sparten stehen und bei mehreren Regionen in Anspruch genommen werden. Bedingt durch die Komplexität ist es oftmals schwierig, das exakte Kundenergebnis zu bestimmen.“[46]

Die in der Praxis anzutreffenden Ergebnisrechnungen setzen in der Regel an einem *aktuellen Kundendeckungsbeitrag* der Geschäftsbeziehung an. SCHÜTZ/KRUG haben zuletzt auf die Problematik dieser Größe hingewiesen, die insbesondere

- nur ein stichtagsbezogenes Bild liefert,
- durch die übliche periodische Abgrenzung keine Informationen über „Vorlaufinvestitionen“ in die Beziehung enthält,
- und auch keine Aussage über die Rentabilität des Einsatzes weiterer finanzieller Mittel macht.[47]

Ziel muß es daher sein, in der Planung, Steuerung und Kontrolle einer Geschäftsbeziehung auf einen laufend ermittelten „*Lifetime Value*“ abzustellen[48], also einen auf den Kalkulationszeitpunkt auf- bzw. abgezinsten Barwert der vergangenen und zukünftigen Ergebnisse.

Hiervon sind die meisten deutschen Kreditinstitute aber noch ein gutes Stück entfernt. Nach einer intensiven Methodendiskussion in den achtziger Jahren gehört zwar die sogenannte „Marktzinsmethode“ immerhin zum Standard des internen Rechnungswesens. Danach werden die Zinssätze am Geld- bzw. Kapitalmarkt zur „Benchmark“ für Kredit- und Einlagengeschäfte. Über die Aggregation der Differenz zwischen Kunden- und Marktzinssätzen („Margen“) läßt sich der Erfolg von Kundenbetreuern, Produkten und eben auch Kundenbeziehungen sachgerechter ermitteln als in der zuvor verbreiteten

[46] H. Steinmann, Generaldirektor Schweizerische Bankgesellschaft, (1995, S. 500f.).

[47] Vgl. Schütz/Krug (1996).

[48] Meyer/Oevermann (1995), Sp. 1345; vgl. weiterhin in diesem Sinne Oggenfuß (1993), S. 6 - 14.

„Schichtenbilanzmethode".[49] Doch liegt dem Grundmodell der Marktzinsmethode eine nur einperiodige Betrachtungsweise zugrunde.

Kaum Umsetzung gefunden hat bisher die in der Literatur vorgeschlagene Erweiterung der Marktzinsmethode durch das *„Barwertkonzept".*[50] Hierbei wird der Versuch gemacht, die Erfolgswirkungen einzelner Bankgeschäfte über ihre gesamte Laufzeit zu berechnen. Statt diese Information insbesondere für die Kalkulation von Geschäftsbeziehungen nutzbar zu machen, beschäftigt sich allerdings auch die Wissenschaft wesentlich intensiver mit der Frage, wie dieser periodenübergreifende - und daher für die auf Dauer angelegte Geschäftsbeziehung einzig aussagekräftige - Barwert mühsam mit den dem engen Korsett des externen Rechnungswesens entstammenden Ergebnisinformationen in Einklang gebracht werden kann.[51]

Bei der Behandlung der über den Zinsanteil hinausgehenden Komponenten der Kundenerfolgsrechnung sind in der Literatur ebenfalls Inkonsistenzen festzustellen. So plädiert SCHIERENBECK in seinem Standardwerk zum Bank-Controlling zwar sachgerecht dafür, den Barwert der (bonitätsbedingten) Risikokosten im Kreditgeschäft anzusetzen, will jedoch mit den Betriebskosten und den Dienstleistungserträgen (z.B. Kontoführungsgebühren) anders verfahren - nämlich diese nicht abzinsen. Für die Personal- und Sachkosten lautet die Begründung, daß *„ein Großteil (dieser Kosten) ohnehin zum Zeitpunkt des Vertragsabschlusses anfällt, sie im weiteren Verlauf relativ niedrig sind und erst gegen Vertragsende wieder ansteigen... Da der überwiegende Kostenteil bei einer Multiplikation mit den exakten Abzinsfaktorn aufgrund seiner Zukunftsnähe nur geringfügig abgezinst würde, sind die möglichen Abweichungen relativ unbedeutend."* Die Dienstleistungserträge werden von ihm ebenfalls nicht diskontiert, *„... zumal ihr Gewicht im bilanzrelevanten Geschäft im Regelfall nur gering sein wird."* SCHIERENBECK gesteht aber zu: *„Wenn man die Berechnung allerdings exakt durchführen will, können die Dienstleistungserträge natürlich auch im Kunden-Cash flow mit aufgeführt und entsprechend abgezinst werden."*[52]

Obwohl diese Argumentation aufgrund der tendenziell enger gewordenen Margen schon im bilanzrelevanten Geschäft auf einer brüchigen Basis steht, ist sie im bilanzindifferenten

---

49 Vgl. St. Paul (1987). - Allerdings ist die Kontroverse um die Marktzinsmethode (insbesondere die Grenzen ihrer Anwendbarkeit) noch immer nicht abgeschlossen: vgl. Adam/Hering/Schlüchtermann (1994).

50 Vgl. Benke/Gebauer/Piaskowski (1991) sowie Schierenbeck/Wiedemann (1993).

51 So bei Schierenbeck (1994), S. 175 - 193.

52 Alle Zitate Schierenbeck (1994), S. 285.

Geschäft kaum noch haltbar. Diejenigen Leistungen aber, über die sich die Kreditinstitute im Privatkundengeschäft besonders profilieren, durch die sie den Kunden mithin gut binden können, sind insbesondere Beratungsleistungen (wie die Vermögensverwaltung), also bilanzirrelevante Provisionsgeschäfte. Gerade diese Leistungen müssen sorgfältig geplant und dann abgezinst Eingang in einen Barwert der Geschäftsbeziehung finden, um diese adäquat zu steuern.[53] Noch werden speziell die Betriebskosten und Dienstleistungserträge in dieser Hinsicht von der Praxis, aber auch der Wissenschaft stiefmütterlich behandelt.

Daß dabei vom Postulat der Genauigkeit Abstriche gemacht werden müssen, ist schon aufgrund der nicht auflösbaren Erlös- und Kostenverbundwirkungen in Banken[54] sowie der sich im Zeitablauf ändernden Prozeß- und damit Kosten- und Erlösstruktur banal. Doch eine Annäherung an das Gesamtergebnis der Geschäftsbeziehung scheint immer noch besser zu sein als eine Steuerung auf Basis periodisierter Zahlen unter bewußter Ausklammerung bestimmter Ergebnisbestandteile bzw. deren ungleicher Einbeziehung.

Darüber hinaus ist der *absolute* Kundendeckungsbeitrag - auch ein über mehrere Perioden berechneter Barwert - allein wenig aussagekräftig[55]. SCHÜTZ/KRUG schlagen daher vor, auf die *Kundenrentabilität* als

$$\frac{\text{Kundendeckungsbeitrag}}{\text{Kundeninvestment}}$$

abzustellen.[56] Das läßt allerdings noch die Frage unbeantwortet, ob schon bei einem positiven Vorzeichen dieses Terms weiter in die Geschäftsbeziehung investiert werden sollte. Will man den Shareholder Value der Bank[57] nicht aus den Augen verlieren, so hat auch für die einzelne Geschäftsbeziehung im Prinzip und auf Dauer dasselbe wie für ganze Geschäftsfelder zu gelten: Die Kundenrentabilität muß die von der Bank angestrebte, als Renditeforderung der Eigenkapitalgeber beispielsweise aus dem Capital Asset Pricing Model abgeleitete Mindestverzinsung überschreiten - nur dann tragen weitere Investitionen in die Beziehung zur Steigerung des Unternehmenswertes bei:

---

53 Vgl. Paul/Siewert (1997), S. 133 - 136.

54 Vgl. Süchting (1992), S. 102.

55 Das ist auch der Haupteinwand gegen die Untersuchung von Sachenbacher (1991), die aber zumindest als eine der wenigen Arbeiten eine periodenübergreifende Erfolgsermittlung anstrebt.

56 Schütz/Krug (1996), S. 193.

57 Vgl. grundsätzlich Süchting (1996).

$$\frac{\text{Gesamt(plan)barwert der Kundenbeziehung}}{\text{Gesamt(plan)investment}} \rangle r_{EK}.$$

Begrenzte Unterschreitungen der Mindestrendite durch den Ist-Barwert können demnach hingenommen werden, wenn begründete Anhaltspunkte für Kompensationen in späteren Perioden vorliegen, so daß der geplante Lifetime Value wiederum die Mindestverzinsung überschreitet.

In diese Planung müssen Annahmen über die Bankloyalität bzw. Kundenbindung eingehen, auf die zumindest näherungsweise z.B. mit Hilfe von Zufriedenheitsstudien und eine Analyse der Kundenbeschwerden geschlossen werden kann.[58] Dabei erweist es sich als Problem, daß die Umfeldbedingungen zunehmend instabil werden, typische Verläufe von Geschäftsbeziehungen also immer seltener ohne Korrekturen in die Zukunft extrapoliert werden können. Dies darf indes nicht in die Aufforderung für das Bank-Controlling münden, vor diesem - zugegeben weiten - Aufgabenfeld zu kapitulieren.

6. Mögliche Strategien der Banken als Reaktion auf den Wandel von Geschäftsbeziehungen im Privatkundengeschäft

Für die Kreditinstitute eröffnen sich mehrere Möglichkeiten, auf die Veränderung der Märkte zu reagieren; eine allgemeine Strategie des Geschäftsbeziehungsmanagements kann es nicht geben. Alle drei Grundtypen von Kunden (Abbildung 2) erfordern eine sorgfältige Behandlung des Kontakts, diese wird aber für die einzelnen Gruppen unterschiedlich aussehen. Nur wenn das Geschäftsbeziehungsmanagement darauf ausgerichtet ist, diesen differenzierten Beziehungen gerecht zu werden, kann die Bank auch unter den veränderten Umfeldbedingungen rentabel bleiben.

Eine für das jeweilige Institut passende Positionierung kann in fünf Schritten erfolgen:

[58] Meyer/Dornach (1993).

1. Identifikation der erreichbaren Zielsegmente[59],
2. Analyse, welches Angebot für die Nachfrager des betreffenden Zielsegments hinsichtlich (vor allem) Qualität und Preis adäquat ist,
3. Analyse des erreichbaren Cash-flows in der Zeit,
4. Auswahl der gemessen am Shareholder Value attraktiven Segmente,
5. Abstimmung der Strategie und des Instrumenten-Mix auf diese Segmente sowie entsprechende Gestaltung der Potentiale.

Eine ***erste Strategie*** könnte darin bestehen, die verbliebenen „Alles-aus-einer-Hand-Kunden" mit einem umfassenden Angebot anzusprechen bzw. mit den Vorteilen eines solchen Angebots derzeitige „Hauptsächlich-bei-einem-Kunden" wieder fester an sich zu binden. Dieses Segment kann attraktiv sein im Hinblick auf zwei unterschiedliche Kundenklassen:

- Zum einen trifft man hier den mäßig vermögenden Nachfrager, der einige wenige Geldgeschäfte tätigt, die er grundsätzlich auf verschiedene Institute verteilen könnte. Da er in Geldfragen sehr unsicher ist, neigt er nicht dazu, über einen Wechsel der Bankverbindung nachzudenken. In diese Geschäftsbeziehungen muß im Vergleich wenig investiert werden, da der Kunde von sich aus die Beziehung nicht in Frage stellt. Daher ist der Nachfrager auch hinsichtlich des Preis/Leistungs-Verhältnisses relativ unsensibel, solange es sich nicht im negativen Sinne deutlich von dem entfernt, was ihm als „normal" oder „angemessen" erscheint. Es ergibt sich dann auch ein vergleichsweise stabiler Cash-flow.

- Zum anderen befindet sich hier auch der vermögende Privatkunde, der von seinem umfangreichen Bedarf an Bankleistungen her erst recht eine Aufteilung auf verschiedene Institute vornehmen könnte. Er tut dies zwar ebenfalls aus Gründen der Risikoaversion und/oder der Bequemlichkeit nicht, stellt aber deutlich höhere Qualitätsansprüche als der Kunde im ersten Fall. Hier sind dementsprechend verstärkt (z.B. Personal-)Investitionen erforderlich, um die notwendige Problemlösungskompetenz sicherzustellen. Angesichts des Ergebnispotentials dieser Kunden muß um eine Amortisation aber nicht gefürchtet werden, denn für die Covenience, die ihnen ein solches Angebot bietet, sind sie bereit, bei einzelnen Teilleistungen einen höheren Preis zu bezahlen, als dies marktüblich ist.

[59] Dabei wird die Loyalität nur ein Segmentierungskriterium unter mehreren sein, allerdings mit einer herausgehobenen - da kaufverhaltensbestimmenden - Bedeutung. Wenn im folgenden nur auf dieses Kriterium zurückgegriffen wird, dient dies lediglich der gedanklichen Vereinfachung.

Ein Kreditinstitut, das auf dieses Segment setzt, muß nicht nur ein umfangreiches Sortiment bereithalten, um dem Nachfrager tatsächlich „alles aus einer Hand“ anbieten zu können. Um das Beziehungsziel *absolut* loyaler Kunden erreichen zu können, ist auch die abgestimmte Vermarktung erforderlich, die es diesen unattraktiv erscheinen läßt, weitere Geschäftsbeziehungen zu anderen Banken zu unterhalten.

Grundlage dieses Sortiments sind - klassisch - die Zeitraumleistungen. Unabhängig vom Grad der Komplexität werden sie so angeboten, daß ein häufiger und zugleich intensiver persönlicher Kontakt besteht. Idealerweise müßte auch außerhalb der Absatzakte im engeren Sinne die Nähe zu den Nachfragern durch ein „Einklinken“ in das persönliche Umfeld (z.B. Vereinsleben, Freizeitveranstaltungen) gesucht werden.

Aus dieser Anforderung an die Zeitraumleistungen ergibt sich die Notwendigkeit, die Potentiale und Prozesse des Anbieters entsprechend zu gestalten. Das bedingt zunächt die Schaffung oder Erhaltung möglichst vieler Kontaktpunkte. Eine solche Bank benötigt ein Geschäftsstellennetz, das zumindest dort, wo regionale Schwerpunkte der Kundschaft identifiziert werden können, sehr eng geknüpft sein sollte. Ergänzend gilt es aber auch in hohem Maße, die Chancen der Integration des Bankkunden als externen Faktor in die Potential- und Prozeßgestaltung zum Zwecke der Bindung zu nutzen. Der integrative Aufbau spezifischer Potentiale[60] besteht z.B. in der Sammlung und systematischen Auswertung der Kundenhistorie sowie des gesamten Umfelds der Geschäftsbeziehung. Auf Mitarbeiterseite muß Interesse für die über die finanziellen hinausgehenden Probleme des Kunden bestehen.[61] In der Prozeßgestaltung kann man die große Eingriffshäufigkeit[62] (der Kunde soll so oft wie nur möglich Kontakt zu seiner Geschäftsstelle aufnehmen) für die Informationssammlung nutzen. Dazu muß sich selbstverständlich eine ausreichende Zahl von Mitarbeitern in der Geschäftsstelle befinden, die diesen Prozeß durchführen können. Dabei sollte man einem Nachfrager dieses Typs auch das Gefühl geben, daß er intensiv in die Prozeßgestaltung eingreifen kann, selbst wenn man ihn schließlich nur zwischen standardisierten Teilelementen wählen läßt. Der Eindruck, mitbestimmen zu können, steigert sein Sicherheitsgefühl in der Beziehung.

---

60 Vgl. Engelhardt/Freiling (1995), S. 908ff..

61 Vgl. Süchting (1994).

62 Zu den Eingriffsdimensionen vgl. Engelhardt/Kleinaltenkamp/Reckenfelderbäumer (1993) und Engelhardt/Freiling (1995), S. 910.

Im Bereich des Kostenmanagements sind Banken bei einer solchen Strategie somit aber enge Grenzen gesetzt, kann man doch bei den hohen Personalkosten im direkten Kundenkontakt dann nur wenig einsparen. Die Rentabilität läßt sich allenfalls steigern durch eine „Entschlackung" der Prozesse jenseits der „Line of visibility", dem Back-office. Hier scheint es sehr sinnvoll, mit Hilfe eines kombinierten Einsatzes von Target Costing und Prozeßkostenrechnung ein integriertes Preis- und Kostenmanagement zu betreiben[63].

Als Abwandlung und gleichzeitig Bindeglied zu einem radikal anderen Vorgehen kann die ***zweite Strategie*** angesehen werden. Hierbei würde versucht, diejenigen Kunden, die zumindest „hauptsächlich bei einer" Bank bleiben wollen, zu halten, bzw. „Grenzfälle" aus den beiden anderen Kundengruppen zu akquirieren.

Für die Sortimentspolitik birgt dies die Aufgabe, einen Kern zu definieren, in dem die Bank ihren Sortimentsschwerpunkt setzen will. Um ihn herum werden diejenigen Leistungen gruppiert, die die Kunden des anvisierten Segments nach Möglichkeit ebenfalls abnehmen sollen, bei denen die Bank sich von der Leistungsqualität her aber allenfalls im Durchschnitt des Marktes bewegt.

Beziehungsziel dieser Kreditinstitute wäre es, eine *prinzipielle* Loyalität zu erzeugen, die sie in den Augen der Nachfrager im Hinblick auf das Kernsortiment zur alleinigen Bezugsquelle, bei den Leistungen „in der zweiten Reihe" zumindest zur ersten Wahl macht. Eine so begrenzte Loyalität, die sich in Abwanderungen zumindest bei bestimmten Leistungen äußert, wird bewußt hingenommen - in der Erkenntnis, daß ein Vollsortiment für diese Banken nicht rentabel darstellbar ist.

Fragt man nach der Art des Kernsortiments, so läßt sich dieses mit Blick auf die Leistungskomplexität „von unten" oder aber „von oben" definieren. Einerseits kann sich eine Bank auf die wenig komplexen Routineleistungen konzentrieren und für die anspruchsvolleren Kundenprobleme lediglich Standardlösungen anbieten. Zum anderen ist als Schwerpunkt das hochkomplexe Geschäft wie die genannte Vermögensbetreuung denkbar; Routineleistungen wie Termingelder würden nur „nebenbei" und in geringer Variantenzahl angeboten.
Im zweiten Fall ist es unmittelbar einsichtig, daß die Zeitraumleistung die Basis der Beziehung bildet, die personalintensiv ausgestaltet werden wird, um eine weitreichende Integration des externen Faktors gewährleisten zu können. Im ersten Fall drängt es sich zunächst auf, die

[63] Vgl. M. Paul/Reckenfelderbäumer (1995).

weniger komplexen Leistungen durch hohen Technikeinsatz zu einem möglichst niedrigen Preis anzubieten. Es wäre allerdings ebenso denkbar, auch hierbei den persönlichen Kontakt zu suchen, zumal bereits solche Banken für derartige Leistungen den anonymeren Weg wählen werden, die in ihrem Kernsortiment auf komplexe Leistungen setzen. Während demnach im zweiten Fall eine Konzentration besonders qualifizierter Mitarbeiter in wenigen Kompetenzzentren bzw. einem Außendienst stattfinden kann, bleibt es für den ersten Fall offen, ob unvermindert ein dichtes Zweigstellennetz erforderlich oder aber dessen Ausdünnung und Kompensation z.B. durch Telefon-, PC- und SB-Banking möglich ist.

Die ***dritte Strategie*** ist die des „Rosinenpickens". Kreditinstitute, die diese Vorgehensweise wählen, nutzen bewußt die Illoyalität einzelner Nachfrager ihren vormaligen „Hausbanken" gegenüber aus. Es werden gezielt einige wenige Leistungen ausgewählt, die in Qualität und/oder Preis wesentlich attraktiver gestaltet werden, als dies am Markt üblich ist. Dabei gelten hinsichtlich der Aufnahme von mehr oder weniger komplexen Leistungen in das Sortiment ähnliche Überlegungen wie bei der zweiten Strategie - mit dem Unterschied, daß das vorsichtige (wenn auch gegenüber der „Alles"- Strategie abgemilderte) „sowohl als auch" zu einem „entweder oder" wird. Insofern handelt es sich um eine Zuspitzung der zweiten Strategie.

Das Beziehungsziel der *selektiven* Loyalität besteht darin, die Nachfrager bei bestimmten Leistungen fest an die jeweilige Bank zu binden, nicht an das Kreditinstitut insgesamt. Das wäre auch wenig sinnvoll, ist doch die diese Strategie wählende Bank nur in sehr begrenztem Umfang in der Lage, über die ausgewählten Leistungen hinaus weitere Angebote kompetent darzustellen. Institute mit dieser strategischen Stoßrichtung haben in erster Linie, aber nicht allein die „Immer-woanders-Kunden" im Visier. Auch das partielle Herausbrechen von Nachfragern der beiden ersten Gruppen aus ihren bestehenden Geschäftsbeziehungen erscheint sinnvoll, je nach dem, ob man hier gegenüber den anderen Anbietern Vorteile preislicher oder qualitativer Art besitzt.

7. Status quo: Konformität statt notwendiger Differenzierung

Es hat den Anschein, daß derzeit noch die Mehrzahl der deutschen Banken unverändert auf die "Alles-bei-einem-Kunden" setzt. Öffentlich-rechtliche Institute, Kreditgenossenschaften aber auch die privaten Großbanken versuchen, die Jagd nach dem absolut loyalen Bankkunden mit einem möglichst umfassenden Leistungsangebot zu gewinnen. Stark vergröbert stellt man fest: Sparkassen und Genossenschaftsbanken streben - mehr oder

weniger intensiv, insgesamt jedoch einem Herdentrieb folgend - in den bisher von ihnen vernachlässigten Bereich der anspruchsvollen privaten Vermögensanlage und wollen sich den Großbanken insofern annähern. Dort wiederum wird das Breitengeschäft weiterhin mit Verve betrieben, etwa wenn die Deutsche Bank ankündigt, nun auch in Supermärkten Präsenz zu zeigen.[64]

Ob diese Strategie erfolgreich - also rentabel - ist, läßt sich extern insofern schwer beurteilen, als die Publizität deutscher Kreditinstitute noch keine Segmentberichterstattung enthält. Erst durch den Einfluß der anglo-amerikanischen auf die deutsche Rechnungslegung sind hier Fortschritte zu erwarten.[65] Allerdings kann von Aussagen der Großbanken, die das inländische Filialgeschäft (das jedoch auch das Firmenkundengeschäft enthält) als „Sorgenkind" bezeichnen, das der Branche „wie ein Mühlstein am Halse hängt", auf sicherlich unterhalb der angestrebten Mindestverzinsung des Eigenkapitals liegende Margen geschlossen werden.[66]

Offenbar gelingt die Darstellung eines Vollsortiments zu einem akzeptablen Preis/Leistungs-Verhältnis in den Augen der Kunden immer schlechter. Im jüngst veröffentlichten Bericht über das „Deutsche Kundenbarometer 1996" schneiden sowohl die Sparkassen (Wert von 2,99) als auch die Deutsche Bank (3,00 = Mitte zwischen „völlig zufrieden" und „unzufrieden") in dieser Beziehung wesentlich schlechter ab als z.B. die Citibank.[67] Diese hat es in den letzten Jahren verstanden, ein eng abgegrenztes Sortiment mit starker Standardisierung und hohem Technikeinsatz „preiswert" anzubieten. In anderen Bankengruppen jedoch führen die Investitionen in die bislang noch nicht angesprochenen Kundengruppen zu hohen Belastungen und damit Deckungsbedarf durch die angestammten Kunden via Quersubventionierung.
Neben diesen schon heute sichtbar werdenden Problemen hatten die vorhergehenden Ausführungen gezeigt, daß das „Alles-bei-einem"- Segment der absolut loyalen Kunden immer weiter erodiert, ja sich zu einer Marktnische entwickelt, in der nur noch wenige Anbieter Platz haben werden. Die hier vertretene These lautet daher: Nur eine schärfere Profilierung durch Konzentration auf die Strategie 2 oder 3 bewahrt die Kreditinstitute davor, gegen Ende dieses Jahrzehnts doch noch die „Stahlindustrie der neunziger Jahre"[68] zu

---

64 Vgl. Deutscher Sparkassen- und Giroverband (1995), S. 49ff. sowie o. V.: Deutsche Bank geht (1996).

65 Vgl. o.V.: „Werkstatt" Vereinsbank (1997).

66 Vgl. o. V.: Die Großbanken (1996), S. 20, o. V.: Filialgeschäft (1996), und Voss (1995).

67 Vgl. Erzweiler/Tilger (1996).

68 U. Cartellieri, Vorstandsmitglied der Deutsche Bank AG, (1990).

werden. Die zunehmende Illoyalität der Kunden eröffnet hierzu den Weg. Durch Preis- und Qualitätssignale muß eine verstärkte *Selbstselektion* der Nachfrager initiiert werden. Stellt ein Kunde fest, daß er bei bestimmten Leistungen nicht (mehr) der „passende" externe Faktor im Rahmen der Leistungserstellung der Bank ist, so wird er schneller bereit sein, zumindest mit Teilen seines Engagements abzuwandern. Dies erspart der Bank weitere Investitionen in (zumindest für sie) unrentable Kundenbeziehungen. Gleichzeitig besteht - umgekehrt - die Möglichkeit, illoyale Kunden anderer Institute anzusprechen.

Für diejenigen Kunden, die bleiben respektive neu hinzukommen sollen, müssen die richtigen Bindungspotentiale aufgebaut werden. Einige Schlaglichter sollen zeigen, wie dies für die unterschiedlichen Gruppen des Kreditgewerbes ansatzweise aussehen könnte:

Der strategische Vorteil der *Großbanken* liegt darin, daß sie frühzeitig ihr Provisionsgeschäft intensiviert haben und im Hinblick auf die komplexen und zugleich besonders zukunftsträchtigen Leistungen „rund um das Wertpapier" Marktführer sind. Als Ausdruck dessen werden etwa 50 % der Depots inländischer Privatpersonen bei ihnen unterhalten.[69] Insbesondere aufgrund der spezifischen Qualifikation ihres Potentialfaktors Mitarbeiter bietet es sich an, auf die Strategie 2 zu setzen und aus den genannten sowie weiteren besonders komplexen Leistungen (dem rechten Strang der Abb. 1) den Kern des Sortiments zu formen. Hier scheint das im Oktober 1996 verkündete, neue Strategieziel der Dresdner Bank konsequent: „Ziel im Privatkundengeschäft (ist) es, sich als Nummer eins für Vermögensanlage und Vermögensaufbau zu positionieren."[70] Ihr neuer Slogan lautet: „Die Beraterbank". - Fraglich bleibt dann noch, inwiefern die Leistungen mit nur geringem Komplexitätsgrad überhaupt und wenn, dann in welcher Form angeboten werden sollen.

Eine wichtige Rolle dürften in diesem Zusammenhang die sogenannten *Direktbanken* spielen, die seit etwa drei Jahren in zunehmender Zahl und Konsequenz, meist als Töchter der Großbanken den Markt betreten haben. Überwiegend wird dabei auf den Vertrieb einiger weniger Standardleistungen mittels Telefon, Fax und den PC gesetzt, eine persönliche Beratung nicht angeboten. Eine Ausnahme macht hier die Advance Bank, Tochter der Vereinsbank, die „Banking für Fortgeschrittene" anpreist und auf die unvermindert mögliche Beratung hinweist.[71] - Noch sind die Erfolgsrechnungen der Direktbanken zu stark durch Vorlaufinvestitionen belastet, um bewerten zu können, ob sie dauerhaft rentabel arbeiten

[69] Vgl. Oehler (1995).

[70] O. V.: Dresdner plant (1996).

[71] Vgl. zum Überblick die Sonderbeilage „Direct Banking" (1996).

werden. Aber auch der Kundenzustrom als Erlösbasis liegt bisher unter den Erwartungen. So hat eine der ersten Direktbanken, die comdirect, Tochter der Commerzbank, statt der anvisierten 90.000 erst 73.000 Kunden gewonnen. Dabei hielt sich der Kannibalisierungseffekt aus dem Kundenstamm der Mutter heraus mit 9 - 10% noch in Grenzen[72]. Die Direktbank der Frankfurter Sparkasse konnte dagegen - selbst mit deutlich über dem Markt liegenden Konditionen für die Geldanlage - nur ein Drittel Neukunden verzeichnen, zwei Drittel waren bisher schon Kunden der Mutter[73]. Prognosen gehen dennoch davon aus, daß mittel- bis langfristig 25 % des Privatkundengeschäfts auf die Direktbanken zulaufen könnte.[74] Unabhängig davon, ob und wann dieses Szenario vollständig Wirklichkeit wird, ist ein Nebeneinander von Direktbanken und Filialnetz in der heutigen Form aber nicht denkbar. Eine noch darüber hinausgehende, „nicht als Konkurrenz, sondern als Parallele zur Filiale“ vorgenommene Eröffnung von „Bankingshops“ in Supermärkten, um „Kundennähe ganz wörtlich (zu) nehmen“[75], wirft die Frage nach der Existenz eines sorgfältigen Ressourcencontrolling auf. Bisherige Erfahrungen mit derartigen Einrichtungen im Handelsbereich geben jedenfalls noch keinen Anlaß zur Euphorie.[76] Darf in der Aussage „Dabei wird die Eröffnung von Bankingshops keinerlei Schließung traditioneller Filialen zur Folge haben.“[77] vor diesem Hintergrund mehr als eine „Beruhigungspille“ für die Arbeitnehmer gesehen werden?

Die Auslagerung von Teilen des Privatkundengeschäfts in die Direktbanken scheint mithin der richtige Weg zu einem rationellen Angebot der Routineleistungen (linker Strang der Abb. 1) durch Großbanken, der jedoch wesentlich konsequenter als bisher gegangen werden sollte. Es kann sich bei den neuen Vertriebswegen nicht um eine schlichte Ergänzung des Geschäftsstellennetzes handeln, sondern es muß langfristig eine Substitution angestrebt werden. Nur auf diese Weise lassen sich die notwendigen Mittel für den Ausbau der Potentiale zum Vertrieb der komplexen Leistungen freisetzen.

Von den Direktbanken bedroht werden die *öffentlich-rechtlichen Institute* und die *Kreditgenossenschaften*. Die bisherigen Erfahrungen zeigen, daß besonders Sparkassen Kunden an

---

72 Vgl. Gloystein (1997).

73 Vgl. o.V.: 1822 testiert (1997).

74 Vgl. o. V.: Direktbanken haben (1995).

75 Zitate von G. Krupp, für das Privatkundengeschäft zuständiges Vorstandsmitglied der Deutsche Bank AG, nach o. V.: Deutsche Bank zeigt (1996), o. V.: Geldgeschäfte im Supermarkt (1996).

76 Vgl. o. V.: Deutsche Bank geht (1996) und Radecki/ Wenninger/Orlow (1996).

77 So B. Pauluhn, Bereichsvorstand Privat- und Geschäftskunden der Deutsche Bank AG, (1997), S. 67.

die Newcomer verlieren.[78] Es dürfte für diese Bankengruppen schwierig sein, einerseits den Preiswettbewerb gegen die Direktbanken zu gewinnen und andererseits ausreichend Ressourcen für die Forcierung des anspruchsvollen Privatkundengeschäfts zur Verfügung zu stellen. Auch hier muß deshalb die Strategie 2 eingeschlagen werden. Den Kern des Sortiments können (im Gegensatz zu den Großbanken) nur die wenig bis mäßig komplexen Leistungen bilden. In diesem Bereich aber sollte zur Abgrenzung von den Direktbanken auf (1) umfassenden, (2) persönlichen Service (3) vor Ort gesetzt werden.

„Umfassend“ (1) meint hier eine breitere und zudem stärker individualisierbare Palette von weniger komplexen Leistungen als diejenige der Groß- und Direktbanken, die die wesentlichen Bedürfnisse der „Hauptsächlich-bei-einem“- Kunden abdeckt. Dazu kommen aber z.B. auch die Baufinanzierung sowie die Immobilienvermittlung, Geschäfte, bei denen sich Sparkassen und Kreditgenossenschaften aufgrund lokaler Informationsvorteile besonders profilieren können. Für noch komplexere Finanzprobleme sollten allerdings nur wenige Standardlösungen angeboten[79], ansonsten aber intensiver die Möglichkeiten des Verbundsystems genutzt werden. Damit könnten auch anspruchsvolle Leistungen durch das Einzelinstitut angeboten, jedoch durch die Landes- bzw. Zentralbanken erstellt werden (z.B. ein Wertpapier-Informationsservice).

Mit der persönlichen Beratung (2) kann wiederum eine Differenzierung gegenüber den anderen genannten Bankengruppen, aber auch im Vergleich mit stark auf neue Vertriebsmedien setzende Institute (wie die Citibank) gelingen. Es werden die Kunden „aufgefangen“, die auf das Beratungsmerkmal Wert legen und daher - in bezug auf die erwähnten Leistungen - von Groß- und Direktbanken langfristig „ausgesteuert“ werden dürften. Diese Personalisierung erscheint aussichtsreicher, als - wie allerdings geplant[80] - ebenfalls in den Direktbankbereich einzutreten, zumal dort eine Profilierung gegenüber der Konkurrenz wesentlich schwieriger sein dürfte. - Dabei spart der Nachfrager Transaktionskosten, wenn die Sparkassen und Genossenschaftsbanken ihre Potentiale in geographischer Hinsicht aufrecht erhalten und weitgehend unvermindert mit einem dichten Zweigstellennetz „vor Ort“ vertreten bleiben (3).

[78] Vgl. o. V.: Abschied von (1996).

[79] Vgl. etwa zu den diesbezüglichen Angeboten der Stadtsparkasse Köln Drewes/Böhm (1993) und o. V.: Zwischen Marmor-Tresen (1993).

[80] Vgl. o. V.: Direktmarkt (1996) sowie die umfangreichen Bemühungen der genossenschaftlichen Bankengruppe mit dem „KontoDirect“, dargestellt im Heft 2/1997 der Zeitschrift „Bankinformation“.

Der Erfolg dieser Strategie wird insbesondere davon abhängen, inwieweit eine ausreichende Zahl von Nachfragern auch zukünftig noch den physischen Kontakt präferiert. Geben sich immer mehr Kunden auch mit einem Kontakt via Bildtelefon zufrieden, so besitzen die Direktbanken mit den bereits aufgebauten bzw. noch im Aufbau befindlichen Potentialen einen Wettbewerbsvorteil, da sie über geeignetere technische Plattformen verfügen.

Für Banken mit keinem oder einem sehr beschränkten Filialnetz bietet sich eine noch weitergehende Sortimentseinengung in Richtung der *Strategie 3* an. Die BHF-Bank kann hier als ein Musterbeispiel genannt werden, da sie sich im Privatkundengeschäft ausschließlich auf die Vermögensberatung konzentriert[81] und entsprechend in den Potentialfaktor des Mitarbeiter-Know-hows investiert. - Auch Institute wie die Vereinsbank und die Bayerische Hypotheken- und Wechsel-Bank, die nur in einem enger begrenzten Gebiet die Möglichkeit zur persönlichen Kundenansprache besitzen, werden über diesen Weg nachdenken müssen. Die eingangs präsentierte Anzeige deutet in die richtige Richtung.

8. Zusammenfassung

Abschließend seien die sieben Kernaussagen noch einmal thesenartig zusammengestellt:

1. Die Zahl der absolut loyalen Bankkunden nimmt stetig ab; dies macht ein differenzierteres Management unterschiedlicher Geschäftsbeziehungen erforderlich.

2. Voraussetzung hierfür ist eine aussagekräftige Kundenergebnisrechnung, mit der der Lifetime Value einer Geschäftsbeziehung geplant, gesteuert und kontrolliert werden kann; auf diesem Gebiet sind bislang allenfalls Ansätze zur Problemlösung erkennbar.

3. Das weitgehend gleichgerichtete strategische Vorgehen von Großteilen der Kreditwirtschaft führt zu einer Konturlosigkeit der einzelnen Institute und dadurch in eine Sackgasse.

4. Am Shareholder Value ausgerichtete Renditeziele lassen sich nur durch eine Abkehr vom „Alles-bei-einem"- Kunden und damit auch vom Vollsortiment erreichen. Notwendig sind

81 Vgl. o. V.: Die BHF-Bank (1995).

dafür eine wesentlich stärkere Fokussierung auf bestimmte Zielgruppen und der Aufbau zu ihnen passender Bindungspotentiale.

5. Für die Großbanken scheint eine Konzentration auf komplexere Problemlösungen unter weitgehender Auslagerung von Standardleistungen angezeigt.

6. Sparkassen und Kreditgenossenschaften müssen dagegen einen Weg der Personalisierung gerade von weniger komplexen Leistungen finden, um nicht langfristig von den Direktbanken verdrängt zu werden.

7. Zunehmende Illoyalität ist dann kein Schicksal, sondern - richtig aufgenommen - eine Chance: Die Kreditinstitute müssen sich systematischer und konsequenter von unattraktiven Kunden trennen und vice versa attraktive Kunden der Konkurrenz akquirieren. Hierfür ist jedoch eine eindeutigere Positionierung am Markt dringend erforderlich.

9. Literatur

Adam, D./**Hering**, Th./**Schlüchtermann**, J.: Die Eignung der Marktzinsmethode als Partialmodell zur Beurteilung der Vorteilhaftigkeit von Investitionen, in: Die Betriebswirtschaft, 54. Jg. (1994), S. 775 - 786

Becker, D.: Bankbetriebliche Zweigstellenexpansion und Standortplanung, Diss. Göttingen 1975

Benke, H./**Gebauer**, B./**Piaskowski**, F.: Die Marktzinsmethode wird erwachsen: Das Barwertkonzept, (I) und (II), in: Die Bank, o. Jg., 8/1991, S. 457 - 468 und 9/1991, S. 514 - 521

Cartellieri, U.: Aktuelle Perspektiven deutscher Banken im internationalen Wettbewerb, in: Süchting, J. (Hrsg.): Semesterbericht Nr. 32 des Instituts für Kredit- und Finanzwirtschaft an der Ruhr-Universität Bochum, Sommersemester 1990, S. 36 - 39

Corsten, H.: Die Produktion von Dienstleistungen: Grundzüge einer Produktionswirtschaftslehre des tertiären Sektors, Berlin 1985

Deutscher Sparkassen- und Giroverband: Jahresbericht, Bonn 1995

Diller, H.: Beziehungsmanagement, in: Tietz, B. (Hrsg.): Handwörterbuch des Marketing, 2. Aufl., Stuttgart 1995, Sp. 285 - 300

Diller, H.: Kundenbindung als Marketingziel, in: Marketing ZFP, 18. Jg. (1996), S. 81 - 94.

Diller, H./**Götz**, P.: Die Kundenportfolioanalyse - ein Instrument zur Steuerung von Kundenbeziehungen, Arbeitspapier Nr. 1 des Lehrstuhls für Marketing an der Universität Erlangen-Nürnberg 1991

Diller, H./**Kusterer**, M.: Beziehungsmanagement. Theoretische Grundlagen und explorative Befunde, in: Marketing ZFP, 10. Jg. (1988), S. 210 - 220

Drewes, W./**Böhm**, St.: Effiziente Vermögensverwaltung durch standardisiertes Management-Depot, in: Sparkasse, 110. Jg. (1993), S. 190 - 192

Engelhardt, W. H.: Erscheinungsformen und absatzpolitische Probleme von Angebots- und Nachfrageverbunden, in: ZfbF, 28. Jg. (1976), S. 69 - 82

Engelhardt, W. H./**Freiling**, J.: Integrativität als Brücke zwischen Einzeltransaktion und Geschäftsbeziehungen, in: Backhaus, K./Diller, H. (Hrsg.): Dokumentation des 1. Workshops der Arbeitsgruppe "Beziehungsmanagement" v. 27./28. 9. 1993, Münster u.a. 1994, S. 53 - 68

Engelhardt, W. H./**Freiling**, J.: Die integrative Gestaltung von Leistungspotentialen, in: ZfbF, 47. Jg. (1995), S. 899 - 918

Engelhardt, W. H./**Freiling**, **J**.: Prekäre Partnerschaften, in: Absatzwirtschaft, 39. Jg. (1996), Sonderheft Oktober, S. 145 -151

Engelhardt, W. H./**Kleinaltenkamp**, M./**Reckenfelderbäumer**, M.: Leistungsbündel als Absatzobjekte, in: ZfbF, 45. Jg. (1993), S. 395 - 426

Engelhardt, W. H./**Schwab**, W.: Die Beschaffung von investiven Dienstleistungen, in: Die Betriebswirtschaft, 42. Jg. (1982), S. 503 - 513

Epple, M. H.: Die Kundenbindung wird schwächer: Vertrieb von Bankprodukten, in: Die Bank, o. Jg., 10/1991, S. 544 - 550

Erzweiler, T./**Tilger**, C.: Störenfried Kunde, in: Capital, 35. Jg. (1996), Nr. 11, S. 48 - 55

Farny, D.: Versicherungsmarketing, in: Tietz, B. (Hrsg.): Handwörterbuch des Marketing, 2. Aufl., Stuttgart 1995, Sp. 2600 - 2612

Gloystein, P.: Erste Erfahrungen mit einer Direktbank, in: Süchting, J./Paul, St. (Hrsg.): Semesterbericht Nr. 45 des Instituts für Kredit- und Finanzwirtschaft an der Ruhr-Universität Bochum, Wintersemester 1996/97, S. 41 - 45

Hallowell, R.: The relationships of customer satisfaction, customer loyality, and profitability: an empirical study, in: International Journal of Service Industry Management, vol. 7 (1996), no. 4, S. 27 - 42

Klages, H.: Indikatoren des Wertewandels, in: von Rosenstiel, L./Einsiedler, H. E./Streich, R. K. (Hrsg.): Wertewandel als Herausforderung für die Unternehmenspolitik, Stuttgart 1987, S. 1 - 16

Kleinaltenkamp, M.: Institutionenökonomische Begründung der Geschäftsbeziehung, in: Backhaus, K./Diller, H. (Hrsg.): Dokumentation des 1. Workshops der Arbeitsgruppe "Beziehungsmanagement" v. 27./28. 9. 1993, Münster u.a. 1994

Kleinaltenkamp, M./**Marra**, A.: Institutionenökonomische Aspekte der Customer Integration, in: Kaas, K. P. (Hrsg.): Kontrakte, Geschäftbeziehungen, Netzwerke: Marketing und neue Institutionenökonomik, ZfbF Sonderheft 35, Düsseldorf 1995, S. 101 - 119

Kleinaltenkamp, M./**Plinke**, W./**Söllner**, A.: Drum prüfe, wer sich ewig bindet, in: Absatzwirtschaft, 39. Jg. (1996), Sonderheft Oktober, S. 152 - 157

Köcher, R.: Zur aktuellen Attraktivität der Direktbanken, in: Bankinformation, 23. Jg. (1997), S. 4 - 6

Kreissparkasse Recklinghausen (Hrsg.): Mitarbeiterzeitschrift "Online", 10/1995

Meyer, A./**Dornach**, F.: Feedback für strategische Vorteile, in: Absatzwirtschaft, 36. Jg. (1993), Sonderheft Oktober, S. 120 - 135

Meyer, A./**Oevermann**, D.: Kundenbindung, in: Tietz, B. (Hrsg.): Handwörterbuch des Marketing, 2. Aufl., Stuttgart 1995, Sp. 1340 - 1351

O. V.: 1822 testiert sich einen „Traumstart", in: Börsen-Zeitung, Nr. 19 v. 29. 1. 1997, S. 9

O. V.: Abschied von der Alleskönner-Bank, in: Börsen-Zeitung, Nr. 41 v. 28. 2. 1996, S. 12

O. V.: Aggressive Strategie im Privatkundengeschäft, in: Börsen-Zeitung, Nr. 244 v. 20. 12. 1995, S. 4

O. V.: Deutsche Bank geht in die Supermärkte, in: Börsen-Zeitung, Nr. 145 v. 31. 7. 1996, S. 4

O. V.: Deutsche Bank zeigt im Supermarkt Flagge, in: Süddeutsche Zeitung, Nr. 253 v. 2./3. 11. 1996, S. 34

O. V.: Deutsche Bank: Regelmäßige Kundenbefragungen, in: Handelsblatt, Nr. 213 v. 4. 11. 1996, S. 16

O. V.: Die BHF-Bank wird ein „High-Quality-Player", in: Börsen-Zeitung, Nr. 182 v. 21. 9. 1995, S. 6

O. V.: Die Großbanken gewähren neue Einblicke in ihr Rechenwerk, in: Frankfurter Allgemeine Zeitung, Nr. 79 v. 2. 4. 1996, S. 20

O. V.: Direktbanken haben den Durchbruch geschafft, in: Börsen-Zeitung, Nr. 216 v. 9. 11. 1995, S. 19

O. V.: Direktmarkt fast schon „overbanked", in: Börsen-Zeitung, Nr 240 v. 12. 12. 1996, S. 8

O. V.: Dresdner plant eigene Direktbank, in: Börsen-Zeitung, Nr. 208 v. 29. 10. 1996, S. 5

O. V.: Filialgeschäft erweist sich als Sorgenkind, in: Handelsblatt, Nr. 62 v. 27. 3. 1996, S. 20

V.: Geldgeschäfte im Supermarkt, in: Westdeutsche Allgemeine Zeitung, Nr. 258 v. 1. 11. 1996, S. 14

O. V.: Sonderbeilage „Direct Banking", in: Börsen-Zeitung, Nr. 212 v. 2. 11. 1996, S. 13 - 18

O. V.: Zwischen Marmor-Tresen und Barfuß-Bankiers, in: Süddeutsche Zeitung v. 22. 3. 1993, S. 20

O.V.: „Werkstatt" Vereinsbank, in: Börsen-Zeitung, Nr. 56 v. 21. 3. 1997, S. 6

OEHLER, A.: Eine Analyse des Wettbewerbs im Privatkundengeschäft der Universalbanken, in: Sparkasse, 112. Jg. (1995), S. 125 - 130

OGGENFUß, C. W.: Keine Betreuung von der Stange, in: Geldinstitute, o. Jg., Heft 1 + 2/1993, S. 6 - 14

PAUL, M./**RECKENFELDERBÄUMER,** M.: Preispolitik und Kostenmanagement - neue Perspektiven unter Berücksichtigung von Immaterialität und Integrativität, in: Kleinaltenkamp, M. (Hrsg.): Dienstleistungsmarketing, Wiesbaden 1995, S. 225 - 260

PAUL, St.: Lenkungssysteme in Filialbanken - Steuerung über Komponenten oder Verrechnungszinsen?, Wiesbaden 1987

PAUL, St.: Bankenintermediation und Verbriefung, Wiesbaden 1994

PAUL, St./**SIEWERT,** K.-J.: Bank-Controlling I: Ertragsmanagement, 2. Aufl., Frankfurt/M. 1997

PAULUHN, B.: Die Bank kommt zum Kunden, in: Die Bank der Zukunft, Sonderbeilage der Frankfurter Allgemeinen Zeitung, Nr. 29 v. 4. 2. 1997, S. 7

PLINKE, W.: Die Geschäftsbeziehung als Investition, in: Specht, G./Silberer, G./Engelhardt, W. H. (Hrsg.): Marketing-Schnittstellen, Festschrift f. H. Raffée, Stuttgart 1989, S. 305 - 325

PLINKE, W.: Ausprägungen der Marktorientierung im Investitionsgüter-Marketing, in: ZfbF, 44. Jg. (1992), S. 830 - 846

PLINKE, W.: Grundlagen des Geschäftsbeziehungsmanagements, in: Kleinaltenkamp, M./Plinke, W. (Hrsg.): Technischer Vertrieb. Bd. 2: Geschäftsbeziehungsmanagement, Berlin u.a. 1997, S. 1-62

PLINKE, W./RESE, M.: Analyse der Erfolgsquellen, in: Kleinaltenkamp, M./Plinke, W. (Hrsg.): Technischer Vertrieb. Bd. 1: Grundlagen, Berlin u.a. 1995, S. 597 - 660

POLAN, R.: Ein Meßkonzept für die Bankloyalität, Investitionen in Bank/Kunde-Beziehungen unter Risikoaspekten, Wiesbaden 1995

RADECKI, L. J./WENNINGER, J./ORLOW, D. K.: Bank Branches in Supermarkets, in: Federal Reserve Bank of New York (Ed.): Current Issues in Economics and Finance, vol. 2, no. 13, december 1996

SACHENBACHER, H. U.: Prospektive Lebensdauerkalkulation von Kundenbeziehungen in Kreditinstituten, München 1991

SCHÄFER, H.: Beziehungsmanagement durch Dialogmarketing: Bankloyalität aus institutionenökonomischer Sicht, in:. Kaas, K. P. (Hrsg.): Kontrakte, Geschäftbeziehungen, Netzwerke: Marketing und neue Institutionenökonomik, ZfbF Sonderheft 35, Düsseldorf 1995, S. 119 - 139

SCHIERENBECK, H.: Ertragsorientiertes Bankmanagement, 4. Aufl., Wiesbaden 1994

SCHIERENBECK, H./WIEDEMANN, A.: Das Treasury-Konzept der Marktzinsmethode, (I): Integration von Grundmodell und Barwertkalkül, in: Die Bank, o. Jg., 11/1993, S. 670 - 676 und (II): Die Messung des Treasury-Erfolges, in: Die Bank, o. Jg., 12/1993, S. 731 - 737

SCHÜTTE, M.: Anforderungen an die Entwicklung von Kundenbetreuern, in: Süchting, J./van Hooven, E. (Hrsg.): Handbuch Bankmarketing, 2. Aufl., Wiesbaden 1991, S. 211 - 232

SCHÜTZ, P./KRUG, H.: Top oder Flop? Kundenbeziehungen profitabel gestalten, in: Absatzwirtschaft, 39. Jg. (1996), Sonderheft Oktober, S. 188 - 193

SEITZ, J.: Die Determinanten der Bankwahl und der Bankloyalität, Diss. Münster 1976

SHARPE, St. A.: Asymmetric Information, Bank Lending, and Implicit Contracts: A Stylized Model of Customer Relationship, in: The Journal of Finance, vol. 45 (1990), S. 1069 - 1087

SPIEGEL-VERLAG (HRSG.): Soll und Haben, Hamburg, 1: 1980, 2: 1985, 3: 1990, 4: 1996

STAUSS, B./NEUHAUS, P.: Das Qualitative Zufriedenheitsmodell (QZM), in: Diller, H. (Hrsg.): Beziehungsmanagement, Nürnberg 1995, S. 137 - 165

Steinmann, H.: Der dreidimensionale Ergebnisausweis als Grundlage der Controllingfunktion, in: Schierenbeck, H./Moser, H. (Hrsg.): Handbuch Bankcontrolling, Wiesbaden 1995, S. 491 - 515

Storbacka, K./Strandvik, T./Grönroos, C.: Managing customer relationships for profit: the dynamics of relationship quality, in: International Journal of Service Industry Management, vol. 5 (1994), no. 2, S. 105 - 115

Süchting, J./Boening, D.: Der personale Produktions- und Verkaufsprozeß von Bankleistungen, in: Bank-Betrieb, 11. Jg. (1971), S. 364 - 370

Süchting, J.: Theorie und Politik des Banksortiments - Grundlagen einer Sortimentslehre der Bank, unveröff. Habilitationsschrift, Frankfurt/M. 1967

Süchting, J.: Die Einkaufswirtschaftlichkeit für Bankleistungen und die Zweigstellenpolitik, in: Bank-Betrieb, 8. Jg. (1968), Nr. 10, S. 277 - 280

Süchting, J.: Die Bankloyalität als Grundlage zum Verständnis der Absatzbeziehungen von Kreditinstituten, in: Kredit und Kapital, 5. Jg. (1972), S. 269 - 300

Süchting, J.: Die Theorie der Bankloyalität - (noch) eine Basis zum Verständnis der Absatzbeziehungen von Kreditinstituten, in: Süchting, J./van Hooven, E. (Hrsg.): Handbuch Bankmarketing, 2. Aufl., Wiesbaden 1991, S. 25 - 43

Süchting, J.: Bankmanagement, 3. Aufl., Stuttgart 1992

Süchting, J.: Vertrieb von Finanzdienstleistungen auf dem Markt für Privatkunden, in: Die Bank, o. Jg., 8/1994, S. 449 - 457

Süchting, J.: Unternehmenssteuerung in Aktienbanken nach dem Shareholder Value-Konzept, in: International Bankers Forum e.V. (Hrsg.): Die Banken auf dem Weg ins 21. Jahrhundert, Wiesbaden 1996, S. 406 - 418

Szallies, R.: Vom Bankkunden zum Finanzverkäufer, in: Absatzwirtschaft, 39. Jg. (1996), Sonderheft Oktober, S. 94 - 101

Voss, G.: Sparwelle: Bankberatung bald nur noch für Betuchte, in: Westdeutsche Allgemeine Zeitung, Nr. 255 v. 1. 11. 1995, S. 23

Wehrli, H. P./**Jüttner**, U.: Relationship Marketing in Value Generating Systems, in: Sheth, J. N./Parvatiyar, A. (Eds.): Relationship Marketing: Theory, Methods and Applications, Atlanta 1994, Section I: Paradigm and Prospectives

WITT, F.-J.: Bankloyalität - eine empirische Untersuchung, in: bank und markt, 15. Jg. (1986), Nr. 1, S. 20 - 23

WÜNSCHE, G./**SWOBODA,** U.: Die Bedeutung von Zielgruppen für die fokussierte Universalbank, in: Die Bank, o. Jg., 5/1994, S. 275 - 279

Matthias Schnittka*

DAS „SCHÖNE-WOCHENENDE-TICKET“ DER DB AG ALS INSTRUMENT DES KAPAZITÄTSMANAGEMENTS

<u>Inhalt</u>

---

* Dipl.-Ök. Matthias Schnittka, Ruhr-Universität Bochum, Lehrstuhl für Angewandte BWL III (Marketing), Prof. Dr.Dr.h.c. Werner H. Engelhardt, Universitätsstraße 150, 44780 Bochum, Tel. 0234 / 700 2897, Fax 0234 / 7094 256

1. Das „Schöne-Wochenende-Ticket“ - Hintergrund und Struktur

1.1. Die Situation des Nahverkehrs der DB AG vor Einführung des SWT

Mit der Umwandlung in eine Aktiengesellschaft ging bei der Deutschen Bahn AG eine Neuorganisation einher. Die Zuständigkeit für den Nahverkehr wurde in einem eigenen Geschäftsbereich zusammengefaßt. Gleichzeitig wurde die Ergebnisverantwortung der Teilbereiche gestärkt, so daß die vorher weitgehend vernachlässigte Kapazitätsauslastung für den Geschäftsbereich „Personennahverkehr“ zunehmend an Bedeutung gewann: Aufgrund des erheblichen Fixkostenanteils der DB AG im Personenverkehr ist der wirtschaftliche Erfolg entscheidend von der Kapazitätsauslastung abhängig. Den verschwindend geringen Grenzkosten eines weiteren Fahrgastes stehen zusätzliche Erlöse gegenüber, die fast vollständig einen zusätzlichen Deckungsbeitrag bedeuten.

Die durchschnittliche Kapazitätsauslastung im Schienenpersonennahverkehr (SPNV) liegt vor Einführung des SWT bei ca. 8%[1] - eine Situation, die auf den ersten Blick bereits einen Handlungsbedarf signalisiert. Noch eklatanter tritt die Problematik zu tage, wenn man die Situation einzelner Züge betrachtet, die selbst von den Verantwortlichen als „Geisterzüge“ bezeichnet werden.[2] Neben der Belastung der Ertragssituation hat eine solche Situation auch negative Auswirkungen auf das Sicherheitsgefühl der Reisenden.

Von den zwei als Basisstrategien des Kapazitätsmanagements bezeichneten Alternativen[3] schied die Anpassung des Angebots an die Nachfrage weitgehend aus: Die Zubringerfunktion zum Fernverkehr ließ eine einschneidende Reduktion des Nahverkehrsangebots nicht realisierbar erscheinen. Vor diesem Hintergrund sollte die Einführung des SWT zusätzliche Nachfrage in Form von Freizeitreisenden akquirieren.

---

1 Vgl. Beiersdorf (1995), S. 1; die DB AG sah sich nicht in der Lage, detailliertere Zahlen zur Verfügung zu stellen.

2 Klaus Daubertshäuser, Vorstandsmitglied DB AG und verantwortlich für den Bereich Nahverkehr, in einem Focus-Interview, Heft 11/1995, S. 37.

3 Vgl. Corsten (1992), S. 241ff.; Armistead/Clark (1994), S. 5ff.

1.2. Konstruktion des SWT

Zur Einführung des SWT am 4. Februar 1995 galt folgende Regelung: Mit den Erwerb eines Tickets können fünf Personen zwischen Samstag, 00.00 Uhr und Sonntag, 24.00 Uhr alle Nahverkehrszüge der DB AG in der 2. Klasse zum Preis von 15,- DM ohne jede Kilometerbegrenzung benutzen. Darüber hinaus gab es noch einen Gruppentarif, der aber sehr schnell wieder abgeschafft wurde.[4]

Diese Tarifkonstruktion läßt sich als eine Kombination von sachlicher[5] und zeitlicher Preisdifferenzierung charakterisieren. Es handelt sich nicht um eine Sonderaktion, die auf einen bestimmten Zeitraum begrenzt ist. Die Tarifgestaltung weicht aber von den üblichen Bahnangeboten ab, da der Fahrpreis nicht entfernungsabhängig berechnet wird. Als Vorbild können die Tagestickets angesehen werden, die von vielen Unternehmen des ÖPNV bereits seit längerem angeboten werden. Im Unterschied zu diesen Tickets ist im SWT jedoch eine Beschränkung enthalten, die bahnspezifisch ist: der Fernreiseverkehr - genauer diejenigen Züge, die primär für den Fernreiseverkehr bestimmt sind - sind nicht zur Benutzung mit dem Wochenendticket freigegeben. Eine solche Beschränkung ist für andere Anbieter im ÖPNV nicht erforderlich, da es sich um reine Nahverkehrsunternehmen handelt.

Die Angebotsgestaltung hat sich seit der Einführung verändert: Der Preis für ein SWT ist in zwei Stufen auf 35,- DM erhöht worden. Damit einhergehend wurde die Gültigkeit des Tikkets auf die Angebote der meisten Verkehrsverbunde erweitert sowie die Gültigkeitsdauer bis zum Montag morgen, 02.00 Uhr, verlängert.

Die DB AG begründet die einschneidende Preiserhöhung mit der sachlichen und zeitlichen Leistungsausweitung[6] - eine Argumentation, die vor dem Hintergrund der Kapazitätsauslastung als Ziel des SWT wenig überzeugt. Vielmehr läßt sich die begründete Vermutung aufstellen, daß die Preiserhöhung eine Reaktion auf den in diesem Ausmaß nicht erwarteten Zuspruch der Kunden darstellt. Am ersten Wochenende im Mai 1995 wurden mehr als 210.000 Tickets verkauft, die gleichbedeutend mit etwa 650.000 Fahrgästen sind.[7] Mit der Preiserhöhung auf 35,- DM sank die Zahl der verkauften Tickets von durchschnittlich 157.000 auf un-

---

[4] Vgl. Franz (1995), S. 94f.

[5] Sachlich deshalb, weil nur Nahverkehrszüge im Angebot enthalten sind. Auf die Diskussion, ob eine sachliche Preisdifferenzierung überhaupt eine Preisdifferenzierung sein kann, soll hier verzichtet werden.

[6] Vgl. Franz (1995), S. 94.

[7] Vgl. Franz (1995), S. 95.

ter 100.000 Stück. Pro Wochenende erzielt die DB AG somit einen Erlös von mehr als 3 Mio. DM.

Im folgenden soll das SWT nicht primär als Erlösträger, sondern in seinen Eigenschaften als Instrument des Kapazitätsmanagements betrachtet werden. Zunächst soll die Frage diskutiert werden, welche Möglichkeiten der Kapazitätssteuerung für integrative Leistungen denkbar sind und wie das SWT darin eingeordnet werden kann. Anschließend wird eine Interpretation der Ergebnisse versucht, die über die Ermittlung von Auslastungskennzahlen hinausgeht.

2. Grundlagen des Kapazitätsmanagements integrativer Leistungen

2.1. Beschaffung externer Faktoren

Unter Kapazität wird weitgehend übereinstimmend die „Leistungsfähigkeit einer wirtschaftlichen oder technischen Einheit beliebiger Art, Größe und Struktur in einem Zeitabschnitt"[8] verstanden. Diese sehr allgemein gehaltene Definition führt zu verschiedenen Kapazitätsarten, wenn man die Begriffe Leistungsfähigkeit, Einheit und Zeitabschnitt mit unterschiedlichen Inhalten belegt.[9]

Das Kapazitätsmanagement als zielgerichtete Gestaltung der Leistungsfähigkeit hat im wesentlichen zwei Aufgaben zu erfüllen: Zunächst muß die Kapazität in qualitativer und quantitativer Hinsicht dimensioniert werden, d.h. es ist eine Entscheidung über den Umfang der Leistungsfähigkeit im weiteren Sinne zu treffen. Die zweite, damit untrennbar verbundene Funktion besteht darin, die Auslastung der bereitgestellten Kapazität im Zeitablauf zu überwachen und zu steuern.[10] Der Grad der Erfüllung dieser Aufgabe wird in der Regel über Beschäftigungskennzahlen zu messen versucht.

Dieses Kapazitätsverständnis basiert auf einer produktionswirtschaftlichen Betrachtung und ist für einen Industriebetrieb entwickelt worden. Noch Gutenberg trennt eindeutig zwischen der Produktion von Sachleistungen und der Bereitstellung von Dienstleistungen.[11] Nachfol-

8 Kern (1962), S. 27.

9 Vgl. Wiegand (1968), S. 27ff., Layer (1979), Sp. 873ff.

10 Vgl. Steven (1996), Sp. 875, die von Kapazitätsgestaltung und Kapazitätsnutzung spricht.

11 Vgl. Gutenberg (1958), S. 19f., Gutenberg (1965), S. 2.

gend ist in der Literatur eine Diskussion darüber geführt worden, inwiefern dieses Kapazitätsverständnis auf Dienstleistungen übertragbar sei. Im Mittelpunkt stand dabei die Frage, ob die Analyse der Dienstleistungsproduktion ein eigenes Faktorsystem erfordere, welches die externen Faktoren als eigene Gruppe berücksichtigt.[12] Gegen ein solches Vorgehen spricht zunächst die Systematik, da sich die Unterscheidung intern-extern ausschließlich an der Verfügbarkeit der Faktoren aus Sicht des Anbieters orientiert, nicht aber das Verhalten während des Leistungserstellungsprozesses berücksichtigt. Externe Faktoren sind als Spiegelbild der herkömmlichen Produktionsfaktoren auf Seiten des Nachfragers zu interpretieren. Sie können grundsätzlich in denselben Ausprägungen wie interne Faktoren auch auftreten. Demzufolge ist es nicht statthaft, die Gruppe der externen Faktoren neben Potential- und Verbrauchsfaktoren zu stellen. Zum anderen muß der Einwand erhoben werden, daß die Gegenüberstellung von Dienstleistungen und Sachleistungen weder trennscharf noch weiterführend ist.[13]

Dennoch ist die Integration externer Faktoren der Ansatzpunkt, um Kapazitätsplanung und Kapazitätssteuerung in vielen Dienstleistungsbranchen mit angemessenen Instrumenten anzugehen. Die Verfügbarkeit über externe Faktoren in entsprechender Qualität und Quantität - nicht ihre fertigungswirtschaftlichen Eigenschaften - ist der Schlüssel zum erfolgreichen Kapazitätsmanagement bei integrativer Leistungserstellung.[14] Über die Integrativität läßt sich die als wesentliches Problem angeführte schwankende Nachfrage bei „Dienstleistungen“ systematisch in das Kapazitätsmanagement einbetten. Die Ursache von Kapazitätsdefiziten ist darin zu sehen, daß das qualitative oder quantitative Verhältnis von internen und externen Faktoren gestört ist. Ist die erforderliche Menge an externen Faktoren nicht erreicht, besteht ein Auslastungsdefizit; im umgekehrten Fall entsteht eine Überlastung, die sich auf verschiedene Art und Weise äußern kann.

Gelingt es einem Anbieter, die Beschaffung externer Faktoren[15] zu optimieren, so ist das Absatzproblem in Form einer schwankenden Nachfrage ebenfalls gelöst. Dabei darf der technische Ausdruck der Beschaffung nicht darüber hinwegtäuschen, daß es sich keinesfalls um einen Kaufvertrag handelt. Zum einen ist die Beschaffung eines externen Faktors immer unmittelbar mit dem Absatz der Leistung verbunden. Zum anderen ist die Verfügungsgewalt

---

12 Vgl. hierzu vor allem Corsten (1985) und die dort angegebene Literatur.

13 Vgl. Engelhardt / Kleinaltenkamp / Reckenfelderbäumer (1993), S. 395ff.

14 Die Übertragung der Konzeption und Instrumente von Just-in-time Systemen liefert wichtige Ansatzpunkte, vgl. Harvey (1989), Duclos / Siha / Lummus (1995), Schnittka (1996).

15 Vgl. hierzu Kleinaltenkamp (1993), der die Beschaffung externer Faktoren für das Investitionsgütermarketing untersucht hat; vgl. zur Übertragung auf die Kapazitätplanung in Dienstleistungsunternehmen Schnittka (1996), S. 22ff.; eine branchenspezifische Betrachtung findet sich bei Paul / Schnittka (1996).

über diesen Faktor immer zeitlich begrenzt, und zwar in der Regel auf die Dauer des Leistungserstellungsprozesses. Ein Nachfrager wird nur dann bereit sein, die in seiner Verfügung befindlichen Faktoren bereitzustellen, wenn zuvor über das mit der Leistungserstellung bezweckte Ergebnis Einigung erzielt werden konnte.

Beide Teilgebiete des Kapazitätsmanagements sind primär unter der Fragestellung zu betrachten, welchen Einfluß eine bestimmte Maßnahme auf die Art und Weise der Beschaffung bzw. Anlieferung externer Faktoren hat.

Die zu Erstellung einer integrativen Leistung erforderliche Beschaffung externer Faktoren ist für den Nachfrager immer auch mit Kosten verbunden. Aus seiner Sicht handelt es sich dabei um die Übernahme einer Zulieferfunktion, die neben unmittelbaren Kostenwirkungen auch einen Verzicht auf die uneingeschränkte Verfügbarkeit über den einzubringenden Faktor während der Leistungserstellung bedeutet. Die Aufgabenverteilung zwischen Anbieter und Nachfrager kann über den Erfolg einer integrativen Leistung entscheiden.[16]

Eine stärkere Differenzierung dieser Aussagen ist im Rahmen dieses Beitrags nicht möglich.[17] Dies gilt auch für die Berücksichtigung der Art externer Faktoren, die zu beschaffen sind. Im vorliegenden Beispiel handelt es sich in erster Linie um die Person des Reisenden, daneben aber auch um Informationen hinsichtlich Reiseziel und Reisedauer. Im folgenden Abschnitt soll der Leistungserstellungsprozeß im Nahverkehr der Bahn betrachtet werden.

2.2. Der SPNV als kollektive Dienstleistung

Ein Fahrgast im Nahverkehr der DB AG kommt mit der Bereitstellungsleistung auf vielfältige Art und Weise direkt in Kontakt. Ein Blueprinting[18], wie es vor allem für das Qualitäts- und Kostenmanagement durchgeführt wird, zeigt die zahlreichen Kontaktpunkte auf. Im Hinblick auf das Kapazitätsmanagement führt dieser Umstand dazu, daß die Kapazität nicht nur objektiv erfaßt werden muß, sondern auch einer subjektiven Bewertung durch den Nachfrager unterzogen wird.[19] In Ermangelung eines fertigen Leistungsergebnisses gewinnt die Bereitstel-

---

16 Vgl. zum Verhältnis von Absatz und Produktion bei integrativen Leistungen Meyer / Blümelhuber (1994).

17 Vgl. vor allem Corsten (1985); Gerhardt (1987).

18 Vgl. hierzu Shostack (1982), Vavra (1993), S. 97ff., Gersch (1995), S.55ff.

19 Vgl. zur Qualitätsermittlung im Personenverkehr Klaus (1984), insb. S. 58ff.

lungsleistung aus Sicht des Nachfragers den Charakter eines Sortiments.[20] Die Verwandtschaft dieser beiden auf den ersten Blick sehr verschiedenen Begriffe zeigt sich auch bei der Gegenüberstellung zweier gängiger Definitionen.

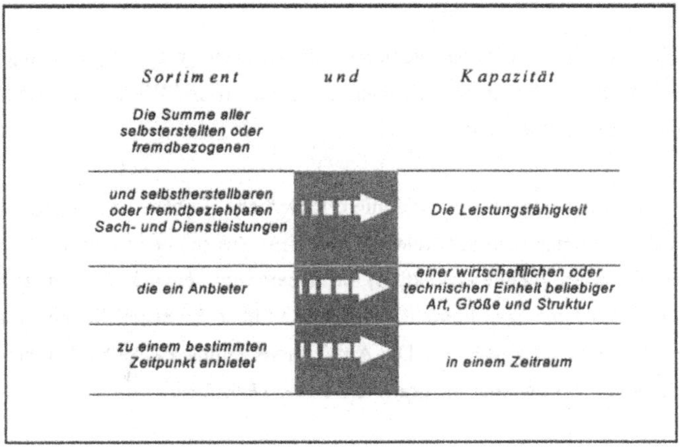

Abb. 1: Kapazität und Sortiment[21]

Einerseits ist der Sortimentsbegriff umfassender als der Kapazitätsbegriff, finden in ihm doch auch die bereits erstellten Leistungen Berücksichtigung. Gerade dieser Sortimentsbestandteil ist jedoch bei integrativen Leistungen dann nicht vorhanden, wenn man bedenkt, daß zur Fertigstellung einer Leistung immer eine Mitwirkung des Nachfragers erforderlich ist. Das Angebot von Leistungsfähigkeiten - häufig als Charakteristikum von Dienstleistungen bezeichnet - schließt diesen Sortimentsbestandteil aus.

Dann aber kann der Sortimentsbegriff als Unterfall oder Spezifizierung des Kapazitätsbegriffs interpretiert werden. Auch der scheinbare Widerspruch zwischen der Zeitpunktbetrachtung des Sortiments und der Zeitraumbetrachtung der Kapazität steht dem nicht entgegen. In vielen Branchen ist es durchaus üblich, daß nicht alle angebotenen Leistungen ohne zeitliche Verzögerung dem Nachfrager zur Verfügung gestellt werden. Eine pragmatische Interpretation des

20 Vgl. zu differierenden Erwartungen zwischen Anbieter und Nachfragern und Möglichkeiten ihrer Ermittlung Hubbert / Sehorn / Brown (1995).

21 Vgl. Schnittka (1996), S. 32

Zeitpunktbegriffs im Sortiment muß aus der Perspektive des Nachfragers und seiner Toleranz bezüglich einer zeitlichen Verzögerung erfolgen.[22]
Das Charakteristikum kollektiver Leistungen liegt in dem Verhältnis der Nachfrager untereinander begründet. Ein Fahrgast wird in der Regel die Zugfahrt - also den Leistungserstellungsprozeß - mit anderen Nachfragern gemeinsam erleben. Im Rahmen des Qualitätsmanagements ist diese Tatsache bereits ausführlich diskutiert worden.[23] Für das Kapazitätsmanagement ergeben sich ebenfalls wichtige Rückschlüsse:
Zunächst läßt sich am Beispiel eines Zuges die als dienstleistungstypisch angesehene Kostenstruktur hoher Fixkosten bei minimalen variablen Kosten exemplifizieren. Die Grenzkosten eines zusätzlichen Fahrgastes sind annähernd null, sofern die Kapazitätsauslastung unter 100% liegt. Diesem Umstand hat es die DB AG zu verdanken, daß das SWT trotz des geringen Preises einen hohen Deckungsbeitrag erzielt.

Kollektive Dienstleistungen sind aber auch dadurch gekennzeichnet, daß der Nachfrager nicht nur die Bereitstellungsleistung, sondern auch die Auslastung der Bereitstellungsleistung wahrnimmt. Auch dies läßt sich wiederum nicht für den einzelnen Nachfrager isoliert betrachten: Ist ein Zug überfüllt, so sind alle Fahrgäste in diesem Zug davon betroffen. Übersteigt die Auslastung 100% - aufgrund der Flexibilität der Kapazität eines Zuges ist das ohne weiteres möglich - sind nicht nur die zusätzlichen Fahrgäste, sondern alle Reisenden davon betroffen.

Gleichzeitig ergibt sich hieraus ein weiterer Hinweis auf die Relevanz einer subjektiven Kapazitätsbetrachtung. Eine vollständig ausgelastete Kapazität bedeutet aus Nachfragersicht zunächst, daß er entweder Wartezeiten akzeptieren muß oder aber - wie im vorliegenden Fall - Unannehmlichkeiten und Qualitätseinbußen in Kauf zu nehmen hat.

Eine intersubjektiv unterschiedliche Beurteilung wird aus der Konkurrenzsituation der Nachfrager um die Kapazität des Anbieters verständlich. Reisende in einem überfüllten Zug werden sich hinsichtlich der Frage, ob die bereitgestellte Kapazität ausreicht anders äußern, als die Fahrgäste in einem Geisterzug[24]. Extremsituationen ergeben sich dann, wenn einzelne Fahrgäste - wie durch die Einführung des SWT geschehen - wegen Überfüllung des Zuges am Bahnsteig zurückgelassen werden müssen. Neben die Beschäftigungsdimension tritt eine Sortimentsdimension, die die Beurteilung der Kapazität aus Sicht der Nachfrager widerspiegelt.

---

22 Vgl. zum Sortimentsbegriff vor allem Gümbel (1963), S. 17ff.

23 Vgl. Klaus (1984), S. 59ff.; Pranter / Martin (1991); Meyer / Westerbarkey (1991).

24 Auf intersubjektiv unterschiedliche Beurteilungen derselben Kapazitätsauslastung wird an dieser Stelle nicht eingegangen.

Auf den Zusammenhang beider Dimensionen sowie auf die Konsequenzen für die Kapazitätsmessung und -gestaltung wird im folgenden näher eingegangen.

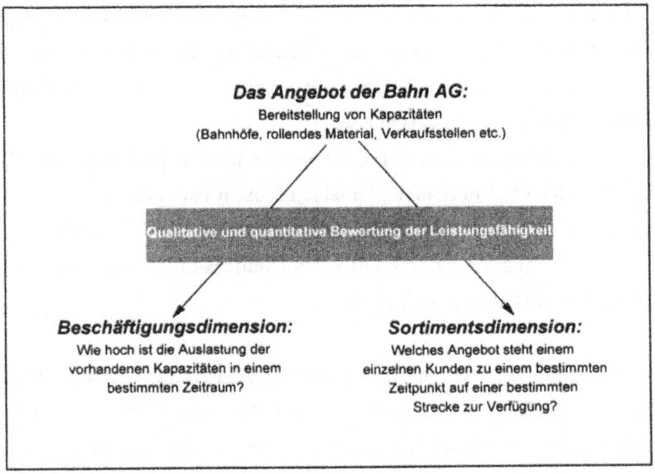

Abb. 2: Kapazität und Sortiment der Deutschen Bahn AG

2.3. Steuerungsmechanismen des SWT

Die Beschaffung externer Faktoren und damit die Steuerung der Kapazitätsauslastung kann auf unterschiedliche Art und Weise erfolgen. Zur Klassifizierung sollen zwei Merkmale herangezogen werden:

1. Zunächst ist eine Entscheidung darüber zu treffen, ob und in welcher Form eine Anmeldung der Nachfrager erfolgt. Ist eine Anmeldung vorgesehen, so nimmt der Anbieter eine Zuordnung der Kapazitäten zu den externen Faktoren vor. Damit ist ein zweiseitiger Informationsfluß verbunden, indem der Nachfrager den Anbieter über seine Reisewünsche informiert, der Anbieter im Gegenzug freie Kapazitäten darstellt und die Nutzung dieser Kapazitäten reserviert. Für den Anbieter resultiert aus einem solchen System in erster Linie ein Dispositionsvorteil, der sich aus dem der Leistungserstellung zeitliche vorgelagerten Informationsfluß ergibt.

2. Weiterhin besteht die Möglichkeit, hinsichtlich der Art der externen Faktoren zu differenzieren. Basierend auf einer Marktsegmentierung lassen sich Gruppen von Nachfragern - und damit auch externen Faktoren - bilden, die eine gegebene Leistungsfähigkeit in unterschiedlichem Ausmaß oder auf unterschiedliche Art und Weise in Anspruch nehmen.

Für das SWT ist zu konstatieren, daß weder eine Anmeldung erfolgt noch eine Differenzierung in der Integration der externen Faktoren vorgenommen wird. Zwar nimmt nicht jeder Nachfrager des SWT die Leistung im selben Umfang in Anspruch, grundsätzlich wird aber jedem Reisende ein identisches Angebot unterbreitet. Der Weg über ein Reservierungssystem wird offensichtlich nicht beschritten. Ohne hier auf Einzelheiten eingehen zu können, mögen folgende Gründe hierfür ausschlaggebend gewesen sein: Der Aufbau eines Reservierungssytems ist zunächst mit erheblichen Kosten verbunden, die durch die Schaffung der informationstechnischen Voraussetzungen sowie die Umsetzung und Überwachung eines derartigen Systems zurückzuführen sind. Gleichzeitig ist ein zeitlicher Vorlauf erforderlich, der kurzfristige Verbesserungen der Kapazitätsauslastung unmöglich macht. In dieser Beziehung hat das SWT sicherlich Vorteile.

Anders ausgedrückt: Die Lieferung externer Faktoren wird vollständig dem Nachfrager überlassen. Es erfolgt weder eine Absprache des Lieferzeitpunkts noch eine Übernahme bestimmter Teilaufgaben durch den Anbieter.[25] Damit handelt es sich um ein undifferenziertes Go-show-System im Sinne des Systematisierungsansatzes in Abb. 3.

Zum anderen wird mit einem Reservierungssystem gleichzeitig der Anspruch beim Nachfrager herausgebildet, daß die Kapazitätsauslastung vom Anbieter zu steuern sei. Der mit einer Reservierung verbundene Platzanspruch erfordert zwangsläufig eine viel höhere Genauigkeit der Planung, die zumindest im Nahverkehrsbereich nur mit erheblichem Aufwand realisiert werden kann. Bei Nichteinhaltung eines Reservierungsversprechens ist im Vergleich zur bisherigen Situation eine weitaus schärfere Reaktion des Nachfragers zu erwarten, da ein Reservierungssystem zu einer differierenden Erwartungsbildung des Nachfragers führt. Die Bahn steht in diesem Fall vor der Frage, ob sie das mit einer Reservierung verbundene Versprechen auch einzulösen in der Lage ist.

[25] Der Service des Gepäcktransports von Tür zu Tür stellt einen solchen Ansatzpunkt dar. Für den SPNV, insbesondere für die Inhaber eines SWT, ist dieser Service aber nicht relevant.

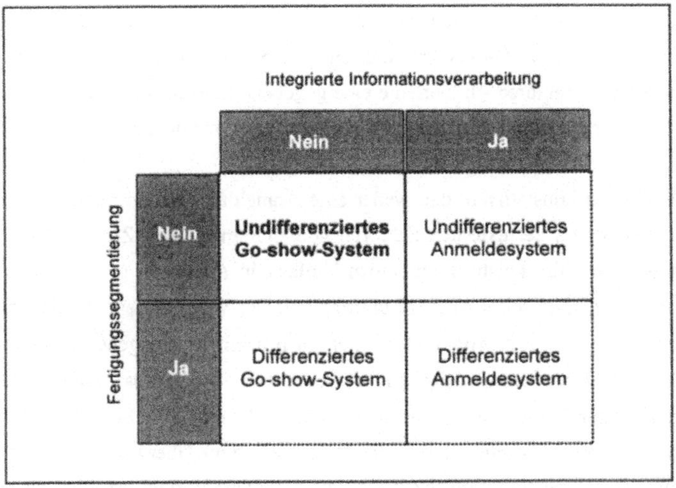

Abb. 3: JIT-Systemelemente bei externen Faktoren

Der mit dem SWT verbundene Informationsfluß im Hinblick auf die Kapazität ist eindimensional: mit dem Nahverkehrsfahrplan gibt die DB AG Auskunft über die Leistungen, die mit dem SWT in Anspruch genommen werden können. Dabei handelt es sich um eine pauschale Information, die keinerlei Angaben darüber machen, ob zu einem bestimmten Zeitpunkt in einem bestimmten Zug auf einer bestimmten Strecke noch eine Reisemöglichkeit für einen bestimmten Fahrgast besteht. Mit dem SWT ist eine Kapazitätsinformation verbunden, die auf ein ungenutztes Angebot am Wochenende hindeutet.

Auf Basis dieser Informationen ist der potentielle Fahrgast angehalten, sich im Wege der Selbstselektion das für ihn passende Angebot herauszusuchen. Im folgenden soll nun untersucht werden, welchen Einfluß der Nachfrageanstieg auf die Beschaffung externer Faktoren einerseits, die Kapazitätsauslastung in Beschäftigungs- und Sortimentsdimension andererseits gehabt hat.

3. Die Auslastungsrechnung der DB AG

Die durchschnittliche Auslastung der Nahverkehrszüge am Wochenende beträgt mittlerweile ca 40% - ein Wert, der die positive Resonanz der Nachfrage auf das SWT eindrücklich unterstreicht. Mit der - in den Grenzen des Nahverkehrs - ausschließlich zeitabhängigen Nutzungs-

begrenzung des Tickets wurde eine Tarifkonstruktion gewählt, die einfach und verständlich ist sowie dem Nachfrager eine hohe Flexibilität in der Nutzung gewährt. Mit ähnlichen Angeboten hatten andere Anbieter im Bereich des ÖPNV bereits einen ähnlichen Erfolg.

Mit Einführung des SWT entstanden jedoch eine Reihe von Schwierigkeiten. Diese resultieren vor allem daher, daß einige Züge mit einer Auslastung von 180 % fahren.[26] In erster Linie sind die Fahrgäste von diesen Zuständen betroffen, wenn man sich vor Augen hält, daß bei einer derartigen Auslastung auf einen sitzenden Fahrgast fast ein stehender Reisender kommt. Auch für die Mitarbeiter der DB AG sind negative Folgen spürbar: so klagten beispielsweise die Zugbegleiter, daß in vielen überfüllten Zügen eine Fahrkartenkontrolle nicht möglich sei. Eine Überprüfung wird dadurch zusätzlich erschwert, daß bis zu fünf Personen mit einem Ticket reisen dürfen. Darüber hinaus bekamen die Zugbegleiter vielfach den Unmut der Reisenden zu spüren.

Diese Extremauslastung hat weitere Konsequenzen: Das rollende Material ist erheblichen Beanspruchungen ausgesetzt, die in jedem Fall zu einer erhöhten Verschmutzung führen. Gleiches ist für viele Bahnhöfe zu konstatieren. Nicht zuletzt zeitigt das SWT auch Wirkungen auf andere Leistungsangebote der Bahn: die Zubringer- und Verteilfunktion des Nahverkehrs für die Fernreiseverkehr ist ebenfalls betroffen. Dies ist besonders bedenklich, weil damit nicht nur die Inhaber von „Billigtickets" in überfüllten Zügen reisen müssen, sondern unter Umständen auch langjährige und zahlungskräftige Kunden, die viel Geld für eine Fernreise bezahlt haben.

Die Reaktion der Bahn eröffnet einen Hinweis darauf, wie Kapazitätsmanagement für integrative Leistungen häufig betrieben wird. Zwar werden die Einzelprobleme gesehen und teilweise auch abgestellt, eine Berücksichtigung der Interdependenz von Beschäftigungs- und Sortimentsdimension unterbleibt jedoch. In erster Linie ist dies auf die Indikatoren zurückzuführen, die die Beschäftigung widerspiegeln sollen.

Mit den Zuständen in einigen Zügen auf besonders belasteten Strecken konfrontiert, machen die Verantwortlichen der DB AG folgende Rechnung auf:[27] Bei einer wochenenddurchschnittlichen Auslastung im Nahverkehr von 40 % seien lediglich 2% der Züge einer Überla-

---

[26] Vgl. Beiersdorf (1995), S. 1; teilweise wird sogar von Auslastungszahlen in Höhe von 230% berichtet. Es drängt sich jedoch die Frage auf, wie solche Zahlen zu ermitteln sind.

[27] Vgl. zu den folgenden Aussagen sowie zu den Zahlen Daubertshäuser (1995), S. 37f.; Franz (1995), S. 95; Neuhaus (1996), S. 24.

stung in der o.g. Größenordnung ausgesetzt. Die nachfolgende Abbildung verdeutlicht, welche Perspektive dieser Argumentation zugrunde liegt.

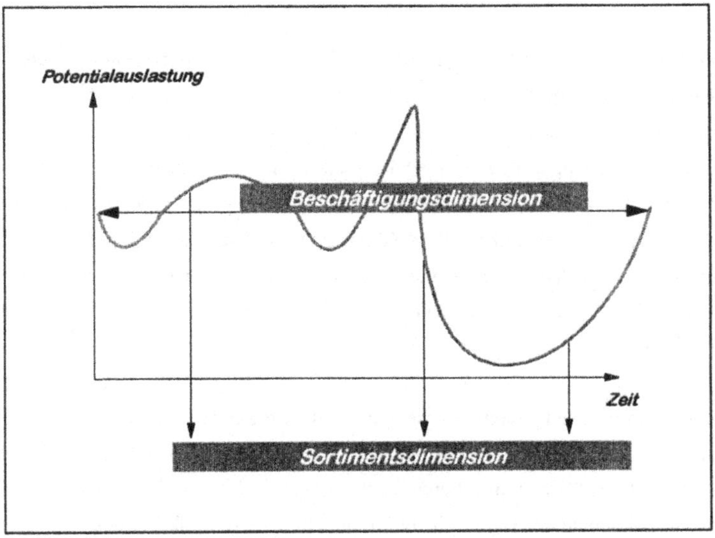

Abb. 4: Perspektiven der Auslastungsbetrachtung

Die vollständige Vernachlässigung der Sortimentsdimension ist auf eine verkürzte Analyse zurückzuführen, die ausschließlich die Beschäftigung der internen Faktoren zum Maßstab erhebt. Diese Sicht der Dinge kann aus Marketing-Sicht nicht befriedigen, was wie folgt begründet werden kann.

Die Sinnhaftigkeit der Kapazitätsfestlegung muß angesichts der Tatsache bezweifelt werden, daß sie offenbar fast problemlos um das 1,8fache überschritten werden kann. Ohne auf die Diskussion um Maximal- und Normalkapazität im einzelnen einzugehen, kann konstatiert werden, daß die Bestimmung der Leistungsfähigkeit ausschließlich anhand der Sitzplätze eines Zuges zu kurz greift. Nicht berücksichtigt werden die Ein- und Ausstiegskapazitäten, die bereits bei einer Auslastung unterhalb 100% zum Engpaß werden und neben Unannehmlichkeiten auch Verspätungen verursachen können.

Weiterhin kann eine Bewertung einer bestimmten Kapazitätsauslastung nur dann erfolgen, wenn zuvor eine Zielgröße formuliert worden ist. Dabei muß der Verdrängungseffekt berücksichtigt werden, der dazu führt, daß ein vollständig ausgelasteter Zug keine weiteren Fahrgäste mehr zu transportieren in der Lage ist. Die Informationsfunktion des Fahrplans wird damit nachhaltig gestört: er verliert seinen Sortimentscharakter zumindest für die Reisenden, die am Bahnhof zurückbleiben müssen. Aber auch für diejenigen, die im Zug reisen dürfen, geht im Hinblick auf zukünftige Fahrten die Planungssicherheit verloren, müssen sie doch damit rechnen, beim nächsten mal weniger Glück zu haben. Der Nutzen, der aus der Möglichkeit resultiert, die Leistung der Bahn nach Maßgabe des Fahrplans jederzeit in Anspruch nehmen zu können, geht teilweise oder vollständig verloren. Dieser Umstand betrifft unmittelbar das Kapazitätsmanagement und darf bei einer Auslastungsbetrachtung keinesfalls vernachlässigt werden. An dieser Stelle ergibt sich die Notwendigkeit, den vielfach hervorgehobenen Nutzen der Bereitstellungsleistung an sich einer Operationalisierung zu unterziehen.[28] Überdies täuschen die Zahlen über das tatsächliche Ausmaß der Kapazitätsspitzen hinweg, wie eine einfache Rechnung zeigt:

Auslastungsgrad	*Zahl der Züge*	*Zahl der Fahrgäste*
0,37	49.000	3.626.000
1,8	1.000	360.000
Summe	50.000	3.986.000
Durchschnittliche Auslastung	0,98 * 0,37 + 0,02 * 1,8 = **40 %**	
Anteil Fahrgäste in überfüllten Zügen	360000 / 3.986.000 = **9%**	

Tab. 1: Auslastungskennzahlen[29]

Auf Basis der vorliegenden Beschäftigungskennzahlen sowie einiger, im Hinblick auf die Gleichverteilung sogar noch sehr optimistischer Annahmen stellt sich heraus, daß 9% aller Fahrgäste in völlig überfüllten Zügen reisen. Dieser Umstand ist nicht verwunderlich, sind doch für eine hohe Kapazitätsauslastung mehr Fahrgäste vonnöten als für einen Geisterzug.

28 Vgl. vor allem Oettle (1970).

29 Pro Wochenende verkehren etwa 50.000 Züge im Nahverkehr, vgl. Franz (1995), S. 94. Zusätzlich wird die Annahme getroffen, daß jeder Zug über 200 Sitzplätze verfügt.

Potentialüberlastung und Zahl der Fahrgäste in überlasteten Zügen stehen in einem Verhältnis von 1:4,5. Dieser eklatante Unterschied in den Auslastungszahlen kann für kollektive integrative Leistungen als typisch angesehen werden. Dies liegt in dem o.g. Kumulationseffekt begründet, der durch die folgende Graphik illustriert werden soll.

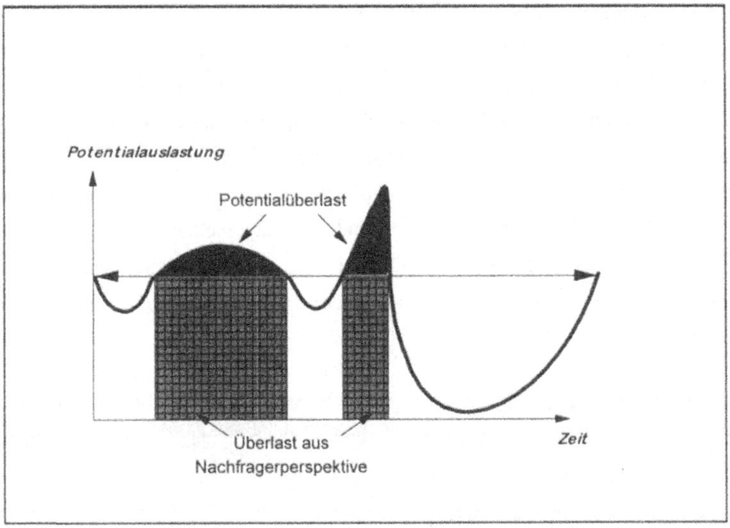

Abb. 5: Kumulationseffekt der Kapazitätsauslastung

Die Auslastungsrechnung der DB AG bringt die ausschließlich intern orientierte, von Kostenüberlegungen dominiert Sichtweise der Kapazität zum Ausdruck. Zudem erfolgt eine Beschränkung der Beschäftigungsbetrachtung auf ein Element der Leistungserstellung. Zwar mag dies aus Anbietersicht deshalb gerechtfertigt erscheinen, weil über die Disposition des rollenden Materials ein erheblicher Teil der Kosten disponiert wird. Die Kennzahlen in Tabelle 1 lassen jedoch erkennen, daß eine potentialorientierte Auslastungsbetrachtung unter Berücksichtigung der externen Faktoren deutlich andere Ergebnisse zeigt.

Im Zentrum der Überlegungen der DB AG steht eindeutig die Steigerung der Durchschnittsauslastung. Damit wird eine Verrechnung von Kapazitätsspitzen und -tälern vorgenommen, die dem Schicksal des einzelnen Reisenden keinerlei Bedeutung zumißt. Zudem signalisiert die Operationalisierung der Kapazitätsspitzen in der Form „Zahl der überfüllten Züge“ nur einen geringen Handlungsbedarf. Vergegenwärtigt man sich, daß die Nachfrager mit ihren Wahlentscheidungen die Kapazitätsauslastung maßgeblich bestimmen, so wiegt das

Fehlen einer Berücksichtigung der Nachfragerperspektive im Rahmen der Auslastungsanalyse besonders schwer.

Eine Durchschnittsauslastung stellt im Extremfall einen Wert dar, der für einen einzelnen Zug niemals zu beobachten ist. Diese Problematik des arithmetischen Mittels ist seit langem bekannt.[30] Die Argumentation mit diesem Wert der Öffentlichkeit gegenüber bleibt unverständlich. Die einseitige Konzentration auf Auslastungstäler - in diesem Fall „Nahverkehrszüge am Wochenende“ - läßt eine Sensibilität für Auslastungsspitzen vermissen, die nicht nur wenig kundenfreundlich, sondern auch sehr kurzsichtig ist. Um dies zu unterstreichen, soll im folgenden Abschnitt die Sortimentsdimension der Kapazität bei integrativen Leistungen näher betrachtet werden. Im Unterschied zu den bisher angestellten Betrachtungen geht es jetzt um eine Argumentation aus der Perspektive des einzelnen Nachfragers.

4. Die Sortimentsdimension der Kapazität

4.1. Informationswirkung und Informationsbedarf

Das Sortiment der DB AG äußert sich in dem veröffentlichten Fahrplan, der alle Verbindungen enthält.[31] Jeder Nachfrager, der einen gültigen Fahrschein besitzt, ist zur Benutzung jedes im Fahrplan aufgeführten Zuges berechtigt. Das Angebot des SWT beinhaltet ausdrücklich diesen Teil des gesamten Leistungsangebots der DB AG.

Vor diesem Hintergrund bedeutet ein überfüllter Zug, der einige Reisende am Bahnhof zurückläßt, für die Betroffenen eine Verminderung des Sortiments. Im günstigsten Fall verlängert sich die Dauer der gesamten Reise, im ungünstigsten Fall kann eine derartige Verzögerung den gesamten Reiseplan eines Fahrgastes obsolet werden lassen. Der Bereithaltungsnutzen wird an dieser Stelle sichtbar, wenn auch nur dadurch, daß er offensichtlich durch die Kapazitätsauslastung geschmälert wird.

Dieser Fall wird die absolute Ausnahme bleiben, wird er doch nur dann Wirklichkeit, wenn die Auslastung so extreme Formen annimmt, daß selbst ein Stehplatz nicht mehr zu haben ist.

---

30 Gleichzeitig werden durch Kompensationseffekte Probleme verdeckt, vgl. Corsten (1994), S. 51.

31 Vgl. zu dieser Interpretation des Sortimentsbegriffs Schnittka (1996), S. 31ff.; dem Verfasser ist keine weiterführende Literatur zum Sortiment von Dienstleistungsunternehmen bekannt.

Die Informationswirkung solcher Einzelfälle darf dennoch nicht unterschätzt werden. Multipliziert durch die Medien läßt Sie den potentiellen Reisenden gewahr werden, daß durchaus die Gefahr besteht, einen bestimmten Zug nicht benutzen zu können. Damit verliert die Bereitstellungsleistung, wie sie durch den Fahrplan dargestellt wird, erheblich an Glaubwürdigkeit. Je nach Anlaß der Reise führt dies zu einer Änderung der Reisplanung, die zur Sicherstellung einer bestimmten Ankunftszeit gewisse Polster einkalkulieren wird. Abgesehen von den damit verbundenen Unannehmlichkeiten für den Reisenden ergeben sich hieraus Verschiebungen im zeitlichen Nachfrageanfall, die nicht nötig wären und eventuell sogar wieder neue Probleme hervorrufen. Die Beinträchtigung hängt nicht direkt von der tatsächlichen Kapazitätsauslastung ab, sondern primär von der Einschätzung des Nachfragers im Hinblick auf die Verfügbarkeit der Bereitstellungsleistung.

Diesem vom einzelnen Reisenden in unterschiedlichem Ausmaß verspürten Informationsdefizit begegnet die DB AG mit der beruhigenden Aussage, lediglich für 2% der Züge seien Engpässe zu befürchten. Wie oben geschildert, täuscht diese Angabe über die wahren Verhältnisse hinweg. Zudem ist sie nicht geeignet, ex-ante darüber Informationen zu liefern, ob der einzelne Reisende auf einer bestimmten Strecke von dieser Überlast betroffen sein könnte.

Konzipiert man ein Kapazitätsmanagement auf Basis der Selbstselektion, wie es im vorliegenden Fall geschehen ist, so steht und fällt der Erfolg des Systems mit validen Informationen, die dem Nachfrager als Basis für eine Entscheidung dienen können.

Die Situation im Nahverkehr am Wochenende ist dadurch gekennzeichnet, daß insbesondere die Ausflugsstrecken von einer Vielzahl von Nachfragern frequentiert werden. Gleiches gilt für den Einkaufs- und Besorgungsverkehr sowie im Falle von Sonderveranstaltungen im sportlichen und kulturellen Bereich.[32] Es ist also wenig zutreffend, von *der* Auslastung des SPNV am Wochenende zu sprechen.

In der Öffentlichkeit muß aber der Eindruck entstehen, die vielen negativen Erlebnisse seien bis zu einem gewissen Maße eine Situation, die jedem Benutzer auf jeder Strecke widerfahren könne. Dies ist insbesondere deshalb zu befürchten, weil mit dem SWT gezielt Neukunden angesprochen werden sollen[33], die mangels Erfahrung die Auslastung auf den für sie relevanten Strecken kaum antizipieren können. Welche Schlußfolgerungen für Kapazitätsmessung

[32] Vgl. Franz (1995), S. 95

[33] Vgl. Franz (1995), S. 96, der die Zahl der durch das SWT gewonnenen Neukunden mit 40% beziffert.

und Kapazitätssteuerung aus diesen Erkenntnissen zu ziehen sein könnten, soll im folgenden Abschnitt untersucht werden.

4.2. Umsetzung in Kapazitätsmessung und Kapazitätssteuerung

4.2.1. Outputbezogene Kapazitätsmessung

Im Rahmen der produktionswirtschaftlich ausgerichteten Diskussion um Kapazität und Kapazitätsmessung ist immer wieder die Frage aufgeworfen worden, in welchen Einheiten die Leistungsfähigkeit zu messen sei.[34] Diese Frage besitzt immer dann Relevanz, wenn verschiedene Teileinheiten zum Entstehen eines Leistungsergebnisses beitragen. Um zu einer einheitlichen Maßgröße zu kommen und damit die Maßgrößen der Leistungsfähigkeit der Teileinheiten gleichnamig zu machen, ist das Leistungsergebnis als Maßstab zu wählen.

Die o.g. Angaben der DB AG haben jedoch einen anderen Hintergrund: In Anlehnung an den Begriffsursprung[35] wird Kapazität als Fassungsvermögen, hier bezogen auf einen Zug, verstanden. Damit wird der Prozeßcharakter der Leistung in doppelter Hinsicht negiert.

Zum einen fehlt bei einer derartigen Größe der dynamische Charakter der Kapazität. Wie in der Definition zum Ausdruck kommt, erstreckt sich eine Leistungsfähigkeit immer auf einen bestimmten Zeitabschnitt, dessen Länge im Hinblick auf unterschiedliche Analyseziele variiert werden kann. Die Zahl der Plätze in einem Zug ist dann nur als Eingangsgröße zu verstehen, die mit der Dauer der Fahrt und der Auslastung auf unterschiedlichen Teilstrecken erst zu einer sinnvollen Kapazitätsgröße verbunden werden kann. Als Einheit hierfür kommt nur die Beförderungsleistung zwischen unterschiedlichen Haltepunkten in Betracht. Das würde dazu führen, daß die Kapazität in Verbindungen ausgedrückt wird, wie es dem Ziel des Bahnangebots - vereinfacht als Ortsveränderung zu bezeichnen - und in der Regel auch dem Empfinden des Nachfragers entspricht. Wie unschwer zu erkennen ist, hätte eine solche Kapazitätsangabe den Vorteil, daß die Folgewirkungen eines überfüllten Zuges sehr viel besser erfaßt werden könnten. Jeder Bahnreisende wird aus eigener Erfahrung die teilweise gravierenden Auswirkungen eines verpaßten Anschlußzuges, oder - wie in diesem Fall - eines überfüllten An-

---

34 Vgl. Betge (1996); Kern (1993) sowie die dort zitierte Literatur.

35 Vgl. Clar (1964), S. 28; Henzel (1967), S. 76; Wiegand (1968), S. 5; Selchert (1970), S. 681; Schmitt (1981), S. 49; Kern (1975), Sp. 2083.

schlußzuges bestätigen können. Auf die Wirkungen des SWT angewendet resultiert daraus, daß ein überfüllter und damit häufig auch gleichzeitig verspäteter Zug eine erhebliche Reduzierung der Kapazität der DB AG in bezug auf mehrere Verbindungen haben kann.

Zum anderen führt nur eine Kapazitätsmessung der Größe „Mögliche Fahrgäste zwischen zwei Orten in einem Zeitabschnitt" dazu, daß der Sortimentsdimension der Kapazität Rechnung getragen werden kann. Auch aus Sicht des Nachfragers ist es der Prozeß des Reisens und sein Ergebnis, die die Leistung der DB AG ausmachen.

4.2.2. Berücksichtigung der Sortimentsdimension der Kapazität

Wie oben bereits geschildert, stellt die Summe der Züge im Nahverkehr das Sortiment der DB AG für diesen Bereich dar. Aus Sicht des einzelnen Reisenden ist die Frage nach der verfügbaren Kapazität anders zu formulieren. Seine Anforderungen sind in der Regel auf eine bestimmte Verbindung, bestehend aus einem oder mehreren Zügen, die er zu einem bestimmten Zeitpunkt oder Zeitraum in Anspruch nehmen möchte. Die folgende Abbildung unternimmt den Versuch, diesen Aspekt der Kapazität aus einem intern orientierten, ausschließlich potentialbezogenen Kapazitätsverständnis abzuleiten. Es handelt sich dabei insofern noch um eine Vereinfachung, als Umsteigevorgänge nicht betrachtet werden.

Wie bereits ausgeführt, läßt sich eine enge Verbindung von Kapazität und Sortiment feststellen,[36] der im vorliegenden Fall auf folgende Weise dargestellt werden kann. Eine Verkürzung des Zeitraums der Kapazitätsmessung bringt unterschiedliche Leistungsfähigkeiten im Zeitablauf zum Ausdruck. Riebel trägt diesem Umstand Rechnung, indem er zwischen der generellen Leistungsfähigkeit und einer sofort verfügbaren Leistungsbereitschaft unterscheidet.[37] Damit verbunden ist eine Spezifizierung des Zeitraums, wie sie in Abb. 6 durch Datum und Uhrzeit zum Ausdruck kommt.

[36] Vgl. die Ausführungen in Abschnitt 2.2 auf den Seiten 127ff.

[37] Vgl. Riebel (1954), S. 14.

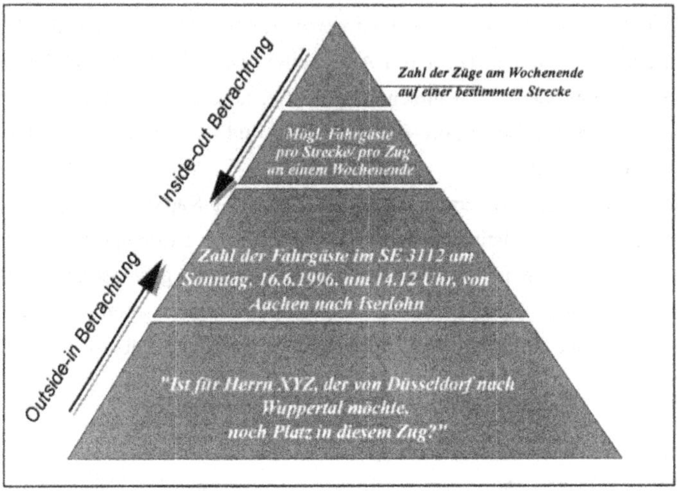

Abb. 6: Kapazitätsstufen[38]

Für die Sortimentsdimension der Kapazität - und damit für das dem einzelnen Nachfrager zur Verfügung stehende Angebot - ist es jedoch unerheblich, ob ihm ein Angebot aufgrund einer zu geringen Kapazität oder einer zu hohen Kapazitätsauslastung nicht zur Verfügung steht. Die Sortimentsdimension der Kapazität ergibt sich demzufolge erst dann, wenn Kapazitätsdimensionierung und Kapazitätsauslastung simultan betrachtet werden. Für die Auswahl bestimmter Angebote aus dem Sortiment sind die Erwartungen des Nachfragers hinsichtlich der Leistungsqualität maßgebend. Das Urteil des Nachfragers äußert sich aber nicht nur in der Inanspruchnahme bestimmter Bahnleistungen, sondern eben auch in der bewußten Entscheidung gegen die DB AG. Eine vollständige Messung von Kapazität und Kapazitätsauslastung muß diesen Umstand berücksichtigen. Die folgende Abbildung zeigt mögliche Ansatzpunkte auf.

Die Kapazitätsmessung beschränkt sich häufig auf den Punkt 4, in dem eine einfache Beschäftigungskennzahl ermittelt wird, die zudem bei Anbietern integrativer Leistungen nicht selten inputorientiert vorgenommen wird.[39] Ähnlich wie für den Qualitätsbegriff kann jedoch davon ausgegangen werden, daß Kapazität und Kapazitätsauslastung immer dann zu einer Erfahrungsgröße werden, wenn die Nachfrager im Rahmen eines Selbstselektionsprin-

38 Vgl. Schnittka (1996), S. 41.

39 Hotelkapazitäten werden in der Regel über die Bettenzahl erfaßt; Theaterkapazitäten in Sitzplätzen ausgedrückt. Vgl. hierzu Franz (1969), S. 71ff.; Schulz (1955), S. 65.

zips direkt mit der Leistungsfähigkeit konfrontiert werden. Das Angebot der DB AG wird vom Einzelnen immer nur in Form von Ausschnitten wahrgenommen werden können. Mit jeder Reise geht eine selektive Wahrnehmung der Leistungsqualität, aber auch der Kapazität und Kapazitätsauslastung einher, die ein bestimmtes Bild beim Nachfrager entstehen lassen. Die Meßpunkte 1 bis 3 in

***Abb.** 7* geben einen Hinweis darauf, in welcher Weise das Kapazitätsimage eines Anbieters erfaßt werden könnte.[40] Relativ einfach zu operationalisieren ist Meßpunkt 1: Neben den Bedürfnissen der Nachfrager in bezug auf Art und Zeitpunkt der gewünschten Leistungserstellung muß erfaßt werden, welche und wieviel potentielle Kunden aufgrund einer Diskrepanz zwischen Angebot und Nachfrage nicht zu Nachfragern werden konnten.

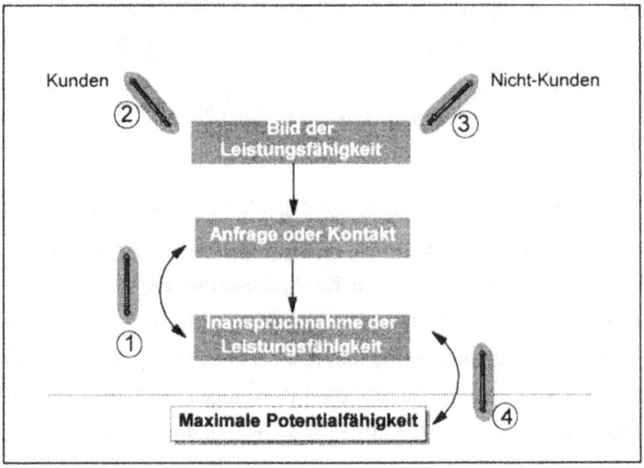

Abb. 7: Meßpunkte von Kapazität und Kapazitätsauslastung

In jedem Fall liegt es nahe, daß Kapazitätsspitzen und -täler nicht isoliert voneinander betrachtet werden können.[41] Der Reisende in einem überfüllten Nahverkehrszug wird sein Bild von der qualitativen und quantitativen Leistungsfähigkeit der DB AG durch dieses Erlebnis verändern. Ohne dies hier im Detail nachweisen zu können, kann eine Veränderung des Nachfrageverhaltens als sehr wahrscheinlich angesehen werden. Diese Auswirkungen müssen im Rahmen des Kapazitätsmanagements in Rechnung gestellt werden.

---

40 Nicht geleugnet werden kann, daß die Meßpunkte 1 und 2 noch einer Operationalisierung bedürfen.

41 Vgl. analog für die Produktivitätsmessung Corsten (1994), S. 50ff.

Zwischen Kapazität und Qualität bestehen vielfältige Interdependenzen, wie das Beispiel eines überfüllten Zuges deutlich macht. Vor diesem Hintergrund stellt sich die Frage, wie diese Interdependenzen berücksichtigt werden können. Die erste Aufgabe besteht in der Definition einer Normalkapazität, deren Inanspruchnahme einer Beschäftigung von 100% entspricht. Im Hinblick auf die Leistungsqualität bietet es sich an, diejenige Kapazität als 100% zu bezeichnen, bei deren Inanspruchnahme noch keine negativen Auswirkungen auf die Leistungsqualität zu befürchten sind. Damit müssen sowohl aus der Auslastung resultierende Unannehmlichkeiten als auch Verspätungen, beispielsweise in Folge zu langer Ein- und Ausstiegszeiten auf den Bahnhöfen ausgeschlossen werden.

Unabhängig davon, ob man auf diese Weise verfährt, ist die explizite Formulierung eines Kapazitätsauslastungsziels erforderlich, das bisher zu fehlen scheint. Dabei kann es nicht darum gehen, jeden Platz in jedem Zug auszulasten. Die Interdependenz zwischen der Auslastung verschiedener Züge müssen in einer solchen Zielformulierung ihren Niederschlag finden. Nur dann kann verhindert werden, daß Groß- und Stammkunden zugunsten von Gelegenheitskunden zurücktreten müssen.

Im Rahmen der Zielformulierung ist es problematisch, daß eine Beeinträchtigung der Leistungsqualität durch eine zu hohe Kapazitätsauslastung intersubjektiv verschieden wahrgenommen wird. Hinzu kommt, daß negative Konsequenzen auf die wahrgenommene Leistungsqualität auch bei einer zu geringen Auslastung entstehen können. Anders ausgedrückt: Kapazitätsmanagement besteht nicht nur darin, eine bestimmte Zahl von Nachfragern für ein bestimmtes Leistungsangebot zu gewinnen, sondern muß auch darauf achten, um welche Nachfrager es sich handelt. An dieser Stelle wird der Unterschied zwischen dem Absatz einer Leistung und der Beschaffung externer Faktoren besonders deutlich.

Eine aktive Selektion der Nachfrager und gezielter Einsatz eines Kompatibilitätsmanagements ist im Nahverkehr kaum möglich, da sich eine dafür erforderliche Anmeldung und Reservierung nicht wird durchsetzen lassen. In konsequenter Anwendung des Prinzips der Selbstselektion kann die Aufgabe der DB AG dann nur darin bestehen, denjenigen Nachfragern, für die die Kapazitätsauslastung eines Zuges ein Auswahlkriterium darstellt, die nötigen Informationen zur Verfügung zu stellen. Würde die DB AG innerhalb des Fahrplans oder als Zusatzinformation auf Anfrage mitteilen, welche Verbindungen zur welcher Zeit wie stark frequentiert werden, könnten zwei Ziele zugleich erreicht werden:

1. Zumindest eine Tendenz zur Gleichverteilung ist anzunehmen, auch wenn ein gewisser kontraproduktiver Effekt zu befürchten ist.[42]
2. Gerade diejenigen Nachfrager, die durch eine besondere Sensibilität im Hinblick auf die Kapazitätsauslastung gekennzeichnet sind, könnten ein für sie besonders negatives Erlebnis eher vermeiden, als dies bisher der Fall ist. Auf diese Weise wird der Heterogenität der Nachfrage Rechnung getragen.

Für die Umsetzung dieser Maßnahme sollte es ausreichend sein, Kategorien zu bilden, die verschiedene Auslastungsklassen angeben. Der Reisende wäre aufgrund dieser Angaben sehr viel besser in der Lage, seine Reise zu planen und an die bereitgestellten Kapazitäten anzupassen. Damit hätte die Bahn ein Instrument in der Hand, um die Vorstellungen ihrer Kunden über ihre Kapazitätsauslastung aktiv zu beeinflussen. Gleichzeitig würde transparent, wo Auslastungsspitzen und -täler im Detail zu finden sind.

In diesem Zusammenhang könnte auch der Einsatz neuer Medien einen Ansatzpunkt für das Kapazitätsmanagement darstellen. Die immer weitere Verbreitung findenden elektronischen Fahrplananzeigen sowie die Großbildschirme, die in ausgewählten Bahnhöfen der Kategorie A installiert worden sind, könnten für die Übermittlung von Kapazitätsauslastungsinformationen genutzt werden. Ihr Vorteil gegenüber dem Fahrplan als Informationsinstrument liegt in ihrer Flexibilität, die eine höhere Aktualität der Kapazitätsangaben gewährleisten könnte.

5. Fazit: Kapazitätsmanagement als Informationsmanagement

Das SWT stellt einen Versuch dar, mit dem Instrument der Preispolitik die Auslastung der Kapazitäten in einem bestimmten Teilbereich zu steuern. Der scheinbare Erfolg, wie er sich in Verkaufszahlen und Durchschnittsauslastung widerspiegelt, erscheint in einem anderen Licht, wenn man die zahlreichen Nebeneffekte dieses Bahnangebots berücksichtigt. Da sich mit der Preiserhöhung auf DM 35,- ein spürbarer Nachfragerückgang eingestellt hat, sind einige der oben geschilderten Effekte mittlerweile nicht mehr in gleicher Intensität anzutreffen. Im Zentrum der Diskussion stand deshalb eher die grundsätzliche Eignung der Vorgehensweise, wie sie die DB AG zur Verbesserung der Kapazitätsauslastung gewählt hat.

[42] In diesem Zusammenhang kann man von einer „self destroying prophecy“ für den Fall sprechen, daß sehr viele Nachfrager ihr Verhalten an den Kapazitäts- und Beschäftigungsgrößen ausrichten und somit eine Umkehrung der vorher ermittelten Verhältnisse entsteht. Selbst dann wäre einem solchen Vorgehen noch etwas Positives abzugewinnen, da die DB AG zuverlässige Informationen über die Sensibilität ihrer Kunden in bezug auf die Kapazitätsauslastung sowie die Flexibilität in bezug auf Reisezeiten gewinnen würde.

Der intendierte Imagegewinn für den Nahverkehr sowie ein beabsichtigter positiver Imagetransfer auf die DB AG muß zumindest in Frage gestellt werden.[43] Die anfänglich durchweg positive Beurteilung durch die Öffentlichkeit ist zunehmend negativen Schlagzeilen und Erlebnisberichten gewichen. Zusätzlich ist davon auszugehen, daß einige Kunden in einer Weise verärgert worden sind, die nicht ausschließt, daß sie sich durch negative Propaganda als „Terroristen“[44] betätigen. Ebenfalls nicht auszuschließen ist, daß es sich bei diesen Kunden um - vormalige - Stammkunden handelt. Diese Zielgruppe wurde bei der Konzeption des Tikkets vernachlässigt.
Auch dann, wenn man von einer qualitätsorientierten zu einer quantitativ orientierten Betrachtung übergeht, lassen sich erhebliche Zweifel an der Zweckmäßigkeit eines SWT anmelden. Im Ergebnis ist allenfalls die Kapazitätsschwankung auf ein höheres Niveau gehoben worden, eine Beseitigung oder Glättung der Spitzen ist jedoch nicht erreicht worden.

Die Interpretation der Ergebnisse läßt darauf schließen, daß die notwendige Analyse bereits im Vorfeld unterblieben ist. Die Zielformulierung „Steigerung der Kapazitätsauslastung im Nahverkehr am Wochenende“ ist für ein effektives Kapazitätsmanagement nicht geeignet, weil sie sowohl sachlich als auch zeitlich zu undifferenziert ist. Zahlreiche Informationen, deren Einfluß auf Kapazität und Beschäftigung in diesem Beitrag nachgewiesen werden sollte, finden keinen Niederschlag in den Betrachtungen der Bahn. Allenfalls werden sie als Nebeneffekte betrachtet, die nicht unmittelbar dem Kapazitätsmanagement zuzuordnen sind.

Die Konstruktion des SWT kann ebenfalls nicht vollständig überzeugen, da sie einen Konflikt enthält, der vielen Ansätzen inhärent ist, die über preispolitische Maßnahmen eine Steuerung der Beschäftigung erreichen wollen. Ein großer Vorteil des SWT wird in seiner einfachen und verständlichen Tarifkonstruktion gesehen. Im Unterschied zu vielen anderen Angeboten der DB AG sind Geltungsbereich und -dauer für jeden Nachfrager verständlich formuliert worden. Damit geht zwangsläufig ein Verzicht auf ein Differenzierung einher, die für einen Abbau von Kapazitätsspitzen und -tälern unerläßlich ist. Diese Differenzierung kann aber bei der Gestaltung der Preispolitik nur auf Kosten der Übersichtlichkeit der Tarifgestaltung vorgenommen werden. Insofern ist mit der Wahl des Steuerungsinstruments, wie sie die DB AG getroffen hat, bereits ein Konflikt zwischen kundenfreundlicher Preisgestaltung und effektiver Kapazitätsauslastungssteuerung angelegt.

---

[43] Vgl. zu diesen Zielformulierungen Franz (1995), S. 94.

[44] Vgl. Heskett et.al. (1994), S. 52f.

Dieser Konflikt offenbart den Unterschied zwischen dem Absatz der Leistung und der Beschaffung externer Faktoren: mit dem Absatz des Tickets wird die Kapazitätsauslastung keinesfalls sichergestellt. Vielmehr besteht einer der Kaufanreize in der Möglichkeit, aus der Vielzahl der bereitgestellten Kapazitäten individuell und unabhängig eine Auswahl treffen zu können. Eine gleichmäßige Kapazitätsauslastung kann nur dann sichergestellt werden, wenn unter Berücksichtigung möglicher Kriterien der Auswahlentscheidung des Nachfragers eine Äquivalenz von internen und externen Faktoren herbeigeführt wird.[45]

Der Einsatz der Preispolitik ist noch aus einem anderen Grund kritisch zu betrachten: Er legt den Verdacht nahe, daß unter Verzicht auf eine detaillierte Analyse dem Aktionismus das Feld überlassen wird. Die im Hinblick auf eine Selbstselektion der potentiellen Reisenden ausgesendeten Signale dieses Vorgehens sind nicht geeignet, eine Verstetigung der Kapazitätsauslastung zu unterstützen. Damit werden die Kapazitätsinformationen von einem preispolitischen Anreiz überlagert, der notwendigerweise weniger differenziert wirkt.

Besonders schwer wiegt, daß gerade diejenigen Anreize ungenutzt bleiben, die aus den Interessen und Bedürfnissen der Nachfrager heraus auf ein Gleichgewicht hinwirken. Diese könnten dann nutzbar gemacht werden, wenn den Nachfragern auslastungsrelevante Informationen zur Verfügung gestellt würden, die zunächst den potentiellen Reisenden Transparenz über die Auslastung einzelner Züge oder Verbindungen schafft. Im Anschluß daran ist die Veränderung der Kapazitätsauslastung in der Zeit zu erfassen und zu bewerten.
Sollten die verbleibenden Auslastungsspitzen und -täler in den Augen der Verantwortlichen nicht akzeptabel sein, könnte sich ein weiterer Schritt anschließen. Offensichtlich sind dann die Eigeninteressen der Nachfrager nicht stark genug, um die Ziele der DB AG zu erreichen. Dann ist zu überlegen, ob zusätzliche Anreize in Form preispolitischer Zugeständnisse zweckmäßig sein könnten. Ein Erfolg ist aber nur dann zu erwarten, wenn vorhandene Bedürfnisse beim Nachfrager verstärkt werden, nicht aber dann, wenn eine Verstetigung der Kapazitätsauslastung gegen Nachfragerpräferenzen durchgesetzt werden soll.

Die Gestaltung des Tarifsystems in einfacher und damit kundenfreundlicher Art und Weise ist eine positiv zu beurteilende Absicht. Vor diesem Hintergrund ist die Einführung des SWT sicherlich zu begrüßen. Man darf allerdings an dieses Instrument nicht Erwartungen stellen, die es aufgrund seiner Konzeption niemals erfüllen kann.

---

45 Vgl. Schnittka (1996), S. 23ff.

6. Literatur

ANDREASSEN, Tor Wallin (1995): (Dis-)satisfaction with public services: the case of public transportation, in: Journal of services marketing, 9. Jg. (1995), Nr. 5, S. 30 - 41

ARMISTEAD, Colin G. / CLARK, Graham (1994): The „coping" capacity management strategy in services and the influence on quality performance, in: International journal of service industry management, 5. Jg. (1994), Nr. 2, S. 5 - 22

BEIERSDORF, Wilfried (1995): Schönes Wochende der Bahn wird teurer, in: Westdeutsche Allgemeine Zeitung, Nr. 104 vom 5.5.1995, S. 1

BETGE, Peter (1996): Kapazität und Beschäftigung, in: Kern, Werner / Schröder, Hans-Horst / Weber, Jürgen (Hrsg.), Handwörterbuch der Produktionswirtschaft, 2. Auflage, Stuttgart 1996, Sp. 852 - 861

CLAR, Peter (1964): Die Kapazitätsausnutzung in der Industrieunternehmung, Berlin 1964

CORSTEN, Hans (1985): Die Produktion von Dienstleistungen, Berlin 1985

CORSTEN, Hans (1992): Kapazitätsplanung in Dienstleistungsunternehmen, in: Corsten et.al. (Hrsg.), Kapazitätsmessung, -gestaltung, -optimierung: eine betriebswirtschaftliche Kernfrage, Stuttgart 1992, S. 229 - 254

CORSTEN, Hans (1994): Produktivitätsmanagement bilateraler personenbezogener Dienstleistungen, in: Corsten, Hans / Hilke, Wolfgang (Hrsg.), Dienstleistungsproduktion, Schriften zur Unternehmensführung Band 52, Wiesbaden 1994, S. 43 - 77

DAUBERTSHÄUSER, Klaus (1995): Interview im Nachrichtenmagazin Focus, Heft 11/1995, S. 37ff.

DUCLOS, Leslie K. / SIHA, Samia / LUMMUS, Rhonda R. (1995): JIT in services: a review of current practices and future directions for research, in: International journal of service industry management, 6. Jg. (1995), S. 36 - 52

ENGELHARDT, Werner H. / KLEINALTENKAMP, Michael / RECKENFELDERBÄUMER, Martin (1993): Leistungsbündel als Absatzobjekte, in: ZfbF, 45. Jg. (1993), S. 395 - 426

FRANZ, Jürgen (1969): Die Labilität der Nachfrage bei investitionsintensiven, kundenpräsenzbedingten Dienstleistungsbetrieben und die Möglichkeit einer betriebspolitischen Anpassung, Diss. München 1969

FRANZ, Hans-Werner (1995): Das „Schöne-Wochenende-Ticket" - die Erfolgsstory der DB AG, in: Der Nahverkehr, 13. Jg. (1995), Heft 10, S. 94 - 96

GERHARDT, Jürgen (1987): Dienstleistungsproduktion, Bergisch-Gladbach 1987

GERSCH, Martin (1995): Die Standardisierung integrativ erstellter Leistungen, Arbeitsbericht Nr. 57 des Instituts für Unternehmungsführung und Unternehmensforschung der Ruhr-Universität Bochum, Bochum 1995

GÜMBEL, Rudolf (1963): Die Sortimentspolitik in den Betrieben des Wareneinzelhandels, Beiträge zur betriebswirtschaftlichen Forschung Band 21, Köln/Opladen 1963

GUTENBERG, Erich (1958): Einführung in die Betriebswirtschaftslehre, Wiesbaden 1958

GUTENBERG, Erich (1965): Grundlagen der Betriebswirtschaftslehre, Band 1: Die Produktion, 11. Auflage, Berlin 1965

HARVEY, Jean (1989): Just-in-time health and human service: a client approach, in: Public productivity and management review, 13. Jg. (1989), S. 77 - 88

HENZEL, Friedrich (1967): Kosten und Leistung, 4. Auflage, Essen 1967

HESKETT, James L. et. al. (1994): Dienstleister müssen die ganze Service-Gewinn-Kette nutzen, in: Harvard manager, 24. Jg. (1994), S. 50 - 61

HUBBERT, Amy R. / **SEHORN**, Annette G. / **BROWN**, Stephen, W.: Service expectations: the consumer versus the provider, in: International journal of service industry management, 6. Jg. (1995), Nr. 1, S. 6 - 21

KERN, Werner (1962): Die Messung industrieller Fertigungskapazitäten und ihrer Ausnutung, Köln/Opladen 1962

KERN, Werner (1975): Kapazität und Beschäftigung, in: Grochla, Erwin / Wittmann (Hrsg.), HWB, 4. Auflage (1975), Sp. 2083-2090

KERN, Werner (1993): Kapazität, in: Chmielewicz, Klaus / Schweitzer, Marcell (Hrsg.), Handwörterbuch des Rechnungswesens, 3. Auflage, Stuttgart 1993, Sp 1055 - 1063

KLAUS, Peter G. (1984): Service-Qualität im öffentlichen Personenverkehr: ein retrograder Ansatz zur Analyse und Veränderung, in: Zeitschrift für öffentliche und gemeinwirtschaftliche Unternehmen, 1. Jg. (1984), Nr. 7, S. 54 - 73

KLEINALTENKAMP, Michael (1993): Investitionsgütermarketing als Beschaffung externer Faktoren, in: Thelen, Eva / Mairamhof, Gabi (Hrsg.), Dienstleistungsmarketing, Tagungsband zum 2. Workshop für Dienstleistungsmarketing, Frankfurt et.al. 1993, S. 101 - 126

LAYER, Manfred (1979) : Kapazität: Begriff, Arten und Messung, in: Kern, Werner (Hrsg.), Handwörterbuch der Produktionswirtschaft, Stuttgart 1979, Sp. 1636 - 1647

MEYER, Anton / BLÜMELHUBER, Christian (1994): Interdependenzen zwischen Absatz und Produktion in Dienstleistungsunternehmen und ihre Auswirkungen auf konzeptionelle Fragen des Absatzmarketing, in: Corsten, Hans / Hilke, Wolfgang (Hrsg.), Dienstleistungsproduktion, Schriften zur Unternehmensführung Band 52, Wiesbaden 1994, S. 5 - 41

MEYER, Anton / WESTERBARKEY, Peter (1991): Bedeutung der Kundenbeteiligung für die Qualitätspolitik von Dienstleistungsunternehmen, in: Bruhn, Manfred / Stauss, Bernd (Hrsg.), Dienstleistungsqualität, Konzepte, Methoden, Erfahrungen, Wiesbaden 1991, S. 83 - 103

NEUHAUS, Heinz (1995): „Bahn frei in die Freizeit", Interview in Mobil, Heft 4/1995, S. 22 - 24

OETTLE, Karl (1970) : Die Dienstbereitschaft in einzelwirtschaftlicher und gesamtwirtschaftlicher Sicht, in: Linhardt, H. / Petzkofer, P. / Scherpf, P. (Hrsg.), Dienstleistungen in Theorie und Praxis, Stuttgart 1970, S. 16 - 36

PAUL, Michael / SCHNITTKA, Matthias (1996): Der Handel mit immateriell-integrativen Leistungen: Implikationen für das Marketing von Reiseveranstaltern, in: Meyer, Anton (Hrsg.), Grundsatzfragen und Herausforderungen des Dienstleistungsmarketing, Wiesbaden 1996, S. 233 - 273

PRANTER, Charles A. / MARTIN, Charles L. (1991): Compatibility management: roles in service performers, in: The journal of services marketing, 5. Jg. (1991), Nr. 2, S. 43 - 53

RIEBEL, Paul (1954): Die Elastizität des Betriebes. Eine produktions- und marktwirtschaftliche Untersuchung, Köln/Opladen 1954

SCHMITT, W.M. (1981): Die Problematik von Leistung, Kapazität, Kosten und Erträgen in der Containerlinienschiffahrt, Frankfurt a.M. 1981

SCHNITTKA, Matthias (1996): Dienstleistungskapazität als Gegenstand des Marketing - Überlegungen auf Basis eines subjektiven Kapazitätsbegriffs, Arbeitsbericht Nr. 62 des Instituts für Unternehmungsführung und Unternehmensforschung der Ruhr-Universität Bochum, Bochum 1996

SCHULZ, H. (1955) : Kapazität, Beschäftigungsgrad und Betriebsgröße im Hotelgewerbe, Jahrbuch für Fremdenverkehr, 4. Jg. (1955/56), Heft 2, S. 62 - 75

SELCHERT, Friedrich W. (1970): Lagerkapazitäten und die Möglichkeit ihrer Messung, in: ZfbF, 22. Jg. (1970), S. 681 - 693

SHOSTACK, Lynn G. (1982): How to design a service, in: European Journal of Marketing, 16. Jg. (1982), Heft 1, S. 49 - 63

STEVEN, Marion (1996): Kapazitätsgestaltung und -optimierung, in: Kern, Werner / Schröder, Hans-Horst / Weber, Jürgen (Hrsg.), Handwörterbuch der Produktionswirtschaft, 2. Auflage, Stuttgart 1996, Sp. 874 - 883

VAVRA, Terry G. (1992): Aftermarketing: How to keep customers for life through relationship marketing, Homewood 1992

WIEGAND, Bernd (1968): Darstellung und Vergleich der Berechnungsmethoden industrieller Kapazitäten und deren Auslastungsgrad, Diss. Darmstadt 1968

Reinhard Hünerberg/Andreas Mann*

STRATEGISCHE IMPLIKATIONEN DES SERVICE-MARKETING IN INDUSTRIEUNTERNEHMEN

Konzeptionelle Überlegungen und empirische Befunde

Inhalt

* Prof. Dr. Reinhard Hünerberg, Lehrstuhl Marketing an der Universität Gesamthochschule Kassel; Dipl.-Oec. Andreas Mann, wissenschaftlicher Assistent am Lehrstuhl

1. Bedeutung des Customer Service

Serviceleistungen werden von immer mehr Unternehmen in unterschiedlichen Wirtschaftszweigen und Branchen eingesetzt, um sich von Wettbewerbern zu differenzieren sowie Kunden zu gewinnen, zufriedenzustellen und zu binden[1]. In Abbildung 1 sind wesentliche Einflußfelder auf die Unternehmensführung und Ansatzpunkte für die Servicepolitik dargestellt, die besonders für industrielle Anbieter relevant sind.

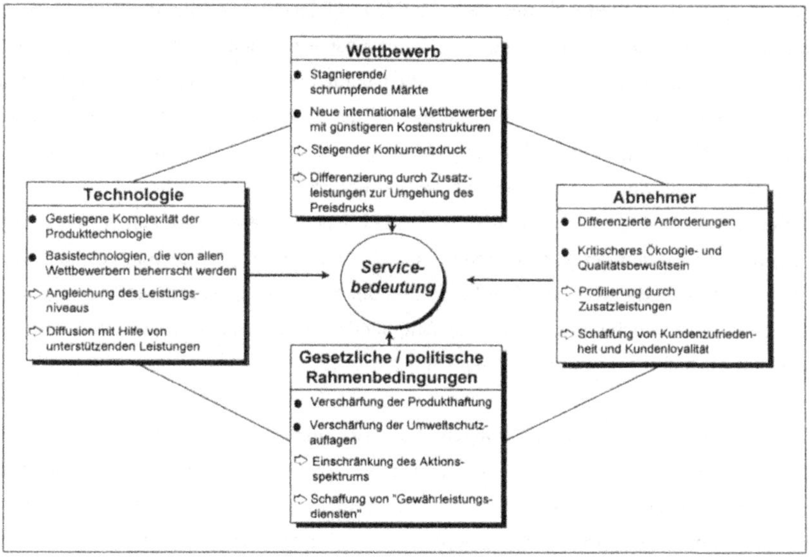

Abb. 1: Bedeutungszunahme des Customer Service

Als Service werden dabei alle **Sekundärdienstleistungen** verstanden, die zusätzlich zu einer Kernleistung angeboten werden. Hierzu gehören beispielsweise personen-/abnehmerbezogene Leistungen wie Kundenberatung und -information, Schulungen, Anwendungs- und Wirtschaftlichkeitsstudien sowie kernleistungs-/produktbezogene Services wie Installation, Wartung, Reparatur, technologisches Upgrading und Recycling. Das Spektrum der Serviceleistungen ist also sehr vielfältig und kann sowohl zur akquisitorischen Funktion vor dem Kauf (Pre-

[1] Vgl. z.B. Davidow/Uttal (1989), S. 26ff.; Horovitz (1989), S. 31ff.; Horovitz/Panak (1993), S. 107ff.; Simon (1993), S. 10f.; Singh (1990), S. 193f.

Sales-Services) als auch zur Kundenbindung und Sicherstellung der Funktionsfähigkeit von Kernleistungen nach dem Kauf (After-Sales-Services) angeboten werden.

Bei der Kern-/Primärleistung kann es sich sowohl um materielle Sachleistungen als auch um immaterielle Dienstleistungen handeln. Dabei werden produktbezogene Services in der Regel nur bei Sachleistungen angeboten. Personenbezogene Serviceleistungen sind hingegen auch im Dienstleistungsbereich einsetzbar, wenngleich sie sich oft nur schwer von den Teilleistungen des Kernangebots abgrenzen lassen und sich deshalb bei der Vermarktung nicht grundlegend von der eigentlichen Leistung unterscheiden. Anders ist die Situation beim Marketing und Management von Serviceleistungen in Industrieunternehmen, die Massen- und Seriengüter produzieren und absetzen. Hier kommen die Charakteristika von Sekundärdienstleistungen bei der Erstellung eines Absatzkonzeptes und bei der Durchführung von Markttransaktionen besonders zum Tragen. Während die Kernleistungen in diesem Fall weitgehend ohne besondere Einbeziehung der Kunden erbracht werden können und aufgrund der tangiblen Eigenschaften lager- und transportierbar sind, ist das bei Serviceleistungen wegen der notwendigen Kundenintegration und der Immaterialität nicht der Fall[2]. Dadurch ergeben sich zum Teil erhebliche Unterschiede zwischen dem Marketing der Kernleistung (Produkt) und den Serviceleistungen sowie gleichzeitig spezifische Aufgaben, die im Sinne eines integrierten Marketing-Konzepts aufeinander abzustimmen sind[3].

Durch das Angebot von Serviceleistungen lassen sich also nicht ohne weiteres Synergieeffekte für den Marktauftritt und -erfolg von Industrieunternehmen realisieren. Häufig determinieren Serviceleistungen - aufgrund ihrer dienstleistungsspezifischen Charakteristika - vielmehr die Vermarktung der Kernleistung in besonderer Weise und schränken unter Umständen das absatzstrategische Handlungsspektrum eines Unternehmens ein.

Obwohl in Praxis und Wissenschaft immer häufiger die Bedeutung von Serviceleistungen für den Erfolg beim Absatz industrieller Güter erkannt und herausgestellt wird[4], fehlt es dennoch weitgehend an theoretischen und empirischen Ergebnissen über den Einfluß von Serviceleistungen auf konzeptionelle und strategische Entscheidungen im Marketing von Industrieunternehmen. Meist wird der Service implizit mit Kundendienst gleichgesetzt und als Bestand-

---

2 Vgl. insbesondere die Ausführungen von Engelhardt/Kleinaltenkamp/Reckenfelderbäumer (1993), S. 418ff.; Corsten (1989), S. 24 ff.; Meffert/Bruhn (1995), S. 61ff.

3 Vgl. hierzu auch Zeithaml/Parasuraman/Berry (1985), S. 34.

4 Siehe insbesondere den Überblick bei Homburg/Garbe (1996), S. 263ff.

teil der Produktpolitik[5] oder - bei einer weitergehenden Begriffsabgrenzung - als gleichrangiger Bestandteil des Marketing-Mix und damit eher operativ gesehen[6].

Ziel des Beitrags ist es, einige grundsätzliche Überlegungen über die strategischen Wirkungen des Service vorzustellen. Hierbei handelt es sich sowohl um den Einfluß der Servicepolitik auf strategische Basisentscheidungen im Marketing als auch um die Bedeutung von Serviceleistungen als Wettbewerbs- und Profilierungsinstrument. Auf der Basis empirischer Befunde einer explorativen Studie bei 320 Unternehmen der be- und verarbeitenden Industrie, die zur Jahreswende 1995/96 von den Autoren durchgeführt wurde, sollen dabei einige Einflußbereiche und -wirkungen des Service auf das strategische Marketing exemplarisch aufgezeigt werden. Die Befragung wurde in schriftlicher Form durchgeführt und basiert auf einer Zufallsauswahl von 2.000 Unternehmen aus der Hoppenstedt Datenbank für Groß- und mittelständische Unternehmen. Es wurden lediglich Unternehmen aus der be- und verarbeitenden Industrie in die Stichprobe einbezogen. Ausgeschlossen wurden Dienstleistungs- und Handelsbetriebe mit Blick auf die oben skizzierte Grundhypothese, daß die Vermarktung von (Sekundär-)Dienstleistungen gerade in Industrieunternehmen besondere Anforderungen stellt. Die Fragen wurden hauptsächlich in geschlossener Form unter Verwendung von Rating-Skalen gestellt. Die abgefragten Items wurden auf Grundlage einer Literaturauswertung sowie auf Basis von einigen Pre-Interviews mit Praktikern generiert und geprüft.

In Abbildung 2 ist die branchenbezogene Zusammensetzung der befragten Unternehmen wiedergegeben (Rücklaufquote = 16%). Die Branchenverteilung des Rücklaufs entspricht aber bei einer hohen Irrtumswahrscheinlichkeit nur annähernd der Struktur der Grundgesamtheit ($A^2 = 7{,}4154$ bei 8 DF und $p = 0{,}4925$). Unternehmen aus der Chemie- und Pharmaindustrie sowie aus dem Lebensmittelsektor sind geringfügig unterrepräsentiert. Dafür sind Unternehmen aus der Elektronikbranche etwas überproportional im Rücklauf vertreten.

---

5 Vgl. z.B. Bruhn (1995a) S. 125 und S. 148ff.; Meffert (1986), S. 411ff.; Nieschlag/Dichtl/Hörschgen (1994), S. 157f.

6 Vgl. z.B. Fassott (1996), S. 77.

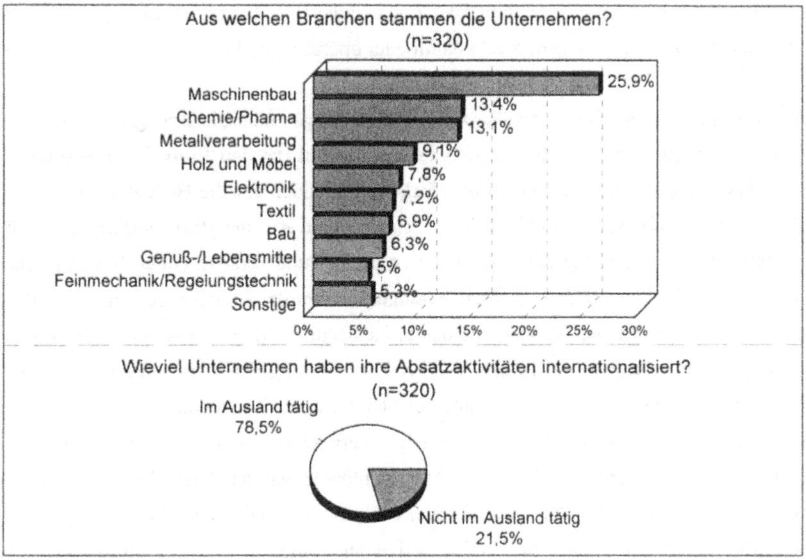

Abb. 2: Rücklaufstruktur der Befragung

2. Einfluß von Serviceleistungen auf strategische Markt- / Marketingentscheidungen

Als strategische Marktentscheidungen sollen vor allem die drei Basisbereiche Marktselektion bzw. -segmentierung, Marktimplantation bzw. -expansion und Marktverhalten hervorgehoben werden. Sie bilden den grundlegenden strategischen Rahmen für die Marketingaktivitäten eines Unternehmens[7]. Dabei werden diese drei Strategiefelder auch im internationalen Kontext analysiert, da Unternehmen ihre Absatzaktivitäten immer häufiger länderübergreifend durchführen[8]. So zeigt sich bei der Untersuchung, daß 78,5 % der analysierten Unternehmen auch im Ausland ihre Produkte direkt oder indirekt mit Hilfe von heimischen oder ausländischen Absatzmittlern absetzen.

7 Vgl. ähnlich auch Raffée (1989), S. 17ff.

8 Vgl. hierzu auch Hünerberg/Mann (1996), S. 98.

2.1. Kopplung zwischen Serviceleistung und Produkt als Determinante der Strategieformulierung

Ausgangspunkt des Strategieeinflusses ist die Verbundenheit und Abhängigkeit von Kern-/ Primärleistung und den Serviceleistungen auf der einen Seite sowie die Bedeutung des Service für die Marktbearbeitung auf der anderen Seite. Grundsätzlich läßt sich feststellen, daß mit zunehmender Verbundenheit von Produkt und Serviceleistungen eine isolierte Planung der Kernprodukt-Strategie und -Politik schwieriger wird[9]. Generell ist dies bei produktbezogenen Serviceleistungen per Definition gegeben. Sie werden deshalb häufig als obligatorische Serviceleistungen bezeichnet. Doch auch eine Vielzahl personengerichteter Services (z.B. Beratungs- und Finanzierungsleistungen) sollen den Absatz der Kernleistung fördern und sind in bestimmtem Grad damit verbunden. Es ist aber bei personenbezogenen Serviceleistungen möglich, daß sie für die Vermarktungsfähigkeit einer Kernleistung nicht notwendig und daher fakultativ sind[10]. Abhängig von dem Bedeutungsgrad der Serviceleistung kann bei einer engen Leistungsverbundenheit der Einfluß des Service auf die Strategieformulierung sehr stark sein. Wie Abbildung 3 zeigt, lassen sich vier generelle Gestaltungsmuster für das Marketing von Serviceleistungen feststellen:

- Bei einer geringen bzw. bei keiner Leistungsverbundenheit zwischen Service und Kernprodukt sowie einer geringen Bedeutung von Serviceleistungen für die Marktbearbeitung lassen sich Produktangebote völlig unabhängig von Serviceleistungen vermarkten (**„Produkt-Marketing“**). Diese Situation ist in der Regel sehr selten, da selbst im internationalen Kontext länderspezifische Gewährleistungspflichten des Verkäufers bestehen, die bestimmte Muß-Serviceleistungen, wie z.B. Reparaturen, zwangsläufig erfordern.
- Haben Serviceleistungen eine große Marktbedeutung und eine geringe Kernleistungsverbundenheit, dann lassen sich Serviceleistungen isoliert gestalten und absetzen. In diesen Fällen ist der Service eigentlich keine Zusatzleistung mehr, sondern stellt eine eigene Marktleistung dar, die als solche auch im Leistungsangebot des Unternehmens positioniert werden kann (**„isoliertes Service-Marketing“**).

9 Vgl. hierzu grundsätzlich Engelhardt (1976), S. 78ff.

10 Vgl. Engelhardt (1996), S. 75.

- Ist die Leistungsverbundenheit zwischen Kernprodukt und Service zwar sehr stark, die Markt- und Marketingbedeutung des Service jedoch gering, dann wird die Kernleistung im Absatzkonzept dominierend sein. Hierbei werden die Serviceleistungen als Zusatzleistungen um das Kernleistungsangebot gruppiert und daran ausgerichtet (**„produktdominiertes Service-Marketing“**).
- Anders ist die Situation, wenn bei einem hohen Leistungsverbund der Service zusätzlich eine große Markt- und Wettbewerbsbedeutung hat. In diesem Fall handelt es sich um ein Systemangebot, das aufeinander abgestimmt werden muß. Das kann sogar soweit gehen, daß die Servicekomponenten den eigentlichen „Kern“ der Leistung darstellen, an denen das Produkt auszurichten ist (**„integriertes System-Marketing“**)[11].

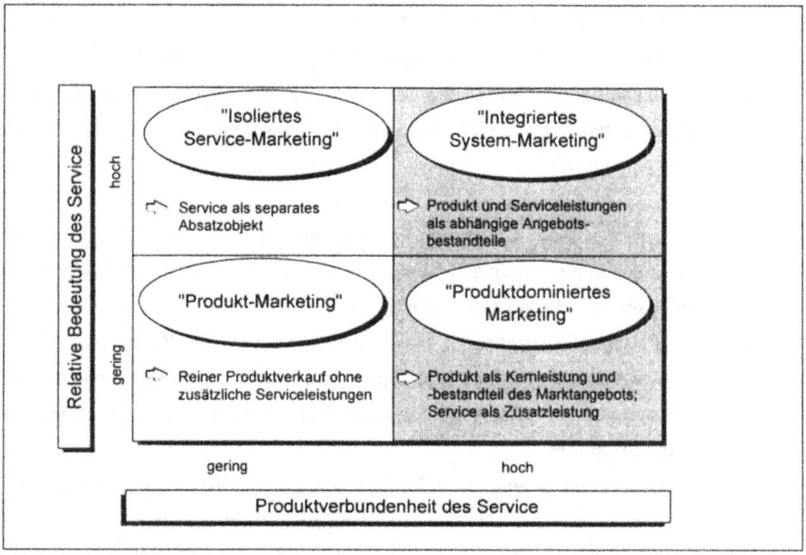

Abb. 3: Verbundenheit zwischen Kernleistung und Service

Insbesondere beim Systemverkauf sind die strategischen Implikationen des Service auf die Marketingplanung besonders evident und nachhaltig. Wie Abbildung 4 zeigt, sind in diesem Fall die Serviceleistungen nicht einfach aus den allgemeinen Marketingzielen und den verfolgten Basisstrategien abzuleiten. Vielmehr können Servicenotwendigkeiten und spezifische

[11] Vgl. auch Wimmer/Zerr (1994), S. 225f.

Servicebesonderheiten strategische Grundentscheidungen beeinflussen und revidieren. Gerade beim Systemverkauf ist deshalb eine integrierte Planung von Servicepolitik und Produktpolitik als Grundlage der Marktbearbeitung erforderlich. Diese muß sowohl auf Geschäftsfeldebene als auch auf Unternehmensebene erfolgen, wenn die Leistungen unter einem gemeinsamen Markendach abgesetzt werden. Hierdurch sollen Irritationen und negative Imagetransformationen vermieden werden, die durch eine zersplitterte, nicht aufeinander abgestimmte Vorgehensweise entstehen können. Damit zeigt sich, daß Service im Systemgeschäft mehr ist als ein additives Marketing-Instrument mit operativem Charakter, es handelt sich um ein strategierelevantes Entscheidungsfeld.

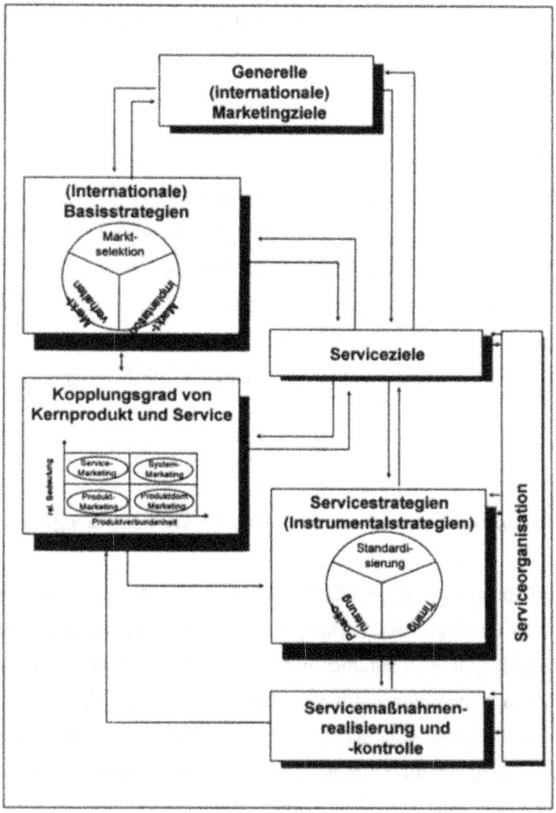

Abb. 4: Gestaltungs- und Einflußbereiche einer Servicekonzeption

Auch beim „produktdominierten Service-Marketing“ sind diese Zusammenhänge tendenziell gegeben, wenngleich die Intensität nicht so stark ausgeprägt ist. Die Leistungsverbundenheit macht jedoch eine Berücksichtigung der Servicebesonderheiten und -anforderungen bei der Planung von Marketingstrategien und -programmen notwendig.

In unserer Untersuchung zeigte sich - auf Basis einer Kreuztabellierung - , daß die deutschen Unternehmen auf dem heimischen Markt vor allem ein „integriertes System-Marketing“ (46,2 %) verfolgen . Ein „produktdominiertes Marketing“ wird von 40,2 % verfolgt. Ein reines „Produkt-Marketing“ und ein „isoliertes Service-Marketing“ werden eher selten realisiert (5,4 % und 8,2 %). Auf den Auslandsmärkten ergibt sich ein ähnliches Bild. 49,4 % der deutschen Unternehmen betreiben hier ein „integriertes System-Marketing“, 35,8 % ein „produktdominiertes Marketing“, 5,1 % ein reines „Produkt-Marketing“ und 9,7 % ein „isoliertes Service-Marketing“.

Es ist durchaus denkbar, daß - bezogen auf das Gesamtangebot eines Unternehmens - eine Kombination der skizzierten „Service-Marketing-Facetten“ möglich ist. Das ist dann gegeben, wenn beispielsweise eine Zielgruppe ein Systemangebot erwartet, eine andere Zielgruppe allerdings nur an spezifischen Dienstleistungen des Anbieters interessiert ist. Insbesondere bei internationalen Absatzaktivitäten können sich länderspezifisch oder auch -übergreifend unterschiedliche Vermarktungsmuster von Kern- und Serviceleistungen ergeben, wenn beispielsweise in einem Land die Notwendigkeit einer Bündelung stärker gegeben ist als in einem anderen.

2.2. Servicepolitik und (internationale) Basisstrategien

Basisstrategien bilden den grundlegenden Rahmen für den Einsatz von Marketinginstrumenten im Unternehmen und legen die Wirkungsrichtung der verschiedenen Marketingaktivitäten fest. Die aus den Basisstrategien resultierenden Entscheidungen stellen den strategischen Kern der marktorientierten Unternehmensführung dar. Sie umfassen die Auswahl von Marktsegmenten und die Festlegung von spezifischen Zielgruppen (Marktselektion), die Art des Markteintritts (Marktimplantation) sowie die grundsätzliche inhaltliche und formelle Marktbearbeitung (Marktverhalten). Serviceaktivitäten werden ebenfalls von diesen Entscheidungen determiniert. Allerdings können auch Serviceleistungen aufgrund ihrer Besonderheiten - gerade in Industrieunternehmen - erhebliche Auswirkungen auf die strategischen Basisentscheidungen haben, die es frühzeitig zu erkennen und zu berücksichtigen gilt.

2.2.1. Service und Marktselektion

Marktselektionsentscheidungen führen zur Festlegung von zeitlich-räumlich und sachlich definierten Zielgruppen bei gleichzeitiger Angebotsabstimmung. In Abbildung 5 ist das Entscheidungsfeld in Form eines Segmentierungswürfels dargestellt. Diese Darstellung macht deutlich, daß die Abgrenzung und Auswahl von Segmenten im Prinzip eine simultane Entscheidung nach den drei Dimensionen erfordert. Die hieraus resultierende Komplexität ist jedoch selbst mit Computerunterstützung kaum beherrschbar, so daß in praxi regelmäßig ein mehrstufiges Vorgehen angewendet wird. Im allgemeinen geht man hierbei so vor, daß, von übergeordneten Segmenten ausgehend, zunehmend spezifischere Segmente gebildet werden. Grundlage bilden meistens Marktleistungen, die an geeignete Kundengruppen abgesetzt werden sollen. Die Frage lautet dann: Welche Käufer kommen für unser Produkt in Frage? Zur Beantwortung werden zunächst häufig sozio-demographische und -ökonomische Kriterien (z.B. Geschlecht, Alter, Beruf, Bildung, Einkommen, Haushaltsgröße) herangezogen. In weiteren Schritten werden die daraus gebildeten Segmente dann weiter analysiert, z.B. nach psychographischen Kriterien, räumlicher Verteilung etc., bis schließlich die Kundengruppen festgelegt sind, die mit einem spezifischen Kommunikations-, Distributions- und auch Service-Mix zu bearbeiten sind.

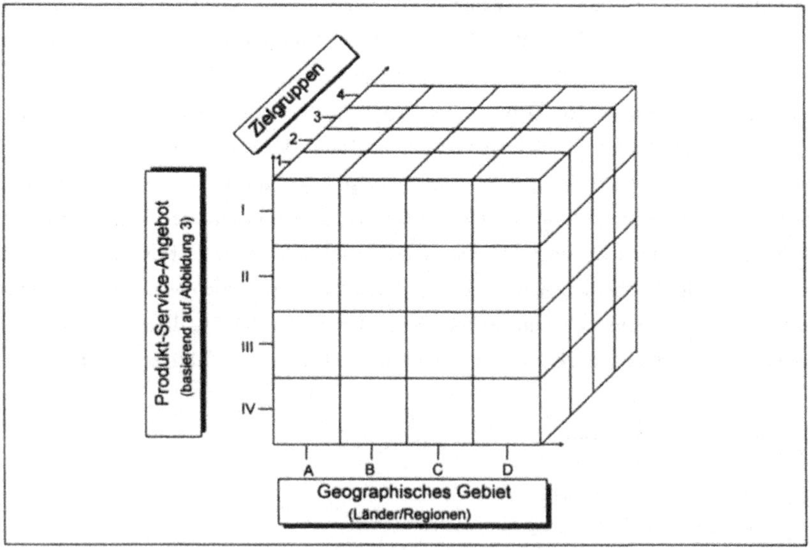

Abb. 5: Segmentierungswürfel

Im internationalen Marketing geht man meist von einer groben Länderauswahl aus, bei der nach bestimmten länderspezifischen Rahmenbedingungen (z.B. ökonomische, juristische, kulturelle, technische und soziale Faktoren) zunächst solche Ländermärkte selektiert werden, die - bezogen auf die zugrunde gelegten Bewertungskriterien - die aufgestellten Anforderungen erfüllen[12]. Diese bilden dann die Grundlage für die oben angedeutete intranationale Feinsegmentierung nach spezifischen Markt- und Abnehmerkriterien, bei der im Ergebnis Detailsegmente verbleiben, die es zu bearbeiten gilt[13]. Dabei kann es durchaus sinnvoll sein, die in den einzelnen Ländern gebildeten und ausgewählten Zielgruppen zu transnationalen Segmenten zusammenzufassen, wenn es sich um gleichartige Kundengruppen handelt[14]. Sind mehrere Ländermärkte für eine Feinsegmentierung geeignet, ist auch ein integrales Vorgehen möglich, bei dem Ländergrenzen und -besonderheiten völlig ignoriert werden und sofort mit einer Segmentierung auf der Abnehmerebene begonnen wird[15].

Sowohl bei der Bildung als auch bei der Bearbeitung von nationalen und inter- oder transnationalen Segmenten können Serviceleistungen einen erheblichen Einfluß haben[16]. Bei der Segmenterfassung und -abgrenzung können Serviceleistungen, z.B. beim Systemverkauf, als eigenständiges Segmentierungskriterium die generelle Zielgruppenbildung und -auswahl sogar dominieren. Dabei kann bei zunehmender Bedeutung des Service als Absatz- und Wettbewerbsinstrument der Einfluß auf die Marktselektion so stark sein, daß nicht erfüllbare Serviceanforderungen bestimmter Segmente deren Bearbeitung verhindern. Für Unternehmen, die ihre Absatzaktivitäten internationalisieren wollen, kann ein notwendiges Serviceniveau und ein erforderlicher Servicestil in bestimmten Ländern sogar zu einem Ausschlußkriterium bei der Länderauswahl werden. Daß es unterschiedliche Serviceniveaus in den Ländermärkten gibt, zeigen unsere Untersuchungsergebnisse. Für 21,8 % der befragten Unternehmen ist das Serviceniveau im Ausland geringer bzw. sehr viel geringer, für 64,5 % gibt es keine Unterschiede und 13,8 % der befragten Unternehmen schätzen nach eigener Erfahrung das Serviceniveau höher oder sehr viel höher ein als in Deutschland. Zu den serviceintensiven Märkten zählen sie Nord-Amerika, Asien und auch Osteuropa. Auf diesen Märkten wird das Serviceniveau als signifikant höher angesehen als in Ländern der EU. Für die analysierten Unternehmen ist der Service jedoch im Durchschnitt nur teilweise ein wichtiges Kriterium für die

12 Vgl. Hünerberg (1994), S. 108.

13 Vgl. Meffert/Bolz (1994), S. 104ff.

14 Vgl. Heise/Hünerberg (1995), S. 100f.

15 Vgl. Kreutzer (1991), S. 4ff; Hassan 1991, S. 7ff.

16 Vgl. Vandermerwe/Chadwick (1991), S. 50ff.

nationale und internationale Marktsegmentierung (MW = 56 % bzw. MW = 53,7 % Zustimmung, daß Service ein wichtiges oder sehr wichtiges Segmentierungskriterium ist).

Neben der kombinierten Segmentierung nach Produkt-, Service- und Abnehmer-Kriterien zur Festlegung von generellen Marktsegmenten lassen sich selbstverständlich ganz gezielt auch servicebezogene Segmente definieren, die einen gezielten Einsatz von Serviceleistungen ermöglichen. Es geht um die Festlegung, welche Serviceleistungen, wem (Abnehmergruppe), wozu (Produktgruppe), wo (geographischer Raum) angeboten werden. Dabei können sich hier völlig andere Segmente ergeben als auf Basis der Kernprodukte. Insbesondere wenn Serviceleistungen differenzierter betrachtet werden, z.B. nach dem Bezugsobjekt (personen- versus produktbezogene Serviceleistungen) oder nach dem Zeitbezug (Pre-Sales-Services versus After-Sales-Services), läßt sich eine sehr feine Segmentierung durchführen. Im internationalen Kontext wird dieser Prozeß noch komplexer, da zusätzlich nach Ländern segmentiert werden kann. Im Ergebnis sind dann über ausgewählte Ländermärkte hinweg durchaus unterschiedliche Produkt- und Servicesegmente zu bearbeiten. Wie jedoch die Untersuchungsergebnisse zeigen, sind die Zielgruppen von Kern- und Serviceleistungen im Inland (MW=70,6 % Gleichheitsgrad zwischen Zielgruppen für Produkt und Serviceleistung) und auch bei der Auslandsmarktbearbeitung (MW=71,2 % Gleichheitsgrad) weitgehend identisch. Serviceleistungen werden also kaum als eigenständige Marktleistung zur Zielgruppenausweitung eingesetzt.

Die vorgestellten Ergebnisse sind für die international tätigen Betriebe vor dem Hintergrund zu sehen, daß die überwiegende Zahl der befragten Unternehmen (= 42,5 %) ihre Auslandsaktivitäten über Absatzmittler im indirekten Export abwickeln und die Serviceleistungen gegenüber der eigentlichen Zielgruppe für die Marktsegmentierung und -bearbeitung eine eher untergeordnete Rolle spielen. Damit wird direkt zum nächsten strategischen Entscheidungsfeld übergeleitet, zur Marktimplantation.

2.2.2. Service und Marktimplantation

Die Marktimplantation umfaßt Entscheidungen darüber, wie der Markteintritt und die Markteroberung bzw. -verteidigung grundsätzlich ablaufen sollen. Es handelt sich hierbei vor allem um die Festlegung der formalen Expansionsstrategie (Wachstum aus eigener Kraft versus Wachstum durch Kooperationen, Akquisitionen/Fusionen). In diesem Zusammenhang ist zu

klären, wer die Servicefunktionen übernimmt, wenn überhaupt Serviceleistungen angeboten werden sollen bzw. müssen. Grundsätzlich ist es hierbei möglich, daß die Leistungen

- vom Unternehmen selbst erbracht und angeboten werden (make and sell),
- vom Unternehmen zwar angeboten werden, aber von anderen (spezialisierten) Anbietern (aus dem Dienstleistungsbereich) erbracht werden (buy and sell),
- vom Unternehmen lediglich vermittelt werden, also weder im eigenen Namen und auf eigene Rechung angeboten noch erstellt werden (arrange),
- in Kooperation mit anderen Unternehmen (z.B. mit Absatzmittlern) gemeinsam angeboten und erstellt werden (cooperated make and sell) [17].

Die Entscheidung über die Trägerschaft des Service wird von einer Vielzahl unterschiedlicher Kriterien determiniert, wie z.B. Kosten, Know-How, Kapazitäten und strategische Bedeutung bestimmter Serviceleistungen[18]. Diese Einflußfaktoren gelten sowohl im nationalen als auch im internationalen Kontext. Grundsätzlich ist hierbei zu berücksichtigen, daß die Entscheidungen über die Service-Trägerschaft auch die Unternehmenskonfiguration und -struktur als Ganzes betreffen. So sind beispielsweise mit Partnerunternehmen (z.B. Handelsunternehmen) Service-Netzwerke oder eigenständige Serviceeinheiten (z.B. als Profit-Center) aufzubauen, die zu einer veränderten Ressourcenallokation sowie Führungs- und Steuerungsstruktur im Unternehmen führen können.

Auch bei internationalen Markteintrittsentscheidungen können länderbedingte Servicenotwendigkeiten die Wahl des Marktengagements wesentlich beeinflussen. So geben 44,9 % der Unternehmen in unserer Studie an, daß der anzubietende Service einen starken bzw. sehr starken Einfluß auf die Wahl der Markteintrittsform hatte. Lediglich bei 14,2 % der Betriebe wurde die Markteintrittsentscheidung ohne, bei 23,1 % der Unternehmen mit einem geringen und bei 17,8 % der Firmen mit einem mittleren Einfluß getroffen. Insbesondere bei der Errichtung von Niederlassungen vor Ort ist der Serviceeinfluß bei den befragten Unternehmen besonders groß (MW = 70,5 %) und unterscheidet sich signifikant von der Einflußstärke bei der Gründung von Joint Ventures im Ausland (MW = 20 %) sowie von der Durchführung eines direkten Exports (MW = 42,8 %) und eines indirekten Exports (MW = 42,8 %). Ein eigenständiger Markteintritt für die Vermarktung und Erstellung von Serviceleistungen wurde - wie Abbildung 6 zeigt - nur von 4,8 % der untersuchten Unternehmen gewählt.

17 Vgl. insbesondere Engelhardt/Reckenfelderbäumer (1993), S. 268ff.

18 Vgl. u.a. Engelhardt (1996), S. 75.

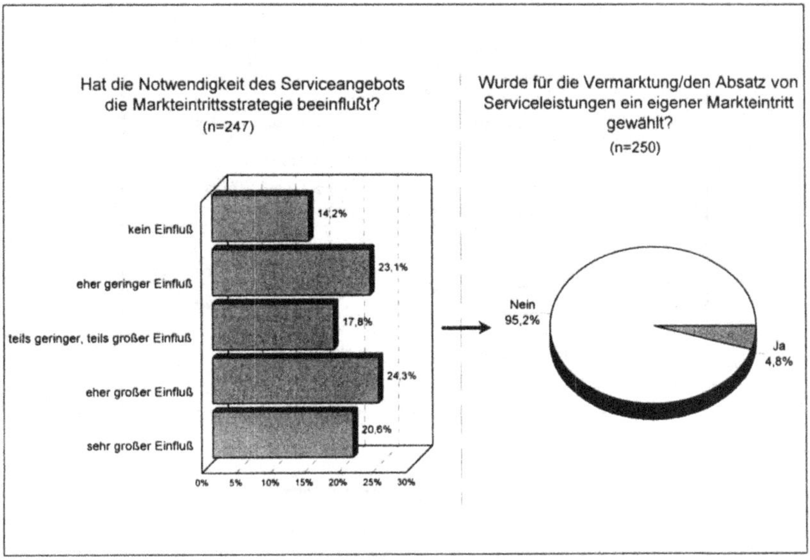

Abb. 6: Serviceeinfluß auf die Marktimplantation

Die Gründe für den servicebedingten Einfluß auf die Form des Marktengagements liegen - aus theoretischer Sicht - in der Immaterialität von Serviceleistungen und der notwendigen Kundenintegration bei deren Erstellung[19]. Lassen sich Serviceleistungen nämlich nicht auf Speicher- und Trägermedien materialisieren, dann ist beispielsweise ein Export nicht möglich. Unternehmen sind also in einer derartigen Situation in ihrem Handlungsspektrum eingeschränkt; für sie stehen nur Direktinvestitionen als Markteintrittsalternativen zur Disposition, wenn sie das Handling von strategisch wichtigen Serviceleistungen nicht an externe Partner vor Ort aus der Hand geben wollen. Abbildung 7 zeigt - entsprechend der Sampson-Snape-Box - die Markteintrittsoptionen, die für Anbieter von (Sekundär-) Dienstleistungen bestehen[20].

19 Vgl. Simon (1992), S. 408.

20 Vgl. hierzu insbesondere auch Stauss (1995), S. 455; Sampson/Snape (1985), S. 171ff.

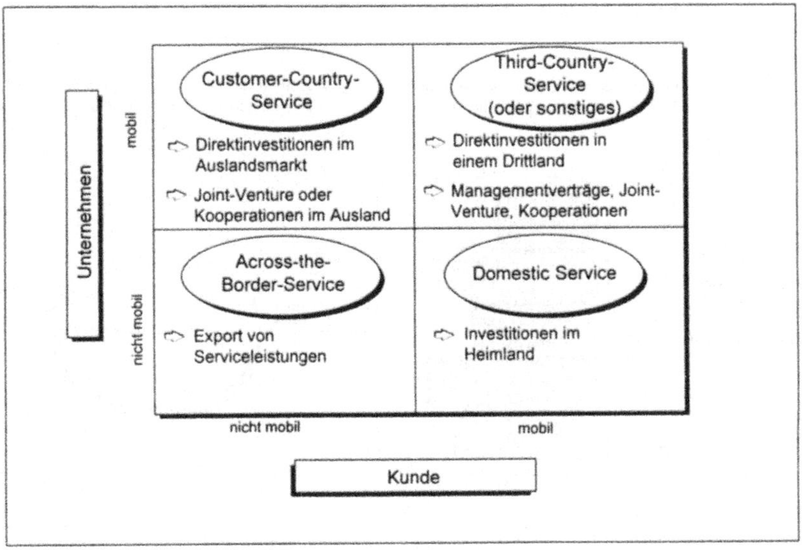

Abb. 7: Kundenintegration und Markteintritt

Abhängig von der für die Kundenintegration notwendigen Mobilität bzw. Mobilitätsbereitschaft des einheimischen Anbieters und der/den ausländischen Zielgruppe(n), sind also vier grundsätzliche Service-Situationen denkbar:

- Beim **„Across-the-Border-Service"** wird von keiner der beiden Parteien eine Mobilität gefordert. Die Serviceleistungen werden in diesem Falle bei gegebenen Bedingungen der Speicherbarkeit „exportiert".
- Der **„Customer-Country-Service"** erfordert vom Anbieter ein gewisse Mobilität, da der Service - aufgrund der Immobilität der Kunden und der Nicht-Exportierbarkeit der Leistungen - im Abnehmerland erstellt werden muß. Hiermit sind dann in der Regel Direktinvestitionen verbunden, die allein oder gemeinsam mit anderen (einheimischen) Unternehmen getätigt werden müssen. Es ist auch möglich, die Servicefunktionen völlig auf externe Servicepartner vor Ort zu übertragen.
- Direktinvestitionen sind auch im Falle des **„Domestic-Service"** notwendig. Allerdings werden sie im Heimland des Anbieters getätigt, da nur der Nachfrager mobil ist.
- Sind beide Parteien mobil, ist ein **„Third-Country-Service"** möglich. Da die Mobilität in diesem Fall keine Restriktion darstellt, sind auch die anderen angesprochenen „internationalen" Service-Engagements möglich, die das gesamte Spektrum von Eintritts-

strategien umfassen. Die konkrete Entscheidung für eine Markteintrittsstrategie hängt hierbei von der jeweiligen Verhandlungsstärke der beiden Service-Parteien ab.

Servicecharakteristika und Marktimplantationsentscheidungen stehen also in einem engen Zusammenhang. Entsprechende Interdependenzen sind deshalb frühzeitig im Rahmen von Internationalisierungsentscheidungen festzustellen.

2.2.3. Service und Marktverhalten

Beim Marktverhalten geht es um das generelle Vorgehen bei der inhaltlichen und formalen Marktbearbeitung. Bei der inhaltlichen Ausrichtung wird festgelegt, worin die Schwerpunkte der Marktbearbeitung liegen und auf welchen Feldern der Wettbewerb geführt wird (Kostenorientierung/-führerschaft und/oder Qualitätsorientierung/-führerschaft).

Das formale Marktverhalten umfaßt insbesondere den Grad der Aggressivität und die Dominanz beim Einsatz der Marketinginstrumente. Entscheidet sich ein Unternehmen jedoch dazu, Kann-Serviceleistungen ganz bewußt wettbewerbsstrategisch einzusetzen, dann ist zu entscheiden, ob es sich hierbei um ein offensives oder ein defensives Wettbewerbsinstrument handeln soll. Im internationalen Kontext ist dabei gleichzeitig festzulegen, inwieweit die Verhaltensstrategie über sämtliche Ländermärkte gleichmäßig angewandt werden kann. Die Existenz globaler Konkurrenten kann dazu führen, daß der Servicewettbewerb im globalen Rahmen zu sehen ist und nicht allein auf bestimmte Ländermärkte beschränkt bleibt.

Die Ergebnisse unserer Studie zeigen, daß Serviceleistungen auf den Auslandsmärkten und im Inland häufig ganz gezielt zur Erlangung von Wettbewerbsvorteilen eingesetzt werden (MW-Ausland = 65,1 % und MW-Inland = 67,2 % Zustimmungsgrad). Dies belegt die strategische Bedeutung des Service im Wettbewerb aus Sicht der Unternehmen. Möglichkeiten der konkurrenzbezogenen Nutzung von Serviceleistungen in Abhängigkeit von ihrem Neuigkeitsgrad in dem Markt(-segment) und der Aggressivität ihres Einsatzes sind in Abbildung 8 wiedergegeben[21].

---

[21] Vgl. Hünerberg/Mann (1996), S. 100f.

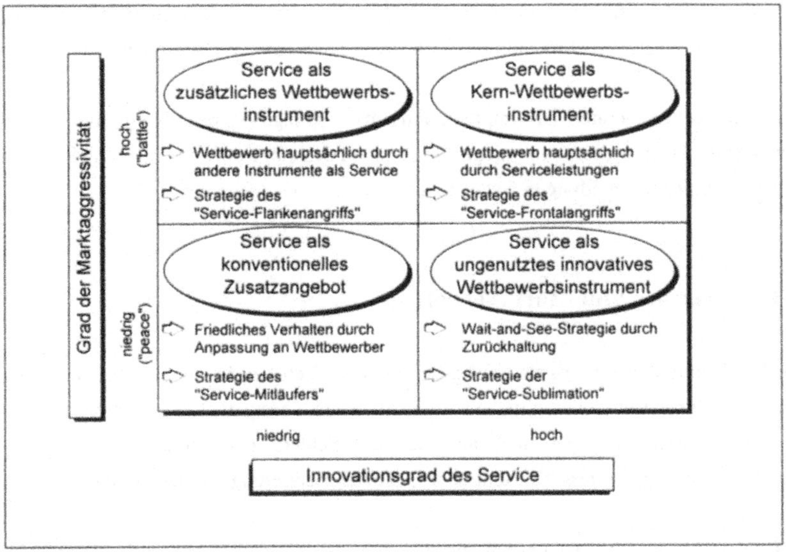

Abb. 8: Service als Wettbewerbsinstrument

Werden Muß- sowie landes- und branchenübliche Soll-Serviceleistungen angeboten, ohne sie bewußt zur Wettbewerbsführung einzusetzen, wird die **„Strategie des Service-Mitläufers"** gewählt. Der Service ist hierbei kein besonderer Wettbewerbsparameter, sondern wird neben den anderen Marketinginstrumenten konventionell eingesetzt. Wie die Ergebnisse einer Kreuztabellierung zeigen, wenden 29,6 % der analysierten Betriebe diese Strategie in Deutschland an. 31,7 % der Unternehmen wählen diese Vorgehensweise auf dem ausländischen Markt.

Ebenfalls friedlich verhalten sich Unternehmen, die eine **„Strategie der Service-Sublimation"** wählen. Auch hat der Service bei dieser Vorgehensweise keinen besonderen Stellenwert im Wettbewerb, wenngleich die Unternehmen in diesem Fall innovative Kann-Serviceleistungen zur Marktbearbeitung heranziehen. Sie werden jedoch meist eingesetzt, um die Kundenzufriedenheit bei bestehenden Abnehmern zu erhöhen und die Kundenbindung zu verstärken. Service wird hierbei also zur Absicherung von angestammten Marktarealen und Kundengruppen angewandt. Von den befragten Unternehmen verfolgen 27,4 % im Inland und 20,4 % auf den Auslandsmärkten diese Strategie.

Service wird als „Waffe“ zur Neukundengewinnung beim **„Frontalangriff“** herangezogen. Der Service ist hierbei das wichtigste Marketinginstrument im Wettbewerb. Bei dieser Vorgehensweise werden vor allem Kann-Leistungen ganz bewußt zur Erzielung von Wettbewerbsvorteilen eingesetzt. In gesättigten Märkten mit ausgereiften Produkt- und Verfahrenstechnologien sind sie neben dem Preis häufig eines der wenigen Marketinginstrumente, die der Profilierung am Markt und der Differenzierung gegenüber Konkurrenten dienen können[22]. Von den befragten Unternehmen setzen 24 % auf dem Inlandsmarkt und 23,4 % auf den ausländischen Märkten Serviceleistungen für den Frontalangriff ein.

Beim **„Service-Flankenangriff“** werden konventionelle Serviceleistungen aggressiv gegenüber den Wettbewerbern eingesetzt. Entsprechend dem Motto „try harder the same“ versucht man beispielsweise, durch eine bessere Servicequalität und/oder günstigere Servicepreise/-kosten gegenüber den Konkurrenten Vorteile zu erzielen. Allerdings wird der Wettbewerb bei dieser Strategie primär über andere Marketing-Instrumente als den Service ausgetragen. Der Service ist also lediglich ein zusätzliches Wettbewerbsinstrument. Im Inland setzen 19 % der untersuchten Unternehmen den Service dementsprechend ein, im Ausland sind es 24,5 %.

2.3. Strategische Entscheidungen bei der Gestaltung der (internationalen) Servicepolitik

Instrumentalstrategien bilden die Handlungskanäle für den konkreten Einsatz der einzelnen Marketing-Mix-Bereiche. Insbesondere Positionierungs-, Standardisierungs- und Timingentscheidungen sind zu treffen. Diese Festlegungen gelten auch für den Service als Marketinginstrument.

2.3.1. Positionierung von Serviceleistungen

Positionierung umfaßt dabei die grundlegende Einordnung von absatzpolitischen Instrumenten in das Marketing. Hierbei ist zwischen interner und externer Positionierung zu unterscheiden. Bei der **internen Positionierung** geht es darum, welcher Stellenwert einem Marketinginstrument im Rahmen des Marketing-Mix beigemessen wird. Dieser kann sich beispielsweise

22 Vgl. Olemotz (1995), S. 81ff.; siehe auch Meffert (1994a), S. 234ff.; derselbe (1994b), S. 98ff. für rezessive Märkte.

an dem absoluten oder relativen Ressourceneinsatz für ein Marketing-Instrument niederschlagen. Dabei können auch die Kosten, die für den Einsatz entstehen, als Indikator herangezogen werden. In unserer Studie zeigt sich, daß die **Servicekosten** nach Einschätzung der befragten Unternehmen im Durchschnitt 11,1 % der gesamten Produktkosten im Inland betragen. In Abbildung 9 ist die Kostenverteilung nach Klassen auf die Unternehmen dargestellt. Der Modalwert, also der Wert, der am häufigsten genannt wurde, liegt bei einem Kostenanteil von 5 %. So haben 21,3 % der Unternehmen den Kostenanteil des Service an den Gesamtproduktkosten eben auf diese 5 % beziffert. Signifikante Unterschiede nach Branchen konnten hierbei nicht festgestellt werden.

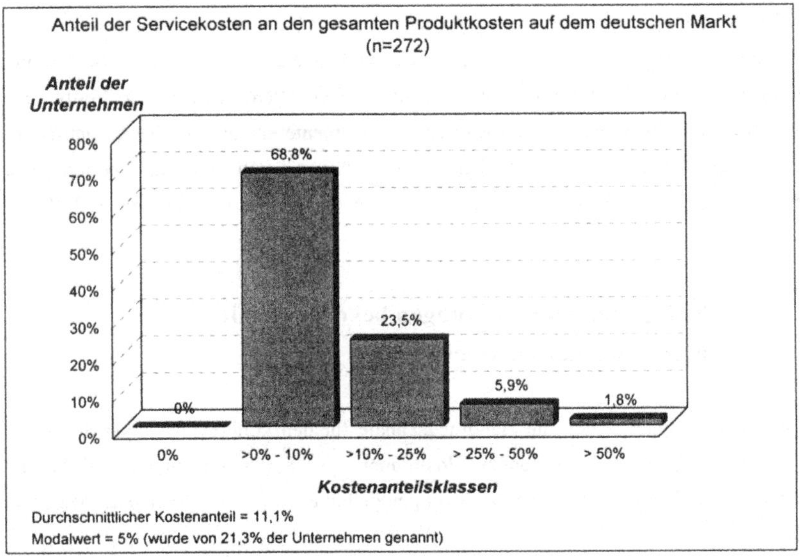

Abb. 9: Anteil der Servicekosten an den gesamten Produktkosten (im Inland)

Im internationalen Kontext ist im Rahmen der internen Positionierung auch zu entscheiden, ob die Ressourcenallokation auf ein Marketinginstrument in jedem Land gleich oder unterschiedlich verteilt werden soll. In unserem Fall zeigt sich anhand des Servicekostenanteils, daß dieser - wie in Abbildung 10 dargestellt - im Ausland geringer ist als im Inland. Im Durchschnitt aller befragten Unternehmen mit Absatzaktivitäten im Ausland liegt er bei 9,5 %. 18 % der Unternehmen haben den Modalwert von 8 % als Servicekostenanteil angegeben. Der Kostenunterschied kann vielfältige Gründe haben, z.B. geringere Faktorkosten für die Serviceerstellung im Ausland und/oder ein weniger umfassendes Serviceangebot der Unter-

nehmen. Auch hier konnten keine signifikanten Unterschiede zwischen Branchen festgestellt werden. Außerdem zeigt sich, daß deutsche Unternehmen, die im Ausland tätig sind, auf dem deutschen Heimmarkt signifikant höhere Kostenanteile für den Service haben (MW = 10,5 %) als auf den jeweiligen Auslandsmärkten (MW = 9,4 %).

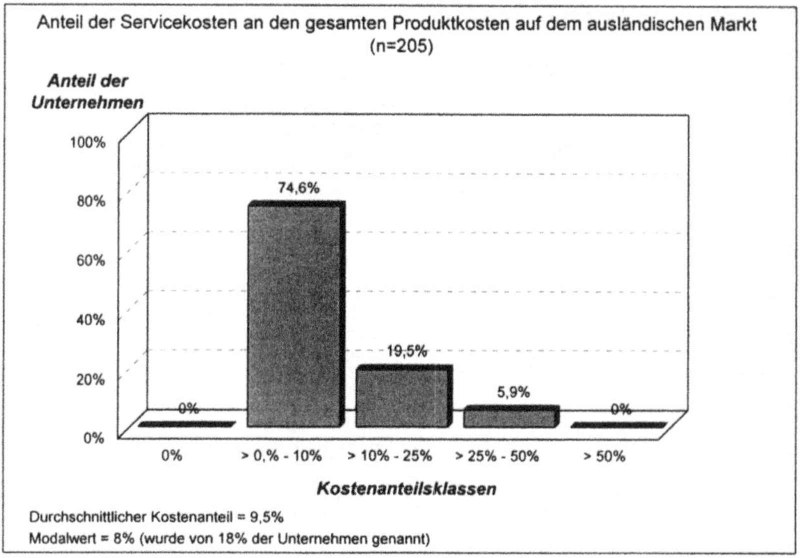

Abb. 10: Anteil der Servicekosten an den Gesamtproduktkosten bei der Auslandsmarktbearbeitung

Im Rahmen der **externen Positionierung** ist zu entscheiden, welche Bedeutung die Marketinginstrumente für die Markbearbeitung haben sollen. Es geht also vor allem darum, Bedeutung, Neuartigkeit und Image des spezifischen Instrumentaleinsatzes, wie z.B. des Service, für die Marktbearbeitung festzulegen. Bezüglich der Bedeutung des Service gaben die Unternehmen der Studie an, daß er für verschiedene Kriterien der Inlands- und Auslandmarktbearbeitung einen hohen Stellenwert einnimmt (siehe Abbildung 11). Unternehmen, die in den USA tätig sind, attestieren dem Service für den Markt-Unternehmenserfolg und speziell als Differenzierungsinstrument im Wettbewerb eine signifikant höhere Bedeutung als Unternehmen, die Geschäfte in Ost-Europa tätigen (MW = 83 % Wichtigkeit versus MW = 64 % Wichtigkeit). Das mag daran liegen, daß das generell höhere Serviceniveau in den USA zu höheren Erwartungen bei den Kunden und zu einem stärkeren Servicewettbewerb zwischen den Unternehmen führt. Das ist jedoch nur eine Vermutung, für die keine signifikanten Ergebnisse

gefunden werden konnten. Bei Unternehmen mit unterschiedlicher Marktbearbeitungsstrategie (z.B. Nischenanbieter versus Mehrsegmentbearbeiter versus Massenmarktanbieter) konnten weder in Deutschland noch im internationalen Geschäft signifikante Unterschiede festgestellt werden. Service hat also - bezogen auf die abgebildeten Kriterien - für alle abgefragten Arten der nationalen und internationalen Marktbearbeitung bei Unternehmen mit differenzierter Marktbearbeitung die gleiche Bedeutung.

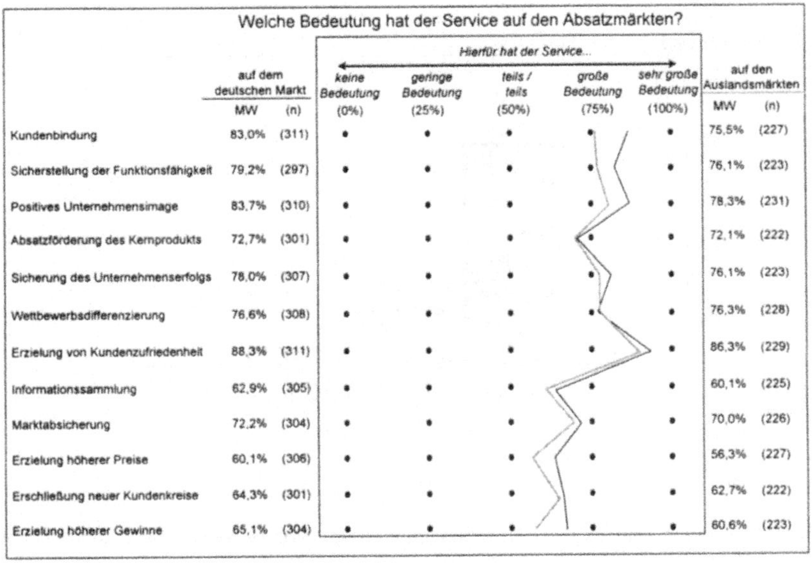

Abb. 11: Bedeutung des Service

Interessant ist, daß die Befragten dem Service für die Erreichung und Sicherstellung von Kundenzufriedenheit einen recht hohen Stellenwert beimessen (MW = 88,3 % im Inland und MW = 86,3 % im Ausland), dieser für die Erzielung höherer Preise jedoch nur einen eher mittleren Stellenwert hat (MW = 60,1 % im Inland und MW = 56,3 % im Ausland). Das ist umso erstaunlicher, als gerade der Service implizit als Differenzierungsinstrument einen Preisspielraum schaffen soll[23]. Ein Grund für dieses Ergebnis könnte darin liegen, daß die o.g. Servicekosten selbst vom Preis der Primärleistung getragen werden müssen. Allerdings ist hierbei zu berücksichtigen, daß vor allem fakultative Serviceleistungen, die einen echten Added-Value für die Kunden liefern, über den Nutzenzuwachs auch die Preisbereitschaft er-

[23] Vgl. z.B. Läbe/Stolpmann (1994), S. 97.

höhen. Im anderen Fall ist das Serviceangebot lediglich ein „Frill-Angebot", das die Kunden weder erwarten noch nachfragen[24]. Sie werden für derartige Serviceangebote dann auch nicht bereit sein, ein Entgelt zu entrichten. Für das Unternehmen wächst dadurch die Gefahr eines „Service-Wildwuchses"[25], der lediglich ein Kostentreiber ist und die Wettbewerbsposition - genau entgegen der eigentlichen Zielsetzung - im negativen Sinne nachhaltig beeinflussen kann. Es ist daher genau zu prüfen, welche Serviceleistungen den Kunden angeboten werden sollen und müssen.

Vergleicht man (für den deutschen Absatzmarkt) die international tätigen Unternehmen mit den Betrieben, die ausschließlich in Deutschland tätig sind, dann zeigt sich, daß für die nur national ausgerichteten Anbieter der Service auf dem deutschen Markt in einigen Bereichen einen höheren Stellenwert hat als für die Unternehmen mit Auslandserfahrung. So messen die Heimmarktbearbeiter dem Service generell eine höhere Bedeutung für den Unternehmenserfolg zu (MW = 81 % versus MW = 77,3 %). Gleiches gilt für die Schaffung von Kundenzufriedenheit (MW = 92 % versus MW = 87,4 %), für die Durchsetzung höherer Preise (MW = 69,4 % versus MW = 57,4 %) und für die Erzielung höherer Gewinne (MW = 72 % versus MW = 63,1 %). Diese Ergebnisse können darin begründet sein, daß der deutsche Markt für die international tätigen Unternehmen - aufgrund der geographischen Streuung des Absatzrisikos - in Relation zu den ausschließlich nationalen Heimanbietern weniger im Mittelpunkt des Interesses steht.

Interessante Ergebnisse bringt in diesem Zusammenhang auch eine vergleichende Analyse der Servicebedeutung des deutschen Marktes und der ausländischen Märkte für die international tätigen Unternehmen. Hier läßt sich feststellen, daß diese Unternehmen einigen Servicebereichen auf dem deutschen Markt eine signifikant höhere Bedeutung zumessen als auf Auslandsmärkten. Hierzu zählen die Kundenbindung (MW = 84,7 % versus 75,8 %), der Unternehmenserfolg (MW = 76,8 % verus 75,1 %) und die Informationssammlungsfunktion des Service (MW = 62,6 % versus MW=60,4 %). Damit zeigt sich, daß auch für die international tätigen Unternehmen der Service auf dem deutschen Markt generell eine recht große Bedeutung hat, wenngleich, wie oben beschrieben, das deutsche Serviceniveau von den meisten Unternehmen gemessen an den Auslandsmärkten als identisch angesehen wird.

---

24 Vgl. Meyer/Blümelhuber (1995), S. 30.

25 Sebastian/Hilleke (1994), S. 50.

Bei den Unternehmen in der Untersuchung werden die angebotenen Serviceleistungen in der Regel nicht oder nur selten separat in Rechnung gestellt. Das gilt sowohl im Inland (43,9 %) als auch für die Auslandsmarktbearbeitung (46,6 %). In der Textil- und Chemieindustrie ist dieser „kostenlose" Service für die Kunden im Ausland signifikant häufiger verbreitet als im Maschinenbau. Für den deutschen Markt konnten in dieser Hinsicht aber keine branchenbezogenen Unterschiede festgestellt werden.

Ein weiterer Aspekt der externen Marktpositionierung ist eng mit dem Marktverhalten verbunden. Es ist festzulegen, welche Ausrichtung das Unternehmen gegenüber Wettbewerbern einnehmen will. Hierbei ist zwischen einer **Folger-/Anpassungs-** oder einer **Differenzierungs-/Abhebungsstrategie** hinsichtlich des Instrumentaleinsatzes zu unterscheiden. Bezogen auf den Umfang des Servicespektrums geben 49,7 % der Unternehmen an, daß sie - nach eigener Einschätzung - ein umfangreicheres Serviceangebot aufweisen als ihre Wettbewerber. Nur 7,5 % sind nach eigener Einschätzung in diesem Bereich schlechter, 42,8 % schätzen sich gleich stark ein. Auch gegenüber den Wettbewerbern auf den Auslandsmärkten schätzen sich 43,5 % der Unternehmen besser ein. Lediglich 11,3 % sehen sich hier in einer schlechteren Position, während 45,2 % keine Unterschiede konstatieren.

Bei der angebotenen Servicequalität gehen 54,3 % der befragten Unternehmen davon aus, daß sie gegenüber der Konkurrenz einen hochwertigeren Service anbieten, 3,6 % schätzen sich hier schlechter und 42,1 % gleich gut ein. Ein ähnliches Bild ergibt sich bei der Positionsbeurteilung gegenüber den Wettbewerbern im Ausland. Nur 4,3 % der Unternehmen glauben, schlechter zu sein als ihre Konkurrenten. 47 % haben nach eigener Auffassung das gleiche Niveau bei der Servicequalität und 48,7 % sehen sich hier sogar in einer besseren Position. Die vorstehenden Ergebnisse sind jedoch dahingehend zu relativieren, daß es sich um eigene Einschätzungen der Unternehmen handelt. Aussagefähige Ergebnisse können letztlich nur Kundenbefragungen liefern, die in Unternehmen immer noch relativ selten durchgeführt werden.

Stellt man die beiden Dimensionen der wettbewerbsbezogenen Qualität und Quantität des Serviceangebots in einer Matrix gegenüber, dann lassen sich - wie in Abbildung 12 dargestellt - neun typische Wettbewerbspositionen und -strategien im Service ableiten[26].

[26] Vgl. in Anlehnung an Perlitz (1988), S. 48.

Servicequantität \ Servicequalität	besser	gleich	schlechter
schlechter	Service-Premiumstrategie Inland: 2 % Ausland: 2,2 %	Service-Hoffnungsstrategie Inland: 3,7 % Ausland: 5,3 %	Service-Problemstrategie Inland: 2 % Ausland: 3,9 %
gleich	Service-Qualitätsführer Inland: 9,2 % Ausland: 8,7 %	Service-Patt Inland: 32 % Ausland: 36 %	Service-Hoffnungsstrategie Inland: 1,7 % Ausland: 0,4 %
besser	Service-Meisterstrategie Inland: 43 % Ausland: 38,1 %	Service-Mengenführer Inland: 6,4 % Ausland: 5,3 %	Service-Massenstrategie Inland: 0 % Ausland: 0 %

(Inland: n = 300; Ausland: n = 228)

Abb. 12: Servicewettbewerb in der Praxis

Nach eigener Einschätzung gehen die meisten Unternehmen sowohl im Inland (43 %) als auch im Ausland (38,1 %) davon aus, daß sie als **„Service-Meister"** in qualitativer und in quantitativer Hinsicht ein besseres Serviceangebot liefern als ihre Wettbewerber. Wird dies von den Abnehmern ebenfalls so gesehen, dann kann diese Strategie gerade in serviceintensiven Märkten sehr erfolgreich sein. In einem **„Service-Patt"** befinden sich - als zweithäufigste Situation - im Inland 32 % und im Ausland 36 % der Unternehmen. Sie unterscheiden sich im Serviceangebot nicht von ihren Konkurrenten. Eine problematische Situation kann sich für Unternehmen ergeben, die sowohl in qualitativer als auch in quantitativer Richtung schlechter sind als ihre Mitbewerber. Vor allem auf Märkten, bei denen Serviceleistungen einen wichtigen Einfluß auf die Kaufentscheidungen der Abnehmer haben, kann sich eine derartige **„Service-Problemsituation"** negativ auf den Unternehmensbestand auswirken. In unserer Studie waren 2 % der Unternehmen auf den Inlandsmarkt und 3,9 % auf dem Auslandsmarkt davon betroffen, obwohl sie die Bedeutung des Service als Differenzierung- und Profilierungsinstrument im Durchschnitt als sehr hoch einschätzen. Unternehmen, die sich in einer nationalen oder internationalen Service-Problemsituation befinden, verteilen sich relativ gleichmäßig über alle Branchen hinweg.

Änliches gilt auch für die **„Service-Hoffnungsstrategien“**, bei denen die Unternehmen in einer Dimension schlechter abschneiden als ihre Konkurrenten und in der anderen Dimension gleich gut sind. Während jedoch bei der Problemstrategie das Servicemanko für die Kunden in der Regel sofort auffällig ist, kann es bei den Hoffnungsstrategien durchaus vorkommen, daß die negative Abweichung der einen Dimension gegenüber den Wettbewerberangeboten nicht sofort wahrgenommen wird. Im übrigen ist auch immer zu beachten, wie wichtig die jeweils schlechtere Dimension aus Kundensicht ist, um die wettbewerbsbezogene Relevanz dieser vermeintlichen Schwäche zu beurteilen. Interessant ist, daß bei den beiden Hoffnungsstrategien nur selten der Nachteil gegenüber den Konkurrenten bei der Servicequalität liegt (1,7 % der Unternehmen im Inland und 0,4 % im Ausland). Häufiger liegt die Schwäche hingegen bei der Quantität des Servicespektrums (3,7 % der Unternehmen auf dem Inlandsmarkt und 5,3 % auf den ausländischen Märkten), wobei wiederum zu beachten ist, daß umfassendere Serviceangebote von Konkurrenten häufig aus „Frill-Leistungen“ bestehen, die lediglich kostentreibend, aber für die Abnehmer nicht nutzenstiftend sind. Es ist eben genau zu prüfen, ob ein umfassendes Serviceangebot auch tatsächlich mit einer Wertsteigerung für die Kunden einhergeht oder ob es sich lediglich um ein aufgeblähtes Leistungsprogramm handelt, das aus Abnehmersicht weder attraktivitäts- noch zufriedenheitssteigernd ist[27]. Eine durchaus sinnvolle Vorgehensweise kann deshalb darin bestehen, sich auf wesentliche Serviceanforderungen der Abnehmer zu beschränken und diese im Rahmen einer **„Service-Prämienstrategie“** dann mit einem erheblich besseren Qualitätsniveau zu erfüllen als die Wettbewerber. Das setzt allerdings voraus, daß die Kundenanforderungen eindeutig erhoben werden und der angebotene Kundennutzen der Serviceleistungen klar kommuniziert wird. Bei den Unternehmen in unserer Untersuchung wird diese Vorgehensweise von 2 % im Inland und 2,2 % im Ausland zugrunde gelegt.

Mehr Unternehmen verfolgen hingegen im Inland (9,2 %) und im Ausland (8,7 %) die Strategie eines **„Service-Qualitätsführers“**, indem sie zwar vom Umfang her ein gleiches Serviceprogramm anbieten, dafür aber versuchen, eine insgesamt bessere Qualität der Leistungen zu erreichen. Wichtig für diese Strategie ist, daß der hiermit angestrebte höhere Kundennutzen auch die eventuellen Mehrkosten des Serviceangebots ausgleicht. Da gerade bei Standard-Serviceleistungen von den Kunden auf jeden Fall eine einwandfreie und herausragende Qualität verlangt wird, bezieht sich die Ausdehnung der „Qualitätsführerschaft“ vor allem auf alle anderen Soll- und Kann-Leistungen des Service. Ohne eine segmentbezogene Analyse der Kundenerwartungen an verschiedene Servicebereiche kann es auch hier schnell über eine

[27] Vgl. Meyer/Blümelhuber (1996), S. 320ff.

„Over-Quality“ zu einer exorbitanten Kostensteigerung kommen, die sich nicht pretial abwälzen läßt.

Eine ähnliche Gefahr ergibt sich auch für den **„Service-Mengenführer“**, der in eine Kostenfalle laufen kann, wenn aus dem dominierenden Angebot eine unkontrollierte Vielfalt erwächst. Immerhin 6,4 % der Unternehmen setzen im Inland und 5,3 % im Ausland auf diese Strategie.

Eine **„Service-Massenstrategie“**, bei der die Servicequalität schlechter und der Umfang des Servicespektrums besser ist, wird von keinem der befragten Unternehmen auf dem inländischen Markt oder den ausländischen Absatzmärkten realisiert.

2.3.2. Standardisierung von Serviceleistungen

Im Rahmen der **Standardisierung** geht es um den Grad der Vereinheitlichung von Marketing-Maßnahmen bezogen auf bearbeitete Marktsegmente. Bei internationalen Absatzaktivitäten ist diese Entscheidung in besonderem Maße von Bedeutung. Hier ist festzulegen, ob beispielsweise Serviceleistungen bzw. -programme länderübergreifend einheitlich angeboten werden können und sollen. Dabei stellt diese Entscheidung bei Serviceleistungen - aufgrund der notwendigen Kundenbeteiligung - ein erhebliches Problem dar, denn man kann davon ausgehen, daß mit zunehmendem Integrationsgrad und stärkerer Immaterialität der Serviceleistungen die Servicemaßnahmen individueller ausfallen. Deshalb ist zumindest auf der Ergebnisebene eine Standardisierung von derartigen Serviceleistungen besonders problematisch. Darüber hinaus sind im internationalen Rahmen die üblichen Standardisierungsbarrieren zu berücksichtigen.

In Abbildung 13 sind die aus Sicht der befragten Unternehmen wichtigsten Hemmnisse für eine internationale Vereinheitlichung der Servicepolitik dargestellt. 27,7 % der Unternehmen haben ihre Serviceaktivitäten auf dem deutschen Markt und den ausländischen Absatzmärkten nicht standardisiert. Die Gründe hierfür sehen sie vor allem darin, daß[28]

- sie unterschiedliche Marketingstrategien auf den Märkten verfolgen (53,8 %),
- sie unterschiedliche Vertriebskanäle mit einem anderen Leistungs-/Servicepotential nutzen (49,2 %),

[28] Siehe auch Hünerberg/Mann (1996), S. 102.

- die wirtschaftlichen Rahmenbedingungen auf den Märkten verschieden sind (44,6 %),
- eine andere Wettbewerbsstruktur vorliegt (41,5 %) und
- die rechtlichen Bedingungen unterschiedlich sind (32,3 %).

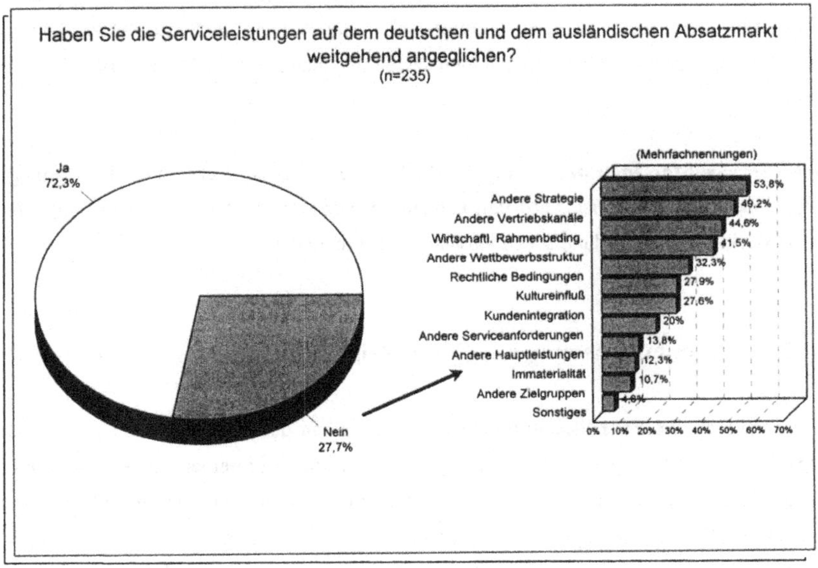

Abb. 13: Standardisierung von Serviceleistungen

Es sind also vor allem markt- und umfeldbezogene Faktoren, die gegen eine Standardisierung von Serviceleistungen sprechen. Die Servicecharakteristika Immaterialität und Kundenintegration spielen aus Sicht der befragten Unternehmen eine eher untergeordnete Rolle. Allerdings ist hierbei die Tatsache zu berücksichtigen, daß - wie bereits beschrieben - eine Vielzahl der Unternehmen (= 42,5 %) ihre Auslandsaktivitäten über den indirekten Export durchführen, so daß die Serviceaufgaben gegenüber den eigentlichen Kunden bzw. Endkunden häufig auf inländische oder ausländische Absatzmittler übertragen werden. Da von den befragten Unternehmen auch im Inland häufig indirekte Absatzwege genutzt werden (59,4 %), scheint das Ergebnis einleuchtend, daß die Mehrzahl (= 72,3 %) die „Serviceleistungen" bzw. die Übertragung der Servicefunktion auf den Handel vereinheitlicht hat. Gleichzeitig bedeutet das aber auch, daß der Hersteller nur indirekt auf die Servicepolitik des Absatzmittlers Einfluß nimmt und damit auch das strategische Profilierungs- und Differenzierungspotential des Service auf der Zielgruppenebene nur mittelbar nutzen kann.

2.3.3. Timing von Serviceleistungen

Timingstrategien betreffen den Zeitpunkt, die Dauer und die Häufigkeit des Einsatzes von Marketing-Instrumenten. Timingstrategien sind häufig eng mit Positionierungsentscheidungen verbunden, so daß sie sowohl auf die zeitliche Verteilung des Ressourceneinsatzes einwirken als auch auf die zeitliche Abfolge von Marktbearbeitungsmaßnahmen.

Bezüglich des **Zeitpunktes** können Serviceleistungen bereits vor der eigentlichen Markteinführung des Kernproduktes im Sinne eines Prä-Marketing eingesetzt werden, um den Take-Off einer Produktinnovation vorzubereiten[29], oder auch als After-Marketing-Instrument nach der Produktelimination bzw. beim Marktaustritt Anwendung finden[30]. Darüber hinaus lassen sich Serviceleistungen auch unmittelbar vor oder nach dem Kaufakt als stimulierende Pre-Sales-Leistungen oder als nachbetreuende und zufriedenheitsschaffende After-Sales-Leistungen heranziehen. Allerdings ist bei einer derartigen temporären Betrachtung zu berücksichtigen, daß im Rahmen einer ganzheitlichen Marketing-Perspektive jede After-Sales-Aktivität darauf ausgerichtet sein sollte, eine langfristige Kundenbeziehung aufzubauen oder zu stärken und damit Wiederholungs- bzw. Folgekäufe vorzubereiten[31]. Vor diesem Hintergrund ist after-sales immer auch pre-sales. In Abbildung 14 ist deshalb bewußt auf Service-Prä- und -After-Marketing abgestellt worden. Zu den Leistungen des **Service-Prä-Marketing** gehören typischerweise Informationsdienste, Dummypräsentationen, Aufstellung und Demonstration von Präferenzanlagen sowie Kundenschulungen[32]. Zu dem **Service-After-Marketing** gehören beispielsweise Wartungs-, Reparatur-, De-Installations- und Recyclingmaßnahmen sowie sonstige Serviceleistungen aus Gewährleistungsansprüchen der Kunden.

In Abbildung 14 sind der Prä- und Aftermarketing-Einsatz des Service dargestellt. Wie ersichtlich ist, setzen die befragten Unternehmen ihre Servieceleistungen eher selten als Prä-Marketing-Maßnahmen ein. Das gilt sowohl für die nationale als auch für die internationale Marktbearbeitung. Damit werden Akquisitionspotentiale und Möglichkeiten zum Aufbau von Markteintrittsbarrieren gegenüber Wettbewerbern nicht in vollem Maße genutzt. Ein ähnliches Bild ergibt sich beim gezielten After-Marketing-Einsatz des Service. Allerdings zeigt sich im Auslandsgeschäft, daß Unternehmen, die eine differenzierte Marktbearbeitung von

29 Vgl. Möhrle (1995), S. 69ff.

30 Vgl. Vavra (1992), S. 15f.

31 Vgl. auch Engelhardt (1996), S. 74.

32 Vgl. Hünerberg/Mann (1996), S. 102f.

wenigen Segmenten verfolgen, signifikant häufiger ein Service-Prä-Marketing durchführen (MW = 44,5 %) als standardisiert vorgehende Segmentbearbeiter (MW = 33,3%) und standardisiert vorgehende Massenmarktbearbeiter (MW = 24,4 %). Außerdem konnte ermittelt werden, daß international tätige Unternehmen auf dem deutschen Heimmarkt signifikant häufiger Serviceleistungen als After-Marketing-Maßnahmen einsetzen als auf den Auslandsmärkten (MW = 39,3 % versus MW = 37,3 %). Das kann beispielsweise daran liegen, daß in Deutschland die Anforderungen an Garantieleistungen umfassender und langfristiger ausgelegt sind als in einigen Auslandsmärkten. Ursachen hierfür wurden in der Studie allerdings nicht erhoben.

Mit der **Dauer** des Serviceeinsatzes wird nicht nur die Frage angesprochen, in welchem Zeitraum bestimmte Serviceleistungen angeboten werden sollen, es geht auch darum, wie lange die strategische Wirkung von Serviceleistungen am Markt genutzt werden kann. Beide Dimensionen hängen dabei im wesentlichen von den Kundenerwartungen und Wettbewerberaktivitäten ab. Aber auch rechtliche Vorschriften (z.B. zur Länge von Gewährleistungspflichten), kulturelle Eigenheiten (z.B. typische Zeitdauer von Serviceangeboten und -erstellungsprozessen) und die Art der abgesetzten Produkte (z.B. technisch-komplexe Produkte versus Low-Tech-Güter) haben hierauf einen Einfluß.

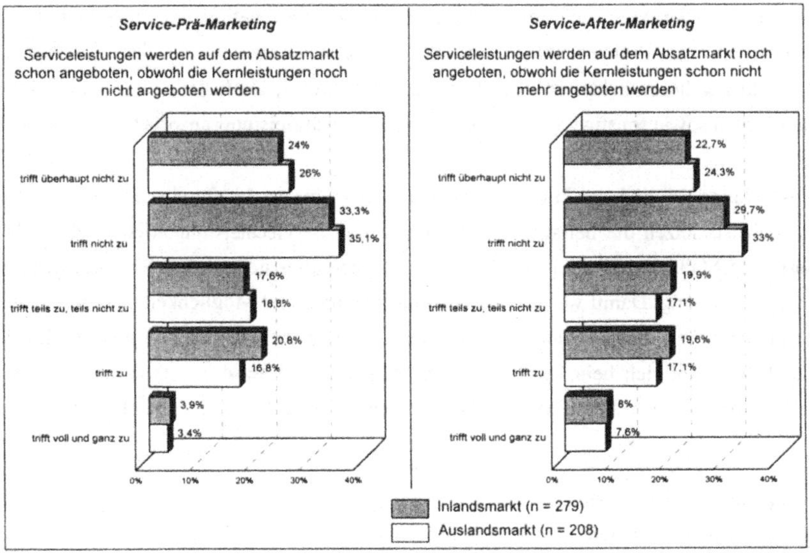

Abb. 14: Service-Timing

Insbesondere die sich im Zeitablauf ergebenden Veränderungen der Wettbewerbsintensität können dazu führen, daß auch der Profilierungscharakter von Serviceleistungen einer dynamischen Entwicklung unterliegt. So werden aus innovativen Kann-Leistungen häufig Soll-Leistungen, wenn nach einiger Zeit auch andere Wettbewerber diese Services anbieten. Haben sich Soll-Leistungen weitgehend als obligatorische Muß-Serviceangebote durchgesetzt, dann ist das Profilierungspotential weitgehend ausgeschöpft. Im Zeitablauf kommt es also zu einer Abnutzung der strategischen Bedeutung von Kann-Leistungen. Während sie anfangs noch die Möglichkeit aufweisen, durch ihre Neuartigkeit Wettbewerbsvorteile zu erzielen, können durch ihr Angebot zu einem späteren Zeitpunkt, wenn sie zu Muß-Leistungen geworden sind, höchstens Wettbewerbsnachteile vermieden werden. Betrachtet man die Serviceleistungen, die von den befragten Unternehmen am häufigsten eingesetzt werden, dann erhält man den Eindruck, daß es sich hierbei vor allem um Muß- und Soll-Leistungen handelt (siehe Abb. 15).

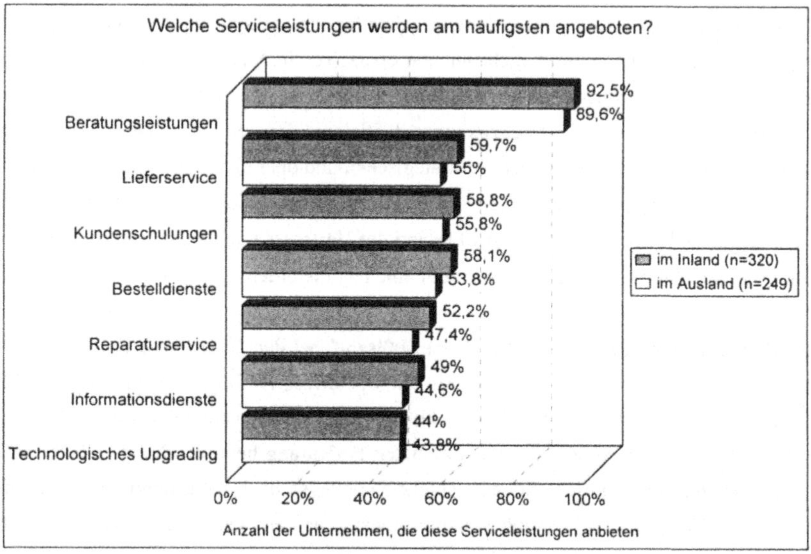

Abb. 15: Die am häufigsten eingesetzten Serviceleistungen

Für die unterschiedlichen Serviceleistungen bzw. -leistungskategorien entsteht ein Lebenszyklus, der die Bedeutungsverschiebungen wiedergibt. Bei produktbezogenen Serviceleistungen ist dieser abhängig von dem Verlauf und der Länge des Produktlebenszyklus[33]. In der Regel

[33] Vgl. Potts (1988), S. 32ff.

ist der Lebenszyklus für produktbezogene Serviceleistungen dem Produktlebenszyklus nachgelagert. Im internationalen Kontext können sich jedoch aufgrund zeitlich versetzter Entwicklungen in den jeweiligen Ländermärkten ganz unterschiedliche nationale Servicelebenszyklen ergeben[34]. In diesem Fall kann es zu einer Verlängerung des gesamten (länderübergreifenden) Servicezyklus kommen. Letztlich handelt es sich bei der Entstehung internationaler Servicelebenszyklen um eine zeitliche Dimension der Standardisierung von Serviceleistungen, die bereits vorstehend angesprochen wurde.

3. Integriertes Service-Management als Herausforderung in Industrieunternehmen

Die skizzierten Interdependenzen zwischen Marketingstrategien und dienstleistungsspezifischen Besonderheiten von Serviceleistungen haben bereits gezeigt, daß der Service im Marketing von Industrieunternehmen nicht nur ein operatives Instrument im Geflecht von Marketingmaßnahmen ist, sondern ein strategisches Entscheidungsfeld darstellt[35]. Zur Nutzung von Profilierungs- und Differenzierungspotentialen des Service ist ein Service-Handlungsrahmen zu entwickeln, der die strategischen und operativen Gestaltungsmöglichkeiten aufzeigt sowie Implementierungs- und Umsetzungshilfen liefert. Das ist bisher in der Praxis und in der Wissenschaft nach Auffassung der Verfasser noch nicht hinreichend - in einem integrierten Ansatz - geschehen und stellt eine Herausforderung für beide Seiten dar.

Grundsätzlich geht es darum, das „Servicebewußtsein“ bei den (Industrie-) Unternehmen zu schärfen, um die strategischen Möglichkeiten und operativen Anforderungen richtig zu erkennen. Die oben skizzierten Ergebnisse, z.B. hinsichtlich der Internationalisierungsanforderungen von Serviceleistungen oder der unterschätzten Bedeutung bei Umgehung eines pretialen Wettbewerbs, machen deutlich, daß eine solche Sichtweise noch nicht dominiert. Auch hinsichtlich der Wirkung und Nutzung situationsabhängiger Servicestrategien sowie ihrer tatsächlichen Erfolgsträchtigkeit liegen in den Unternehmen kaum Erkenntnisse vor. Allerdings sind hier auch von Seiten der Wissenschaft noch keine ausreichenden Informationen verfügbar (z.B. in Verbindung mit strategischen Gruppen oder mit der Internationalisierung)[36]. Das liegt nicht zuletzt daran, daß bisher noch kein ausgefeiltes Service-Controlling-Konzept vor-

34 Vgl. auch Hünerberg (1994), S. 159

35 Vgl. auch die Ergebnisse zur strategischen Bedeutung des Service bei Simon (1993), S. 10ff. und bei Olemotz (1995), S. 193ff.

36 Vgl. auch die Aussagen von Homburg/Garbe (1996), S. 273ff.

liegt, das Kostenwirkungen, monetäre Erträge sowie außermonetären Nutzen von Serviceleistungen erfaßt und einen effizienten Einsatz von Serviceleistungen ermöglicht[37].

Außerdem ist auch eine stärkere Berücksichtigung von organisatorischen und personellen Aspekten in der Service-Implementierung im Unternehmen erforderlich. Durch die notwendige Kundenintegration sind beispielsweise Organisationsformen zu schaffen, die es erlauben, eine hohe Servicequalität - auch länderübergreifend - zu erarbeiten. Hier lassen sich durch Benchmarking-Projekte mit Dienstleistungsunternehmen für die Industriebetriebe Erkenntnisse über Implementierungsanforderungen, -instrumente und -probleme gewinnen. Dabei ist zu berücksichtigen, daß letztlich in allen Wertschöpfungsphasen eines Unternehmens Servicepotentiale bestehen. So wird beispielsweise bereits in der FuE der Wartungs- und Reparaturbedarf von Produkten festgelegt, und die Verwendung von ökologisch verträglicheren Komponenten in der Produktion kann Recycling-Services beeinflussen[38].

Darüber hinaus erfordert eine angestrebte hohe Servicequalität motivierte Servicemitarbeiter, die im Rahmen eines internen Marketing für den direkten Kundenkontakt zu qualifizieren sind[39]. Damit verbunden ist die Bereitschaft des Managements, die Mitarbeiter an der „Servicefront" auch zu „empowern", damit sie flexibel auf die unterschiedlichen Einbringungsqualitäten des externen Faktors reagieren können. Die Schaffung einer Servicekultur ist dafür gerade in Industrieunternehmen eine unabdingbare Voraussetzung. Alle diese Faktoren sind in einem umfassenden (kunden-/service-, mitarbeiter-, kultur-, qualitäts- und effizienzorientierten) Marketingkonzept zu berücksichtigen und in einem Guß zu realisieren. Dabei ergeben sich gerade bei internationaler Unternehmenstätigkeit erhebliche Anforderungen, die es zu erkennen und zu meistern gilt. Inwieweit dies gelingt, hängt nicht zuletzt von einer ausreichenden Informationsbasis über Wirkungszusammenhänge und Restriktionen zwischen spezifischen Service- und konstitutiven Marketingentscheidungen ab.

---

37 Siehe hierzu die Überlegungen von Engelhardt (1996), S. 85ff. und die Arbeit von Reckenfelderbäumer (1995).

38 Vgl. Crown/Nuño (1991), S. 92f.; Mann (1996), S. 37.

39 Vgl. Bruhn (1995b), S. 28; Berry/Parasuraman (1995), S. 95ff.

4. Literatur

Berry, Leonard L./**Parasuraman**, Anantharanthan (1995): Dienstleistungsmarketing fängt beim Mitarbeiter an, in: Bruhn, Manfred (Hrsg.), Internes Marketing, Wiesbaden, S. 87-110

Bruhn, Manfred (1995a): Marketing - Grundlagen für Studium und Praxis, 2. Aufl., Wiesbaden

Bruhn, Manfred (1995b): Internes Marketing als Forschungsgebiet der Marketingwissenschaft, in: Bruhn, Manfred (Hrsg.), Internes Marketing, Wiesbaden, S. 13-61

Corsten, Hans (1989): Dientsleistungsmarketing - Elemente und Strategien, in: Jahrbuch der Absatz- und Verbrauchsforschung, 35. Jg., Heft 1, S. 23-40

Crown, Thomas J./**Nuño**, Jose Pablo (1991): Deciding Manufactoring Priorities - Flexibilty, Cost, Quality and Service, in: Long Range Planning, Vol. 24, No. 6, S. 88-95

Davidow, William H./**Uttal**, Bro (1989): Total Customer Service - The Ultimative Weapon, New York

Engelhardt, Werner Hans (1976): Erscheinungsformen und absatzpolitische Probleme von Angebots- und Nachfrageverbunden, in: Zeitschrift für betriebswirtschaftliche Forschung, 28. Jg., Heft 1, S. 77-90

Engelhardt, Werner Hans (1996): Effiziente Customer Integration im industriellen Service Management, in: Kleinaltenkamp, Michael/Fließ, Sabine/Jacob, Frank (Hrsg.), Customer Integration, Wiesbaden, S. 73-89

Engelhardt, Werner Hans/**Kleinaltenkamp**, Michael/**Reckenfelderbäumer**, Martin (1993): Leistungsbündel als Absatzobjekte, in: Zeitschrift für betriebswirtschaftliche Forschung, 45. Jg., Heft 5, S. 395-427

Engelhardt, Werner Hans/**Reckenfelderbäumer**, Martin (1993): Trägerschaft und organisatorische Gestaltung industrieller Dienstleistungen, in: Simon, Hermann (Hrsg.), Industrielle Dienstleistungen, Stuttgart, S. 263-293

Fassott, Georg (1996): Dienstleistungspolitik industrieller Unternehmen, in: der markt, 35. Jg., Heft 2, S. 75-85

Hassan, Salah S. (1991): Strategic Competitiveness in the Globalizing Consumer Markets, in: Journal of International Consumer Marketing, Vol. 3, No. 4, S. 7-14

HEISE, Gilbert/**HÜNERBERG**, Reinhardt (1995): Globale Segmentierung - Herausforderung für das Automobilmarketing, in: Hünerberg, Reinhard/Heise, Gilbert/Hoffmeister, Mike (Hrsg.), Internationales Automobilmarketing - Wettbewerbsvorteile durch marktorientierte Unternehmensführung, Wiesbaden, S. 83-119

HOMBURG, Christian/**GARBE**, Bernd (1996): Industrielle Dienstleistungen - Bestandsaufnahme und Entwicklungsrichtungen, in: Zeitschrift für Betriebswirtschaft, 66. Jg., Heft 3, S. 253-282

HOROVITZ, Jacques (1989): Service entscheidet - Im Wettbewerb um den Kunden, Frankfurt/New York

HOROVITZ, Jacques/**PANAK**, Michele Jurgens (1993): Marktführer durch Service, Frankfurt/New York

HÜNERBERG, Reinhard (1994): Internationales Marketing, Landsberg/Lech

HÜNERBERG, Reinhard/MANN, Andreas (1996): Internationales Servicemarketing - Die neue Dimension im industriellen Wettbewerb, in: der markt, 35. Jg., Heft 2, S. 95-106

KREUTZER, Ralf (1991): Länderübergreifende Segmentierungskonzepte - die Antwort auf die Globalisierung der Märkte, in: Jahrbuch der Absatz- und Verbrauchsforschung, 37. Jg., Heft 1, S. 4-23

LÄBE, Stefan M./**STOLPMANN**, Frank N. (1994): Service-Wege zu neuen Geschäftspotentialen und hoher Kundenbindung, in: Becker, Lutz/Lukas, Andreas (Hrsg.), Effizienz im Marketing, Wiesbaden, S. 95-116

MANN, Andreas (1996): Grundlagen einer strategischen Service-Konzeption, in: Weber, René (Hrsg.), Service-Management (Loseblattsammlung), 19. NL., Landsberg/Lech, Kap. V.6.1

MEFFERT, Heribert (1986): Marketing - Grundlagen der Absatzpolitik, 7. Aufl., Wiesbaden

MEFFERT, Heribert (1994a): Marketing-Management, Wiesbaden

MEFFERT, Heribert (1994b): Erfolgreiches Marketing in der Rezession, Wien

MEFFERT, Heribert/**BOLZ**, Joachim (1994): Internationales Marketing-Management, 2. Aufl., Stuttgart et al.

MEFFERT, Heribert/**BRUHN**, Manfred (1995): Dienstleitungsmarketing, Wiesbaden

MEYER, Anton/**BLÜMELHUBER**, Christian (1995): No Frills! Service-Konzepte ohne Wildwuchs und Schnickschnack, in: absatzwirtschaft, 38. Jg., Sondernummer 10, S. 30-40

MEYER, Anton/BLÜMELHUBER, Christian (1996): McDonalds, Aldi, Fielmann, Southwest Airlines, Continental lite, DAB, comdirect bank - Ist weniger mehr?, in: Meyer, Anton (Hrsg.), Grundsatzfragen und Herausforderungen des Dienstleistungsmarketing, Wiesbaden 1996, S. 315-334

MÖHRLE, Martin (1995): Prämarketing - Zur Markteinführung neuer Produkte, Wiesbaden

NIESCHLAG, Robert/DICHTL, Erwin/HÖRSCHGEN, Hans (1994): Marketing, 17. Aufl., Berlin

OLEMOTZ, Thomas (1995): Strategische Wettbewerbsvorteile durch industrielle Dienstleistungen, Frankfurt/Main et al.

PERLITZ, Manfred (1988): Instrumente zur Schaffung von Wettbewerbsvorteilen, in: Simon, Hermann (Hrsg.), Wettbewerbsvorteile und Wettbewerbsfähigkeit, Stuttgart, S. 47-65

POTTS, George W. (1988): Exploit Your Product's Service Life Circle, in: Harvard Business Review, Vol. 66, No. 5 (September-October), S. 32-36

RAFFÉE, Hans (1989): Grundfragen und Ansätze des strategischen Marketing, in: Raffée, Hans/Wiedmann, Klau-Peter (Hrsg.), Strategisches Marketing, 2. Aufl., Stuttgart, S. 3-33

RECKENFELDERBÄUMER, Martin (1995): Marketing-Accounting im Dienstleistungsbereich, Wiesbaden

SAMPSON, Gary P./SNAPE, Richard H. (1985): Identifying the Issues in Trade in Services, in: The World Economy, Vol. 8, S. 171-181

SEBASTIAN, Karl-Heinz/HILLEKE, Klaus (1994): Rückzug ohne Risiko, Teil 1, in: absatzwirtschaft, 37. Jg., Heft 1, S. 50-55

SIMON, Hermann (1992): Service Policies of German Manufacturers - Critical Factros in International Competition, in: European Management Journal, Vol. 10, No. 4, S. 404-411

SIMON, Hermann (1993): Industrielle Dienstleistungen und Wettbewerbsstrategie, in: Simon, Hermann (Hrsg.), Industrielle Dienstleistungen, Stuttgart, S. 3-22

SINGH, M.P. (1990): Service as a Marketing Strategy - A Case Study at Reliance Electric, in: Industrial Marketing Management, Vo. 19, No. 2, S. 193-200

STAUSS, Bernd (1995): Internationales Dienstleistungsmarketing, in: Hermanns, Arnold/Wißmeier, Urban Kilian (Hrsg.), Internationales Marketing-Management, München, S. 437-474

VANDERMERWE, Sandra/**CHADWICK**, Michael (1991): The Internationalization of Service, in: Lovelock, Christopher H. (Hrsg.), Services Marketing, 2. Aufl., Englewood Cliffs, S. 48-58

VAVRA, Terry G. (1992): Aftermarketing, Burr Ridge

WIMMER, Frank/**ZERR**, Konrad (1994): Systemplanung als Aufgabe des Systemmarketing, in: Marketing - ZFP, 16. Jg., Heft 4, S. 221-233

ZEITHAML, Valerie A./**PARASURAMAN**, Anantharanthan/**BERRY**, Leonard L. (1985): Problems and Strategies in Service Marketing, in: Journal of Marketing, 49. Jg., Nr. 2, S. 33-46

Michael Ehret*

NUTZUNGSPROZESSE ALS AUSGANGSPUNKT DES INNOVATIONSMANAGEMENTS

Inhalt

---

* Michael Ehret, Freie Universität Berlin, Institut für Allgemeine Betriebswirtschaftslehre, Altensteinstraße 48 D - 14195 Berlin, Tel.: 030/ 838-2493, Fax: 030/ 8325746; e-mail: michael.ehret@ccmailer.wiwiss.fu-berlin.de

1. Einführung in die Problemstellung: Angebote ohne Nachfrager, Prozesse ohne Anbieter - Zentrale Herausforderungen für das Dienstleistungsmarketing

Virtual Reality, Multimedia, Internet - diese Schlagworte aus der derzeitigen Innovationspalette in der Branche der Informations- und Kommunikationstechnologien wecken bei dem Betrachter aus der Marketing-Perspektive äußerst widersprüchliche Assoziationen:

– Wie so häufig bei der Einführung neuer Technologien herrscht eine breite Skepsis, nicht nur über den Sinn oder die befürchteten gesellschaftlichen Folgen dieser Technologien, sondern gerade bezüglich des Nutzens und der Marktattraktivität der innovativen Angebote. „Technik sucht Anwendung"[1], mit diesem Schlagwort wird der fehlende Durchbruch auf den innovativen Kommunikationsmärkten treffend beschrieben. Vor allem die Aussichten des interaktiven Fernsehens[2] und einer ganzen Reihe weiterer Datenaustauschdienste[3] werden mit immer größeren Fragezeichen versehen. Eine Vielzahl von Wissenschaftlern haben die sich abzeichnenden Nachfrageprobleme nach der Erklärung des Mißerfolgs der „totgeborenen Kinder"[4] des Innovationsmanagements bereits antizipiert und Modelle zur Erklärung der Akzeptanz von Multi-Media-Angeboten[5] entworfen. Die Akzeptanzforschung gründet ihre Aktivitäten dabei auf den meist unausgesprochenen Verdacht, daß die beobachtbaren Marketing-Aktivitäten die Integration der Kundenanfor-

---

1 So der Titel des 1995'er Jahrbuch Telekommunikation und Gesellschaft (Kubicek et al. (Hrsg.) (1995). Ähnlich titelt Dieter Klumpp, Leiter der Stabsabteilung 'Technik und Gesellschaft' bei Alcatel SEL ein Kapitel seines Buches über die Infrastrukturvoraussetzungen für Multimedia-Applikationen: „Techniklösungen auf Problemsuche?" und leitet es folgendermaßen ein: „Ein Gespenst geht um in Europa, Japan und den USA. Es ist das Gespenst des Anwenders der vielfältigen infrastrukturellen und der konsumorientierten Informations- und Kommunikationstechnik." (Klumpp 1996), S. 36.

2 Erste Ergebnisse einer Akzeptanzstudie zu interaktivem Fernsehen finden sich bei: Weiber/ Kollmann (1995), insbes. S. 24-32.

3 Zu einem Überblick vgl. Kubiceck/ Reimers (1996), insbes. S. 60-62.

4 Dieser Ausdruck stammt von Jean Paul Arie, einem Vertriebsingenieur und ehemaligen Teilnehmer des Weiterbildenden Studiums Technischer Vertrieb der Freien Universität Berlin, der in seinem Berufsleben den Vertrieb für so manche aussichtslose innovative Kommunikationstechnik durchführen mußte.

5 Grundlegende Überlegung zur Konzeption der Akzeptanzforschung für Multi-Media-Angebote finden sich bei Backhaus/ Voeth/ Bendix (1995) und Kollmann (1996). Vor allem der Ansatz von Kollmann stellt eine vielversprechende Weiterentwicklung der Akzeptanzforschung dar, da er explizit die Dimension der Nutzungsakzeptanz als Problemfeld begreift. Vgl. Kollmann (1996), S. 72-84.

derungen in die Unternehmensprozesse nicht bewältigen und daher die Ursachen im Hinblick auf die Verbesserung der Marketing-Aktivitäten analysiert werden müssen[6].

- Diesem eher pessimistischen Bild stehen verblüffende Erfolge bei der Diffusion neuer Kommunikationstechnologien gegenüber, die kaum auf gezielte Marketing-Aktivitäten zurückzuführen sind und scheinbar von einer „unsichtbaren Hand" gelenkt werden: Im Internet bilden sich User-Groups aus Mitgliedern, denen eher ein technologiefernes bis technologiefeindliches Image nachgesagt wurde[7]. Konzerne organisieren, ohne vorher erkennbare Marketing-Anstrengungen der Anbieter, nach dem Vorbild des Internets unternehmenseigene Netze, sogenannte Intranets, die meist über eine Schnittstelle zum Internet verfügen und somit auch der Kommunikation mit Lieferanten und Kunden dienen. Intranet-Anwendungen stellen inzwischen die wichtigsten Kunden der ursprünglich auf das Internet fixierten Hersteller professioneller Netz-Software dar.[8] Es ist bereits von der „Killerapplikation"[9] die Rede. Online-Dienste, die bis vor kurzem noch zu den „Fragezeichen"-Anwendungen des vorigen Absatzes gehörten, haben durch die Schaffung von Internet-Schnittstellen eine Autobahn zu ihren Kunden gefunden.

Beide Phänomene legen ein Marketing-Versagen bei der Einführung innovativer Leistungsangebote nahe: Im ersten Fall werden Produktinnovationen entwickelt, deren Akzeptanz und tatsächliche Nutzung durch die Kunden zumindest fraglich ist. In dem zweiten Fall manifestiert sich ein Marketing-Versagen in der Form, daß Kunden Prozeßinnovationen und damit Nachfrage nach neuen Technologien entwickeln, die außerhalb der Vorstellungskraft der Marketing-Abteilungen ihrer Anbieter lagen. *Dieter Klumpp*, Leiter der Stabsabteilung 'Technik und Gesellschaft' bei Alcatel SEL, macht darauf aufmerksam, daß die traditionelle Sicht, die Technologie sei den Anwendern voraus, den Blick auf deren produktive Potentiale versperrt:

---

6 Dabei bleibt sie meist in einer passiv beobachtenden Rolle verhaftet, statt in einer aktiv gestalterischen. Dieter Klumpp schreibt treffend über die Rolle der Aktzeptanzforschung in der aktuellen Multimediadiskussion: „Dies hat dazu geführt, daß sich die -nach wie vor vorhandene - Notwendigkeit eines Diskurses auf das Ingangsetzen von modernistischen Kolloquien beschränkt, in denen typischerweise der 'Diskurs' *über* die Kirch-Gruppe, die Telekom oder Bertelsmann, über IBM, Siemens, Alcatel, Microsoft, *über* die privaten oder geschäftlichen Nutzer geführt wird anstatt der Diskurs mit diesen über etwas." (Klumpp (1996), S. 88.

7 Thomas Wetzstein charakterisiert in seiner Studie über die Entwicklung von Nutzungsmustern in Computernetzn folgendermaßen: „Es findet - wie eingangs erwähnt- eine 'informelle Technikaneignung' statt, die sowohl hinsichtlich des Erlernens wie auch des Gebrauchs tendenziell auf 'Vorfabriziertes' verzichtet und statt dessen Eigentätigkeit in den Mittelpunkt stellt." (Wetzstein (1995, S. 137).

8 Eine exponierte Rolle nimmt dabei „die" Internet Firma Netscape ein. Vgl. Bödel/ Stein (1996).

9 Vgl.: Böndel/ Stein (1996), S.84.

„Mit der Möglichkeit, daß sich der Anwender weiterdreht und die kommunikationstechnische Anwendungswelt gleichsam stehenbleibt, rechnet die Branche in Europa offensichtlich nicht."[10]

Die ökonomische Entwicklung, die *Alvin Toffler* schon vor fast zwanzig Jahren beschrieb, scheint sich auch bei der Entwicklung innovativer Leistungsangebote zu bewahrheiten:

„We see a progressive blurring of the line that separates producer from consumer. We see the rising significance of the prosumer."[11]

Die zentrale These, der im folgenden nachgegangen werden soll, lautet dabei folgendermaßen: Innovationen im Leistungsangebot erfordern die Neugestaltung von Nutzungsprozessen und somit Prozeßinnovationen auf Seiten der Kunden. Das Verständnis von Prozeßinnovationen ist somit der entscheidende Schritt zu einer ökonomischen Erklärung des Erfolgs von innovativen Leistungsangeboten.

Dienstleistungen gewinnen in diesem Zusammenhang eine strategische Bedeutung für Unternehmen, die sich in Innovationsprozessen befinden. Begreift man Dienstleistungen als Prozesse der Integration von Produktionsfaktoren der Nachfrager in die Leistungserstellung der Anbieter, so wird schnell die Chance deutlich, die Dienstleistungen für beide Tauschparteien mit sich bringen: Da hier die Produktionsprozesse von Anbieter und Nachfrager direkt in einem integrierten Leistungserstellungsprozeß miteinander verknüpft werden, bietet sich für beide die Chance, durch die mit diesem Prozeß verbundenen Informationen Ansatzpunkte für das erfolgreiche Management von Innovationen zu erschließen.

Die Untersuchung beginnt mit grundlegenden Überlegungen zu der Rolle von Anwendern in Innovationsprozessen (Abschnitt 2). Anschließend wird anhand der Gütertheorie von Menger und dessen Weiterentwicklung durch die mikroökonomische Haushaltstheorie die Perspektive einer Theorie der Innovation entwickelt, die die Rolle innovativer Nutzungsprozesse explizit berücksichtigt. Im vierten Teil wird anhand eines informationsökonomischen Ansatzes

---

[10] Klumpp (1996), S. 37.

[11] Toffler (1980), S. 284. Ein erster Ansatz zur Integration des „Prosumer"-Phänomens in das Marketing kann in der Analyse der „Leistungsbündel als Absatzobjekte" von Engelhardt/ Kleinaltenkamp/ Reckenfelderbäumer gesehen werden. Vgl. dazu Engelhardt/ Kleinaltenkamp/ Reckenfelderbäumer (1993), S. 402.

gezeigt, wie Anbieter innovative Nutzungsprozesse für die strategische Weiterentwicklung ihres Angebots nutzen können.

Abschließend wird ein zusammenfassender Überblick gegeben und vor allem offene Fragen für die weitere Forschung aufgezeigt.

2. Die Entdeckung der aktiven Rolle des Nachfragers im Innovationsprozeß

2.1. Das anbieterzentrierte Phasenmodell des Innovationsprozesses

Wenngleich heute kaum mehr Beiträge zum F&E- oder Innovationsmanagement zu finden sind, die nicht die entscheidende Rolle des Marktes oder der Kunden für den Erfolg von Innovationen betonen,[12] steht im Kern der meisten Phasenmodelle[13] ein anbieterzentriertes Modell des Innovationsprozesses. [14]

Als eine exemplarische Beschreibung des anbieterzentrierten Innovationsprozesses kann die Definition von *Pay* dienen:

> *„Eine Innovation ist eine Unternehmensaktivität, die durch Forschung neue Ideen in das Unternehmen einführt, durch Entwicklung diese Ideen weiterverarbeitet und sie anschließend im Produktionsprozeß und auf dem Absatzmarkt verwertet.“*[15]

Dabei sind die Funktionen Forschung, Entwicklung, Produktion und Vermarktung exklusiv bei den anbietenden Unternehmen angesiedelt, während auf der Marktebene, im Sinne eines Stimulus-Response-Modells,[16] lediglich die Marktreaktionen auf die verschiedenen Aktivitä-

---

12 Z.B. Kleinschmidt/ Geschka/ Cooper (1996), insbesondere S.1-50.

13 Zu einem zusammenfassenden Überblick und umfangreichen Quellenangaben zu Phasenmodellen des Innovationsprozesses s. Weiber/ Pohl (1996), S. 9-11.

14 Die gängigen Versuche, die einzelnen Schritte dieses Modells kundenorientierter zu gestalten, werden im Abschnitt 2.2. dieses Beitrags beschrieben.

15 Pay (1989), S. 85 und sinngemäß ebd. S. 8.

16 Eine zusammenfassende Darstellung des Stimulus-Response-Paradigmas aus Marketing-Sicht findet sich bei Nieschlag/ Dichtl/ Hörschgen (1991), S. 102-104. Zur mangelnden Eignung des Stimulus-Response-

ten dieses Unternehmens betrachtet werden, nicht aber produktive Beiträge der Nachfrager zur Gestaltung des Innovationsprozesses (vgl. auch Abb.1).

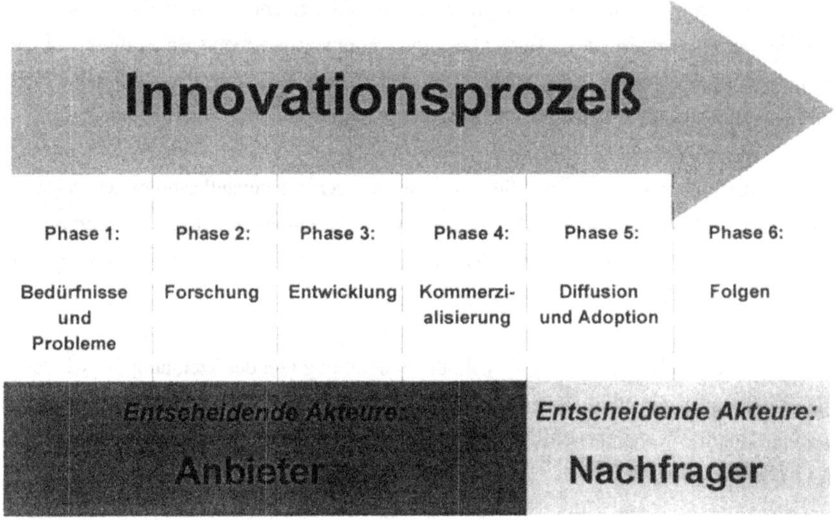

Abb. 1: Anbieterzentriertes Innovationsmodell

nach Rogers (1983), S. 136

Dieses anbieterzentrierte Modell findet seine Entsprechung in dem Forschungszweig, der sich gezielt mit der Marktentwicklung im Zuge von Innovationsprozessen auseinandersetzt, nämlich in der Diffusionsforschung beziehungsweise der Diffusionstheorie.[17] Auch hier wird der Innovationsprozeß in Phasen unterteilt, wobei in den Phasen vor der Markteinführung die

Paradigmas für Problemstellungen das Investitionsgütermarketing vgl.: Backhaus (1992), S. 5 u. S. 107-111. Zum Stimulus-Response-Paradigma in der Verhaltensforschung s. Kroeber-Riehl (1992), S. 322-342.

17 Das Grundlagenwerk der Diffusionsforschung wie auch der Theorie ist Rogers (1983). Die Diffusionsforschung hat dabei zumindest in der Konzeption von Rogers die Funktion des Zulieferers des empirischen Materials für eine induktive Theoriebildung, die aufbauend auf der Diffusionstheorie den Entwurf einer allgemeinen Theorie des sozialen Wandels ermöglichen soll. Vgl. hierzu v.a. Rogers/ Shoemaker (1971), S. 45.

Aktivitäten der Anbieter von Innovationen maßgeblich sind, in den Phasen des Diffusionsprozesses nach der Markteinführung hingegen die Aktivitäten der Nachfrager.[18]

Gemeinsames Kennzeichen der anbieterzentrierten Modelle ist die strikte Trennung zwischen der eigentlichen Innovation und deren Diffusion, deren Scheidepunkt durch den Zeitpunkt der Markteinführung markiert ist. Im Bereich des Innovationsmanagements findet diese Anbieterorientierung beispielsweise ihren Ausdruck in dem Ansatz von *Bierfelder*, der seine Arbeit nach Innovationstheorien, Diffusionstheorien und Adoptionstheorien untergliedert.[19]

In einem zusammenfassenden Überblick zu Betrachtungen des hersteller-dominierten Innovationsprozesses identifiziert *Gemünden* als Leitfigur eine Unternehmung, die aufgrund ihrer überlegenen Technologie und ihres überlegenen Marketing den Innovationsprozeß steuere und somit die treibende Kraft eines Technologie-Push darstelle.[20]

Im Grunde genommen zeichnet dieses Bild die Vorstellung von der Trennung der wirtschaftlichen Funktionen von Produzenten und Konsumenten nach,[21] wie es für das Zeitalter der Massenproduktion[22] charakteristisch war und heute noch allenfalls auf hochstandardisierten Märkten zu finden ist.[23]

---

18 Rogers wollte mit der gemeinsamen Betachtung die Begrenzungen sowohl der technologieorientierten als auch der marktorientierten Ansätze aufzeigen (Vgl. insbesondere Rogers (1983), S. 134-135). Betrachtet man nun beide Ansätze als Zugänge eines integrierten Innovationsprozesses, entsteht zumindest der Eindruck, daß durch die Trennung der Innovatinonsfunktionen während der einzelnen Phasen die jeweiligen Grenzen eher zementiert als aufgelöst werden.

19 Bierfelder (1989), S.7-81.

20 Vgl.: Gemünden (1990), S. 7.

21 Grundlegend für die Rolle der Arbeitsteilung und die Entstehung von Märkten aus ökonomischer Perspektive: Smith (1982), S. 109-126.

22 Eine hervorragende zusammenfassende Analyse der Wechselwirkungen zwischen ökonomischen, politischen und gesellschaftlichen Strukturen im Zeitalter der Massenproduktion findet sich bei Toffler (1980), S. 35-140.

23 Zumindest die zunehmende Entwicklung von strategischen Konzepten zur stärkeren Integration des Kunden in die Anbieterprozesse kann als Indikator für diese Entwicklung gesehen werden. S. Peppers/ Rogers (1993), insbes.S. 3-50, Jacob (1995), insbes. S. 3-48, Pine (1993), paradigmatisch S.3-75, Kleinaltenkamp (1996).

2.2. Die Integration von kunden- und marktbezogenen Aktivitäten in den Innovationsprozeß zur Sicherung des Markterfolges von Innovationen

Daß Markt- beziehungsweise Kundenorientierung die entscheidenden Impulse für ein erfolgreiches Innovationsmanagement geben, darüber besteht in der einschlägigen Literatur kein Zweifel. *Brockhoff* schreibt in dem einleitenden Kapitel zu seinem Grundlagenwerk:

> *„Immer wieder finden sich Fallbeispiele dafür, daß **reine Technikorientierung zu Unternnehmenskrisen führt**“*[24]

Die Vorstellung, daß technologische Neuerungen die treibende Kraft für die Entstehung neuer Märkte darstellen, weicht immer stärker vor der Erkenntnis des Marktes als Schiedsrichter über den Erfolg der Technologie zurück. Unter den grundlegenden Werken zu dem Innovations- oder F&E -Management gibt es kaum eines, das nicht zumindest die Möglichkeit eines Nachfragesoges („demand pull“)[25] als Erklärungsgrund für die Entstehung innovativer Technologien anführt.

Fallstudien zu den Erfolgsfaktoren von Innovationsprozessen weisen regelmäßig die kunden-, nachfrage- und marktbezogenen Kriterien als entscheidende Einflüsse auf den Markterfolg aus. So finden sich unter den acht Erfolgsfaktoren für Produktinnovationen, *die Kleinschmidt/ Geschka/ Cooper* ermittelten, gleich vier mit explizitem Nachfragebezug[26] :

- Ein überlegenes Produkt, das dem Kunden einzigartigen Nutzen bietet,
- Marketingsynergie,
- Ausführungsqualität der Marketingaktivitäten,
- Marktattraktivität.

Der heutige Stand der Diskussion schlägt sich im wesentlichen darin nieder, daß man den Entscheidungsträgern der Anbieter rät, stets in den einzelnen Phasen des Innovationsprozesses

---

24 Brockhoff (1992), S. 11.

25 Vgl. beispielhaft Specht/ Beckmann, S. 32-33; Weiber/ Pohl (1996), S. 37, Brockhoff (1992), S. 28-35.

26 Kleinschmidt/ Geschka/ Cooper (1996), S. 9-25. Auch Kupsch/ Marr/ Picot (1991), S. 1080-1081 nennen an erster Stelle der „Innovationswirtschaftlichen Erfolgefaktoren“ die „Marktgerechtheit der Innovation“.

die Markterfordernisse zu berücksichtigen. Der Markt soll die Inputs für den Innovationsprozeß liefern. *Roberts* formuliert dies folgendermaßen:

„*The product development cycle should be organized ... to bring market inputs into design repeatedly during the early product and again during active prototyping through active involvement of selected customers.*"[27]

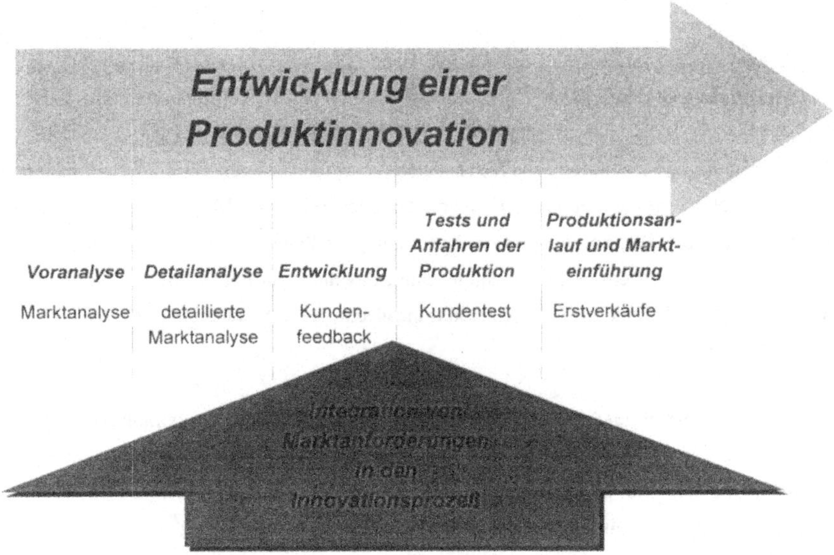

Abb. 2: Integration von Marktanforderungen im Standardprozeß von Kleinschmidt/ Geschka/ Cooper anhand ausgewählter Beispiele.

Quelle: *Kleinschmidt/ Geschka/ Cooper* (1996), S. 52-53

Verdeutlicht werden kann dies an dem Phasenschema von *Kleinschmidt/ Geschka/ Cooper* (vgl. Abb.2). Das anbieterzentrierte Phasenschema wird beibehalten, in jeder Phase sind aber markt- beziehungsweise kundenorientierte Aktivitäten, wie Marktanalysen oder Kundentests vorgesehen, die die Koordination der Unternehmensprozesse mit den Anforderungen des Marktes bzw. der Kunden sicherstellen sollen.

27 Roberts (1987), S. 10.

2.3. Die aktive Rolle der Nutzer im Innovationsprozeß

Nimmt man das anbieterzentrierte Schema des Innovationsprozesses als Referenzmodell, so erscheint die Integration von marktbezogenen Aktivitäten in die einzelnen Schritte des Innovationsprozesses[28] zunächst einmal als die konsequente Umsetzung der Kundenorientierung. Allerdings haben die empirischen Innovationsstudien, *die Eric von Hippel* am *Massachusetts Institute for Technology* durchführte[29], Ergebnisse zu Tage gebracht, die das Referenzmodell als Ganzes in Frage stellen.

Ausgangspunkt seiner Arbeit war eine Studie über Innovationen im Bereich der wissenschaftlichen Meßgeräte,[30] die in vorwiegend naturwissenschaftlich ausgerichteten Forschungslabors eingesetzt werden. Markantes Ergebnis dieser Studie war, daß in 77% der untersuchten Fälle die Schritte der Problemidentifikation, der Forschung, der Entwicklung und der Anwendungskonzeption von den Nutzern übernommen wurden. Die Hersteller der Geräte traten lediglich als „Übernehmer“ in Erscheinung, die die neuen Geräte dann kommerziell vermarkten konnten.[31]

Dieses Phänomen stellt nun aber die genaue Umkehrung des, wenn auch inzwischen verfeinerten, anbieterzentrierten Innovationsmodells dar: Tritt bei diesem der Nutzer erst in der Diffusionsphase in Erscheinung, sind bei dem nutzerinduzierten Innovationsprozeß die Anbieter in den eigentlichen Innovationsphasen abwesend und übernehmen erst in der Kommerzialisierung im Zuge des Diffusionsprozesses eine aktive Rolle. Dies veranlaßt *Hippel* zur Formulierung eines nutzeraktiven Paradigmas des Innovationsprozesses (vgl. Abb. 3), das er dem herstelleraktiven Paradigma gegenüberstellte.[32]

---

28 Vgl. Abschnitt 2.2. dieses Beitrags.

29 Diese finden sich zusammengefaßt in Hippel (1988).

30 Es handelte sich dabei um Innovationen in folgenden Bereichen: Gas-Chromatographen, Nukleare magnetische Resonanz-Spektrometer, Ultraviolett-Absorptions-Spektrometer, Übertragungs-Elektronenmikroskop. Ursprünglich wurde die Studie veröffentlicht als Hippel (1976).

31 Vgl. Hippel (1988), S. 13-19.

32 Vgl. v.a.: Hippel (1978), S. 40-44. In der deutschen Literatur wurde dieses Paradigma aufgegriffen von: Biegel (1988) und Kleinaltenkamp/ Staudt (1991).

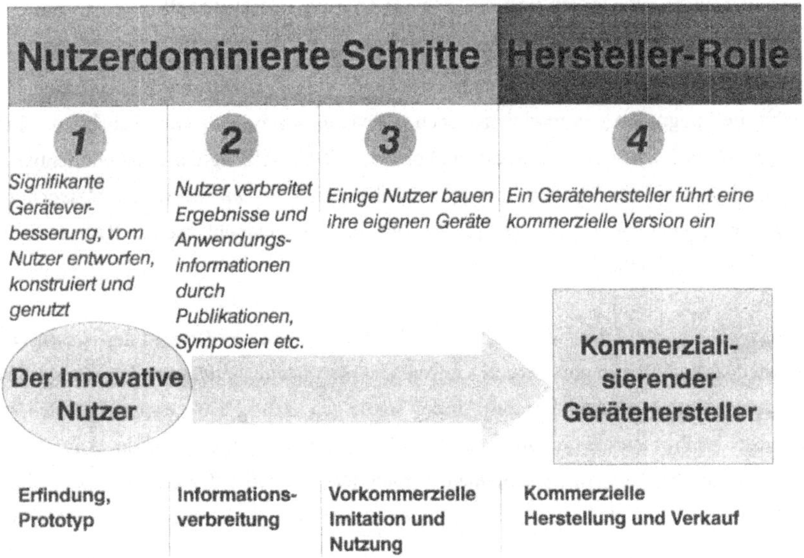

Abb. 3: Typischer nutzerdominierter Innovationsprozeß bei wissenschaftlichen Meßgeräten

Quelle: Hippel (1988), S. 19

Hippel fand auch eine einfache Erklärung dafür, warum die Anbieter innovativer Produkte so häufig als die treibende Kraft im Innovationsprozeß Innovatoren erscheinen: Sie haben als Agenten im Vermarktungsprozeß ein aktives Interesse an breitenwirksamer Werbung und Öffentlichkeitsarbeit für die Innovation, um latente Nachfrage für die neuen Leistungen zu erschließen. Daher werden sie häufig im öffentlichen Bewußtsein eher als die Schöpfer dieser Innovation angesehen, während sie eigentlich 'nur' die Vermarkter sind.[33]

Die Ergebnisse dieser Studie veranlaßten *Hippel* die Arbeit fortzusetzen, um eine umfassendere Strukturierung von Innovationsprozessen durchführen zu können. Auch hier führte er jeweils branchenbezogene Fallstudien durch, mit dem Ziel, die Quellen von Innovationen zu identifizieren. Drei typische Quellen fand er dabei heraus: den Nutzer, den Hersteller und den Zulieferer (des Herstellers).

[33] Vgl. Hippel (1988), S. 25.

Wenngleich diese Ergebnisse weiterführen als die Unterstellungen des „Technology push" und des „Demand Pull"[34], so sind sie letztendlich nicht sonderlich aussagekräftig, da im Prinzip jeder Teilnehmer am ökonomischen Geschehen eine potentielle Quelle von Innovationen ist.

Hippel versucht diesem Dilemma mit einer ökonomischen Erklärung zu entgehen: Danach entscheiden die Gewinnerwartungen der Akteure im Innovationsprozeß darüber, wer die Quelle einer Innovation wird. Eine nutzerinduzierte Innovation erklärt *Hippel* also dadurch, daß in diesem Fall die Nutzer die besten Verwertungsmöglichkeiten für Neuerungen sehen, während die Hersteller diese erst wahrnehmen, wenn die Konzeption entwickelt und kommerzialisierbar ist.

Die Erklärung der Gewinnerwartungen ist dabei eine recht unbefriedigende:

- Sie ermöglicht lediglich eine ex-post Erklärung der Übernahme der Innovationsquelle: Erst in einem fortgeschrittenen Stadium ist es möglich festzustellen, wer den Innovationsprozeß vorantreibt. Innovierende Unternehmer, die sich ihrer Sache sicher sind, brauchen diese Erklärung nicht für ihre Entscheidungsfindung, während solche, die sich unsicher sind, in dem frühen Stadium von dieser Erklärung im Stich gelassen werden.
- Unterstellt man den Akteuren im Innovationsprozeß ein ökonomisches Kalkül, so ist die Feststellung der Gewinnerwartungen keine neue Erklärung für die Handlungsmotive der Innovationsbetreiber.
- Sie stellt letztlich eine Tautologie dar: Eine Innovation wird in der ökonomischen Theorie als eine Aktion zur Erzielung von entsprechenden „Innovationsrenten"[35] gesehen.

Vor allem aber hilft diese Feststellung kaum bei der Problemlösung in aktuellen Innovationsprozessen: Da stehen die Entscheidungsträger in der Regel nicht vor der Frage, wer sich die meisten Profite von einem Innovationsprojekt verspricht. Können sie ihre Profiterwartungen bezüglich eines Innovationsprojektes nennen, dann haben sie eigentlich kein Entscheidungs-

---

34 Auch bei der Erklärung des Demand Pull als treibende Kraft im Innovationsprozeß wird letztlich doch unterstellt, daß die eigentlichen Innovationsaktivitäten auf der Herstellerseite stattfinden. Auch wenn die Arbeiten von Hippel häufig zur Erklärung eines Demand Pull herangezogen werden, ist dies nicht der Kern der Ergebnisse dieser Arbeiten.

35 Vgl. hierzu die Ausführungen in Abschnitt 3 dieses Beitrags.

problem mehr. Es stellt sich vielmehr die Frage nach Kriterien für den ökonomischen Erfolg von Innovationen. Bei dieser Frage werden sie aber von *Hippel* im Stich gelassen.

Mit seinen empirischen Innovationsstudien hat *Hippel* eine neue Perspektive auf den Innovationsprozeß ermöglicht, die vor allem neue Wege für Innovationsstrategien aufzeigt. Gleichzeitig ist die ökonomische Erklärung der Innovationsquellen aus den genannten Gründen unbefriedigend. Im folgenden Abschnitt werden Ansätze zu solch einer ökonomischen Erklärung präsentiert.

3. Ansätze zu einer ökonomischen Erklärung von Innovationsprozessen: Die Rolle von Nutzungsprozessen

3.1. Schumpeters Begriff der „Schöpferischen Zerstörung" als Ansatzpunkt für eine ökonomische Theorie der Innovation

Den entscheidenden Zugang zur ökonomischen Rolle der Innovation legte *Schumpeter* mit seiner Arbeit über die Überlebensbedingungen von Wirtschaftssystemen „Kapitalismus, Sozialismus und Demokratie" frei. Hier stellt er als das Wesensmerkmal des Kapitalismus den Prozeß der „schöpferischen Zerstörung" heraus.[36] Er besteht in der Durchsetzung neuer Konsumgüter, neuer Produktions- oder Transportmethoden, der Erschließung neuer Märkte sowie der Schaffung neuer Formen der industriellen Organisation.[37]

Mit diesen spezifischen Formen von Innovationen versuchen deren Verfechter den Preiswettbewerb zu bekämpfen und Monopole zur Durchsetzung ihrer ökonomischen Interessen zu errichten.[38]

Das Wesen der kapitalistischen Konkurrenz wird daher, so *Schumpeter*, in der Lehrbuch-Ökonomie nur unzureichend erfaßt:[39]

---

[36] Vgl. Schumpeter (1950), S. 134-142.

[37] Vgl. Schumpeter (1950), S. 137.

[38] Dieser Gedanke wurde von der Neuen Österreichischen Schule zu deren Marktprozeßtheorie weiterentwickelt.

[39] Schumpeter (1950), S. 140. Zudem sah Schumpeter in der Analyse dieses Prozesses den eigentlichen Schlüssel zu dem Verständnis von ökonomischen Phänomenen: „Gewöhnlich wird nur das Problem

> *„In der kapitalistischen Wirklichkeit jedoch, im Unterschied zu ihrem Bild in den Lehrbüchern, zählt nicht diese Art von Konkurrenz (*gemeint ist der Preiswettbewerb innerhalb bestehender Marktstrukturen, M.E.*), sondern die Konkurrenz der neuen Ware, der neuen Technik, der neuen Versorgungsquelle, des neuen Organisationstyps (zum Beispiel der größtdimensionierten Unternehmenseinheit) - jene Konkurrenz, die über einen entscheidenden Kosten- oder Qualitätsvorteil gebietet und die bestehenden Firmen nicht an den Profit- und Produktionsgrenzen, sondern in ihren Grundlagen, ihrem eigentlichen Lebensmark trifft.“*

Mit Hilfe dieses Innovationsbegriffes gelingt es *Schumpeter,* die Bedeutung von Innovationen im Marktprozeß unabhängig von der eingesetzten Technologie zu beleuchten. So betonte er, daß es für das Verständnis von Innovationsprozessen wichtig sei, zwischen der Rolle des Erfinders („inventor“) und der des Unternehmers („entrepreneur“) zu unterscheiden:[40]

> *„The inventor produces ideas, the entrepreneur „gets things done“, which may, but need not embody anything that is scientifically new. Moreover, an idea or scientific principle is not, by itself, of any importance for economic practice: The fact that Greek science had probably produced all that is necessary in order to construct a steam engine did not help the Greeks or Romans to build a steam engine;...“*

Ökonomische Prozesse, deren handelnde Akteure die Unternehmer sind, entscheiden nach *Schumpeters* Auffassung letztlich darüber, welche Ideen in die Praxis umgesetzt werden. Als Ergebnis der *Schumpeter'schen* Analyse von Innnovationsprozessen kann daher festgehalten werden:

- Die technologische Neuheit einer Innovation ist kein ausreichender Indikator für deren ökonomischen Erfolg.
- Es sind ökonomisch erfolgreiche Innovationen denkbar und beobachtbar, die nicht auf technologisch Neuem beruhen, beispielsweise durch die Neuorganisation von Produktionsprozessen.

betrachtet, wie der Kapitalismus mit bestehenden Strukturen umgeht, während das relevante Problem darin besteht, wie er sie schafft und zerstört“ (Schumpeter (1950), S. 139.

[40] Schumpeter (1947), S. 152.

Diese Ergebnisse können aber letztlich nur der Beginn einer ökonomischen Analyse der Innovation darstellen. Sie werfen nämlich die Frage auf, welche Bedingungen für den ökonomischen Erfolg von Innovationen ausschlaggebend sind. Diese wurden erstmals von *Carl Menger* formuliert.

3.2. Der Güterbegriff von Menger als Grundlage für die Analyse ökonomischer Prozesse

Wenngleich *Mengers* Werk kaum explizite Beiträge zur Analyse wirtschaftlicher Prozesse enthält, schuf er durch seine Werttheorie die Grundlage für die Prozeßbetrachtung in den Wirtschaftswissenschaften, auf die seine Schüler der „Österreichischen Schule" aufbauen konnten. Der entscheidende Schritt *Mengers* bestand darin, den wirtschaftlichen Wert nicht anhand der objektiven Eigenschaften der betrachteten Güter zu analysieren,[41] sondern Bedingungen zu suchen, unter denen Phänomene der Objektwelt einen wirtschaftlichen Wert erhalten.[42] Diese Methode vereinfacht die Analyse ökonomischer Prozesse nicht zuletzt im Falle von Innovationen: Gelingt es nämlich solche Bedingungen zu finden, können sich zwar die **Phänomene der Objektwelt** ändern, also die betrachteten Güter und Prozesse, die **Kriterien für den ökonomischen Erfolg von Innovationen** hingegen ändern sich nicht.

Ausgangspunkt von *Mengers* Betrachtungen ist die menschliche Bedürfnisbefriedigung, die er als Ziel allen wirtschaftlichen Handelns ansieht. Güter sind bei *Menger* Dinge,[43] die der Mensch in seiner Umwelt vorfindet und zu seiner Bedürfnisbefriedigung einsetzt. Grundlegend ist dabei die Beziehung zwischen Mensch und Objektwelt. Diese charakterisiert er durch vier Kriterien, die erfüllt sein müssen, damit aus einem Ding ein Gut wird:[44]

---

41 Diese Methode hatte sich in den physikalischen Wissenschaften als erfolgreich erwiesen und führte zu ähnlichen Ansätzen in den Wirtschaftswissenschaften. Einen hervorragenden Überblick zu diesem Zusammenhang findet sich in Hayek (1968).

42 Diesen Aspekt der Menger'schen Theorie hebt Hayek hervor und sieht darin das Charakteristische der Österreichischen Schule indem er schreibt: „The Austrians, on the other hand, made the full analysis of the **conditions of valuation** (Hervorhebung von M.E.), independent of the possibility of exchange, so much their central task that later they had to defend themselves against the misunderstanding that they believed marginal utility porvided a direct explanation of price". (Hayek (1968), S. 458-459).

43 Dieser Begriff umfaßt auch zeitlich begrenzte Nutzungen von Gütern und Diensten.

44 Menger (1923), S. 11.

- „die Erkenntnis, beziehungsweise die Voraussicht eines menschlichen Bedürfnisses,
- solche objektive Eigenschaften des Dinges, welche es tauglich machen, die Befriedigung des Bedürfnisses zu bewirken,
- die Erkenntnis dieser Tauglichkeit,
- die Verfügung über dieses Ding: ein solches Verhältnis des Dinges zu uns, daß dasselbe zur Befriedigung eines menschlichen Bedürfnisses (wenngleich eines künftigen und nur mit Hilfe von anderen Gütern) herangezogen werden kann.“

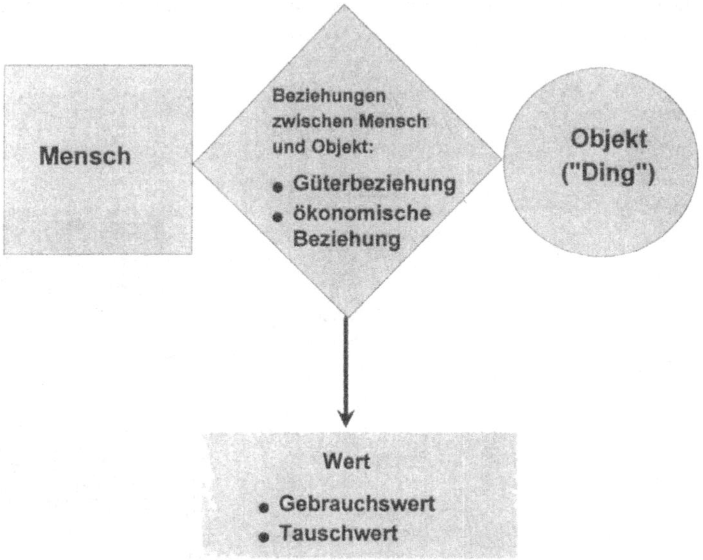

Abb. 4: Mengers Erklärung der Wertentstehung aus den Beziehungen zwischen Mensch und Objektwelt.

Vgl.: Menger (1923), S. 1-31 sowie S. 64-72

Dies ist aber nur die notwendige Bedingung für das Entstehen eines wirtschaftlichen Wertes eines Gutes. Erst wenn ein Gut für den Menschen knapp wird,[45] führt dieser wirtschaftliche

---

[45] Mit diesem Ansatz gelang Menger die Lösung des Wertparadoxons: Bis dahin fehlte eine befriedigende Erklärung dafür, daß Wasser ein unverzichtbares Gut für den Menschen ist, aber weitgehend kostenlos

Aktivitäten durch. Die beiden grundlegenden Prozesse hierfür sind die Produktion und der Tausch, die zur Lösung des Problems der Knappheit durchgeführt werden. Somit können Güter einen Gebrauchswert haben, der sich durch die Nutzung in der Produktion darstellt, oder einen Tauschwert, soweit sie den Bezug von für die Produktion benötigten Gütern ermöglichen (vgl. Abb.4).[46]

Mit Hilfe dieses Instrumentariums gelang es *Menger* zudem, die Rolle der Technologie in der Wirtschaft zu illustrieren: Technik ist nur insofern von ökonomischen Interesse, soweit sie zum Gegenstand der ökonomischen Disposition wird. Technik, die nicht in den Prozeß der menschlichen Bedürfnisbefriedigung eingeht, ist wirtschaftlich wertlos und vom ökonomischen Standpunkt betrachtet uninteressant (vgl. Abb. 5).[47]

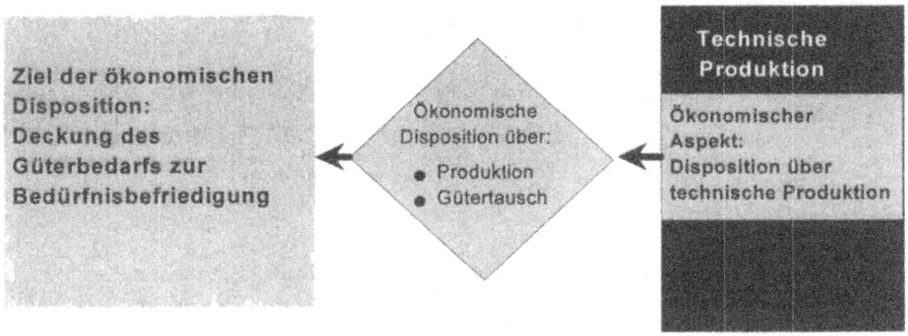

Abb. 5: Rolle der Technik in Mengers Werttheorie

Vgl. Menger (1923), S. 72-74

erhältlich ist. Diese Grenznutzenerklärung, die neben Menger auch Jevons und Walras unabhänig voneinnader präsentierten, ermöglichte es Menger gleichzeitig, auch Bedingungen zu finden, unter denen Wasser sehr wohl einen hohen Wert erfahren kann, beispielsweise in einer Oase in der Wüste.

46 Mit diesem Ansatz gelang Menger auch die Analyse der ökonomischen Rolle des Geldes, dessen wirtschaftliche Funktion die Vereinfachung des Gütertauschs ist. Vgl.: Menger (1970).

47 Die Ausführungen des Abschnitts 3.3. werden dies noch genauer beleuchten.

Die Ergebnisse von *Mengers* Analysen haben zwei wichtige Konsequenzen für die Analyse von Innovationsprozessen:

- Erst die grundlegenden Bedingungen, unter denen Objekte einen Gütercharakter und darüber hinaus einen Wert erlangen, ermöglichen die Analyse von ökonomischen Prozessen. Innovationsprozesse müssen also vor dem Hintergrund der Problemstellung betrachtet werden, wie neuartige Leistungen den Charakter eines Gutes annehmen und darüber hinaus auch noch einen ökonomischen Wert erlangen.
- *Menger* gelang es mit diesem Ansatz, eine ökonomische Erklärung für die wirtschaftliche Rolle der Technologie aufzuzeigen: Nur Technologien, die den Kriterien der Wertentstehung genügen, bringen für deren Anbieter und Anwender einen ökonomischen Wert.

Diese ist sind gleichzeitig die Grundlage für die Entwicklung der Güterordnung von Menger, die von der modernen mikroökonomischen Haushaltstheorie aufgegriffen wurde.

3.3. Die Rolle der Gestaltung von Nutzungsprozessen für die Wertbildung von Gütern in Mengers Gütertheorie

Ein weiterer Gedanke von *Menger* wurde für die Entwicklung der mikroökonomischen Haushaltstheorie aufgegriffen.[48] *Menger* sah zwei grundlegende Wege der menschlichen Bedürfnisbefriedigung:

- Güter, die unmittelbar der Bedürfnisbefriedigung dienen, findet der Mensch quasi genußbereit vor. Darunter kann man sich eine fertig zubereitete Mahlzeit, ein fahrbereites Auto auf einer funktionsfähigen, leergefegten Straße genauso vorstellen, wie ein Fernsehsystem, bestehend aus Fernseher, Antenne und einem laufenden attraktiven Programmangebot. Güter, die der unmittelbaren Bedürfnisbefriedigung dienen, nennt *Menger* Güter erster Ordnung.
- Darüber hinaus gibt es Güter, die dem Menschen nur mittelbar zur Bedürfnisbefriedigung dienen: Der Mensch muß diese erst durch einen Produktionsprozeß in Güter umformen, die für seine unmittelbare Bedürfnisbefriedigung geeignet sind. *Menger* nennt diese Güter höherer Ordnung. Nach der Anzahl der Produktionsprozesse, die für die Umformung in

[48] Vgl. hierzu Abschnitt 3.4.

Güter für die unmittelbare Bedürfnisbefriedigung notwendig sind, richtet sich denn auch die Ordnungsziffer eines bestimmten Gutes: So sind Mehl, Wasser und ein Backofen Güter zweiter Ordnung für die Produktion eines Brotes, das in diesem Fall ein Gut erster Ordnung ist. Das Getreide für die Produktion von Mehl wäre bei Menger dann ein Gut dritter Ordnung.

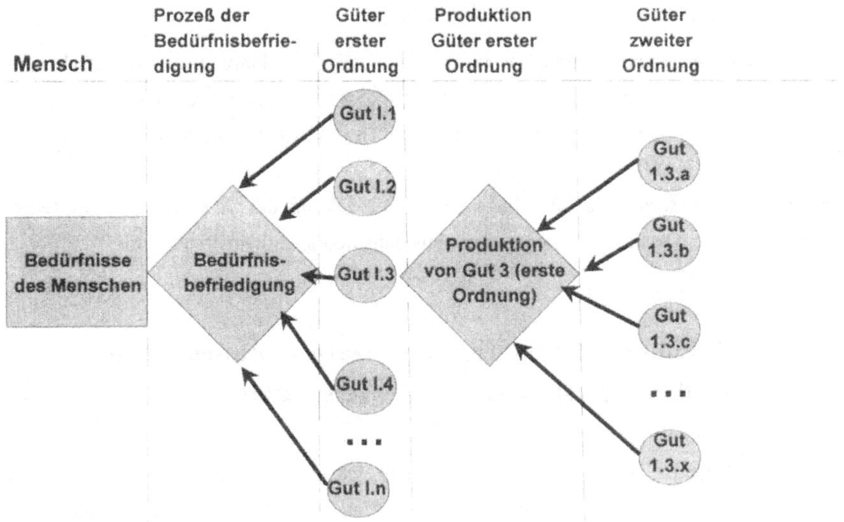

Abb. 6: Die Güterordnung Mengers und die Rolle des Wirtschaftens für die Bedürfnisbefriedigung des Menschen.

Vgl.: Menger (1923), S.20-23

Somit gelingt *Menger* der Entwurf eines Grundmusters für die Analyse gesamtwirtschafticher Prozesse (Vgl. Abb.6). Der Wirtschaftskreislauf stellt sich bei *Menger* als eine Verknüpfung von Produktionsprozessen dar[49]. Die in diesen Prozessen produzierten Güter erfahren nur insofern einen Wert, als sie in die nächste, konsumnähere Produktionsstufe eingehen und insofern die gesamte Kette der Produktionsstufen tatsächlich in die unmittelbare Bedürfnisbe-

[49] Ein änliches Modell der gesamtwirtschaftlichen Güterproduktion auf der Basis von Verarbeitungsstufen entwerfen *Engelhardt/ Günter* (1981), S. 28 zur Kategorisierung der Investitionsgüter.

friedigung des Menschen mündet. Dieses Kriterium gilt auch für die in den Produktionsprozessen eingesetzte Technologie, was *Menger* ausdrücklich betonte.[50]

Die Dispositionen zur Deckung des Güterbedarfs vollziehen sich nach *Menger* in zwei Dimensionen: Zum einen in der „technisch-ökonomischen Disposition",[51] „welche den Produktionsmitteln Ziel und Richtung auf die Deckung unseres endlichen Güterbedarfs gibt"[52] und als **Effektivitätsdimension** der Disposition anzusehen ist. Zum anderen in der „sparenden (der ökonomisierenden) Richtung"[53] der wirtschaftlichen Disposition,[54] die auf die Ermittlung immer **effizienterer** Wege zur Gestaltung der Güterproduktion gerichtet ist.[55] In doppelter Hinsicht ist die Gestaltung von Nutzungsprozessen dabei als Bezugspunkt für diese beiden eben skizzierten Richtungen der ökonomischen Disposition relevant:

- Die Nutzungsprozesse der Endkonsumenten sind, soweit man *Menger* folgt, die Meßlatte für die Bewertung der Leistungsergebnisse der vorgelagerten Produktionsstufen: Erst durch die Nutzung der Endprodukte, also der Güter erster Ordnung, bestimmt sich der Wert der für ihre Produktion eingesetzten Vorprodukte. *Menger* illustriert dies an dem Gesetz der „Bedingtheit der Güter höherer Ordnung durch die Güterqualität der entsprechenden Güter niedrigerer Ordnung"[56].
- Erst die Verwertung der Leistungsergebnisse der Nutzungsprozesse, sei es zum Endkonsum oder für nachgelagerte Produktionsstufen, führt zu der Bildung eines Wertes für die

---

50 Hierzu schreibt Menger (1923), S. 63: „Auch die technische Produktion ist mit der Wirtschaft nicht zu verwechseln. Das Ziel der Wirtschaft ist die Sicherstellung der Befriedigung unserer Bedürfnisse durch den entsprechenden Güterbesitz; das Ziel der technischen Produktion dagegen ist die Herstellung bestimmter Produkte, nicht notwendig die Sicherstellung unseres Güterbedarfs. Es gibt technische Produktion, die überhaupt nicht auf die Erzeugung von Gütern, andere, welche doch nicht auf die Deckung des Güterbedarfs gerichtet sind...".

51 Vgl. Menger (1923), S. 72-74.

52 Menger (1923), S. 73.

53 Menger (1923), S. 76.

54 Vgl. Menger (1923), S. 74-77.

55 Nach Plinke (1995) sind Effektivität und Effizienz die beiden grundlegenden Bausteine in dem Konstrukt des Wettbewerbsvorteils: Sie schlagen sich in Nutzenvorsprüngen, Kostenvorsprüngen oder in der simultanen Schaffung beider Vorteilsdimensionen nieder. Vgl. Plinke (1995), S. 82-87.

56 Vgl.: Menger (1923), S. 26-28. Im Wortlaut lautet das „Gesetz": „Es ergibt sich somit das Gesetz, daß die Güter überhaupt (ohne Unterschied ihrer Ordnung) in ihrer Güterqualität durch das Vorhandensein der Bedürfnisse geprägt sind, zu deren Befriedigung sie dienen, beziehungsweise **daß die Güter höherer Ordnung in Rücksicht auf ihre Güterqualität durch jene der Güter niederer Ordnung bedingt sind, zu deren Hervorhebung sie dienen.**" (Menger (1923), S. 27).

in diesen Prozessen eingesetzten Güter. Der Gütereinsatz muß durch die ökonomische Disposition so koordiniert werden, daß die Leistungsergebnisse optimal in den folgenden Produktionsstufen verwendet werden können und letztlich der Bedarfsdeckung der Endkonsumenten dienen. *Menger* illustriert dies durch das Gesetz der komplementären Güter. Dieses besagt im Kern, daß ein Gut seinen Wert verliert, wenn nur eines der komplementären Güter auf einer Produktionsstufe nicht verfügbar ist.[57]

Zusammenfassend läßt sich sagen, daß in *Mengers* gesamtwirtschaftlicher Betrachtung Nutzungsprozesse in zweierlei Hinsicht die entscheidende Rolle spielen: Die Nutzungsprozesse der Endkonsumenten sind letztlich die Quelle für den Wert aller im Wirtschaftsprozeß zirkulierenden Güter. Zudem läßt sich die Wertbildung von Gütern nur durch ihre Verwendung in den entsprechenden Produktionsstufen erklären. Sie erfahren nie einen Wert um ihrer selbst Willen, sondern sind Mittel zu dem Ziel der Bedürfnisbefriedigung. Die Preisbildung auf den Gütermärkten kann daher ohne eine Analyse der Nutzungsstrukturen der Güter nicht erklärt werden. Dies ist der zentrale Gedanke, den die mikroökonomische Haushaltstheorie von *Menger* aufgegriffen hat.

3.4. Nutzungsprozesse in der mikroökonomischen Haushaltstheorie

Mit Hilfe der Werttheorie *Mengers* gelang es der Mikroökonomie, ihre Erklärungsdefizite für die Phänomene der Substitutions- und Komplementaritätsbeziehungen innerhalb der Güternachfrage zu beseitigen. Diese wurden umso dringlicher, je stärker das Modell des monopolistischen Wettbewerbs eine zunehmende Akzeptanz erfuhr, und somit nicht nur Preise, sondern auch die unterschiedliche Gestaltung von Produkten, Distributionswegen und Kommunikationsinstrumenten in die Analyse ökonomischer Prozesse integriert werden mußten[58].

---

57 Vgl.: Menger (1923), S. 23-.26. Das „Gesetz" im Wortlaut: „In diesem umfassenderen Sinne ist das Gesetz zu verstehen, **daß die Güterqualität der einzelnen Produktionsfaktoren dadurch bedingt ist, daß wir über die komplementären Güter derselben verfügen.**" (Menger (1923), S. 24).

58 Chamberlins Grundthese des monopolistischen Wettbewerbs läßt sich folgendermaßen formulieren: Im Sinne der mikroökonomischen Preistheorie streben Unternehmen Monopole an. Um höhere Preise durchsetzen zu können, treten sie in einen Differenzierungswettbewerb. Insofern lassen sich in Marktprozessen also monopolistische wie auch Wettbewerbselemente finden. Zur Grundthese Vgl. Chamberlin (1948), S. 3-10, zur Rolle der Differenzierung für die Wertbildung und den monopolistischen Wettbewerb Vgl. Chamberlin (1948), S. 71-116. Zu den Konsequenzen der Theorie des monopolistischen Wettbewerbs für die mikroökonomische Nachfragetheorie Vgl. Lancaster (1990), S. 192-195 sowie Thisse/ Norman (1994), S. X.

Lancaster faßte die Probleme der traditionellen Mikroökonomie, die die Nachfrage schlicht durch gegebene Präferenzen zu erklären suchte, im fortgeschrittenen Stadium prägnant zusammen:[59]

> „*In the case of new commodities, the theory is particularly helpless. We have to expand from a commodities space of dimension n to dimension n+1, replacing the old utility function by a completely new one, and even a complete map of the consumers preferences among the n goods provides absolutely no information about the new preference map. A theory which can make no use of so much information is a remarkable empty one.*"

Die Einführung eines neuen Produktes erfordert für die traditionelle Theorie eine völlig neue Ermittlung der Präferenzen der Nachfrager, während in einer gegebenen Präferenzstruktur doch viele relevante Informationen für die Ermittlung zumindest zu vermuten sind.

Zudem war die traditionelle Erklärung der Komplementärbeziehungen zwischen Gütern heftig umstritten. Solange die traditionelle Theorie sich im Rahmen der statischen Gleichgewichtsanalyse bewegte, führte dies zu Erklärungen der Komplementarität, die jeder Alltagserfahrung widersprechen. Kurioses Ergebnis der Analyse von Komplementärbeziehungen im Rahmen des statischen Nachfragergleichgewichts war, daß die Preiserhöhung eines Gutes X zu einer Preisreduktion dessen Komplementärgutes Y zur Folge hat.[60]

Das Ergebnis dieser Analyse führte zu heftigen Kontroversen. *Fritz Machlup* brachte die Kritik an *Hicks* als dem Vertreter der traditionellen Theorie in einer Buchbesprechung folgendermaßen auf den Punkt:[61]

---

[59] Lancaster (1966) S, 133.

[60] Der Theorie zufolge führt eine Preiserhöhung von Gut X zu einer Reduzierung der Nachfrage nach Gut Y. Dies deutet auf eine Komplementaritätsbeziehung zwischen X und Y hin. Die reduzierte Nachfrage nach Y erklärt sich aus der reduzierten Nachfrage nach X. Unter sonst gleichen Umständen führt dies zu einer Reduzierung des Marktpreises für Y: Die geringere Nachfrage nach Y zwingt die Anbieter zur Reduktion ihrer Preise. Im Falle der Komplementarität zwischen X und Y führt also bei der statischen Betrachtung die Preiserhöhung von X zu einer Preisreduktion von Y. Neben der im folgenden skizzierten Lösung dieses Problems durch die Einführung der Produktionsfunktion des Haushaltes in die Erklärung des Nachfrageverhaltens entwickelte Oskar Lange eine Lösung mit Hilfe der komparativen Statik, bei der die Komplementaritätsbeziehung durch parallele Verschiebungen der Präferenzen bezüglich der komplementären Güter dargestellt wird. Offen blieb aber weiterhin die Frage, was für diese Verschiebung verantwortlich ist. Die Erklärung der Komplementarität zweier Güter durch einen gemeinsamen Produktionsvektor in der Produktionsfunktion des Haushaltes, liefert hier die weitergehende Erklärung.

[61] Machlup (1940), S. 286.

„The reader, in despair, asks himself why in the world the people who want tea instead of coffee would not want complementary lemon with their tea; and if so, why lemons would not rise in price along with tea"

Paradoxien wie diese wurden als Anzeichen der Schwäche der traditionellen auf die Bestimmung von Preis-Mengen-Relationen in Gleichgewichtszuständen fixierten traditionellen Theorie gesehen. *Cairncross* spricht in diesem Zusammenhang gar von einer „Ökonomischen Schizophrenie"[62], der die Ökonomen dadurch unterliegen, daß sie eine scharfe Linie zwischen Produzenten und Konsumenten ziehen.[63] Betrachte man die Ausstattung der damals modernen amerikanischen Haushalte, könne man deren Nachfrageverhalten dann am besten erklären, wenn man es analog zu dem einer kleinen Fabrik betrachte:

„Is it not, in fact, a close approximation to the truth to regard the average American home as a small factory, highly equipped with labour-saving devices, where the housewive puts in a very long working week and her husband a rather short one?"[64]

Doch nicht nur Aktivitäten in dem Haushalt seien mit denen einer Fabrik zu vergleichen. In der Tat, so *Cairncross*, würden die Beschäftigten einer Fabrik auch unmittelbaren Nutzen aus ihren Tätigkeiten ziehen: Auch Beschäftigung habe also einen 'Konsumaspekt'. Aktivitäten in Firmen und Haushalten hätten daher einiges gemeinsam, und Ökonomen könnten die Aktivitäten in Firmen besser verstehen, wenn Sie die Haushaltsaktivitäten analysieren würden. Dies könnte zu einem verbesserten Verständnis ökonomischen Verhaltens führen, denn:

*„Economic behaviour does not consist exclusively in responding to price incentives, in exchanging this for that, in market-oriented activity, but embraces much that goes on **within** the firms that produce and **within** the households that consume. In the market there is an obvious antithesis between firms and households; but the antithesis disappears when the two are looked at as administrative units."*[65]

Eine ökonomische Theorie des Haushalts wäre, so *Cairncross* mit einem Verweis auf die Haushaltstheorie des *Aristoteles,* der Grundstein für das Verständnis der Management- und

---

[62] Cairncross (1958).

[63] Cairncross (1958), S. 15.

[64] Cairncross (1958), S. 17.

[65] Cairncross (1958), S. 16.

Dispositionsaktivitäten, die erst die Grundlage für die Erklärung von Marktphänomenen darstellen:[66]

„If, following Aristotle, economists had sought first to understand the acitvities of the household and then studied the firm as a special type of household, they would have been less seriously in error. They would certainly have done fuller justice to the activity we call management.“

Der Weg, den *Cairncross* für die Weiterentwicklung vorschlug, enthielt nichts weniger als die Forderung des Wechsels vom Markt- zum Haushaltsparadigma. Während im Marktparadigma im Zentrum der Analyse der Austauschprozeß steht und der Nachfrager auf die Rolle des „Purchasing Agent“ begrenzt ist, steht in der Haushaltstheorie der Nutzungsprozeß im Blickpunkt, und der Nachfrager wird in seiner Eigenschaft als Produzent oder auch als Prosument betrachtet (vgl. Tab.1)

Vergleichskriterien	**Marktparadigma**	**Haushaltsparadigma**
Gegenstand der Analyse	Austauschprozeß	Nutzungsprozeß
Rolle des Nachfragers	"Purchasing Agent"	Produzent/ Prosument
Beziehung unterschiedlicher Leistungen	Netzeffekte	Inputs in den Nutzungsprozeß
Erscheinungsform des Nutzens einer Leistung	Marktsignale	Leistungsergebnis des Nachfragers

Tab. 1: Markt- vs. Haushaltsparadigma im Vergleich

Dem von *Cairncross* skizzierten Weg entsprachen eine ganze Reihe von Ökonomen. Nicht die Präferenzen in bezug auf Leistungsangebote standen im Mittelpunkt der ökonomischen Erklärung des Nachfragerverhaltens, sondern die Mittel-Zweck-Beziehungen, die diese durch den Nutzungsprozeß des Nachfragers erfahren. Oder mit einem Schlagwort formuliert: „De gustibus non est disputandum!“[67], nicht in unterschiedlichen Präferenzen sind die Bestim-

---

[66] Cairncross 1958, S. 16.

[67] So der Titel eines haushaltstheoretischen Beitrags von Stigler/ Becker (1977) , in dem sie zeigen, wie sich auch bei stabilen Präferenzen untschiedliche Nachfragestrukturen der Haushalte erklären lassen.

mungsgründe der Nachfrage zu suchen, sondern in den unterschiedlichen Produktionsaktivitäten der Haushalte.

Markower/ Baumol zeigten, daß Substitutions - und Komplementaritätsbeziehungen ebenso für Produktionsentscheidungen eine Rolle spielten wie in der Nachfragetheorie. In der Folgezeit wurden eine ganze Reihe von Nachfragemodellen entwickelt, die explizit auf der Produktionsfunktion des nachfragenden Haushalts basieren.[68]

Etabliert wurde die Theorie der Haushaltsproduktion durch das Modell von *Lancaster*, das auf zentralen Aussagen des *Menger*'schen Ansatzes[69] aufbaut. So betont auch *Lancaster*, daß Güter nicht um ihrer selbst willen nachgefragt werden, sondern weil sie Eigenschaften besitzen, die für die Bedürfnisbefriedigung des Nachfragers relevant sind.[70] Der Nachfrager fragt also nicht die Güter selbst nach, sondern deren Eigenschaften. Dies führt zu folgenden zentralen Thesen von *Lancasters* Nachfragetheorie:[71]

„*1. The good, per se, does not give utility to the consumer; it possesses characteristics, and these characteristics give rise to utility.*

2. In general, a good will possess more than one characteristic, and many characteristics will be shared by more than one good.

3. Goods in combination may possess characteristics different pertaining to the goods separately."

Ausgangspunkt des *Lancaster*-Modells ist, wie auch in den klassischen Modellen, die Nutzenmaximierung des Nachfragers (vgl. Abb.7). Im Gegensatz zu den klassischen Modellen wählt er dazu nicht Produkte, sondern Eigenschaften aus (Eigenschaftsvektor z). Diese Eigenschaften produziert der Nachfrager durch seine eigenen Aktivitäten. Im Modell wird die Beziehung zwischen Aktivitäten und Eigenschaften durch die Prozeßmatrix A dargestellt. Welche Eigenschaften in welchem Ausmaß produziert werden, wird durch die Wahl der Aktivitätsniveaus bestimmt (Aktivitätsvektor y). Welche Güter für welche Aktivität in

---

68 Morishima entwarf ein erstes Modell der Haushaltsproduktion zur Klärung des oben dargestellten Paradoxons der Komplementarität aufgrund einer Darstellung der Menger'schen Gütertheorie von Hicks. Muth schließlich entwarf ein ähnliches Modell.

69 Es ist nicht sicher, ob Lancaster dies bei der ersten Formulierung schon bewußt war. In der Buchfasstung seiner Nachfragetheorie gibt Lancaster allerdings ausdrücklich Menger als den 'Vater' dieses Gedankens an.

70 Zu den Konsequenzen für das Marketing: Kaas (1987), S. 231-232 und Gümbel (1996), S. 121-143.

71 Lancaster 1966, S. 134.

welcher Menge benötigt werden, wird in der Prozeßmatrix B festgehalten. Diese bestimmt die tatsächliche Güternachfrage, die in dem Gütervektor x nachgefragt wird.

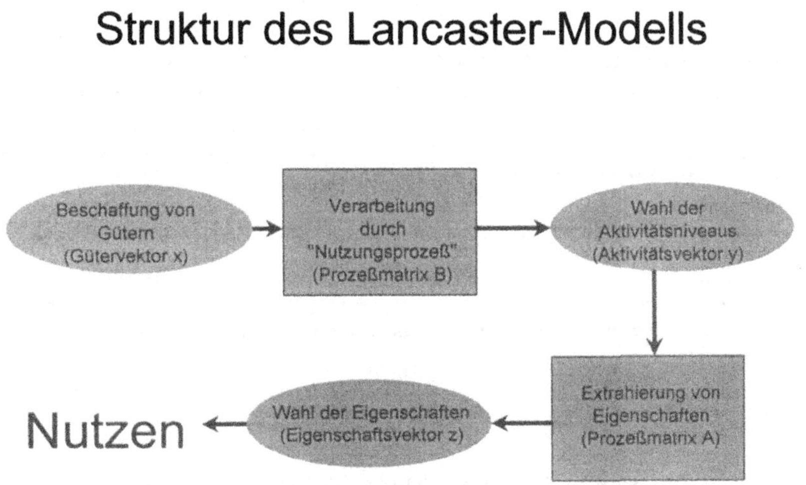

Abb. 7: Struktur des Lancaster-Modells

Durch die Einbeziehung der Nutzungsprozesse in die Analyse gewinnt das *Lancaster*-Modell gegenüber dem Marktmodell einen direkteren Zugang zur Erklärung der Wertentstehung von Gütern: Relevant sind hierfür im Lancaster-Modell die Eigenschaften von Produkten, die Produktionsaktivitäten der Nachfrager und ihre Konsumtechnologie. Dies ermöglicht einen Vergleich der Komplementär- und Substitutionsbeziehungen von nachgefragten Gütern: Gleiche Eigenschaften deuten auf Substitutionsbeziehungen hin, die gemeinsame Verwendung von Gütern in einer Aktivität deutet auf eine Komplementärbeziehung hin.

	Klassisches Marktmodell	**Haushaltsmodell von Lancaster**
Nutzenentstehung	Durch Produkte	Eigenschaften von Produkten
Beziehung zwischen Produkt und Nutzen	bestimmt durch Präferenzen	bestimmt durch Präferenzen und Produktionsaktivitäten
Produktionsleistung des Nachfragers	keine	Zweistufiges Produktionsmodell
Bewertung von Innovationen	Vergleich nur von Güterkörben möglich	Durch Ergebnisse der Konsumtechnologie

Tab. 2: Klassisches Marktmodell und das Lancaster-Modell der Haushaltsproduktions im Vergleich

3.5. Innovation im Lancaster Modell der Haushaltsproduktion

Lancaster ermittelt vier grundlegende Formen von Innovationen in der Konsumtechnologie[72] :

1. „Magic Wand"-Effekte, bei denen eine spezifische Input-Kombination auf unerklärliche Weise plötzlich einen höheren Output erzeugt.
2. Eine Verbesserung der Fähigkeiten oder eine Verbesserung der Effizienz der Nachfrager, deren Produktivität unter dem bekannten technologischen Potential liegt. Dies ist nach der Lancaster-Diktion keine Änderung der Technologie im strengen Sinne, wirkt sich aber genauso aus wie diese.
3. Eine technische Veränderung durch die Einführung neuer Aktiviäten.
4. Eine Veränderung in der Struktur der verwendeten Eingangsgüter, wie die Einführung neuer Kapitalgüter, neue Qualifikationen der Beschäftigten oder neue Management-Fähigkeiten.

[72] Lancaster 1966a, S. 18.

Die Verbesserung der Effizienz erklärt er sich durch die Verbreitung von produktbezogenen Informationen und Wissen. Somit birgt ein Produkt ein verborgenes Potential in sich, das durch die Aktivierung dieses Wissens zur Verbesserung der Nutzungsprozesse genutzt werden kann. Der Nutzen eines Produktes für seine Nachfrager kann also durch die Verbesserung ihres Informationsstandes vergrößert werden, ohne daß dieses selbst verändert werden muß.

Die Innovationen innerhalb der Konsumtechnologie, verstanden als die Einführung neuer Aktivitäten in der Haushaltsproduktion, sieht *Lancaster* als die essentielle Form von Innovation:

> *„Innovation in the true sense occurs in the technology of consumption, and this takes place primarily through the introduction ot new products or new variants and product differentiation.“*[73]

Neue Produkte wie auch neue Varianten werden in *Lancaster's* Modell durch neue Aktivitäten in die Konsumtechnologie integriert. Sie erweitern so das Spektrum der Wege für die Prosumer, ihre gewünschten Eigenschaften zu produzieren.

Als Ergebnis kann festgehalten werden, daß Produktinnovationen und Innovationen in der Konsumtechnologie eng miteinander verknüpft sind.

Innovative Leistungsangebote erfordern stets die Entwicklung neuer Nutzungsprozesse der Anbieter und führen zur Bildung eines neuen Aktivitätsvektors zu der Konsumtechnologie. Es sind aber auch Veränderungen der Konsumtechnologie denkbar, die nicht auf die Einführung neuer Produkte zurückgehen: Diese liegen im wesentlichen im Erwerb neuen Wissens zur Gestaltung der Nutzungskonzeption, so daß sich hier die Eingangsgüter zwar nicht ändern, wohl aber ihre Kombination im Aktivitätsvektor.

Die Ergebnisse der empirischen Studien von Innovationsprozessen *von Abernathy/ Utterback*[74] stützen *Lancasters* These des Zusammenhangs zwischen Produktinnovationen der Anbieter und Prozeßinnovationen der Nachfrager. Entscheidendes Ergebnis der Arbeiten war, daß in unterschiedlichen Entwicklungsphasen eines Unternehmens jeweils andere Innovationsaktivitäten dominieren. Die Gründungsphase stützt sich nach *Abernathy/*

---

[73] Lancaster 1966a, S. 20.

[74] Vgl. zusammenfassend Abernathy/ Utterback (1978).

Utterback dabei stets auf Produktinnovationen. Erschließt das Unternehmen mit deren Hilfe Massenmärkte, gewinnen die Prozeßinnovationen vor allem im Hinblick auf die Reduzierung der Kosten und auf die Errichtung von Markteintrittsbarrieren an Bedeutung.[75] Das für die Bedeutung der Nutzungsprozesse spannende Ergebnis dieser Arbeit ist aber die Feststellung, daß Unternehmen, die Prozeßinnovationen betreiben, bei der Reorganisation ihrer Prozesse auf die Angebote von Produktinnovatoren zurückgreifen. Strukturiert man aufgrund der Studie von *Abernathy/ Utterback* eine Branche nach dem Innovationsverhalten ihrer Akteure, treffen hier stets die Anbieter von Produktinnovationen auf Nachfrager, die diese Innovationen zur Neugestaltung ihrer Prozesse beziehen.[76] Folgt man diesen Ausführungen *Abernathy/ Utterbacks*, gründet sich der Erfolg der Anbieter von Produktinnovationen stets auf den Erfolg von Prozeßinnovationen ihrer Nachfrager.

Als entscheidendes Ergebnis der mikroökonomischen Analyse von Innovationsprozessen ist festzuhalten, daß innovative Leistungsangebote nur bei einer Prozeßinnovation in der Konsumtechnologie auf Nachfrage stoßen. Im Gegenzug sind Innovationen in der Konsumtechnologie nicht unbedingt auf innovative Leistungsangebote angewiesen, sondern können durch neue Kombinationen der bisher beschafften Eingangsgüter bewirkt werden.

Auch für die Gestaltung von Innovationsprozessen zeigt *Lancaster* mit seinem Beitrag Anknüpfungspunkte. Wichtig sind hier vor allem die Punkte 2 und 4. In beiden Fällen spielt neues Know-how die entscheidende Rolle bei der Innovation in der Haushaltsproduktion. Zum einen können auch mit den bestehenden Eingangsgütern durch Lerneffekte neue, verbesserte Produktionsmethoden entwickelt werden (s. Punkt 2). Zum anderen wird für die Verwendung neuer Eingangsgüter das entsprechende Management-Know-how für die Entwicklung der Nutzungskonzeption benötigt. Erst dann wird die Einführung neuer Inputs (Punkt 3) wirklich für die Neugestaltung der Nutzungsprozesse greifen. Von „Magic-Wand"-Effekten

---

75 Bezogen auf die Rolle der unterschiedlichen Innovationstypen in der Entwicklungsgeschichte von Unternehmen schreiben Abernathy/ Utterback (1978), S. 42: „These two patterns of innovation may be taken to represent extreme types - in one case involving incremental change to a rigid, efficient production system specifically designed to produce standardized product, and in the other case involving radical innovation with product variety in flux. They are not in fact rigid, independent categories. Several examples will make it clear that organizations currently considered in the specific category - where incremental innovation is now motivated by cost reduction - were at their origin small, „fluid" units intent on new product innovation.".

76 Am Beispiel der Halbleiterindustrie verdeutlichen sie diesen Zusammenhang: „The established units responded to competition from the newcomers by emphasizing prodcess innovations. Meanwhile the latter sought entry and strength through product innovation" (Abernathy/ Utterback (1978), S. 43).

soll in diesem Beitrag abgesehen werden, da sie einer wissenschaftlichen Betrachtung nicht zugänglich sein dürften.

Dies alles deutet auf die besondere Bedeutung des Wissens des Haushalts für die Gestaltung seiner Produktion hin, die *Lancaster* zwar diskutiert, nicht aber explizit in sein Modell integriert.

3.6. Die Rolle des Wissens und der Information bei der Neugestaltung der Nutzungsprozesse

3.6.1. Wissen als Menge der Produktionsmöglichkeiten einer Organisation

Der entscheidende neue Beitrag der mikroökonomischen Haushaltstheorie besteht in der Anwendung der Produktionsfunktion zur Erklärung der Güternachfrage des Haushaltes. Die Rolle des Wissens für die Konsumtechnologie ist daher die gleiche wie in der Produktionstheorie.

Bahnbrechend für die Erkenntnis der Rolle des Wissens für die Gestaltung von Produktionsprozessen waren dabei die Studien von *Machlup* zur Wissensproduktion. Dabei untersuchte er nicht nur, wie Wissen „produziert" wird, sondern auch welche Folgen diese Wissensproduktion auf das Wachstum und die Produktivität der US-amerikanischen Wirtschaft nach sich zog. Resultat seiner Studien: Investitionen in das Humankapital in Form von Ausbildung, Forschung und Entwicklung führen zu einer Veränderung der Beschäftigungstruktur[77] und zu wissensintensiverer Produktion.[78] Diese Neu-Strukturierung der Produktionsprozesse vollzieht sich entlang des Wachstumspfades mit einem im Vergleich zum „Gross National Product" überdurchschnittlichen Anstieg der Wissensproduktion. Wirtschaftliches Wachstum erfordert Investitionen in die „Wissens-Branchen", so *Machlups* Fazit. Volkswirtschaften, die

[77] Machlup resümiert aus seinen Studien folgendermaßen: „In particuolar it seems safe to conclude that technological progress has been such as to favor the employment of knowledge-producing labor; that shifts of demand for final products have been such as to increase the demand for such labor over the demand for unskilled manual labor, and that the supply suitable for knowledge-producing occupations has increased, presumably as a result of more widespread school attendance" (Machluß (1962), S. 396).

[78] Vgl. Machlup (1962), S. 362-376.

den Wachstumspfad beschreiten wollen, müssen daher in die Produktion von Wissen investieren.

In einer Folgestudie illustrierte *Machlup* den Zusammenhang zwischen dem Wissen und der Produktionsfunktion. In einem Vergleich des „production function approach“ mit dem „human capital approach“ kommt er dabei zu folgendem Schluß:[79]

> *„One may wonder wether these are rival approaches. They are not. There is no contradiction between the two. ... If several factors (inputs) determine the product (earnings) it is logically impossible to estimate the contribution of one or two of them - the human capital embodied in the workers through their past schooling and training - separately from the contribution of other factors“*

Wissen wird also ebenso für die Kombination der übrigen Produktionsfaktoren benötigt, wie es selbst ohne weitere Inputs nicht in einen Produktionsprozeß einfließt.

Nelson/ Winter machen deutlich, daß in der traditionellen Theorie die Produktionsfunktionen den Stand des gegebenen Wissens über realisierbare Input-Output-Relationen repräsentieren:

> *„What determines a firm's production set? Why is it what it is? On the surface, at least, orthodoxy is relatively clear about this. It is a state of knowledge that the production set is supposed to characterize - not, for example, the ultimate limits imposed by physical law, or the limits imposed by the actual conditions of input availability.“*[80]

An der traditionellen Theorie kritisieren sie dabei, daß diese das Wissen als gegeben hinnimmt und die Rolle des Wissenserwerbs für die Neugestaltung der Produktion vernachlässigt[81].

In ihrem eigenen Ansatz ist ein gegebener Wissensstand in Form von „Routinen“ verfügbar, die in dem organisationalen Gedächtnis gespeichert sind[82]. Die entscheidende ökonomische

---

[79] Machlup (1984), S. 521.

[80] Nelson/ Winter (1982), S. 60.

[81] Vgl. Nelson/ Winter (1982), S. 59-65, insbesondere schreiben sie zur Rolle des technologischen Fortschritts in der traditionellen Theorie: „In turn, the technological progress may be viewed as exogenous, or as the consequence of a costly activity called 'research and development'.“ (Nelson/ Winter (1982), S. 61.

Funktion von Routinen nach *Nelson/ Winter* ist die Speicherung von Wissen zur Steuerung von Produktionsprozessen:

> *„Basically, we claim that organizations* ***remember*** *by* ***doing*** *...“*[83]

Für Innovationen folgern *Nelson/ Winter* schließlich in ihrem Ansatz, daß diese durch eine Veränderung der Routinen charakterisiert sind:

> *„Both, in customary usage and in our techical use of the term, 'innovation' involves change in routine.“*[84]

In dem Ansatz von *Nelson/ Winter* tätigen Unternehmen also Innovationsaktivitäten zur Neugestaltung der Routinen. Der Antrieb zur Entwicklung neuer Routinen kommt dabei aus der Umwelt des Unternehmens: Die Innovationsaktivitäten werden beispielsweise verstärkt, wenn sich die Marktposition eines Unternehmens verschlechtert.

3.6.2. Die Entwicklung von Prozeßkompetenz im Zuge des Adoptions- und des Diffusionsprozesses

Soweit man Wissen als die entscheidende Determinante der Produktionsmöglichkeiten von Wirtschaftseinheiten versteht, ist der Erwerb von neuem Wissen die Voraussetzung für die Entwicklung innovativer Nutzungsprozesse. Wissen, das für die erfolgreiche Gestaltung von Prozessen notwendig ist, wird im folgenden als **Prozeßkompetenz** bezeichnet. Sie beschreibt das Wissen, das ein Wirtschaftssubjekt benötigt, um aus Ressourcen im Zuge eines Leistungserstellungsprozesses vorteilhafte Leistungsergebnisse zu gestalten.

Somit ist der Erwerb von Prozeßkompetenz bei der Entwicklung innovativer Nutzungsprozesse das entscheidende Ziel: Erst wenn diese Kompetenz erreicht ist, kann ein Anwender mit Hilfe eines innovativen Prozesses seine Wertschöpfung verbessern.

---

[82] Vgl. Nelson/ Winter (1982), S. 99-107.

[83] Nelson/ Winter (1982), S. 99.

[84] Nelson/ Winter (1982), S. 128.

Mit Hilfe dieser Kompetenz kann der Nutzer entscheiden, ob und welche innovativen Leistungsangebote er nachfragt.

Der Erwerb von innovativer Prozeßkompetenz zur Neugestaltung von Nutzungsprozessen ist dabei das Ergebnis eines Lernprozesses. Schon im Rahmen der Diffusionstheorie, die sich mit der Ausbreitung von Innovationen in sozialen Systemen beschäftigt, wurde diese Zielposition beschrieben. Zentral ist im Rahmen der Diffusionstheorie der Begriff der Adoption, den *Rogers* wie folgt definiert:[85]

> *„**Adoption** is a decision to make full use of an innovation as **the best course of action available** (Hervorhebung von m.e.).“*

Diese Adoption steht der Diffusionstheorie zufolge am Ende des Lernprozesses von Individuen, nämlich des Adoptionsprozesses. Bemerkenswert ist dabei, daß auch *Rogers* die Entwicklung von verbesserten Prozessen („best course of action available“) als das entscheidende Kriterium für den Erfolg von Innovationsprozessen betrachtet.

Adoptions- und Diffusionsprozeß sind in diesem Sinne als Informationsverarbeitungsprozesse zu verstehen, in denen Informationen über die Eigenschaften der Innovationen[86] gesammelt werden, was schließlich zur Annahme oder Ablehnung der Innovation führt. Der Adoptionsprozeß beschreibt in diesem Zusammenhang die Informationsverarbeitungsprozesse von Individuen.[87] die zur Annahme oder Ablehnung von Innovationen führen. Da im Falle der Adoption diese die beste verfügbare Praxis darstellt, kann der Adoptionsprozeß durchaus als ein Entwicklungspfad individueller Prozeßkompetenz interpretiert werden.

Der Diffusionsprozeß hingegen entsteht dadurch, daß sich Individuen an dem Verhalten anderer Mitglieder des sozialen Systems orientieren. *Rogers* postuliert anhand der Zeitpunkte der Adoptionsentscheidung fünf Adopterkategorien, die sich in ihrem Innovationsverhalten

---

85 Rogers (1983), S. 172. Siehe auch ebd. S. 21 u. S. 176.

86 Rogers strukturiert diese als diffusionsrelevante Eigenschaften eines innovativen Leistungsangebotes, die das Diffusionsverhalten der Innovation maßgeblich beeinflussen (Dies sind: der relative Vorteil, die Kompatibilität, die Komplexität, die Erprobbarkeit und die Kommunizierbarkeit), vgl.: Rogers (1983), S. 210- 232. Zu dem Versuch der Bildung einer Hierarchie der Innovationseigenschaften s. Schmalen/ Pechtl (1996), insbes. S. 822-825.

87 Diese spielen sich nach Rogers auf fünf Ebenen ab: Die Wissensebene, die Entscheidungsfindungsebene, die Entscheidungsebene, die Implementierungsebene und die Bestätigungsebene (Vgl. Rogers (1983), S. 163-197. Zur Interpretation dieser Ebenen als Phasenmodell s. Pohl (1996), S. 47-54.

signifikant unterscheiden: Während die Innovatoren eine Innovation schon fast nur wegen ihres Neuheitsgrades anstreben, kann die konservativste Gruppe der Nachzügler nur durch den zunehmenden sozialen Druck zur Annahme der Innovation bewegt werden. Entscheidend ist dabei der Diffusionseffekt[88] : Im Zuge des Diffusionsprozesses verbreitet sich in dem sozialen System Wissen, das die individuellen Adoptionsprozesse beschleunigt.[89]

Der Diffusionsprozeß kann also als die Verbreitung von innovativer Prozeßkompetenz in einem sozialen System angesehen werden.

Mit Hilfe der Diffusionstheorie ist es mithin möglich, die Entwicklung von Prozeßkompetenz sowohl auf individueller als auch auf gesellschaftlicher Ebene zu analysieren. Allerdings birgt die Diffusionstheorie schwerwiegende Widersprüche in sich, die in den Grundlagen des Konzepts begründet sind und die sie als fragwürdiges Instrument für die Analyse innovativer Nutzungsprozesse erscheinen lassen.

Das zentrale Dilemma der Diffusionstheorie besteht folglich darin, daß sie zwar ausdrücklich als Erfolgsbedingung für Innovationsprozesse die **überlegene Nutzungskonzeption** postuliert, hingegen die **aktive Rolle der Nachfrager bei der Entwicklung** nicht nur der Nutzungskonzeption selbst, sondern auch unter Umständen zentraler Leistungsmerkmale der Anbieter, keinen Raum in diesem Theoriegebäude findet. Die Konzeption folgt dem S-O-R-Paradigma, wobei die Innovationsaktivitäten des Anbieters den Stimulus darstellen, die Adoptions- und Diffusionsprozesse den Organismus beschreiben, die letztlich zur Annahme oder Ablehnung auf Nachfragerseite führen.

Tatsächlich ist die Bandbreite der Handlungsmöglichkeiten der Nachfrager in Innovationsprozessen viel breiter als die, die ihnen die Diffusionstheorie zuschreibt, und geht bis hin zur Konzeption der innovativen Leistungen der Anbieter.[90] Um dieser Rolle des Nachfragers

---

88 Vgl. Rogers (1983), S. 234-236. Rogers beschreibt den Diffusions-Effekt folgendermaßen: „The Diffusions Effect is the culminative increasing degree of influence upon an individual to adopt or reject an innovation, resulting from the peer networks about an innovation in a social system." (Rogers (1983), S. 234.

89 Der Diffusionsprozeß beeinflußt dabei die indivudellen Adoptionsentscheidungen durch zwei Wirkungsmechanismen: Zum einen werden durch die Ausbreitung der Innovation Informationen über deren Nutzungspotentiale verbreitet. Zum anderen geht eine zunehmende Diffusion mit der Bildung von Standards einher (Vgl. hierzu Kleinaltenkamp (1993), insbes. S. 111-.117). Standards stellen Institutionen dar, die Einzeltransaktionen ermöglichen, deren positive Netzeffekte Einzeltransaktionen begünstigen (zu Netzeffekten: Katz/ Shapiro (1986), zur Funktion von Standards als Instiutionen und ihre Wirkung auf Einzeltransaktionen im Zuge von Marktprozessen vgl. Marra (1995) insbes. S. 53-56.

90 Vgl. dazu die Ausführungen im Abschnitt 2.3. dieses Beitrages.

gerecht zu werden, wird daher ein Konzept benötigt, das diese produktiven Beiträge der Nachfrager im Innovationsprozeß erfassen kann.

4. Integration der Kunden als Weg zur Entwicklung innovativer Leistungsangebote

4.1. Dienstleistungsprozesse, die Entwicklung von Prozeßkompetenz und deren Verwertung im Marktprozeß

Für die Analyse der aktiven Beiträge der Nachfrager im Verlaufe des Innovationsprozesses wird ein Konzept benötigt, das explizit die Potentiale des Kunden als Produktionsfaktoren mit einbezieht.

Am ehesten kann ein solches Konzept aus der Dienstleistungsperspektive entwickelt werden. Herausragendes Merkmal von Dienstleistungen ist, daß deren Anbieter stets Produktionsfaktoren ihrer Kunden benötigen, um diese tatsächlich effektiv durchführen zu können.[91] Diese Integration der Produktionsfaktoren der Kunden in die Wertschöpfung der Anbieter wird im Dienstleistungsgeschäft zu den „Momenten der Wahrheit“[92] für deren Anbieter.

Absatzobjekte sind hier im Gegensatz zum Produktgeschäft keine „fertigen“ Leistungsergebnisse, sondern Leistungserstellungsprozesse.[93] Der Anbieter wird quasi zum ‘Ko-Produzenten’[94] des Nachfragers. Der Nachfrager nimmt als ‘Prosument’[95] aktiven Einfluß auf die Prozesse des Anbieters: durch Informationen zur Steuerung des Prozesses, durch die Überlassung von Produktionsfaktoren, an denen die Dienstleistungen erbracht werden sollen, und nicht zuletzt durch die aktive Mitarbeit bei der Umsetzung[96].

---

[91] Vgl.: Lovelock (1991), S. 7-8; Kleinaltenkamp (1996), S. 15-16, Meyer (1994), S. 21-23.

[92] Grönroos zeigen sich die Momente der Wahrheit durch die Integration der Dienstleistungsproduktion mit dem Konsumprozeß. Vgl. Grönroos (1990), S. 201-220.

[93] Vgl. z.B. Lovelock (1991), S. 13–14.

[94] Schade (1996), S.74–88 entwirft ein Modell der Ko-Produktion.

[95] Toffler (1980), S. 282–305.

[96] Vgl. Kleinaltenkamp (1996), S. 15-16.

Dies verdeutlicht die Perspektiven, die der Dienstleistungsansatz für die Entwicklung von Innovationen mit sich bringt. Soweit tatsächlich die überlegene Nutzungskonzeption das entscheidende Erfolgskriterium für Innovationsprozesse ist, können Nachfrager durchaus innovativ sein, ohne Anbieter in die Entwicklung miteinzubeziehen. Nicht so die Anbieter: Sie müssen in den Dimensionen der Wertschöpfung ihrer Kunden denken, um erfolgreich innovative Leistungsangebote entwickeln und absetzen zu können

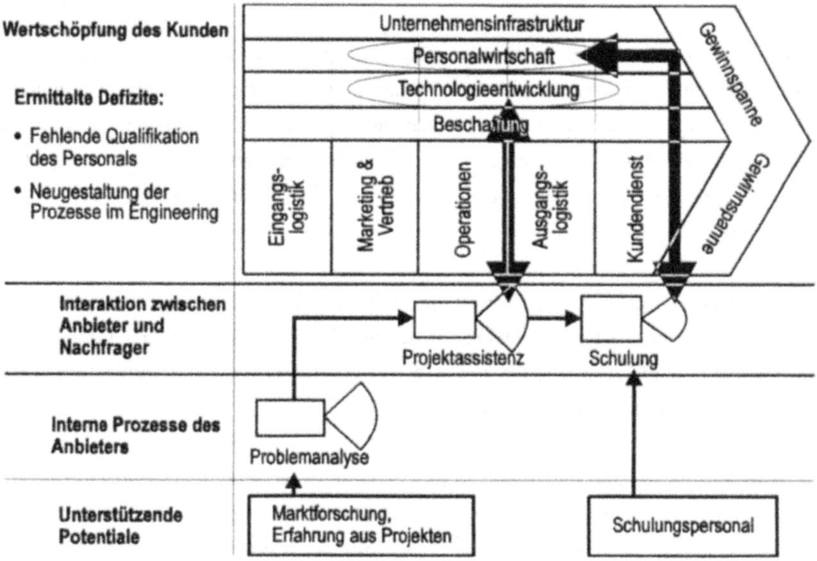

Abb. 8: Analyse der Wertkette für die Entwicklung neuer Leistungsangebote am Beispiel von Computer Aided Engineering (CAE).

Ehret/ Glogowsky (1996), S. 205 in Anlehnung an Porter (1992), S. 62 und Shostack (1991)

Dies erfordert zunächst die Analyse der Wertschöpfung der Nachfrager. Ziel ist die Ermittlung von Verbesserungspotentialen in der Nachfrager-Wertkette. Auf dieser Grundlage können dann die Leistungserstellungsprozesse des Anbieters definiert und die dafür benötigen Potentiale disponiert werden. Als Hilfsmittel für die Analyse der Nachfragerprozesse scheint die Wertkette von *Porter* geeignet. Für die Darstellung von Dienstleisungsprozessen hat sich die Methode des Blueprinting etabliert. Abbildung 8 zeigt diese Vorgehensweise beispielhaft für die Entwicklung von Computer Aided Engineering Systemen (CAE). In diesem Fall wurden in der Problemanalyse bei einem Kunden der Bedarf eines Redesigns des Engineering-Bereichs und fehlende Qualifikationen des Personals festgestellt. Aufgrund dieser Analyse

wird mit dem Kunden ein problemadäquates Angebot für die Bereiche Technologieentwicklung und Personalwirtschaft entwickelt. Erst mit Hilfe dieser Problemanalyse wurden im Bereich der Technologieentwicklung innovative Hardware-Komponenten beschafft.

Hier steht eindeutig die Entwicklung von Prozeßkompetenz im Vorgergrund. Erst das Wissen über die Wertschöpfung der Kunden und somit den Nutzungskontext für potentielle Leistungsangebote ermöglicht dem Anbieter die Entwicklung von Innovationen.

Die geschilderte Vorgehensweise ist ein mustergültiges Beispiel für die Integration des Kunden in den Leistungserstellungsprozeß des Anbieters. Diese Integration kann nur kundengerecht bewerkstelligt werden, wenn der Anbieter die relevanten Informationen zur Steuerung seines Leistungserstellungsprozesses erhält. Diese Informationen, die den integrativen Leistungserstellungsprozeß steuern, können mithin als die entscheidenden Produktionsfaktoren des Innovationsprozesses gelten.

Für den Aufbau von Prozeßkompetenz müssen diese Informationen auch für Folgetransaktionen zur Verfügung stehen: Sie müssen also gespeichert werden. Gespeichertes Wissen ist nun aber die Basis für die Verwertung der erworbenen Prozeßkompetenz gegenüber Nachfragern mit vergleichbaren Problemen.

Diese Vorgehensweise läßt sich anhand des Lead-User-Konzeptes von *Hippel* illustrieren. Lead User sind nach *Hippel* Nachfrager, deren Bedürfnisse als beispielhaft für die künftige Marktentwicklung gelten können und die einen besonderen Nutzen aus auf diesen Bedarf zielenden Angeboten ziehen können.[97] Infolge der Arbeiten *Hippels* wird innovativen Anbietern zusehends zur Kooperation mit Lead-Usern geraten.[98] Das Potential wird vor allem in dem Zugang zu strategisch relevanten Informationen für den Innovationsprozeß gesehen.[99] Das Lead-User Konzept läßt sich am besten als ein Weg zum Aufbau von Prozeßkompetenz verstehen. In dem integrativen Leistungserstellungsprozeß entwerfen der Lead User und der Anbieter gemeinsam das Design für eine innovative Nutzungskonzeption und das Design der hierfür benötigten innovativen Leistungsangebote. Gelingt die angestrebte Verbesserung der Wertschöpfung des Lead Users, kann der Anbieter die so erworbene Prozeßkompetenz bei

---

97 Vgl. Hippel (1986), S. 796 und Kleinaltenkamp/ Staudt (1991), S. 61.

98 S. hierzu Kleinaltenkamp/ Staudt (1991), S. 69-70, zu einer empirischen Studie von Lead-User Kooperation bei der Entwicklung von elektronischen Leiterplatten vgl. Nagel (1993), insbes. S. 87-117.

99 Vgl. hierzu vor allem Kirchmann (1994), S. 7-9, der Innovationsprozesse primär als Informationsprozesse betrachtet.

den Nachfragern verwerten, die den Erfolg des Lead Users imitieren möchten. Die ursprünglich für den Anbieter nur im Zuge der Integration des Nachfragers zugänglichen Informationen zur Nutzungskonzeption, stellen für ihn nun, da er die Prozeßkompetenz erlangt hat, autonom verfügbare Informationen dar, über die er selbst verfügen kann und die ihm zur Gestaltung seiner Wettbewerbsvorteile dienen. Zwei wichtige Beschränkungen wurden dabei schon aufgezeigt: Erstens muß die Problemstellung des Lead Users tatsächlich repräsentativ für die Problemstellungen der imitierenden Nachfrager sein.

Die zweite wichtige Voraussetzung ist die Speicherung der im Innovationsprozeß gewonnenen integrativen Informationen, ihr Ausbau zur Prozeßkompetenz und ihre Nutzung als autonom verfügbare Informationen im sich nun entwickelnden Marktprozeß.

Der strategische Aufbau von innovativer Prozeßkompetenz und deren Nutzung erfordert daher ein Konzept, das das gewonnene Wissen in der anbietenden Organisation speichert und zur Steuerung der relevanten Prozesse verfügbar macht.

Ein anschauliches Beispiel stellt der japanische Fahrradhersteller National Bycicle Industrial Company (NBIC) dar. Dieser betreibt zwei Geschäftsfelder, eines zur kundenindividuellen Massen-Fertigung („mass-customization") und eines zur traditionellen standardisierten Massenproduktion. Diese beiden Geschäftsfelder sind strategisch verknüpft: Durch Informationssysteme, durch Job-Rotation und durch Bildung von gemeinsamen Entwicklungsteams.[100]

Die kundenindividuelle Fertigung ermöglicht es der NBIC im Zuge der direkten Interaktion mit den Kunden Informationen für das Design der Fahrräder des standardisierten Geschäftsfelds zu erlangen. Sofern die Kunden der individuellen Werkstattfertigung repräsentativ für die Massenmarktentwicklung sind, hat die NBIC also wertvolle Informationsvorsprünge gegenüber der Konkurrenz eben durch die strategische Nutzung der im Dienstleistungsprozeß erlangten Informationen.

[100] Vgl. Kotha (1995), S. 28-36.

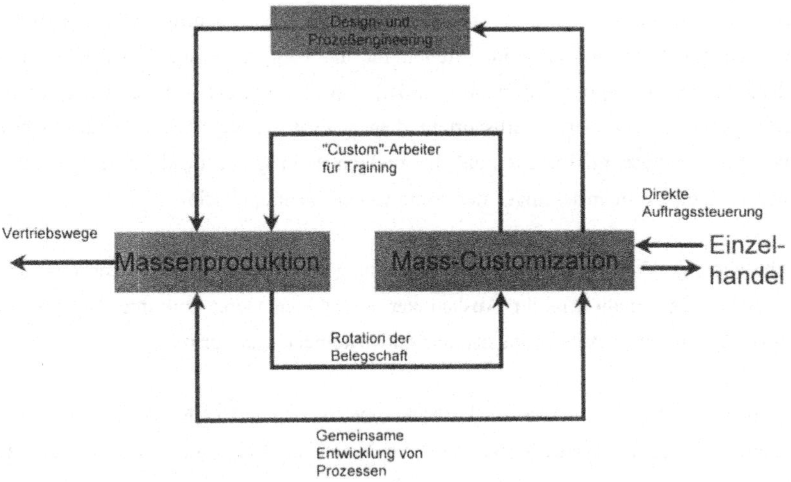

Abb. 9: Aufbau von Prozeßkompetenz durch Verwandlung von integrativen in autonome Informationen am Beispiel der National Bycicle Industrial Company, Japan

Vgl.: Kotha, Suresh: Mass Customization: Implementing the Emerging Paradigm for Competitive Advantage. In: Strategic Management Journal 1995, S,21-42, S. 33

4.2. Interpretation der Ergebnisse im Sinne des Ansatzes von Menger

Innovationsprozesse bedeuten innerhalb *Mengers* Gütertheorie, daß Anbieter einer betrachteten Produktionsstufe neue Leistungen an Nachfrager der darauffolgenden Stufe vermarkten. Mit Hilfe von *Mengers* Gütertheorie können nun die Bedingungen für den ökonomischen Erfolg von Innovationsstrategien aufgezeigt werden. Dies läßt sich zunächst anhand von *Mengers* Güterordnung demonstrieren: Im Ergebnis müssen im Zuge des Innovationsprozesses die Produktionsprozesse der nachfragenden Produktionsstufe verbessert werden. Sie muß sich also in verbesserten Nutzen- oder Kostenstrukturen niederschlagen. Dies bedeutet vor allem, daß für die innovativen Leistungen Nutzungskonzeptionen entwickelt werden müssen. In *Mengers* Gütertheorie geschieht dies im Zuge des Produktionsprozesses der Nachfrager, wo die innovativen Leistungen immer auch mit Komplementärgütern kombiniert werden müssen. Prozeßkompetenz, verstanden als die Fähigkeit, diese Integration zu bewerkstelligen, ist somit entscheidend für den erfolgreichen Verlauf des Innovationsprozesses.

Dienstleistungsprozesse sind dabei das entscheidende Instrument zur Entwicklung innovativer Leistungsangebote durch die Anbieter: Im Zuge der Integration externer Faktoren, die mit den Dienstleistungsprozessen immer verbunden ist, erhalten die Anbieter integrative Informationen. Haben sie diese gespeichert, verfügen sie über die nötige Prozeßkompetenz, die sie in die Lage versetzt, ihre Leistungen in die Wertschöpfungskette ihrer Nachfrager zu integrieren.

Auf diesem Weg gelingt es den innovativen Anbietern, die vier notwendigen Bedingungen für die Wertentstehung ihrer angebotenen Leistungen zu erfüllen:

- Die Erkenntnis bzw. Voraussicht eines menschlichen Bedürfnisses wird im Zuge der Problemdefinition und Lösungskonzeption innerhalb des Dienstleistungsprozesses ermöglicht. Entscheidend ist hierbei, daß auf der Nachfragerseite Problemevidenz entsteht. Diese besteht in der Wahrnehmung von latenten Verbesserungspotentialen durch den Nachfrager. Diese Problemevidenz kann sowohl durch Nachfrager als auch durch Anbieter hergestellt werden. Verfügt der Anbieter über eine überlegene Prozeßkompetenz, so hat er das Potential, dem Nachfrager Verbesserungsmöglichkeiten in seiner Wertschöpfung aufzuzeigen und so einen anbietergetriebenen Innovationsprozeß anzustoßen. Prozeßkompetenz auf seiten des Nachfragers ermöglicht hingegen nachfrageraktive Innovationsprozesse. Auch in diesem Fall können Dienstleistungsangebote den Anbietern zu einem Know-how-Transfer verhelfen.
- Die objektiven Eigenschaften bedeuten für das Innovationsmanagement, daß die angestrebten Vorteilspositionen auch realisiert werden müssen. Innovationsprozesse, in denen nicht nachweisbare Verbesserungen erreicht werden, sind daher zum Scheitern verurteilt.
- „Die Erkenntnis der Tauglichkeit" ist als die nötige Prozeßkompetenz zu verstehen, die Anbieter oder Nachfrager in die Lage versetzt, die notwendige Integration auf der vorliegenden Produktionsstufe zu bewältigen. Sie ist das ökonomisch relevante Wissen für die Gestaltung des Innovationsprozesses. Wie bereits geschildert, entscheidet dieses Wissen über die Rollenverteilung im Innovationsprozeß.
- Die Verfügbarkeit schließlich wird durch die Produktionsprozesse der Anbieter hergestellt: Während die Prozeßkompetenz die Informationen für die Konzeption der innovativen Leistungen erforderlich ist, müssen diese Konzepte auch umgesetzt werden, wenn die Verbesserung der Wertschöpfung tatsächlich durchgesetzt werden soll.

Dies sind die Bedingungen dafür, daß im Zuge des Innovationsprozesses Güter entstehen, also Objekte, die für die Nutzung im Zuge der menschlichen Bedürfnisbefriedigung tauglich sind.

Daß ein Wert entsteht und wie dieser verteilt wird, dafür ist nach *Menger* das Gesetz der Knappheit relevant. Auch hier ist die Prozeßkompetenz entscheidend: Verfügt ein Marktteilnehmer über eine herausragende Prozeßkompetenz, so ist das gleichzeitig die Basis für seine Verhandlungsposition bei der Verteilung des im Zuge des Innovationsprozesses geschöpften Mehrwerts.

4.3. Bezug zu etablierten Marketing-Konzepten

Der hier vorgestellte Ansatz ist nicht der erste Versuch, aus den Nutzungsprozessen der Nachfrager Informationen für die Leitusngserstellung der Anbieter zu gewinnen. Auch *Alderson* sah das Verständnis der Nutzungsprozesses als grundlegend für eine Theorie des Käuferverhaltens an. So schreibt er:

> *„Eventually marketing will have to look beyond consumer purchase to the stream of activities in which goods are consumed in order to achiueve a more fundamental understanding of consumption requirements"*[101]

Von dem industriellen Marketing erhoffte er sich am ehesten Beiträge zur Klärung dieser Problemstellung, die er aber auch für das Konsumgütermarketing als paradigmatisch ansah:

> *„In fact, this is one point where industrial marketing can help clarify our thinking about consumer goods marketing."*[102]

Ein Blick gerade in die Beiträge des Investitionsgüter- beziehungsweise des Business-to-Business-Marketing zeigt allerdings, daß die Wissenschaft auch dreißig Jahre nach *Aldersons* Vorüberlegungen kaum nennenswerte Beiträge zu der Produzentenrolle der Nachfrager geleistet hat. Die wesentlichen Beiträge zum industriellen Käuferverhalten beziehen sich vor allem auf Buying-Center-Modelle und die besondere Rolle der Geschäftsbeziehungen.[103]

---

[101] Alderson (1965), S. 144.

[102] Alderson (1965), S. 145.

[103] Zu diesem Ergebnis gelangt man auf Grund des Überblicks über die Anätze zum organisationalen Käuferverhalten bei Johnston/ Lewin (1996). Zu einer Einführung in das industrielle Käuferverhalten: Fließ (1995).

Bisher gibt es allerdings eine ganze Reihe von Konzepten, die implizit auf die Produzentenrolle des Nachfragers abstellen: Im Konsumgütermarketing ist hier vor allem der Means-End-Chain Ansatz von *Gutman* zu nennen.[104] Von der formalen Struktur her, erinnert dieser an die Güterlehre von *Menger*. Ziel dieses Ansatzes ist es, die Verbindung zwischen den Werten der Konsumenten und den Produkteigenschaften zu ermitteln.[105] Im Means-End-Chain-Ansatz wird daher nach Zusammenhängen zwischen den Werten, den Nutzungs-Situationen, der Produktkategorisierung durch die Konsumenten und letztlich deren Bewertungen der Folgen der Nutzung geforscht.[106] Der Zusammenhang zu den Nutzungsprozessen liegt auf der Hand. Allerdings steht bei dem Forschungskonzept das mentale Abbild der Nutzungsprozesse bei den Nutzern im Vordergrund und bietet somit vor allem für die empirische Erforschung aktueller Nutzungsstrukturen wichtige Anknüpfungspunkte. Es bietet aber wenig Raum für die dynamische Weiterentwicklung von Nutzungsprozessen im Zuge des Innovationsmanagements, da es immer auf die Wahrnehmung und das Wissen der Konsumenten beschränkt ist. Die Konsumenten sind zwar die relevanten Entscheider, gleichwohl sind sie gerade in Innovationsprozessen nicht im Besitz aller relevanten Informationen für die innovative Gestaltung ihrer Prozesse.

Einen expliziten Rückgriff auf die Nutzungsprozesse stellt das Produktpositionierungskonzept von *Fennell* dar.[107] Als relevanter Bezugspunkt für Positionierungsaktiviäten der Anbieter wird die Nutzungssituation, wie sie die Nachfrager erfahren, dargestellt. Als Konsequenz für die Produktdifferenzierung stellt *Fennell* dabei fest:

> *„Meaningful difference, rather than product differentiation for its own sake, seems to be the key; and the criterion of meaningfulness is consumer want satisfaction."*[108]

Auch hier steht allerdings weniger die Analyse der Nutzungsstrukturen, sondern die Erforschung des mentalen Abbildes der Nutzungssituation in dem Bewußtsein der Konsumenten im Mittelpunkt, was wichtig für die Ermittlung der gegebenen Nutzungsstrukturen ist, aber wesentliche Entwicklungsmöglichkeiten in der Nutzungsstruktur ausklammert.

---

104 Vgl. Gutman (1982) u. Gutman (1991).

105 Vgl. Gutman (1982); S. 60-62.

106 Als spezielle Interviewtechnik für die Gestaltung von Konsumentenbefragungen entwarf Gutman die „Leiter"- („laddering") Technik, die den Weg von der Kaufentscheidung zu den Konsumentenwerten nachzeichnen soll. (Vgl. Gutman (1991), S. 143-144.

107 Fennell (1978).

108 Fennell (1978), S. 46.

In mehreren Beiträgen haben *MacMillan* und *McGrath* das produktive Potential aufgezeigt, das durch die Analyse von Nutzungsprozessen erschlossen werden kann:

> *„Observing customers as they buy and use a product is the first step in discovering its salient attributes.“*[109]

Anhand einer Reihe eindrucksvoller Beispiele zeigen sie, daß durch eine an den Nutzungsprozessen orientierte Kommunikationspolitik deren Wertschöpfung verbessert werden kann, ohne daß das „Produkt“ im engeren Sinne stark geändert werden müßte.[110]

Im Dienstleistungsmarketing haben die Nutzungsprozesse der Kunden traditionell eine hohe Beachtung gefunden. Da Dienstleistungsprozesse die Integration von Produktionsfaktoren der Kunden erfordern, treffen hier die Produktionsleistung des Anbieters und die Nutzungsprozesse des Nachfragers unmittelbar aufeinander. Dieses Aufeinandertreffen wird zum Moment der Wahrheit für die Leistungserstellung des Anbieters. Daher stehen Konzepte zum Management der Arbeit mit dem Kunden stets im Mittelpunkt des Dienstleistungsmarketing. Dies ist auch ein Hinweis für das produktive Potential, das das Dienstleistungsmarketing für ein tieferes Verständnis von Produktionsprozessen birgt. Dies kann trotzdem nicht darüber hinwegtäuschen, daß auch das Dienstleistungsmarketing den Focus auf die Nutzungsprozesse der Kunden sehr eng legt. Beispielsweise werden im Blueprinting die Prozesse des unmittelbaren Kundenkontaktes zum Mittelpunkt der Betrachtung gestellt. Die Wertschöpfung jenseits der „Line of visibility“ wird nur auf Anbieterseite reflektiert, die Rolle für des Dienstleistungsprozesses für die Nutzungsprozesse der Kunden hingegen vernachlässigt.[111] Auch im Bereich des Service-Marketing gibt es also durchaus noch Forschungsbedarf für die Analyse des Nutzungskontextes, der unter anderem dann relevant wird, wenn ursprünglich produktorientierte Angebote in Form von Dienstleistungen vermarktet werden.

---

109 MacMillan/ McGrath (1996), S. 59.

110 Rührend sind dabei die Erfahrungen, die die Walt Disney Company bei der Vermarktung von CD-ROMS im Weihnachtsgeschäft gemachtc hat. Die erste CD-ROM „Der König der Löwen“ wurde für die Firma zum Ärgernis auf dem amerikanischen Markt: Viele Eltern mit wenig Computererfahrung hatten Probleme mit der Installation des Programms, was zur Ungeduld und zum Unmut der beschenkten Kinder und zu einem Zusammenbruch der Telefon-Hotline bei Walt Disney führte. Im folgenden Jahr verkaufte der Konzern die CD-ROM „Pocahontas“ mit dem Rat an die Eltern, die CD-ROM bereits vor dem Fest auszuprobieren und legte noch spezielles Geschenkpapier bei. (Vgl. MacMillan/ MacGrath (1996), S. 60).

111 Grundlegend zum Blueprinting: Shostack (1991).

5. Fazit und Ausblick

Als entscheidender Faktor für den Erfolg von Innovationsprozessen konnte in diesem Beitrag die Entwicklung von Prozeßkompetenz ermittelt werden. In Innovationsprozessen zeigt sich die Prozeßkompetenz in Wissen, das eine Verbesserung der Wertschöpfung der Nachfrager ermöglicht. Diese Prozeßkompetenz kann beim Nachfrager wie beim Anbieter liegen. Die Verteilung von Prozeßkompetenz bringt unterschiedliche Problemstellungen für Innovationsprozesse mit sich.

Nachfragergetriebene Innovationsprozesse sind ein Indiz dafür, daß die Anwender in der Prozeßkompetenz Vorsprünge gegenüber den Anbietern haben. Diesem Marketingproblem können die Anbieter durch den Erwerb von Prozeßkompetenz im Zuge von integreativen Leistungserstellungsprozessen begegnen.

Anbietergetriebene Innovationsprozesse führen nur zum Erfolg, wenn Wege für die Entwicklung der Prozeßkompetenz gefunden werden. Keinesfalls ist eine fortschrittliche Technologie für sich ausreichend, um neue Nutzenpotentiale zu erschließen. Anderenfalls droht hier das klassische Marketing-Problem der „Lösungen auf der Suche nach Problemen". Auch hier bieten integrative Leistungserstellungsprozesse die Chance, neue Potentiale für tragfähige Problemlösungen zu erschließen. Prozeßkompetenz dokumentiert sich hier in der Integrationsfähigkeit des Anbieters. Diese muß den Anforderungen des Sinnbildes des „T-förmigen Wissens" genügen:[112] Stellt man sich den Stamm des T's als das Technologie-Know-how eines Anbieters vor und das Dach des T als die Nutzung dieses Know-hows im Leistungserstellungsprozeß des Nachfragers, so wird schnell klar, daß erst durch die Prozeßkompetenz die Technologie für die Verbesserung der Nutzungsprozesse erschlossen wird.

Dies bedeutet, daß Dienstleistungen eine strategische Querschnittsfunktion für Unternehmen gleich welcher Branche bekommen: Sie bieten die Möglichkeiten, mit dem Kunden zu arbeiten und von ihm zu lernen, sei es „nur die Nutzungskonzeption" für eine innovative Technologie, sei es ein komplett vom Kunden entwickeltes Technologiekonzept.

Die hier vorgestellten Konzepte können dabei nur ein Startpunkt für die Forschung sein und sollten vor allem die Perspektiven des Denkens in Nutzungsprozessen aufzeigen: So bietet die Haushaltstheorie einen wesentlichen Zugang zur Analyse von Wertschöpfungsprozessen. Der

---

[112] Vgl.: o.V. (1995).

Fokus auf die Wertbildung von Gütern verhindert einen Rückfall in Autarkie-Denken: Haushaltstheorie in dem hier angewendeten Sinne bedeutet nicht etwa Abkehr von dem Markt- und Marketing-Denken. Es baut vielmehr auf dem Bedarf nach der Erklärung der Grundlagen für die Wertbildung ökonomischer Leistungen auf, und diese können ohne die Nutzungsstrukturen nicht verstanden werden. Daher werden in den nächsten Schritten dieses Projektes die Operationalisierung und die empirische Validierung der vorgestellten Konzepte im Vordergrund stehen. Gleichzeitig soll dieses Projekt dazu dienen, die ökonomische Fundierung des Marketing im Hinblick auf die Analyse von Marktprozessen weiter voranzutreiben.

6. Literatur

ABERNATHY, William J./ **UTTERBACK**, James M. (1978): Patterns of Industrial Innovation. In: Technology Review. June/ July 1978, S. 41-47

ALDERSON, Wroe (1965): Dynamic Marketing Behavior. A Functionalist Theory of Marketing. Pennsylvania (Richard D. Irwin) 1965

BACKHAUS, Klaus (1992): Investitionsgütermarketing. 3. Auflage, München (Vahlen) 1992

BACKHAUS, Klaus/ **VOETH**, Markus/ **BENDIX**, Kai Boris (1995): Die Akzeptanz von Mulimedia-Diensten. Konzeptionelle Anmerkungen und empirische Ergebnisse. Arbeitspapier Nr. 19/ 1995. Institut für Anlagen und Systemtechnologien, Westfälische Wilhelms-Universität Münster. Münster 1995

BIEGEL, Udo (1988): Erfolgreiche Neuprodukte durch anwenderorienierte Entwicklungsarbeit. In: Die Betriebswirtschaft 46/ 1988, S. 2319-2322

BIERFELDER, Wilhelm H. (1989): Innovationsmanagement. 2. unwesentlich veränderte Auflage, München/ Wien (Oldenbourg) 1989

BÖNDEL, Burkhard/ **STEIN**, Isidor: Wie Legosteine. In: Wirtschaftswoche 11/ 1996, S. 84-94

BROCKHOFF, Klaus (1992): Forschung und Entwicklung. Planung und Kontrolle.3., überarbeitete und erweiterte Auflage, München/ Wien (Oldenbourg) 1992

CAIRNCROSS, A. K. (1958): Economic Schizophrenia. In: Scottish Journal of Political Economy, February 1958, S. 15-21

CHAMBERLIN, Edward Hastings (1948): The Theory of Monopolistic Competition. A Re-orientation of the Theory of Value. Sixth edition, London (Oxford University Press) 1948

EHRET, Michael/ **GLOGOWSKY**, Andreas (1996): Customer Integration im industriellen Dienstleistungsmanagement. In: Kleinaltenkamp, Michael/ Fließ, Sabine/ Jacob, Frank (1996): Customer Integration. Von der Kundenorientierung zur Kundenintegration. Wiesbaden (Gabler) 1996, S. 203-218

ENGELHARDT, Werner H./ **GÜNTER**, Bernd (1981): Investitionsgüter-Marketing. Anlagen, Einzelaggregate, Teile, Roh- und Einsatzstoffe, Energieträger. Stuttgart (Kohlhammer) 1981

ENGELHARDT, Werner H./ **KLEINALTENKAMP**, Michael/ **RECKENFELDERBÄUMER**, Martin (1993): Leistungsbündel als Absatzobjekte. Ein Ansatz zur Überwindung der Dichotomisierung von Sach- und Dienstleistungen. In: Zeitschrift für betriebswirtschaftliche Forschung 5/1993, S. 395-425

FENNELL, Geraldine (1978): Consumers' Perceptions of the Product-Use Situation. A conceptual framework for identifying consumer wants and formulating positioning options. In: Journal of Marketing, April 1978, S. 38-47

FLIEß, Sabine (1995): Industrielles Kaufverhalten. In: Kleinaltenkamp, Michael/ Plinke, Wulff (1995): Technischer Vertrieb. Grundlagen. Berlin et al. (Springer) 1995), S. 287-395

GEMÜNDEN, Hans Georg (1990): Innovationen in Geschäftsbeziehungen und Netzwerken. Arbeitspapier des Instituts für Angewandte Betriebswirtschaftslehre und Unternehmensführung der Universität Fridericana zu Karlsruhe (TH). Karlsruhe 1990

GRÖNROOS, Christian (1990): Service Management and Marketing. Managing the Moments of Truth in Service Competition. Lexington (Lexington Books) 1990

GÜMBEL, Rudolf (1996): Betriebswirtschaftslehre und ökonomische Theorie. Stuttgart (Schäffer-Poeschel) 1996

GUTMAN, Jonathan (1982): A Means-End Chain Model Based on Consumer Categorization Processes. In: Journal of Marketing Vol. 46 (Spring 1982), S. 60-72

GUTMAN, Jonathan (1991): Exploring the Nature of Linkages Between Consequences and Values. In: Journal of Business Research Vol. 22 (1991), S. 143-148

HAYEK, Friedrich A. von: (1968): The Austrian School. In: Sills, David L. (Hrsg.): International Encyclopedia of the social science. London (Macmillan) 1968, S. 458-467

HIPPEL, Eric von (1976): The Dominant Role of Users in the Scientific Instrument Innovation Process. Research Policy Vol. 5 (1976), No.3, S. 212-239

HIPPEL, Eric von (1978): Successful Products from Customer Ideas. Presentation of a new customer-active paradigm with evidence and implications. In: Journal of Marketing Vol. 42 (1978), S. 39-49

HIPPEL, Eric von (1988): Lead Users: A Source of Novel Product Concepts. In: Management Science Vol. 32, No.7, July 1988, S. 791-805

Hippel, Eric von (1988): The Sources of Innovation. New York/ Oxford (Oxford University Press) 1988

Jacob, Frank (1995): Produktindividualisierung. Ein Ansatz zur innovativen Leistungsgestaltung im Business-to-Business-Bereich. Wiesbaden (Gabler) 1995

Johnston, Wesley J./ **Lewin**, Jeffrey E. (1996): Organizational Buying Behavior: Toward an Integrative Framework. In: Journal of Business Research Vol. 35 (1996), S. 1-15

Kaas, Klaus Peter (1987): Nachfragemodelle im Marketing. In: Marketing ZFP, Heft 4/ November 1987, S. 229-236

Katz, Michael/ **Shapiro**, Carl (1986): Technology Adoption in the Presence of Network Externalities. In: Journal of Political Economy, No. 4 Vol 94 (1986), S. 822-841

Kirchmann, Edgar M.W. (1994): Innovationskooperation zwischen Herstellern und Anwendern. Wiesbaden (Deutscher Universitäts Verlag) 1994

Kleinaltenkamp, Michael (1993): Standardisierung und Marktprozeß. Entwicklungen und Auswirkungen im CIM-Bereich. Wiesbaden (Gabler) 1993

Kleinaltenkamp, Michael (1996): Customer Integration - Kundenintegration als Leitbild für das Business-to-Business-Marketing. In: Kleinaltenkamp, Michael / Fließ, Sabine/ Jacob, Frank (1996): Customer Integration. Von der Kundenorientierung zur Kundenintegration. Wiesbaden (Gabler) 1996, S. 13-24

Kleinaltenkamp, Michael/ **Staudt**, Meike (1991): Kooperationen zwischen Investitionsgüter-Herstellern und führenden Anwendern („Lead User"). In: Hilbert, Josef/ Kleinaltenkamp, Michael/ Nordhause-Janz, Jürgen/ Widmaier, Brigitta (1991): Neue Kooperationsformen in der Wirtschaft. Können Konkurrenten Partner werden? Opladen (Westdeutscher Verlag) 1991, S. 59-70

Kleinschmidt, Elko J./ **Geschka**, Horst/ **Cooper**, Robert G. (1996): Erfolgsfaktor Markt. Kundenorientierte Produktinnovation. Berlin et al. (Springer) 1996

Klumpp, Dieter (1996): Marktplatz Multimedia. Praxisorientierte Strategien für die Informationsgesellschaft. Mössingen-Talheim (Talheimer) 1996

Kollmann, Tobias (1996): Die Akzeptanz technologischer Innovationen - eine absatztheoretische Fundierung am Beispiel von Multimedia-Systemen. Arbeitspapier zum Marketing Nr.7, Universität Trier 1996

KOTHA, Suresh (1995): Mass Customization: Implementing the Emerging Paradigm for Competitive Advantage. In: Strategic Management Journal 1995, S. 21-42

KROEBER-RIEL, Werner (1992): Konsumentenverhalten. 5. überarbeitete und ergänzte Auflage. München (Vahlen) 1992

KUBICEK, Herbert/ **MÜLLER**, Günter/ **NEUMANN**, Karl-Heinz/ **RAUBOLD**, Eckart/ **ROßNAGEL**, Alexander (1995) (Hrsg.): Jahrbuch Telekommunikation und Gesellschaft. Multimedia - Technik sucht Anwendung. Heidelberg (R.v.Decker) 1995

KUBICEK, Herbert/ **REIMERS**, Kai (1996): Hauptdeterminanten der Nachfrage nach Datenkommunikationsdiensten. Abstimmungsprozesse vs. Kritische Massen. In: Marketing ZFP, Heft 1, 1. Quartal 1996, S. 55-57

KUPSCH, Peter Uwe/ **MARR**, Rainer/ **PICOT**, Arnold (1991): Innovationswirtschaft. In: Heinen, Edmund (Hrsg.) (1991): Industriebetriebslehre. Entscheidungen im Industriebetrieb. 9. vollständig neu bearbeitete und erweiterte Auflage, Wiesbaden (Gabler) 1991, S. 1069-1156

LANCASTER, Kelvin J. (1966): A New Approach to Consumer Theory. In: Journal of Political Economy, Vol. 74 (1966), S. 132-157

LANCASTER, Kelvin J. (1966a): Change and Innovation in the Technology of Consumption. In: American Economic Journal, Papers and Proceedings (1966), S. 14-23

LANCASTER, Kelvin J. (1971): Consumer Demand. A New Approach. New York, London (Columbia University Press) 1971

LANCASTER, Kelvin J. (1990): The Economics of Product Variety: A Survey. In: Marketing Science, Vol. 9, No.3, Summer 1990, S. 189-206

LOVELOCK, Christopher H. (1991): Services Marketing. Second edition, Englewood Cliffs (Prentices Hall) 1991

MACHLUP, Fritz (1962): The Production and Distribution of Knowledge in the United States. Princeton/ New Jersey (Princeton University Press) 1962

MACHLUP, Fritz (1984): Knowledge: Its Creation, Distribution and Economic Significance. Vol. III: The Economics of Information and Human Capital. Princeton/ New Jersey (Princeton University Press) 1984

MACHLUP, Fritz (1940): Professor Hicks' Statics. In: Quarterly Journal of Economics, February 1940, S. 286

MacMillan, Ian C./ **McGrath**, Rita Gunther (1996): Discover Your Products' Hidden Potential. In: Harvard Business Review, May-June 1996, S. 58-73

Marra, Andreas (1995): Marktprozeß und Einzeltransaktion. Eine institutionen- und informationsökonomische Analyse am Beispiel von Standardisierungsprozessen. Arbeitspapier Nr. 8 der Berliner Reihe „Business-to-Business-Marketing" (Herausgeber: Michael Kleinaltenkamp), Berlin 1995

McGrath, Rita Gunter/ **MacMillan**, Ian C. (1995): Discovery Driven Planning. New Ventures require a new way to plan. In: Harvard Business Review, July-August 1995, S. 44-54

Menger, Carl (1923): Grundsätze der Vokswirtschaftslehre. Wien/ Leipzig (Hölder-Pichler-Tempsky/ Freytag) 1923, zweite Auflage

Menger, Carl (1970): Geld. In: Menger, Carl (1970): Gesammelte Werke. Zweite Auflage, Band IV. Schriften über Geld und Währungspolitik. Tübingen (J.C.B. Mohr) 1970, S. 1-116 (Ursprünglich erschienen in: Handwörterbuch der Staatswissenschaften. 3.Auflage, Band IV, Jena 1909)

Meyer, Anton (1994): Dienstleistungs-Marketing. Erkenntnisse und praktische Beispiele. 6. unveränd. Auflage, München (FGM) 1994

Nagel, Rolf (1993): Lead User Innovationen. Entwicklungskooperationen am Beispiel der Industrie elektronischer Leiterplatten. Wiesbaden (Deutscher Universitäts Verlag) 1993

Nelson, Richard R./ **Winter**, Sidney G. (1982): An Evolutionary Theory of Economic Change. Cambridge/ Massachusetts, London/ England (Belknap) 1982

Nieschlag, Robert/ **Dichtl**, Erwin/ **Hörschgen**, Hans (1991): Marketing. Sechzehnte, durchgesehene Auflage, Berlin (Duncker & Humblot) 1991

o.V. [1995]: The Knowledge; in: The Economist, November 11th 1995, S. 75.

Pay, Diana de (1989): Die Organisation von Innovationen. Ein transaktionskostentheoretischer Ansatz. Wiesbaden (Gabler) 1989

Peppers, Don/ Rogers, Martha (1993): The One to One Future. Building Relationships One Customer at a Time. New York et al. (Doubleday) 1993

Pine, Joseph B. (1993): Mass Customization. The New Frontier in Business Competition. Boston/ Massachusetts (Harvard University Press) 1993

Plinke, Wulff (1995): Grundlagen des Marktprozesses. In: Kleinaltenkamp, Michael/ Plinke, Wulff (1995): Technischer Vertrieb. Grundlagen. Berlin et al. (1995), S. 3-95

Pohl, Alexander (1996): Leapfrogging bei technologischen Innovationen. Ein Erklärungsansatz auf Basis der Theorie des wahrgenommenen Risikos. Wiesbaden (Gabler) 1996

Porter, Michael (1992): Wettbewerbsvorteile. Spitzenleistungen erreichen und behaupten. Dritte Auflage Frankfurt a.M. (Campus) 1992, deutsche Ausgabe von: Competitive Advantagel. New York (The Free Press) 1985

Roberts, Edward B. (1987): Managing Technological Innovation - A Search for Generalizations. In: Roberts, Edward B. (Hrsg.): Generating Technological Innovation. New York/ Oxford (Oxford University Press) 1987, S. 3-21

Rogers, Everett M./ **Shoemaker**, F. Floyd (1971): The Communication of Innovations. A Cross-Cultural Approach. New York (Free Press) 1971 (zweite Auflage von: Rogers, Everett M.: The Diffusion of Innovations)

Rogers, Everett M. (1983): Diffusion of Innovations. Third Edition, New York (Free Press) 1983

Schade, Christian (1996): Marketing für Unternehmensberatungen. Ein institutionenökonomischer Ansatz. Wiesbaden (Gabler) 1996

Schmalen, Helmut/ **Pechtl**, Hans (1996): Die Rolle der Innovationseigenschaften als Determinanten im Adoptionsverhalten. In: Zeitschrift für betriebswirtschaftliche Forschung 48 (9/1996), S. 816-836

Schumpeter, Joseph A. (1947): The Creative Response in Economic History. In: Journal of Economic History. Vol VII (1947), No.2, S. 149-159

Schumpeter, Joseph A. (1950): Kapitalismus, Sozialismus und Demokratie. Zweite, erweiterte Auflage, Bern (Francke) 1950, deutschsprachige Ausgabe von: Capitalism, Socialism and Democracy. New York (Harper & Brothers) 1942

Shostack, G. Lynn (1991): Service Positioning Through Structural Change. In: Lovelock, Christopher H. (Hrsg.) (1991): Services Marketing. Second edition, Englewood Cliffs (Prentice Hall) 1991, S. 147-160

Smith, Adam (1986): The Wealth of Nations. Books I-III. London (Penguin) 1986 (Erscheinungsjahr der Originalausgabe: 1776)

SPECHT, Günter/ **BECKMANN**, Christoph (1996): F&E-Management. Stuttgart (Schäffer-Poeschel) 1996

STIGLER, George J./ **BECKER**, Gary S. (1977): De Gustibus Non Est Disputandum. In: The American Economic Review, Vol. 67, No.2, S. 76-90

THISSE, Jacques-Francois/ **NORMAN**, George (Hrsg.)(1994): The Economics of Product Differentiation. Vol. I. Aldershot (Edward Elgar) 1994

TOFFLER, Alvin (1980): The Third Wave. London et al.(Collins) 1980

WEIBER, Rolf/ **KOLLMANN**, Tobias (1995): Die Vermarktung von Multimedia-Diensten: Akzeptanzprobleme bei interaktivem Fernsehen. Voruntersuchung. Forschungsbericht zum Marketing Nr. 3, Universität Trier 1995

WEIBER, Rolf/ **POHL**, Alexander (1996): Einführung technologischer Innovationen. Lehrbrief des Weiterbildenden Studiums Technischer Vertrieb, Freie Universität Berlin 1996

WETZSTEIN, Thomas (1995): Informelle Aneignung von Computernetzwerken. Ergebnisse einer empirischen Untersuchung. In: Kubicek, Herbert/ Müller, Günter/ Neumann, Karl-Heinz/ Raubold, Eckart/ Roßnagel, Alexander (1995) (Hrsg.): Jahrbuch Telekommunikation und Gesellschaft. Multimedia - Technik sucht Anwendung. Heidelberg (R.v.Decker) 1995, S. 124-139

Martin Reckenfelderbäumer*

WETTBEWERBSVORTEILSORIENTIERTES MANAGEMENT ZENTRALER SERVICE-BEREICHE

Entwicklung eines konzeptionellen Rahmens

Inhalt

---

* Wiss. Ass. Dr. Martin Reckenfelderbäumer, Ruhr-Universität Bochum, Lehrstuhl für Angewandte Betriebswirtschaftslehre III (Marketing), Universitätsstr. 150, 44780 Bochum, Tel.: 0234/700-2895, Fax: 0234/7094-256

1. Zentrale Service-Bereiche als Gegenstand aktueller Management-Diskussionen - begriffliche und inhaltliche Einführung in die Thematik

Dienstleistende Tätigkeiten dominieren heute nicht nur in den Unternehmungen des Tertiären Sektors, sondern gewinnen auch in der Industrie mehr und mehr an Bedeutung[1]. Dabei spielen nicht nur auf den Absatzmarkt gerichtete „reine" oder „produktbegleitende" Dienstleistungen eine wichtige Rolle. Vielmehr muß ein dienstleistungsorientiertes Management auch die Vielzahl von Leistungen einbeziehen, die eine Unternehmung zum Aufbau und zur Aufrechterhaltung ihrer Handlungsfähigkeit benötigt. Häufig werden diese Leistungen als „interne Dienstleistungen" durch innerhalb der Unternehmung[2] institutionalisierte Abteilungen, Stellen oder Personen erbracht. Das Spektrum derartiger interner Services reicht dabei von Kostenrechnung und Controlling über Marktforschung und Lagerhaltung bis hin zu Kantine und Werksfeuerwehr.

Häufig sind derartige Leistungen in Unternehmens- oder Konzernzentralbereichen angesiedelt. Nicht nur, aber ganz besonders dann wird ihre Existenzberechtigung im Zuge „aktueller" Management-Konzepte wie Lean Management oder Busniss Reengineering immer wieder in Frage gestellt. Die Vorwürfe der Unwirtschaftlichkeit und fehlenden Kundenorientierung sind weit verbreitet[3] und vielfach sehr berechtigt. Allerdings fehlt es allzu oft an kritischen Reflexionen der relevanten Sachverhalte, insbesondere aber an einer fundierten Analyse, ob und - wenn ja - unter welchen Umständen interne Services und die sie anbietenden Bereiche entgegen anderes propagierenden Thesen möglicherweise doch zur Erzielung von Wettbewerbsvorteilen beitragen können. Letzteres nämlich muß im Sinne einer marktorientierten Unternehmungsführung der Maßstab für die Beurteilung der betreffenden Leistungen und ihrer Anbieter sein.

Ausgehend von dieser Feststellung erscheint es angebracht zu untersuchen, inwieweit potentielle Vorteile, die einmal zur Institutionalisierung interner Services geführt haben[4], heute noch gegeben sind und mit Hilfe welcher Maßnahmen die entsprechenden Chancenpotentiale

---

1 Vgl. z.B. Gruhler (1993), S. 29.

2 Als eine Unternehmung wird dabei im folgenden auch der Konzern aufgefaßt. Zwischen Konzernunternehmen nach § 18 AktG erbrachte Dienstleistungen stellen insofern im Sinne des vorliegenden Beitrags interne Services dar.

3 Vgl. beispielhaft Bühner (1996), S. 227ff., Vandermerwe/Gilbert (1989), S. 83ff.

4 Vgl. z.B. Connell (1996), S. 55ff., Kreikebaum (1992), Sp. 2603ff.

aktiviert und zur Erzielung von Wettbewerbsvorteilen genutzt werden können. In diesem Sinne wird im vorliegenden Beitrag ein konzeptioneller Rahmen zur Planung, Steuerung und Kontrolle interner Service-Bereiche entwickelt.

Zwei im Kontext der Thematik wichtige Fragen, nämlich diejenige **der Eigenerstellung oder des Fremdbezugs**[5] der betreffenden Leistungen sowie diejenige **des optimalen (De)Zentralisationsgrades**[6] ihrer organisatorischen Institutionalisierung, werden dabei bewußt in den Hintergrund gestellt. Vielmehr wird aus Gründen der Überschaubarkeit von einer gegebenen Organisationsform ausgegangen, an deren Beispiel die relevanten Sachverhalte verdeutlicht werden sollen. Zudem wird ein bestimmter Typus interner Services herausgegriffen, für den die Überlegungen besonders bedeutsam erscheinen. Diese institutionelle und funktionale Eingrenzung sei im folgenden kurz spezifiziert[7].

Bei der Abgrenzung in **funktionaler Hinsicht** kann die in Abb. 1 wiedergegebene Typologie interner Services hilfreich sein. Eine Eingrenzung soll an dieser Stelle dahingehend erfolgen, daß eine Konzentration auf „**Support and Advice Services**", d.h. auf unterstützende und beratende Leistungen, erfolgt. Neben den in Abb. 1 genannten zählen hierzu z.B. Tätigkeitsfelder wie Fuhrpark, Werkskantine, Rechenzentrum, Schulung und Training, Volkswirtschaft oder Hauspost. Eine Auseinandersetzung mit diesen Leistungen bietet sich deshalb an, weil bei ihnen regelmäßig Alternativen hinsichtlich der organisatorischen Trägerschaft bestehen, sie deshalb aber auch in besonderem Maße Gegenstand der Optimierungsdiskussionen sind.

---

5 Vgl. dazu z.B. Männel (1981), Schneider/Baur/Hopfmann (1994), aber auch die zahlreichen Publikationen zum Outsourcing, z.B. aktuell Horchler (1996), Koppelmann (1996). Auch die damit verknüpfte und gegenwärtig vielfach diskutierte Frage nach der „richtigen" oder „effizienten" Unternehmensgrenze soll daher hier nicht aufgegriffen werden; vgl. dazu und zu neuen Organisations-und Kooperationsformen „zwischen Markt und Hierarchie" Picot/Reichwald/Wigand (1996); siehe auch Wagner (1994).

6 Vgl. hierzu als eine frühe grundlegende Arbeit Bleicher (1966) sowie den aktuelleren Überblick bei Beuermann (1992), Sp. 2611ff. Siehe aber auch den wissenschaftlichen Disput in der Zeitschrift „Die Betriebswirtschaft", Hefte 1 und 2/1996.

7 Verzichtet werden muß und kann in diesem Beitrag auf eine Diskussion der Begriffe „interner Service" und „interne Dienstleistung"; vgl. zu derartigen Begriffsfassungen z.B. Cramer (1987), S. 1f., Davis (1991), S. 5, Stauss (1995a), S. 65. Zu idealtypischen Charakteristika interner Services siehe z.B. Stauss (1995a), S. 72ff., Witt (1985), S. 163. Die terminologische Diskussion ist weitgehend unabhängig von der hier behandelten Problematik und wird an anderer Stelle aufzugreifen sein.

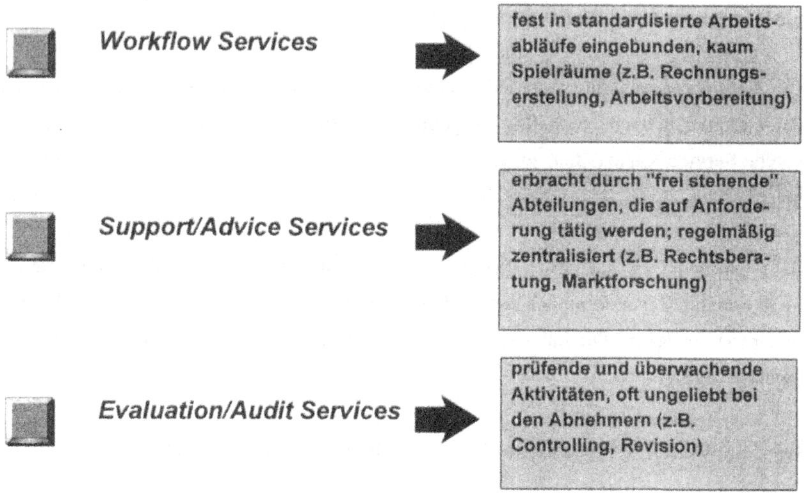

Abb. 1: Erscheinungsformen interner Services

Quelle: basierend auf Davis (1993), S. 304ff., Stauss (1995a), S. 65ff., zurückgehend auf Sayles (1964)

Bei der **institutionellen Eingrenzung** soll eine Konzentration auf Zentralbereiche[8] erfolgen, und zwar auf solche, die direkt unterhalb der Unternehmungsleitung angesiedelt sind. Derartige Zentralbereiche haben in divisionalisierten Unternehmungen eine besonders große Bedeutung[9]; daher erfolgt eine Beschränkung auf diese Organisationsform[10]. Zentralbereiche erfüllen allerdings oft Aufgaben, die nicht dem Typus der unterstützenden und beratenden Dienstleistungen zuzuordnen sind[11]. Daher sollen im folgenden nur diejenigen Zentralbereiche her-

8 In diesem Zusammenhang sei darauf hingewiesen, daß die Zentralbereichsproblematik die Betriebswirtschaftslehre zwar schon seit langem beschäftigt; vgl. etwa Altfelder (1965), Arbeitskreis Dr. Krähe (1952), Schmalenbach (1959), sie aber im Lichte neuer theoretischer und praktischer Erkenntnisse einer modifizierten Betrachtung bedarf.

9 Vgl. in diesem Sinne Kreisel (1995), S. 11ff.

10 Dabei wird von einem stark vereinfachten, für die vorliegenden Zwecke aber völlig ausreichenden Unternehmungsmodell mit drei Gruppen von Beteiligten (Unternehmungsleitung, Geschäftsbereiche, Zentralbereiche) auf nur zwei hierarchischen Ebenen ausgegangen.

11 Zu den generellen Aufgaben von Zentralbereichen vgl. z.B. Frese/von Werder (1993), S. 4, Kreikebaum (1992), Sp. 2606.

ausgegriffen werden, die nach dem sogenannten „**Service-Modell**" organisiert sind[12], da dieses am ehesten dem Charakter der unterstützenden und beratenden Services entspricht. Folgende Kennzeichen sind für das Service-Modell typisch:

- Die **Nachfrage** nach den durch den Zentralbereich angebotenen Leistungen erfolgt seitens der Geschäftsbereiche **freiwillig**. Regelmäßig verfügen die Geschäftsbereiche auch über eigene Service-Kapazitäten, so daß sie vor einer internen Make-or-Buy-Entscheidung stehen.

- Sehr häufig haben die Geschäftsbereiche die Möglichkeit, die angebotenen Leistungen nicht nur intern, sondern auch **extern** bei außerhalb der Unternehmung angesiedelten Anbietern **zu beziehen**. Die internen Dienstleister stehen somit in einer Konkurrenzbeziehung zu den externen.

- Die Zentralbereiche haben **keine Weisungsbefugnisse** gegenüber den Geschäftsbereichen.

- Oft wird der Versuch unternommen, derartigen Zentralbereichen eine **eigene Erfolgs-**, zumindest aber **Kostenverantwortlichkeit** zuzuordnen.

Insofern erfüllen nach dem Service-Modell organisierte Zentralbereiche im Unterschied zu anderen Zentralbereichstypen überwiegend Service-, aber kaum oder gar nicht Steuerungsaufgaben[13]; nicht zuletzt deshalb wird ihre Notwendigkeit besonders häufig hinterfragt. Nach dem Service-Modell organisierte Zentralbereiche sollen im folgenden als „**zentrale Service-Bereiche**" bezeichnet werden. Sofern diese für die Erbringung unterstützender und beratender Services zuständig sind, bilden sie den Untersuchungsgegenstand des vorliegenden Beitrags[14]. Dabei wird das wettbewerbsvorteilsorientierte Management zentraler Service-Bereiche weniger von der Anwendungsseite als vielmehr von seinen theoretisch-konzeptionellen Grundlagen her behandelt. So wird im folgenden Kapitel 2 die Lehre von den

---

12 Zu diesen und anderen Organisationsformen für Zentralbereiche siehe Frese/von Werder (1993), S. 36ff., Kreisel (1995), S. 116ff. Letzterer verwendet für die hier interessierende Organisationsform den Begriff „Wettbewerbsmodell".

13 Vgl. dazu Kreisel (1995), S. 118ff.

14 Hingewiesen sei an dieser Stelle noch darauf, daß zwischen den zentralen Service-Bereichen und ihren Abnehmern ein Sonderfall der sogenannten „**internen Kunden-Lieferanten-Beziehungen**" besteht, deren Besonderheiten für das Management zentraler Service-Bereiche gleichsam von Bedeutung sind; vgl. dazu z.B. Gremler/Bitner/Evans (1994), S. 34ff., Hart (1995), S. 81, McDermott/Emerson (1991), S. 61, Pfau/Detzel/Geller (1991), S. 9, Reynoso/Moores (1995), S. 64ff., Sanfilippo (1990), S. 26. Siehe aber insbesondere auch die ausführliche Auseinandersetzung bei Neuhaus (1996), S. 5ff.

Unternehmerfunktionen als eine mögliche theoretische Fundierung zur Diskussion gestellt. Kapitel 3 verbindet diese Theorierichtung mit Überlegungen zur Erlangung von Wettbewerbsvorteilen, indem Gestaltungsfelder für das Management systematisiert und strukturiert werden. Kapitel 4 schließlich zeigt anhand einiger weniger Beispiele, wie die zuvor erarbeiteten Gestaltungsfelder mit konkreten Inhalten gefüllt werden können.

2. Perspektiven einer theoriebasierten Annäherung an die Thematik: Erklärungs- und Gestaltungsnutzen der Lehre von den Unternehmerfunktionen

2.1. Einführung in die Lehre von den Unternehmerfunktionen

Verschiedene Zweige der ökonomischen und ökonomienahen Theorie bieten auf den ersten Blick Ansatzpunkte für eine theoretische Untermauerung bzw. Begründung des wettbewerbsvorteilsorientierten Management zentraler Service-Bereiche. Insofern stellt sich an dieser Stelle die Frage, welche Denk- und Forschungsrichtung am besten geeignet erscheint, die relevanten Sachverhalte abzubilden und zu durchdringen[15]. Die vorliegende Thematik bringt es mit sich, daß sie - u.a. - organisatorische, absatzwirtschaftliche, rechnungswesenbezogene, führungsspezifische und personalwirtschaftliche Aspekte miteinander verbindet. Dadurch bedingt muß die Suche nach der geeigneten Theorie an sehr unterschiedlichen Stellen und in verschiedenen Bereichen der Betriebswirtschaftslehre ansetzen; genau genommen sollte die entsprechende Theorie mit Blick auf eine „Allgemeine Betriebswirtschaftslehre“ konzipiert sein, um für alle Detailfragen der Problematik grundlegende Relevanz zu besitzen. Im Rahmen des vorliegenden Beitrags können nicht alle potentiell Aussagekraft besitzenden theoretischen Ansätze vorgestellt und hinsichtlich ihrer Tragfähigkeit geprüft werden. Ohne damit andere Ansätze - wie z.B. die Neue Institutionenökonomik oder die Verhaltenswissenschaften[16] - abwerten zu wollen, soll daher ein in der Betriebswirtschaftslehre bis heute noch wenig

---

15 Vgl. in diesem Zusammenhang die Untersuchung von Föhr (1991), die die Vielzahl möglicher Konzepte anzudeuten vermag.

16 Ohne Zweifel bieten auch diese und andere Theorierichtungen vielfältige Ansatzpunkte für die vorliegende Thematik. Auf ihre Behandlung sei aber deshalb verzichtet, um den für eine eingehende Auseinandersetzung mit der Anwendbarkeit der Lehre von den Unternehmerfunktionen erforderlichen Raum zu gewinnen. Weitere Überlegungen werden zeigen müssen, ob und in welcher Form die Lehre von den Unternehmerfunktionen ergänzende oder ersetzende theoretische Grundlagen herangezogen werden müssen. Auch der Klärung dieser Frage dient der vorliegende Beitrag.

beschrittener Weg eingeschlagen und zur Diskussion gestellt werden: derjenige über die Lehre von den Unternehmerfunktionen.

Diese erfüllt wichtige Anforderungen: Sie verbindet den Marktbezug mit der internen, in die Unternehmung hinein gerichteten Perspektive, sie bildet aufgrund ihrer umfassenden Ausrichtung eine geeignete Basis für die Analyse der vielfältigen betriebswirtschaftlichen Fragestellungen im Kontext zentraler Service-Bereiche, sie verfügt über einen im Vergleich zu anderen Theorien höheren Novitäts- und Originalitätsgrad und beläßt insofern schließlich interessante Gestaltungsspielräume, die es sinnvoll auszufüllen gilt. Zudem liefert sie adäquate Anknüpfungspunkte für die Verbindung zum Streben nach Wettbewerbsvorteilen[17]. Bevor dieser Schritt vollzogen werden kann, bedarf es eines zusammenfassenden Abrisses zentraler Inhalte der Lehre von den Unternehmerfunktionen, wie sie im folgenden zugrunde gelegt werden soll.

Die Wurzeln der Lehre von den Unternehmerfunktionen liegen vor bzw. in der Zeit der ökonomischen Klassik[18]. Als älteste bekannte Quelle wird regelmäßig die Schrift von Cantillon aus dem Jahre 1755 zitiert[19]. Trotz dieser langen Tradition hat sich bis heute keine einheitliche Theorie herausgebildet[20], die von den einzelnen Vetretern herausgestellten Funktionen des Unternehmers divergieren teilweise sehr deutlich, wie Abb. 2 zeigt[21].

---

17 Hier sei auch auf die Verbindungsmöglichkeiten mit einem weiteren theoretischen Konzept, dem Resource Based View bzw. der ressourcenorientierten Unternehmungsführung, aufmerksam gemacht; so sieht Schneider (1996), S. 1112, in der Lehre von den Unternehmerfunktionen eine Möglichkeit, die Umsetzung von Ressourcen in Strategien zu untermauern. Zum Resource Based View vgl. in knapper Form, z.B. Bamberger/Wrona (1996), S. 130ff., Rasche/Wolfrum (1994), S. 501ff.

18 Vgl. Schneider (1985), S. 1238.

19 Vgl. Cantillon (1755); Schneider (1995), S. 35, nennt als Ursprung dieser Überlegungen die Zeit um das Jahr 1725.

20 Vgl. Schneider (1995), S. 157, der explizit darauf verweist, daß eine Theoriebildung über das Ausüben von Unternehmerfunktionen erst in wenigen Ansätze vorliegt.

21 So macht die Tabelle etwa auch deutlich, daß eine Auseinandersetzung mit den Unternehmerfunktionen auch bei den Vertretern der Neuen Institutionenökonomik stattfindet, vgl. z.B. Coase (1937), Williamson (1975). Casson (1982) verbindet die Lehre von den Unternehmerfunktionen mit Transaktions- bzw. Koordinationskostenüberlegungen. U. a. Schneider (1985), S. 1238, schließlich betont die Verknüpfung der Unternehmerfunktionen mit den Modern Austrian Economics. An anderer Stelle bezeichnet er die Lehre von den Unternehmerfunktionen explizit als dem Denkstil der Modern Austrian Economics zuordenbar; vgl. Schneider (1995), S. 254.

Berücksichtigte Unternehmerfunktionen	Vertreter
Risikoträger bei Ungewißheit/Spekulant/Grundlegender Disponent	Cantillon (1755), Knight (1921), v. Thünen (1826), Shackle (1955)
Innovator/Durchsetzer neuer Kombinationen/schöpferischer Zerstörer/Marktentwickler	Schumpeter (1911), Heuss (1965), Weber (1905)
Vertragschließender	Bentham (1793)
Auserwählter (protestantische Ethik)	Weber (1905)
Arbitrageur/Informationsverwerter/Nutzer und Beseitiger von Ungleichgewichten	Kirzner (1973), v. Mises (1949), v. Hayek (1937), Cantillon (1755), Walras (1886)
Entscheidungsträger/Verteiler von Ressourcen zwischen unterschiedlichen Verwendungsrichtungen	Cantillon (1755), Keynes (1944), Shackle (1955), Cole (1946), Schultz (1975)
Industrielenker/Captain of Industry/Wirtschaftskapitän	Say (1803), Sombart (1913), Schumpeter (1911), Redlich (1956)
Organisator/Koordinator/Kombinierer von Produktionsfaktoren/Haftender/Eigner des Produkts	Say (1803), Clark (1934), Schmoller (1923), Davenport (1908), Hawley (1907)
Unternehmer = Unternehmung = Firma	Stauss (1944)
Beseitiger von Ineffizienzen/Nutzer organisatorischer Unzulänglichkeiten anderer Unternehmen (Unternehmer)	Leibenstein (1978)
Entscheidungsträger mit überdurchschnittlichem Urteilsvermögen	Casson (1982), Hébert/Link (1988)
Transaktionskostenminimierer/Pendant zum Marktpreissystem/Nutzer von Marktunvollkommenheiten durch Vertragsabschlüsse	Coase (1937), Williamson (1975), Casson (1982), Penrose (1959), Alchian/Demsetz (1972), Jensen/Meckling (1976)

Abb. 2: Sichtweisen von (dynamischen) Unternehmerfunktionen in der Literatur[22]

Quelle: Schoppe et al. (1995), S. 283

Allerdings ist in jüngerer Zeit eine Tendenz dahingehend auszumachen, daß insbesondere drei Funktionen betont werden[23] :

[22] Zu den in der Abbildung genannten Quellen vgl. - sofern sie im Text des vorliegenden Beitrags nicht gesondert zitiert sind - das Literaturverzeichnis bei Schoppe et al. (1995).

[23] Vgl. in diesem Sinne und zu entsprechenden Erläuterungen etwa Picot/Reichwald/Wigand (1996), S. 29, Schoppe et al. (1995), S. 285, Wieandt (1994), S. 20, Windsperger (1991), S. 1414.

- Arbitragefunktion,
- Innovationsfunktion,
- Koordinationsfunktion.

Im Unterschied zur neoklassischen Gleichgewichtstheorie geht die Lehre von den Unternehmerfunktionen von **unvollständigem und ungleich verteiltem Wissen** der Individuen aus[24], sie nimmt eine dynamische Perspektive ein, bei der Innovation und Wandel den Wettbewerb prägen, und sie löst sich vom Denken in Marktgleichgewichten: Ungleichgewichte sind die Regel[25].

Im folgenden wird die **Konzeption der Lehre von den Unternehmerfunktionen nach Dieter Schneider als Grundlage** herangezogen, da dieser Ansatz als der auf dem gegenwärtigen Stand der Forschung ausgereifteste und für die Zwecke der vorliegenden Untersuchung tragfähigste erscheint. Insofern ergibt sich allerdings eine von der oben aufgeführten Dreiteilung partiell abweichende Systematik der Unternehmerfunktionen (siehe Abb. 3), die Schneider als **Grundlage einer Einzelwirtschaftstheorie der Institutionen** verwendet[26].

Von anderen Einteilungen hebt sich die letztgenannte insbesondere dadurch positiv ab, daß die einzelnen Unternehmerfunktionen nicht unverbunden analysiert, sondern zu einer konsistenten Gesamtheit kombiniert werden. Wichtig ist in diesem Zusammenhang nämlich, daß die drei Funktionen keinesfalls in einem Gleichordnungsverhältnis nebeneinander stehen, sondern in einer **hierarchischen Beziehung** zueinander, entsprechend der Reihenfolge in Abb. 3: Die Übernahme von Einkommensunsicherheit ist die grundlegende Unternehmerfunktion, der die Erzielung von Arbitragegewinnen nachgeordnet ist. Die Durchsetzung von Änderungen ist wiederum der Arbitrageerzielung nachgeordnet, da erstere sich an letzterer ausrichten muß[27]. Insofern werden die weiteren Ausführungen aber auch deutlich machen, daß die einzelnen Unternehmerfunktionen nicht isoliert voneinander betrachtet werden kön-

---

24 Schneider (1995), S. 7, verdichtet dies auf die beiden Kernsätze „*Das Wissen über das, was sein wird, ist unvollständig.*" und „*Wissen, Wollen und Können sind zwischen den Menschen höchst ungleich verteilt.*" (Kursivdruck im Original). Siehe in diesem Zusammenhang aber auch die informationsökonomische Sichtweise bei Spremann (1990), S. 561ff.

25 Vgl. Schoppe et al. (1995), S. 283.

26 Vgl. Schneider (1995), S. 30.

27 Vgl. Schneider (1995), S. 114f.

nen, da sie zum Teil eng miteinander verzahnt sind[28]. Alle drei Funktionen sind auf historische Wurzeln zurückzuführen. Im folgenden seien die einzelnen Aspekte kurz erläutert[29]:

institutionenbegründende Funktion:

Übernahme von Einkommensunsicherheiten anderer Menschen

- ***einseitig***
- ***gegenseitig***

institutionenerhaltende Funktion nach außen:

Erzielung von Arbitragegewinnen

- ***Arbitrage i.e.S.***
- ***räumliche Arbitrage***
- ***zeitliche Arbitrage***
- ***Produktionsstufen-Arbitrage***
- ***Arbitrage gegen Regulierungen***

institutionenerhaltende Funktion nach innen:

Durchsetzen von Änderungen in wirtschaftlicher Führerschaft

- ***Innovationsfunktion***
- ***Organisations- und Koordinationsfunktion***

Abb. 3: Systematik der Unternehmerfunktionen

Quelle: zusammengestellt nach Schneider (1995), S. 30ff.

- Institutionen - so auch Unternehmungen - werden dadurch begründet, daß Individuen sich bereit erklären, anderen **Individuen Unsicherheiten im Hinblick auf den Einkommenserwerb abzunehmen**. Diese Unsicherheiten wiederum resultieren aus der Unvollständigkeit und Ungleichverteilung von Wissen. Dabei wird davon ausgegangen, daß jeder Mensch hinsichtlich der Unsicherheit im Einkommenserwerb „Unternehmer seines Wissens, seiner Arbeitskraft und seines sonstigen Vermögens"[30] ist, somit Unternehmerfunktionen ausübt, allerdings in sehr unterschiedlichem Maße. In diesem Sinne beschäftigen

28 Zudem bringt es die Vielschichtigkeit und fehlende inhaltliche Geschlossenheit der Lehre von den Unternehmerfunktionen zwangsläufig mit sich, daß bestimmte Begriffe je nach Autor mit zum Teil divergierenden Inhalten verwendet werden. Sofern erforderlich, wird darauf an den entsprechenden Textstellen hingewiesen.

29 Hier seien tatsächlich nur die für die vorliegende Untersuchung wichtigsten Aspekte angesprochen. Ausführlich dazu vgl. Schneider (1995), S. 30ff.

30 Schneider (1995), S. 31.

Arbeitgeber ihre Angestellten, um für sich selbst die Voraussetzungen des Einkommenserwerbs zu verbessern; gleichzeitig nehmen sie jedoch - im theoretischen Grenzfall unbeabsichtigt - diesen Angestellten - z.B. durch die vertragliche Zusicherung fester Gehälter - einen Teil ihrer Unsicherheit ab. Es lassen sich in diesem Zusammenhang zwei Grundformen der Übernahme von Einkommensunsicherheit unterscheiden[31] : Als **einseitige Übernahme** von Einkommensunsicherheit wird etwa der Fall dargestellt, daß ein selbständiger Handwerksmeister Gesellen beschäftigt, eine **gegenseitige Übernahme** liegt z.B. im Falle von Kooperationen zwischen zwei Personen (oder auch Unternehmungen) vor, die Chancen und Risiken miteinander teilen. Zwischen diesen Grundformen finden sich zudem zahlreiche Mischungen.

- Das **Erzielen von Arbitragegewinnen** wird durch das Ausnutzen von Preisunterschieden zwischen Beschaffungs- und Absatzmärkten ermöglicht[32] , die der Unternehmer aufgrund von Wissensvorsprüngen zu erkennen vermag. Insofern handelt es sich um eine nach außen - auf die Märkte - gerichtete Funktion, die der Erhaltung von Institutionen, speziell Unternehmungen, dient. „Ein Unternehmer als Anbieter sucht Arbitragegewinne durch Absatz von Gütern, wenn die Preisobergrenzen, die einzelne Nachfrager zu zahlen bereit sind, höher liegen als das, was der Unternehmer für die Güter aufgewandt hat. Ein Unternehmer als Nachfrager sucht Arbitragegewinne durch Beschaffung auf demselben Markt, wenn nach Einrechnung seiner Kosten die Preisuntergrenzen, die einzelne Anbieter einräumen, niedriger als einzelne, nicht allen bekannte Absatzpreise sind."[33] Neben dieser als **Arbitrage i.e.S.** zu bezeichnenden Form lassen sich als Grundformen **räumliche Arbitragen** (resultierend aus Preisunterschieden zur gleichen Zeit an unterschiedlichen Orten) und **zeitliche Arbitragen** (beruhend auf Preisunterschieden an einem bestimmten Ort zu unterschiedlichen Zeitpunkten) sowie **Produktionsstufenarbitragen** (begründet durch Preisunterschiede zwischen Produktionsfaktoren und aus diesen hergestellten Produkten) unterscheiden. Zu ergänzen ist diese Aufzählung schließlich um die **Arbitragen gegen Regulierungen**, d.h. vorteilsversprechende Ausweichhandlungen gegenüber insbesondere staatlichen und gesetzlichen Regulierungen. Die Realität ist geprägt durch Mischungen dieser Grundformen: So zielt letztlich jede Form der Leistungserstellung auf Produktionsstufenarbitragen ab, denn insbesondere in Unternehmungen werden stets Produktionsfaktoren

---

31 Vgl. Schneider (1995), S. 33f.

32 Vgl. Schneider (1995), S. 36ff. In den Mittelpunkt seiner Überlegungen stellt diese Unternehmerfunktion in neuerer Zeit vor allem Kirzner (1978).

33 Schneider (1995), S. 37.

kombiniert, um zu absetzbaren Produkten bzw. Leistungsbündeln zu gelangen[34]. Diese Arbitragen werden regelmäßig ergänzt durch das Ausnutzen räumlicher und/oder zeitlicher Preisunterschiede. Arbitragen, die durch Absatz und Beschaffung zur gleichen Zeit am gleichen Ort realisiert werden können, dürfen wiederum nur als theoretischer Grenzfall ohne praktische Relevanz gelten.

- Bei der Behandlung der nach innen gerichteten Funktion der Institutionenerhaltung, dem **Durchsetzen von Änderungen in wirtschaftlicher Führerschaft**, werden die in der Literatur oft getrennten Inhalte der **Innovations-** und der **Organisations- bzw. Koordinationsfunktion** angesprochen[35]. Grundlegenderen Charakter hat die Innovationsfunktion, die zwar nicht erstmals von Schumpeter erwähnt wurde[36], die dieser jedoch besonders in den Vordergrund stellt: „Diese wirtschaftliche Führerschaft betätigt sich also an Aufgaben, die sich in folgenden Typen fassen lassen: 1. Die Erzeugung und Durchsetzung neuer Produkte oder neuer Qualitäten von Produkten, 2. Die Einführung neuer Produktionsmethoden, 3. Die Schaffung neuer Organisationen der Industrie (Vertrustung z.B.), 4. Die Erschließung neuer Absatzmärkte, 5. Die Erschließung neuer Bezugsquellen."[37]. Das Durchsetzen von Änderungen wird aber nicht nur in derartig grundlegenden Tätigkeiten spürbar, sondern auch innerhalb des durch diese grundsätzlichen Weichenstellungen vorgegebenen Rahmens durch die „Tätigkeit des Organisators, der Planungen durch Anordnungen und Kontrollen verwirklicht, Mängel abstellt"[38]. Anpassungen an gewandelte Markt- und Umfeldbedingungen sind somit in verschiedener Hinsicht erforderlich, um das Überleben einer Unternehmung sicherzustellen[39]. Ihren Charakter als Ausübung von Unternehmerfunktionen er-

---

[34] Siehe in diesem Sinne auch Schneider (1995), S. 38.

[35] Vgl. Schneider (1995), S. 39ff. Die Trennung findet sich etwa bei Wieandt (1994), S. 20, Windsperger (1991), S. 1414.

[36] Zu den Ursprüngen vgl. Schneider (1995), S. 40f.

[37] Schumpeter (1928), S. 483. Diese Aufzählung, die sich etwas anders strukturiert auch bei Schneider (1995), S. 41, wiederfindet, macht unmittelbar die enge Verbindung der institutionenerhaltenden Funktion nach innen mit der nach außen gerichteten Arbitragefunktion deutlich: Letztlich muß die Erschließung neuer Absatzmärkte ebenso wie die Aufdeckung neuer Bezugsquellen als nach außen, zum Markt hin orientierte Tätigkeit des Unternehmers interpretiert werden, denn beide Teilbereiche der Innovationsfunktion stellen gleichzeitig unmittelbare Beiträge zur Aufdeckung von Arbitragemöglichkeiten dar. Insofern erscheint es wenig sinnvoll, die Innovationsfunktion im Sinne Schumpeters einseitig und vollständig der Unternehmerfunktion des Durchsetzens von Änderungen zu subsumieren. Im folgenden wird der Terminus „Innovationsfunktion" daher anders als bei Schumpeter nur auf die mit der Ausübung der nach innen gerichteten Unternehmerfunktion verbundenen Tätigkeiten bezogen.

[38] Schneider (1995), S. 40.

[39] In diesem Sinne verweist auch Casson (1996), S. 81, darauf, daß Unternehmertum nicht nur für die Gründung einer Unternehmung benötigt wird, sondern auch für deren Erhalt - eben durch flexibles Reagieren auf veränderte Rahmenbedingungen.

halten derartige Tätigkeiten jedoch erst durch das Hinzutreten der wirtschaftlichen Führerschaft, so daß nicht jede Aktivität in einer Unternehmung als Ausübung von Unternehmerfunktionen interpretiert werden kann und darf. Die Trennung in Innovations- und Organisationsfunktion kann dabei wiederum nicht als trennscharf angesehen werden, da auch in diesem Zusammenhang die Übergänge fließend sind[40]: Es fehlt an Kriterien, die eine Einordnung ermöglichen, ob bestimmte Tätigkeiten grundlegenden Charakter (im Sinne der Innovation) oder eher umsetzenden Charakter (im Sinne der Organisation bzw. Koordination) besitzen[41]. Insofern erscheint es zweckmäßig, die institutionenerhaltende Funktion nach innen im Hinblick auf Unternehmungen allgemeiner so zu umschreiben, daß Träger von Unternehmerfunktionen innerhalb der Unternehmung notwendige Änderungen durchsetzen, um den externen Anforderungen des Marktes und des sonstigen Umfeldes Rechnung zu tragen[42]. Weniger sinnvoll erscheint es dagegen häufig, die in Konzepten einzelner Verfasser herausgestellten Funktionen des Unternehmers dieser oder anderen Funktionen in der Schneider'schen Dreiteilung subsumieren zu wollen, was die in den zurückliegenden Ausführungen angesprochenen Abgrenzungsprobleme deutlich gemacht haben mögen.

Festzuhalten bleibt, daß die Lehre von den Unternehmerfunktionen, basierend auf der zentralen Prämisse unvollständigen und ungleich verteilten Wissens, eine umfassende Klammer um die unternehmerischen Tätigkeiten ermöglicht, dabei aber im Sinne der drei genannten Funktionen auch unterschiedliche Betrachtungsweisen bzw. Schwerpunktlegungen erlaubt. Festzuhalten bleibt jedoch auch, daß die drei Funktionen sinnvollerweise nicht dem Versuch unterzogen werden sollten, bestimmte Tätigkeiten innerhalb einer Unternehmung zweifelsfrei der

---

40 Vgl. in diesem Zusammenhang z.B. die weite Fassung der Koordinationsfunktion des Unternehmers bei Casson (1982), zusammengefaßt bei Wieandt (1994), S. 22f. Hier werden wiederum die Nachteile bzw. Unschärfen der angesprochenen Einteilung in Arbitrage-, Innovations- und Koordinationsfunktion deutlich, denn die bei Casson als dem vielleicht zentralen Vetreter der Koordinationsfunktion genannten Tätigkeiten des „Market-making" - siehe die Übersicht bei Wieandt (1994), S. 23 - weisen unübersehbare Parallelitäten zu den beiden anderen Funktionen auf: So dient etwa das Führen von Preisverhandlungen dem Erzielen von Arbitragegewinnen, das Suchen nach Käufern läßt sich als Erschließung neuer Absatzmöglichkeiten im Sinne der Innovationsfunktion einordnen.

41 Die Auffassung von Niman (1991), S. 172, daß der Unternehmer für die notwendigen Veränderungen bestehender Organisationsstrukturen sorgt, während der Manager innerhalb gegebener Organisationsstrukturen agiert, muß daher als nicht nachvollziehbar gelten. Hier ist eher Schneider (1995), S. 32 („Manager heißt eine Person, auf die Unternehmerfunktionen übertragen werden."), zu folgen, der von dieser Gegensätzlichkeit von Unternehmer und Manager in sinnvoller Weise Abstand nimmt.

42 Ähnlich auch die grundlegende Charakterisierung bei Schneider (1995), S. 39. Dennoch wird sich weiter unten zeigen, daß sich ungeachtet dieser Abgrenzungs- bzw. Zuordnungsproblematik eine Unterteilung der unternehmenserhaltenden Funktion nach innen in die beiden Teilfunktionen Innovation und Organisation/Koordination aus Verdeutlichungs- und Anschauungsgründen zumindest vorläufig teilweise anbietet.

ersten, zweiten oder dritten Funktion zuordnen zu wollen. Dieser Versuch muß scheitern und kann weder den praktischen Gegebenheiten in der Unternehmung noch dem Theoriekonzept der Lehre von den Unternehmerfunktionen gerecht werden. Dennoch erschließt sich mit letzteren ein Analysefeld, das im folgenden im Hinblick auf die in diesem Beitrag aufgegriffene Problemstellung weiter zu differenzieren ist.

2.2. Management zentraler Service-Bereiche als Ausübung von Unternehmerfunktionen - eine Zwei-Ebenen-Betrachtung

Der vorliegende Abschnitt dient der Herstellung der Beziehung zwischen dem theoretischen Ansatz der Lehre von den Unternehmerfunktionen zum Management zentraler Service-Bereiche, insbesondere der Frage, wie sich die Ausübung von Unternehmerfunktionen in letzterem wiederfindet.

Der Begriff **Management** hat sich im betriebswirtschaftlichen Sprachgebrauch und Schrifttum durchgesetzt und wird daher aus Gründen der Verständlichkeit der Ausführungen auch in diesem Beitrag verwendet. Inhaltlich verbirgt sich dahinter *„die Tätigkeit des Ausübens von Unternehmerfunktionen in Handlungssystemen“*[43], so auch und vor allem in Unternehmungen[44]. Insofern - und das ist im vorliegenden Zusammenhang von besonderer Bedeutung - läßt sich Management in drei Handlungsbereiche unterteilen, nämlich entsprechend den Unternehmerfunktionen in die Übernahme von Einkommensunsicherheit für andere Personen bzw. Personengruppen, das Streben nach Arbitragegewinnen[45] durch Ausschöpfen von Preisunterschieden auf den externen Märkten sowie das Durchsetzen von Änderungen innerhalb der Unternehmung. Dabei kann ein Manager[46] je nach spezifischer Aufgabenstellung seine

---

43 Schneider (1995), S. 33 (Hervorhebung im Original), der damit das umgangssprachliche Verständnis von Management sinnvoll einengt. Vgl. aber in diesem Zusammenhang auch die grundlegende Kritik an einer „Betriebswirtschaftslehre als angewandte interdisziplinäre Managementwissenschaft“ bei Schneider (1995), S. 140ff. Von einer grundlegenden Diskussion der Zweckmäßigkeit der Begriffe „Management“ und „Manager“ sei an dieser Stelle im Sinne einer im Vordergrund stehenden Auseinandersetzung mit stärker inhaltlich geprägten Aspekten Abstand genommen.

44 Zur Einordnung der Unternehmung als Handlungssystem vgl. Schneider (1995), S. 99.

45 Von „Streben nach“ ist anstelle des „Erzielen von“ Arbitragegewinnen präziser die Rede, denn auch die Manager einer Unternehmung, die Verluste schreibt, üben Unternehmerfunktionen aus. So spricht auch Schneider (1995), z.B. S. 33, teilweise treffender von der „Suche“ nach denn vom „Erzielen“ von Arbitragegewinnen.

46 Manager heißt - wie erwähnt - eine Person, auf die Unternehmerfunktionen übertragen werden; vgl. Schneider (1995), S. 32. Ergänzend sei darauf hingewiesen, daß Unternehmerfunktionen nicht nur durch Einzel-

Arbeitszeit mit unterschiedlichen Schwergewichten auf die einzelnen Unternehmerfunktionen verteilen: Während der Leiter eines Zentralbereiches „Organisation“ überwiegend mit der Funktion des Durchsetzens von Änderungen befaßt ist, obliegt dem Verkaufsleiter vor allem die Erbringung eines Beitrags zur Erzielung von Arbitragegewinnen, indem er mit seinem unternehmerischen Wissen Absatzchancen aufzuspüren und auszunutzen weiß.

Aufbauend auf dieser allgemeinen Charakterisierung des Management-Begriffs läßt sich der im Titel dieses Beitrags verwendete Terminus **wettbewerbsvorteilsorientiertes Management** als das Ausüben von Unternehmerfunktionen mit dem Zweck der Erzielung von Wettbewerbsvorteilen umreißen. Zumindest werden der Aufbau und die Erhaltung von Wettbewerbsfähigkeit als Ziele verfolgt. Beides erscheint jedoch nur möglich, wenn wenigstens zeitweise und partiell Wettbewerbsvorteile erreicht werden. Besonders deutlich wird das Streben nach Wettbewerbsvorteilen in der Arbitragefunktion[47]: Das Aufspüren von Arbitragemöglichkeiten ist verbunden mit der Ansammlung und Ausnutzung von Wissen über Sachverhalte, die für die Gewinnerzielung von hervorgehobener Bedeutung sind. Es wird sich aber zeigen, daß auch die beiden anderen Unternehmerfunktionen bedeutend zur Erzielung von Wettbewerbsvorteilen beitragen können.

Ein solcher **Wettbewerbsvorteil** entsteht dementsprechend als Ergebnis einer im Vergleich zur Konkurrenz erfolgreicheren Ausübung von Unternehmerfunktionen[48]. Nur im Vergleich zur Konkurrenz nämlich läßt sich feststellen, ob ein Wettbewerbsvorteil vorliegt oder nicht[49]. Entscheidend ist dabei allerdings, daß die Kunden diesen Vorteil als solchen wahrnehmen bzw. ihn durch ihre mengen- und/oder preismäßige Abnahmebereitschaft honorieren[50].
Geht man des weiteren davon aus, daß Wettbewerbsvorteile somit aus der im Konkurrenzvergleich besseren bzw. erfolgreicheren Ausübung von Unternehmerfunktionen resultieren, so liegt der Schluß nahe, daß

---

personen, sondern auch durch Gruppen von Individuen wahrgenommen werden können; vgl. Plinke (1995), S. 60.

47 Vgl. dazu auch die Erwähnung des Wettbewerbsvorteils bei Schneider (1995), S. 38.

48 Spezifischer drückt es Casson (1996), S. 61, aus, der nachhaltige Wettbewerbsvorteile als Folge der komparativ besseren Handhabung (Aufdeckung und Ausnutzung) von vorhandenen Informations- bzw. Wissensvorsprüngen einordnet.

49 Vgl. z.B. Plinke (1995), S. 61 i.V.m. S. 68, Porter (1986), S. 31. Backhaus (1992), S. 17, spricht deshalb auch vom „Komparativen Konkurrenzvorteil“; kritisch zu diesem Begriff und seinem Inhalt vgl. aber Plinke (1995), S. 88.

50 Genauer zum Wettbewerbsvorteil vgl. den folgenden Abschnitt 3.1.

1. die **Gelegenheit zum Unternehmertum** (d.h. zur adäquaten Ausübung von Unternehmerfunktionen) für das Management-Personal (verstanden als die Gesamtheit von Personen innerhalb einer Unternehmung, die einzeln oder in Gruppen Unternehmerfunktionen ausüben) eine **notwendige Bedingung** für die Erzielung von Wettbewerbsvorteilen darstellt und
2. die Wettbewerbsvorteile **um so ausgeprägter und dauerhafter ausfallen werden, je besser** die Unternehmungsleitung die einzelnen Glieder der Unternehmung (Personen, Abteilungen, Bereiche) zum Unternehmertum zu befähigen versteht.

Mit anderen Worten werden insbesondere diejenigen Unternehmungen Wettbewerbsvorteile erzielen können, die über eine Unternehmungsleitung verfügen, die besondere Fähigkeiten darin besitzt, **auf einer ersten Stufe** die Ausübung der Unternehmerfunktionen innerhalb ihrer Organisation durch Aufgaben- und Stellenzuweisungen angemessen zu delegieren sowie **auf einer zweiten Stufe** diejenigen, denen Unternehmerfunktionen übertragen wurden, auch zu deren zum Wohle der gesamten Unternehmung erfolgreichen Ausübung zu befähigen[51]. Beide Stufen sind dabei eng miteinander verbunden: Unternehmertum im individuellen Bereich der einzelnen Person fördert das unternehmensweite Unternehmertum und begünstigt damit das Streben nach Wettbewerbsvorteilen[52]. Je erfolgreicher die Unternehmungsleitung unternehmerische Anreize im Hinblick auf nachgelagerte Hierarchieebenen einsetzt, desto besser wird die Gesamtleistung der Unternehmung[53].

Legt man das für die vorliegende Untersuchung ausreichende vereinfachte Unternehmungsmodell zugrunde[54], werden Unternehmerfunktionen insbesondere auf Geschäftsbereiche und Zentralbereiche, speziell zentrale Service-Bereiche, delegiert: Die zentralen Service-Bereiche stellen **Auftragshandelnde der Unternehmungsleitung** dar, die mit speziellen Aufgaben, eben der Erbringung der betreffenden internen Services, betraut werden, verbunden mit der Übertragung der entsprechenden Unternehmerfunktionen. Diese ihnen zugewiesenen Aufgaben sollen die Service-Bereiche im Interesse der Gesamtunternehmung erfüllen, d.h. sie müs-

---

51 Vgl. in diesem Sinne auch Stevenson/Jarillo (1990), S. 24f.

52 Vgl. in diesem Zusammenhang auch die Unterscheidung „between the independent autonomous an the corporate entrepreneur" bei Shils/Zucker (1979), S. 195.

53 In diesem Zusammenhang sei auf das in jüngerer Zeit vermehrt diskutierte Intrapreneurship-Konzept verwiesen, das für Unternehmertum innerhalb der Unternehmung sorgen soll; vgl. dazu etwa Bitzer (1991) sowie die dort angegebene Literatur. Die Bedeutung des Intrapreneurship-Konzeptes für sekundäre Aktivitäten und damit für zentrale Service-Bereiche heben z.B. Nielsen/Peters/Hisrich (1985), S. 182, hervor.

54 Vgl. Kapitel 1. Danach besteht die Unternehmung wie ausgeführt aus Unternehmungsleitung, Geschäftsbereichen und Zentralbereichen.

sen die ihnen obliegenden Unternehmerfunktionen in adäquater Weise wahrnehmen und durch bereichsspezifisches Unternehmertum zum organisationsweiten Unternehmertum beitragen. Auf diese Weise leisten die Service-Bereiche ihren Beitrag zur Erzielung von Wettbewerbsvorteilen.

Aus der Delegation von Unternehmerfunktionen erwächst das Problem des Auftragshandelns als „*die Kernfrage einer Lehre von den Innenbeziehungen einer Organisation schlechthin*“[55]. Bei genauer Betrachtung sind zentrale Service-Bereiche zudem nicht nur Auftragshandelnde der Unternehmungsleitung, sondern auch Auftragshandelnde der Geschäftsbereiche, also **Auftragshandelnde in doppelter Hinsicht**. Während die erste Beziehung durch ein Nach- bzw. Überordnungsverhältnis permanenter Art geprägt ist, findet sich in der zweiten Beziehung jedoch ein Gleichordnungsverhältnis - im Sinne der Abwesenheit von Weisungsbefugnissen einer gegenüber der anderen Seite -, das fallweise im Hinblick auf einzelne Aufträge aktiviert wird, mithin grundsätzlich diskreter Natur ist. Das komplexe Geflecht von Auftragsbeziehungen innerhalb einer Unternehmung wird schon in dem hier verwendeten einfachen Modell deutlich, wenn zudem bedacht wird, daß die Geschäftsbereiche ihrerseits Auftragshandelnde der Unternehmungsleitung sind. Unter Berücksichtigung der Vielzahl von Zentral- und Geschäftsbereichen einer größeren Unternehmung ergibt sich ein oft kaum noch überschaubares Bild[56].

Im Hinblick auf zentrale Service-Bereiche und angesichts ihres Charakters als Auftragshandelnde in doppelter Hinsicht muß die Untersuchung von Gestaltungsansätzen eines wettbewerbsvorteilsorientierten Management zentraler Service-Bereiche zumindest an zwei Stellen - genauer: auf zwei Ebenen - ansetzen. Die Ausübung von Unternehmerfunktionen auf beiden Ebenen ist zu analysieren und zu optimieren. Bei den angesprochenen Ebenen handelt es sich um die folgenden[57]:

- Die **Unternehmungsleitung** übt Unternehmerfunktionen aus der Perspektive der Gesamtunternehmung aus und versucht, für diese Wettbewerbsvorteile zu realisieren. Die Delegation von Unternehmerfunktionen auf nachgelagerte Einheiten, z.B. auf zentrale

---

55 Schneider (1995), S. 49 (Hervorhebung im Original).

56 Dabei sei einmal ganz davon abgesehen, daß sich innerhalb eines Bereiches wiederum verschiedene Personen finden, die mit anderen Personen innerhalb und außerhalb ihres Bereiches ein Auftragsverhältnis verbindet.

57 Auf die vielfältigen Detailprobleme und -anforderungen, die auf beiden Ebenen bewältigt werden müssen, kann im Rahmen dieses Beitrags nicht eingegangen werden. Dies sei nachfolgenden Untersuchungen vorbehalten. Lediglich einige wenige Aspekte werden exemplarisch in diesem und in den folgenden Abschnitten, speziell in Kapitel 4, kurz angesprochen.

Service-Bereiche, muß den Ansprüchen des Strebens nach Wettbewerbsvorteilen für die Gesamtunternehmung genügen: Die Unternehmungsleitung muß die zentralen Service-Bereiche zur wettbewerbsvorteilsorientierten Erfüllung ihrer Aufgaben befähigen. Insofern stellt sich aus der Sicht der Unternehmungsleitung die Frage, wie vorhandene Ressourcen und Kompetenzen optimal auf die nachgelagerten Ebenen verteilt werden sollten bzw. welche Ressourcen und Kompetenzen bei der Leitung verbleiben sollten. Die Gestaltung adäquater Anreiz- und Kontrollmechanismen, die die Ausübung der Unternehmerfunktionen auf allen Ebenen plan-, steuer- und kontrollierbar machen, stellt in diesem Zusammenhang eine zentrale Frage dar. Im vorliegenden Kontext interessiert dabei speziell der Aspekt der Schaffung entsprechender Instrumentarien im Hinblick auf zentrale Service-Bereiche[58].

- Die **zentralen Service-Bereiche** selbst bilden die zweite Untersuchungsebene. Sie leisten mit der Ausübung der ihnen übertragenen Unternehmerfunktionen einen Beitrag zum organisationsweiten Unternehmertum, sind in diesem Zusammenhang aber auch bemüht, durch diesen Beitrag ihre eigene Existenz zu sichern. Insofern müssen die zentralen Service-Bereiche ihren Blick auf die Frage richten, wie sie sich mit ihrem Service-Angebot gegenüber alternativen Formen der Bedarfsdeckung[59] behaupten und auf diese Art einen - wenn man so will - „internen Wettbewerbsvorteil" erzielen können.

Will man diesen Begriff verwenden, finden sich auf beiden Ebenen **interne Märkte**[60], die gestaltet werden müssen: Die Unternehmungsleitung ist Anbieter auf einem internen Markt für Ressourcen und Kompetenzen, auf dem Geschäftsbereiche und Zentralbereiche als Nach-

---

58 Für dieses spezielle Problem sind Konzepte bisher allenfalls in Ansätzen vorhanden. Allerdings gibt es eine Vielzahl allgemeinerer Überlegungen im Hinblick auf Steuerungs- und Lenkungsmechanismen, insbesondere auch Anreizsysteme, deren Überprüfung für die vorliegenden Zwecke im Detail noch aussteht; vgl. etwa zum Überblick Becker (1995), Sp. 34ff., Küpper (1991), S. 175ff., Küpper (1995), Sp. 1595ff. Speziell zu agencytheoretischen Ansätzen vgl. Breid (1995), S. 821ff.

59 Zu nennen sind hier insbesondere der externe Bezug der Services durch die Geschäftsbereiche als potentielle Kunden der Zentralbereiche, aber auch das Make durch die Geschäftsbereiche unter Einsatz ihrer eigenen Kapazitäten; vgl. auch Witt (1988), S. 77ff., sowie Abschnitt 3.1.

60 Die Existenzberechtigung des Terminus „interner Markt" ist allerdings - darauf sei ausdrücklich hingewiesen - umstritten. Legt man etwa der Suche nach dem optimalen Transaktionsdesign die Alternativen „Markt **oder** Hierarchie (bzw. Unternehmung)" zugrunde, kann es Märkte innerhalb von Unternehmungen prinzipiell nicht geben; auf dieser Ausgangsfragestellung basieren insbesondere ältere Transaktionskostenbetrachtungen, kritisch dazu vgl. z.B. Schneider (1985), S. 1237ff. Andere Quellen wiederum betonen die Notwendigkeit der Schaffung von Marktbedingungen u.a. für interne Services, wollen externe Marktbedingungen so weit wie möglich auf innerbetriebliche Austauschbeziehungen übertragen wissen und verwenden den Begriff des internen Marktes explizit; vgl. z.B. Davis (1991), S. 6, Magidson/Polcha (1992), S. 37, Schütz (1993), S. 195. Auch im Bereich der ökonomischen Theorie findet der Begriff Verwendung, z.B. bei Casson (1982), S. 187. Letztlich handelt es sich hier ausschließlich um ein terminologisches Problem, denn inhaltlich besteht weitgehend Einigkeit bezüglich der relevanten Sachverhalte: Es sind jeweils Austauschprozesse zu beobachten, an denen Anbieter und Nachfrager beteiligt sind und in denen Leistung und Gegenleistung einander gegenüberstehen.

frager agieren. Beide Seiten sind daran interessiert, ein für sich möglichst günstiges Ergebnis zu erzielen: Die Unternehmungsleitung möchte die Ressourcen und Kompetenzen denjenigen Nachfragen zugänglich machen, die diese am besten zum Wohl der Unternehmung einzusetzen wissen; die nachfragenden Einheiten sind bestrebt, ihre Vorstellungen hinsichtlich der optimalen Ressourcen- und Kompetenzausstattung zu verwirklichen, um ihren spezifischen Zielen nachgehen zu können. Eine weitere Form interner Märkte sieht die zentralen Service-Bereiche als Anbieter ihrer Dienstleistungen, die Nachfrage wird durch die Geschäftsbereiche repräsentiert. Auf diesen internen Märkten finden sich allerdings vielfach auch externe Konkurrenten, nämlich immer dann, wenn die Geschäftsbereiche die Möglichkeit des externen Bezugs der betreffenden Services haben.

Die Delegation von Unternehmerfunktionen bzw. das Auftragshandeln sorgen daher dafür, daß im Hinblick auf zentrale Service-Bereiche zwei Ebenen von Wettbewerbsvorteilen relevant sind: solche auf externen Märkten aus der Perspektive der Gesamtunternehmung bzw. der für diese verantwortlichen Unternehmungsleitung und solche auf internen Märkten aus dem Blickwinkel der zentralen Service-Bereiche bzw. deren Managern[61] . Beide Sorten von Wettbewerbsvorteilen werden durch das Ausüben von Unternehmerfunktionen ermöglicht. Für eine tiefergehende Analyse ist das Phänomen des Wettbewerbsvorteils allerdings weiter zu präzisieren.

61 Damit sind die internen Absatzmärkte für die erbrachten Services gemeint, nicht die internen Märkte für Ressourcen und Kompetenzen, da deren Bedeutung für die Suche nach Wettbewerbsvorteilen hier der Ebene der Unternehmungsleitung zuzurechnen ist.

3. Zentrale Service-Bereiche und Wettbewerbsvorteile - Gestaltungsfelder auf der Basis der Ausübung von Unternehmerfunktionen

3.1. Arten von Wettbewerbsvorteilen im Kontext zentraler Service-Bereiche

Im vorhergehenden Abschnitt wurde herausgearbeitet, daß die Erzielung von Wettbewerbsvorteilen im Hinblick auf das Management zentraler Service-Bereiche auf zwei Ebenen untersucht werden muß: auf externen Märkten, auf denen die Unternehmung für sich nach Wettbewerbsvorteilen strebt, und auf internen Märkten, auf denen die zentralen Service-Bereiche nach der Erzielung von Wettbewerbsvorteilen gegenüber ihren internen Konkurrenten streben. Unabhängig von der Betrachtungsebene sind jedoch zunächst verschiedene Arten von Wettbewerbsvorteilen zu differenzieren.

Prinzipiell lassen sich gemäß Abb. 4 zwei Arten von Wettbewerbsvorteilen unterscheiden, die ein Anbieter in Relation zu seinen Konkurrenten realisieren kann[62] :

- **Kostenvorteile** realisiert ein Anbieter, wenn er ein vergleichbares Produkt (oder allgemeiner: eine vergleichbare Leistung) zu geringeren Kosten hervorbringen kann als seine Wettbewerber. Diese Art des Wettbewerbsvorteils wird auch als **Anbietervorteil** bezeichnet, da sie aus der Betrachtung der Kostensituationen verschiedener Anbieter resultiert und die Wahrnehmung der Nachfrager zunächst vernachlässigt bzw. diese nur mittelbar berücksichtigt.

- **Nettonutzenvorteile** äußern sich auf der Nachfragerseite und werden daher auch als **Kundenvorteile** bezeichnet. Diese entstehen, wenn ein Nachfrager der Leistung eines bestimmten Anbieters eine günstigere Kosten- (genauer: Preis-)/Nutzen-Relation beimißt als den konkurrierenden Leistungen anderer Anbieter.

---

62 Vgl. dazu Plinke (1995), S. 61ff., der eine verbreitete Einteilung, die in ähnlicher Form bei Porter (1986), S. 31, zur Systematisierung unterschiedlicher Wettbewerbsstrategien Verwendung findet, aufgreift und differenziert auch formal ausarbeitet. Im Rahmen des vorliegenden Beitrags erfolgt eine Beschränkung auf die wesentlichen Sachverhalte.

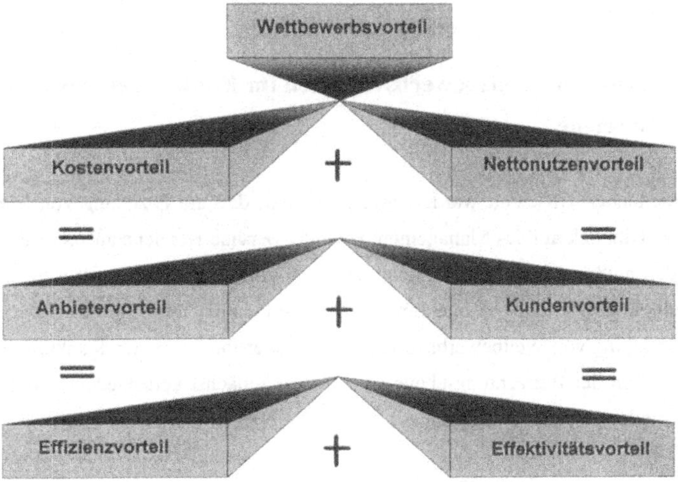

Abb. 4: Arten des Wettbewerbsvorteils

Quelle: nach Plinke (1995), S. 76ff.

Kostenvorteil und Nettonutzenvorteil zusammengenommen machen den Wettbewerbsvorteil aus. Dieser läßt sich, wie Abb. 4 gleichfalls zeigt, auf zwei zentrale ökonomische Größen zurückführen: Effektivität und Effizienz[63] :

- **Effektivität** wird demnach verstanden als externes Leistungsmaß, das angibt, inwieweit eine Unternehmung den Erwartungen und Ansprüchen ihrer Kunden gerecht wird.

---

[63] Vgl. Plinke (1995), S. 85. Dieser Begrifflichkeit hinsichtlich Effektivität und Effizienz wird im weiteren gefolgt. Allerdings bedarf es an dieser Stelle des Hinweises, daß Plinke mit Effektivität und Effizienz zwei Begriffe heranzieht, die in der ökonomischen Literatur außerordentlich vielfältig verwendet werden und die Gegenstand vieler wissenschaftlicher Abhandlungen waren und sind. Da es hier keinesfalls weiterführend wäre, diese Diskussion aufzugreifen und zu vertiefen, sei lediglich zum Überblick verwiesen auf Bohr (1993), Sp. 855ff., Scholz (1992), Sp. 533ff., Strehl (1985), S. 499ff. Für das Marketing hebt die Bedeutung von Effektivität und Effizienz als Zielgrößen bereits Kotler (1972), S. 50, hervor. Etwas anders verwendet die Begriffe - in Anlehnung an Barnard (1938) - Meyer (1995), S. 45f. Dort wird zwischen Effektivität als Ziel der Unternehmungsorganisation und Effizienz als Ziel der internen Mitarbeiter unterschieden (diese Einteilung wird später, S. 144, übertragen auf Netzwerkorganisationen, worauf an dieser Stelle nicht einzugehen ist).

- **Effizienz** ist im Unterschied dazu als internes Leistungsmaß zu interpretieren, das das Verhältnis von Output zu Input angibt.

Die Arten des Wettbewerbsvorteils können einzeln (Effektivitäts- oder Effizienzvorteile), gemeinsam (Effektivitäts- und Effizienzvorteile) oder gar nicht (weder Effektivitäts- noch Effizienzvorteile) auftreten. Je nach Ausprägung der beiden Arten ergibt sich insgesamt ein unterschiedlich großer Wettbewerbsvor- oder -nachteil[64]. Insbesondere läßt sich der Kostenvorteil auch in einen Nettonutzenvorteil umsetzen, wenn nämlich die Kostenvorteile des Anbieters über Preisvorteile ganz oder teilweise an die Nachfrager weitergegeben werden.

Diese beiden Arten von Wettbewerbsvorteilen, die hinsichtlich ihrer Entstehung und Ausgestaltung an dieser Stelle ebensowenig näher analysiert werden sollen wie im Hinblick auf mögliche detailliertere Unterteilungen[65], sind für die Zwecke der vorliegenden Untersuchung ergänzend hinsichtlich ihres Geltungsbereiches (externer oder interner Markt[66]) zu untersuchen, d.h. der Blick auf mögliche Wettbewerbsvorteile muß sowohl aus der Perspektive der Gesamtunternehmung[67] als auch aus derjenigen des betreffenden zentralen Service-Bereichs erfolgen. Es ergibt sich dann die in Abb. 5 dokumentierte Systematik.

Die Matrix rastert grob die grundlegenden Ansatzpunkte für ein wettbewerbsvorteilsorientiertes Management zentraler Service-Bereiche. Bevor dieses Konzept im folgenden Abschnitt vertieft und verfeinert wird, seien die einzelnen Felder kurz erläutert:

---

64 Ergänzend und der Abrundung halber sei an dieser Stelle angemerkt, daß Plinke (1995), S. 68, Kostenunterschiede auf Potential- und Prozeßunterschiede der Anbieter zurückführt, Nettonutzenunterschiede dagegen primär auf Programmunterschiede, die allerdings durch Potential- und Prozeßunterschiede unterstützt werden. Interessant ist in diesem Zusammenhang die ressourcenorientierte Perspektive, die sich etwa bei Hunt/Morgan (1996), S. 109, findet: Hier werden - bei expliziter Erwähnung - beide Arten von Wettbewerbsvorteilen (oder gegebenenfalls auch Wettbewerbsnachteilen) im Sinne der ressourcenorientierten Unternehmungsführung auf die Ressourcen der Organisation zurückgeführt. Damit kommt den Potentialen eine deutlich exponiertere Bedeutung zu als bei Plinke.

65 Vgl. in diesem Zusammenhang auch Day/Wensley (1988), S. 1ff., Simon (1988), S. 461ff.

66 Vgl. zur Herleitung dieser Unterscheidung Abschnitt 2.2.

67 Die Perspektive der Gesamtunternehmung schließt dabei den Sachverhalt mit ein, daß die Wettbewerbsvorteile im Regelfall nicht für die gesamte Unternehmung gelten, sondern durch die einzelnen Geschäftsbereiche in bestimmten Geschäftsfeldern realisiert werden - im Interesse und zum Nutzen der Gesamtunternehmung.

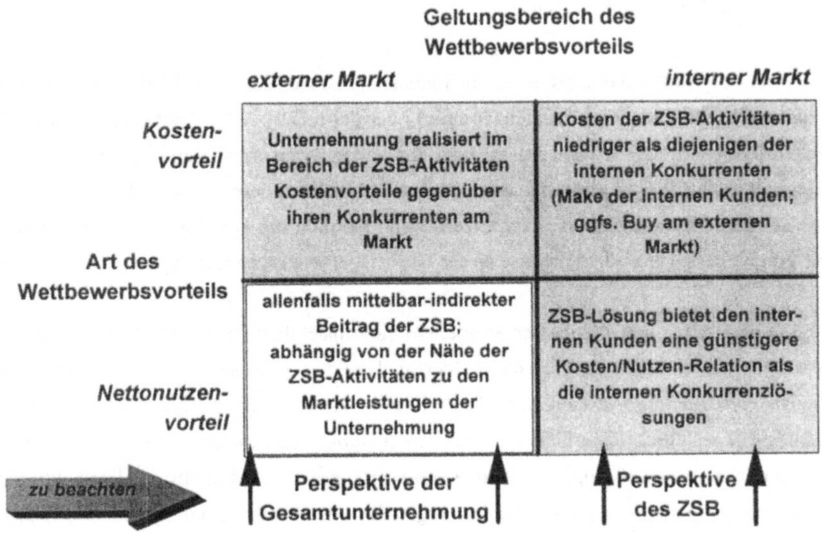

Abb. 5: Das Wettbewerbsvorteils-"Spielfeld" der zentralen Service-Bereiche

- **Kostenvorteile am externen Markt** können mit Hilfe zentraler Service-Bereiche entstehen, wenn die Zentralbereiche die betreffenden Services zu Kosten erbringen, die niedriger sind als die Kosten, die die externe Konkurrenz für die Selbsterstellung oder den Fremdbezug der betreffenden Services aufbringen muß. Ein solcher Vorteil ist etwa dann gegeben, wenn ein zentraler Service-Bereich im Konkurrenzvergleich zwischen zwei Industriebetrieben kostengünstigere Fuhrparkleistungen anbieten kann.

- **Nettonutzenvorteile am externen Markt** sind für die Unternehmung über das Management zentraler Service-Bereiche allenfalls mittelbar realisierbar, denn der Charakter der internen Services bringt es mit sich, daß diese nicht unmittelbar gegenüber dem Kunden erbracht werden, so daß dieser deren relatives Niveau im Konkurrenzvergleich nicht direkt wahrnehmen kann. Je nach der Enge des Bezugs der internen Services zu den Marktleistungen der Unternehmung ergeben sich allerdings unterschiedliche Intensitäten des Einwirkens zentraler Service-Bereiche auf das Erzielen von externen Nettonutzenvorteilen. So fördern etwa zeitlich zuverlässige innerbetriebliche Transporte die Möglichkeit der pünkt-

lichen Bereitstellung einer Leistung für den Kunden und damit letztlich indirekt auch dessen Zufriedenheit mit der Leistung. Ebenso ist vorstellbar, daß eine besonders eingehende und qualitativ hochwertige Marktforschungsstudie in außerordentlich bedarfsgerechte Produkte umgesetzt wird, die zu Nettonutzenvorteilen führen.

- **Kostenvorteile auf seinen internen Absatzmärkten** kann ein zentraler Service-Bereich dann erzielen, wenn er seine Services im Konkurrenzvergleich kostengünstiger erstellen kann, d.h. die Kosten der Service-Bereiche müssen sowohl unter denen der internen Selbsterstellung durch die Geschäftsbereiche als auch unter denen der am externen Markt (insbesondere durch spezialisierte Dienstleister) angebotenen Services liegen. Im Falle des Fuhrparkbeispiels bedeutet das z.B., daß kein am externen Markt tätiger Spediteur einen Transport kostengünstiger erbringen kann als der zentrale Service-Bereich.

- **Interne Nettonutzenvorteile** schließlich realisiert ein zentraler Service-Bereich dann, wenn er seinen internen Nachfragern (also den Geschäftsbereichen) in deren Augen eine gegenüber den genannten Konkurrenzformen günstigere Preis-/Nutzen-Relation zu bieten vermag. Dabei lassen sich die Kostenvorteile wiederum durchaus in Nettonutzenvorteile umsetzen. Nettonutzenvorteile realisiert ein zentraler Marktforschungsbereich etwa dann, wenn er sein spezifisches Wissen einsetzt, um eine exakt auf den auftraggebenden Geschäftsbereich zugeschnittene Studie zu erstellen, die diesem kein externer Anbieter zu einem vergleichbaren Preis hätte bieten können und zu deren Erstellung der Geschäftsbereich auch selbst nicht in der Lage gewesen wäre.

Im folgenden ist zu zeigen, wie diese unterschiedlichen Wettbewerbsvorteile mit Hilfe der Ausübung der Unternehmerfunktionen angestrebt werden können.

3.2. Idealtypische Systematisierung der Gestaltungsfelder eines wettbewerbsvorteilsorientierten Management zentraler Service-Bereiche

Die sich aus den bisherigen Überlegungen ergebende Kernfrage lautet: **Auf welche Art und Weise kann die Ausübung der einzelnen Unternehmerfunktionen zur Realisierung von Wettbewerbsvorteilen auf beiden Gestaltungsebenen - auf externen wie auf internen Märkten - beitragen?**

Es ist somit zu untersuchen, inwiefern die Ausübung von Unternehmerfunktionen als Ansatz und Voraussetzung der Erzielung der verschiedenen aufgezeigten Formen von Wettbewerbsvorteilen betrachtet werden kann. Dabei wird im folgenden als Analyseschema die in Abb. 6 wiedergegebene Sechzehn-Felder-Matrix verwendet und zur Diskussion gestellt.

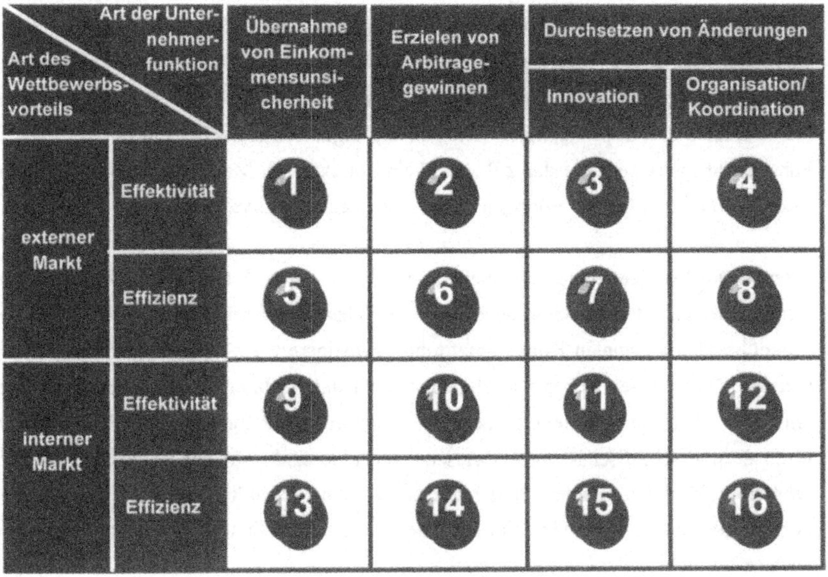

Abb. 6: Idealtypische Gestaltungsfelder des wettbewerbsvorteilsorientierten Management zentraler Service-Bereiche

Die Basisannahme, die dieser Einteilung zugrunde liegt, ist, daß mit der Ausübung jeder der Unternehmerfunktionen die Möglichkeit besteht, einen mehr oder weniger großen Beitrag zur Erzielung jeder Art von Wettbewerbsvorteil zu leisten. Es wird im folgenden deutlich werden, daß diese potentiellen Beiträge sich im Einzelfall sehr stark unterscheiden können, die Grundannahme bleibt davon jedoch unberührt. Insofern handelt es sich um eine Verfeinerung der im Laufe dieses Beitrags herausgearbeiteten Aussage, daß Wettbewerbsvorteile dann erzielt werden, wenn Unternehmerfunktionen besser ausgeübt werden als durch die Konkurrenz bzw. daß Wettbewerbsvorteile das Resultat der im Konkurrenzvergleich erfolgreicheren Ausübung von Unternehmerfunktionen sind.

Jedes der sechzehn Felder repräsentiert eine Wettbewerbsvorteils-/Unternehmerfunktions-Kombination[68]. Allerdings sei deutlich darauf hingewiesen, daß die Abbildung nicht den Eindruck vermitteln soll, als seien die einzelnen Felder jeweils völlig isoliert voneinander zu betrachten. Im Gegenteil: Die Tatsache, daß die Unternehmerfunktionen wie ausgeführt in einem Über-/Unterordnungsverhältnis zueinander stehen, macht eine derartige Isolierung ebenso unmöglich wie der Sachverhalt, daß insbesondere Effizienz- in Effektivitätsvorteile umgesetzt werden können. Zudem soll das Streben nach internen Wettbewerbsvorteilen durch die zentralen Service-Bereiche bekanntlich im Sinne eines organisationsweiten Unternehmertums auch zur Erzielung externer Wettbewerbsvorteile beitragen[69]. Insofern steht das Streben nach internen Wettbewerbsvorteilen in einer Mittel-Ziel-Beziehung zum Hinarbeiten auf externe Wettbewerbsvorteile.

Unter Berücksichtigung der genannten Zusammenhänge sind Interdependenzen und Überschneidungen zwischen den Gestaltungsfeldern nicht nur unvermeidbar, sondern im Sinne eines abgestimmten Management ist deren explizite Beachtung und Nutzung sogar zwingend erforderlich. Im folgenden wird zu zeigen sein, daß einzelne Management-Maßnahmen regelmäßig mehrere Felder betreffen, daß die Matrix aber dennoch ein Instrumentarium darstellt, mit dessen Hilfe diese Maßnahmen systematisiert und vor einem theoretischen Hintergrund eingeordnet und erklärt werden können. Die betreffenden Maßnahmen dienen der Konkretisierung der Ausübung der Unternehmerfunktionen bzw. deren Umsetzung in praktisches Handeln. Sie tragen gleichzeitig zur Erfüllung der eher allgemein formulierten Unternehmerfunktionen mit betriebswirtschaftlichem „Leben“ bei und unterstützen somit die Nutzbarkeit dieses theoretischen Konzeptes für praktische Probleme der Unternehmungsführung.

Prinzipiell ist im Hinblick auf einen bestimmten zentralen Service-Bereich zu überprüfen, ob die Ausfüllung der einzelnen Gestaltungsfelder mit konkreten Maßnahmen dazu beitragen kann, daß die potentiellen Wettbewerbsvorteile aufgedeckt, erschlossen und ausgeschöpft werden können - oder ob dies möglicherweise sogar schon geschehen ist. **Es ist zu analysieren, ob und in welcher Form mit welcher Unternehmerfunktion ein Beitrag zu welcher Art von Wettbewerbsvorteil möglich ist.** Stellt sich dabei heraus, daß der betreffende Service-Bereich über keine oder keine ausreichenden Wettbewerbsvorteilspotentiale verfügt, die

---

68 Dabei wurde im Hinblick auf das Durchsetzen von Änderungen trotz der in Abschnitt 2.1. aufgezeigten Abgrenzungsprobleme die Unterscheidung in Innovations- und Organisations- bzw. Koordinationsfunktion berücksichtigt, da auf diese Weise detailliertere Aussagen ermöglicht werden.

69 Vgl. hierzu Stevenson/Jarillo (1990), S. 24f., aber auch die in Abschnitt 4.2. angestellten Überlegungen zum internen Marketing.

ausgeschöpft werden können, ist er aufgrund seiner Unterlegenheit gegenüber alternativen Lösungen (z.B. externer Zukauf des Service) zu eliminieren. Ansonsten sind die betreffenden Maßnahmen zur Ausschöpfung und Absicherung der Wettbewerbsvorteile sowohl durch die Unternehmungsleitung im Hinblick auf den externen Markt als auch durch das Management des zentralen Service-Bereichs im Hinblick auf die internen Märkte einzuleiten.

Maßnahmen der Unternehmungsleitung zielen somit unmittelbar auf die Gestaltungsfelder 1 bis 8 ab, bedeuten aber gleichzeitig eine Weichenstellung für die Felder 9 bis 16, auf die die Maßnahmen der zentralen Service-Bereiche primär ausgerichtet sind; letztere wirken sich aber mittelbar auch wiederum auf die erstgenannten Gestaltungefelder aus, wie sich unten zeigen wird. Im folgenden nämlich wird zu jedem der sechzehn Felder **ein knappes Beispiel** gegeben, welche Art von Maßnahme der Ausfüllung des betreffenden Gestaltungsfeldes dienen könnte, ohne daß dabei ein Anspruch auf Vollständigkeit oder Repräsentativität erhoben werden soll oder kann:

- **Feld 1**: Durch die Ausgestaltung der Arbeitsverträge mit den Zentralbereichsmitarbeitern hat die Unternehmungsleitung die Möglichkeit, durch Übernahme von Einkommensunsicherheit besonders qualifizierte Kräfte an sich zu binden und damit die Basis für Effektivitätsvorteile zu schaffen.

- **Feld 2**: Die Erbringung qualifizierter Marktforschungsleistungen durch einen Zentralbereich ermöglicht der Unternehmung die Erstellung besonders bedarfsgerechter Produkte, für die am Markt Arbitragegewinne erzielt werden können. Aufgabe der Unternehmungsleitung ist es, die Voraussetzungen eines entsprechenden Einsatzes der Marktforschung zu schaffen.

- **Feld 3**: Durch die Umstrukturierung, Elimination und Neuschaffung von Service-Bereichen kann die Unternehmungsleitung eine bedarfsgerechtere Leistungserstellung unterstützen.

- **Feld 4**: Die Unternehmungsleitung sorgt für eine bedarfsgerechtere Leistungserstellung, indem sie adäquate Koordinationsmechanismen, z.B. Verrechnungspreismodelle, für die zentralen Service-Bereiche einsetzt und deren Funktionieren überwacht.

- **Feld 5**: Durch die vertragliche Bindung der Arbeitskräfte sichert die Unternehmungsleitung sich eine im Konkurrenzvergleich kostengünstigere Erbringung der zentralen Services.

- **Feld 6**: Die zentralen Service-Bereiche erbringen die Services kostengünstiger als es in Konkurrenzunternehmen der Fall ist. Auf Basis dieser Kostenvorteile erhöhen sich die Gewinnpotentiale der Unternehmung.

- **Feld 7**: Die Unternehmungsleitung beschließt die Eliminierung eines zentralen Service-Bereichs, da sich die externe Beschaffung der betreffenden Leistungen als kostengünstiger herausgestellt hat.

- **Feld 8**: Die Unternehmungsleitung setzt Mechanismen ein, die die Kostengünstigkeit der zentralen Service-Bereiche überwachen helfen, z.B. entsprechende Controlling-Instrumente.

- **Feld 9**: Zentraler Service-Bereich und Geschäftsbereich arbeiten zusammen und nehmen sich dadurch gegenseitig einen Teil ihrer Einkommensunsicherheit ab. Aus der engen Zusammenarbeit resultiert für den Zentralbereich die Möglichkeit, besonders bedarfsgerechte Lösungen für seinen internen Kunden anzubieten.

- **Feld 10**: Der zentrale Service-Bereich „vermarktet" seine Leistungen erfolgreich und erzielt entsprechende Erfolge.

- **Feld 11**: Innerhalb eines Zentralbereichs werden neue Services entwickelt, die auf die Bedürfnisse der internen Kunden besser zugeschnitten sind als verfügbare Konkurrenzangebote.
- **Feld 12**: Innerhalb des Service-Bereiches wird die kundenorientierte Erstellung der Leistungen überwacht und koordiniert.

- **Feld 13**: Durch die längerfristige Zusammenarbeit im Zuge der gegenseitigen Übernahme von Einkommensunsicherheit entstehen kundenspezifische Lerneffekte beim zentralen Service-Bereich, in deren Folge die Kosten sinken und unter denen interner oder externer Alternativlösungen liegen.

- **Feld 14**: Durch Kostensenkungsbemühungen kann der zentrale Service-Bereich seine Arbitragemöglichkeiten verbessern.

- **Feld 15**: Innerhalb des zentralen Service-Bereichs werden kostengünstigere Leistungsprozesse entwickelt und eingesetzt.

- **Feld 16**: Die Führung des zentralen Service-Bereiches überwacht die Einhaltung von Kostenvorgaben und greift gegebenenfalls regulierend ein.

Es hat sich gezeigt, daß die Anknüpfungspunkte des Management zwar nicht für alle Gestaltungsfelder als gleichwertig bzw. gleich offensichtlich anzusehen sind, daß jedoch für jedes der Felder zumindest Ansatzpunkte zu erkennen sind, was möglicherweise als Hinweis auf die Tragfähigkeit des hier vorgestellten Systematisierungsansatzes gewertet werden kann[70]. Eine intensivere Auseinandersetzung mit dieser Problematik soll allerdings späteren, tiefergehenden Untersuchungen vorbehalten bleiben. Um die sich bietenden Möglichkeiten etwas plastischer zu machen, seien im folgenden Kapitel 4 lediglich drei Beispiele herausgegriffen, an Hand derer zumindest ansatzweise detailliertere Gestaltungsmöglichkeiten angedeutet werden sollen. Dabei werden jeweils mehrere Gestaltungsfelder zusammengefaßt, um den aufgezeigten Interdependenzen Rechnung zu tragen. Oder anders gesagt: Konzepte zur Umsetzung der Unternehmerfunktionen in konkretes Handeln werden mit Hilfe der in Abb. 6 aufgespannten Matrix hinsichtlich ihrer wettbewerblichen Stoßrichtung positioniert und strukturiert.

---

[70] Möglicherweise bietet es sich zukünftig an, so etwas wie eine Hierarchie der einzelnen Felder herauszuarbeiten und auch abbildungstechnisch zu berücksichtigen, die Ziel-Mittel-Beziehungen bzw. Über-/Unterordnungs-Verhältnisse aufgreift und dokumentiert. Davon sei jedoch in diesem vergleichsweise frühen Stadium der Überlegungen zunächst noch abgesehen.

4. Von der Konzeption zur Anwendung: ausgewählte Beispiele zur inhaltlichen Umsetzung der Gestaltungsfelder

4.1. Beispiel 1: Ausstattung eines zentralen Service-Bereichs mit Verfügungsmöglichkeiten über Ressourcen und Kompetenzen

Dieses Beispiel betrifft vor allem die Felder 3 und 7 in Abb. 6. Es geht um die Ausstattung eines Service-Bereichs mit Personal und sonstigen Ressourcen sowie um die Kompetenzen, die dem Bereich hinsichtlich der Verfügungsmöglichkeiten über diese Ressourcen eingeräumt werden sollten. Insofern steht in diesem Zusammenhang die Entscheidung an, in welchem Umfang das Service- bzw. Wettbewerbsmodell in seiner reinen Form tatsächlich realisiert werden soll. Diese Ausstattung mit Ressourcen und Kompetenzen fällt in den Bereich der Unternehmerfunktion des Durchsetzens von Änderungen, speziell in den Bereich der Innovationsfunktion[71].

Mit der Schaffung von Verfügungsmöglichkeiten für die zentralen Service-Bereiche zwangsläufig einhergehend, legt die Unternehmungsleitung Regelungen für Anreiz- und Kontrollmechanismen fest. Insbesondere Mitarbeitern, die über einzigartige Informationen bzw. spezifische Kenntnisse verfügen, muß die Unternehmungsleitung Anreize bieten, die sicherstellen, daß die entsprechenden Kenntnisse innerhalb der Unternehmung genutzt werden können und die im Hinblick auf ihr Wissen als Unternehmer agierenden Mitarbeiter[72] dieses Wissen nicht außerhalb der Unternehmung und gegebenenfalls zu deren Nachteil einsetzen. Insofern müssen die internen unternehmerischen Anreize für derartige Mitarbeiter mindestens so groß sein wie auf dem externen Markt[73]. Daher bietet sich das Service- bzw. Wettbewerbsmodell of-

---

71 Es handelt sich hier gleichsam um eine Spezialform des von Schumpeter (1928), S. 483, genannten Falls der Schaffung neuer Organisationen.

72 Ähnlich wie Schneider (1995), S. 31, sieht Casson (1982), S. 259, die Individuen als Unternehmer ihres Wissens.

73 In dieser Weise argumentiert Casson (1982), S. 258f. Damit befindet er sich in einem gewissen Konflikt mit den üblichen Aussagen vieler Vertreter des Transaktionskostenansatzes. Diese sehen bei hoher Spezifität - und die liegt im Falle dieser besonderen Kenntnisse der Mitarbeiter, die auch in einzigartige Leistungen münden können, vor - prinzipiell marktferne Einbindungsformen als adäquat an; vgl. z.B. Picot (1991), S. 346. Casson, der in seinen Überlegungen selbst auf die Minimierung von Koordinationskosten abstellt, vgl. dazu auch Wieandt (1994), S. 22, und einen Brückenschlag zwischen Transaktionskostenüberlegungen und Unternehmerfunktionen versucht, betont dagegen die Notwendigkeit der Schaffung marktähnlicher Bedingungen innerhalb der Unternehmung im Falle des Vorliegens spezifischer Informationen bei den betreffenden Mitarbeitern. Handelt es sich dagegen um standardisierte Routine-Informationen, hält er derartige unternehmerische Anreize für weniger bedeutsam; siehe Casson (1982), S. 259. Siehe aber in diesem Zusammenhang auch die aktuellen Überlegungen zu den Transaktionskostenwirkungen der sogenannten „Modularisierung“ der Unternehmung bei Picot/Reichwald/Wigand (1996), S. 234ff.

fenbar gerade für solche Services an, für deren Erstellung spezielle Kenntnisse erforderlich sind, die sich nicht problemlos anderweitig extern am Markt finden lassen. Ähnliche Empfehlungen zum „Hereinholen des Marktes in die Unternehmung" lassen sich auch aus allgemeineren Überlegungen zur Schaffung neuartiger Organisationsformen ableiten[74]. Im Hinblick auf standardisierte Leistungen, für die keine besonderen Kenntnisse erforderlich sind, kommt dagegen auch im Bereich der internen Services der Fremdbezug als naheliegende Alternative in Betracht, da die Unternehmung - bzw. ihre Mitarbeiter - über keine spezifischen Fähigkeiten verfügt, die sich in Leistungsvorteile umsetzen lassen.

Ein wichtiger Aspekt in diesem Zusammenhang ist, daß ein angemessenes Gleichgewicht zwischen den Koordinations- und Motivationswirkungen der Ausstattung der Service-Bereiche gefunden wird. Gerade beim Service- bzw. Wettbewerbsmodell nämlich muß davon ausgegangen werden, daß es zwar die Motivation der betreffenden Mitarbeiter fördert, daß die unternehmensweite Koordination aber erschwert wird[75].

Entsprechend dem Grad an Notwendigkeit der Schaffung unternehmerischer Freiräume für die Service-Bereiche muß die Unternehmungsleitung aus dem grundsätzlich verfügbaren Spektrum betriebswirtschaftlicher Steuerungs- und Lenkungsmechanismen organisationsinterner Kooperation auswählen[76]. Abb. 7 gibt einen charakterisierenden Überblick über wichtige Verfahren, der deutlich macht, daß Profit-Center-Systeme[77] - mit sehr deutlichen Abstrichen auch bis zu einem gewissen Grade Lenkungspreissysteme[78] - marktähnliche Verhältnisse simulieren helfen.

---

74 Vgl. stellvertretend Frese/von Werder (1994), S. 6ff., bei deren Kennzeichnung der Gestaltungsprinzipien aktueller Reorganisationen die Schaffung marktähnlicher Verhältnisse eine große Rolle spielt.

75 Vgl. Frese/von Werder (1993), S. 24ff., Kreisel (1995), S. 145ff. Dort ist jeweils von „Koordinations- und Motivationseffizienz" die Rede. Diese organisationstheoretischen Begriffe werden hier allerdings nicht verwendet, um Unschärfen gegenüber der Effizienz als Art des Wettbewerbsvorteils zu vermeiden. Eine intensivere Auseinandersetzung mit dem Effizienzbegriff, als sie Gegenstand der vorliegenden Untersuchung sein kann, wird sich allerdings auch mit dieser Fragestellung beschäftigen müssen.

76 Vgl. zu einem differenzierten Überblick über wichtige Verfahren Küpper (1991), S. 175ff. Vgl. aber auch Connell (1996), S. 56.

77 Vgl. dazu z.B. Frese (1990), S. 137ff., Neuhof (1982), S. 11ff., Schweitzer (1992), Sp. 2078ff. Zu einer Kurzcharakterisierung unterschiedlicher „Center-Konzepte" vgl. Friedrich (1996), S. 988.

78 Vgl. in diesem Zusammenhang zur Gestaltung von Verrechnungspreisen z.B. Drumm (1989), Sp. 2168ff., Schimmelpfennig (1994), S. 93ff., Treyer (1990), S. 247ff., aber auch vor allem Wagenhofer (1995), S. 281ff.

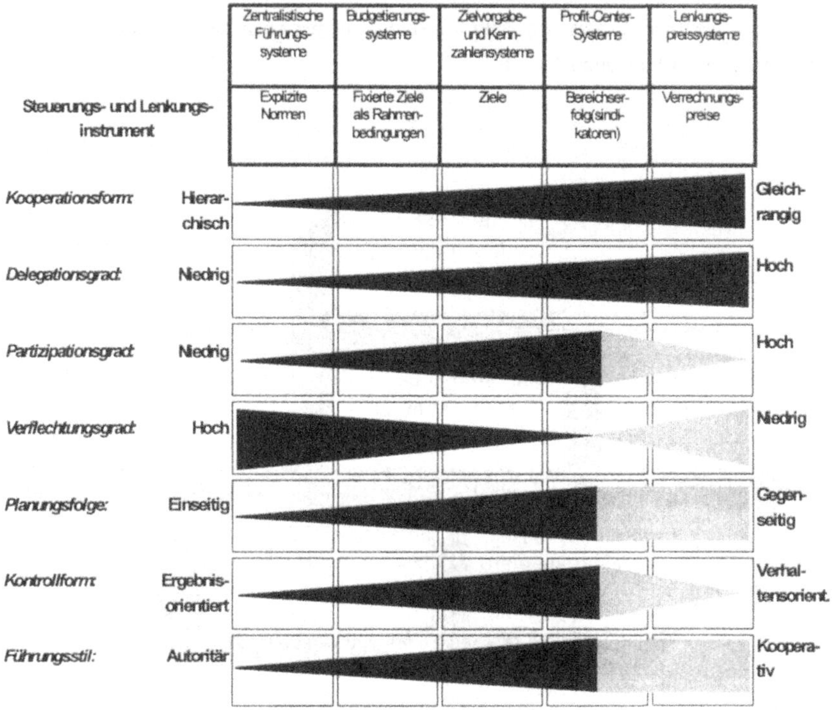

Abb. 7: Charakterisierung betriebswirtschaftlicher Steuerungs- und Lenkungssysteme

Quelle: Küpper (1991), S. 193

Die weitere Auseinandersetzung mit der Thematik wird es erforderlich machen, diejenigen Mechanismen herauszuarbeiten und gegebenenfalls weiterzuentwickeln, die eine Unternehmung implementieren muß, um eine optimale Verteilung und Ausnutzung der Ressourcen durch die zentralen Service-Bereiche zu gewährleisten.

4.2. Beispiel 2: Die Vermarktung interner Services als Spezialfall des internen Marketing

Die folgenden Überlegungen beziehen sich auf die Ausgestaltung des Feldes 10 i.V.m. den Feldern 11 und 12 in Abb. 6. Hier sind Fragestellungen der Vermarktung der internen Servi-

ces durch die Zentralbereiche gegenüber ihren innerbetrieblichen Abnehmern zu untersuchen. Abb. 8 macht deutlich, daß es sich beim Marketing interner Dienstleistungen um einen Spezialfall des internen Marketing handelt[79].

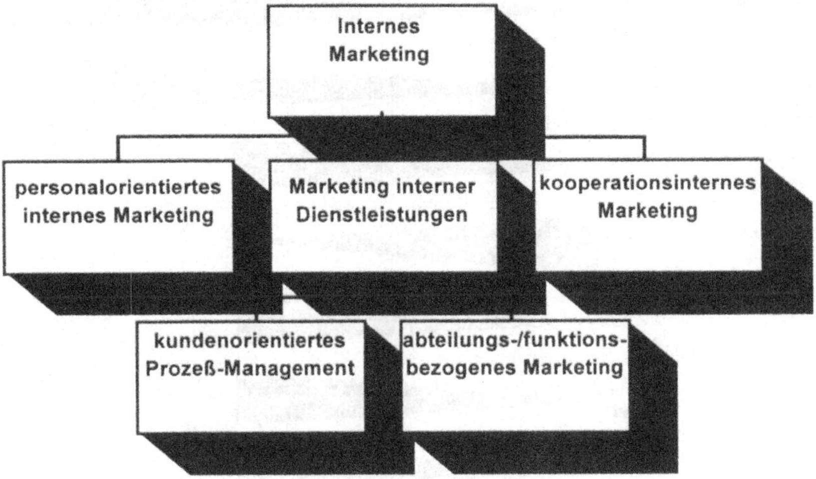

Abb. 8: Erscheinungsformen des internen Marketing

Quelle: abgeleitet aus Stauss (1995b), Sp. 1046

Internes Marketing beinhaltet im hier zugrundeliegenden Sinne „die planmäßige Gestaltung der unternehmerischen Austauschbeziehungen mit internen Systemelementen zu absatzmarktorientierten Zwecken“[80]. Im Konzept des internen Marketing findet sich durchgängig das schon angesprochene Denken in internen Kunden-Lieferanten-Beziehungen wieder: Jeder Mitarbeiter sollte sich als Lieferant anderer Mitarbeiter bzw. Abteilungen verstehen, die in diesem Sinne seine Kunden darstellen und die er zufriedenstellen muß. Dies ist die in der Li-

[79] Dabei werden die beiden anderen Formen, das personalorientierte interne Marketing, das den traditionellesten und am intensivsten ausgearbeiteten Zweig darstellt, und das kooperationsinterne Marketing, im Rahmen des vorliegenden Beitrags nicht weiter behandelt; vgl. zum Überblick Bruhn (1995), S. 13ff., Stauss (1995b), Sp. 1045ff., Stauss/Schulze (1990), S. 149ff., Varey (1995a), S. 40ff.

[80] Stauss (1994), S. 477.

teratur vielfach betonte Forderung[81]. Dabei - und das macht obige Definition deutlich - darf diese interne Kundenorientierung nicht um ihrer selbst willen erfolgen[82], sondern sie muß unter dem Primat der (externen) Absatzorientierung stehen. Mit anderen Worten: Internes Marketing hat die Aufgabe, das externe Marketing zu unterstützen, die externen Marktchancen sollen durch internes Marketing verbessert werden[83]. Insofern soll internes Marketing unmittelbar der Erzielung von Wettbewerbsvorteilen am externen Markt dienen.

Für die Marketing-Bemühungen interner Service-Bereiche bedeutet dies, daß sie durch das Streben nach internen Wettbewerbsvorteilen durch das auf ihre internen Abnehmer gerichtete Marketing gleichsam „automatisch" zur Erzielung externer Wettbewerbsvorteile beitragen sollten. An dieser Stelle wird der schon mehrfach betonte Mittel-Ziel-Bezug zwischen den beiden Betrachtungsebenen der vorliegenden Untersuchung wiederum deutlich[84].

Gemäß Abb. 8 umfaßt das Marketing interner Services die kundenorientierte Optimierung der Service-Prozesse[85] sowie - hier interessanter - das abteilungs- bzw. funktionsbezogene Marketing, das als innerbetriebliche Vermarktung im engsten Sinne angesehen werden kann. Die zentralen Service-Bereiche müssen - um nur einige wichtige Punkte herauszuheben - z.B.[86]

- interne Marktforschung betreiben, und zwar im Hinblick auf
  - □ die internen Kunden und ihre Bedürfnisse,
  - □ die Konkurrenten auf dem internen Markt, d.h. externe Spezialisten und Selbsterstellungsmöglichkeiten der Geschäftsbereiche;

---

81 Vgl. als kleine Auswahl Chung (1993), S. 26, George (1990), S. 67ff., Hauser/Simester/Wernerfelt (1996), S. 270, Piercy/Morgan (1991), S. 84, Stauss/Neuhaus (1995), S. 577ff., Töpfer (1995), S. 547ff.

82 Vgl. in diesem Zusammenhang wiederum die Kritik am Konzept des internen Kunden bei Harari (1991), S. 41ff., Harari (1993), S. 30ff. Dort werden die Gefahren einer überzogenen Betonung der Orientierung am internen Kunden bei gleichzeitiger Vernachlässigung der externen Markterfordernisse aufgezeigt.

83 Vgl. z.B. Comm (1989), S. 41, Davis (1992), S. 34, Flipo (1990), S. 5ff., Heskett et al. (1994), S. 51, Tansuhaj/Randall/McCullough (1988), S. 31ff., Varey (1995b), S. 41ff.

84 Interessant ist an dieser Stelle aber auch der Sachverhalt, daß sich mit der Unterordnung des nach innen gerichteten internen unter das nach außen gerichtete externe Marketing eine bemerkenswerte Parallelität zur Hierarchie der Unternehmerfunktionen findet, wie sie in Abschnitt 2.1. herausgestellt wurde: Auch dort nämlich besitzt die nach außen gerichtete Arbitragefunktion Priorität gegenüber der nach innen gerichteten Funktion des Durchsetzens von Änderungen. Daraus läßt sich eine grundlegende Verträglichkeit des Konzeptes des Marketing als marktorientierte Unternehmungsführung mit der Lehre von den Unternehmerfunktionen ablesen.

85 Die Optimierung erfolgt hier vor allem mit Blick auf die Befriedigung der Bedürfnisse externer Kunden; vgl. Stauss (1995b), Sp. 1052.

86 Vgl. dazu insbesondere Davis (1993), S. 301ff., Gremler/Bitner/Evans (1994), S. 34ff., Harrell/Fors (1992), S. 299ff., McDermott/Emerson (1991), S. 61ff., Reynoso/Moores (1995), S. 64ff., Stauss (1995a), S. 62ff., Vandermerwe/Gilbert (1989), S. 83ff., Vandermerwe/Gilbert (1991), S. 50ff., Witt (1985), S. 162ff.

- Leistungsangebote bedürfnisgerecht gestalten, z.B. durch segmentspezifische Leistungsbündel oder durch den Einsatz interner Service-Garantien;
- für Nachfragerevidenz bezüglich ihrer Services sorgen, indem sie mittels des Einsatzes kommunikationspolitischer Instrumente oder auch von Gesprächsrunden mit potentiellen Kunden die angebotenen Leistungen bekannt machen;
- ein gezieltes Qualitäts-Management betreiben, einschließlich Kundenzufriedenheitsuntersuchungen, Beschwerdeanalysen und Benchmarking.

Diese und andere Instrumente werden durch die zentralen Service-Bereiche vielfach zu wenig genutzt, obwohl gerade der Nachweis der erfolgreichen Vermarktung der betreffenden Leistungen ein wichtiges Argument gegen etwaige Eliminierungs- bzw. Outsourcing-Überlegungen sein kann. Auch im Hinblick auf diese Gestaltungsfelder kann eine tiefergehende Analyse wichtige Erkenntnisse für das wettbewerbsvorteilsorientierte Management zentraler Service-Bereiche liefern.

4.3. Beispiel 3: Prozeß-Management innerhalb zentraler Service-Bereiche

Das Management der zentralbereichsinternen Service-Prozesse berührt effektivitäts- und effizienzorientierte Aspekte und ist daher primär in den Feldern 11, 12, 15 und 16 von Abb. 6 anzusiedeln: Die Prozesse sollen im Hinblick auf die Bedürfnisse der internen Kunden und deren Nutzen sowie im Hinblick auf die Kosten optimiert werden[87]. Dabei sind einige gravierende Unterschiede zwischen Fertigungs- und Service-Prozessen zu beachten, die das Prozeß-Management im Service-Bereich vor besondere Herausforderungen stellen. Abb. 9 gibt einen - idealtypisch polarisierenden - Überblick hinsichtlich der wichtigsten Unterschiede.

---

[87] Diese Verbindung von Kunden- und Kostenorientierung ist vielfach genanntes charakteristisches Merkmal des Prozeß-Management, vgl. z.B. Bullinger (1995), S. 784f., Fischer (1996), S. 222, Hinterhuber (1994), S. 59, Striening (1995), S. 168. Vgl. in diesem Zusammenhang auch die interessanten Überlegungen zu einer ressourcenorientierten Perspektive eines wettbewerbsvorteilsorientierten Prozeß-Management bei Gaitanides/Sjurts (1995), S. 61ff.

Merkmale	Fertigungsprozeß	Service-Prozeß
Prozeß-Gesamtverantwortung	vorhanden	unklar
Prozeß-Definition	eindeutig	fraktioniert
Schnittstellenidentifikation	definiert	unklar
Ein-/Ausgabe-Beziehungen	quantifiziert	verbal
Dokumentation/Arbeitsanweisungen	präzise	unvollständig
Meßpunkte	festgelegt	nicht bzw. selten vorhanden
statistische Messungen	regelmäßig	nicht bzw. selten vorhanden
Produktivitätsmaßstab	Ausbeute, Durchlaufzeit	Bearbeitungszeit
Korrekturen/Modifikationen	präventiv/planvoll	reaktiv/sporadisch

Abb. 9: Unterschiede zwischen Fertigungs- und Service-Prozessen

Quelle: Striening (1988), S. 18

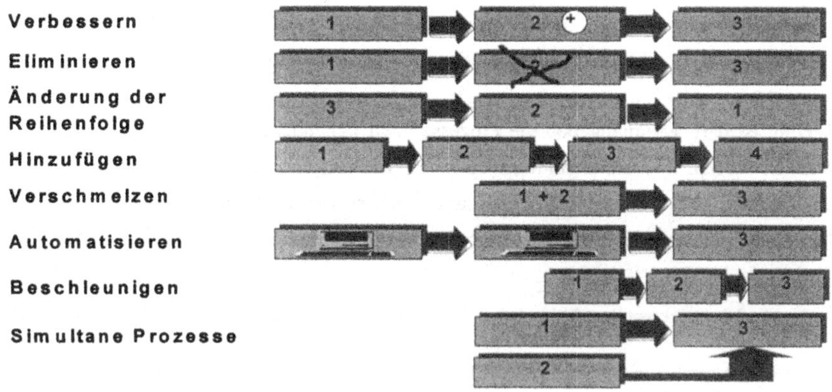

Abb. 10: Ansatzpunkte der Prozeß-Optimierung

Quelle: Lohoff/Lohoff (1993), S. 251

Ohne im einzelnen darauf eingehen zu müssen, macht Abb. 10 deutlich, daß es eine Reihe von Ansatzpunkten zur Prozeß-Optimierung gibt. Welcher gewählt wird, bleibt dem jeweiligen Einzelfall vorbehalten: Die Regel wird jedoch eine Kombination unterschiedlicher Teilaspekte sein.

Im einzelnen stellt das Prozeß-Management zur Unterstützung dieser Verbesserungsmaßnahmen ein breites Spektrum unterschiedlicher Instrumente und potentieller Maßnahmen zur Verfügung, wobei für die internen Services die aus Dienstleistungsunternehmungen vorliegenden Kenntnisse genutzt werden sollten[88]. Als beispielhafte Gestaltungsoptionen seien an dieser Stelle nur drei genannt, ohne näher auf deren spezifische Vor- und Nachteile eingehen zu können:

- Die Durchführung von **Prozeßanalysen** erlaubt eine detaillierte Betrachtung von Zeit, Qualität und Kosten als Erfolgsfaktoren im Hinblick auf jeden einzelnen Teilprozeß innerhalb des Service-Bereichs, aber auch auf die Erstellung bestimmter Services insgesamt. Wichtige Instrumente sind in diesem Zusammenhang das Service-Blueprinting[89] sowie die eng damit verwandte Prozeßwertanalyse[90].
- Zur Klärung der Service-Verantwortlichkeiten sind **Prozeßverantwortliche**[91] zu benennen. Ergänzend können **Verantwortlichkeitscharts**[92] eingesetzt werden, die deutlich machen, wer für welchen Teilschritt innerhalb der Service-Bereiche zuständig ist.
- Schließlich können **Prozeß-Portfolios**[93], die die einzelnen Teilprozesse nach unterschiedlichen Kriterien systematisieren und strukturieren, als Visualisierungs- und Analysehilfe herangezogen werden. In dieser Funktion können sie zwar keine Entscheidungen vorwegnehmen, die Entscheidungsfindung jedoch wirksam unterstützen.

Wichtig ist darüber hinaus, daß die Prozesse nicht nur innerhalb des Service-Bereiches hinsichtlich Kosten und Kundennutzen optimiert werden, sondern daß auch eine nachhaltige Abstimmung mit den unternehmensweiten Prozeßstrukturen erfolgt, damit der Beitrag des Service-Bereichs zur Erzielung externer Wettbewerbsvorteile ermöglicht und gefördert wird.

---

88 Entsprechende Erkenntnisse finden sich z.B. bei Kastner/Bohnenkamp (1991), S. 35ff., Melan (1985), S. 52ff.

89 Zu einem Überblick vgl. z.B. Shostack (1984), S. 93ff.

90 Vgl. Beischel (1990), S. 53ff.

91 Vgl. Striening (1988), S. 164ff.

92 Vgl. Davis (1991), S. 8.

93 Vgl. z.B. Fröhling (1992), S. 341ff.

Diese Abstimmung auf und Integration in die zentralbereichsübergreifenden Abläufe obliegt allerdings nicht primär den Service-Bereichen selbst, sondern der Unternehmungsleitung, die auf die Vermeidung von Schnittstellen- und Reibungsverlusten hinwirken muß.

Wie auch die in den Abschnitten 4.1. und 4.2. angesprochenen Aspekte bedarf derjenige des Prozeß-Management der intensiven Vertiefung. Als knapper Aufriß hinsichtlich der inhaltlichen Ausgestaltung möglicher Gestaltungsfelder eines wettbewerbsvorteilsorientierten Management zentraler Service-Bereiche mögen diese wenigen Hinweise jedoch an dieser Stelle ausreichen.

5. Fazit: Konsequenzen der vorgestellten Überlegungen und Problemfelder der weiteren Auseinandersetzung mit der Thematik

Im vorliegenden Beitrag wurde ein konzeptioneller Rahmen herausgearbeitet, mit dem systematisiert und erklärt werden soll, wie durch die Ausübung von Unternehmerfunktionen im Hinblick auf zentrale Service-Bereiche (als Ausschnitt aus der Gesamtheit denkbarer Institutionalisierungsformen interner Dienstleistungen) Wettbewerbsvorteile erzielt werden können, indem Perspektiven unternehmerischen Verhaltens auf unterschiedlichen Betrachtungsebenen Berücksichtigung finden.

Dabei lag der Schwerpunkt der Überlegungen auf der Herleitung und Fundierung dieses konzeptionellen Rahmens; weitgehend im Hintergrund mußte seine Ausgestaltung durch konkrete Handlungsmaßnahmen bleiben. Diese Gewichtung wurde gewählt, da das primäre Anliegen dieses Beitrags darin liegt, die Zweckmäßigkeit und Tragfähigkeit des dargestellten Ansatzes einer fundierten Überprüfung zugänglich zu machen. Diese Frage nämlich kann zum gegenwärtigen Zeitpunkt noch nicht als beantwortet angesehen werden, da insbesondere die Heranziehung der Lehre von den Unternehmerfunktionen einige Probleme aufwirft, die nicht verschwiegen werden können und die der kritischen Hinterfragung bedürfen. Insbesondere sind in diesem Zusammenhang folgende Aspekte erwähnenswert:

- Die Lehre von den Unternehmerfunktionen ist bis heute mehr eine heterogene Mischung unterschiedlicher Komponenten, die aus verschiedenen ökonomischen Richtungen beigesteuert wurden und werden, als eine zumindest in Ansätzen geschlossene theoretische Konzeption. Insofern stellt sich die Frage, ob die Heranziehung heterogener Bausteine zur Errichtung eines geschlossenen Fundaments ausreichen kann. Im vorliegenden Beitrag

wurde versucht, eine gewisse Stimmigkeit der Ausführungen durch die Fokussierung auf die Konzeption von Dieter Schneider herbeizuführen.

- Ein weiteres Problemfeld in Verbindung mit der Lehre von den Unternehmerfunktionen besteht darin, daß dieser Ansatz zwar vieles zu erklären vermag, im Hinblick auf die Formulierung konkreter Handlungsempfehlungen bis heute aber hinter z.B. der Neuen Institutionenökonomik deutlich zurückhängt. Hier stellt sich die schwer zu beantwortende Frage, ob darin eher die Chance der Suche nach Neuem oder die Gefahr der Vernachlässigung anderweitig bereits vorhandener brauchbarer Erkenntnisse gesehen werden sollte.

- Erachtet man die Lehre von den Unternehmerfunktionen als tragfähig und angemessen für die theoretische Fundierung eines wettbewerbsvorteilsorientierten Management zentraler Service-Bereiche, so stellt sich zumindest die Frage, inwieweit es zulässig sein kann, die Erkenntnisse anderer Theoriezweige zur Füllung vorhandener Lücken in einer auf den Unternehmerfunktionen basierenden Theorie der Unternehmung heranzuziehen. Wichtig wird dabei sein, die der Lehre von den Unternehmerfunktionen zugrundeliegenden Prämissen nicht zu verletzen.

In jedem Fall - das sei abschließend festgehalten - eröffnet die Lehre von den Unternehmerfunktionen interessante Einblicke in die Thematik, die durch das Verlassen weitgehend ausgetretener Pfade der Theorie ermöglicht werden. Die Anknüpfungspunkte zwischen den Unternehmerfunktionen und dem marktorientierten Denken in Kategorien des Wettbewerbsvorteils dürften in den zurückliegenden Ausführungen nachvollziehbar hervorgetreten sein[94]. Der entscheidende „Knackpunkt" ist daher nicht in der Frage der **generellen** Verträglichkeit von marktorientierter Unternehmungsführung und Unternehmerfunktionen zu sehen, sondern in der Frage, ob die Unternehmerfunktionen **genügend** Ansatzpunkte für die Auseinandersetzung mit Problemstellungen im Kontext der marktorientierten Unternehmungsführung - hier diskutiert am Spezialfall des Management zentraler Service-Bereiche - bieten. Anstöße zur Auseinandersetzung mit und Hinweise zur Beantwortung dieser Frage zu liefern, war das Anliegen des vorliegenden Beitrags.

---

[94] Vgl. dazu auch einzelne Versuche zur Verknüpfung von Marketing und Theorie des Unternehmertums, wie sie sich etwa bei Reekie/Savitt (1982), S. 55ff., oder insbesondere in dem von Hills (1994) herausgegebenen Sammelband finden. Auffällig ist, daß von derartigen Überlegungen in der deutschsprachigen Literatur bisher kaum Notiz genommen wurde. Offen ist allerdings derzeit noch die generelle Frage, inwieweit entsprechende Untersuchungen zu Marketing und Unternehmertum mit dem hier vorgestellten Konzept theoretisch „kompatibel" sind. Auch die Beantwortung dieser Frage muß Gegenstand weiterer Analysen sein.

6. Literatur

ALTFELDER, Klaus (1965): Stabsstellen und Zentralabteilungen als Formen der Organisation der Führung, Berlin 1965

ARBEITSKREIS DR. KRÄHE (1952): Konzern-Organisation, Köln/Opladen 1952

BACKHAUS, Klaus (1992): Investitionsgütermarketing, 3. Aufl., München 1992

BAMBERGER, Ingo/WRONA, Thomas (1996): Der Ressourcenansatz und seine Bedeutung für die Strategische Unternehmensführung, in: Zeitschrift für betriebswirtschaftliche Forschung, 48. Jg. (1996), S. 130-153

BARNARD, Chester I. (1938): The Functions of the Executive, Cambridge/Mass. 1938

BECKER, Fred G. (1995): Anreizsysteme als Führungsinstrumente, in: Kieser, Alfred/Reber, Gerhard/Wunderer, Rolf (Hrsg.): Handwörterbuch der Führung, 2. Aufl., Stuttgart 1995, Sp. 34-45

BEISCHEL, Mark E. (1990): Improving Production with Process Value Analysis, in: Journal of Accountancy, Vol. 17 (1990), September, S. 53-57

BEUERMANN, Günter (1992): Zentralisation und Dezentralisation, in: Frese, Erich (Hrsg.): Handwörterbuch der Organisation, 3. Aufl., Stuttgart 1992, Sp. 2611-2615

BITZER, Marc (1991): Intrapreneurship - Unternehmertum in der Unternehmung, Stuttgart 1991

BLEICHER, Knut (1966): Zentralisation und Dezentralisation von Aufgaben in der Organisation der Unternehmungen, Berlin 1966

BOHR, Kurt (1993): Effizienz und Effektivität, in: Wittmann, Waldemar et al. (Hrsg.): Handwörterbuch der Betriebswirtschaft, 5. Aufl., Bd. 1, Stuttgart 1993, Sp. 855-869

BREID, Volker (1995): Aussagefähigkeit agencytheoretischer Ansätze im Hinblick auf die Verhaltenssteuerung von Entscheidungsträgern, in: Zeitschrift für betriebswirtschaftliche Forschung, 47. Jg. (1995), S. 821-854

BRUHN, Manfred (1995): Internes Marketing als Forschungsgebiet der Marketingwissenschaft, in: Bruhn, Manfred (Hrsg.): Internes Marketing, Wiesbaden 1995, S. 13-61

BÜHNER, Rolf (1996): Die Größe von Konzernzentralen - eine Benchmarking Studie, in: Zeitschrift Führung + Organisation, 65. Jg. (1996), S. 227-236

BULLINGER, Hans-Jörg (1995): Prozeßmanagement, in: Corsten, Hans/Reiß, Michael (Hrsg.): Handbuch Unternehmungsführung, Wiesbaden 1995, S. 779-790

CANTILLON, Richard (1755): Essai sur la nature du commerce en général, London 1755

CASSON, Mark (1982): The Entrepreneur: An Economic Theory, Oxford 1982

CASSON, Mark (1996): The Nature of the Firm Reconsidered: Information Synthesis and Entrepreneurial Organisation, in: Buckley, Peter J. (Hrsg.): International Business Theory, Wiesbaden 1996 (Management International Review, Vol. 36, Special Issue 1996/1), S. 55-94

CHUNG, Ronald K. (1993): TQM: Internal Client Satisfaction, in: Business Credit, Vol. 95 (1993), H. 4, S. 26-28

COASE, Ronald H. (1937): The Nature of the Firm, in: Economica, Vol. 4 (1937), S. 386-405

COMM, Clare L. (1989): The Internal Marketing of Demand Intensive Services by Companies Can Lead to Better External Marketing, in: Journal of Professional Services Marketing, Vol. 5 (1989), H. 1, S. 41-46

CONNELL, Regina (1996): Learning to Share, in: Journal of Business Strategy, Vol. 17 (1996), H. 2, S. 55-58

CRAMER, Birgit (1987): Marketing für innerbetriebliche Weiterbildungsleistungen, Frankfurt a.M. et al. 1987

DAVIS, Tim R.V. (1991): Internal Service Operations: Strategies for Increasing Their Effectiveness and Controlling Their Cost, in: Organizational Dynamics, Vol. 20 (1991), Autumn, S. 5-22

DAVIS, Tim R.V. (1992): Satisfying Internal Customers: The Link to External Customer Satisfaction, in: Planning Review, Vol. 20 (1992), H. 1, S. 34-37

DAVIS, Tim R.V. (1993): Managing Internal Service Delivery in Organizations, in: Swartz, T.A./Bowen, D.E./Brown, S.W. (Hrsg.): Advances in Services Marketing and Management, Vol. 2, Greenwich/Conn. 1993, S. 301-321

DAY, George S./**WENSLEY**, Robin (1988): Assessing Advantage: A Framework for Diagnosing Competitive Superiority, in: Journal of Marketing, Vol. 52 (1988), April, S. 1-20

DRUMM, Hans Jürgen (1989): Verrechnungspreise, in: Szyperski, Norbert/Winand, Udo (Hrsg.): Handwörterbuch der Planung, Stuttgart 1989, Sp. 2168-2177

FISCHER, Joachim (1996): Prozeßorientiertes Controlling: Ein notwendiger Paradigmenwechsel?, in: Controlling, 8. Jg. (1996), S. 222-231

FLIPO, Jean-Paul (1990): Service Firms: Interdependence of External and Internal Marketing Strategies, in: European Journal of Marketing, Vol. 20 (1990), H. 8, S. 5-14

FÖHR, Silvia (1991): Ökonomische Analyse der internen Organisation, Wiesbaden 1991

FRESE, Erich (1990): Das Profit-Center-Konzept im Spannungsfeld von Organisation und Rechnungswesen, in: Ahlert, Dieter/Franz, Klaus-Peter/Göppl, Hermann (Hrsg.): Finanz-und Rechnungswesen als Führungsinstrument, Wiesbaden 1990, S. 137-155

FRESE, Erich/VON WERDER, Axel (1993): Zentralbereiche - Organisatorische Formen und Effizienzbeurteilung -, in: Frese, Erich, von Werder, Axel/Maly, Werner (Hrsg.): Zentralbereiche, Stuttgart 1993, S. 1-50

FRESE, Erich/VON WERDER, Axel (1994): Organisation als strategischer Wettbewerbsfaktor - Organisationstheoretische Analyse gegenwärtiger Umstrukturierungen -, in: Frese, Erich/Maly, Werner (Hrsg.): Organisationsstrategien zur Sicherung der Wettbewerbsfähigkeit, Zeitschrift für betriebswirtschaftliche Forschung, Sonderheft 33/1994, S. 1-27

FRIEDRICH, Rainer (1996): Der Centeransatz zur Führung und Steuerung dezentraler Einheiten, in: Bullinger, Hans-Jörg/Warnecke, Hans Jürgen (Hrsg.): Neue Organisationsformen im Unternehmen, Berlin et al. 1996, S. 984-1014

FRÖHLING, Oliver (1992): Prozeßorientiertes Portfolio-Management, in: Die Betriebswirtschaft, 52. Jg. (1992), S. 341-358

GAITANIDES, Michael/SJURTS, Insa (1995): Wettbewerbsvorteile durch Prozeßmanagement, in: Corsten, Hans/Will, Thomas (Hrsg.): Unternehmungsführung im Wandel, Stuttgart/Berlin/Köln 1995, S. 61-82

GEORGE, William R. (1990): Internal Marketing an Organizational Behavior: A Partnership in Developing Customer-Conscious Employees at Every Level, in: Journal of Business Research, Vol. 20 (1990), S. 63-70

GREMLER, Dwayne D./BITNER, Mary Jo/EVANS, Kenneth R. (1994): The Internal Service Encounter, in: International Journal of Service Industry Management, Vol. 5 (1994), H. 2, S. 34-56

Gruhler, Wolfram (1993): Gesamtwirtschaftliche Bedeutung und einzelwirtschaftlicher Stellenwert industrieller Dienstleistungen, in: Simon, Hermann (Hrsg.): Industrielle Dienstleistungen, Stuttgart 1993, S. 23-40

Harari, Oren (1991): Should Internal Customers Exist?, in: Management Review, Vol. 80 (1991), H. 7, S. 41-43

Harari, Oren (1993): Internal Customer, R.I.P., in: Management Review, Vol. 82 (1993), H. 6, S. 30-32

Harrell, Gilbert D./**Fors**, Matthew F. (1992): Internal Marketing of a Service, in: Industrial Marketing Management, Vol. 21 (1992), S. 299-306

Hart, Christopher W.L. (1995): Vom Nutzen interner Qualitätsgarantien, in: Harvard Business Manager, 17. Jg. (1995), H. 3, S. 78-86

Hauser, John R./**Simester**, Duncan I./**Wernerfelt**, Birger (1996): Internal Customers and Internal Suppliers, in: Journal of Marketing Research, Vol. 33 (1996), S. 268-280

Heskett, James L. et al. (1994): Dienstleister müssen die ganze Service-Gewinn-Kette nutzen, in: Harvard Business Manager, 16. Jg. (1994), H. 4, S. 50-61

Hills, Gerald E. (Hrsg.) (1994): Marketing and Entrepreneurship, Westport/London 1994

Hinterhuber, Hans H. (1994): Paradigmenwechsel: Vom Denken in Funktionen zum Denken in Prozessen, in: Journal für Betriebswirtschaft, 44. Jg. (1994), H. 2, S. 58-75

Horchler, Hartmut (1996): Outsourcing, Köln 1996

Hunt, Shelby D./**Morgan**, Robert M. (1996): The Resource-Advantage Theory of Competition: Dynamics, Path Dependencies, and Evolutionary Dimensions, in: Journal of Marketing, Vol. 60 (1996), October, S. 107-114

Kastner, Karl-Heinz/**Bohnenkamp**, Peter (1991): Das Aktivitäten-Management-System (AMY), in: Office Management, 39. Jg. (1991), H. 7/8, S. 35-40

Kirzner, Israel M. (1978): Wettbewerb und Unternehmertum, Tübingen 1978

Koppelmann, Udo (Hrsg.) (1996): Outsourcing, Stuttgart 1996

Kotler, Philip (1972): A Generic Concept of Marketing, in: Journal of Marketing, Vol. 36 (1972), H. 2, S. 46-54

Kreikebaum, Hartmut (1992): Zentralbereiche, in: Frese, Erich (Hrsg.): Handwörterbuch der Organisation, 3. Aufl., Stutgart 1992, Sp. 2603-2610

KREISEL, Henning (1995): Zentralbereiche, Wiesbaden 1995

KÜPPER, Hans-Ulrich (1991): Betriebswirtschaftliche Steuerungs- und Lenkungsmechanismen organisationsinterner Kooperation, in: Wunderer, Rolf (Hrsg.): Kooperation, Stuttgart 1991, S. 175-203

KÜPPER, Hans-Ulrich (1995): Steuerungsinstrumente von Führung und Kooperation, in: Kieser, Alfred/Reber, Gerhard/Wunderer, Rolf (Hrsg.): Handwörterbuch der Führung, 2. Aufl., Stuttgart 1995, Sp. 1995-2005

LOHOFF, Petra/**LOHOFF**, Heinz-Günter (1993): Verwaltung im Visier, in: Zeitschrift Führung + Organisation, 62. Jg. (1993), S. 248-254

MÄNNEL, Wolfgang (1981): Die Wahl zwischen Eigenfertigung und Fremdbezug, 2. Aufl., Stuttgart 1981

MAGIDSON, Jason/**POLCHA**, Andrew A. (1992): Creating Market Economies Within Organizations: A Conference on „Internal Markets"

MCDERMOTT, Lynda C./**EMERSON**, Michael (1991): Quality and Service for Internal Customers, in: Training & Development Journal, Vol. 45 (1991), H. 1, S. 61-64

MELAN, Eugene M. (1985): Process Management in Service and Administrative Operations, in: Quality Progress, Vol. 8 (1985), June, S. 52-59

MEYER, Margit (1995): Ökonomische Organisation der Industrie, Wiesbaden 1995

NEUHAUS, Patricia (1996): Interne Kunden-Lieferanten-Beziehungen, Wiesbaden 1996

NEUHOF, B. (1982): Profit Center-Organisation - Grundkonzeption und praxisorientierte Modifizierungen, in: Das Wirtschaftsstudium, 11. Jg. (1982), S. 11-15 (Teil I) und S. 61-66 (Teil II)

NIELSEN, Richard P./**PETERS**, Michael P./**HISRICH**, Robert D. (1985): Intrapreneurship Strategy for Internal Markets - Corprate, Non-profit and Government Institution Cases, in: Strategic Management Journal, Vol. 6 (1985), S. 181-189

NIMAN, Neil B. (1991): The Entrepreneurial Function in the Theory of the Firm, in: Scottish Journal of Political Economy, Vol. 38 (1991), S. 162-176

PFAU, Bruce/**DETZEL**, Denis/**GELLER**, Andrew (1991): Satisfying Your Internal Customers, in: The Journal of Business Strategy, Vol. 12 (1991), H. 6, S. 9-13

PICOT, Arnold (1991): Ein neuer Ansatz zur Gestaltung der Leistugstiefe, in: Zeitschrift für betriebswirtschaftliche Forschung, 43. Jg. (1991), S. 336-357

PICOT, Arnold/**REICHWALD**, Ralf/**WIGAND**, Rolf T. (1996): Die grenzenlose Unternehmung, 2. Aufl., Wiesbaden 1996

PIERCY, Nigel/**MORGAN**, Neil (1991): Internal Marketing - The Missing Half of the Marketing Programme, in: Long Range Planning, Vol. 24 (1991), H. 2, S. 82-93

PLINKE, Wulff (1995): Grundlagen des Marktrprozesses, in: Kleinaltenkamp, Michael/Plinke, Wulff (Hrsg.): Technischer Vertrieb, Berlin et al. 1995, S. 3-95

PORTER, Michael E. (1986): Wettbewerbsvorteile, Frankfurt a.M. 1986

RASCHE, Christoph/**WOLFRUM**, Bernd (1994): Ressourcenorientierte Unternehmensführung, in: Die Betriebswirtschaft, 54. Jg. (1994), S. 501-517

REEKIE, W. Duncan/**SAVITT**, Ronald (1982): Marketing Behavior and Entrepreneurship: A Synthesis of Alderson and Austrian Economics, in: European Journal of Marketing, Vol. 10 (1982), H. 7, S. 55-66

REYNOSO, Javier/**MOORES**, Brian (1995): Towards the Measurement of Internal Service Quality, in: International Journal of Service Industry Management, Vol. 6 (1995), H. 3, S. 64-83

SANFILIPPO, Barbara (1990): 8 Ideas to Stimulate Internal Service, in: Bank Marketing, Vol. 22 (1990), H. 12, S. 26-29

SAYLES, L.R. (1964): Managerial Behavior, New York et al. 1964

SCHIMMELPFENNIG, Katja (1994): ZP-Stichwort: Verrechnungspreise, in: Zeitschrift für Planung, 5. Jg. (1994), S. 93-96

SCHMALENBACH, Eugen (1959): Über Dienststellengliederung im Großbetriebe, Köln/Opladen 1959

SCHNEIDER, Dieter (1985): Die Unhaltbarkeit des Transaktionskostenansatzes für die „Markt oder Unternehmung"-Diskussion, in: Zeitschrift für Betriebswirtschaft, 55. Jg. (1985), S. 1237-1254

SCHNEIDER, Dieter (1995): Betriebswirtschaftslehre, Band 1: Grundlagen, 2. Aufl., München/Wien 1995

SCHNEIDER, Dieter (1996): Biologische Vorbilder für eine evolutorische Theorie der Unternehmung?, in: Zeitschrift für betriebswirtschaftliche Forschung, 48. Jg. (1996), S. 1098-1114

SCHNEIDER, Dietram/**BAUR**, Cornelius/**HOPFMANN**, Lienhard (1994): Re-Design der Wertkette durch Make or Buy, Wiesbaden 1994

SCHOLZ, Christian (1992): Effektivität und Effizienz, organisatorische, in: Frese, Erich (Hrsg.): Handwörterbuch der Organisation, 3. Aufl., Stuttgart 1992, Sp. 533-552

SCHOPPE, Siegfried G. et al. (1995): Moderne Theorie der Unternehmung, München/Wien 1995

SCHÜTZ, Peter (1993): Marketing interner Dienstleister - Marketing ohne Markt?, in: Thelen, Eva M./Mairamhof, Gaby B. (Hrsg.): Dienstleistungsmarketing, Frankfurt a.M. et al. 1993, S. 193-201

SCHUMPETER, Joseph (1928): Unternehmer, in: Handwörterbuch der Staatswissenschaften, Bd. 8, 4. Aufl., Jena 1928, S. 476-487

SCHWEITZER, Marcell (1992): Profit Center, in: Frese, Erich (Hrsg.): Handwörterbuch der Organisation, 3. Aufl., Stuttgart 1992, Sp. 2078-2089

SHILS, Edward B./ZUCKER, William (1979): Developing a Model for Internal Corporate Entrepreneurship, in: Social Science, Vol. 54 (1979), S. 105-203

SHOSTACK, G. Lynn (1984): Planung effizienter Dienstleistungen, in: Harvard Manager, 6. Jg. (1984), H. 3, S. 93-99

SIMON, Hermann (1988): Management strategischer Wettbewerbsvorteile, in: Zeitschrift für Betriebswirtschaft, 58. Jg. (1988), S. 461-480

SPREMANN, Klaus (1990): Asymmetrische Information, in: Zeitschrift für Betriebswirtschaft, 60. Jg. (1990), S. 561-586

STAUSS, Bernd (1994): Internes Marketing, in: Diller, Hermann (Hrsg.): Vahlens Großes Marketing Lexikon, München 1994, S. 477-479

STAUSS, Bernd (1995a): Internal Services: Classification and Quality Management, in: International Journal of Service Industry Management, Vol. 6 (1995), H. 2, S. 62-78

STAUSS, Bernd (1995b): Internes Marketing, in: Tietz, Bruno/Köhler, Richard/Zentes, Joachim (Hrsg.): Handwörterbuch des Marketing, 2. Aufl., Stuttgart 1995, Sp. 1045-1056

STAUSS, Bernd/NEUHAUS, Patricia (1995): Interne Kundenzufriedenheit als Zielgröße des Total Quality Management: Dargestellt am Beispiel einer Abteilung Personalmanagement, in: Bruhn, Manfred (Hrsg.): Internes Marketing, Wiesbaden 1995, S. 575-609

STAUSS, Bernd/SCHULZE, Henning S. (1990): Internes Marketing, in: Marketing ZFP, 12. Jg. (1990), S. 149-158

STEVENSON, Howard H./JARILLO, J. Carlos (1990): A Paradigm of Entrepreneurship: Entrepreneurial Management, in: Strategic Management Journal, Vol. 11 (1990), S. 17-27

STREHL, Franz (1985): Organisatorische Effektivität - ein Modellvergleich, in: Bühler, Wilhelm et al. (Hrsg.): Die ganzheitliche Betrachtung der sozialen Leistungsordnung, Wien/New York 1985, S. 599-519

STRIENING, Hans-Dieter (1988): Prozeß-Management, Frankfurt a.M. et al. 1988

STRIENING, Hans-Dieter (1995): Möglichkeiten und Grenzen des Prozeßmanagement, in: Corsten, Hans/Will, Thomas (Hrsg.): Unternehmungsführung im Wandel, Stuttgart/Berlin/Köln 1995, S. 161-178

TANSUHAJ, Patriya/RANDALL, Donna/MCCULLOUGH, Jim (1988): A Services Marketing Management Model: Integrating Internal and External Marketing Functions, in: The Journal of Services Marketing, Vol. 2 (1988), H. 1, S. 31-38

TÖPFER, Armin (1995): Anforderungen des Total Quality Management an Konzeption und Umsetzung des Internen Marketing, in: Bruhn, Manfred (Hrsg.): Internes Marketing, Wiesbaden 1995, S. 545-573

TREYER, Oscar A.G. (1990): Verrechnungspreise für dezentrale Organisationen, in: Die Unternehmung, 44. Jg. (1990), S. 247-272

VANDERMERWE, Sandra/GILBERT, Douglas J. (1989): Making Internal Services Market Driven, in: Business Horizons, Vol. 31 (1989), H. 6, S. 83-89

VANDERMERWE, Sandra/GILBERT, Douglas J. (1991): Internal Services: Gaps in Needs/Performance and Prescriptions for Effectiveness, in: International Journal of Service Industry Management, Vol. 2 (1991), H. 1, S. 50-60

VAREY, Richard J. (1995a): Internal Marketing: A Review and Some Interdisciplinary Research Challenges, in: International Journal of Service Industry Management, Vol. 6 (1995), H. 1, S. 40-63

VAREY, Richard J. (1995b): A Model of Internal Marketing for Building and Sustaining a Competitive Servce Advantage, in: Journal of Marketing Management, Vol. 11 (1995), S. 41-54

WAGENHOFER; Alfred (1995): Verhaltenssteuerung durch Verrechnungspreise, in: Scheer, August-Wilhelm (Hrsg.): 16. Saarbrücker Arbeitstagung 1995 Rechnungswesen und EDV, Heidelberg 1995, S. 281-301

Wagner, Ralph (1994): Die Grenzen der Unternehmung, Heidelberg 1994

Wieandt, Axel (1994): Die Theorie der dynamischen Unternehmerfunktionen, in: Wirtschaftswissenschaftliches Studium, 23. Jg. (1994), S. 20-24

Williamson, Oliver E. (1975): Markets and Hierarchies - Analysis and Antitrust Implications, New York/London 1975

Windsperger, Josef (1991): Der Unternehmer als Koordinator, in: Zeitschrift für Betriebswirtschaft, 61. Jg. (1991), S. 1413-1429

Witt, Frank-Jürgen (1985): Marketing für innerbetriebliche Leistungen, in: Betriebswirtschaftliche Forschung und Praxis, 35. Jg. (1985), S. 162-175

Witt, Frank-Jürgen (1988): Unternehmensinterne Make-or-Buy-Entscheidungen, in: Controller Magazin, 13. Jg. (1988), S. 77-82

Zahn, Erich (1996): Kernkompetenzen, in: Kern, Werner/Schröder, Hans-Horst/Weber, Jürgen (Hrsg.): Handwörterbuch der Produktionswirtschaft, 2. Aufl., Stuttgart 1996, Sp. 883-894

Made in the USA
Las Vegas, NV
13 November 2024

11639434R00167